A Place of Hiding

A Place
of
Hiding

Elizabeth George

BANTAM BOOKS

RANDOM HOUSE
LARGE PRINT

This is a book about siblings
and I dedicate it to my own

Robert Rivelle George

with love and with admiration for his
talent, wit, and wisdom

In one respect, indeed, our employment
may be reckoned dishonest, because,
like great Statesmen,
we encourage those who betray their friends.

The Beggar's Opera
John Gay

November 10
2:45 P.M.

MONTECITO, CALIFORNIA

SANTA ANA WINDS WERE no friends of photography, but that was something you could not tell an egomaniacal architect who believed his entire reputation rested upon capturing for posterity—and for *Architectural Digest*—fifty-two thousand square feet of unfinished hillside sprawl *today*. You couldn't even try to tell him that. Because when you finally found the location after making what felt like two dozen wrong turns, you were already late, he was already ticked off, and the arid wind was already throwing up so much dust that all you wanted to do was get out of there as fast as possible, which wasn't going to *be* possible if you argued with him over whether you were going to take the pictures in the first place. So you took them, never mind the dust, never mind the tumbleweeds that seemed to have been imported by a special-effects team to make several million dollars' worth of California ocean-view real estate look like Barstow in August, and never mind the fact that the grit got under your contact lenses and the air made your skin feel like peach pits and your hair like burnt hay. The job was everything; the job was all. And since China River supported herself by doing the job, she did it.

But she wasn't happy. When she completed the work, a patina of grime lay on her clothes and against her skin, and the only thing she wanted—other than a tall glass of the coldest water she could find and a long soak in a very cool tub—was to be out of there: off the hillside and closer to the beach. So she said, "That's it, then. I'll have proofs for you to choose from the day after tomorrow. One o'clock? Your office? Good. I'll be there," and she strode off without giving the man a chance to reply. She didn't much care about his reaction to her abrupt departure, either.

She drove back down the hillside in her ancient Plymouth, along a smoothly paved road, potholes being permanently banned in Montecito. The route took her past houses of the Santa Barbara super-rich who lived their shielded privileged lives behind electronic gates, where they swam in designer swimming pools and toweled themselves off afterwards on terrycloth as thick and white as a Colorado snow bank. She braked occasionally for Mexican gardeners who sweated behind those protective walls and for teenage girls on horseback who bounced along in tight-fitting blue jeans and skimpy T-shirts. The hair on these girls swung in the sunlight. On every last one of them it was long and straight and shiny like something lit it from within. Their skin was flawless and their teeth were perfect, too. And not a single one of them carried an ounce of unwanted flesh anywhere. But then, why would they? Weight wouldn't have had the moral fortitude to linger upon them any longer than the time it took them to stand on the bathroom scale, get hysterical, and fling themselves at the toilet afterwards.

They were so pathetic, China thought. The whole coddled, undernourished crowd of them. And what was worse for the little twits: Their mothers probably looked exactly like them, doing their part to be role models for a lifetime of personal trainers, plastic surgery, shopping excursions, daily massages, weekly manicures, and regular sessions with a shrink. There was *nothing* like having a gold-plated meal ticket, courtesy of some idiot whose only requirement of his women was zeroed in on the looks department.

Whenever China had to come to Montecito, she couldn't wait to get *out* of Montecito, and today was no different. If anything, today the wind and the heat made the urgency to put this place behind her worse than normal, like something gnawing at her mood. Which was bad enough already. An overall uneasiness had been sitting on her shoulders since the moment her alarm had rung early that morning.

Nothing else had rung. That was the problem. Upon waking, she'd made that automatic three-hour leap in time to ten-A.M.-in-Manhattan-so-why-hasn't-he-called, and while the hours passed till the one at which she had to leave for her appointment in Montecito, she'd mostly watched the phone and stewed, something that was easy enough to do since it was nearly eighty degrees by nine A.M.

She'd tried to occupy herself. She'd watered the

entire front yard by hand and she'd done the same to the back, right down to the grass. She'd talked over the fence to Anita Garcia—Hey, girl, is this weather killing you? Man oh man, it's destroying me—and sympathised with her neighbour's degree of water retention in this last month of her pregnancy. She'd washed the Plymouth and dried it as she went, managing to stay one step ahead of the dust that wanted to adhere to it and turn into mud. And she leaped inside the house twice when the phone rang, only to find those unctuous, obnoxious telephone solicitors on the line, the kind who always wanted to know what kind of day you were having before they launched into their spiels about changing your long-distance telephone company which would, of course, also change your life. Finally, she'd had to leave for Montecito. But not before she picked up the phone one last time to make sure she had a dial tone and not before she double-checked her answering machine to make sure it would take a message.

All the time she hated herself for not being able just to *dismiss* him. But that had been the problem for years. Thirteen of them. God. How she hated love.

Her cell phone was the phone that finally did the ringing towards the end of her drive home to the beach. Not five minutes away from the uneven lump of sidewalk that marked the concrete path to her own front door, it chimed on the passenger seat and China grabbed it up to hear Matt's voice.

"Hey, good-looking." He sounded cheerful.

"Hey yourself." She hated the instant relief she

felt, like she'd been uncorked of carbonated anxiety. She said nothing else.

He read that easily. "Pissed?"

Nothing from her end. Let him hang, she thought.

"I guess I've blown my wad with this one."

"Where've you been?" she demanded. "I thought you were calling this morning. I waited at the house. I *hate* it when you do that, Matt. Why don't you get it? If you're not going to call, just say that in the first place and I can deal with it, okay? Why didn't you call?"

"Sorry. I meant to. I kept reminding myself all day."

"And . . . ?"

"It's not going to sound good, China."

"Try me."

"Okay. A real bitch of a cold front moved in last night. I had to spend half the morning trying to find a decent coat."

"You couldn't call from your cell while you were out?"

"Forgot to take it. I'm sorry. Like I said."

She could hear the ubiquitous background noises of Manhattan, the same noises she heard whenever he called from New York. The blare of horns reverberating through architectural canyons, jack hammers firing like heavy armaments against cement. But if he'd left his cell phone in the hotel, what was he doing on the street with it now?

"On my way to dinner," he told her. "Last meeting. Of the day, that is."

She'd pulled to the sidewalk at a vacant spot about thirty yards down the street from her house. She hated stopping because the air conditioning in her car was too weak to make much of a dent in the stifling interior so she was desperate to get out, but Matt's last remark made the heat suddenly less important and certainly far less noticeable. All her attention shifted to his meaning.

If nothing else, she'd learned to keep her mouth shut when he dropped one of his small verbal incendiary bombs. There'd been a time when she'd jump all over him at a remark like "Of the day, that is," to weed specifics out of his implications. But the years had taught her that silence served just as well as demands or accusations. It also gave her the upper hand once he finally admitted what he was trying to avoid saying.

It came in a rush. "Here's the situation. I've got to stay here another week. I've got a chance to talk to some people about a grant, and I need to see them."

"Matt. Come on."

"Wait, babe. Listen. These guys dumped a fortune on a filmmaker from NYU last year. They're looking for a project. Hear that? They're actually *looking*."

"How do you know?"

"That's what I was told."

"By who?"

"So I called them and I managed to get an appointment. But not till next Thursday. So I've got to stay."

"Goodbye Cambria, then."

"No, we'll do it. We just can't next week."

"Sure. Then when?"

"That's just it." The street sounds on the other end of the cell phone seemed to grow louder for a moment, as if he were throwing himself into the midst of them, forced off the sidewalk by the congestion of the city at the end of a workday.

She said, "Matt? Matt?" and knew a moment of irrational panic when she thought she'd lost him. Damn phones and damn signals, always fading in and out.

But he came back on the line and it was quieter. He'd ducked inside a restaurant, he said. "This is make or break for the film. China, this one's a festival winner. Sundance for sure, and you know what that can mean. I hate letting you down like this, but if I don't make a pitch to these people, I'm not going to be worth taking you anywhere. To Cambria. To Paris. Or to Kalamazoo. That's just how it is."

"Fine," she told him, but it was not and he would know that by the flat sound of her voice. It had been a month since he'd managed to carve two days away from pitch-meetings in LA and funding-scavenges across the rest of the country, and before that it had been six weeks while she cold-called potential clients for herself and he continued to pursue the horizon of his dream. "Sometimes," she said, "I wonder if you'll ever be able to put it together, Matt."

"I know. It seems like it takes forever to get a film going. And sometimes it does. You know the stories. Years in development and then—*wham!*—instant box office. But I want to do this. I need to do it. I'm just sorry it seems like we end up apart more than we're together."

China heard all this as she watched a toddler trundle along the sidewalk on his tricycle, trailed by his watchful mother and even more watchful German shepherd. The child came to a spot where the cement was uneven, lifted on an angle by the root of a tree, and his wheel rammed into the resulting eruption. He tried to move his pedals against it, but he could do nothing till Mom came to his aid. The sight of this filled China with unaccountable sadness.

Matt was waiting for her response. She tried to think of some new variation on expressing disappointment, but she could come up with nothing. So she said, "I wasn't really talking about putting together a film, Matt."

He said, "Oh."

Then there was nothing more to discuss because she knew that he would stay in New York to keep the appointment he'd fought so hard to get and she would have to fend for herself, another date broken, another wrench thrown in the works of the great Life Plan.

She said, "Well, good luck with your meeting."

He said, "We'll talk. All week. All right? You okay with this, China?"

"What choice do I have?" she asked him and said goodbye.

She hated herself for ending their conversation like that, but she was hot, miserable, dispirited, depressed . . . Call it what you wanted to call it. In any event, she had nothing more to give.

She loathed the part of herself that was unsure of the future, and most of the time she could keep that side of her character subdued. When it got away from her and gained dominance in her life like an overconfident guide into chaos, it never led to anything good. It reduced her to adhering to a belief in the importance of the sort of womanhood she had long detested, one defined by having a man at any cost, lassoing him into marriage, and plugging up his life with babies ASAP. She would not go there, she told herself repeatedly. But a fraction of her wanted it anyway.

This led her to asking questions, making demands, and turning her attention to an *us* instead of keeping it focused on a *me.* When that occurred, what flared up between her and the man in question—who had always been Matt—was a replay of the debate they'd been having for five years now. This was a circular polemic on the subject of marriage that had so far achieved the same result: his obvious reluctance—as if she actually *needed* to see it and hear it—followed by her furious recriminations, which were then followed by a break-up initiated by whoever felt most exasperated with the differences that cropped up between them.

Those same differences kept bringing them back together, though. For they charged the relationship with an undeniable excitement that so far neither one of them had found with anyone else. He had

probably tried. China knew that. But she had not.
She didn't need to. She'd known for years that
Matthew Whitecomb was right for her.

China had arrived at this conclusion yet again by
the time she reached her bungalow: one thousand
square feet of 1920 architecture that had once served
as the weekend getaway of an Angeleno. It sat
among other similar cottages on a street lined with
palm trees, close enough to the beach to reap the
benefit of the ocean breeze, far enough from the water to be affordable.

It was definitely humble, comprising five small
rooms—if you counted the bathroom—and only
nine windows, with a wide front porch and a rectangle of lawn in the front and the back. A picket
fence fronted the property, shedding flakes of white
paint into the flowerbeds and onto the sidewalk, and
it was to the gate in this fence that China lumbered
with her photography equipment once she ended
her conversation with Matt.

The heat beat down, only less marginally intense
than it had been on the hillside, but the wind wasn't
as fierce. The palm fronds rattled like old bones in
the trees, and where lavender lantana grew against
the front fence, it hung listlessly in the bright sunlight, with flowers like purple asterisks, growing out
of ground that was thoroughly parched this afternoon, as if it hadn't been watered this morning.

China lifted the lopsided gate and swung it open,
her camera cases weighting down her shoulder and
her intention to head for the garden hose and drag it
over to soak the poor flowers. But she forgot this in-

tention in the sight that greeted her: A man, naked down to his Skivvies, was lying on his stomach in the middle of her lawn with his head pillowed on what appeared to be the ball of his blue jeans and a faded yellow T-shirt. No shoes were in evidence, and the soles of his feet were black beyond black and so calloused at the heels that the skin was canyoned. If his ankles and elbows were anything to go by, he appeared to be someone who eschewed bathing, too. But not eating or exercising, since he was well built without being fat. And not drinking, since at the moment his right hand clutched a sweating bottle of Pellegrino.

Her Pellegrino by the look of it. The water she'd been looking forward to downing.

He turned over lazily and squinted up at her, resting on his dirty elbows. "Your security sucks the big one, Chine." He took a long swig from the bottle.

China glanced at the porch where the screen door hung open and the front door gaped wide. "God damn it," she cried. "Did you break into my house again?"

Her brother sat up and shaded his eyes. "What the hell are you dressed like that for? Ninety frigging degrees and you look like Aspen in January."

"And you look like an arrest for exposure waiting to happen. Good grief, Cherokee, show some sense. There're little girls in this neighbourhood. One of them walks by and sees you like that, you'll have a squad car here in fifteen minutes." She frowned. "D'you have sunblock on?"

"Didn't answer my question," he pointed out.

"What's with the leather? Delayed rebellion?" He grinned. "If Mom got a look at those pants, she'd have a real—"

"I wear them because I like them," she cut in. "They're comfortable." And I can afford them, she thought. Which was more than half the reason: owning something lush and useless in Southern California because she *wanted* to own it, after a childhood and adolescence spent trolling the racks in Goodwill for clothes that simultaneously fit, were not completely hideous, and—for the benefit of her mother's beliefs—had no scrap of animal skin anywhere on them.

"Oh sure." He scrambled to his feet as she passed him and went onto the porch. "Leather in the middle of a Santa Ana. Real comfortable. That makes sense."

"That's my last bottle of Pellegrino." She dropped her camera cases just inside the front door. "I was looking forward to it all the way home."

"From where?" When she told him, he chuckled. "Oh, I get it. Doing a shoot for an *architect*. Loaded and at loose ends? I hope so. Available also? This is cool. Well, let me see how you look, then." He upended the bottle of water into his mouth and examined her while he did so. When he was sated, he handed the bottle to her and said, "You can have the rest. Your hair looks like crap. Whyn't you stop bleaching it? Not good for you. Sure not good for the water table, all those chemicals going down the drain."

"As if you care about the water table."

"I've got my standards."

"One of which obviously isn't waiting for people to get home before you raid their houses."

"You're lucky it was only me," he said. "It's pretty dumb to go off and leave the windows open. Your screens are complete shit. A pocket knife. That's all it took."

China saw her brother's means of access into her house since, in Cherokee's typical fashion, he'd done nothing to hide how he'd managed to enter. One of the two living room windows was without its old screen, which had been easy enough for Cherokee to remove since only a metal hook and eye had held it in place against the sill. At least her brother had had enough sense to break in through a window that was off the street and out of sight of the neighbours, any one of whom would have willingly called the police.

She went through to the kitchen, the bottle of Pellegrino in her hand. She poured what was left of the mineral water into a glass with a wedge of lime. She swirled it round, drank it down, and put the glass in the sink, unsatisfied and annoyed.

"What're you doing here?" she asked her brother. "How'd you get up here? Did you fix your car?"

"That piece of crap?" He padded across the linoleum to the refrigerator, pulled it open, and browsed through the plastic bags of fruit and vegetables inside. He emerged with a red bell pepper, which he took to the sink and meticulously washed off before scoring a knife from a drawer and slicing the pepper in half. He cleaned both halves and handed one of

them to China. "I've got some things going so I won't
need a car anyway."

China ignored the hook implied in his final remark. She knew how her brother cast his bait. She
set her half of the red bell pepper on the kitchen
table. She went into her bedroom to change her
clothes. The leather was like wearing a sauna in this
weather. It looked terrific, but it felt like hell.
"Everyone needs a car. I hope you haven't come up
here thinking you're going to borrow mine," she
called out to him. "Because if you have, the answer
is no in advance. Ask Mom. Borrow hers. I assume
she's still got it."

"You coming down for Thanksgiving?" Cherokee called back.

"Who wants to know?"

"Guess."

"Her phone doesn't work all of a sudden?"

"I told her I was coming up. She asked me to ask
you. You coming or what?"

"I'll talk to Matt." She hung the leather trousers
in the closet, did the same with the vest, and tossed
her silk blouse into the dry-cleaning bag. She threw
on a loose Hawaiian dress and grabbed her sandals
from the shelf. She rejoined her brother.

"Where *is* Matt, anyway?" He'd finished his half
of the pepper and had started on hers.

She removed it from his hand and took a bite.
The meat was cool and sweet, a modest anodyne to
the heat and her thirst. "Away," she told him.
"Cherokee, would you put your clothes on, please?"

"Why?" He leered and thrust his pelvis at her. "Am I turning you on?"

"You're not my type."

"Away where?"

"New York. He's on business. Are you going to get dressed?"

He shrugged and left her. A moment later she heard the bang of the screen door as he went outside to retrieve the rest of his clothes. She found an un-cooled bottle of Calistoga water in the musty broom closet that served as her pantry. At least it was something sparkling, she thought. She rooted out ice and poured herself a glassful.

"You didn't ask."

She swung around. Cherokee was dressed, as requested, his T-shirt shrunk from too many washes and his blue jeans resting low on his hips. Their bottoms grazed the linoleum, and as she looked her brother over, China thought not for the first time how misplaced he was in time. With his too-long sandy curls, his scruffy clothes, his bare feet, and his demeanour, he looked like a refugee from the summer of love. Which would doubtless make their mother proud, make his father approve, and make her father laugh. But it made China . . . well, annoyed. Despite his age and his toned physique, Cherokee still looked too vulnerable to be out on his own.

"So you didn't ask me," he said.

"Ask you what?"

"What I've got going. Why I won't be needing a

car anymore. I thumbed, by the way. Hitchhiking's gone to crap, though. Took me since yesterday lunchtime to get here."

"Which is why you need a car."

"Not for what I've got in mind."

"I've already said. I'm not lending you my car. I need it for work. And why aren't you in class? Have you dropped out again?"

"Quit. I needed more free time to do the papers. *That's* taken off in a very big way. I've got to tell you, the number of conscienceless college students these days just boggles the mind, Chine. If I wanted to do this for a career, I'd probably be able to retire when I'm forty."

China rolled her eyes. *The papers* were term papers, take-home essay tests, the occasional master's thesis, and, so far, two doctoral dissertations. Cherokee wrote them for university students who had the cash and who couldn't be bothered to write the papers themselves. This had long ago raised the question of why Cherokee—who'd never received less than a B on something he'd written for payment—couldn't himself get up the steam to remain in college. He'd been in and out of the University of California so many times that the institution practically had a revolving door with his name above it. But Cherokee had a facile explanation for his exceedingly blotted college career: "If the UC system would just pay me to do my work what the students pay me to do *their* work, I'd do the work."

"Does Mom know you've dropped out again?" she asked her brother.

"I've cut the strings."

"Sure you have." China hadn't had lunch, and she was beginning to feel it. She pulled out the fixings for a salad from the refrigerator and from the cupboard took down one plate, a subtle hint that she hoped her brother would take.

"So, ask me." He dragged a chair out from the kitchen table and plopped down. He reached for one of the apples that a dyed basket held in the centre of the table and he had it all the way to his mouth before he seemed to realise it was artificial.

She unwrapped the romaine and began to tear it onto her plate. "Ask you what?"

"You know. You're avoiding the question. Okay. I'll ask it for you. 'What's the big plan, Cherokee? What've you got going? Why won't you be needing a car?' The answer: because I'm getting a boat. And the boat's going to provide it all. Transportation, income, and housing."

"You just keep thinking, Butch," China murmured, more to herself than to him. In so many ways Cherokee had lived his thirty-three years like that Wild West outlaw: There was always a scheme to get rich quick, have something for nothing, and live the good life.

"No," he said. "Listen. This is sure-fire. I've already found the boat. It's down in Newport. It's a fishing boat. Right now it takes people out from the harbour. Big bucks a pop. They go after bonita. Mostly it's day trips, but for bigger bucks—and I'm talking significant big ones here—they go down to Baja. It needs some work but I'd live on the boat while I fixed it up. Buy what I need at marine chandleries—don't need a car for that—and I'd take people out year-round."

"What d'you know about fishing? What d'you know about boating? And where're you getting the money, anyway?" China chopped off part of a cucumber and began slicing it onto the romaine. She considered her question in conjunction with her brother's propitious arrival on her doorstep and said, "Cherokee, don't even go there."

"Hey. What d'you think I am? I said that I've got something going, and I do. Hell. I thought you'd be happy for me. I didn't even ask Mom for the money."

"Not that she has it."

"She's got the house. I could've asked her to sign it over to me so I could get a second on it and raise the money that way. She would've gone for it. You know she would."

There was truth in that, China thought. When hadn't she gone for one of Cherokee's schemes? *He's asthmatic* had been her excuse in childhood. It had simply mutated through the years to *he's a man*.

That left China herself as the choice of a source. She said, "Don't think of me, either, okay? What I've got goes to me, to Matt, and to the future."

"As if." Cherokee pushed away from the table. He walked to the kitchen door and opened it, resting his hands on the frame and looking out into the sun-parched back yard.

"As if what?"

"Forget it."

China washed two tomatoes and began to chop them. She cast a glance at her brother and saw that he was frowning and chewing on the inside of his lower lip. She could read Cherokee River like a billboard at fifty yards: There were machinations going on in his mind.

"I've got money saved," he said. "Sure, it's not enough but I've got a chance to make a little bundle that'll help me out."

"And you're saying that you haven't hitchhiked all the way up here to ask me to make a contribution? You spent twenty-four hours on the side of the road in order to make a social call? To tell me your plans? To ask me if I'm going to Mom's for Thanksgiving? This isn't exactly computing, you know. There're telephones. E-mail. Telegrams. Smoke signals."

He turned from the doorway and watched her brushing the dirt from four mushrooms. "Actually," he finally said, "I've got two free tickets to go to Europe and I thought my little sister might like to tag along. That's why I'm here. To ask you to go. You've never been, have you? Call it an early Christmas present."

China lowered her knife. "Where the hell did you get two free tickets to Europe?"

"Courier service."

He went on to explain. Couriers, he said, transported materials from the United States to points around the globe when the sender didn't trust the post office, Federal Express, UPS, or any other carrier to get them to their destination on time, safely, or undamaged. Corporations or individuals provided a prospective traveler with the ticket he needed to get to a destination—sometimes with a fee as well—and once the package was placed into the hands of the recipient, the courier was free to enjoy the destination or to travel onward from there.

In Cherokee's case, he'd seen a posting on a notice board at UC Irvine from someone—"Turned out to be an attorney in Tustin"—looking for a courier to take a package to the UK in return for payment and two free airline tickets. Cherokee applied, and he was selected, with the proviso that he "dress more businesslike and do something about the hair."

"Five thousand bucks to make the delivery," Cherokee concluded happily. "Is this a good deal or what?"

"What the *hell*? Five thousand dollars?" In China's experience, things that seemed too good to be true generally were. "Wait a minute, Cherokee. What's in the package?"

"Architectural plans. That's one of the reasons I thought of you right off for the second ticket. Architecture. It's right up your alley." Cherokee returned to the table, swung the chair around this time, and straddled it backwards.

"So why doesn't the architect take the plans over himself? Why doesn't he send them on the Internet? There's a program for that, and if no one has it at the other end, why doesn't he send the plans over on a disk?"

"Who knows? Who cares? Five thousand bucks

and a free ticket? They can send their plans by row-boat if they want to."

China shook her head and went back to her salad. "It sounds way fishy. You're on your own."

"Hey. This is *Europe* we're talking about. Big Ben. The Eiffel Tower. The frigging Colosseum."

"You'll have a great time. If you're not arrested at customs with heroin."

"I'm telling you this is completely legit."

"Five thousand dollars just to carry a package? I don't think so."

"Come on, China. You've *got* to go."

There was something in his voice when he said that, an edge that tried to wear the guise of eagerness but tilted too closely to desperation. China said warily, "What's going on? You'd better tell me."

Cherokee picked at the vinyl cord around the top of the seatback. He said, "The deal is . . . I have to take my wife."

"What?"

"I mean the courier. The tickets. They're for a couple. I didn't know that at first but when the at-torney asked me if I was married, I could tell he wanted a yes answer so I gave him one."

"Why?"

"What difference does it make? How's anyone going to know? We have the same last name. We don't look alike. We can just pretend—"

"I mean why does a couple have to take the pack-age over? A couple wearing business clothes? A couple that've done 'something to their hair'? Some-thing to make them look innocuous, legitimate, and above suspicion? Good grief, Cherokee. Get some brains. This is a smuggling scam and you'll end up in jail."

"Don't be so paranoid. I've checked it out. This is an attorney we're talking about."

"Oh, *that* gives me buckets of confidence." She lined the circumference of her plate with baby carrots and tossed a handful of pepitas on top. She sprinkled the salad with lemon juice and carried the plate to the table. "I'm not going for it. You'll need to find someone else to play Mrs. River."

"There *is* no one else. And even if I could find someone that fast, the ticket has to say River and the passport has to match the ticket and . . . Come *on*, China." He sounded like a little boy, frustrated because a plan that had seemed so simple to him, so easily set up with a trip to Santa Barbara, was proving to be otherwise. And that was one hundred percent Cherokee: I've got an idea and surely the world will go along with it.

But China wouldn't. She loved her brother. Indeed, despite the fact that he was older than she, she'd spent part of her adolescence and most of her childhood mothering him. But regardless of her devotion to Cherokee, she wasn't going to accommodate him in a scheme that might well raise easy money at the same time as it put both of them at risk.

"No way," she told him. "Forget it. Get a job. You've got to join the real world sometime."

"That's what I'm trying to do here."

"Then get a *regular* job. You'll have to eventually. It might as well be now."

"Oh, great." He surged up from his chair. "That's really *terrifically* great, China. Get a regular job. Join the real world. So I'm trying to do that. I have an idea for a job and a home and money all at once, but that's apparently not good enough for you. It has to be the real world and a job on exactly your terms." He strode to the door and flung himself out into the yard.

China followed him. A birdbath stood in the centre of the thirsty lawn, and Cherokee dumped out its water, took up a wire brush at its base, and furiously attacked the ridged basin, scrubbing away its film of algae. He marched to the house, where a hose lay coiled, and turned it on, tugging it over to refill the basin for the birds.

"Look," China began.

"Forget it," he said. "It sounds stupid to you. I sound stupid to you."

"Did I say that?"

"I don't want to live like the rest of the world— eight-to-five working for the man and a lousy pay-check—but you don't approve of that. You think there's only one way to live and if anyone has a different idea, it's bullshit, stupid, and liable to end them up in jail."

"Where's all this coming from?"

"What I'm *supposed* to do, according to you, is work for peanuts, save the peanuts, and put enough of the peanuts together so I can end up married with a mortgage and kids and a wife who will maybe be *more* of a wife and a mother than Mom was to anyone. But that's *your* life plan, okay? It isn't mine." He flung the burbling hose to the ground, where water flowed onto the dusty lawn.

"This has nothing to do with anyone's life plan. It's basic sense. Look at what you're proposing, for God's sake. Look at what's been proposed to you."

"Money," he said. "Five thousand dollars. Five thousand dollars that I God damn need."

"So you can buy a boat you know nothing about running? To take people out fishing God only knows where? Think things through for once, okay? If not the boat then at least the courier idea."

"Me?" He barked a laugh. "I should think things through? Just when the hell're *you* going to do that?"

"Me? What—"

"It's really amazing. You can tell me how to live my life while yours is a running joke and you don't even know it. And here *I* am, giving you a decent chance to get out of it for the first time in what . . . ten years? more? . . . and all you—"

"What? Get out of what?"

"—can do is put *me* down. Because you don't like the way I live. And you won't see the way you live is worse."

"What do you know about the way I live?" She felt her own anger now. She *hated* the way her brother turned conversations. If you wanted to have a discussion with him about the choices he'd made or wanted to make, he invariably turned the spotlight onto you. That spotlight always became an attack in which only the nimble-footed could emerge unscathed. "I haven't seen you for months. You show up here, break into my house, tell me you need my help in some shady deal, and when I don't cooperate the way you expect me to, suddenly everything becomes *my* fault. But I'm not going to play that game."

"Sure. You'd rather play the one Matt's got going."

"What's that supposed to mean?" China demanded. But at the mention of Matt, she couldn't help it: She felt the skeletal finger of fear touch her spine.

"God, China. You think *I'm* stupid. But when the hell're *you* going to figure things out?"

"Figure what things? What are you talking about?"

"All this about Matt. Living for Matt. Saving your money 'for me and Matt and the future.' It's ludicrous. No. It's sure-as-hell pathetic. You're standing right in front of me with your head so far up your butt that you haven't figured out—" He stopped himself. It seemed as if he suddenly remembered where he was, with whom he was, and what had gone before to bring them both to this place. He stooped and grabbed up the hose, carrying it back to the house and turning the water off. He coiled the hose back to the ground with too much precision.

China watched him. It seemed to her suddenly that all that was her life—her past and her future— was reduced by fire to this single moment. Knowing and not, simultaneously.

"What do you know about Matt?" she asked her brother.

Part of the answer she knew already. For the three of them had been teenagers together in the same ramshackle neighbourhood in a town called Orange where Matt was a surfer, Cherokee his acolyte, and China a shadow cast by both. But part of the answer she had never known because it had been hidden in the hours and the days that the two boys had gone alone to ride the waves in Huntington Beach.

"Forget it." Cherokee moved past her and returned to the house.

She followed him. But he didn't stop in the kitchen or the living room. Instead, he walked straight through, swung the screen door open, and stepped onto the warped front porch. There he stopped, squinting out at the bright dry street where the sun beat down on the cars parked there and a gust of wind *whoosh*ed dead leaves against the pavement.

"You'd better tell me where you're heading with this," China said. "You started something. You might as well finish it."

"Forget it," he said.

"You said pathetic. You said ludicrous. You said a game."

"It slipped out," he said. "I was pissed off."

"You talk to Matt, don't you? You must still see him when he visits his parents. What do you know, Cherokee? Is he . . ." She didn't know if she could actually say it, so reluctant was she in truth to know. But there were his lengthy absences, his trips to

New York, the cancellation of their plans together. There was the fact that he lived in LA when he wasn't traveling and there were all the times when he was at home but still too busy with his work to make a weekend with her. She'd told herself all this meant nothing, placed in the scales against which she measured their years together. But her doubts had grown, and now they stood before her, asking to be embraced or obliterated.

"Does Matt have another woman?" she asked her brother.

He blew out a breath and shook his head. But it didn't seem so much a reply to her question as it was a reaction to her having asked it in the first place.

"Fifty bucks and a surfboard," he said to his sister. "That's what I asked for. I gave the product a good guarantee—just be nice to her, I said, she'll cooperate with you—so he was willing to pay."

China heard the words but for a moment her mind refused to assimilate them. Then she remembered the surfboard all those years ago: Cherokee bringing it home and his triumphant crow, "Matt *gave* it to me!" And she remembered what followed: seventeen years old, never had a date much less been kissed or touched or the rest and Matthew Whitecomb—tall and shy, good with a surfboard but at a loss with girls—coming by the house and stammering an embarrassed request for a date except it wasn't embarrassment at all, was it, that first time, but rather the sweaty-palmed anticipation of collecting what he'd paid her brother to possess.

"You *sold*—" She couldn't complete the sentence.

Cherokee turned to look at her. "He likes to fuck you, China. That's what it is. That's all it is. End of story."

"I don't believe you." But her mouth was dry, drier than her skin felt in the heat and the wind that came off the desert, drier even than the cracked scorched earth where the flowers wilted and the rain worms hid.

She felt behind her for the rusty knob of the old screen door. She went into the house. She heard her brother following, his feet shuffling sorrowfully in her wake.

"I didn't want to tell you," he said. "I'm sorry. I never meant to tell you."

"Get out," she replied. "Just go. *Go.*"

"You know I'm telling you the truth, don't you? You can feel it because you've felt the rest: that something's not right between you and hasn't been for a while."

"I don't know anything of the sort," she told him.

"Yeah, you do. It's better to know. You can cut him loose now." He came up behind her and put his hand—so tentative a gesture, it seemed—on her shoulder. "Come with me to Europe, China," he said quietly. "It'll be a good place to start forgetting."

She shook his hand off and turned to face him. "I wouldn't even step out of this house with you."

December 5
6:30 A.M.

ISLAND OF GUERNSEY
ENGLISH CHANNEL

Ruth Brouard woke with a start. Something in the house wasn't right. She lay motionless and attended to the darkness as she'd learned to do all those years ago, waiting for the sound to repeat so as to know whether she was safe in her hiding place or whether she should flee. What the noise had been she couldn't have said in this moment of strained listening. But it hadn't been part of the nighttime noises she was used to hearing—the creak of the house, the rattle of a window in its frame, the soughing of wind, the call of a gull roused out of its sleep—so her pulse quickened as she worried her ears and forced her eyes to discriminate among the objects in her room, testing each one out, comparing its position in the gloom with where it stood in daylight, when neither ghosts nor intruders would dare disturb the peace of the old manor house in which she lived.

She heard nothing more, so she ascribed her sudden waking to a dream she couldn't remember. Her jangled nerves she ascribed to imagination. That and the medication she was taking, the strongest painkiller her doctor would give her that wasn't the morphine her body needed.

She grunted in her bed, feeling a bud of pain that flowered from her shoulders and down her arms. Doctors, she thought, were modern-day warriors. They were trained to battle the enemy within till the last corpuscle gave up the ghost. They were programmed to do that, and she was grateful for it. But there were times when the patient knew better than the surgeon, and she understood she'd arrived at one of those times. Six months, she thought. Two weeks until her sixty-sixth birthday, but she'd never see her sixty-seventh. The devil had made it from her breasts to her bones, after a twenty-year respite during which she'd got sanguine.

She shifted her position from her back to her side, and her gaze fell on the red digital numbers of the clock at her bedside. It was later than she'd thought. The time of year had utterly beguiled her. She'd assumed from the darkness that it was two or three in the morning, but it was half past six, only an hour from her usual time of rising.

From the room next to hers, she heard a sound. But this time it wasn't a noise out of place, born of dream or imagination. Rather, it was the movement of wood upon wood as a wardrobe door was opened and closed and a drawer in the chest was handled likewise. Something thudded quietly on the floor, and Ruth pictured the trainers accidentally falling from his hands in his haste to get them on.

He would already have gyrated his way into his bathing suit—that insignificant triangle of azure

Lycra that she thought so unsuitable for a man of his age—and his track suit would be covering it for now. All that remained of his bedroom preparations were the shoes he would wear on his walk to the bay, and those he was putting on at the moment. A creak of the rocking chair told Ruth that.

She smiled as she listened to her brother's movements. Guy was as predictable as the seasons. He'd said last night that he intended to swim in the morning, so swim he would, as he did every day: tramping across the grounds to gain access to the outer lane and then fast-walking down to the beach to warm up, alone on the narrow switchback road that carved a tunneled zigzag beneath the trees. It was her brother's ability to adhere to his plans and to make them successful that Ruth admired more than anything else about him.

She heard his bedroom door closing. She knew exactly what would come next: Through the darkness, he'd feel his way to the airing cupboard and pull out a towel to take with him. That procedure would take ten seconds, after which he'd use up five minutes to locate his swimming goggles, which he'd have placed yesterday morning in the knife box or draped over the canterbury in his study or shoved without thought into that corner dresser that listed against the wall in the breakfast room. With the goggles in his possession, he'd be off to the kitchen to brew his tea, and when he had it in hand—because he always took it with him for afterwards, his steaming ginkgo-and-green reward for another successful dip into water too cold for ordinary mortals—he'd be out of the house and striding across the lawn towards the chestnuts, beyond them the drive and beyond that the wall that defined the edge of the property. Ruth smiled at her brother's predictability. It was not only what she loved best about him; it was also what had long given her life a sense of security that by rights it shouldn't have had.

She watched the numbers on her digital clock change as the minutes passed and her brother made his preparations. Now he would be at the airing cupboard, now descending the stairs, now rustling round for those goggles and cursing the lapses of memory that were becoming more frequent as he approached seventy. Now he would be in the kitchen, she thought, perhaps even sneaking a pre-swim snack.

At the point at which Guy's morning ritual would be taking him out of the house, Ruth rose from bed and wrapped her dressing gown round her shoulders. She padded to the window on bare feet and pulled aside the heavy curtains. She counted down from twenty, and when she hit five, there he was below her, coming out of the house, dependable as the hours of the day, as the December wind and the salt it blew off the English Channel.

He was wearing what he always wore: a red knitted cap pulled low on his forehead to cover his ears and his thick greying hair; the navy running suit stained at the elbows, the cuffs, and the thighs with the white paint he'd used on the conservatory last summer; trainers without socks—although she couldn't see that, merely knew her brother and how he dressed. He carried his tea. He had a towel slung round his neck. The goggles, she guessed, would be in a pocket.

"Have a good swim," she said into the icy window pane. And she added what he'd always said to her, what their mother had cried out long ago as the fishing boat pulled away from the dock, taking them from home in the pitch-black night, *"Au revoir et adieu, mes chéris."*

Below her, he did what he always did. He crossed the lawn and headed for the trees and the drive beyond them.

But this morning, Ruth saw something else as well. Once Guy reached the elms, a shadowy figure melted out from beneath them and began to follow her brother.

Ahead of him, Guy Brouard saw that the lights were already on in the Duffys' cottage, a snug stone structure that was, in part, built into the boundary wall of the estate. Once the collection point for rent from tenants of the privateer who'd first built *Le Reposoir* in the early eighteenth century, the steep-roofed cottage now served to house the couple who helped Guy and his sister maintain the property: Kevin Duffy on the grounds and his wife, Valerie, inside the manor house.

The cottage lights indicated that Valerie was up seeing to Kevin's breakfast. That would be exactly like her: Valerie Duffy was a wife beyond compare. Guy had long thought that the mould had been broken after Valerie Duffy's creation. She was the last of a breed, a wife from the past who saw it as her job and her privilege to take care of her man. If Guy himself had had that sort of wife from the first, he knew he wouldn't have had to spend a lifetime sampling the possibilities out there in the hope of finally finding her.

His own two wives had been true to tedious type. One child with the first, two children with the second, good homes, nice cars, fine holidays in the sun, nannies, and boarding schools . . . It hadn't mattered: You work too much. You're *never* at home. You love your miserable *job* more than me. It was an endless variation on a deadly theme. No wonder he'd not been able to keep himself from straying.

Out from beneath the bare-branched elms, Guy followed the drive in the direction of the lane. It was quiet still, but as he reached the iron gates and swung one of them open, the first warblers stirred from within the bramble, the blackthorn, and the ivy that grew along the narrow road and clung to the lichened stone wall that edged it.

It was cold. December. What could one expect? But as it was early, there was still no wind, although a rare southeast promised for later that day would make swimming impossible after noon. Not that anyone other than he would likely be swimming in December. That was one of the advantages of having a high tolerance for cold: One had the water all to oneself.

That was how Guy Brouard preferred it. For swimming time was thinking time, and he generally had much to think about.

Today was no different. The wall of the estate to his right, the tall hedgerows of the surrounding farmland to his left, he strode along the lane in the dim morning light, heading for the turn that would take him down the steep hillside to the bay. He considered what he had wrought in his life in the past few months, some of it deliberately and with plenty of forethought, some of it as a consequence of events no one could have anticipated. He'd engendered disappointment, confusion, and betrayal among his closest associates. And because he'd long been a man who kept his own counsel in matters closest to his heart, none of them had been able to comprehend— let alone to digest—the fact that their expectations of him had been so wildly off the mark. For nearly a decade he'd encouraged them to think of Guy Brouard as a permanent benefactor, paternal in his concern for their futures, profligate in the manner in which he assured those futures were secure. He hadn't meant to mislead any of them with this. To the contrary, he'd all along fully intended to make everyone's secret dream come true.

But all that had been before Ruth: that grimace of pain when she thought he wasn't looking and what he knew that grimace meant. He wouldn't have realised, of course, had she not started slipping away for appointments she called "opportunities for exercise, *frère*" along the cliffs. At Icart Point, she said, she was taking inspiration for a future needlepoint from the crystals of feldspar in the flaky gneiss. At Jerbourg, she reported, the patterns of schist in the stone formed unequal grey bands that one could follow, tracing the route that time and nature used to lay silt and sediment into ancient stone. She sketched the gorse, she said, and she described with her pencils the thrift and sea-campion in pink and white. She picked ox-eye daisies, arranged them on the ragged surface of a granite outcrop, and made a drawing of them. She clipped bluebells and broom, heather and gorse, wild daffodils and lilies as she went along, depending on the season and her inclination. But the flowers never quite made it home. "Too long on the car seat, I had to throw them out," she'd claim. "Wild flowers never last when you pick them."

Month after month, this had gone on. But Ruth wasn't a walker of cliffs. Nor was she a picker of flowers or a student of geology. So all of this made Guy naturally suspicious.

He'd foolishly thought at first that his sister finally had a man in her life and was embarrassed to tell him so. The sight of her car at Princess Elizabeth Hospital had brought him round, however. That in conjunction with her grimaces of pain and her lengthy retreats to her bedroom had forced him to realise what he didn't want to face.

She had been the only constant in his life from the night they'd set off from the coast of France, making good an escape left far too late, on a fishing boat, hidden among the nets. She'd been the reason he himself had survived, her need for him a spur to maturity, to laying plans, and to ultimate success.

But this? He could do nothing about this. From this that his sister suffered now, there would be no fishing boat in the night.

So if he had betrayed, confused, and disappointed the others, it was nothing in light of losing Ruth.

Swimming was his morning release from the overwhelming anxiety of these considerations. Without his daily swim in the bay, Guy knew that the thought of his sister, not to mention his absolute impotence to change what was happening to his sister, would consume him.

The road he was on was steep and narrow, thickly wooded on this east side of the island. The rarity of any harsh wind from France had long allowed the trees to prosper here. Where Guy walked beneath them, the sycamores and chestnuts, ash and beech, made a skeletal arc that was grey etched on pewter in the pre-dawn sky. The trees rose on sheer hillsides held back by stone walls. At the base of these, water flowed eagerly from an inland spring, chirping against stones as it raced to the sea.

The way switched back and forth on itself, past a shadowy water mill and a misplaced Swiss chalet hotel that was closed for the season. It ended in a minuscule car park, where a snack bar the size of a misanthrope's heart was boarded and locked, and the granite slipway once used to give horses and carts access to the *vraic* that was the island's fertiliser was slick with seaweed.

The air was still, the gulls unroused from their nighttime cliff-top resting places. In the bay the water was tranquil, an ashen mirror reflecting the colour of the lightening sky. There were no waves in this deeply sheltered place, just a gentle slapping of water on pebbles, a touch that seemed to release from the seaweed the constrasting sharp odours of burgeoning life and decay.

Near the life ring that hung from a spike long ago driven into the cliffside, Guy set down his towel and placed his tea on a flat-surfaced stone. He kicked off his shoes and removed his track suit's trousers. He reached into his jacket pocket for his swimming goggles.

His hand came into contact with more than just the goggles, however. Inside his pocket was an object that he took out and held in the palm of his hand.

It was wrapped in white linen. He unfolded this and brought forth a circular stone. It was pierced in the middle in the fashion of a wheel, for a wheel was what it was supposed to be: *énne rouelle dé faïtot*. A fairy's wheel.

Guy smiled at the charm, at the memory it evoked. The island was a place of folklore. To those born and bred here, of parents and grandparents born and bred here, carrying the occasional talisman against witches and their familiars was something that might be scoffed at publicly but not so lightly dismissed privately. *You ought to carry one of these, you know. Protection's important, Guy.*

Yet the stone—fairy wheel or not—had not been nearly enough to protect him in the single way he'd thought he was protected. The unexpected still occurred in everyone's life, so he could not rightfully call himself surprised when the unexpected had occurred in his.

He wrapped the stone back in its linen and returned it to his pocket. Shrugging out of his jacket, he removed his knitted cap and stretched the goggles round his head. He picked his way across the narrow beach and without hesitation, he entered the water.

It came at him like a knife's blade. In the midst of summer the Channel was no tropical bath. In the tenebrous morning of fast-approaching winter, it felt glacial, dangerous, and forbidding.

But he didn't think of that. Instead, he moved resolutely forward and as soon as he had enough depth to make it safe to do so, he pushed off from the bottom and began to swim. He dodged patches of seaweed in the water, moving fast.

In this manner, he swam a hundred yards out, to the toad-shaped granite outcropping that marked the point where the bay met the English Channel. Here he stopped, right at the toad's eye, a creation of guano collected in a shallow recess of the stone. He turned back to the beach and began to tread water, the best way he knew to keep in shape for the coming ski season in Austria. As was his habit, he removed his goggles to clear his view for a few minutes. He idly inspected the cliffs in the distance and the heavy foliage that covered them. Through this means, his gaze traveled downward on an uneven, boulder-strewn journey to the beach.

He lost count of his kicks.

Someone was there. A figure, mostly in shadow but obviously watching him, stood on the beach. To one side of the granite slipway, it wore dark clothing with a flash of white at the neck, which was what must have caught his attention in the first place. As Guy squinted to bring the figure into better focus, it stepped away from the granite and moved across the beach.

There was no mistaking its destination. The figure glided over to his discarded clothes and knelt among them to pick up something: the jacket or the trousers, it was difficult to tell at this distance.

But Guy could guess what the figure was after, and he cursed. He realised that he should have emptied his pockets before setting out from the house. No ordinary thief, of course, would have been interested in the small pierced stone that Guy Brouard habitually carried. But no ordinary thief would ever have anticipated finding a swimmer's belongings in the first place, unguarded on the beach so early on a December morning. Whoever it was knew who was swimming in the bay. Whoever it was either sought the stone or fingered through his clothing as a feint devised to get Guy back to shore.

Well, damn it, he thought. This was *his* time in solitude. He didn't intend to get into it with anyone. What was important to him now was only his sister and how his sister would meet her end.

He resumed swimming. He traversed the width of the bay twice. When at last he looked to the beach another time, he was pleased to see that whoever had encroached on his peace was gone.

He swam to shore and arrived there breathless, having covered nearly twice the distance that he usually covered in the morning. He staggered out and hurried over to his towel, his body a mass of chicken flesh.

The tea promised quick relief from the cold, and

he poured himself a cup from his Thermos. It was strong and bitter and most especially hot, and he gulped down all of it before whipping off his swim suit and pouring himself another. This he drank more slowly as he toweled himself off, rubbing his skin vigorously to restore some heat to his limbs. He put his trousers on and grabbed his jacket. He slung it round his shoulders as he sat on a rock to dry his feet. Only after he'd donned his trainers did he put his hand in his pocket. The stone was still there.

He thought about this. He thought about what he had seen from the water. He craned his neck and searched the cliffside behind him. Nothing stirred anywhere, that he could see.

He wondered then if he'd been mistaken about what he'd assumed was on the beach. Perhaps it had not been a real person at all but, rather, a manifestation of something going on in his conscience. Guilt given flesh, for example.

He brought out the stone. He unwrapped it once more and with his thumb traced the shallow initials carved into it.

Everyone needs protection, he thought. The tricky part was knowing from whom or what.

He tossed back the rest of his tea and poured himself another cup. Full sunrise was less than an hour off. He would wait for it right here this morning.

December 15
11:15 P.M.

LONDON

Chapter 1

THERE WAS THE WEATHER to talk about. That was a blessing. A week of rain that had hardly ceased for more than an hour *was* something to remark upon, even by dreary December standards. Added to the previous month's precipitation, the fact that most of Somerset, Dorset, East Anglia, Kent, and Norfolk were under water—not to mention three-quarters of the cities of York, Shrewsbury, and Ipswich—made avoiding a post mortem of a Soho gallery's opening exhibit of black-and-white photography practically de rigueur. One couldn't entertain a discussion about the small handful of friends and relatives who had comprised the opening's meagre turnout when people outside of London were homeless, animals were displaced by the thousands, and property was destroyed. Not dwelling upon the natural disaster seemed nothing short of inhuman.

At least, that was what Simon St. James kept telling himself.

He recognised the inherent fallacy in this line of thinking. Nonetheless, he persisted in thinking it. He heard the wind rattle the window panes, and he grabbed on to the sound like a drowning swimmer finding salvation in a half-submerged log.

"Why don't you wait for a break in the storm?" he asked his guests. "It's going to be deadly driving home." He could hear the earnestness in his voice. He hoped they put it down to his concern for their welfare and not to the rank cowardice it was. Never mind the fact that Thomas Lynley and his wife lived less than two miles northeast of Chelsea. No one should be out in this downpour.

Lynley and Helen already had their coats on, however. They were three steps short of St. James's front door. Lynley clasped their black umbrella in hand, and its condition—which was dry—told the tale of how long they'd already been gathered by the fire in the ground-floor study with St. James and his wife. At the same time, Helen's condition—plagued at eleven o'clock at night by what in her case could only euphemistically be called *morning* sickness this second month into her pregnancy—suggested a departure that was imminent, rain or not. Still, St. James thought, there was always hope.

"We've not even talked about the Fleming trial yet," he told Lynley, who'd been the Scotland Yard officer investigating that murder. "CPS got it to court quick enough. You must be pleased."

"Simon, *stop* this," Helen Lynley said quietly. But she gentled her words with a fond smile. "You can't avoid things indefinitely. Talk to her about it. It's not like you to avoid."

It was, unfortunately, *exactly* like him, and had St. James's wife heard Helen Lynley's comment, she would have been the first to make that declaration. The undercurrents of life with Deborah were treacherous. Like an inexperienced boatman in an unfamiliar river, St. James habitually steered clear of them.

He looked over his shoulder at the study. The firelight and the candles within provided the only illumination there. He should have thought to brighten the room, he realised. While the subdued lighting could have been construed as romantic in other circumstances, in these circumstances it seemed downright funereal.

But we have no corpse, he reminded himself. This isn't a death. Just a disappointment.

His wife had worked on her photographs for nearly twelve months leading up to this night. She'd accumulated a fine array of portraits taken across London: from fishmongers posing at five in the morning at Billingsgate to upmarket boozers stumbling into a Mayfair nightclub at midnight. She'd captured the cultural, ethnic, social, and economic diversity that was the capital city, and it had been her hope that her opening in a small but distinguished Little Newport Street gallery would be well enough attended to garner her a mention in one of the publications that fell into the hands of collectors looking for new artists whose work they might decide to buy. She just wanted to plant the seed of her name in people's minds, she'd said. She didn't expect to sell many pieces at first.

What she hadn't taken into account was the miserable late-autumn-verging-on-winter weather.

The November rain hadn't concerned her much. The weather was generally bad that time of year. But as it had segued relentlessly into the ceaseless downpour of December, she'd begun to voice misgivings. Maybe she ought to cancel her show till spring? Until summer, even, when people were out and about well into the night?

St. James had advised her to hold firm to her plans. The bad weather, he told her, would never last until the middle of December. It had been raining for weeks, and statistically speaking if nothing else, it couldn't go on much longer.

But it had done exactly that. Day after day, night after night, until the city parks began to resemble swamps, and mould started growing in cracks in the pavement. Trees were toppling out of the saturated ground and basements in houses close to the river were fast becoming wading pools.

Had it not been for St. James's siblings—all of whom attended with their spouses, partners, and children in tow—as well as his mother, the only attendees at his wife's gala exhibit opening would have been Deborah's father, a handful of personal friends whose loyalty appeared to supersede their prudence, and five members of the public. Many hopeful glances were cast in the direction of this latter group until it became obvious that three of them were individuals seeking only to get out of the rain while two others were looking for relief from the queue that was waiting for a table at Mr. Kong's.

St. James had attempted to put a good face on all this for his wife, as had the gallery's owner, a bloke called Hobart, who spoke Estuary English as if the letter T did not exist in his alphabet. Deborah was "No' 'o worry, darling," Hobart said. "Show will be up for a month and i' *is* quality, love. Look how many you've sold already!" To which Deborah had replied with her typical honesty, "And look how many of my husband's relatives are here, Mr. Hobart. If he'd only had more than three siblings, we'd be sold out."

There was truth in that. St. James's family had been generous and supportive. But their purchase of her pictures couldn't mean to Deborah what a stranger's purchase would have meant. "I feel like they bought because they pity me," she had confided in despair during the taxi ride home.

This was largely why the company of Thomas Lynley and his wife was so welcome to St. James at the moment. Ultimately, he was going to have to act the part of advocate to his wife's talent in the wake of the night's disaster, and he didn't yet feel equipped to do so. He knew she wasn't going to believe a word he said, no matter how much he believed his own assertions. Like so many artists, she wanted some form of outside approbation for her talent. He wasn't an outsider, so he wouldn't do. Nor would her father, who'd patted her on the shoulder and said philosophically, "Weather can't be helped, Deb," on his way up to bed. But Lynley and Helen somewhat qualified. So when he finally got round to bringing up the topic of Little Newport Street with Deborah, St. James wanted to have them there.

It wasn't to be, however. He could see that Helen was drooping with fatigue and that Lynley was determined to get his wife home. "Mind how you go, then," St. James told them now.

" 'Coragio, bully-monster,' " Lynley said with a smile.

St. James watched them as they headed up Cheyne Row through the downpour to their car. When they reached it safely, he closed the door and girded himself for the conversation awaiting him in his study.

Aside from her brief remark in the gallery to Mr. Hobart, Deborah had put up an admirably brave front until that cab ride home. She'd chatted to their friends, greeted her in-laws with exclamations of delight, and taken her old photographic mentor Mel Doxson from picture to picture to listen to his praise and to receive his astute criticism of her work. Only someone who'd known her forever—like St. James himself—would have been able to see the dull glaze of dejection in her eyes, would have noted from her quick glances to the doorway how much she had foolishly pinned her hopes on an imprimatur that was given by strangers whose opinion she wouldn't have cared a half fig for in other circumstances.

He found Deborah where he'd left her when he'd accompanied the Lynleys to the door: She stood in front of the wall on which he always kept a selection of her photographs. She was studying those that hung there, her hands clasped tightly behind her back.

"I've thrown away a year of my life," she announced. "I could have been working at a regular job, making money for once. I could have been taking wedding pictures or something. A debutante's ball. Christenings. Bar mitzvahs. Birthday parties. Ego portraits of middle-aged men and their trophy wives. What else?"

"Tourists standing with cardboard cutouts of the Royal Family?" he ventured. "That probably would've brought in a few quid had you set yourself up in front of Buckingham Palace."

"I'm *serious*, Simon," she said, and he could tell by her tone that levity on his part wasn't going to get them through the moment, nor was it going to make her see that the disappointment of one night's showing was in reality just a momentary setback.

St. James joined her at the wall and contemplated her pictures. She always let him choose his favourites from every suite she produced, and this particular grouping was among the best she'd done, in his unschooled opinion: seven black-and-white studies at dawn in Bermondsey, where dealers in everything from antiques to stolen goods were setting up their wares. He liked the timelessness of the scenes she'd captured, the sense of a London that never changed. He liked the faces and the way they were lit by street lamps and distorted by shadows. He liked the hope on one, the shrewdness on another, the wariness, the weariness, and the patience of the rest. He thought his wife was more than merely talented with her camera. He thought she was gifted in ways only very few are.

He said, "Everyone who wants to make a stab at

this sort of career begins at the bottom. Name the photographer you admire most and you'll be naming someone who started out as someone's assistant, a bloke carrying floodlights and lenses for someone who'd once done the same. It would be a fine world if success were a matter of producing fine pictures and doing nothing more than gathering accolades for them afterwards, but that's not how it is."

"I don't want accolades. That's not what this is about."

"You think you've spun your wheels on ice. One year and how many pictures later . . . ?"

"Ten thousand three hundred and twenty-two. Give or take."

"And you've ended up where you started. Yes?"

"No closer to anything. Not one step further. Not knowing if any of this . . . this kind of life . . . is even worth my time."

"So what you're saying is that the experience alone isn't good enough for you. You're telling yourself—and me, not that I believe it, mind you—that work counts only if it produces a result you've decided you want."

"That isn't it."

"Then what?"

"I need to believe, Simon."

"In what?"

"I can't take another year to dabble at this. I want to be more than Simon St. James's arty wife in her dungarees and her combat boots, carting her cameras for a lark round London. I want to make a contribution to our life. And I can't do that if I don't *believe*."

"Shouldn't you start with believing in the process, then? If you looked at every photographer whose career you've studied, wouldn't you see someone who began—"

"That's not what I mean!" She swung to face him. "I don't need to learn to believe that you start from the bottom and work your way upwards. I'm not such a fool that I think I'm supposed to have a show one night and the National Portrait Gallery demanding samples of my work the next morning. I'm not *stupid,* Simon."

"I'm not suggesting you are. I'm just trying to point out that the failure of a single showing of your pictures—*which,* for all you know, will not be a failure at all, by the way—is a measurement of nothing. It's just an experience, Deborah. No more. No less. It's how you interpret the experience that gets you into trouble."

"So we're not supposed to interpret our experiences? We're just supposed to have them and go on our way? Something ventured, nothing gained? Is that what you mean?"

"You know it isn't. You're getting upset. Which is hardly going to avail either of us—"

"*Getting* upset? I'm *already* upset. I've spent months on the street. Months in the darkroom. A fortune in supplies. I can't keep doing that without believing that there's a point to it all."

"Defined by what? Sales? Success? An article in the *Sunday Times Magazine?*"

"No! Of course not. That's not what *any* of this is about, and you know it." She pushed past him, crying, "Oh, why do I bother?" and she would have left the room, flying up the stairs and leaving him no closer to understanding the character of the demons she confronted periodically. It had always been this way between them: her passionate, unpredictable nature set against his phlegmatic constitution. The wild divergence in the way they each viewed the world was one of the qualities that made them so good together. It was also, unfortunately, one of the qualities that made them so bad as well.

"Then tell me," he said. "Deborah. *Tell* me."

She stopped in the doorway. She looked like Medea, all fury and intention, with her long hair rain-sprung round her shoulders and her eyes like metal in the firelight.

"I need to believe in myself," she said simply. It sounded as if she despaired the very effort to speak, and he understood from this how much she loathed the fact that he had failed to understand her.

"But you've got to know your work is good," he said. "How can you go to Bermondsey and capture it like this"—with a gesture towards the wall—"and not know that your work is good? Better than good. Good God, it's brilliant."

"Because knowing all that happens here," she replied. Her voice had become subdued now and her posture—so rigid a moment before—released its tension so that she seemed to sag in front of him. She pointed to her head upon the word *here* and she placed her hand beneath her left breast as she said, "But believing all that happens here. So far I've not been able to bridge the distance between the two.

And if I can't do that . . . How can I weather what I *have* to weather to do something that will prove me to myself?"

There it was, he thought. She didn't add the rest, for which he blessed her. Proving herself as a woman through childbirth had been denied his wife. She was looking for something to define who she was.

He said, "My love . . ." but had no other words. Yet those alone seemed to comprise more kindness from him than she could bear because the metal of her eyes went to liquid in an instant, and she held up a hand to prevent him from crossing the room to comfort her.

"All the time," she said, "no matter what happens, there's this voice inside me whispering that I'm deluding myself."

"Isn't that the curse of all artists? Aren't those who succeed the ones who're able to ignore their doubts?"

"But I haven't come up with a way not to listen to it. You're playing at pictures, it tells me. You're just pretending. You're wasting your time."

"How can you think you're deluding yourself when you take pictures like these?"

"You're my husband," she countered. "What else can you say?"

St. James knew there was no real way to argue against that point. As her husband, he wanted her happiness. Both of them knew that—aside from her father—he'd be the very last person to utter a word that might destroy it. He felt defeated, and she must have read that defeat on his face, because she said,

"Isn't the real proof in the pudding? You saw it for yourself. Next to no one came to see them."

They were back to that again. "That's owing to the weather."

"It *feels* like more than the weather to me."

How it did and didn't feel seemed like a fruitless direction to take, as amorphous and groundless as an idiot's logic. Always the scientist, St. James said, "Well, what result did you hope for? What would have been reasonable for your first showing in London?"

She considered this question, running her fingers along the white door-jamb as if she could read the answer there in Braille. "I don't know," she finally admitted. "I think I'm too afraid to know."

"Too afraid of what?"

"I can see my expectations were out of kilter. I know that even if I'm the next Annie Leibovitz, it's going to take time. But what if everything else about me is like my expectations? What if everything else is out of kilter as well?"

"Such as?"

"Such as: What if the joke's on me? That's what I've been asking myself all evening. What if I'm just being humoured by people? By your family. By our friends. By Mr. Hobart. What if they're accepting my pictures on suffrage? Very nice, Madam, yes, and we'll hang them in the gallery, they'll do little enough harm in the month of December, when no one's considering art shows anyway in the midst of their Christmas shopping and besides, we need *some-*

thing to cover our walls for a month and no one else is willing to exhibit. What if that's the case?"

"That's insulting to everyone. Family, friends. Everyone, Deborah. And to me as well."

The tears she'd been holding back spilled over then. She raised a fist to her mouth as if she knew fully well how childish was her reaction to her disappointment. Yet, he knew, she couldn't help herself. At the end of the day, Deborah simply was who Deborah was.

"She's a terribly sensitive little thing, isn't she, dear?" his mother had remarked once, her expression suggesting that proximity to Deborah's emotion was akin to exposure to tuberculosis.

"You see, I *need* this," Deborah said to him. "And if I'm not to have it, I want to know, because I do need something. Do you understand?"

He crossed the room to her and took her in his arms, knowing that what she wept for was only remotely connected to their dismal night in Little Newport Street. He wanted to tell her that none of it mattered, but he wouldn't lie. He wanted to take her struggle from her, but he had his own. He wanted to make their life together easier for both of them, but he had no power. So instead, he pressed her head against his shoulder.

"You have nothing to prove to me," he said into her springy copper hair.

"If only it was as easy as knowing that" was her reply.

He started to say that it was as easy as making each

day count instead of casting lines into a future neither of them could know. But he got only as far as drawing breath, when the doorbell rang long and loud, as if someone outside had fallen against it.

Deborah stepped away from him, wiping her cheeks as she looked towards the door. "Tommy and Helen must have forgotten . . . Did they leave something here?" She looked round the room.

"I don't think so."

The ringing continued, rousing the household dog from her slumber. As they went to the entry, Peach came barreling up the stairs from the kitchen, barking like the outraged badger hunter she was. Deborah scooped up the squirming dachshund.

St. James opened the door. He said, "Have you decided—" but he cut off his own words when he saw neither Thomas Lynley nor his wife.

Instead, a dark-jacketed man—his thick hair matted by the rain and his blue jeans soaked against his skin—huddled in the shadows against the iron railing at the far side of the top front step. He was squinting in the light and he said to St. James, "Are you—?" and nothing more as he looked beyond to where Deborah was standing, the dog in her arms, just behind her husband. "Thank God," he said. "I must've gotten turned around ten times. I caught the Underground at Victoria, but I went the wrong way and didn't figure it out till . . . Then the map got soaked. Then it blew away. *Then* I lost the address. But now. Thank *God* . . ."

With that, he moved fully into the light, saying

only, "Debs. What a frigging miracle. I was starting to think I'd never find you."

Debs. Deborah stepped forward, hardly daring to believe. The time and the place came back to her in a rush. As did the people from that time and that place. She set Peach on the floor and joined her husband at the door to have a better look. She said, "Simon! Good Lord. I don't believe . . ." But instead of completing her thought, she decided to see for herself what seemed real enough, no matter how unexpected it was. She reached for the man on the step and drew him inside the house. She said, "Cherokee?" Her first thought was how could it be that the brother of her old friend would come to be standing in her front doorway. Then, seeing it was true, that he was actually there, she cried, "Oh my God, Simon. It's Cherokee River."

Simon seemed nonplussed. He shut the door behind them as Peach scooted forward and sniffed their visitor's shoes. Apparently not liking what she discovered there, she backed off from him and began to bark.

Deborah said, "Hush, Peach. This is a friend."

To which remark, Simon said, "Who . . . ?" as he picked up the dog and quieted her.

"Cherokee River," Deborah repeated. "It *is* Cherokee, isn't it?" she asked the man. For although she was fairly certain it was he, nearly six years had passed since she'd last seen him, and even during the period of their acquaintance, she'd met him only half a dozen times. She didn't wait for him to reply, saying, "Come into the study. We've a fire burning. Lord, you're *soaked*. Is that a cut on your head? What are you *doing* here?" She led him to the ottoman before the fire and insisted that he remove his jacket. This might have at one time been water resistant, but that time had passed and now it shed rivulets onto the floor. Deborah tossed it on the hearth, where Peach went to investigate.

Simon said reflectively, "Cherokee River?"

"China's brother," Deborah said in reply.

Simon looked at the man, who'd begun to shiver. "From California?"

"Yes. China. From Santa Barbara. Cherokee, what on earth . . . ? Here. *Do* sit down. Please sit by the fire. Simon, is there a blanket . . . ? A towel . . . ?"

"I'll fetch them."

"Do hurry!" Deborah cried, for stripped of his jacket Cherokee had begun to shake like a man who was bordering on convulsions. His skin was so white that it was cast with blue, and his teeth had bitten a tear in his lip that was starting to ooze blood onto his chin. This was in addition to a nasty-looking cut on his temple, which Deborah examined, saying, "This needs a plaster. What's *happened* to you, Cherokee? You've not been mugged?" Then, "No. Don't answer. Let me get you something to warm you up first."

She hurried to the old drinks trolley that sat beneath the window overlooking Cheyne Row.

There, she poured a stiff glass of brandy, which she took to Cherokee and pressed upon him.

Cherokee raised the glass to his mouth, but his hands were shaking so badly that the glass merely chattered against his teeth and most of the brandy spilled down the front of his black T-shirt, which was wet like the rest of him. He said, "Shit. Sorry, Debs." Either his voice, his condition, or the spilling of the drink seemed to disconcert Peach, for the little dog left off sniffing Cherokee's drenched jacket and began to bark at him again.

Deborah hushed the dachshund, who wouldn't be still till she'd hauled her from the room and sent her to the kitchen. "She thinks she's a Doberman," Deborah said wryly. "No one's ankles are safe around her."

Cherokee chuckled. Then a tremendous shudder took his body, and the brandy he was holding sloshed round inside the glass. Deborah joined him on the ottoman and put her arm round his shoulders. "Sorry," he said again. "I got really freaked out."

"Don't apologise. Please."

"I've been wandering around in the rain. Smacked into a tree branch over near the river. I thought the bleeding stopped."

"Drink the brandy," Deborah said. She was relieved to hear that he'd not fallen into some sort of trouble on the street. "Then I'll see to your head."

"Is it bad?"

"Just a cut. But it does need seeing to. Here." She had a tissue in her pocket and she used this to dab at the blood. "You've given us a surprise. What're you doing in London?"

The study door opened and Simon returned. He carried both a towel and a blanket. Deborah took them from him, draping one round Cherokee's shoulders and using the other on his dripping hair. This was shorter than it had been during the years that Deborah had lived with the man's sister in Santa Barbara. But it was still wildly curly, so different to China's, as was his face, which was sensuous with the sort of heavily lidded eyes and full-lipped mouth that women pay surgeons mightily to create on them. He'd inherited all of the desirability genes, China River had often said of her brother, while she'd ended up looking like a fourth-century ascetic.

"I called you first." Cherokee clutched the blanket tightly. "At nine, this was. Chine gave me your address and number. I didn't think I'd need them, but then the plane was delayed because of the weather. And when there was finally a break in the storm, it was too damn late to go to the embassy. So I called you, but no one was here."

"The embassy?" Simon took Cherokee's glass and replaced his spilled brandy with more. "What's happened exactly?"

Cherokee took the brandy, nodding his thanks. His hands were steadier. He gulped at the drink but began to cough.

"You need to get out of those clothes," Deborah said. "I expect a bath'll do the trick. I'm going to run one for you and while you're soaking, we'll throw your things in the dryer. All right?"

"Hey, no. I can't. It's . . . hell, what time is it?"

"Don't worry about the time. Simon, will you take him to the spare room and help him with his clothes? And no arguments, Cherokee. It isn't any trouble."

Deborah led the way upstairs. While her husband went in search of something dry for the man to wear when he was finished bathing, she turned the taps on in the tub. She laid out towels, and when Cherokee joined her—clothed in an old dressing gown of Simon's with a pair of Simon's pyjamas draped over his arm—she cleaned the cut on his head. He winced at the alcohol she dabbed on his skin. She held his head more firmly and said, "Grit your teeth."

"You don't provide bullets to bite?"

"Only when I'm doing surgery. This doesn't count." She tossed the cotton wool away and took up a plaster. "Cherokee, where've you come from tonight? Not Los Angeles, surely. Because you've no . . . Have you any luggage?"

"Guernsey," he said. "I came over from Guernsey. I set off this morning. I thought I'd get everything taken care of and get back there by tonight, so I didn't bring anything with me from the hotel. But I ended up spending most of the day at the airport, waiting for the weather to clear."

Deborah homed in on a single word. "Everything?" She fitted a plaster over his cut.

"What?"

"Getting everything taken care of today. What's everything?"

Cherokee's gaze flicked away from her. It was just for a moment but long enough for Deborah to feel trepidation. He'd said his sister had given him their Cheyne Row address, and from this Deborah had first assumed she'd provided it to her brother before he left the States, as one of those gestures one person makes to another when an upcoming journey is mentioned in passing. *Going to London as part of your holiday? Oh, do call on my good friends there.* Except when she really thought it out, Deborah had to admit how unlikely this scenario was in a situation in which she hadn't had contact with Cherokee's sister in the last five years. That made her think that if Cherokee himself wasn't in trouble but if he'd come in a rush from Guernsey to London with their address in his possession and the express purpose of going to the American embassy . . .

She said, "Cherokee, has something happened to China? Is that why you're here?"

He looked back at her. His face was bleak. "She's been arrested," he said.

"I didn't ask him anything more." Deborah had found her husband in the basement kitchen, where, prescient as always, Simon had already gone to put soup on the cooker. Bread was toasting as well, and the scarred kitchen table where Deborah's father had prepared a hundred thousand meals over the years was set with one place. "I thought after his bath . . . It seemed better to let him recover a bit. That is, before he tells us . . . If he *wants* to tell us . . ." She frowned, running her thumbnail along the edge of the work top where a splinter in the wood felt like a pinprick in her conscience. She tried to tell herself that she had no reason to feel it, that friendships came and went in life and that's just how it was. But she was the one who'd stopped replying to letters from the other side of the Atlantic. For China River had been a part of Deborah's life that Deborah had wanted very much to forget.

Simon shot her a look from the cooker, where he was stirring tomato soup with a wooden spoon. He appeared to read worry into her reluctance to speak, because he said, "It could be something relatively simple."

"How on earth can an arrest be simple?"

"Not earth-shattering, I mean. A traffic accident. A misunderstanding in Boots that looks like shoplifting. Something like that."

"He can't have meant to go to the American embassy over shoplifting, Simon. And she's not a shoplifter anyway."

"How well do you actually know her?"

"I know her well," Deborah said. She felt the need to repeat it fiercely. "I know China River perfectly well."

"And her brother? Cherokee? What the dickens sort of name is that anyway?"

"The one he was given at birth, I expect."

"Parents from the days of Sergeant Pepper?"

"Hmm. Their mother was a radical . . . some sort

of hippie . . . No. Wait. She was an environmental-ist. That's it. This was early on, before I knew her. She sat in trees."

Simon cast a wry look in her direction.

"To keep them from being cut down," Deborah said simply. "And Cherokee's father—they have different fathers—he was an environmentalist as well. Did he . . . ?" She thought about it, trying to remember. "I think he may have tied himself to railway tracks . . . somewhere in the desert?"

"Presumably to protect them as well? God knows they're fast becoming extinct."

Deborah smiled. The toast popped up. Peach scooted out from her basket in the hope of fallout while Deborah crafted soldiers.

"I don't know Cherokee all that well. Not like China. I spent holidays with China's family when I was in Santa Barbara, so I know him that way. From being with her family. Dinners at Christmas. New Year. Bank holidays. We'd drive down to . . . Where did her mother live? It was a town like a colour . . ."

"A colour?"

"Red, green, yellow. Ah. Orange, it was. She lived in a place called Orange. She would cook tofu turkey for the holidays. Black beans. Brown rice. Seaweed pie. Truly horrible things. We'd try to eat them, and then afterwards we'd find an excuse to go out for a drive and look for a restaurant that was open. Cherokee knew some highly questionable—but always thrifty—places to eat."

"That's commendable."

"So I'd see him then. Ten times altogether? He

did come up to Santa Barbara once and spend a few nights on our sofa. He and China had a bit of a love-hate relationship back then. He's older but he never acted it, which exasperated her. So she tended to mother-hen him, which exasperated him. Their own mother . . . well, she wasn't much of a *mother* mother, if you see what I mean."

"Too busy with the trees?"

"All sorts of things. There but not there. So it was a . . . well, rather a bond between China and me. Another bond, that is. Beyond photography. And other things. The motherless bit."

Simon turned down the burner beneath the soup and leaned against the cooker, watching his wife. "Tough years, those," he said quietly.

"Yes. Well." She blinked and offered him a quick smile. "We all muddled through them, didn't we?"

"We did that," Simon acknowledged.

Peach raised her nose from snuffling around the floor, head cocked and ears at the ready. On the window sill above the sink, the great grey Alaska—who'd been indolently studying the worm tracks of rain against the glass—rose and gave a languid feline stretch, with his eyes fixed on the basement stairs which descended right next to the old dresser on which the cat frequently spent his days. A moment later, the door above them creaked and the dog barked once. Alaska leaped down from the window sill and vanished to seek slumber in the larder.

Cherokee's voice called, "Debs?"

"Down here," Deborah replied. "We've made you soup and soldiers."

Cherokee joined them. He looked much improved. He was shorter than Simon by an inch or two and more athletic, but the pyjamas and dressing gown sat on him easily, and the trembles had gone. His feet were bare, however.

"I should have thought of slippers," Deborah said.

"I'm fine," Cherokee replied. "You've been great. Thanks. To both of you. It must be a real freak-out, me showing up like this. I appreciate being taken in." He nodded to Simon, who took the pan of soup to the table and ladled some into the bowl.

"This is something of a red-letter day, I must tell you," Deborah said. "Simon's actually opened a carton of soup. He'll usually do only tins."

"Thank you very much," Simon remarked.

Cherokee smiled, but he looked exhausted, like someone operating from the last vestiges of energy at the end of a terrible day.

"Have your soup," Deborah said. "You're stopping the night, by the way."

"No. I can't ask you—"

"Don't be silly. Your clothes are in the dryer and they'll be done in a while, but you surely didn't expect to go back out on the streets to find a hotel at this time of night."

"Deborah's right," Simon agreed. "We've plenty of room. You're more than welcome."

Cherokee's face mirrored relief and gratitude despite his exhaustion. "Thanks. I feel like . . ." He shook his head. "I feel like a kid. You know how they get? Lost in the grocery store except they don't know that they're lost till they look up from what they're doing—reading a comic book or something—and they see their mom's out of sight and then they flip out. That's what it feels like. What it *felt* like."

"Well, you're quite safe now," Deborah assured him.

"I didn't want to leave a message on your machine," Cherokee said. "When I phoned. It would have been a real downer to come home to. So I decided to try to find the house instead. I got totally screwed up on that yellow line on the subway and ended up at Tower Hill before I could figure what the hell I'd done wrong."

"Ghastly," Deborah murmured.

"Bad luck," Simon said.

A little silence fell among them then, broken only by the sounds of the rain. It splattered on the flagstones outside the kitchen door and slid in ceaseless rivulets down the window. There were three of them—and a hopeful dog—in the midnight kitchen. But they were not alone. The Question was there, too. It squatted among them like a palpable being, breathing noisome breath that could not be ignored. Neither Deborah nor her husband asked it. But as things turned out, neither needed to do so.

Cherokee dipped his spoon into his bowl. He raised it to his mouth. But he lowered it slowly without tasting the soup. He stared into the bowl for a moment before he raised his head and looked from Deborah to her husband.

"Here's what happened," he said.

• • •

He was responsible for everything, he told them. If it hadn't been for him, China wouldn't have gone to Guernsey in the first place. But he'd needed money, and when this deal came up to carry a package from California to the English Channel and to get paid for carrying it *and* to have the airline tickets provided . . . well, it seemed too good to be true.

He asked China to go because there were two tickets and the deal was that a man and woman had to carry the package over together. He thought Why not? And why not ask Chine? She never went anywhere. She'd never even been out of California.

He had to talk her into it. It took a few days, but she'd just broken up with Matt—did Debs remember China's boyfriend? the filmmaker she'd been with forever?—and she decided she wanted a break. So she called him and told him she wanted to go, and he made the arrangements. They carried the package from Tustin, south of LA, where it had originated, to a place on Guernsey outside of St. Peter Port.

"What was in the package?" Deborah pictured a drug bust at the airport, complete with dogs snarling and China and Cherokee backed into the wall like foxes seeking shelter.

Nothing illegal, Cherokee told her. He was hired to carry architectural plans from Tustin to the English Channel island. And the lawyer who had hired him—

"A lawyer?" Simon queried. "Not the architect?"

No. Cherokee was hired by a lawyer, and that had

sounded fishy to China, fishier even than being paid to carry a package to Europe as well as being given the airline tickets to do so. So China insisted that they open the package before they agreed to take it anywhere, which was what they did.

It was a good-size mailing tube, and if China had feared it was packed with drugs, weapons, explosives, or any other contraband that would have put them both in handcuffs, her fears were allayed when they unsealed it. Inside were the architectural plans that were supposed to be there, which set her mind at rest. His mind, too, Cherokee had to admit. For China's worries had unnerved him.

So they went to Guernsey to deliver the plans, with the intention of heading from there to Paris and onwards to Rome. It wouldn't be a long trip: Neither of them could afford that, so they were doing only two days in each place. But on Guernsey, their plans changed unexpectedly. They'd thought they'd make a quick exchange at the airport: paperwork for the promised payment and—

"What sort of payment are we talking about?" Simon asked.

Five thousand dollars, Cherokee told them. At their expressions of incredulity, he hastened to say that yeah, it was outrageous as all get-out and the amount of the payment was the number-one reason China had insisted they open the package because who the heck would give someone two free tickets to Europe *and* five thousand dollars just to carry something over from LA? But it turned out that doing outrageous stuff with money was what this whole deal was about in the first place. The man who wanted the architectural plans was richer than Howard Hughes, and he evidently did outrageous stuff with his money all the time.

However, they weren't met at the airport by someone with a cheque or a briefcase filled with cash or anything remotely resembling what they'd expected. Instead, they were met by a near-mute man called Kevin Something who hustled them to a van and drove them to a very cool spread a few miles away.

China was freaked out by this turn of events, which admittedly was disconcerting. There they were, enclosed in a car with a total stranger who didn't say fifteen words to them. It was very weird. But at the same time, it was like an adventure, and for his part Cherokee was intrigued.

Their destination turned out to be an awesome manor house sitting on God only knew how much acreage. The place was ancient—and completely re-stored, Debs—and China shifted into photographic mode the moment she laid eyes on it. Here was a whole *Architectural Digest* spread just waiting for her to shoot it.

China decided then and there that she wanted to do the photographs. Not only of the house but of the estate itself, which contained everything from duck ponds to prehistoric whatevers. China knew she'd been presented with an opportunity she might never get again, and although it meant taking the photographs on spec, she was willing to invest the time, the money, and the effort because the place was that sensational.

This was fine by Cherokee. She thought it would take only a couple of days and he'd have time to explore the island. The only question was whether the owner would go for the idea. Some people don't like their homes showing up in magazines. Too much inspiration for your B-and-E types.

Their host turned out to be a man called Guy—rhymed with *key*—Brouard, who was happy enough with the idea. He urged Cherokee and China to spend the night or perhaps a few days or whatever it took to get the photographs right. My sister and I live alone here, he told them, and visitors are always a diversion for us.

The man's son was also there as things turned out, and Cherokee thought at first that Guy Brouard might be hoping that China and the son would hook up. But the son was a disappearing type who showed up only at mealtimes and otherwise kept to himself. The sister was nice, though, and so was Brouard. So Cherokee and China felt right at home.

For her part, China connected big with Guy. They shared a common interest in architecture: hers because photographing buildings was her job, his because he was planning to put up a building on the island. He even took her to see the site and showed her some of the other structures on the island that were important historically. China should photograph all of Guernsey, he told her. She should do an entire book of pictures, not just enough for a magazine article. For so tiny a place it was steeped in history, and every society that had ever dwelt upon it had left its imprint in the form of buildings.

For their fourth and final night with the Brouards, a party had long been scheduled. It was a dressed-to-the-nines blowout that appeared to involve a cast of thousands. Neither China nor Cherokee knew what it was for, until midnight, when Guy Brouard gathered everyone together and announced that the design for his building—it turned out to be a museum—had finally been chosen. Drum rolls, excitement, champagne corks popping, and fireworks afterwards as he named the architect whose plans Cherokee and China had carried from California. A water colour of the place was brought out on an easel, and the partyers oohed, aahed, and went on drinking the Brouards' champagne until something like three in the morning.

The next day, neither Cherokee nor his sister was surprised when no one was up and about. They made their way to the kitchen around eight-thirty and browsed until they found the cereal, the coffee, and the milk. They assumed it was okay to make their own breakfast while the Brouards slept off the previous night's drunk. They ate, phoned for a taxi, and left for the airport. They never saw anyone from the estate again.

They flew to Paris and spent two days seeing the sights they'd only gazed upon in pictures. They were set to do the same in Rome, but as they went through customs at Da Vinci airport, Interpol stopped them.

The police packed them back to Guernsey, where they were wanted, they were told, for questioning. When they asked, Questioning about what? all they were told was that "a serious incident requires your presence on the island at once."

Their presence, it turned out, was required at the police station in St. Peter Port. They were held alone in separate cells: Cherokee for twenty-four pretty bad hours and China for three nightmarish days that turned into an appearance in front of the magistrate and a trip to the remand section of the prison, where she was now being held.

"For what?" Deborah reached across the table for Cherokee's hand. "Cherokee, what are they charging her with?"

"Murder," he replied hollowly. "It's completely insane. They're charging China with killing Guy Brouard."

Chapter 2

DEBORAH TURNED BACK THE covers on the bed and fluffed up the pillows. She realised that she'd seldom felt quite so useless. There was China sitting in a prison cell on Guernsey and here was she bustling round the spare room, drawing curtains and fluffing up *pillows*—for God's sake—because she didn't know what else to do. Part of her wanted to take the next plane to the Channel Islands. Part of her wanted to dive into Cherokee's heart and do something to calm his anxiety. Part of her wanted to draw up lists, devise plans, give instructions, and take an immediate action that would allow both Rivers to know they were not alone in the world. And part of her wanted someone *else* to do all of this because she didn't feel equal to any of it. So she uselessly fluffed pillows and turned down the bed.

Then, because she wanted to say something to China's brother, she turned to him where he stood awkwardly by the chest of drawers. "If you need anything in the night, we're just on the floor below."

Cherokee nodded. He looked dismal and very

alone. "She didn't do it," he said. "Can you see China hurting a fly?"

"Absolutely not."

"We're talking about someone who used to get me to carry spiders from her bedroom when we were kids. She'd be up on the bed yelling because she'd seen one on the wall and I'd come in to get rid of it and *then* she'd start yelling, 'Don't hurt him! Don't hurt him!' "

"She was like that with me, as well."

"God, if I'd only let it be, not asked her to come. I've got to do something and I don't know what."

His fingers twisted the tie of Simon's dressing gown. Deborah was reminded of how China had always seemed like the older sibling of the two. Cherokee, what am I going to do with you, she'd ask him. When are you *ever* growing up?

Right now, Deborah thought. With circumstances demanding a kind of adulthood that she wasn't sure Cherokee even possessed.

She said to him because it was the only thing she could say, "You sleep now. We'll know better what to do in the morning," and she left him.

She was heavy at heart. China River had been the closest of friends to her during the most difficult moments of her life. She owed her much but had repaid her little. That China would now be in trouble and that she would be in that trouble alone . . . Deborah only too well understood Cherokee's anxiety about his sister.

She found Simon in their bedroom, sitting on the straight-backed chair that he used when he removed his leg brace at night. He was in the midst of tearing back the brace's Velcro strips, his trousers puddling down round his ankles and his crutches on the floor next to his chair.

He looked childlike, as he generally looked in this vulnerable posture, and it had always taken all the discipline she could muster for Deborah not to go to his assistance when she came upon her husband like this. His disability was, for her, the great leveling force between them. She hated it for his sake because she knew he hated it, but she'd long ago accepted the fact that the accident that had crippled him in his twenties had also made him available to her. Had it not occurred, he'd have married while she was a mere adolescent, leaving her far behind. His time in hospital and then convalescing and then the black years of depression that followed had put paid to that.

He didn't like to be seen in his awkwardness, though. So she went straight to the chest of drawers, where she made a pretence of removing what few pieces of jewellery she wore while she waited for the sound of the leg brace clunking to the floor. When she heard it, followed by the grunt he gave as he rose, she turned. He had his crutches snapped round his wrists, and he was watching her fondly.

"Thank you," he said.

"Sorry. Have I always been so obvious?"

"No. You've always been so kind. But I don't think I've ever thanked you properly. That's what comes from a marriage too happy for its own good: taking the beloved for granted."

"Do you take me for granted, then?"

"Not intentionally." He cocked his head to one side and observed her. "Frankly, you don't give me the chance." He made his way across the room to her, and she put her arms round his waist. He kissed her gently and then kissed her long, one arm holding her to him, till she felt the wanting that stirred in them both.

She looked up at him then. "I'm glad you can still do that to me. But I'm gladder I can do it to you."

He touched her cheek. "Hmm. Yes. Yet all things considered, it's probably not the time . . ."

"For what?"

"For exploring some interesting variations of this 'it' you were speaking of."

"Ah." She smiled. "That. Well, perhaps it is the time, Simon. Perhaps what we learn every day is how quickly life changes. Everything that's important can be gone in an instant. So it is the time."

"To explore . . . ?"

"Only if we're exploring together."

Which was what they did in the glow of a single lamp that burnished their bodies gold, darkened Simon's grey-blue eyes, and turned to crimson the otherwise hidden pale places where their blood beat hot. Afterwards, they lay in the tangle of the counterpane, which they hadn't bothered to remove from the bed. Deborah's clothes were scattered wherever her husband had tossed them and Simon's shirt draped from one of his arms like an indolent tart.

"I'm glad you hadn't gone to bed," she said against his chest, where she rested her cheek. "I thought you might have done. It didn't seem right to just deposit him in the spare room without staying for a moment. But you were looking so tired in the kitchen that I thought you might've decided to sleep. I'm glad you didn't, though. Thank you, Simon."

He caressed her hair as was his habit, moving his hand into the heavy mass of it till his fingers came into contact with her head. He played them warmly against her scalp, and she felt her body relax in response. "He's all right?" Simon asked. "Is there anyone we can phone, just in case?"

"Just in case what?"

"Just in case he doesn't get what he wants from the embassy tomorrow. I expect they've already been in contact with the police on Guernsey. If they've not sent someone over there . . ." Deborah felt her husband shrug. "Chances are good there's nothing else they intend to do."

Deborah rose from his chest. "You aren't thinking China actually committed this murder, are you?"

"Not at all." He brought her back to his arms. "I'm only pointing out that she's in the hands of a foreign police force. There'll be protocols and procedures to be followed and that might be the extent of what the embassy is going to involve itself with. Cherokee needs to be prepared for that. He might also need someone to lean on if that turns out to be the case. That might be why he's come, in fact."

Simon said this last more quietly than the rest. Deborah raised her head to look at him again. "What?"

"Nothing."

"There's more, Simon. I can hear it in your voice."

"Just this. Are you the only person he knows in London?"

"Probably."

"I see."

"I see?"

"He might well need you, then, Deborah."

"And does that bother you if he does?"

"Not bother. No. But are there other family members?"

"Just their mum."

"The tree-sitter. Yes. Well, it might be wise to phone her. What about the father? You said China has a different father to Cherokee's?"

Deborah winced. "Hers is in prison, my love. At least he was when we lived together." And when she saw the concern on Simon's face—expressing nothing so much as *like father, like daughter?*—she went on to say, "It was nothing serious. I mean, he didn't *kill* anyone. China never talked about him much, but I know it had something to do with drugs. An illegal lab somewhere? I think that was it. It's not like he pushed heroin on the street, though."

"Well, that's comforting."

"She's *not* like him, Simon."

He made a grumbling sound, which she took for his hesitant agreement. They lay in silence then, content with each other, her head back on his chest and his fingers once again in her hair.

Deborah loved her husband differently in

moments like this. She felt more his equal. The sensation came not only from their quiet conversation but also—and perhaps more important for her—from what had preceded their conversation. For the fact that her body could give him such pleasure always seemed to balance the scales between them and that she could be a witness to that pleasure allowed her to feel even momentarily her husband's superior. Because of this, her own pleasure had long been secondary to his, a fact that Deborah knew would horrify the liberated women of her world. But that's just how it was.

"I reacted badly," she finally murmured. "Tonight. I'm sorry, my love. I do put you through it."

Simon had no trouble following the line of her thinking. "Expectations destroy our peace of mind, don't they? They're future disappointments, planned out in advance."

"I did have it all planned out. Scores of people with champagne glasses in their hands, standing awestruck in front of my pictures. 'My God, she's a genius,' they declare to each other. 'The very idea of taking a Polaroid . . . Did *you* know they could be black and white? And the *size* of them . . . Heavens, I must own one at once. No. Wait. I must have at least ten.' "

" 'The new flat in Canary Wharf demands them,' " Simon added.

" 'Not to mention the cottage in the Cotswolds.' "

" 'And the house near Bath.' "

They laughed together. Then they were silent. Deborah shifted her position to look at her husband.

"It still stings," she admitted. "Not as much. Not nearly. But a bit. It's still there."

"Yes," he said. "There's no quick panacea for being thwarted. We all want what we want. And not getting it doesn't mean we cease to want it. I do know that. Believe me. I know."

She looked away from him quickly, realising that what he was acknowledging traveled a much greater distance than comprised the brief journey to this night's disappointment. She was grateful that he understood, that he'd always understood no matter how supremely rational logical cool and incisive were his comments on her life. Her eyes ached with tears, but she wouldn't allow him to see them. She wanted to give him the momentary gift of her tranquil acceptance of inequity. When she'd managed to displace sorrow with what she hoped would sound like determination, she turned back to him.

"I'm going to sort myself out properly," she said. "I may strike out in a whole new direction."

He observed her in his usual manner, an unblinking gaze that generally unnerved lawyers when he was testifying in court and always reduced his university students to hopeless stammers. But for her the gaze was softened by his lips, which curved in a smile, and by his hands, which reached for her again.

"Wonderful," he said as he pulled her to him. "I'd like to make a few suggestions right now."

• • •

Deborah was up before dawn. She'd lain awake for hours before falling asleep, and when she'd finally nodded off, she'd tossed and turned through a series of incomprehensible dreams. In them she was back in Santa Barbara, not as she'd been—a young student at Brooks Institute of Photography—but rather as someone else entirely: a sort of ambulance driver whose apparent responsibility it was not only to fetch a recently harvested human heart for transplant but also to fetch it from a hospital she could not find. Without her delivery, the patient—lying for some reason not in an operating theatre but in the car repair bay at the petrol station behind which she and China had once lived—would die within an hour, especially since his heart had already been removed, with a gaping hole left in his chest. Or it might have been *her* heart instead of his. Deborah couldn't tell from the partially shrouded form that was raised in the repair bay on a hydaulic lift.

In her dream, she drove desperately through the palm-lined streets to no avail. She couldn't remember a single thing about Santa Barbara and no one would help her with directions. When she woke up, she found that she'd thrown off the covers and was so damp with sweat that she was actually shivering. She looked at the clock and eased out of bed, padding over to the bathroom, where she bathed the worst of the nightmare away. When she returned to the bedroom, she found Simon awake. He said her name in the darkness and then, "What time is it? What are you doing?"

She said, "Terrible dreams."

"Not art collectors waving their chequebooks at you?"

"No, sad to say. Art collectors waving their Annie Leibovitzes at me."

"Ah. Well. It could have been worse."

"Really? How?"

"It could have been Karsch."

She laughed and told him to go back to sleep. It was early yet, too early for her dad to be up and about, and she herself certainly wasn't going to trip up and down the stairs with Simon's morning tea as her father did. "Dad spoils you, by the way," she informed her husband.

"I consider it only a minor payment for having taken you off his hands."

She heard the rustle of the bedclothes as he changed his position. He sighed deeply, welcoming back sleep. She left him to it.

Downstairs, she brewed herself a cup of tea in the kitchen, where Peach looked up from her basket by the cooker and Alaska emerged from the larder, where, from the snow-tipped look of him, he doubtless had spent the night on top of a leaking flour bag. Both animals came across the red tiles to Deborah, who stood at the draining board beneath the basement window while her water heated in the electric kettle. She listened to the rain continue to fall on the flagstones of the area just outside the back door. There had been only a brief respite from it during the night, sometime after three, as she lay awake listening not only to the wind and the waves of rainfall hitting the window but also to the committee in her head that was shrilly advising her what to do: with her day, with her life, with her career, and above all with and for Cherokee River.

She eyed Peach as Alaska began to saunter back and forth meaningfully between her legs. The dog hated going out in the rain—walkies became carries whenever there was so much as a drop of precipitation—so a walk was out of the question. But a quick dash up into the back garden to do the necessary was completely in order. Peach seemed to read Deborah's mind, however. The dachshund beat a hasty retreat back into her basket as Alaska began to mew.

"Don't plan on a lengthy lie-in," Deborah told the dog, who watched her mournfully, making her eyes go diamond-shaped in that way she had when she wanted to look especially pathetic. "If you don't go out right now for me, Dad shall take you on a march to the river. You do know that, don't you?"

Peach seemed willing to risk it. She deliberately lowered her head to her paws and let her eyes sink closed. Deborah said, "Very well," and shook out the cat's daily allotment of food, placing it carefully out of the reach of the dog who, she knew, would appropriate it the instant her back was turned, feigned sleep notwithstanding. She made her tea and carried it upstairs, feeling her way in the dark.

It was frigid in the study. She eased the door shut and lit the gas fire. In a folder on one of the bookshelves she'd been assembling a set of small Polaroids that represented what she wanted to photograph next. She carried this to the desk, where she sat in

Simon's worn leather chair and began to flip through the pictures.

She thought about Dorothea Lange and wondered if she herself had what it took to capture in a single face that was the *right* face one unforgettable image that could define an era. She had no 1930s dust bowl America whose hopelessness etched itself on the countenance of a nation, though. And to be successful in capturing an image of this, her own age, she knew she would have to think beyond the box that had long been defined by that remarkable aching arid face of a woman, accompanied by her children and a generation of despair. She thought she was up to at least half of the work: the thinking part of it. But she wondered if the rest was what she really wanted to do: spend another twelve months on the street, take another ten or twelve thousand photographs, always attempting to look beyond the mobile-phone-dominated fast-paced world that distorted the truth of what was really there. Even if she managed all that, what would it gain her in the long run? At the moment, she simply didn't know.

She sighed and placed the pictures on the desk. She wondered not for the first time if China had chosen the wiser path. Commercial photography paid the rent, bought food, and put clothes on one's body. It didn't necessarily have to be a soulless endeavour. And despite the fact that Deborah was in the fortunate position of not *having* to pay the rent, buy the food, or put clothes upon anyone, the very fact of that caused her to want to make a contribution somewhere else. If she wasn't needed to assist in their economic situation, then at least she could use her talent to contribute to the society in which they lived.

But could turning to commercial photography actually do that? she wondered. And what kind of commercial pictures would she take? At least China's pictures related to her interest in architecture. She'd actually set out to be a photographer of buildings, and professionally doing precisely what she had set out to do was not in any way selling out, not as Deborah would consider herself selling out if she took the easier route and went commercial. And if she *did* sell out, what on earth would she take pictures of? Toddlers' birthday parties? Rock stars being released from gaol?

Gaol . . . Lord. Deborah groaned. She rested her forehead in her hands and closed her eyes. How important was any of this, measured against China's situation? China, who had been there in Santa Barbara, a caring presence when she needed one most. *I've seen the two of you together, Debs. If you tell him the truth, he'll take the next plane back. He'll want to marry you. He wants to already.* But not like this, Deborah had told her. It can't be like this.

So China had made the necessary arrangements. China had taken her to the necessary clinic. Afterwards, China had sat by her bed so when she opened her eyes, the first person she saw was China herself, simply waiting. Then saying, "Hey, girl," with such an expression of kindness that Deborah thought in the span of her life she would never again have such a friend.

That friendship was a call to action. She could not allow China to believe, any longer than possible, that she was alone. But what to do was the question, because—

A floor board creaked somewhere in the corridor outside the study. Deborah raised her head. Another board creaked. She got up, crossed the room, and pulled open the door.

In the diffused light that came from a lamp still lit outside on the early-morning street, Cherokee River was removing his jacket from the radiator, where Deborah had placed it to dry overnight. His intention seemed unmistakable.

"You can't be leaving," Deborah said incredulously.

Cherokee whirled round. "Jeez. You scared the *hell* out of me. Where'd you come from like that?"

Deborah indicated the study door, where behind her the lamp shone on Simon's desk and the gas fire dipped and bobbed a soft glow against the high ceiling. "I was up early. Sorting through some old pictures. But what are you doing? Where are you going?"

He shifted his weight, ran his hand through his hair in that characteristic gesture of his. He indicated the stairs and the floors above. "Couldn't sleep. I swear I won't be able to again—anywhere—till I get someone over to Guernsey. So I figured the embassy . . ."

"What time is it?" Deborah examined her wrist

to discover she'd not put on her watch. She hadn't glanced at the clock in the study, but from the gloom outside—even exacerbated by the insufferable rain—she knew it couldn't be much later than six. "The embassy won't be open for hours."

"I figured there might be a line or something. I want to be first."

"You still can be, even if you have a cup of tea. Or coffee if you like. And something to eat."

"No. You've done enough already. Letting me stay here last night? *Inviting* me to stay? The soup and the bath and everything? You bailed me out."

"I'm glad of it. But I'm not going to hear of your going just now. There's no point. I'll drive you over there myself in plenty of time to be first in line if that's what you want."

"I don't want you to—"

"You don't have to want me to anything," Deborah said firmly. "I'm not offering. I'm insisting. So leave the jacket there and come with me."

Cherokee appeared to think this over for a moment: He looked at the door where its three window panes allowed the light to come through. Both of them could hear the persistent rain, and as if to emphasise the unpleasantness he would face if he ventured out, a gust of wind shot like a prize fighter's blow from the Thames and cracked loudly within the branches of the sycamore just along the street.

He said reluctantly, "All right. Thanks."

Deborah led him downstairs to the kitchen. Peach looked up from her basket and growled.

Alaska, who'd taken up his normal daytime position on the window sill, glanced over, blinked, and went back to his perusal of the patterns the rain was making on the panes.

Deborah said, "Mind your manners," to the dog and established Cherokee at the table, where he studied the scars that knife marks had made upon the wood and the burnt rings left from the assault of too-hot pans upon it. Deborah once again set the electric kettle to work and took a teapot from the ancient dresser. She said, "I'm making you a meal as well. When did you last have a real meal?" She glanced over at him. "I expect not yesterday."

"There was the soup."

Deborah snorted her disapproval. "You can't help China if you fall apart." She went to the fridge for eggs and bacon; she took tomatoes from their basket near the sink and mushrooms from the dark corner near the outside door, where her father kept a large paper sack for them, hanging from a hook among the household's macs.

Cherokee got up and walked over to the window above the sink, where he extended his hand to Alaska. The cat sniffed his fingers and, head lowered regally, allowed the man to scratch behind his ears. Deborah glanced over to see Cherokee gazing round the kitchen as if absorbing every one of its details. She followed his gaze to register what she took for granted: from the dried herbs that her father kept hanging in neatly arranged bunches to the copper-bottomed pots and pans that lined the wall within reach above the hob, from the old worn tiles on the floor to the dresser that held everything from serving platters to photographs of Simon's nieces and nephews.

"This is a cool house, Debs," Cherokee murmured.

To Deborah, it was just the house in which she'd lived from childhood, first as the motherless daughter of Simon's indispensable right-hand man, then however briefly as Simon's lover before becoming Simon's wife. She knew its draughts, its plumbing problems, and its exasperating lack of electrical outlets. To her, it was simply home. She said, "It's old and draughty and it's mostly maddening."

"Yeah? It looks like a mansion to me."

"Does it?" She forked nine rashers of bacon into a pan and set them cooking beneath the grill. "It actually belongs to Simon's whole family. It was quite a disaster when he took it over. Mice in the walls and foxes in the kitchen. He and Dad spent nearly two years making it livable. I suppose his brothers or his sister could move in with us now if they wanted to since it's everyone's house and not just ours. But they wouldn't do that. They know he and Dad did all the work."

"Simon has brothers and sisters, then," Cherokee remarked.

"Two brothers in Southampton . . . where the family business is . . . shipping . . . His sister's in London, though. She used to be a model but now she's campaigning to be an interviewer of obscure celebrities on an even more obscure cable channel that no one watches." Deborah grinned. "Quite the character, is Sidney. That's Simon's sister. She drives her mum mad because she won't settle down. She's had dozens of lovers. We've met one after another at holidays and each one is always the man of her dreams at last at last."

"Lucky," Cherokee said, "to have family like that."

A wistfulness in his voice prompted Deborah to turn from the cooker. "Would you like to ring yours?" she asked. "Your mum, I mean. You can use the phone on the dresser there. Or the one in the study if you'd like privacy. It's . . ." She looked at the wall clock and did the maths. "It's only ten-fifteen last night in California."

"I can't do that." Cherokee returned to the table and dropped into a chair. "I promised China."

"But she does have the right—"

"China and Mom?" Cherokee cut in. "They don't . . . Well, Mom was never much of a mom, not like other moms, and China doesn't want her to know about this. I think it's because . . . you know . . . other moms would catch the next plane out, but our mom? No way. There might be an endangered species to save. So why tell her in the first place? At least, that's what China's thinking."

"What about her father? Is he . . . ?" Deborah hesitated. The subject of China's father had always been a delicate one.

Cherokee raised an eyebrow. "Locked up? Oh yeah. He's inside again. So there's no one to call."

A step sounded on the kitchen stairs. Deborah put plates on the table and heard the uneven nature of someone's cautious descent. She said, "That'll be Simon." He was up earlier than usual, far before her father, which Joseph Cotter wouldn't like. He'd cared for Simon throughout his long-ago convalescence from the drunken road crash that had crippled him, and he didn't like it if Simon denied him the chance to hover protectively over him.

"Fortunately, I'm making enough for three," Deborah said as her husband joined them.

Simon looked from the cooker to the table where she had laid crockery. "I hope your father's heart is strong enough to sustain this shock," he said.

"Most amusing."

Simon kissed her and then nodded at Cherokee. "You look much better this morning. How's the head?"

Cherokee fingered the plaster near his hairline. "Better. I had a pretty good nurse."

"She knows what she's doing," Simon said.

Deborah poured the eggs into the pan and set about scrambling them efficiently. "He's definitely drier," she pointed out. "After we eat, I've said I'll pop him over to the American embassy."

"Ah. I see." Simon glanced at Cherokee. "Guernsey police haven't notified the embassy already? That's unusual."

"No. They have," Cherokee said. "But the embassy didn't send anyone. They just phoned to make sure she had a lawyer to speak for her in court. And then it was Good, that's fine, she's being represented then, phone us if you need anything else. I said I *do* need you. I need you here. I told them we weren't even on the island when it happened. But they said the police would have their evidence and there was really nothing else they could do till things got played out. That's what they said. *Till things got played out.* Like this was a basketball game or something." He moved away from the table abruptly. "I need someone from the embassy *over* there. This whole thing's a set-up, and if I don't do something to stop it from happening, there's going to be a trial and a sentence before the month's up."

"Can the embassy do anything?" Deborah put their breakfast on the table. "Simon, do you know?"

Her husband considered the question. He didn't work often for embassies, more often instead for the CPS or for barristers who were mounting a criminal defence in court and required an outside expert witness to offset the testimony of someone from one police laboratory or another. But he knew enough to be able to explain what the American embassy would doubtless offer Cherokee when he put in his appearance in Grosvenor Square.

"Due process," he said. "That's what the embassy works to ensure. They'll make certain that the laws of the land are applied to China's situation."

"That's all they can do?" Cherokee asked.

"Not much more, I'm afraid." Simon sounded regretful, but he went on in a more reassuring tone. "I expect they'll make sure she has good representation. They'll check the lawyer's credentials and make sure he wasn't called to the bar just three weeks ago. They'll see to it that anyone in the States whom China wants to have informed will be informed.

They'll get her post sent to her in good time and they'll make her part of their regular round of visitations, I expect. They'll do what they can." He observed Cherokee for a moment and then added kindly, "It's early days yet, you know."

"We weren't even there when all this came down," Cherokee said numbly. "When it all happened. I kept telling them that but they wouldn't believe me. They have to have records at the airport, don't they? Records of when we left? They have to have records."

"Of course," Simon said. "If the day and the the time of death conflict with your departure, that's something that'll come out quickly." He toyed with his knife, tapping it against his plate.

Deborah said, "What? Simon, what?"

He looked at Cherokee and then beyond him to the kitchen window, where Alaska sat alternately washing his face and stopping to press his paw against the rain tracks on the glass as if he could prevent them from coursing downward. He said carefully, "You have to look at this with a level head. This isn't a third world country we're talking about. It's not a totalitarian state. The police on Guernsey aren't about to make an arrest without evidence. So"—he set his knife to one side—"the reality is this: Something definite has actually led them to believe they've got the killer they want." He looked at Cherokee then and he studied his face in his usual dispassionate scientist's fashion, as if seeking reassurance that the other man could handle what he was about to conclude with. "You need to prepare yourself."

"For what?" Cherokee reached as if unconsciously towards the table's edge.

"For whatever your sister may have done, I'm afraid. Without your knowledge."

Chapter 3

"Winklewater, Frankie. 'At's what we called it. Never mentioned that, did I? Never talked much of how bad things got round the subject of food, did I, lad? Don't much like to think about those times. Bloody Krauts . . . What they did to this island . . ."

Frank Ouseley slipped his hands gently through his father's armpits as the old man maundered on. He eased him off the plastic chair in the bath and guided his left foot onto the tattered mat that covered the cold linoleum. He'd turned the radiator up as far as it would go this morning, but it still seemed frigid in the bathroom to him. So, one hand on his father's arm to keep him steady, he grabbed the towel from its rail and shook it out. He tucked it snugly round his father's shoulders, which were wizened as was the rest of him. Graham Ouseley's flesh was ninety-two years old, and it hung upon his frame like stringy bread dough.

"Threw everything into the pot in those days," Graham went on, leaning his whippet's frame against Frank's own somewhat rounded shoulder. "Shredded up parsnips, we did, boy, when we could get 'em. Baked 'em first, o' course. Camellia leaves too, lime blossoms and lemon balm, lad. And then we threw bicarb in the pot to make the leaves go longer. Winklewater was what we called it. Well, we couldn't rightly call it tea." He chuckled and his fragile shoulders shook. The chuckle segued into a cough. The cough turned into a wrestle for air. Frank grabbed his father to keep him upright.

"Steady on, Dad." He grasped Graham's fragile body firmly, despite his own fear that one day clutching on to him to keep him from falling was going to do worse damage than any fall he might actually take, snapping his bones like a dunlin's legs. "Here. Let's get you onto the toilet."

"Don't have to pee, boy," Graham protested, trying to shake himself free. "Wha's the matter with you? Mind going, or something? Peed before we got into the bath."

"Right. I know that. I just want you to sit."

"Nothing wrong with my legs. I c'n stand with the best of them. Had to do that when the Krauts were here. Stand still and look like you're queuing for meat. *Not* passing 'long the news, no sir. No radio receiver in *your* dung hill, son. Look like you'd just a'soon *heil* Mr. Dirty Moustache as say God save the King, and they didn't bother you. So you could do what you liked. If you were careful."

"I remember that, Dad," Frank said patiently. "I remember your telling me about it." Despite his father's protest, he lowered him onto the toilet seat, where he began to pat his body dry. As he did so, he listened with some concern to Graham's breathing, waiting for it to return to normal. Congestive heart failure, his doctor had said. There's medication, naturally, and we'll put him on it. But truth to tell, at his advanced age, it's only a matter of time. It's an act of God, Frank, that he's lived this long.

When he'd first received the news, Frank had thought, No. Not now. Not yet and not until. But now he was ready to let his father go. He'd long ago realised how lucky he was to have had him around well into his own sixth decade, and while he'd hoped to have Graham Ouseley alive some eighteen months longer, he'd come to understand—with a grief that felt like a net from which he could never escape—that it was just as well this was not to be.

"*Did* I?" Graham asked, and he screwed up his face as he sorted through his memory. "Did I tell you all that afore, laddie? When?"

Two or three hundred times, Frank thought. He'd been listening to his father's World War II stories since his childhood, and most of them he could repeat by heart. The Germans had occupied Guernsey for five years, preparatory to their foiled plan to invade England, and the deprivations the populace had endured—not to mention the myriad ways they had attempted to thwart German aims on the island—had long been the stuff of his father's conversation. While most children nursed from their mother's breasts, Frank had long suckled at the teat of Graham's reminiscence. Never forget this, Frankie. Whatever else happens in your life, my boy, you must never forget.

He hadn't, and unlike so many children who might have grown weary of the tales their parents told them on Remembrance Sunday, Frank Ouseley had hung upon his father's words and had wished he'd managed to get himself born a decade earlier so that even as a child he could have been part of that troubled and heroic time.

They had nothing to match it now. Not the Falklands or the Gulf—those abbreviated, nasty little conflicts that were fought about next to nothing and geared to stimulate the populace into flag-waving patriotism—and certainly not Northern Ireland, where he himself had served, ducking sniper fire in Belfast and wondering what the hell he was doing in the middle of a sectarian struggle promoted by thugs who'd been taking murderous pot shots at each other since the turn of the last century. There was no heroism in any of that because there was no single enemy who could be identified and against whose image one could fling himself and die. They weren't like World War II.

He steadied his father on the toilet seat and reached for his clothes, which lay in a neatly folded stack on the edge of the basin. He did the laundry himself, so the undershorts and the vest weren't as white as they might have been but, as his father's eyesight was growing steadily worse, Frank was fairly certain Graham wouldn't notice.

Dressing his dad was something he did by rote, always easing his father into his clothing in the exact same order. It was a ritual that he had once found reassuring, giving a sameness to his days with Graham that made the promise, however false, that those days would continue indefinitely. But now he watched his father warily, and he wondered if the catch in his breath and the waxy nature of his skin presaged an end to their time together, a time that had now exceeded fifty years. Two months ago he would have quailed at that thought. Two months ago all he wanted was enough time to establish the Graham Ouseley Wartime Museum so his father could proudly cut the ribbon on its doors on the morning it finally opened. The passage of sixty days had changed everything unrecognisably, though, and that was a pity because gathering every memento that represented the years of German occupation on the island had been the mortar of Frank's relationship with his father for as long as he could remember. It was their shared life's work and their mutual passion, done for a love of history and a belief that the present and future populations of Guernsey should be educated about what their forebears had endured.

That their plans would likely come to nothing now was something which Frank didn't want his father to know just yet. Since Graham's days were numbered, there seemed no sense in dashing a dream that he would not even have had in the first place had Guy Brouard not walked into their lives.

"Wha's up for today?" Graham asked his son as Frank pulled the track-suit trousers up round his shriveled bum. " 'Bout time to walk the construction site, i'n't it? Breaking earth any day now, a'n't they, Frankie? You'll be there for that, won't you,

lad? Turning over the ceremonial shovelful? Or's
that something Guy's wanting for himself?"

Frank avoided the entire set of questions, indeed
the entire subject of Guy Brouard. He'd so far managed to keep from his father the news of their friend
and benefactor's gruesome death, as he hadn't yet
decided whether the information would be too bur-
densome for his health. Besides, they were playing a
waiting game at the moment whether his father
knew it or not: There was no news about how Guy's
estate was being settled.

Frank said to his father, "I thought to check
through the uniforms this morning. It looked to me
like the damp's getting to them." This was a lie, of
course. The ten uniforms they had—from the dark-
collared overcoats worn by the *Wehrmacht* to the
threadbare coveralls used by *Luftwaffe* anti-aircraft
crews—were all preserved in airtight containers and
acid-free tissue against the day that they would be
placed in glass cases designed to keep them forever.
"I can't think how it happened, but if it has, we need
to get on to it before they start to rot."

"Damn rights, that," his father agreed. "You take
care, Frankie. All that clobber. Got to keep it mint,
we do."

"That we do, Dad," Frank replied mechanically.

His father seemed satisfied with this. He allowed
his sparse hair to be combed and himself to be
helped to the lounge. There Frank tucked him into
his favourite armchair and handed him the television
remote. He had no worries that his father might
tune in to the island station and hear the very news

about Guy Brouard which he was attempting to keep from him. The only programmes Graham Ouseley ever watched were cooking shows and the soaps. The former he took notes from, for reasons that never were clear to his son. The latter he studied completely enthralled and spent his daily dinner hour discussing the troubled individuals on them as if they were his next-door neighbours.

There were none of those where the Ouseleys lived. Years ago there had been: two other families living in the line of cottages that grew like an appendage, out from the old water mill called *Moulin des Niaux*. But over time, Frank and his father had managed to purchase these dwellings when they came up for sale. Now they held the vast collection that was supposed to fill the wartime museum.

Frank took his keys and, after checking the radiator in the lounge and setting up the electric fire when he didn't like the modest warmth coming from the old pipes, he walked over to the cottage next to the one in which he and his father had lived forever. They were all in a terrace and the Ouseleys lived in the farthest one from the water mill itself, whose ancient wheel was known to creak and groan at night if the wind whistled up the stream-carved glen that was the Talbot Valley.

The cottage door stuck when Frank pushed upon it because the old stone floor had been laid uneven and neither Frank nor his father had thought to correct the problem in the years they'd owned the place. They were using it for storage primarily, and a sticking door had always seemed a small matter compared to the other challenges that an ageing building presented to someone who wanted to use it as a storage facility. It was more important to keep the roof weatherproof and the windows free of draughts. If the heating system worked and a balance could be maintained between dryness and humidity, the fact that a door was a bother to open was something one could easily overlook.

Guy Brouard hadn't done that, though. The door was the first thing he mentioned when he paid his initial call upon the Ouseleys. He'd said, "The wood's got swollen. That means damp, Frank. Are you guarding against it?"

"It's the floor, actually," Frank had pointed out to him. "Not the damp. Although we've got that as well, I'm afraid. We try to keep the heat in here constant, but in the winter . . . I expect it's the proximity to the stream."

"You need higher ground."

"Not easy to come by on the island."

Guy hadn't disagreed. There were no extreme elevations on Guernsey save perhaps for the cliffs on the south end of the island, which dropped precipitously down to the Channel. But the presence of the Channel itself with its salt-laden air made the cliffs unsuitable as a place to which the collection could be moved . . . if they even could find a building in which to house it, an unlikely prospect.

Guy hadn't suggested the museum at once. He hadn't at first comprehended the breadth of the Ouseleys' collection. He'd come to the Talbot Valley as the result of an invitation extended by Frank at the coffee-and-biscuits conclusion of a presentation at the historical society. They'd assembled above the market square of St. Peter Port, in the old assembly room that had long since been usurped by an extension to the Guille-Alles Library. There they gathered to listen to a lecture about the 1945 Allied investigation of Hermann Göring, which had turned out to be a dry recitation of the facts gleaned from something called The Consolidated Interrogation Report. Most of the members were nodding off a mere ten minutes into the talk, but Guy Brouard had appeared to hang upon the speaker's every word. This told Frank that he might be a worthwhile confederate. So few people really cared any longer about events that happened in another century. Thus, he'd approached him at the lecture's conclusion, not knowing who he was at first and learning to his surprise that he was the gentleman who'd taken the derelict Thibeault Manor between St. Martin and St. Peter Port and engineered its renaissance as *Le Reposoir*.

Had Guy Brouard not been an easy man to know, Frank might have exchanged a few pleasantries with him that night and gone on his way. But the truth was that Guy had displayed an interest in Frank's avocation that Frank had found flattering. So he'd extended the invitation for a call upon *Moulin des Niaux*.

Guy had doubtless come thinking that the invitation was the sort of polite gesture which a dilettante makes to someone evidencing a suitable degree of curiosity about his area of dabbling. But when he'd seen the first room of boxes and crates, of shoeboxes filled with bullets and medals, of armaments half a century old, of bayonets and knives and gas masks and signaling equipment, he'd given a low, appreciative whistle and he'd settled in for a lengthy browse.

This browsing had taken more than one day. Indeed, it had taken more than one week. Guy Brouard had shown up at *Moulin des Niaux* for two months to sift through the contents of the two other cottages. When he'd finally said, "You need a museum for all this, Frank," the seed had been planted in Frank's mind.

It had seemed like a dream at the time. How odd it was to consider now that such a dream could have slowly transmuted into a nightmare.

Inside the cottage, Frank went to the metal filing cabinet in which he and his father had been storing relevant wartime documents as they came across them. They had old identity cards by the dozens, ration cards, and driving permits. They had German proclamations of death for such capital offences as releasing carrier pigeons and German declarations on every conceivable topic to control the islanders' existence. Their most prized objects were a half-dozen examples of *G.I.F.T.,* the underground daily news-sheet that had been printed at the cost of three Guernseymen's lives.

It was these that Frank lifted out of the filing cabinet now. He carried them to a rotting cane-bottomed chair and sat, gingerly holding them on his lap. They were single sheets, typed upon onion-skin paper with as many carbons beneath them as could fit through the platen of an ancient typewriter. They were so fragile that it was nothing short of miraculous that they had survived a month, let alone more than half a century, each of them a micro-millimetre's statement about the bravery of men who would not be cowed by Nazi proclamations and threats.

Had Frank not spent his life being schooled in the importance of history, had he not spent every one of his formative years right on into his solitary adult-hood being taught the inestimable value of every-thing remotely related to Guernsey's time of trial, he might have thought that only one of these sheets of wartime gossamer would suffice as a representation of a people's resistance. But one of anything was never enough for a collector with a passion, and when that collector's passion was for fostering re-membrance and exposing truth so that *never again* took on a meaning that would stand the test of time, having too much or too many of any item was sim-ply not an issue.

A rattle outside the cottage prompted Frank to walk to the grimy window. He saw that a cyclist had just squeaked to a stop, and its youthful rider was in the process of dismounting and setting the kickstand into place. He was accompanied by the thatch-furred dog who was his constant companion.

It was young Paul Fielder and Taboo.

Frank frowned at their presence, wondering what they were doing here, all this way from the Bouet, where Paul lived with his disreputable family in one of the dismal terraces that the Douzaine of the parish had voted to have constructed on the east side of the island to accommodate those whose incomes would never match their propensity to reproduce. He had been Guy Brouard's special project—Paul Fielder—and he'd come with him often to *Moulin des Niaux* to squat by the boxes stored in the cottages and to explore their contents with the two older men. But he'd never come to the Talbot Valley on his own before, and Frank felt a clutch in his gut at the sight of the boy.

Paul started to head for the Ouseleys' cottage, readjusting a dirty green rucksack that he wore on his back like a hump. Frank stepped to one side of the window so as not to be seen. If Paul knocked on the door, Graham would never answer. At this time of morning, he'd be mesmerised by the first of his soaps and oblivious of anything beyond the telly. Getting no reply, Paul Fielder would go. That was what Frank depended on.

But the mongrel had other plans. As Paul walked diffidently in the direction of the last cottage, Taboo headed directly for the door behind which Frank skulked like a dim-witted burglar. The dog sniffed round the base of the door. Then he barked, which caused Paul to change routes.

As Taboo whined and scratched at the door, Paul knocked. It was a hesitant tap, irritatingly like the boy himself.

Frank replaced the copies of *G.I.F.T.* in their folder and shoved this back into the filing drawer. He closed the cabinet, wiped his palms along his trousers, and swung the cottage door open.

He said heartily, "Paul!" and looked beyond him to the bike with a pretence of surprise. "Good Lord. Did you *ride* all this way?" As the crow flew, of course, it was no great distance from the Bouet to the Talbot Valley. Nothing was a great distance from anything else as the crow flew on the island of Guernsey. But taking the narrow serpentine roads added considerably to the journey. He'd never made it before, and Frank wouldn't have bet money on the boy's knowing how to get to the valley on his own, anyway. He was not too bright.

Paul blinked up at him. He was short for his sixteen years, and markedly feminine in appearance. He was just the sort of lad who would have taken the stage by storm during the Elizabethan age, when young boys who could pass for women were in high demand. But in their own age, things would be mightily different. The first time Frank had met the boy he'd registered how difficult his life had to be, particularly at school where a peach-skin face, wavy ginger hair, and eyelashes the colour of corn silk were not the sort of qualities that guaranteed someone immunity from bullying.

Paul made no reply to Frank's specious effort at a genial welcome. Instead, his milky grey eyes filled with tears, which he rubbed away by lifting his arm and scoring his face with the overworn flannel of his shirt. He wore no jacket, which was second cousin to insanity in this weather, and his wrists hung out from his shirt like white parentheses finishing off arms the size of sycamore saplings. He tried to say something but he gave a strangled sob instead. Taboo took the opportunity to enter the cottage unbidden.

There was nothing for it but to ask the boy in. Frank did so, sitting him down on the cane-bottomed chair and shoving the door closed against the December cold. But as he turned, he saw Paul was on his feet. He'd shrugged his rucksack off as if it were a burden he hoped someone would take from his shoulders, and he was bent forward against a stack of cardboard boxes in the attitude of someone either embracing their contents or exposing his back for scourging.

Frank thought it was a little of both. For the boxes represented one of the bonds that Paul Fielder had with Guy Brouard at the same time as they would serve to remind him that Guy Brouard was gone forever.

The boy would doubtless be devastated by Guy's death regardless of what he knew or didn't know of the terrible manner in which he'd met it. Living as he probably did in circumstances where he was one of many with parents ill-suited for any undertaking beyond boozing and bonking, he'd certainly have blossomed under the attention Guy Brouard had showered upon him. True, Frank himself had never actually seen evidence of that blossoming in the times Paul had attended Guy at *Moulin des Niaux,* but then again, he hadn't known the taciturn boy *before* Guy's advent in his life. The near-silent watchfulness that appeared to be the hallmark of Paul's character whenever the three of them were sorting through the wartime contents of the cottages might have actually been an astounding evolution from an abnormal and absolute mutism that had gone before.

Paul's thin shoulders trembled and his neck, against which his fine hair curled like the locks of a Renaissance putto, looked too delicate to support his head. This he dropped forward to rest on the top box in the stack. His body heaved. He gulped convulsively.

Frank felt out of his depth. He approached the boy and patted him awkwardly on the shoulder, saying, "There, there," and wondering how he would reply if the boy said, "Where, where?" in reply. But Paul said nothing, merely continued in his pose. Taboo came to sit at his feet and watched him.

Frank wanted to say that he mourned the passing of Guy Brouard with equal depth, but despite his desire to comfort the boy, he knew how unlikely it was that anyone on the island save the man's own sister felt a grief akin to Paul's. Thus, he could offer Paul one of two things: completely inadequate words of comfort or the opportunity to carry on with the work that he, Guy, and the boy himself had been engaged in. The first Frank knew he couldn't carry off. As to the second, he couldn't bear the thought. So the only option was to send the teenager on his way.

Frank said, "See here, Paul, I'm sorry you're upset. But shouldn't you be at school? It's not end of term yet, is it?"

Paul raised a flushed face to Frank. His nose was running and he wiped it on the heel of his hand. He looked simultaneously so pathetic and so hopeful that it came to Frank all in a rush exactly why the boy had come to see him.

Good God, he was looking for a *replacement,* seeking another Guy Brouard to show an interest in him, to give him a reason to . . . what? Dream his dreams? Persevere in their attainment? What, exactly, had Guy Brouard promised this pitiful boy? Certainly nothing that Frank Ouseley—forever childless—could help him acquire. Not with a ninety-two-year-old father to care for. And not with the burdens he himself was trying to carry: of expectations that had run fast and headlong into an incomprehensible reality.

As if in confirmation of Frank's suspicions, Paul snuffled and stilled his spasmodically heaving chest. He wiped his nose a final time along his flannel sleeve, and he looked round him as if only then he'd become aware of where he was. He sucked in on his lip, his hands plucking at the tattered hem of his shirt. Then he went across the room to where a stack of boxes stood, with *to be sorted* written in black felt pen on the top and sides of each.

Frank's spirits sank. It was as he thought: The boy was here to bond with him and carry on with the work as a sign of that bond. This wouldn't do.

Paul pulled the top box from the stack and gingerly set it down on the floor as Taboo joined him. He squatted next to it. With Taboo sinking into his usual posture of blowsy head on paws and devoted eyes fixed on his silent master, Paul carefully opened the box as he'd seen Guy and Frank do a hundred times. The contents constituted a jumble of wartime medals, old belt buckles, boots, *Luftwaffe* and *Wehrmacht* caps, and other items of apparel worn by those enemy troops in the distant past. He did as Guy and Frank had themselves done: He spread a polythene sheet on the stone floor, and he began to set the items out upon it, preparatory to cataloguing each of them in the three-ring notebook that they had been using.

He rose to get the notebook from its storage place, which was at the back of the filing drawer from which Frank had only moments before pulled the copies of *G.I.F.T.* Frank saw his opportunity.

He cried out, "Hey! See here, young man!" and he shot across the room to slam the filing drawer shut as the boy pulled it open. He moved so quickly and spoke at such a volume that Taboo leaped up and began to bark.

Frank seized the moment. "Just what the hell are you doing?" he demanded. "I'm working in here. You can't barge in and take over like this. These are priceless items. They're fragile, and once they're destroyed, they're gone. D'you understand?"

Paul's eyes widened. He opened his mouth to speak but nothing came out. Taboo continued to bark.

"And get that mongrel out of here, damn it," Frank continued. "You don't have the sense of a monkey, boy. Bringing him in here where he might . . . Just *look* at him. Destructive little beast."

Taboo, for his part, had hackles raised at the source of the commotion, so Frank used this as well.

He raised his voice another degree to shout, "Get him out of here, boy. Before I throw him out myself." When Paul shrank back further but made no other move to depart, Frank looked round frantically for something to spur him into action. His eyes lit on the boy's rucksack and he picked it up, swinging it menacingly at Taboo, who backed off, yelping.

The threat to the dog was what did it. Paul gave a strangled, inarticulate cry and raced for the door with Taboo at his heels. He paused only long enough to grab the rucksack from Frank. He threw it over his shoulder as he ran.

Through the window, his heart hammering, Frank watched them go. The boy's bike was a relic that at best would probably only have squeaked along at little above a walking pace. But he managed to pedal it furiously, so that in record time he and dog had vanished round the side of the water mill, teetering beneath the overhead weed-clogged sluice in the direction of the road.

When they were safely gone, Frank found that he could breathe again. His heart had been pounding in his ears and this had prevented him from hearing a second pounding, from the wall that joined this cottage to the one in which Frank and Graham lived.

He dashed back to see why his father was calling for him. He found Graham tottering back to the armchair from which he'd struggled, a wooden mallet in his hand. He said, "Dad? You all right? What is it?"

"Man can't get any peace in his own home?" Graham demanded. "Wha's the matter with you this

A.M., lad? Can't even hear the bloomin' telly over all your racket."

"Sorry," Frank said to his father. "That boy came round alone. Without Guy. You know the one I mean. Paul Fielder? Well, we can't have that, Dad. I don't want him prowling round here by himself. Not that I don't trust him, but some of what we've got is valuable and as he's from . . . well, rather deprived circumstances . . ." He knew he was talking too fast, but he couldn't help himself. "I don't like to take the chance he might nick something and sell it. He opened one of the boxes, you see. He just dived right in without a how-do-you-do and I—"

Graham took up the remote for the television and raised the volume to a level that assaulted Frank's eardrums. "You go about your damn business," he ordered his son. "I trust you c'n bloody well see for yourself I got my own here."

Paul pedaled like a madman, Taboo running along at his side. He made no stop to breathe, to rest, or even to think. Instead, he shot along the road out of the Talbot Valley, skirting too close for safety to the ivy-grown wall that held back the hillside into which the road was carved. Had he been able to think clearly, he might have stopped where a lay-by gave access to a path up the hill. He could have parked his bike there and followed that path upwards and along the fields where the tawny dairy cows grazed. No one would walk there at this time of year, so he would have been safe, and the solitude would have given him a chance to ponder what to do next. But all he had in his mind was escape. Bellowing was the precursor to violence, in his experience. Flight had long been his only option.

So he coursed up the valley and ages later, when he finally came round to wondering where he was, he saw that his legs had taken him to the single place he'd ever found safety and bliss. He was at the iron gates of *Le Reposoir*. They stood open as if in expectation of his arrival, as they had done so many times in the past.

He braked. At his knee, Taboo was panting. Paul felt a sudden excruciating bolt of guilt as he recognised the little dog's unwavering devotion to him. Taboo had barked to protect Paul from Mr. Ouseley's anger. He'd exposed himself to a stranger's wrath. Having done that, he'd then run half way across the island without hesitation. Paul dropped his bike with an indifferent crash and fell to his knees to hug the dog. Taboo responded by licking Paul's ear, as if he hadn't been ignored and forgotten in his master's flight. Paul choked back a cry at the thought of this. In his entire life's experience, no one but a dog could have offered Paul more love. Not even Guy Brouard.

But Paul didn't want to think of Guy Brouard at the moment. He didn't want to consider what the past had been with Mr. Brouard and even less did he want to contemplate the future with Mr. Brouard gone from his life.

So he did the only thing he could do: He carried on as if nothing had changed.

This meant that, as he was at the gates to *Le Reposoir,* he picked up his bicycle and entered the grounds. Rather than ride this time, however, he pushed the bike along beneath the chestnut trees with Taboo trotting happily beside him. In the distance, the pebbly drive fanned out before the stone manor house, and its line of windows seemed to wink their welcome in the dull December morning sun.

At one time, he would have gone round the back to the conservatory and entered there, stopping in the kitchen where Valerie Duffy would say, "Now, here's a pleasant sight for a lady in the morning," and smile at him and offer him a snack. She'd have a homemade scone for him or perhaps a tea cake, and before she'd let him find Mr. Brouard in his study or the gallery or elsewhere, she'd say, "You sit down and tell me if this is up to scratch, Paul. I don't want to have Mr. Brouard taste it without you giving me the high sign, all right?" And she'd add, "You wash it down with this," and she'd present him with milk or tea or a cup of coffee or on occasion a cup of hot chocolate so rich and thick that his mouth would water at the smell of it. She'd have something for Taboo as well.

But Paul didn't go to the conservatory this morning. Everything had changed with Mr. Guy's death. Instead, he went to the stone stables beyond the house, where in an old tack room Mr. Guy kept the tools. While Taboo snuffled round the delectable odours that the tack room and the stable provided, Paul gathered up the tool box and the saw, shoul-

dered up the planks of wood, and trudged back outside. He whistled for Taboo and the mongrel came
running, dashing on ahead to the pond that lay some
distance beyond the northwest side of the house. To
get to it, Paul had to pass the kitchen, and he could
see Valerie Duffy through the window when he
glanced that way. When she waved at him, though,
he ducked his head. He moved resolutely forward,
scuffling his feet through the gravel in the way he
liked, just to hear the crunch made by the pebbles
against the soles of his shoes. He had long liked that
sound, especially when the two of them walked together: he and Mr. Guy. They sounded just the
same, like two blokes setting off to work, and the
sameness of the sound they made had always assured
Paul that anything was possible, even growing up to
be another Guy Brouard.

Not that he wanted to duplicate Mr. Guy's life.
He had different dreams. But the fact that Mr. Guy
had started out with nothing—a refugee child from
France—and had actually gone from that nothing to
become a giant in his chosen life's path made the
promise to Paul that he could do likewise. Anything
was possible if one was willing to work.

And Paul was willing, had been so from the first
moment he'd met Mr. Guy. Twelve years old at the
time, a skinny kid in his older brother's clothes
which would soon enough be handed down to the
next brother in line, Paul had shaken the hand of the
gentleman in jeans, and all he'd been able to say at
the time was "White, that" as he stared with abject
admiration at the pristine condition of the T-shirt

that Mr. Guy wore beneath his perfect V-necked navy sweater. Then he flushed so hotly that he thought he'd faint. Stupid stupid, the voices shrieked in his head. As sharp as a tack without a point and just about as useful, you are, Paulie.

But Mr. Guy knew exactly what Paul was talking about. He'd said, It's not my doing, this. It's down to Valerie. She does the laundry. Last of her kind, she is. A real housewife. Not mine, unfortunately. She's spoken for by Kevin. You'll meet them both when you come to *Le Reposoir.* That is, if you want to. What d'you think? Shall we try each other out?

Paul didn't know how to reply. His third-form teacher had sat him down in advance and explained the special programme to him—adults from the community doing something with kids—but he hadn't listened as well as he might have done because he'd been distracted by a gold filling in the woman's mouth. It was close to the front and when she spoke, it glittered in the overhead lights in the classroom. He kept trying to see if there were more. He kept wondering how much her mouth was worth.

So when Mr. Guy talked about *Le Reposoir* and Valerie and Kevin—as well as his baby sister, Ruth, whom Paul had actually expected to *be* a baby when he finally met her—Paul took it all in and nodded because he knew that he was supposed to nod and he always did what he was supposed to do because to do anything else sent him directly into panic and confusion. Thus, Mr. Guy became his mate and together they embarked upon their friendship.

This consisted mostly of messing about together

on Mr. Guy's estate, because aside from fishing, swimming, and walking the cliff paths, there wasn't much else for two blokes to do on Guernsey. Or at least that had been the case until they'd begun the museum project.

But the museum project needed to be dismissed from his mind. Not to do that meant to relive those moments alone with Mr. Ouseley's shouting. So instead, he plodded over to the pond where he and Mr. Guy had been rebuilding the winter shelter for the ducks.

There were only three of them left now: one male and two females. The others were dead. Paul had come upon Mr. Guy burying their broken and bloody bodies one morning, innocent victims of a vicious dog. Or of someone's malice. Mr. Guy had stopped Paul from looking at them closely. He'd said, Stay there, Paul, keep Taboo away, too. And as Paul watched, Mr. Guy had buried each poor bird in a separate grave that he himself dug, saying, Damn. God. The waste, the waste.

There were twelve of them, sixteen ducklings as well, each with a grave and each grave marked, set round with stones and headed by a cross and the entire duck graveyard fenced off officially. We honour God's creatures, Mr. Guy had told him. It behooves us to remember we're just one of them ourselves.

Taboo had to be taught this, however, and teaching him to honour God's ducks had been something of a serious project for Paul. But Mr. Guy promised that patience would pay off and so it had done. Taboo was now gentle as a lamb in a dream with the three ducks that remained, and this morning they might have not been at the pond at all for the degree of indifference the dog showed them. He trotted off to investigate the smells among the stand of reeds that grew near a footbridge which spanned the water. For his part, Paul took his burden to the east side of the pond, where he and Mr. Guy had been working.

Along with the duck murders, the winter shelters for the birds had been destroyed. These were what Paul and his mentor had been re-building in the days preceding Mr. Guy's death.

Over time Paul had come to understand that Mr. Guy was trying him out on one project or another in an effort to see what he was suited for in life. He'd wanted to tell him that carpentry, brick laying, tiles setting, and painting were all fine and well but not exactly what led one into becoming an RAF fighter pilot. But he'd been reluctant to admit to that dream aloud. So he'd happily cooperated with every project presented him. If nothing else, the hours he spent at *Le Reposoir* were hours away from home, and that escape was fine by him.

He dropped the wood and the tools a short distance from the water and he shrugged out of his rucksack as well. He made sure Taboo was still within sight before he opened the tool case and studied its contents, trying to remember the exact order in which Mr. Guy had instructed him when building something. The boards were cut. That was good. He wasn't much use with a saw. He reckoned the nailing part came next. The only question was what got nailed to where.

He spied a folded sheet of paper beneath a carton of nails, and he remembered the sketches Mr. Guy had made. He reached for this and unfolded it on the ground, kneeling over it to study the plans.

Large A circled meant here's where you begin. Large B circled meant do this next. Large C circled was what followed B and so forth till the shelter was made. As easy as easy could be, Paul thought. He sorted through the wood to find the pieces that corresponded to the letters on the drawing.

This was a problem, though. For the timber pieces had no letters scrawled on them. They had numbers instead, and although there were also numbers on the drawing, some of these numbers were the same as others and *all* of them had fractions as well and Paul had been an utter disaster at fractions: He couldn't ever sort out what the top number meant to the bottom. He knew it had something to do with dividing. Top into bottom or bottom into top, depending on the least common nomination or something like that. But looking at the numbers made his head swim and brought to mind excruciating trips to the chalk board with the teacher demanding that he for heaven's sake just *reduce* the fraction, Paul. No *no*. The numeration and nomination will *change* when you divide them properly, you stupid stupid boy.

Laughter, laughter. Thick as shoe leather. Paulie Fielder. Brains of a cow.

Paul stared at the numbers, and he went on staring till they swam away. Then he grabbed the paper and crumpled it up. Useless, looseless, goose of a git. *Oh, tha's it, cry, li'tle nancy pantsy prick. Bet I know wha' you're crying 'bout, I do.*

"Ah. There you are."

Paul swung round at the sound. Valerie Duffy was coming along the path from the house, her long wool skirt catching against the fern fronds on the way. She was carrying something folded neatly across her palms. As Valerie drew near, Paul saw it was a shirt.

"Hello, Paul," Valerie Duffy said with the sort of good cheer that sounded deliberate. "Where's your four-legged mate this morning?" And as Taboo came bounding round the pond's edge, barking his greeting, she went on with "There you are, Tab. Why didn't you stop for a visit in the kitchen?"

She asked the question of Taboo, but Paul knew she really meant it for him. It was how she often communicated with him. Valerie liked to make her remarks to the dog. She continued to do so now, saying, "We've got the funeral tomorrow morning, Tab, and I'm sorry to say that dogs aren't allowed in church. But if Mr. Brouard was having his say, you'd be there, love. Ducks would, too. I hope our Paul's going, though. Mr. Brouard would've wanted him there."

Paul looked down at his scruffy clothes and knew he couldn't go to a funeral, no matter what. He hadn't the proper kit and even if he had, no one had told him the funeral was tomorrow. Why? he wondered.

Valerie said, "I phoned over to the Bouet yesterday and spoke to our Paul's brother about the funeral, Tab. But here's what I think: Billy Fielder didn't ever give him the message. Well, I should have known, Billy being Billy. I should've phoned again till I got hold of Paul or his mum or his dad. Still, Taboo, I'm glad you've brought Paul by to see us, 'cause now he knows."

Paul wiped his hands on the sides of his jeans. He hung his head and shuffled his feet in the sandy earth at the edge of the pond. He thought of all the dozens and dozens of people who would attend the funeral of Guy Brouard, and he was just as glad that he hadn't been told. It was bad enough to feel how he felt in private now that Mr. Guy was gone. Having to feel it all in public would be more than he could face. All those eyes fastened on him, all those minds wondering, all those voices whispering That's young Paul Fielder, Mr. Guy's special friend. And the looks that would go with those words—*special friend*—the eyebrows-raised, eyes-wide looks telling Paul that something more than words alone was being said by the speakers.

He looked up to see if Valerie had the eyebrows-raised eyes-wide face on her face. But she didn't, which made his shoulders relax. He'd been holding them so tight since fleeing *Moulin des Niaux* that they'd begun to ache. But now it felt like the pincers gripping his collar bone had suddenly been loosed.

"We're setting out at half past eleven tomorrow," Valerie said, but she spoke to Paul himself this time. "You can ride with Kev and me, love. You're not to mind about your clothes. I've brought you a shirt, see. And you're to keep it, mind you. Kev says he's got another two like it and he doesn't need three. As for the trousers . . ." She studied him thoughtfully. Paul felt the heat at each spot that her eyes rested upon his body. "Kev's won't do. You'd be lost inside them. But I think a pair of Mr. Brouard's . . . Now, you're not to *worry* about wearing something of Mr. Brouard's, love. He'd've wanted you to if you had the need. He was that fond of you, Paul. But you know that. No matter what he said or did, he was . . . He was that much fond . . ." She stumbled on the words.

Paul felt her sorrow like a band that pulled, drawing out of him what he wanted to quell. He looked away from Valerie towards the three surviving ducks, and he wondered how everyone was going to cope without Mr. Guy to hold them together, to set them on a course, and to know what ought to be done from now on.

He heard Valerie blow her nose and he turned back to her. She gave him a shaky smile. "Anyway, we'd like you to go. But if you'd rather not, you're not to feel guilty about it. Funerals aren't for everyone and sometimes it's best to remember the living by living ourselves. But the shirt's yours anyway. You're meant to have it." She looked round, seeming to seek a clean spot to set it and saying, "Here we are, then" when she spied the rucksack where Paul had left it on the ground. She made a move to tuck the shirt inside.

Paul cried out and tore the shirt from her hands. He flung it away. Taboo barked sharply.

"Why, Paul," Valerie said in surprise, "I didn't mean to . . . It's not an *old* shirt, love. It's really quite—"

Paul snatched up the rucksack. He looked left and right. The only escape was the way he'd come, and escape was essential.

He tore back along the path, Taboo at his heels, barking frantically. Paul felt a sob escape his lips as he emerged from the pond path out onto the lawn with the house beyond it. He was so tired of running, he realised. It seemed as if he'd been running all his life.

Chapter 4

RUTH BROUARD WATCHED THE boy's flight. She was in Guy's study when Paul emerged from the bower that marked the entrance to the ponds. She was opening a stack of condolence cards from the previous day's post, cards that she hadn't had the heart to open until now and she heard the dog barking first and then saw the boy himself pounding across the lawn beneath her. A moment later Valerie Duffy emerged, in her hands the shirt she'd taken to Paul, a limp and rejected offering from a mother whose own boys had fledged and flown far before she had been prepared for them to do either.

She should have had more children, Ruth thought as Valerie trudged back towards the house. Some women were born with a thirst for maternity that nothing could slake, and Valerie Duffy had long seemed like one of them.

Ruth watched Valerie's progress till she disappeared through the door to the kitchen, which was beneath Guy's study, where Ruth had taken herself directly after breakfast. It was the one place she felt that she could be close to him now, surrounded by

the evidence that told her, as if in defiance of the terrible manner in which he'd died, that Guy Brouard
had lived a good life. That evidence was everywhere
in her brother's study: on the walls and the bookshelves and sitting on a fine old credence table in
the centre of the room. Here were the certificates,
the photographs, the awards, the plans, and the documents. Filed away were the correspondence and
the recommendations for worthy recipients of the
well-known Brouard largesse. And displayed promi-
nently was what should have been the final jewel
needed to complete the crown of her brother's
achievements: the carefully constructed model of a
building that Guy had promised the island which
had become his home. It would be a monument to
the islanders' suffering, Guy had called it. A monument built by one who had suffered as well.

Or such had been his intention, Ruth thought.

When Guy hadn't come home from his morning
swim, she'd not worried at first. True, he was always punctual and predictable in his habits, but
when she descended the stairs and didn't find him
dressed and in the breakfast room, listening intently
to Radio News as he waited for his meal, she
merely assumed that he'd stopped at the Duffys'
cottage for coffee with Valerie and Kevin after his
swim. He would do that occasionally. He was fond
of them. That was why, after a moment's consideration, Ruth had carried her coffee and her grapefruit
to the telephone in the morning room, where she
rang the stone cottage at the edge of the grounds.

Valerie answered. No, she told Ruth, Mr.

Brouard wasn't there. She hadn't seen him since the early morning when she'd caught a glimpse of him as he went for his swim. Why? Hadn't he returned? He was probably on the estate somewhere . . . perhaps among the sculptures? He'd mentioned to Kev that he wanted to shift them about. That large human head in the tropical garden? Perhaps he was trying to decide where to put it because Valerie knew for certain that the head was one of the pieces that Mr. Brouard wanted to move. No, Kev wasn't with him, Miss Brouard. Kev was sitting right there in the kitchen.

Ruth didn't panic at first. Instead, she went up to her brother's bathroom where he would have changed after his exercise, leaving his swimming trunks and his track suit behind. Neither was there, however. Nor was a damp towel, which would have given further evidence of his return.

She felt it then, a pinch of concern like tweezers pulling at the skin beneath her heart. That was when she remembered what she'd seen from her window earlier as she'd watched her brother set off towards the bay: that figure who'd melted out from beneath the trees close to the Duffys' cottage as Guy had passed.

So she went to the phone and rang the Duffys again. Kevin agreed to set off for the bay.

He'd returned on the run but not to her. It was only when the ambulance finally appeared at the end of the drive that he came to fetch her.

That had begun the nightmare. As the hours passed, it only grew worse. She'd thought at first he'd had a heart attack, but when they wouldn't let her ride to the hospital with her brother, when they said she would have to follow in the car that Kevin Duffy drove silently behind the ambulance, when they whisked Guy away before she could see him, she knew something had dreadfully and permanently changed.

She hoped for a stroke. At least he would still be alive. But at last they came to tell her he was dead, and it was then that they explained the circumstances. From that explanation had come her waking nightmare: Guy struggling, in agony and fear, and all alone.

She would have rather believed that an accident had taken her brother's life. Knowing that he'd been murdered had cleaved her spirit and reduced her to living as the incarnation of a single word: *why*. And then: *who*. But that was dangerous territory.

Guy's life had taught him that he had to grasp for what he wanted. Nothing was going to be given to him. But more than once he had grasped without considering if what he wanted was what he should actually have. The results had brought suffering down upon others. His wives, his children, his associates, his . . . others.

You can't continue like this without someone being destroyed, she'd told him. And I can't stand by and let you.

But he'd laughed at her fondly and kissed her forehead. Headmistress Mademoiselle Brouard, he called her. Will you rap my knuckles if I don't obey?

The pain was back. It gripped her spine like a

spike that was driven through the nape of her neck and then iced till the horrible cold of it began to feel exactly like fire. It sent tentacles downward, each one an undulating serpent of disease. It sent her from the room in search of rescue.

She wasn't alone in the house, but she felt alone, and had she not been in the grip of the devil cancer, she might have laughed. Sixty-six years old and untimely ripped from the womb that a brother's love had provided her. Who would have thought it would come to this on that long-ago night when her mother had whispered, *"Promets-moi de ne pas pleurer, mon petit chat. Sois forte pour Guy."*

She wanted to maintain the faith with her mother that she'd maintained for more than sixty years. But the truth was what she had to deal with now: She couldn't see a way to be strong for anyone.

Margaret Chamberlain hadn't been in her son's presence for five minutes before she wanted to give him instructions: Stand up straight, for the love of God; look people in the eye when you talk to them, Adrian; don't for heaven's sake keep banging my luggage about like that; watch out for that cyclist, darling; *please* signal for your turns, my dear. She managed, however, to hold back this deluge of commands. He was the most beloved and the most exasperating of her four sons—that latter a fact that she put down to his paternity, which was different to the other boys—but since he'd only just lost his father, she decided to overlook the least irritating of his habits. For the moment.

He met her in what went for the arrivals hall at the Guernsey airport. She came through pushing a trolley with her cases piled on it, and she found him lurking by the car hire counter where worked an attractive red-head to whom he could have been chatting like a normal man, had he only been one. Instead, he was making a pretence of studying a map, losing yet another opportunity that life had placed squarely in front of him.

Margaret sighed. She said, "Adrian." And then, "*Adrian,*" when he failed to respond.

He heard her the second time and looked up from his scrutiny. He slunk over to the car hire counter and replaced the map. The red-head asked if she could help him, sir, but he didn't reply. Or even look at her. She asked again. He pulled up the collar of his jacket and gave her his shoulder instead of a reply. "Car's outside," he said to his mother by way of hello as he hoisted her suitcases from the trolley.

"How about 'Nice flight, darling Mum?' " Margaret suggested. "Why don't we just wheel the trolley to the car, dear? It would be easier, wouldn't it?"

He strode off, her cases in hand. There was nothing for it but to follow. Margaret cast an apologetic smile in the direction of the car hire counter in case the red-head was monitoring the welcome she'd received from her son. Then she went after him.

The airport comprised a single building sitting to one side of a single runway just off a series of unploughed fields. It had a car park smaller than her own local railway station's in England, so it was an easy matter to follow Adrian through it. By the time Margaret caught him up, he was shoving her two suitcases into the back of a Range Rover which was, she discovered in very short order, just the wrong sort of car in which to be riding round the thread-like roads of Guernsey.

She'd never been to the island herself. She and Adrian's father had long been divorced by the time he retired from Chateaux Brouard and set up house here. But Adrian had been to visit his father numerous times since Guy's removal to Guernsey, so why he was driving round in something nearly the size of a pantechnicon when what was *clearly* called for was a Mini was beyond her comprehension. As was the case with a number of things that her son did, the most recent being his termination of the only relationship he'd managed to have with a woman in his thirty-seven years. What was *that* all about? Margaret still wondered. All he'd said to her was "We wanted different things," which she didn't believe for a moment, since she knew—from a private and very confidential conversation with the young woman herself—that Carmel Fitzgerald had wanted marriage, and she also knew—from a private and very confidential conversation with her son—that Adrian had considered himself lucky to find someone youthful, moderately attractive, and willing to unquestioningly hook up with a nearly middle-aged man who'd never lived anywhere but in his mother's house. Save, of course, for that dreadful three months on his own while he tried to go to university . . . but the less *that* was thought of the better. So, what had happened?

Margaret knew she couldn't ask that question. At least, not now with Guy's funeral coming fast upon them. But she intended to ask it soon.

She said, "How's your poor aunt Ruth coping, darling?"

Adrian braked for a light at an ageing hotel. "Haven't seen her."

"Whyever not? Is she keeping to her room?"

He looked ahead to the traffic light, all his attention locked on to the moment the amber would show. "I mean I've seen her but I haven't seen her. I don't know how she's coping. She doesn't say."

He wouldn't think to ask her, of course. Any more than he would think to talk to his own mother in something more direct than riddles. Margaret said, "She wasn't the one who found him, was she?"

"That would be Kevin Duffy. The groundsman."

"She must be devastated. They've been together for . . . Well, they've always been together, haven't they."

"I don't know why you wanted to be here, Mother."

"Guy was my husband, darling."

"Number one of four," Adrian pointed out. It was tiresome of him, really. Margaret knew very well how many times she'd been married. "I thought you went to their funerals only if they died while you were still married to them."

"That's an incredibly vulgar remark, Adrian."

"Is it? Good God, we can't have vulgarity."

Margaret turned in her seat to face him. "Why are you behaving like this?"

"Like what?"

"Guy was my husband. I loved him once. I owe him the fact that I have you as a son. So if I want to honour all that by attending his funeral, I intend to do it."

Adrian smiled in a way that indicated his disbelief and Margaret wanted to slap him. Her son knew her only too well.

"You always thought you were a better liar than you actually are," he said. "Did Aunt Ruth think I'd do something . . . hmm . . . what would it be? unhealthy? illegal? just plain mad without you here? Or does she think I've already done that?"

"Adrian! How can you *suggest* . . . even as a joke . . ."

"I'm not joking, Mother."

Margaret turned to the window, unwilling to listen to any more examples of her son's skewed thinking. The light changed and Adrian powered through the intersection.

The route they were following was strung with structures. Beneath the sombre sky, postwar stucco cottages sat cheek by jowl with run-down Victorian terraces which themselves occasionally butted up against a tourist hotel that was shut for the season. The populated areas gave way to bare fields on the south side of the road, and here the original stone farmhouses stood, with white wooden boxes at the edge of their properties marking the sites where their owners would deposit homegrown new potatoes or hot-house flowers for sale at other times of the year.

"Your aunt phoned me because she phoned everyone," Margaret finally said. "Frankly, I'm surprised you didn't ring me yourself."

"No one else is coming," Adrian said in that maddening way he had of altering the course of a conversation. "Not even JoAnna or the girls. Well, I can understand JoAnna . . . how many mistresses did Dad go through while he was married to her? But I thought the girls might come. They hated his guts, of course, but I reckoned sheer greed would light a fire beneath their bums in the end. The will, you know. They'd want to know what they're getting. Big money, no doubt, if he ever got round to feeling guilty about what he did to their mum."

"Please don't talk about your father like that, Adrian. As his only son and the man who will one day marry and have sons to carry on Guy's name, I think you might—"

"But they're not coming." Adrian spoke doggedly and louder now, as if with the wish to drown his mother out. "Still, I thought JoAnna might show up, if only to drive a stake through the old man's heart." Adrian grinned, but it was more to himself than to her. Nonetheless, that grin caused a chill to shoot through Margaret's body. It reminded her too much of her son's bad times, when he pretended all was well while within him a civil war was brewing.

She was reluctant to ask but she was more reluc-

tant to remain in ignorance. So she picked her handbag off the floor and opened it, making a pretence of
searching for a breath mint as she said in an offhand
manner, "I expect the salt air does one a lot of good.
How have your nights gone since you've been here,
darling? Any uncomfortable ones?"

He flicked her a look. "You shouldn't have insisted I come to his bloody party, Mother."

"*I* insisted?" Margaret touched her fingers to her
chest.

" 'You must go, darling.' " He did an uncanny im-
itation of her voice. " 'It's been ages since you've
seen him. Have you even spoken to him on the
phone since last September? No? So there you are.
Your father will be extremely disappointed if you
stay away.' And we couldn't have that," Adrian said.
"Guy Brouard mustn't ever be disappointed when
there's something he wants. Except he didn't want it.
He didn't want me here. You were the one who
wanted that. He told me as much."

"Adrian, no. That's not . . . I hope . . . You . . .
you didn't quarrel with him, did you?"

"You thought he'd change his mind about the
money if I showed up to see him in his moment of
glory, didn't you?" Adrian asked. "I'd parade my
mug at his stupid party and he'd be so damned happy
to see me that he'd finally change his mind and fund
the business. Isn't that what this was all about?"

"I have no idea what you're talking about."

"You aren't suggesting he *didn't* tell you about re-
fusing to fund the business, are you? Last September?
Our little . . . discussion? 'You don't show enough

potential for success, Adrian. Sorry, my boy, but I don't like throwing my money away.' Despite how many buckets of cash he distributed elsewhere, of course."

"Your father said that? 'So little potential'?"

"Among other things. The idea's good, he told me. Internet access can always be improved and this does look like the way to do it. But with your track record, Adrian . . . not that you actually *have* a track record, which means we'll now need to examine all the reasons why you don't."

Margaret felt the outrage slowly spill its acid into her stomach. "Did he actually . . . ? How *dare* he."

"So pull up a chair, son. Yes, do. Ah. You have had your difficulties, haven't you? That incident in the headmaster's garden when you were twelve? And what about the hash you made out of university when you were nineteen? Not exactly what one looks for in an individual in whom one plans to make an investment, my boy."

"He said that to you? He brought those things up? Darling, I'm so sorry," Margaret said. "I could just weep. And you came over anyway after that? You agreed to see him? Why?"

"Obviously, because I'm a stupid lout."

"Don't *say* that."

"I thought I'd give it another try. I thought if I could just get this thing going, Carmel and I might . . . I don't know . . . give it another go. Seeing him—having to put up with whatever he dished out to me—I decided it would be worth it if I could save things with Carmel."

He'd kept his attention determinedly on the road as he admitted all this, and Margaret felt her heart go out to her son despite all the characteristics about him that frequently maddened her. His life had been so much rougher than the lives of his half-brothers, she thought. And she herself was to blame for so much of what had been rough about it. If she'd allowed him to have more time with his father, the time that Guy had wanted, had demanded, had attempted to get . . . That had been impossible, of course. But if she'd allowed it, had taken the risk, perhaps Adrian's way would have been easier. Perhaps she would have less to feel guilty about.

"Did you speak to him again about the money, then? On this visit, dear?" she asked. "Did you ask him to help you with the new business?"

"Didn't have the chance. I couldn't get him alone, what with Miss Melontits hanging all over him, making sure I didn't get a moment to score any of the cash she wanted for herself."

"Miss . . . Who?"

"His latest. You'll meet her."

"That can't be her real—"

Adrian snorted. "It should be. She was always hanging round, thrusting them into his face just in case he started thinking of something that didn't immediately relate to her. Quite the distraction, she provided. So we never talked. And then it was too late."

Margaret hadn't asked before because she hadn't wanted to elicit the information from Ruth, who had sounded on the phone as if she was already suffering enough. And she hadn't wanted to ask her son as soon as she saw him because she'd needed to assess his state of mind first. But now he'd given her an opening, and she took it.

"How exactly did your father die?"

They were entering a wooded area of the island, where a high stone wall richly covered in ivy ran along the west side of the road while the east side grew thick groves of sycamores, chestnuts, and elms. Between these in places the distant Channel showed through, a sheen of steel in the winter light. Margaret couldn't imagine why anyone would have wanted to swim there.

Adrian didn't reply to her question at first. He waited till they'd passed some farmland, and he slowed as they came to a break in the wall where two iron gates stood open. Tiles inset into the wall identified the property as *Le Reposoir*, and here he turned in to a drive. It led in the direction of an impressive house: four storeys of grey stone surmounted by what looked like a widow's walk, the inspiration, perhaps, of a former owner who'd undergone some form of enchantment in New England. Dormer windows rose beneath this balustraded balcony, while beneath these windows the façade of the house itself was perfectly balanced. Guy, Margaret saw, had done quite well for himself in retirement. But that was hardly surprising.

Towards the house, the drive emerged from the trees that tunneled it and circled a lawn at the centre of which stood an impressive bronze sculpture of a young man and woman swimming with dolphins.

Adrian followed this circle and stopped the Range Rover at steps that swept up to a white front door. It was closed and it remained closed as he finally replied to Margaret's question.

"He choked to death," Adrian said. "Down at the bay."

Margaret was puzzled by this. Ruth had said that her brother had not returned from his morning swim, that he had been waylaid on the beach and murdered. But choking to death didn't imply murder at all. *Being* choked did, of course, but *being choked* had not been Adrian's words.

"Choked?" Margaret said. "But Ruth told me your father was murdered." And for a wild moment she considered the fact that her former sister-in-law may have lied to her in order to get her to the island for some reason.

"It was murder, all right," Adrian said. "No one chokes accidentally—or even normally—on what was lodged in Dad's throat."

Chapter 5

"THIS IS JUST ABOUT the last place I thought I'd ever be showing up at." Cherokee River paused for a moment to observe the revolving sign in front of New Scotland Yard. He ran his gaze from the silver metallic letters to the building itself with its protective bunkers, its uniformed guards, and its air of sombre authority.

"I'm not sure if it's going to do us any good," Deborah admitted. "But I think it's worth a try."

It was closing in on half past ten, and the rain had finally begun to abate. What had been a downpour when they'd set off earlier for the American embassy was now a persistent drizzle, from which they sheltered beneath one of Simon's large black umbrellas.

Their sojourn had begun hopefully enough. Despite the desperate quality of his sister's situation, Cherokee possessed that can-do attitude that Deborah recalled being second nature to most Americans she'd met in California. He was a citizen of the United States on a mission to his nation's embassy. As a taxpayer he had assumed that when he entered the embassy and laid out the facts, phone calls would be made and China's release would be effected at once.

At first it had seemed that Cherokee's belief in the embassy's power was perfectly well founded. Once they had established where they were supposed to go—to the Special Consular Services Section, whose entrance was not through the impressive doors and beneath the impressive flag on Grosvenor Square but, rather, round the corner on the much more subdued Brook Street—they gave Cherokee's name at the reception desk, and a phone call into the reaches of the embassy brought an amazingly and gratifyingly quick response. Even Cherokee hadn't expected to be *greeted* by the chief of Special Consular Services. Perhaps ushered into her presence by an underling, but not greeted personally right there in reception. But that was what had happened. Special Consul Rachel Freistat—"It's Ms.," she'd said and her handshake was of the two-fisted sort, designed to reassure—strode into the enormous waiting room and shepherded both Deborah and Cherokee into her office where she offered them coffee and biscuits and insisted they sit near the electric fire to dry out.

It turned out that Rachel Freistat knew everything. Within twenty-four hours of China's arrest, she'd been phoned by the Guernsey police. This, she explained, was regulation, something agreed upon by the nations who'd signed the Hague Treaty. She had, in fact, spoken to China herself by phone, and she'd asked her if she required someone from the embassy to fly over and attend to her on the island.

"She said she didn't need that," the special consul had informed Deborah and Cherokee. "Otherwise we would have sent someone at once."

"But she does need that," Cherokee protested. "She's being railroaded. She knows it. Why would she have said . . . ?" He shoved his hand through his hair and muttered, "I don't get that one at all."

Rachel Freistat had nodded sympathetically, but her expression telegraphed the message that she'd heard the "being railroaded" declaration before. She said, "We're limited as to what we can do, Mr. River. Your sister knows that. We've been in touch with her attorney—her advocate, it's called over there—and he's assured us that he's been present for each one of her interviews with the police. We're ready to make any phone calls to the States that your sister wants made, although she specifically said she wants none right now. And should the American press pursue the story, we'll handle all queries from them as well. The local press on Guernsey is already covering the story, but they're hobbled by their relative isolation and their lack of funds, so they can't do more than just print what few details they're given by the police."

"But that's just it," Cherokee protested. "The police're doing their best to frame her."

Ms. Freistat had taken a sip of her coffee then. She'd looked at Cherokee over the rim of her cup. Deborah could see that she was weighing the available alternatives when it came to delivering bad news to someone, and she took her time before she reached her decision. "The American embassy can't help you with that, I'm afraid," she finally told him. "While it may be true, we can't interfere. If you believe wheels are turning that will steamroll your sister into prison, then you need to get help at once. But it needs to come from within their own system, not from ours."

"What's that supposed to mean?" Cherokee demanded.

"Perhaps some sort of private investigator . . . ?" Ms. Freistat replied.

So they'd left the embassy without attaining the joy they'd hoped for. They'd spent the next hour discovering that finding a private investigator on Guernsey was akin to finding ice cream in the Sahara. That being ascertained, they'd trekked across town to Victoria Street where now they stood with New Scotland Yard rising up before them, grey concrete and glass springing out of the heart of Westminster.

They hurried inside, shaking their umbrella over the rubber rain mat. Deborah left Cherokee staring at the eternal flame while she went to the reception desk and made her request.

"Acting Superintendent Lynley. We don't have an appointment, but if he's in and can see us . . . ? Deborah St. James?"

There were two uniforms behind reception, and they both examined Deborah and Cherokee with an intensity suggesting an unspoken belief that the two of them had come strapped with explosives. One of them made a phone call while the other attended to a delivery being offered by Federal Express.

Deborah waited until the phone caller said to her, "Give it a few minutes," at which point she returned to Cherokee, who said, "D'you think this'll do any good?"

"No way of knowing," she replied. "But we've got to try something."

Tommy came down himself to greet them within five minutes, which Deborah took for a very good sign. He said, "Deb, hullo. What a surprise," and he kissed her on the cheek and waited to be introduced to Cherokee.

They'd never met before. Despite the number of times that Tommy had come to California while Deborah had lived there, his path and the path of China's brother had never crossed. Tommy had heard of him, naturally. He'd heard his name and was unlikely to forget it, so unusual was it when compared to English names. So when Deborah said, "This is Cherokee River," his response was "China's brother," and he offered his hand in that way he had that was quintessentially Tommy: so utterly easy with himself. "Are you giving him a tour of town?" he asked Deborah. "Or showing him you have friends in questionable places?"

"Neither," she said. "May we talk to you? Somewhere private? If you've time? This is . . . It's rather a professional call."

Tommy raised an eyebrow. "I see," he said and within short order, he was whisking them to the lift and floors above to his office.

As acting superintendent, he wasn't in his regular spot. He was instead in a temporary office, which he was inhabiting while his superior officer convalesced from an attempt that had been made on his life in the previous month.

"How *is* the superintendent?" Deborah asked, seeing that Tommy in his good-hearted way hadn't replaced a single photograph that belonged to Superintendent Malcolm Webberly with any of his own.

Tommy shook his head. "Not good."

"That's dreadful."

"For everyone." He asked them to sit and joined them, leaning forward with his elbows on his knees. His posture asked the question What can I do for you? which reminded Deborah that he was a busy man.

So she set about telling him why they had come, with Cherokee adding what salient details he felt were needed. Tommy listened as Tommy had always listened, in Deborah's experience: His brown eyes remained on whoever was speaking and he appeared to shut out all other noises from the offices nearby.

"How well did your sister come to know Mr. Brouard while you were his guests?" Tommy asked when Cherokee had completed the story.

"They spent some time together. They clicked because they were both into buildings. But that was it, as far as I could tell. He was friendly with her. But he was friendly with me. He seemed pretty decent to everyone."

"Perhaps not," Tommy noted.

"Well, sure. Obviously. If someone killed him."

"How exactly did he die?"

"He choked to death. That's what the lawyer found out once China was charged. That's all the lawyer found out, by the way."

"Strangled, d'you mean?"

"No. Choked. He choked on a stone."

Tommy said, "A stone? Good Lord. What sort of stone? Something from the beach?"

"That's all we know right now. Just that it's a stone and he choked on it. Or, rather, my sister somehow choked him *with* it, since she's been arrested for killing him."

"So you see, Tommy," Deborah added, "it doesn't make sense."

"Because how is China supposed to have choked him with it?" Cherokee demanded. "How's *anyone* supposed to have choked him with it? What'd he do? Just open his mouth and let someone shove it down his throat?"

"It's a question that needs to be answered," Lynley agreed.

"It could have been an accident, even," Cherokee said. "He could have put the stone in his mouth for some reason."

"There'd be evidence to show otherwise," Tommy said, "if the police have made an arrest. Someone shoving the stone down his throat would tear the roof of his mouth, possibly his tongue. Whereas if he swallowed it by mistake . . . Yes. I can see how they went straight to murder."

"But why straight to China?" Deborah asked.

"There's got to be other evidence, Deb."

"My sister didn't kill anyone!" Cherokee rose as

he spoke. Restlessly, he walked to the window, then swung to face them. "Why can't anyone see that?"

"Can you do anything?" Deborah asked Tommy. "The embassy suggested we hire someone, but I thought you might . . . Can you ring them? The police? Make them see . . . ? I mean, obviously, they're not evaluating everything as they ought to. They need someone to tell them that."

Tommy steepled his fingers thoughtfully. "This isn't a UK situation, Deb. They're trained here, true, the Guernsey force. And they can request mutual aid, true as well. But as for starting something from this end . . . If that's what you're hoping, it's just not on."

"But . . ." Deborah reached out her hand, knew she was bordering on a plea—which felt utterly pathetic—and dropped her hand to her lap. "Perhaps, if they at least knew there was an interest at this end . . . ?"

Tommy studied her face before smiling. "You don't change, do you?" he asked fondly. "All right. Hang on. Let me see what I can do."

It took only a few minutes to locate the proper number on Guernsey and to track down the investigator in charge of the murder enquiry there. Murder was so uncommon on the island that all Tommy had to mention was the word itself before the connection was being made that put him in touch with the chief investigator.

But there was nothing to be gained from the call. *New Scotland Yard* apparently didn't cut any mustard in St. Peter Port, and when Tommy explained who he was and why he was phoning, making the offer of whatever assistance the Metropolitan police could provide, he was told—as he related to Deborah and Cherokee moments after ringing off—that everything was under control in the Channel, sir. And by the way, if assistance *were* to be required, the Guernsey police would make the request for mutual aid to the Cornwall or Devon Constabulary, as they usually did.

"We've some concern as it's a foreign national you've arrested," Tommy said.

Yes, well, wasn't *that* an interesting bit of a twist that the Guernsey police were also fully capable of handling on their own.

"Sorry," he said to Deborah and to Cherokee at the end of the phone call.

"Then what the hell are we going to do?" Cherokee spoke more to himself than to the others.

"You need to find someone who's willing to talk to the people involved," Tommy said in answer. "If one of my team were on leave or holiday there, I'd suggest you ask them to do some nosing round for you. You can do it yourself, but it would help if you were backed by a force."

"What needs to be done?" Deborah asked.

"Someone needs to start asking questions," Tommy said, "to see if there's a witness that's been missed. You need to find out if this Brouard had enemies: how many, who they are, where they live, where they were when he was killed. You need to have someone evaluate the evidence. Believe me, the police have someone who's doing it for them.

And you need to make sure no evidence has gone overlooked."

"There's no one on Guernsey," Cherokee said. "We tried. Debs and I. We did that before we came to you."

"Then think beyond Guernsey." Tommy leveled a look at Deborah, and she knew what that look meant.

They already had access to the person they needed.

But she wouldn't ask her husband for help. He was far too busy and even if that were not the case, it seemed to Deborah that most of her life had been defined by the countless moments when she had turned to Simon: from that long-ago time as a bullied little schoolgirl when her Mr. St. James—a nineteen-year-old with a well-developed sense of fair play—had frightened the daylights out of her tormentors to the present day as a wife who often tried the patience of a husband who required only that she be happy. She simply couldn't burden him with this.

So they would go it alone, she and Cherokee. She owed that to China but far more than that: She owed it to herself.

For the first time in weeks, sunlight the strength of jasmine tea was striking one of the two scales of justice when Deborah and Cherokee reached the Old Bailey. Neither of them possessed a rucksack or bag of any kind, so they had no trouble gaining admittance. A few questions produced the answer they were looking for: Courtroom Number Three.

The visitors' gallery was up above, and at the moment it was occupied only by four out-of-season tourists wearing see-through rain slickers and a woman clutching a handkerchief. Beneath them, the courtroom spread out like something from a costume drama. Here was the judge—red-gowned and forbidding in wire-rimmed spectacles and a wig that dripped sheep curls down to his shoulders—sitting in a green leather chair, one of five that spread across the top of the room on a dais that separated him from his lessers. These were the black-gowned barristers—defending and prosecuting—lined up along the first bench and table at right angles to the judge. Behind them were their associates: junior members of chambers and solicitors as well. And across from them was the jury with the clerk in between, as if refereeing what might happen in the room. The dock was directly below the gallery, and here the accused sat with an officer of the court. Opposite him was the witness box, and it was to this box that Deborah and Cherokee directed their attention.

The Crown Prosecutor was just concluding his cross-examination of Mr. Allcourt-St. James, expert witness for the defence. He was referring to a many-paged document, and the fact that he called Simon *sir* and *Mr. Allcourt-St. James if you will,* didn't hide the fact that he doubted the opinions of anyone who didn't agree with the police and by extension the CPS conclusions.

"You seem to be suggesting Dr. French's

laboratory work is wanting, Mr. Allcourt–St. James," the Crown Prosecutor was saying as Deborah and Cherokee slid onto a bench at the front of the gallery.

"Not at all," Simon replied. "I'm merely suggesting that the amount of residue taken from the defendant's skin could easily be consistent with his employment as a gardener."

"Are you then also suggesting it's a coincidence that Mr. Casey"—with a nod at the man in the dock the back of whose neck Deborah and Cherokee could study from their position in the gallery—"would have upon his person traces of the same substance that was used to poison Constance Garibaldi?"

"As Aldrin's use is for the elimination of garden insects and as this crime occurred during the height of the season when those same insects are prevalent, I'd have to say that trace amounts of Aldrin on the defendant's skin are easily explainable by his profession."

"His long-standing quarrel with Mrs. Garibaldi not withstanding?"

"That's right. Yes."

The Crown Prosecutor went on for several minutes, referring to his notes and consulting once with a colleague from the row behind the barristers' seats. He finally dismissed Simon with a "thank you, sir," which released him from the witness box when the defence required nothing more of him. He began to step down, which was when he caught sight of Deborah and Cherokee above him in the gallery.

They met him outside the courtroom, where he

said, "What's happened, then? Were the Americans helpful?"

Deborah related to him what they'd learned from Rachel Freistat at the embassy. She added, "Tommy can't help either, Simon. Jurisdiction. And even if that weren't the problem, the Guernsey police ask Cornwall or Devon for assistance when they need it. They don't ask the Met. I got the impression— didn't you, Cherokee?—that they got a bit shirty when Tommy even mentioned the idea of help."

Simon nodded, pulling at his chin thoughtfully. Around them, the business of the criminal court went on, with officials hurrying past with documents and barristers strolling by with their heads together, planning the next move they would make in their trials.

Deborah watched her husband. She saw that he was seeking a solution to Cherokee's troubles, and she was grateful for that. He could so easily have said, "That's it, then. You'll have to go the course and wait for the outcome on the island," but that wasn't his nature. Still, she wanted to reassure him that they hadn't come to the Old Bailey to place further burdens upon him. Rather, they had come to let him know they'd be setting off for Guernsey as soon as Deborah had a chance to pop home and collect some clothes.

She told him as much. She thought he'd be grateful. She was wrong.

St. James reached a swift conclusion as his wife related her intentions to him: He mentally labeled the idea sheer lunacy. But he wasn't about to tell Deborah that. She was earnest and well-intentioned and, more than that, she was worried about her California friend. In addition to this, there was the man to consider.

St. James had been happy to offer Cherokee River food and shelter. It was the least he could do for the brother of the woman who'd been his wife's closest friend in America. But it was quite another situation for Deborah to think she was going to play detectives with a relative stranger or with anyone else. They could both end up in serious trouble with the police. Or worse, if they happened to stumble upon the actual killer of Guy Brouard.

Feeling that he couldn't pop Deborah's balloon so callously, St. James tried to come up with a way merely to deflate it. He guided Deborah and Cherokee to a spot where all of them could sit, and he said to Deborah, "What is it you hope to do over there?"

"Tommy suggested—"

"I know what he said. But as you've already found out, there's no private investigator on Guernsey for Cherokee to hire."

"I know. Which is why—"

"So unless you've already found one in London, I don't see what your going to Guernsey is going to achieve. Unless you want to be there to offer China support. Which is completely understandable, of course."

Deborah pressed her lips together. He knew what she was thinking. He was sounding too reasonable, too logical, too much the scientist in a situation where feelings were called for. And not only feelings but action that was immediate, no matter how ill thought out.

"I don't mean to hire a private investigator, Simon," she said stiffly. "Not at first. Cherokee and I . . . We're going to meet China's advocate. We'll look at the evidence the police have gathered. We'll talk to anyone who'll talk to us. We're not the police ourselves, so people won't be afraid to meet with us, and if someone knows something . . . if the police have missed something . . . We're going to uncover the truth."

"China's innocent," Cherokee added. "The truth . . . It's there. Somewhere. And China needs—"

"Which means someone else is guilty," St. James interrupted. "Which makes the situation inordinately delicate and dangerous as well." He didn't add what he wanted to add at this point. *I forbid you to go.* They didn't live in the eighteenth century. Deborah was—if anything—an independent woman. Not financially, of course. He could stop her there by tightening her purse strings or whatever it was that one did to cut a woman off financially. But he liked to think he was above that kind of machination. He'd always believed that reason could be employed more effectively than intimidation. "How will you locate the people you want to talk to?"

"I expect they have phone books on Guernsey," Deborah said.

"I mean how will you know who to talk to?" St. James asked.

"Cherokee will know. China will know. They were at Brouard's house. They met other people. They'll come up with the names."

"But why would these people want to talk to Cherokee? Or to you, for that matter, once they learn of your connection to China?"

"They won't learn of it."

"You don't think the police will tell them? And even if they do speak to you—to Cherokee as well—and even if you manage that part of the situation, what will you do with the rest?"

"Which . . . ?"

"The evidence. How do you plan to evaluate it? And how will you recognise it if you find more?"

"I hate it when you . . ." Deborah swung to Cherokee. She said, "Will you give us a moment?"

Cherokee looked from her to St. James. He said, "This is making too much trouble. You've done enough. The embassy. Scotland Yard. Let me head back to Guernsey and I'll—"

Deborah cut in firmly. "Give us a moment. Please."

Cherokee glanced from husband to wife then back to husband. He looked inclined to speak again, but he said nothing. He took off to inspect a list of trial dates that was hanging from a notice board.

Deborah turned on St. James furiously. "Why are you *doing* this?"

"I just want you to see—"

"You think I'm bloody incompetent, don't you?"

"That's not the truth, Deborah."

"Incapable of having a few conversations with people who might just be willing to tell us something they haven't told the police. Something that could make a difference. Something that could get China out of gaol."

"Deborah, I don't mean you to think—"

"This is my friend," she persisted in a fierce low voice. "And I mean to help her. She was *there,* Simon. In California. She was the *only* person—" Deborah stopped. She looked ceilingward and shook her head as if this would shake off not only emotion but also memory.

St. James knew what she was recalling. He didn't need a road map to see how Deborah had traveled to her destination. China had been there as soul mate and confessor during the years that he himself had failed Deborah. Doubtless she had been there as well while Deborah fell in love with Tommy Lynley and perhaps she had wept along with Deborah during the aftermath of that love.

He knew this but he could no more bring it up at that moment than he could undress in public and put his body's damage on display. So he said, "My love, listen. I know you want to help."

"Do you?" she asked bitterly.

"Of course I do. But you can't crash round Guernsey just because you want to help. You haven't the expertise and—"

"Oh thank you very much."

"—the police aren't going to be the least bit cooperative. And you have to have their cooperation,

Deborah. If they won't divulge every bit of their evidence, you'll have no way of truly knowing whether China is actually innocent."

"You *can't* think she's a killer! My God!"

"I don't think anything one way or another. I'm not invested as you are. And that's what you need: someone who's not invested either."

Even as he heard his own words, he felt himself becoming committed. She hadn't asked it of him and she certainly wouldn't ask it of him now, after their conversation. But he saw how it was the only solution.

She needed his help, and he had spent over half his lifetime extending his hand to Deborah, whether she reached out for it or not.

Chapter 6

PAUL FIELDER WENT TO his special place when he
fled Valerie Duffy. He left the tools where they
were. He knew this was wrong because Mr. Guy
had explained that at least one part of good work-
manship was the care and maintenance of the work-
man's tools, but he told himself that he'd go back
later when Valerie couldn't see him. He'd sneak
round the other side of the house, the part that
wasn't near to the kitchen, and he'd collect the tools
and return them to the stables. If it felt safe, he might
even work on the shelters then. And he'd check the
duck graveyard and make sure the little plots were
still marked by their circlets of stones and shells. He
knew that he had to do all of that before Kevin
Duffy happened upon the tools, though. If Kevin
happened upon them lying in the damp growth of
weeds, reeds, and grass that surrounded the pond, he
wouldn't be pleased.

Thus, Paul didn't go far in his flight from Valerie.
He just circled round the front of the house and
rode into the woods along the east side of the drive.
There he dove onto the bumpy, leaf-strewn path

beneath the trees and between the rhododendrons and ferns and he followed it till he came to the second fork to the right. Here he dumped his old bike next to a mossy sycamore trunk, part of a tree once felled by a storm and left to become the hollowed home of wild things. The way was too rough to ride the bike forward from this point, so he shouldered his rucksack more firmly and took off on foot with Taboo trotting along beside him, pleased to be out on a morning adventure rather than waiting patiently as he usually did, tied to the ancient *menhir* that stood beyond the wall at the edge of the school yard, a bowl of water at his side and a handful of biscuits to see him through till Paul fetched him at the end of the day.

Paul's destination was one of the secrets he had shared with Mr. Guy. I think we know each other well enough now for something special, Mr. Guy had said the first time he introduced Paul to the spot. If you want to—if you think that you're ready—I have a way that we can seal our friendship, my Prince.

That was what he had called Paul, *my Prince.* Not at first, of course, but later, once they grew to know each other better, once it seemed like they shared an uncommon sort of kinship. Not that they *were* kin and not that Paul would *ever* have thought they could be kin. But there had existed between them a fellowship, and the first time Mr. Guy had called him *my Prince,* Paul was certain the older man felt that fellowship as well.

So he had nodded his assent. He was quite ready to seal his friendship with this important man who'd entered his life. He wasn't altogether sure what it meant to seal a friendship, but his heart was always full to bursting when he was with Mr. Guy and Mr. Guy's words surely indicated *his* heart was full to bursting as well. So whatever it meant, it would be good. Paul knew that.

A place of the spirits was what Mr. Guy called the special place. It was a dome of land like an upended bowl on the earth, grassed over thickly, with a flattened path running round it.

The place of the spirits lay beyond the woods, over a drystone wall, part of a meadow where the docile Guernsey cows once had grazed. It was overgrown with weeds and fast becoming encroached upon by brambles and bracken because Mr. Guy had no cows to eat the undergrowth, and the greenhouses that might have replaced the cattle had themselves been dismantled and carted off when Mr. Guy first purchased the property.

Paul scrambled over the wall and dropped down to the path at its base. Taboo followed. It led through the bracken to the mound itself and there they tripped along another path which wound round to the southwest side. Here, Mr. Guy had once explained, the sunlight would have burned the strongest and the longest for the ancient people who had used this place.

A wooden door of far more recent vintage than the dome itself stood halfway round the circumference of the mound. It was hung from stone jambs beneath a stone lintel, and a combination lock thrust through a hasp on the door kept it safely closed.

Took me months to find a way inside, Mr. Guy had told him. I knew what it was. That was easy enough. What else would a mound of earth be doing in the middle of a meadow? But finding the entrance . . . ? That was the devil, Paul. Debris was piled up—brambles, bushes, the lot—and these entryway stones had long been overgrown. Even when I located the first ones under the earth, telling the difference between the entry and the support stones inside the mound . . . Months, my Prince. It took me months. But it was worth it, I think. I ended up with a special place and believe you me, Paul, every man needs a special place.

That Mr. Guy had been willing to share his special place had caused Paul to blink in surprise. He'd found his throat blocked by a great plug of happiness. He'd smiled like a dolt. He'd grinned like a clown. But Mr. Guy had known what that meant. He said, Nineteen three twenty-seven fifteen. Can you remember that? That's how we get in. I give the combination only to special friends, Paul.

Paul had religiously committed those numbers to memory, and he used them now. He slipped the lock into his pocket, and he shoved the door open. It stood barely four feet from the ground, so he removed his rucksack from his back and clutched it to his chest to give himself more room. He ducked beneath the lintel and crawled inside.

Taboo trotted ahead of him, but he paused, sniffed the air, and growled. It was dark inside—lit only from the door by the shaft of weak December light that did very little to pierce the gloom—and although the special place had been locked, Paul hesitated when the dog seemed uncertain about entering. He knew there were spirits on the island: ghosts of the dead, the familiars of witches, and fairies who lived in hedges and streams. So although he wasn't afraid there was a human within the mound, there could well be something else.

Taboo, however, had no qualms about encountering something from the spirit world. He ventured inside, snuffling the stones that comprised the floor, disappearing into the internal alcove, darting from there into the centre of the structure itself, where the top of the mound allowed a man to stand upright. He finally returned to where Paul still stood hesitantly right inside the door. He wagged his tail.

Paul bent lower and pressed his cheek to the dog's wiry fur. Taboo licked his cheek and bowed deeply into his forelegs. He backed up three paces and gave a yip, which meant he thought they were there to play, but Paul scratched his ears, eased the door shut, and buried them in the darkness of that quiet place.

He knew it well enough to find his way, one hand holding his rucksack to his chest and the other running along the damp stone wall as he crept towards the centre. This, Mr. Guy had told him, was a place of deep significance, a vault where prehistoric man had come to send his dead on their final journey. It was called a dolmen, and it even had an altar—although this looked much like a worn old stone to Paul, raised a mere few inches off the floor—and a secondary chamber where religious rites had been performed, rites they could only speculate upon.

Paul had listened and looked and shivered in the cold that first time he'd come to the special place. And when Mr. Guy had lit the candles that he kept in a shallow depression at the side of the altar, he had seen Paul shaking and had done something about it.

He took him to the secondary chamber, shaped like two palms cupped together, and accessed by squeezing behind an upright stone that stood like a statue in a church and had worn carvings upon its surface. In this secondary chamber Mr. Guy had a collapsible camp bed. He had blankets and a pillow. He had candles. He had a small wooden box.

He said, I come here to think sometimes. To be alone and to meditate. Do you meditate, Paul? Do you know what it is to make the mind go to rest? Blank slate? Nothing but you and God and the way of all things? Hmm? No? Well, perhaps we can work on that, you and I, practise it a bit. Here. Take this blanket. Let me show you round.

Secret places, Paul thought. Special places to share with special friends. Or places where one could be alone. When one needed alone. Like now.

Paul had never been here by himself, however. Today was his very first time.

He crept carefully into the centre of the dolmen and felt his way to the altar stone. Molelike, he ran his hands across its flat surface to the depression at its base, where the candles were. A Curiously Strong Mints tin was tucked into this depression as well as the candles, and inside were the matches, protected from the damp. Paul felt for this and brought it forth. He set his rucksack down and lit the first of the candles, fixing it with wax to the altar stone.

With a little bit of light, he felt less anxious about being alone in this damp, shadowy place. He looked round at the old granite walls, at the curving ceiling, at the pockmarked floor. Incredible that ancient man could build a structure like this, Mr. Guy had said. We think we have everything over the stone age, Paul, with our mobiles, our computers, and the like. Instant information to go along with our instant everything else. But look at this, my Prince, just look at this place. What have we built in the last one hundred years that we can declare will be standing in one hundred thousand more, eh? Nothing, that's what. Here, Paul, take a look at this stone . . .

Which he had done, Mr. Guy's hand warm on his shoulder as the fingers of his other hand followed the marks that hand upon hand upon hand before him had worn into the stone that stood guard to the secondary alcove where Mr. Guy kept his camp bed and blankets. Paul went there now, to that secondary alcove, his rucksack in his hand. He scooted behind the sentinel stone with another candle lit and Taboo at his heels. He placed his rucksack on the floor and his candle on the wooden box where melted wax marked the spot of dozens of candles placed there before it. He took one of the blankets from the camp bed for Taboo, folding it into a dog-sized square and putting it on the cold stone floor. Taboo hopped onto it gratefully and circled three times to make it his own before settling down with a sigh. He lowered his head to his paws and fixed his eyes lovingly on Paul.

That dog thinks I mean you ill, my Prince.

But no. That was just Taboo's way. He knew the important role he played in his master's life—sole friend, sole companion until Mr. Guy had come along—and knowing his role, he liked Paul to *know* he knew his role. He couldn't tell him, so instead he watched him: his every move, in every moment, during every day.

It was the same way Paul had watched Mr. Guy when they were together. And unlike other people in Paul's life, Mr. Guy had never been bothered by Paul's unwavering stare. Find this interesting, do you? he'd ask if he shaved while they were together. And he never poked fun at the fact that Paul himself—despite his age—did not yet need to shave. How short should I have it cut? he'd ask when Paul accompanied him to the barber in St. Peter Port. Have some care with those scissors, Hal. As you can see, I've got my man watching your moves. And he'd wink at Paul and give the signal that meant Friends Till We Die: fingers of his right hand crossed and placed against the palm of his left.

Till We Die had arrived.

Paul felt the tears coming, and he let them come. He wasn't at home. He wasn't at school. It was safe to miss him here. So he wept as much as he wanted to weep, till his stomach hurt and his eyelids were sore. And in the candlelight, Taboo watched him faithfully, in complete acceptance and perfect love.

Cried out at last, Paul realised he had to remember the good things that had come from knowing Mr. Guy: all the things he had learned in his company, all that he had come to value, and all that he had been encouraged to believe. We serve a greater purpose than just getting through life, his friend had told him more than once. We serve the purpose of clarifying the past in order to make the future whole.

Part of their clarifying the past was going to be the museum. To that end, they had spent long hours in the company of Mr. Ouseley and his dad. From them and from Mr. Guy, Paul had learned the significance of items he once might have tossed heedlessly to one side: the odd buckle from a belt found on the grounds of Fort Doyle, hidden among the weeds and buried for decades till a storm beat the earth away from a boulder; the useless lantern from a car boot sale; the rusty medal; the buttons; the dirty dish. This island is a real burial ground, Mr. Guy had told him. We're going to do some exhuming here. Would you like to be a part of that? The answer was easy. He wanted to be a part of anything that Mr. Guy was a part of.

So he threw himself into the museum work with Mr. Guy and Mr. Ouseley. Wherever he went on the island, he kept his eyes open for something to contribute to the vast collection.

He'd finally found something. He'd ridden his bike all the miles southwest to *La Congrelle,* where the Nazis had built one of their ugliest watch towers: a futuristic concrete eruption on the land with slits for their anti-aircraft guns to shoot down anything approaching the shore. He hadn't gone looking for anything related to the five years of German occupation, however. Instead, he'd gone to have a look at the most recent car that had plummeted over the cliff.

La Congrelle possessed one of the few cliff tops on the island that were directly accessible by car. Other cliff tops one had to hike out to from a car park a safe distance away, but at *La Congrelle* one could drive to the very edge. It was a good spot for a suicide that one wished to be seen as an accident, because at the end of the road from *Rue de la Trigale* to the Channel, one merely had to veer to the right and accelerate the last fifty yards through the low-growing gorse and across the grass to the edge of the cliff. A final stomp on the accelerator as the land in front of the bonnet disappeared and the car would shoot over and plunge down to the rocks, end over end till it was stopped by a jagged barrier of granite, exploded into the water itself, or erupted into flames.

The car in question that Paul went to see had met its end by the last method. There was little left of it but twisted metal and one blackened seat, something of a disappointment after the long bike ride in the wind. Had there been something more, Paul might have made the perilous descent to investigate. As there wasn't, he explored the area of the watch tower instead.

A rock fall had occurred, he saw, recent by the look of the stones and the ravaged nature of the ground from which they had become dislodged. The newly bared stones were devoid of thrift and sea campion that grew in tufts along the cliffs. And the boulders that had toppled towards the water below had no guano on them, although their older companion chunks of Icart gneiss were streaked with it.

This was a most dangerous place to be, and as an islander born and bred, Paul knew it. But he'd learned from Mr. Guy that whenever the land opened itself to man, there were secrets that often came into the daylight. For that reason, he scouted round.

He left Taboo on the cliff top and picked his way across the face of the gash left by the rock fall. He was careful to keep a firm hold on a fixed piece of granite whenever he moved his feet, and in this manner he slowly traversed the façade of the cliff, working his way downwards like a crab scouting for a crevice in which to hide.

It was at the midway point that he found it, so encrusted with half a century of soil, dried mud, and pebbles that at first he thought it was nothing more than an elliptical stone. But when his foot dislodged it, he saw the glint of what looked like metal marking a curve that emerged from within the object itself. So he picked it up.

He couldn't examine it there, midway down the cliff, so he carried it tucked between his chin and his chest back to the top. There, with Taboo snuffling at the object eagerly, he used a pocket knife and then his fingers to reveal what the earth had kept secret for so many years.

Who knew how it had come to be there? The Nazis hadn't bothered to clean up their mess once they realised the war was lost and the invasion of England was never going to happen. They merely surrendered, and like the defeated invaders who had occupied the island in times before them, they left behind whatever they found too inconvenient to carry.

So near to a watch tower once occupied by soldiers, it was no wonder that their detritus continued to be unearthed. While this would have been no personal possession of anyone, it certainly would have been something the Nazis might have found useful had the Allies, guerrillas, or Resistance fighters successfully made a landing beneath them.

Now, in the semi-dark of the special place he and Mr. Guy had shared, Paul reached for his rucksack. He'd intended to hand his find over to Mr. Ouseley at *Moulin des Niaux,* his first solo, pride-filled contribution. But he couldn't do that now—not after this morning—so he would keep it here where it would be safe.

Taboo raised his head and watched as Paul unfastened the rucksack's buckles. He reached inside and brought out the old towel in which he'd wrapped his treasure. In the way of all seekers of history's nuggets, he unfolded the towel from round his find to give it a final and rapt inspection before placing it for safekeeping within a place of security.

The hand grenade probably wasn't actually dangerous at all, Paul thought. The weather would have battered it for years before it became buried in the earth and the pin that might have once detonated the explosive within it was most likely rusted immovably in place. But still, it wasn't wise to carry it round in his rucksack. He didn't need Mr. Guy or anyone else to tell him that prudence suggested he put it somewhere that no one would come across it. Just till he decided what else he could do with it.

Within the secondary chamber of the dolmen, where he and Taboo now hid, was the cache. This, too, Mr. Guy had shown him: a natural fissure between two of the stones that comprised the wall of the dolmen. That wouldn't have been here originally, Mr. Guy had said. But time, weather, the movement of the earth . . . Nothing manmade withstands nature completely.

The cache was just to one side of the camp bed and to the uninitiated it appeared to be a simple gap in the stones and nothing more. But sliding a hand deep inside revealed a second, wider gap *behind* the stone that was nearest the camp bed, and this was the cache where secrets and treasures too precious for common view could be kept.

If I show you this, it says something, Paul. Something larger than words. Something bigger than thoughts.

Paul reckoned there was enough room for the grenade within the cache. He'd placed his hand in there before, guided by Mr. Guy's own hand with Mr. Guy's reassuring words spoken softly into his ear: There's nothing in there at the moment, I wouldn't play a nasty trick on you, Prince. Thus he knew there was space for one fist clasped over another, and that was more than enough space for a grenade to occupy. And the depth of the cache was more than sufficient. For Paul hadn't been able to feel the end of it no matter how far he'd managed to stretch his arm.

He moved the camp bed to one side and he set the wooden box with its candle in the middle of the alcove floor. Taboo whined at this alteration in his environment, but Paul patted his head and fondly touched the tip of his nose. Nothing to worry about, his gesture told the dog. We're safe in this place. No one knows about it now but you and me.

Carefully clutching the grenade, he lay on the cold stone floor. He squirreled his arm into the narrow fissure. It widened six or so inches from the opening, and even though he couldn't see far into the interior of the hiding spot, he knew where the second opening was by feel, so he anticipated no problem in depositing the hand grenade there.

But there *was* a problem. Not four inches inside the fissure was something else. He felt his knuckles press against it first, something firm and unmoving and entirely unexpected.

Paul gasped and withdrew his hand, but it was only a moment before he realised that *whatever* it was, it certainly wasn't alive, so there was no reason to be afraid of it. He set the grenade carefully on the camp bed, and he brought the candle closer to the opening of the fissure.

Problem was, he couldn't illuminate the fissure and see inside it at the same time. So he resumed his former position on his stomach and slid his hand, then his arm, back into the hiding place.

His fingers found it, something firm but giving.

Not hard. Smooth. Shaped like a cylinder. He grasped it and began to pull it out.

This is a special place, a place of secrets, and it's our secret now. Yours and mine. Can you keep secrets, Paul?

He could. Oh, he could. He could *better* than could. Because as he pulled it towards him, Paul understood exactly what it was that Mr. Guy had hidden within the dolmen.

The island, after all, was a landscape of secrets and the dolmen itself was a secret place within that larger landscape of things buried, other things unspoken, and memories people wished to forget. It was no wonder to Paul that deep within the ages of an earth that could still yield medals, sabres, bullets, and other items more than half a century old lay buried somewhere something even more valuable, something from the time of the privateers or even further back, but something precious. And what he was pulling from the fissure was the key to finding that long-ago-buried something.

He'd found a final gift from Mr. Guy, who had already given him so very much.

"*Énne rouelle dé faïtot,*" Ruth Brouard said in answer to Margaret Chamberlain's question. "It's used for barns, Margaret."

Margaret thought this reply was deliberately obtuse, so typical of Ruth, whom she'd never particularly come to like despite having had to live with Guy's sister for the entirety of her marriage to the man. She'd clung too much to Guy, Ruth had, and too great a devotion between siblings was unseemly. It smacked of . . . Well, Margaret didn't even want to think of what it smacked of. Yes, she realised that these specific siblings—Jewish like herself but European Jewish during World War II, which gave them certain allowances for strange behaviour, she would grant them that—had lost every single relation to the unmitigated evil of the Nazis and thus had been forced to become everything to each other from early childhood. But the fact that Ruth had never developed a life of her own in all these years was not only questionable and pre-Victorian, it was something that made her an incomplete woman in Margaret's eyes, sort of a lesser creature who'd lived a half life, and that life in the shadows to boot.

Margaret decided patience would be in order. She said, "For barns? I don't quite understand, dear. The stone would have to be quite small, wouldn't it? To have gone into Guy's mouth?" She saw her sister-in-law flinch at the last question, as if talking about it awakened her darkest fantasies of how Guy had met his end: writhing on the beach, clawing uselessly at his throat. Well, it couldn't be helped. Margaret needed information and she meant to have it.

"What use would it have in a barn, Ruth?"

Ruth looked up from the needlework she'd been occupied with when Margaret had located her in the morning room. It was an enormous piece of canvas stretched on a wooden frame that was itself on a stand before which Ruth sat, an elfin figure in black trousers and an overlarge black cardigan that had probably once been Guy's. Her round-framed spectacles had slid down her nose, and she knuckled them back into place with one of her childlike hands.

"It's not used inside the barn," she explained. "It's used on a ring with the keys to the barn. At least, that's what it once was used for. There are few enough barns on Guernsey now. It was for keeping the barn safe from witches' familiars. Protection, Margaret."

"Ah. A charm, then."

"Yes."

"I see." What Margaret thought was These ridiculous islanders. Charms for witches. Mumbojumbo for fairies. Ghosts on the cliff tops. Devils on the prowl. She'd never considered her former husband a man who'd fall for that sort of nonsense. "Did they show you the stone? Was it something you recognised? Did it belong to Guy? I ask only because it doesn't seem like him to carry round charms and that sort of thing. At least, it doesn't seem like the Guy I knew. Was he hoping for luck in some venture?"

With a woman was what she didn't add, although both of them knew the phrase was there. Aside from business—at which Guy Brouard had excelled like Midas and needed no luck at all—the only other venture he had ever engaged in was the pursuit and conquest of the opposite sex, a fact that Margaret hadn't known until she'd found a pair of woman's knickers in her husband's briefcase, playfully tucked there by the Edinburgh flight attendant he'd been shagging on the side. Their marriage had ended the instant Margaret had found those knickers instead of the chequebook she'd been looking for. All that had remained for the next two years was her solicitor meeting with his solicitor to hammer out a deal that would finance the rest of her life.

"The only venture he was involved with recently was the wartime museum." Ruth bent back over the frame that held her needlepoint and she expertly worked the needle in and out of the design she'd rendered there. "And he didn't carry a charm for that. He didn't really need to. It was going well enough, as far as I know." She looked up again, her needle poised for another plunge. "Did he tell you about the museum, Margaret? Has Adrian told you?"

Margaret didn't want to get into Adrian with her sister-in-law or anyone else, so she said, "Yes. Yes. The museum. Of course. I knew about that."

Ruth smiled, inwardly and fondly it seemed. "It made him terribly proud. To be able to do something like that for the island. Something lasting. Something fine and meaningful."

Unlike his life, Margaret thought. She wasn't there to listen to encomia on the subject of Guy Brouard, Patron of Everything and Everyone. She was present only to ensure Guy Brouard had in death established himself additionally as Patron of His Only Son.

She said, "What will happen now? To his plans?"

"I suppose it all depends on the will," Ruth

replied. She sounded careful. Too careful, Margaret thought. "Guy's will, I mean. Well, of course, who else's? I haven't actually had a meeting with his advocate yet."

"Why not, dearest?" Margaret asked.

"I suppose because talking about his will makes everything real. Permanent. I'm avoiding that."

"Would you prefer I talk to his solicitor . . . his advocate, then? If there are arrangements to be made, I'm happy to make them for you, dear."

"Thank you, Margaret. It's good of you to offer, but I must handle it myself. I must . . . and I will. Soon. When . . . when it feels right to do so."

"Yes," Margaret murmured. "Of course." She watched her sister-in-law scoot her needle in and out of the canvas and fix it into place, indicating the conclusion of her work for the moment. She tried to sound like the incarnation of empathy, but inside she was champing at the bit to know exactly how her former husband had distributed his immense fortune. Specifically, she wanted to learn the manner in which he'd remembered Adrian. Because although while living he'd refused their son the money he needed for his new business, Guy's death surely had to benefit Adrian in ways that his life had not. And *that* would bring Carmel Fitzgerald and Adrian back together again, wouldn't it? Which would see Adrian married at last: a normal man leading a normal life with no more peculiar little incidents to worry about.

Ruth had gone to a small drop-front desk, where she'd picked up a delicate shadowbox frame. In this was encased one half of a locket, which she gazed at longingly. It was, Margaret saw, that tedious parting gift from *Maman,* handed over at the boat dock. *Je vais conserver l'autre moitié, mes chéris. Nous le reconstituerons lorsque nous nous retrouverons.*

Yes, yes, Margaret wanted to say. I know you bloody miss her, but we've business to conduct.

"Sooner is better than later, though, dearest," Margaret said gently. "You ought to speak to him. It's rather important."

Ruth set the frame down but continued to look at it. "It won't change things, speaking to anyone," she said.

"But it will clarify them."

"If clarity's needed."

"You do need to know how he wanted . . . well, what his wishes were. You do need to know that. With an estate as large as his is going to be, forewarned is forearmed, Ruth. I've no doubt his advocate would agree with me. Has he contacted you, by the way? The advocate? After all, he must know . . ."

"Oh yes. He knows."

Well, then? Margaret thought. But she said soothingly, "I see. Yes. Well, all in good time, my dear. When you feel you're ready."

Which would be soon, Margaret hoped. She didn't want to have to stay on this infernal island any longer than was absolutely necessary.

Ruth Brouard knew this about her sister-in-law. Margaret's presence at *Le Reposoir* had nothing to do with her failed marriage to Guy, with any sorrow or regret she might feel about the manner in which she and Guy had parted, or even with respect she might have thought appropriate to show at his terrible passing. Indeed, the fact that she'd so far not shown the least bit of curiosity about who had murdered Ruth's brother indicated where her true passion lay. In her mind, Guy had pots of money and she meant to have her ladle-full. If not for herself, then for Adrian.

Vengeful bitch was what Guy had called her. She's got a collection of doctors willing to testify that he's too unstable to be anywhere but with his bloody mother, Ruth. But she's the one ruining the pathetic boy. The last time I saw him, he was covered with hives. *Hives.* At his age. God, she's quite mad.

So it had gone year after year, with holiday visits cut short or canceled till the only opportunity Guy had to meet his son was in his ex-wife's watchful presence. She bloody stands *guard,* Guy had seethed. Probably because she knows if she didn't, I'd tell him to cut the apron strings . . . with a hatchet if necessary. There's nothing wrong with that boy that a few years in a decent school wouldn't sort out. And I'm not talking one of those cold-baths-in-the-morning and straps-on-the-backsides places, either. I'm talking about a *modern* school where he'd learn self-sufficiency which he isn't about to learn as long as she keeps him attached to her side like a barnacle.

But Guy had never won the day over that. The result was poor Adrian as he was now, thirty-seven years old with no single talent or quality upon which he could draw to define himself. Unless an uninterrupted line of failures at everything from team sports to male-female relationships could be deemed a talent. Those failures could be laid directly at the feet of Adrian's relationship with his mother. One didn't need a degree in psychology to arrive at that conclusion. But Margaret would never see it that way, lest she have to take some form of responsibility for her son's enduring problems. And that, by God, she would never do.

That was Margaret to the core. She was a don't-blame-*me,* pull-yourself-up-by-your-bootstraps sort of woman. If you couldn't pull yourself up by the bootstraps you were given, then you damn well ought to cut the bootstraps off.

Poor, dear Adrian, to have had such a mother. That she meant well came to nothing at the end of the day, considering the ill she managed to do along the way.

Ruth watched her now, as Margaret pretended to inspect the single memento she had of her mother, that little half-locket forever broken. She was a big woman, blonde with fiercely upswept hair and sunglasses—in grey December? How extraordinary, really!—perched on the top of her head. Ruth couldn't imagine that her brother had once been married to this woman, but she'd never been able to imagine that. She'd never quite managed to reconcile herself to the image of Margaret and Guy together as husband and wife, not the sex business which of course was part of human nature and could, as a result of that fact, accommodate itself to any sort of strange pairing, but to the emotional part, the sustaining part, the part that she imagined—having never been privileged to experience it herself—to be the fertile earth into which one planted family and future.

As things turned out between her brother and Margaret, Ruth had been quite correct in her assumption that they were wildly unsuited. Had they not produced poor Adrian in a rare moment of sanguinity, they probably would have gone their separate ways at the end of their marriage, one of them grateful for the money she'd managed to excavate from the ruins of their relationship and the other delighted to part with that money as long as it meant he'd be free of one of his worst mistakes. But with Adrian as part of the equation, Margaret had not faded into obscurity. For Guy had loved his son—even if he'd been frustrated by him—and the fact of Adrian made the fact of Margaret an immutable given. Till one of them died: Guy or Margaret herself.

But that was what Ruth didn't want to think of and couldn't bear to speak of, even though she knew she couldn't avoid the topic indefinitely.

As if reading her thoughts, Margaret replaced the locket on the desk and said, "Ruth, dearest, I can't get ten words from Adrian about what happened. I don't want to be ghoulish about it, but I *would* like to understand. The Guy I knew never had an enemy in his life. Well, there were his women, of course, and women don't much like being discarded. But even if he'd done his usual—"

Ruth said, "Margaret. Please."

"Wait." Margaret hurried on. "We simply can't pretend, dear. This is not the time. We both know how he was. But what I'm saying is that even if a woman's been discarded, a woman rarely . . . as revenge . . . You know what I mean. So who . . . ? Unless it was a married woman this time, and the husband found out . . . ? Although Guy did *normally* avoid those types." Margaret played with one of the three heavy gold chains she wore round her neck, the one with the pendant. This was a pearl, misshapen and enormous, a milky excrescence that lay between her breasts like a glob of petrified mashed potato.

"He hadn't . . ." Ruth wondered why it hurt so to say it. She'd *known* her brother. She'd known what he was: the sum of so many parts that were good and only one that was dark, that was hurtful, that was dangerous. "There was no affair. No one had been discarded."

"But hasn't a woman been arrested, dear?"

"Yes."

"And weren't she and Guy . . . ?"

"Of course not. She'd been here only a few days. It had nothing to do with . . . *nothing.*"

Margaret cocked her head, and Ruth could see what she was thinking. A few hours had long been more than enough for Guy Brouard to work his way when it came to sex. Margaret was about to begin probing on this subject. The shrewd expression on her face was enough to communicate that she was seeking a way into it that would look less like morbid curiosity and a belief that her once-philandering husband had finally got what he deserved and more like compassion for Ruth's loss of a brother more beloved to her than her own life. But Ruth was saved from having to enter into that conversation. A hesitant tap sounded against the open morning room door, and a tremulous voice said, "Ruthie? I'm . . . I'm not disturbing . . . ?"

Ruth and Margaret turned to see a third woman standing in the doorway and behind her a gawky teenage girl, tall and not yet used to her height. "Anaïs," Ruth said. "I didn't hear you come in."

"We used our key." Anaïs held it up, a single brass statement of her place in Guy's life lying desolately in the palm of her hand. "I hope that was . . . Oh Ruth, I can't believe . . . still . . . I can't . . ." She began to weep.

The girl behind her looked away uneasily, wiping her hands down the sides of her trousers. Ruth crossed the room and took Anaïs Abbott into her arms. "You're welcome to use the key as long as you like. That's what Guy would have wanted."

As Anaïs wept against her shoulder, Ruth extended her hand to the woman's fifteen-year-old daughter. Jemima smiled fleetingly—she and Ruth had always got on well—but she didn't approach. She looked instead beyond Ruth to Margaret and then to her mother and said, "*Mum*my," in a low but agonised voice. Jemima had never liked displays such as this. In the time Ruth had known her, she'd cringed more than once at Anaïs's propensity for public exhibition.

Margaret cleared her throat meaningfully. Anaïs pulled away from Ruth's arms and fished a packet of tissues from the jacket pocket of her trouser suit. She was dressed in black from head to toe, a cloche covering her carefully maintained strawberry-blonde hair.

Ruth made the introductions. It was an awkward business: former wife, current lover, current lover's daughter. Anaïs and Margaret murmured polite acknowledgements of each other and immediately took stock.

They couldn't have been less alike. Guy liked them blonde—he always had—but beyond that, the two women shared no similarities except perhaps for their background, because if truth were told, Guy had always liked them common as well. And no matter how either of them was educated, how she dressed or carried herself or had learned to pronounce her words, the Mersey still oozed out of Anaïs occasionally and Margaret's charwoman mother emerged from the daughter when she least wanted that part of her history known.

Other than that, though, they were night and day. Margaret tall, imposing, overdressed, and overbearing; Anaïs a little bird of a thing, thin to the point of self-abuse in the odious fashion of the day—aside from her patently artificial and overly voluptuous breasts—but always dressed like a woman who never donned a single garment without obtaining her mirror's approval.

Margaret, naturally, hadn't come all the way to Guernsey to meet, let alone to comfort or entertain, one of her former husband's many lovers. So after murmuring a dignified albeit utterly spurious "So nice to meet you," she said to Ruth, "We'll speak later, dearest," and she hugged her sister-in-law and kissed her on both cheeks and said, "Darling Ruth," as if she wished Anaïs Abbott to know from this uncharacteristic and mildly disturbing gesture that one of them had a position in this family and the other certainly had not. Then she departed, trailing behind her the scent of Chanel No. 5. Too early in the day for such an odour, Ruth thought. But Margaret wouldn't be aware of that.

"I should have been with him," Anaïs said in a hushed voice once the door closed behind Margaret. "I wanted to be, Ruthie. Ever since it happened, I've thought if I'd only spent the night here, I would have gone to the bay in the morning. Just to watch him. Because he was such a joy to watch. And . . . Oh God, oh *God* why did this have to happen?"

To me was what she didn't add. But Ruth was no fool. She hadn't spent a lifetime observing the manner in which her brother had moved in and around and out of his entanglements with women not to know at what point he was in the perpetual game of seduction, disillusionment, and abandonment that he played. Guy had been just about finished with Anaïs Abbott when he died. If Anaïs hadn't known that directly, she'd probably sensed it at one level or another.

Ruth said, "Come. Let's sit. Shall I ask Valerie for coffee? Jemima, would you like something, dear?"

Jemima said hesitantly, " 'V' you got anything I

c'n give Biscuit? He's just out front. He was off his feed this morning and—"

"Duck, darling," her mother cut in, the reproof more than clear in her use of Jemima's childhood nickname. Those two words said everything that Anaïs did not: Little girls concern themselves with their doggies. Young *women* concern themselves with young men. "The dog will survive. The dog, in fact, would have survived very well had we left him at home where he belongs. *As* I told you. We can't expect Ruth—"

"Sorry." Jemima seemed to speak more forcefully than she thought she ought in front of Ruth because she lowered her head at once, and one hand fretted at the seam of her trim wool trousers. She wasn't dressed like an ordinary teenager, poor thing. A summerlong course in a London modeling school in combination with her mother's vigilance—not to mention her intrusion into the girl's clothes cupboard—had taken care of that. She was instead garbed like a model from *Vogue.* But despite her time learning how to apply her makeup, style her hair, and move on the catwalk, she was in truth still gawky Jemima, Duck to her family and ducklike to the world with the same kind of awkwardness a duck would feel thrust into an environment where he was denied water.

Ruth's heart went out to her. She said, "That sweet little dog? He's probably miserable out there without you, Jemima. Would you like to bring him in?"

"Nonsense," Anaïs said. "He's fine. He may be

deaf but there's nothing wrong with his eyes and sense of smell. He knows quite well where he is. Leave him there."

"Yes. Of course. But perhaps he'd like a bit of minced beef? And there's leftover shepherd's pie from lunch yesterday. Jemima, do scoot down to the kitchen and ask Valerie for some of that pie. You can heat it in the microwave if you like."

Jemima's head bobbed up and her expression did Ruth's heart more good than she expected. The girl said, "If it's okay . . . ?" with a glance at her mother.

Anaïs was clever enough to know when to sway with a wind that was stronger than one she herself could blow. She said, "Ruthie. That is so good of you. We don't mean to be the slightest bit of trouble."

"And you aren't," Ruth said. "Go along, Jemima. Let us older girls have a chat."

Ruth didn't intend the term *older girls* to be offensive, but she saw that it had been as Jemima left them. At the age she was willing to declare—forty-six—Anaïs could actually have been Ruth's daughter. She certainly looked it. Indeed, she made every effort to look it. For she knew better than most women that older men were attracted to feminine youth and beauty just as feminine youth and beauty were so frequently and conveniently attracted to the source of the means to maintain themselves. Age didn't matter in either case. Appearance and resources were everything. To speak of age, however, had been something of a faux pas. But Ruth did nothing to smooth over that solecism. She was grieving for her brother, for the love of God. She could be excused.

Anaïs walked over to the needlepoint frame. She examined the design of the latest panel. She said, "What number is this one?"

"Fifteen, I think."

"With how many more to go?"

"As many as it takes to tell the whole story."

"All of it? Even Guy . . . at the end?" Anaïs was red-eyed but she didn't weep again. Instead, she seemed to use her own question to guide them to the point of her call at *Le Reposoir.* "Everything's changed now, Ruth. I'm worried for you. Are you taken care of?"

For a moment, Ruth thought she meant the cancer and how she would face her own imminent dying. She said, "I think I'll be able to cope," whereupon Anaïs's reply disabused her of the notion that the other woman had come to offer shelter, care, or just support in the coming months.

Anaïs said, "Have you read the will, Ruthie?" And as if she actually knew at heart how vulgar the question was, she added, "Have you been able to re-assure yourself that you're taken care of?"

Ruth told her brother's lover what she'd told her brother's former wife. She managed to relay the information with dignity in spite of what she wanted to say about who ought to have a vested interest in the distribution of Guy's fortune and who ought not.

"Oh." Anaïs's voice reflected her disappointment. No reading of a will suggested no sure knowledge of whether, when, or how she was going to be able to pay for the myriad paths she'd followed to keep herself young since meeting Guy. It also meant the wolves were probably ten steps closer to the front door of that overly impressive house that she and her children occupied at the north end of the island near *Le Grand Havre* Bay. Ruth had always suspected Anaïs Abbott was living well above her means. Financier's widow or not—and who knew what that meant anyway: *my husband was a financier,* in these days of stocks worth nothing one week after they were purchased and world markets sitting on top of quicksand? Naturally, he could have been a financial wizard who made other people's money multiply like loaves before the hungry, or an investment broker capable of turning five pounds into five million given enough time, faith, and resources. But on the other hand, he could have just been a clerk at Barclays whose life insurance policy had enabled his grieving widow to move in loftier circles than those into which she had been born and had wed. In either case, gaining entrance to those circles and moving in them took cold, hard cash: for the house, the clothing, the car, the holidays . . . not to mention for little incidentals like food. So it stood to reason that Anaïs Abbott was likely in dire straits at this point. She'd made a considerable investment in her relationship with Guy. For that investment to produce in dividends, the assumption had been that Guy would remain alive and heading towards marriage.

Even if Ruth felt a degree of aversion for Anaïs Abbott because of the Master Plan from which she believed the other woman had always been operating, she knew she had to excuse at least part of her machinations. For Guy had indeed led her to believe in the possibility of a union between them. A legal union. Hand in hand before a minister or a few minutes of smiling and blushing in *Le Greffe*. It had been reasonable for Anaïs to make certain assumptions because Guy had been generous. Ruth knew he'd been the one to send Jemima off to London, and she little doubted that he was also the reason—financial or otherwise—that Anaïs's breasts protruded like two firm perfect symmetrical cantaloupes from a chest too small to accommodate them naturally. But had it all been paid for? Or were there bills outstanding? That was the question. In a moment, Ruth was given the answer.

Anaïs said, "I miss him, Ruth. He was . . . You know I loved him, don't you? You know *how* I loved him, don't you?"

Ruth nodded. The cancer feeding upon her spine was beginning to demand her attention. Nodding was the only thing she could do when the pain was there and she was trying to be its master.

"He was everything to me, Ruth. My rock. My centre." Anaïs bowed her head. A few soft curls escaped her cloche, lying like the evidence of a man's caress against the back of her neck. "He had a way of dealing with things . . . Suggestions he made . . . things he did . . . Did you know it was his idea that Jemima go to London for the modeling course? For confidence, he said. That was so like Guy. Full of such generosity and love."

Ruth nodded again, caught in the grip of her cancer's caress. She pressed her lips together and suppressed a moan.

"Not a single thing he wouldn't do for us," Anaïs said. "The car . . . its maintenance . . . the garden pool . . . There he was. Helping. Giving. What a wonderful man. I'll never meet anyone even close to being . . . He was so good to me. And without him now . . . ? I feel I've lost it all. Did he tell you he paid for school uniforms this year? I know he didn't. He wouldn't because that was part of his goodness, protecting the pride of the people he helped. He even . . . Ruth, this good, dear man was even giving me a monthly allowance. 'You're more to me than I thought a woman could ever be and I want you to have more than you can give yourself.' I thanked him, Ruth, time and time again. But I never stopped to thank him enough. Still, I wanted you to know some of the good he did. The good he did for me. To help me, Ruth."

She could have made her request more blatant only by scrawling it on the Wilton carpet. Ruth wondered how much more tasteless her brother's putative mourners were going to become.

"Thank you for such an elegy, Anaïs," she settled upon saying to the woman. "To know you knew he was goodness itself . . ." And he was, he *was*, Ruth's heart cried out. "It's an act of kindness for you to come here and tell me. I'm terribly grateful. You're very good."

Anaïs opened her mouth to speak. She even drew breath before she appeared to realise there was nothing more to say. She couldn't directly ask for money at this point without appearing grasping and crass. Even if she had no regard for that, she probably wasn't going to be willing any time soon to set aside the pretence that she was an independent widow for whom a meaningful textured relationship was more important than what funded it. She'd been living that pretence too long.

So Anaïs Abbott said nothing more and neither did Ruth as they sat together in the morning room. Really, at the end of the day, what more could they possibly say?

Chapter 7

THE BAD WEATHER CONTINUED to abate during the day in London, and it was this that allowed the St. Jameses and Cherokee River to make the journey to Guernsey. They arrived by late afternoon, circling round the airport to see spread out below them in the fading light grey cotton thread roads unspooling haphazardly, twisting through stony hamlets and between bare fields. The glass of countless inland greenhouses caught the last of the sun, and the leafless trees on valley and hillside marked the areas where winds and storms reached less fiercely. It was a varied landscape from the air: rising to towering cliffs on the east and the south ends of the island, sloping to tranquil bays on the west and in the north.

The island was desolate at this time of year. Holiday makers would fill its tangle of roads in late spring and summer, heading for the beaches, the cliff paths, or the harbours, exploring Guernsey's churches, its castles, its forts. They would walk and swim and boat and bike. They would throng the streets and swell the hotels. But in December, there were three kinds of people who occupied the Channel island: the islanders themselves who were bound to the place by habit, tradition, and love; tax exiles who were determined to shelter as much of their money as was possible from their respective governments; and bankers who worked in St. Peter Port and flew home to England at weekends.

It was to St. Peter Port that the St. Jameses and Cherokee River took themselves. This was the largest town and the seat of government on the island. It was also where the police were headquartered and where China River's advocate had his office.

Cherokee had been loquacious for most of their journey that day. He veered from subject to subject like a man who was terrified of what a silence among them might imply, and St. James had found himself wondering if the constant barrage of conversation was designed to keep them from considering the futility of the mission in which they were engaged. If China River had been arrested and charged, there would be evidence to try her for the crime. If that evidence went beyond the circumstantial, St. James knew there was going to be little or nothing he could do to interpret it differently to the way the police experts had already done.

But as Cherokee had continued his dialogue, it had begun to seem less like distracting them from drawing conclusions about their objective and more like attaching himself to them. St. James played the watcher in all this, a third wheel on a bicycle lurching towards the unknown. He found it a distinctly uneasy ride.

Cherokee chatted most about his sister. Chine— as he called her—had finally learned to surf. Did Debs know that? Her boyfriend, Matt—did Debs ever meet Matt? She must've, right?—well, he finally got her out in the water . . . I mean far *enough* out because she was always freaked out about sharks. He taught her the basics and made her practise and the day she finally stood up . . . She finally got what it was all about, *mentally* got it. The Zen of surfing. Cherokee was always wanting her to come down to surf in Huntington with him . . . in February or March, when the waves could get gnarly, but she would never come because coming to Orange County meant going over to Mom's in her mind and Chine and Mom . . . They had issues with each other. They were just too different. Mom was always doing something wrong. Like the last time Chine came down for a weekend—probably more'n two years ago—it became a major big deal that Mom didn't have any clean glasses in the house. It's not like Chine couldn't wash a glass herself, but Mom should have had them washed in advance because washing the glasses in advance *meant* something. Like I love you or Welcome or I want you to be here. Anyway, Cherokee always tried to stay out of it when they went at it. They were both, you know, really good people, Mom and Chine. They were just so different. However, whenever Chine came to the canyon—Debs knew Cherokee lived in the canyon, didn't she? Modjeska? Inland? That cabin with the logs across the front?—anyway, when Chine came over, believe it, Cherokee put clean glasses everywhere. Not that he had too many of them. But what he *did* have . . . everywhere. Chine wanted clean glasses, and Cherokee gave her clean glasses. But it was weird, wasn't it, the kinds of things that set people off . . .

All the way to Guernsey, Deborah had listened sympathetically to Cherokee's rambling. He'd wandered among reminiscence, revelation, and explanation, and within an hour it seemed to St. James that over and above the natural anxiety the man felt because of his sister's position, he also felt guilt. Had he not insisted that she accompany him, she wouldn't be where she was at the moment. He was at least in part responsible for that. *Shit happens to people* was the way he put it, but it was clear that this particular shit wouldn't have happened to this particular person had Cherokee not wanted her to come along. And he'd wanted her to come along because he needed her to come along, he explained, because that was the only way he himself was going to be able to go in the first place and he'd *wanted* to go because he wanted the money because finally he had a job in mind for himself that he could bear to think about doing for twenty-five years or more and he just needed a down payment to finance it. A fishing boat. That was it in a nutshell. China River was locked behind bars because her asshole brother wanted to buy a fishing boat.

"But you couldn't have known what would happen," Deborah protested.

"I know that. But it doesn't make me feel any better. I've got to get her out of there, Debs." And with an earnest smile at her and then at St. James, "Thank you for helping me out. There's no way I can ever repay you."

St. James wanted to tell the other man that his sister wasn't out of gaol yet and there was a very good chance that even if bail was offered and paid, her freedom at that point would constitute only a temporary reprieve. Instead, he merely said, "We'll do what we can."

To which Cherokee replied, "Thanks. You're the best."

To which Deborah then said, "We're your friends, Cherokee."

At which point the man seemed struck with emotion. It flashed across his face for an instant. He managed only a nod and he gave that odd clenched-fist gesture that Americans tended to use to indicate everything from gratitude to political agreement.

Or perhaps he used it in that moment for something else.

St. James could not keep himself from that thought. Nor had he truly been able to since the moment he'd glanced up to the gallery in Courtroom Number Three and seen his wife and the American above him: the two of them shoulder to shoulder with Deborah murmuring to Cherokee's bent and listening head. Something wasn't right in the world. St. James believed that at a level he couldn't have explained. So the sensation of times out of joint made it difficult for him to affirm his wife's declaration of friendship to the other man. He said nothing, and when Deborah's glance in his direction asked him why, he offered her no answering glance as reply. This wouldn't, he knew, improve things between them. She was still at odds with him about their conversation in the Old Bailey.

When they arrived in town, they established themselves in Ann's Place, where a former government building had long ago been converted into a hotel. There they parted: Cherokee and Deborah to the prison where they hoped to make contact with China in the remand section, St. James to the police station where he wanted to track down the officer in charge of the investigation.

He remained uneasy. He knew very well that he didn't belong there, insinuating himself into a police investigation where he wouldn't be welcome. At least in England, cases existed to which he could refer a police force if he came calling and requesting information from them. You recall the Bowen kidnapping? he could murmur virtually anywhere in England . . . And that strangulation in Cambridge last year? Given enough opportunity to explain who he was and to seek a common river of knowledge in which to swim with the police, St. James had found that the UK officers were generally willing to part with what information they had while remaining unruffled in the face of any attempts he might make to find something more. But here things were different. Garnering if not the cooperation of the police then at least their grudging acceptance of his presence among those people closely connected to the crime would not be a matter of jogging their memories of cases he'd worked on or criminal trials in which he'd been involved. That put him in a place he didn't like to be, relying on his least developed skill to gain admittance into the fraternity of investigators: the ability to establish a connection with another person.

He followed the curve of Ann's Place as it gave onto Hospital Lane and the police station beyond. He pondered the entire idea of connection. Perhaps, he thought, that inability of his which created a chasm between himself and other people—always and ever the cool damn scientist, always and ever looking inward and thinking, always considering, weighing, and observing when other people occupied themselves with just *being* . . . Perhaps that was the source of his discomfort with Cherokee River as well.

"I *do* remember the surfing!" Deborah had said, her face altering in an instant when the shared experience came to her mind. "All three of us went that one time . . . D'you remember? Where were we?"

Cherokee had looked reflective before he'd said, "Sure. It was Seal Beach, Debs. Easier than Huntington. More protected there."

"Yes, yes. Seal Beach. You made me go out and flail round on the board and I kept shrieking about hitting the pier."

"Which," he said, "you weren't *anywhere* close to.

No way were you going to stay on the board long enough to hit anything unless you decided to sleep on it."

They laughed together, another link forged, an effortless instant between two people when they acknowledged that a common chain existed that connected the present to the past.

And that was how it was between everyone who shared any kind of history, St. James thought. That was just how it was.

He crossed the street to the Guernsey police headquarters. It stood behind an imposing wall hewn from a stone that was veined with feldspar, an L-shaped building with four banks of windows climbing its two wings and the flag of Guernsey flying above it. Inside the reception room, St. James gave his name and his card to the special constable. Would it be possible, he asked, to speak with the chief investigating officer on the Guy Brouard murder enquiry? Or, failing that, with the department's Press Officer?

The special constable studied the card, his face a declaration that indicated a few select telephone calls were going to be made across the Channel to ascertain exactly who this forensic scientist on their doorstep was. This was all to the good, because if phone calls were made, they would be made to the Met, to the CPS, or to the university where St. James lectured, and if that were the case, his way would be paved.

It took twenty minutes while St. James cooled his heels in reception and read the notice board half a dozen times. But they were twenty minutes well spent, because at the end of them, Detective Chief Inspector Louis Le Gallez came out personally to lead St. James to the incident room, a vast hammer-beamed former chapel in which departmental exercise equipment vied with filing cabinets, computer tables, bulletin boards, and china boards.

DCI Le Gallez wanted to know, naturally, what interest a forensic scientist from London had in a murder enquiry on Guernsey, especially in an enquiry that was closed. "We've got our killer," he said, arms across his chest and one leg slung over the corner of a table. He rested his weight—which was considerable for a man so short—on the table's edge and he flipped St. James's card back and forth against the side of his hand. He looked curious rather than guarded.

St. James opted for complete honesty. The brother of the accused, understandably shaken by what had happened to his sister, had asked St. James for help after failing to stimulate the American embassy into acting on his sister's behalf.

"The Americans have done their bit," Le Gallez countered. "Don't know what else this bloke's expecting. He was one of the suspects as well, by the way. But then, they all were. Everyone at that party Brouard had. Night before he bought it. Half the island was there. And if that didn't complicate the hell out of matters, nothing did, believe me."

Le Gallez took the lead as if fully aware of where St. James intended to direct the conversation upon that remark about the party. He went on to say that interviews had been conducted with everyone who'd been at the Brouard house on the night before the murder, and nothing had come to light in the days since Guy Brouard's death to alter the investigators' initial suspicion: Anyone who'd ducked out of *Le Reposoir* as the Rivers had done on the morning of the killing was someone who bore looking into.

"All the other guests had alibis for the time of the killing?" St. James asked.

That wasn't what he was implying, Le Gallez responded. But once the evidence was stacked up, what everyone else had been doing on the morning Guy Brouard met his death was germane to nothing related to the case.

What they had against China River was damning, and Le Gallez seemed only too happy to list it. Their four scenes-of-crime officers had worked the location and their forensic pathologist had worked the body. The River woman had left a partial print at the scene—this was a footprint, half of it obscured by a broad blade of seaweed, admittedly, but grains that were the exact match of the coarse sand upon the beach had been imbedded in the soles of her shoes and those same shoes matched the partial print as well.

"She might have been there at some other time," St. James said.

"Might have been. True. I know the story. Brouard gave them the run of the place when he wasn't running them round it himself. But what he didn't do was catch her hair in the zip of the track suit jacket he had on when he died. And I wouldn't put money on him having wiped his head on her wrap, either."

"What sort of wrap?"

"Black blanket affair. One button at the neck, no sleeves."

"A cloak?"

"And his hair was on it, just where you'd expect to find it if you had to lock your arm round him to hold him still. Silly cow hadn't thought to use a clothes brush on it."

St. James said, "The means of the killing . . . It's a bit unusual, wouldn't you say? The stone? His choking? If he didn't swallow it himself by accident—"

Le Gallez said, "Not bloody likely."

"—then someone would have had to thrust it down his throat. But how? When? In the midst of a struggle? Were there signs of a struggle? On the beach? On his body? On the River woman when you brought her in?"

He shook his head. "No struggle. But there wouldn't be the need for one. That's why we were looking for a woman from the first." He went to one of the tables and fetched a plastic container whose contents he dumped into his palm. He fingered through them, said, "Ah. This'll do," and produced a half-open roll of Polos. He thumbed one out, held it up for St. James to see, and said, "Stone in question's just a bit larger than this. Hole in the centre to go on a key ring. Some carving round the sides as well.

Now watch." He popped the Polo into his mouth, tongued it into his cheek, and said, "You c'n pass more than germs when you French it, mate."

St. James understood but was nonetheless doubtful. There was vast improbability implied in the investigator's theory as far as he was concerned. He said, "But she would have had to do more than just pass the stone into his mouth. Yes. I do see it's possible she could have got it onto his tongue if she was kissing him, but surely not down his throat. How would she have managed that?"

"Surprise," Le Gallez countered. "She catches him off guard when the stone goes into his mouth. One hand on the back of his neck while they're lip-locked and he's in the right position. The other on his cheek and in the moment he pulls away from her because she's passed him the stone, she's caught him in the crook of her arm, bent him back, and her hand's down his throat. So's the stone, for that matter. And he's done for."

"You don't mind my saying, that's a bit unlikely," St. James said. "Your prosecutors can't possibly hope to convince . . . D'you have juries here?"

"Doesn't matter. The stone's not intended to convince a soul," Le Gallez said. "It's just a theory. May not even come up in court."

"Why not?"

Le Gallez smiled thinly. "Because we've got a witness, Mr. St. James," he said. "And a witness is worth a hundred experts and their thousand pretty theories, if you know what I mean."

• • •

At the prison where China was being held on remand, Deborah and Cherokee learned that events had moved forward swiftly in the twenty-four hours since he'd left the island to find help in London. China's advocate had managed to get her released on bail and had set her up elsewhere. Prison administration knew where, naturally, but they weren't forthcoming with the information.

Deborah and Cherokee thus retraced their route from the States Prison towards St. Peter Port, and when they found a phone box where Vale Road opened into the wide vista of *Belle Greve* Bay, Cherokee leaped out of the car to ring the advocate. Deborah watched through the phone box glass and could see that China's brother was understandably agitated, rapping his fist against the glass as he spoke. Not adept at lip reading, Deborah could still discern the "Hey, man, *you* listen," when Cherokee said it. Their conversation lasted three or four minutes, not enough time to reassure Cherokee about anything but just enough to discover where his sister had been delivered.

"He's got her in some apartment back in St. Peter Port," Cherokee reported as he climbed back into the car and jerked it into gear. "One of those places people rent out in the summer. 'Only too happy to have her there' was how he put it. Whatever that's supposed to mean."

"A holiday flat," Deborah said. "It would just stand empty till spring, probably."

"Whatever," he said. "He might have gotten a message to me or something. I'm involved here, you know. I asked him why he didn't let me know he was getting her out and he said . . . You know what he said? 'Miss River didn't mention telling anyone her whereabouts.' Like she *wants* to be in hiding."

They wound back to St. Peter Port where it was no easy feat to find the holiday flats where China had been installed, despite being in possession of the address. The town was a warren of one-way streets: narrow tracks that climbed the hillside from the harbour and swooped through a town that had existed long before cars had even been imagined. Deborah and Cherokee made several passes by Georgian town homes and through Victorian terraces before they finally stumbled upon the Queen Margaret Apartments on the corner of Saumarez and Clifton Streets, situated at the crest of the latter. It was a spot that would have afforded a holiday maker the sort of views one pays highly to enjoy during spring and summer: The port spread out below, Castle Cornet stood clearly visible on its spit of land where it once protected the town from invasion, and on a day without the lowering clouds of December, the coast of France would appear to hover on the far horizon.

On this day, however, in the early dusk, the Channel was an ashen mass of liquid landscape. Lights shone on a harbour that was empty of pleasure craft, and in the distance the castle appeared as a series of crosshatched children's blocks, held haphazardly on a parent's palm.

Their challenge at the Queen Margaret Apartments was to find someone who could point them in the direction of China's flat. They finally located an unshaven and odoriferous man in a bed-sitting room at the back of the otherwise deserted property. He appeared to act the part of concierge when he wasn't doing what he was currently doing, which seemed to be taking both sides in a board game that involved depositing shiny black stones into cuplike depressions in a narrow wooden tray.

He said, "Hang on," when Cherokee and Deborah turned up in his single room. "I just need to . . . Damn. He's got me again."

He appeared to be his opponent which was himself, playing from the other side of the board. He cleared this side of its stones in one inexplicable move, whereupon he said, "What c'n I do for you?"

When they told him they'd come to see his tenant-in-the-singular—because it was certainly clear that no one else was occupying any of the Queen Margaret Apartments at this time of year—he feigned ignorance about the whole matter. Only when Cherokee told him to phone China's advocate did he give the slightest hint that the woman charged with murder was staying somewhere in the building. And then all he did was lumber to the phone and punch in a few numbers. When the party answered at the other end, he said, "Someone saying he's the brother . . . ?" And with a glance at Deborah, "Got a red-head with him." He listened for five seconds. He said, "Right, then," and parted with the information. They would find the person they were looking for, he told them, in Flat B on the east side of the building.

It was no far distance. China met them at the

door. She said only, "You came," and she walked directly into Deborah's embrace.

Deborah held her firmly. "Of course I came," she said. "I only wish I'd known from the first that you were in Europe at all. Why didn't you let me know you were coming? Why didn't you phone? Oh, it's so *good* to see you." She blinked against the sting behind her eyelids, surprised by the onslaught of feeling that told her how much she had missed her friend in the years during which they'd lost contact with each other.

"I'm sorry it has to be like this." China gave Deborah a fleeting smile. She was far thinner than Deborah remembered her, and although her fine sandy hair was fashionably cut, it fell round a face that looked like a waif's. She was dressed in clothes that would have sent her vegan mother into a seizure. They were mostly black leather: trousers, waistcoat, and ankle boots. The colour heightened the pallor of her skin.

"Simon's come as well," Deborah said. "We're going to sort this out. You're not to worry."

China glanced at her brother, who'd shut the door behind them. He'd gone to the alcove that served as the flat's kitchen, where he stood shifting from foot to foot and looking like the sort of male who wishes to be in another universe when females are exhibiting emotion. She said to him, "I didn't intend you to bring them back with you. Just to get their advice if you needed it. But . . . I'm glad you did, Cherokee. Thanks."

Cherokee nodded. He said, "You two need . . . ?

I mean, I could go for a walk or something . . . ? You got food here? You know, here's what: I'll go find a store." He took himself out of the flat without waiting for a response from his sister.

"Typical man," China said when he was gone. "Can't deal with tears."

"And we haven't even *got* to them yet."

China chuckled, a sound which lightened Deborah's heart. She couldn't imagine what it would be like, trapped in a country that was not your own and charged with murder. So if she could help her friend not think about the jeopardy she faced, she wanted to do it. But she also wanted to reassure China: about the kinship she still felt for her.

So she said, "I've missed you. I should have written more."

"You should have written period," China replied. "I've missed you, too." She took Deborah into the kitchen alcove. "I'm making us some tea. I can't believe how happy I am to see you."

Deborah said, "No. Let me make it, China. You're not going to start us off by taking care of me. I'm reversing our roles and you're going to let me." She marched the other woman over to a table that stood beneath an east-facing window. A legal pad and a pen lay upon this. The top sheet of the pad bore large block letters of dates and paragraphs beneath them rendered in China's familiar looped scrawl.

China said, "That was a bad time for you back then. It meant a lot to me to do what I could."

"I was quite a pathetic blob," Deborah said. "I don't know how you were able to cope with me."

"You were nowhere near home and in big trouble and trying to figure out what to do. I was your friend. I didn't need to cope with you one way or another. I just needed to care. Which was pretty damn easy, to tell you the truth."

Deborah felt a wash of warmth across her skin, a reaction that she knew had two distinct sources. It originated in part from the pleasure of female-to-female friendship. But it also had a root in a period of her past that was painful to contemplate. China River had been part of that period, nursing Deborah through it in the most literal sense.

Deborah said, "I am *so* . . . What word can I use? Happy to see you? But Lord, that sounds so egocentric, doesn't it? You're in trouble and I'm happy to be here? What a selfish little cod that makes me."

"I don't know about that." China sounded reflective before her contemplative remark segued into a smile. "I mean the real question is: Can a cod *be* selfish?"

"Oh, you know cod," Deborah replied. "A hook in its mouth and all of a sudden it's me, me, me."

They laughed together. Deborah went into the little kitchen. She filled the kettle and plugged it in. She found mugs, tea, sugar, and milk. One of the two cupboards even held a wrapped package of something identified as Guernsey Gâche. Deborah peeled back the covering to find a brick-shaped pastry that appeared to be a cross between raisin bread and fruit cake. It would do.

China said nothing more until Deborah had assembled everything on the table. Then it was only a murmured "I've missed you, too" that Deborah might not have heard had she not been listening earnestly for it.

She squeezed her friend's shoulder. She carried out the rituals of pouring and doctoring their tea. She knew the ceremony likely wouldn't have the power to comfort her friend for long, but there was something in the act of holding a mug of tea, of curving one's palm round the sides of the cup and allowing the heat to penetrate one's hand, that had always possessed a form of magic for Deborah, as if the waters of Lethe and not leaves from an Asian plant had created what steamed from within.

China seemed to know what Deborah intended because she took up her mug and said, "The English and their tea."

"We drink coffee as well."

"Not at a time like this, you don't." China held the mug as Deborah intended her to hold it, palm curved comfortingly round its side. She looked out of the window, where the lights of the town had begun to form a winking palette of yellow on charcoal as the last of daylight deferred to night. "I can't get used to how early it gets dark over here."

"It's the time of year."

"I'm so used to the sun." China sipped the tea and set the mug on the table. With a fork, she picked at a piece of the Guernsey Gâche loaf but she didn't eat. Instead, she said, "I guess I might have to get used to it, though. Lack of sunlight. Being permanently indoors."

"That's not going to happen."

"I didn't do it." China raised her head and looked at Deborah directly. "I didn't kill that man, Deborah."

Deborah felt her insides quiver at the thought that China might believe that she needed convincing of this fact. "My God, of course you didn't. I haven't come here to play see-for-myself. Neither has Simon."

"But they have evidence, see?" China said. "My hair. My shoes. Footprints. I feel like I'm in one of those dreams where you try to shout but no one can hear you because you're not really shouting at all because you *can't* shout because you're in a dream. It's a round-and-round thing. D'you know what I mean?"

"I wish I could drag you out of this. I would if I could."

"It was on his clothes," China said. "The hair. *My* hair. On his clothes when they found him. And I don't know how it got there. I've thought back, but I can't explain it." She gestured to the legal pad. "I've written down every day as best I can remember it. Did he hug me sometime? But why would he hug me, and if he did, why don't I remember? The lawyer wants me to say that there was something between us. Not sex, he says. Don't go that far. But the pursuit, he says. The hope in *his* mind of sex. Stuff between us that might have led to sex. Touching. That kind of thing. But there wasn't and I can't say there was. I mean, it's not like the lying bothers me or anything. Believe me, I'd lie my head off if it would do any good. But who the hell's going to support the story? People saw me with him and he never even put a finger on me. Oh, maybe on my arm or something but that was all. So if I go on the stand and say my hair was on him because he— what? hugged me? kissed me? petted me? what?—it's only my word against everyone else's who'll stand up and say he never looked at me at all. We could counter by putting Cherokee on the stand, but no way am I asking my brother to lie."

"He's desperate to help."

China shook her head in what seemed like resignation. "He's had some sort of scam running all his life. Remember the swap meets at the fairground? Those Indian artifacts he was pawning off on the public every week? Arrowheads, shards of pottery, tools, whatever else he could think of. He almost made *me* believe they were real."

"You're not saying Cherokee . . ."

"No, no. I just mean I should have thought twice—ten times, actually—about coming along on this trip. What seems simple to him, no strings, too good to be true but true anyway . . . ? I should have seen that there had to be something more involved than just carrying some building plans across the ocean. Not something Cherokee had in mind but something that someone *else* was scheming."

"To use you as a scapegoat," Deborah concluded.

"That's all I can figure."

"That means everything about what happened was planned. Even bringing an American over to take the blame."

"Two Americans," China said. "So if one wasn't

likely to be believable as a suspect, there was a good chance the other one would be. That's what's going on, and we walked right into it. Two dumb Californians who'd never even been to Europe before and you *know* they had to be looking for that, too. A couple of naïve oafs who wouldn't have a clue what to do if they got caught up in a mess over here. And the kicker is that I didn't really want to come. I *knew* there was something fishy about it. But I've spent my life being totally incapable of ever saying no to my brother."

"He feels wretched about everything."

"He always feels wretched," China said. "Then *I* feel guilty. He needs a break, I tell myself. I know he'd do the same for me."

"He seemed to think he was doing you a good turn as well. Because of Matt. Time to get away from things for a bit. He told me, by the way. About the two of you. The break-up. I'm quite sorry. I liked him. Matt."

China gave her mug a half turn, staring at it hard and unwaveringly and for so long that Deborah thought she intended to avoid discussing the end of her longtime relationship with Matt Whitecomb. But just as Deborah was about to change the subject, China spoke.

"It was tough at first. Thirteen years is too long to wait for a man to decide he's ready. I think I always knew at some level that we weren't going to work out. It just took me this long to get up my nerve to call it quits. It's the whole idea of going it alone that kept me hanging on to him. What'll I do at New

Year's? Who'll send me a valentine? Where do I go
on the Fourth of July? It's incredible to think how
many relationships must be held together for the purpose of having someone to spend national holidays
with." China picked up her piece of the Guernsey
Gâche and moved it away from her with a little shudder. "Can't eat this. Sorry." And then, "Anyway, I've
got bigger things than Matt Whitecomb to worry
about right now. Why I spent my twenties trying to
massage great sex into marriage, the house, the picket
fence, the SUV, and the kiddies . . . That's one for me
to figure out in my dotage. Right now . . . Funny
how things work out. If I wasn't trapped here with a
prison sentence hanging over my head, I might be
brooding about why it took me so long to see the
truth about Matt."

"Which is?"

"He's permanently scared. It was right in front of
me, but I didn't want to see it. Talk about committing to something more than weekends and vacations together, and he was always out of there. A
sudden business trip. Work piling up at home. A
need for a break to think things through. We split up
so many times in thirteen years that the relationship
started feeling like a recurring nightmare. The relationship, in fact, was starting to be all *about* the relationship, if you know what I mean. Hours talking
about why we're having trouble, why I want one
thing and he wants another, why he backs off and I
rush forward, why he feels suffocated and I feel deserted. What *is* it about men and committing, for
God's sake?" China picked up her spoon and stirred

her tea, clearly something to do with her restlessness and not something that needed to be done. She glanced at Deborah. "Except, you're not the person I ought to ask that question, I guess. Men, you, and committing. It was never a problem you had to face, Debs."

Deborah didn't have the chance to remind her of the facts: that for her three-year stay in America, she'd been completely estranged from Simon. A sharp knock at the door supervened, heralding the return of Cherokee. A duffel bag angled across his shoulder.

He set the duffel on the floor and declared, "I'm out of that hotel, Chine. No way am I letting you stay here all alone."

"There's only one bed."

"I'll sleep on the floor. You need family around you, and that means me."

His tone said *fait accompli*. The duffel bag said there would be no arguing with his decision.

China sighed. She didn't look happy.

St. James found the office of China's advocate on New Street, a short distance from the Royal Court House. DCI Le Gallez had phoned ahead to let the lawyer know he'd be having a caller, so when St. James introduced himself to the man's secretary, he waited less than five minutes before being shown into the advocate's rooms.

Roger Holberry directed him to one of three chairs that encircled a small conference table. There they both sat and St. James laid out for the advocate the facts that DCI Le Gallez had shared with him. Holberry himself would already have these facts, St. James knew. But he needed from the advocate everything that Le Gallez had left out during their interview, and the only way to get it was to allow the other man to note any holes in the blanket of information in order to sew them up.

Holberry seemed only too happy to do this. Le Gallez, he informed him, had shared St. James's credentials in their telephone call. The DCI wasn't a joyful soldier now that it appeared reinforcements had entered the battle on the side of the opposition, but he was an honest man and he had no intention of attempting to thwart them in their efforts to establish China River's innocence. "He made it clear that he doesn't believe you'll be able to do much good," Holberry said. "His case is solid. Or so he thinks."

"What've you got from forensic on the body?"

"What's been combed from it so far. Scrapings from beneath the nails as well. Just the externals."

"No toxicology? Tissue analysis? Organ studies?"

"Too soon for that. We've got to send it all to the UK and then it's a case of join the queue. But the means of the killing is a straightforward business. Le Gallez must have told you."

"The stone. Yes." St. James went on to explain to the advocate that he'd pointed out to Le Gallez how unlikely it was that a woman could have shoved a stone down the throat of anyone older than a child. "And if there were no signs of a struggle . . . What did the nail scrapings show you?"

"Nothing. Other than some sand."

"The rest of the body? Bruised, scraped, banged about? Anything?"

"Not a thing," Holberry replied. "But Le Gallez knows he's got next to nothing. He's hanging this all on the witness. Brouard's sister saw something. God knows what. He's not told us that yet, Le Gallez."

"Could she have done it herself?"

"Possible. But unlikely. Everyone who knows them agrees she was devoted to the victim. They'd been together—lived together, I mean—for most of their lives. She even worked for him when he was getting established."

"As what?"

"Chateaux Brouard," Holberry said. "They made a pile of money and came to Guernsey when he retired."

Chateaux Brouard, St. James thought. He'd heard of the group: a chain of small but exclusive hotels fashioned from country houses throughout the UK. They were nothing flashy, just historic settings, antiques, fine food, and tranquility: the sort of places frequented by those who sought privacy and anonymity, perfect for actors needing a few days away from the glare of the media and excellent for political figures having affairs. Discretion was the better part of doing business, and the Chateaux Brouard embodied that belief.

"You said she might be protecting someone," St. James said. "Who?"

"The son, for starters. Adrian." Holberry explained that Guy Brouard's thirty-seven-year-old son had also been a house guest the night before the murder. Then, he said, there were the Duffys to consider: Valerie and Kevin, who'd been part of life at *Le Reposoir* since the day Brouard had taken the place over.

"Ruth Brouard might lie for any of them," Holberry pointed out. She was known to be loyal to the people she loved. And the Duffys at least, it had to be said, returned the favour. "We're talking about a well-liked pair, Ruth and Guy Brouard. He's done a world of good on this island. He used to give away money like tissues during cold season, and she's been active with the Samaritans for years."

"People without apparent enemies, then," St. James noted.

"Deadly for the defence," Holberry said. "But all is not lost on that front yet."

Holberry sounded pleased. St. James's interest quickened. "You've come up with something."

"Several somethings," Holberry said. "They may turn out to be several nothings, but they bear looking into and I can assure you the police weren't sniffing seriously round anyone but the Rivers from the first."

He went on to describe a close relationship that Guy Brouard had with a sixteen-year-old boy, one Paul Fielder, who lived in what was obviously the wrong side of town in an area called the Bouet. Brouard had hooked up with the boy through a local programme that paired adults from the community with disadvantaged teenagers from the secondary school. GAYT—Guernsey Adults-Youths-Teachers—had chosen Paul Fielder to be mentored by Guy Brouard, and Brouard had more or less adopted the boy, a circumstance which might have been less than thrilling to the boy's own parents or, for that matter, to Brouard's natural son. In either case, passions could have flared and among those passions the basest of them all: jealousy and what jealousy could lead someone to do.

Then there was the fact of that party the night before Guy Brouard met his end, Holberry went on. Everyone had known for weeks it was coming, so a killer prepared to set upon Brouard when he wasn't in top form—as he wouldn't have been after partying till the wee hours of the morning—could have planned in advance exactly how best to carry it off and lay the blame elsewhere. While the party was going on, how difficult would it have been to slip upstairs and plant evidence on clothing and on the soles of shoes or, better yet, even to take those shoes down to the bay to leave a footprint or two that the police could find later? Yes, that party and the death were related, Holberry stated unequivocally, and they were related in more ways than one.

"This whole business with the museum architect needs dissecting as well," Holberry said. "It was unexpected and messy, and when things are unexpected and messy, people get provoked."

"But the architect wasn't present the night of the murder, was he?" St. James asked. "I was under the impression he's in America."

"Not that architect. I'm speaking of the original architect, a bloke called Bertrand Debiere. He's a local man and he, along with everyone else, believed it was his design that would be chosen for Brouard's museum. Well, why not? Brouard had a model of the place he kept showing off for weeks to anyone who was interested and it was Debiere's model, made by his own hands. So when he—this is Brouard—said he was having a party to name the architect he'd chosen for the job . . ." Holberry shrugged. "You can't blame Debiere for assuming he was the man."

"Vengeful?"

"Who's to tell, really? One would think the local coppers might have given him more than a cursory glance, but he's a Guernseyman. So they're not likely to touch him."

"Americans being more violent by nature?" St. James asked. "School-yard shootings, capital punishment, accessible guns, and the rest of it?"

"Not so much that as the nature of the crime itself." Holberry glanced at the door as it creaked open. His secretary eased into the room, *home* written all over her: She carried a stack of papers in one hand and a pen in the other, she wore her coat, and she carried her handbag hooked over her arm. Holberry took the documents from her and began to sign his name as he talked. "There hasn't been a cold start murder on the island in years. No one even knows how long it's been. Not in the memory of anyone at the police department and that goes back quite a way. There've been crimes of passion, naturally. Accidental deaths and suicides, as well. But calculated murder? Not in decades." He completed his signatures, handed the letters back to his secretary, and bade her goodnight. He himself stood and went back to his desk, where he began to sort through paperwork, some of which he shoved into a briefcase on his chair. He said, "That being the situation, the police are, unfortunately, predisposed to believe that a Guernseyman wouldn't be capable of committing a crime like this."

"Do you suspect there are others, then, beyond the architect?" St. James asked. "I mean other Guernseymen with a reason to want Guy Brouard dead?"

Holberry set his paperwork aside as he pondered this question. In the outer office, the door opened then closed as his secretary went on her way. "I believe," Holberry said carefully, "that the surface has barely been scratched when it comes to Guy Brouard and the people of this island. He was like Father Christmas: this charity, that charity, a wing at the hospital, and what do you need? Just see Mr. Brouard. He was the patron of half a dozen artists—painters, sculptors, glassmakers, metal workers—and he was footing the bill on more than one local kid's university education in England. That's who he was. Some called it giving back to a community that had made him welcome. But I wouldn't be surprised to find out others had another name for it."

"When money's paid out, favours are owed?"

"That's about it." Holberry snapped his briefcase closed. "People tend to expect something in return when they hand out money, don't they? If we follow Brouard's cash round the island, I reckon we'll know sooner or later what that something was."

Chapter 8

EARLY IN THE MORNING, Frank Ouseley made arrangements for one of the farmwives from *Rue des Rocquettes* to descend to the valley and look in on his father. He didn't intend to be gone from *Moulin des Niaux* more than three hours, but he really wasn't sure how long the funeral, the burial, and the reception would take. It was inconceivable that he should be absent from any part of the day's proceedings. But leaving his father on his own was too risky to contemplate. So he phoned round till he found a compassionate soul who said she'd bike down once or twice "with something sweet for the old dear. Dad likes his sweeties, doesn't he?"

Nothing was necessary, Frank had assured her. But if she did truly wish to bring Dad a treat, he was partial to anything with apples in it.

Fuji, Braeburn, Pippin? the good woman inquired.

Really, it didn't make a difference.

Indeed, truth to tell, she probably could have made something out of bedsheets and passed it off as apple strudel. His father had eaten worse in his time and had lived to make it a topic of general conversation. It seemed to Frank that as the end of his father's life approached, he talked more and more about the distant past. This was something Frank had welcomed several years previously when it had begun, since aside from his interest in the war in general and the occupation of Guernsey in particular, Graham Ouseley had always been admirably reticent about his own heroics during that terrible time. He'd spent most of Frank's youth deflecting personal questions, saying, "It wasn't about me, boy. It was about all of us," and Frank had learned to cherish the fact that his father's ego needed no bolstering through reminiscences in which he himself played a key role. But as if he knew his time was drawing nigh and wished to leave a legacy of memory for his only son, Graham had started to talk in specifics. Once he had begun this process, it seemed there was no end to what Frank's father was able to remember from the war.

This morning Graham had produced a monologue on the detector-van, a piece of equipment the Nazis had used upon the island to rout out the last of the short-wave radio transmitters that citizens were using to gather information from those labeled enemies, particularly the French and the English. "Last one faced the rifles at Fort George," Graham informed him. "Poor sod from Luxembourg, he was. There're those who say the detector-van got him, but *I* say a quisling pointed the way. And we had those, damn 'em: Jerrybags and spies. Collaborators, Frank. Putting people in front of the firing squad without the blink of a sodding eyelash. God rot their souls."

After that, it was the V for Victory Campaign and all the places that the twenty-second letter of the alphabet not so mysteriously appeared on the island—rendered in chalk, in paint, and in still-wet concrete—to torment the Nazis.

And finally it was *G.I.F.T.*—Guernsey Independent From Terror—Graham Ouseley's personal contribution to a population in peril. His year in prison had its origins in this underground newsletter. Along with three other islanders, for twenty-nine months he'd managed to produce it before the Gestapo came knocking at the cottage door. "I was betrayed," Graham told his son. "Like them short-wave receivers. So don't you ever forget this, Frank: Put to the test, those whose blood runs yellow are afraid of getting cut. Always the same, that, when times are rough. People point fingers if there's something to be gained for themselves. But we shall make them squirm for it in the end. Long time in coming, but they shall pay."

Frank left his father still waxing on this subject, confiding it to the television as he settled into the first of his shows for the day. Frank told him that Mrs. Petit would be looking in on him within the hour and he explained to his father that he himself would be seeing to some pressing business in St. Peter Port. He didn't mention the funeral because he still hadn't mentioned Guy Brouard's death.

Luckily, his father didn't ask the nature of the business. A surge of dramatic music from the telly caught his attention, and within a moment he'd submitted himself to a storyline involving two women, one man, some sort of terrier, and someone's scheming mother-in-law. Seeing this, Frank took his leave.

As there was no synagogue on the island to accommodate what was a negligible Jewish population, and despite the fact that Guy Brouard was not a member of any Christian religion, his funeral service was held in the Town Church, not far from the harbour in St. Peter Port. In keeping with the importance of the deceased and the affection in which he was held by his fellow Guernseymen, the church of St. Martin—in whose parish *Le Reposoir* sat—was deemed too small to hold the number of expected mourners. Indeed, so dear had he become to the people of the island in his nearly ten years as a resident that no fewer than seven ministers of God took part in his funeral.

Frank made it just in time, which was nothing short of a miracle considering the parking situation in the town. But the police had allocated both of the car parks on Albert Pier for the funeral goers, and while Frank was able to find a spot only at the far north end of the pier, by trotting all the way back to the church he managed to get inside just in advance of the coffin and the family.

Adrian Brouard, he saw, had established himself as Chief Mourner. This was his right as Guy Brouard's eldest child and only son. Any friend of Guy's knew, however, that there had been no communication between the two men in at least three months, and what communication had preceded their estrangement had been characterised mostly by a battle of wills. The young man's mother must have had a hand in positioning Adrian directly behind the coffin, Frank concluded. And to make sure he stayed there, she'd positioned *herself* directly behind him. Poor little Ruth came third, and she was followed by Anaïs Abbott and her two children, who'd somehow managed to insinuate themselves into the family for this occasion. The only people Ruth herself had probably asked to accompany her behind her brother's coffin were the Duffys, but the position to which Valerie and Kevin had been relegated— trailing the Abbotts—didn't allow them to offer her any comfort. Frank hoped she was able to take some solace from the number of people who'd shown up to express their affection for her and for her brother: friend and benefactor to so many people.

For most of his life, Frank himself had eschewed friendship. It was enough for him that he had his dad. From the moment his mother drowned at the reservoir, they'd clung to each other—father and son—and having been a witness to Graham's attempts first to rescue and then to revive his wife and then to the terrible guilt Graham had lived with for not having been quick enough at the first or competent enough at the second had bound Frank to his father inextricably. By the time he was forty years old, he'd known too much pain and sorrow, had Graham Ouseley, and Frank decided as a child that he would be the one to put an end to both. He had devoted most of his life to this effort, and when Guy Brouard had come along, the possibility of fellowship with another man for the first time laid itself in front of Frank like an apple from the serpent. He'd bitten at that apple like a victim of famine, never once recalling that a single bite was all condemnation ever took.

The funeral seemed endless. Each minister had to speak his own piece in addition to the eulogy itself, which Adrian Brouard stumbled through, reading off three typed sheets of foolscap. The mourners sang hymns appropriate to the occasion, and a soloist hidden somewhere above them lifted her voice in an operatic farewell.

Then it was over, at least the first part. The interment and the reception came next, both of them scheduled for *Le Reposoir.*

The procession to the property was impressive. It strung all along the Quay, from Albert Pier to well beyond Victoria Marina. It slowly wound up *Le Val des Terres* beneath the thick winter-bare trees skirting along the steep-walled hillside. From there, it followed the road out of town, slicing between the wealth of Fort George on the east with its sprawling modern houses protected behind their hedges and their electric gates and the common housing of the west: streets and avenues thickly built up in the nineteenth century, Georgian and Regency semi-detached dwellings, as well as terraces that had grown decidedly the worse for wear.

Just before St. Peter Port gave way to St. Martin, the cortege turned towards the east. The cars coursed beneath the trees, along a narrow road that gave way to an even narrower lane. Along one side of this ran a high stone wall. Along the other rose an earthen bank from which grew a hedge, gnarled and knotted by the December cold.

A break in the wall made way for two iron gates. These stood open and the hearse pulled onto the expansive grounds of *Le Reposoir.* The mourners followed, with Frank among them. He parked at the side of the drive and made his way along with everyone else in the general direction of the manor house.

Within ten steps, his solitude came to an end. A voice next to him said, "This changes everything," and he looked up to see that Bertrand Debiere had joined him.

The architect looked like hell on diet pills. Always far too thin for his extreme height, he seemed to have lost a full stone since the night of the party at *Le Reposoir.* The whites of his eyes were crisscrossed with spider legs of crimson, and the bones of his cheeks—always prominent anyway—appeared to rise from his face like chicken eggs attempting to escape from beneath his skin.

"Nobby," Frank said with a nod of hello. He used the architect's nickname without a thought. He'd had him as a history student years before at the secondary modern school, and he'd never made it a habit to stand on ceremony when it came to anyone he'd formerly taught. "I didn't see you at the service."

Debiere gave no indication if he was bothered by Frank's use of his nickname. As he'd never been called anything else by his intimates, he probably hadn't noticed. He said, "Don't you agree?"

"To what?"

"To the original idea. To my idea. We'll have to return to it now, I dare say. Without Guy here, we can't expect Ruth to spearhead things. She won't know the first thing about this sort of building, and I can't imagine she'll want to learn. Can you?"

"Ah. The museum," Frank said.

"It'll still go forward. Guy would want that. But as to the design, that'll have to change. I talked to him about it, but you probably know that already, don't you? I know you were thick as thieves, you and Guy, so he probably told you that I cornered him. That night, you know. Just the two of us. After the fireworks. I had a closer look at the elevation drawing and I could see—well, who couldn't if you know anything about architecture?—that this bloke from California had got everything wrong. You'd expect that from someone who designed without having a look at the site, wouldn't you? Pretty ego-driven, if you ask me. Nothing I would have done, and I told Guy that. I know I was starting to bring him round, Frank."

Nobby's voice was eager. Frank glanced at him as they followed the procession that was wending its way to the west side of the house. He didn't reply, although he could tell that Nobby was desperate for him to do so. The faint sheen on his upper lip betrayed him.

The architect continued. "All those windows, Frank. As if there's a spectacular view at St. Saviour's that we're supposed to make use of, or something. He would have *known* there wasn't if he'd come to see the site in the first place. And think what that's going to do to the heating, all those great long windows. It'll cost a bloody fortune to keep the place open out of season when the weather's bad. I presume you want it open out of season, don't you? If it's for the island more than just for the tourists, then it has to be open when local people can get there, which they're not likely even to attempt in the middle of summer when the crowds are here. Don't you agree?"

Frank knew he had to say something because maintaining silence in this situation would be odd, so he said, "Mind you don't put the cart first, Nobby. It's time to go easy, I expect."

"But you're an ally, aren't you?" Nobby demanded. "F-Frank, you *are* on m-my side in this?"

The sudden stammering marked the level of his anxiety. It had done the same when he was a boy in school, called on in class and unable to bluff his way through a recitation. His speech problem had always made Nobby seem more vulnerable than the other boys, which was appealing, but at the same time it cursed him to truth at any cost, removing from him the ability that other people possessed to disguise what they were feeling.

Frank said, "It's not a question of allies and enemies, Nobby. This whole business"—with a nod at the house to indicate what had gone on inside of it, the decisions taken and the dreams destroyed—"it's nothing to do with me. I didn't have the means to become involved. At least, not as you're thinking I might have been involved."

"B-but he'd settled on me. Frank you *know* he'd settled on m-me. On my design. My plan. And, l-l-*listen*. I've g-g-got to have that commi-com-commi-com*miss*ion." He spat the last word out. His entire face had grown shiny with the effort. His voice had become louder, and several mourners on the path to the grave site looked their way curiously.

Frank stepped out of the procession and drew Nobby with him. The coffin was being carried past the side of the conservatory and in the direction of the sculpture garden northwest of the house. A grave site there would be more than suitable, Frank realised as he saw this, Guy surrounded in death by the artists he'd patronised during his life.

His hand on Nobby's arm, Frank led him round the front of the conservatory and out of the view of those who were heading to the burial. "It's too soon to talk about all this," he told his former student. "If there's been no allocation in his will, then—"

"There's been no architect n-named in the will," Nobby said. "You can depend on that." He mopped a handkerchief against his face, and this movement seemed to help him bring his speech back under control. "Given enough time to think about things, Guy would have changed to the Guernsey plans, believe me, Frank. You know his loyalty was to the island. The idea that he'd choose a non-Guernsey architect is ridiculous. He would have seen that eventually. So now it's just a matter of our sitting down and drawing up a coherent reason why the choice of the architect has to be changed, and that can't be difficult, can it? Ten minutes with the plans and I can point out every problem he's got in his design. It's more than just the windows, Frank. This American didn't even understand the nature of the collection."

"But Guy already made the choice," Frank said. "It dishonours his memory to alter it, Nobby. No, don't speak. Listen for a moment. I know you're disappointed. I know Guy's choice is one you don't like. But it was Guy's choice to make, and it's up to us to live with it now."

"Guy is dead." Nobby punched every syllable into his palm as he said it. "So regardless of *whatever* he decided about the look of the place, we can now build the museum the way we see fit. *And* the way that's most practical and suitable. This is your project, Frank. It's always been your project. You have the exhibits. Guy just wanted to give you a place to house them."

He was very persuasive for all his oddity of appearance and speech. In any other circumstance Frank might have found himself being swayed to Nobby's way of thinking. But in the present circumstance, he had to remain firm. There would be hell to pay if he didn't.

He said, "I just can't help you, Nobby. I'm sorry."

"But you could talk to Ruth. She'd listen to you."

"That might be the case, but I actually wouldn't know what to say."

"I'd prepare you in advance. I'd give you the words."

"If you have them, you must say them yourself."

"But she won't listen to me. Not the way she'd listen to you."

Frank held out his hands, empty, and said, "I'm sorry. Nobby, I'm sorry. What more can I say?"

Nobby looked deflated, his last hope gone. "You can say you're sorry enough to do something to change things. But I suppose that's far too much for you, Frank."

It was actually far too little, Frank thought. It was because things had changed that they were standing where they were standing right now.

St. James saw the two men duck out of the procession heading towards the grave site. He recognised the intensity of their conversation, and he made a mental note to learn their identities. For the moment, however, he followed the rest of the mourners to the grave.

Deborah walked beside him. Her reticence all morning told him that she was still smarting from their breakfast conversation, one of those senseless confrontations in which only one person clearly understands the topic under discussion. He hadn't been that person, unfortunately. He'd been talking about the wisdom of Deborah's ordering only mushrooms and grilled tomatoes for her morning meal while she'd appeared to be reviewing the course of their entire history together. At least, that was what he finally assumed after listening to his wife accuse him of "manhandling me in *every* way, Simon, as if I'm completely incapable of taking a single action on my own. Well, I'm tired of that. I'm an adult, and I wish you'd start treating me like one."

He'd blinked from her to the menu, wondering how they'd managed to get from a discussion of protein to an accusation of heartless domination. He'd foolishly said, "What are you talking about, Deborah?" And the fact that he hadn't followed her logic had set them on the path to disaster.

It was disaster only in his eyes, though. In hers it was clearly a moment in which suspected but unnamable truths were finally being revealed about their marriage. He'd hoped she might share one or two of them with him during their drive to the funeral and the burial afterwards. But she hadn't done so, so he was relying upon the passage of a few hours to settle things down between them.

"That must be the son," Deborah murmured to him now. They were at the back of the mourners on a slight slope of land that rose to a wall. Inside this wall a garden grew, separated from the rest of the estate. Paths meandered haphazardly, through carefully trimmed shrubs and flowerbeds, beneath trees that were bare now but thoughtfully placed to shade concrete benches and shallow ponds. Among all this, modern sculptures stood: a granite figure curled foetally; a cupreous elf—seasoned by verdigris—posing beneath the fronds of a palm; three maidens in bronze trailing seaweed behind them; a marble sea nymph rising out of a pond. Into this setting at the top of five steps, a terrace spread out. Along the far end of it, a pergola ran, trailing vines and sheltering a single bench. It was here on the terrace that the grave had been dug, perhaps so that future generations could simultaneously contemplate the garden and consider the final resting-place of the man who had created it.

St. James saw that the coffin had already been lowered and the final parting prayers had been said. A blonde woman, incongruously wearing sunglasses as if in attendance at a Hollywood burial, was now shooing forward the man at her side. She did it verbally first, and when that didn't work, she gave him a little push towards the grave. Next to this was a mound of earth out of which poked a shovel with black streamers hanging from it. St. James agreed with Deborah: This would be the son, Adrian Brouard, the only other inhabitant of the house aside from his aunt and the Rivers siblings on the night before his father had been murdered.

Brouard's lip curled in reaction. He brushed his mother off and approached the mound of earth. In the absolute hush of the crowd round the grave, he scooped up a shovelful of soil and flipped it on top of the coffin. The thud as the earth hit the wood below it resounded like the echo of a door being slammed.

Adrian Brouard was followed in this action by a birdlike woman so diminutive that from the back she could easily have been mistaken for a preadolescent boy. She handed the shovel solemnly over to Adrian Brouard's mother who likewise poured earth into the grave. When she herself would have returned the shovel to the mound next to the grave site, yet another woman came forward and grasped the handle before the sunglassed blonde could release it.

A murmur went through the onlookers at this, and St. James studied the woman more intently. He could see little of her, for she wore a black hat the approximate size of a parasol, but she had a startling figure that she was making the most of in a trim charcoal suit. She did her bit with the shovel and handed it over to a gawky adolescent girl, curve-shouldered and weak-ankled in platform shoes. This girl made her bow at the grave and tried to give the shovel next to a boy round her age, whose height, colouring, and general appearance suggested that he was her brother. But instead of performing his part in the ritual, the boy abruptly turned away and shoved through those standing closest to the grave. A second murmur went up at this.

"What's that all about?" Deborah asked quietly.

"Something that needs looking at," St. James said. He saw the opportunity given to him in the teenager's actions. He said, "D'you feel easy sussing him out, Deborah? Or would you rather head back to China?"

He hadn't met her yet, this friend of Deborah's, and he wasn't sure he wanted to, although he couldn't quite put his finger on the reason for his reluctance. He knew their meeting was inevitable, however, so he told himself that he wanted to have something hopeful to report to her when they were finally introduced. In the meantime, though, he wanted Deborah to have the freedom to go to her friend. She hadn't done that yet today, and there was little doubt the American and her brother would be wondering what their London friends were managing to accomplish.

Cherokee had phoned them early in the morning, afire to know what St. James had learned from the police. He'd kept his voice determinedly cheerful at his end of the line as St. James told him what little there was to tell, and from that it was clear that the other man was making the call in the presence of his sister. At the conclusion of their conversation, Cherokee signaled his intention to attend the funeral. He was firm in his desire to be part of what he called "the action," and it was only when St. James tactfully pointed out that his presence might provide an unnecessary distraction that would allow the real killer to fade into the crowd that he agreed reluctantly to remain behind. He'd be waiting to hear what they were able to uncover, though, he told them. China would be waiting, too.

"You can go to her if you like," St. James said to his wife. "I'll be sniffing round here for a while. I can get a ride back into town with someone. It shouldn't be a problem."

"I didn't come to Guernsey just to sit and hold China's hand," Deborah replied.

"I know. Which is why—"

She cut him off before he could finish. "I'll see what he has to say, Simon."

St. James watched her stride away in pursuit of the boy. He sighed and wondered why communicating with women—particularly with his wife—was frequently a case of speaking about one thing while trying to read the subtext of another. And he pondered how his inability to read women accurately was going to affect his performance here on Guernsey, where it was looking more and more as if the circumstances surrounding Guy Brouard's life and his death were crawling with significant females.

When Margaret Chamberlain saw the crippled man approach Ruth near the end of the reception, she knew he wasn't a legitimate member of the congregation who'd been at the funeral and the burial. First of all, he hadn't spoken to her sister-in-law earlier at the grave site as had everyone else. Besides that, he'd spent the reception afterwards wandering from open room to open room in the house in a manner that suggested speculation. Margaret had at first thought he was a burglar of some sort, despite the limp and the leg brace, but when he finally introduced himself to Ruth—going so far as to hand her his card—she realised he was something else altogether. What that something was had to do with Guy's death. If not that, then with the distribution of his fortune which they were *finally* going to learn about as soon as the last of the mourners left them.

Ruth hadn't wanted to see Guy's solicitor before then. It was as if she was aware that there was bad news coming, and she was trying to spare everyone from having to hear it. Everyone or someone, Margaret thought shrewdly. The only question was who.

If it was Adrian whose disappointment she was hoping to postpone, there was definitely going to be hell to pay. She'd drag her sister-in-law to court and shake out every piece of dirty laundry there was if Guy had disinherited his only son. Oh, she knew there'd be excuses aplenty coming from Ruth if that's what Adrian's father had done. But let them just *try* to accuse her of undermining the relationship between father and son, let them just *make* a single attempt to depict her as the responsible party for Adrian's loss . . . There'd be a real season in hell coming when she trotted out all the reasons she'd kept them apart. They each had a name and a title, those reasons, although not quite the kind of title that redeems one's transgressions in the eyes of the public: Danielle the Air Hostess, Stephanie the Pole Dancer, MaryAnn the Dog Groomer, Lucy the Hotel Maid.

They were the reason that Margaret had kept the son from the father. What sort of example was the boy to see? she could easily demand of anyone who asked her. What sort of role model did she have a duty to provide an impressionable lad of eight, or ten, or fifteen? If his father lived a life that made lengthy visits from his son unsuitable, was it the son's fault? And should he now be deprived of what he was owed by blood because his father's daisy chain of mistresses throughout the years had gone unbroken?

No. She had been within her rights to keep them well apart, doomed to quick or interrupted visits only. After all, Adrian was a sensitive child. She owed him the protection of a mother's love, not exposure to a father's excess.

She watched her son now as he lurked at the edge

of the stone hall, where most of the post-burial reception was being conducted in the warmth of two
fires that burned at either end of the room. He was
trying to edge his way to the door, either to escape
altogether or to duck along to the dining room
where an enormous buffet spread across the fine mahogany table. Margaret frowned. This would not do.
He should have been mingling. Rather than creeping along the wall like an insect, he should have been
doing something to act like the scion of the wealthi-
est man the Channel Islands had ever seen. How
could he expect his life to be anything more than it
already was—confined and described by his mother's
house in St. Albans—if he didn't put himself out, for
God's sake?

Margaret wove her way through the remaining
guests and intercepted her son at the door to the passage that led to the dining room. She put her arm
through his and ignored his effort to pull away, saying with a smile, "*Here* you are, darling. I knew
there was someone who could point out the people
I've still to meet. One can't hope to know them all,
of course. But surely there are important individuals
I ought to meet for future reference?"

"What future?" Adrian put his hand on hers to
disengage her, but she caught his fingers, squeezed
them, and continued smiling as if he weren't trying
to escape.

"Yours, of course. We must set about making certain it's secure."

"Must we, Mother? How d'you propose to do
that?"

"A word here, a word there," she said airily. "It's amazing the kind of influence one can have once one knows the proper person to talk to. That glowering gentleman over there, for instance? Who is he?"

Instead of replying, Adrian started to move away from his mother. But she had the advantage of height over him—of weight as well—and she held him where he was. "Darling?" she asked him brightly. "The gentleman? The one with the patches on his elbows? Attractive in an overnourished-Heathcliff sort of way?"

Adrian gave the man a cursory glance. "One of Dad's artists. The place is crawling with them. They're all here to grease the way with Ruth on the chance she's been left most of the bundle."

"When they should be greasing the way with you? How very strange," Margaret said.

He gave her a look that she didn't like to interpret. "Believe me. No one's that stupid."

"About what?"

"About where Dad left his money. They know he wouldn't have—"

"Darling, that makes no difference at all. Where he may have *wanted* his money to go and where it shall end up might very well be two different places. Wise is the man who realises that and acts accordingly."

"Wise is the woman as well, Mother?"

He sounded hateful. Margaret couldn't understand what she had done to deserve that sort of tone from him. She said, "If we're speaking of your father's latest dalliance with this Mrs. Abbott, I think I can safely say that—"

"You know damn well we're not."

"—your father's bent for younger women being what it was—"

"Yeah. That's just bloody it, Mother. Would you God damn *listen* to yourself for once?"

Margaret stopped, confused. She tracked back through their last exchange. "What I was saying? About what?"

"About Dad. About Dad's women. About his *younger* women. Just think, all right? I'm sure you can put the pieces together."

"Darling, what pieces? I honestly don't know—"

" 'Take her to meet your father so she *sees,* my darling,' " her son recited tersely. " 'No woman will walk away from that.' Because she'd started to have second thoughts about me and you saw that clear enough, didn't you? God knows you probably even expected it. You thought if she knew just how much money was on the horizon if she played her cards right, she'd decide to stay with me. As if I'd bloody want her then. As if I bloody want her now."

Margaret felt an icy wind chill her neck. "Are you saying . . . ?" but she knew that he was. She glanced round them. Her smile felt like a death mask. She drew her son out of the hall. She led him down the passage and beyond the dining room to the butler's pantry, where she shut the door upon them. She didn't like to think where their conversation was heading. She didn't *want* to think where their conversation was heading. Less did she like or want to think what where it was heading might imply about the recent past. But she couldn't stop the force of things she herself had brought into motion, so she spoke.

"What are you telling me, Adrian?" She kept her back to the door of the butler's pantry so he couldn't escape her. There was a second door—this one to the dining room—but she felt confident that he wouldn't go there. The murmur of voices beyond it told them both that the room was occupied. And he'd started to twitch—his eyes beginning to unfocus—which heralded a state he wouldn't want strangers to observe. When he didn't reply at once, Margaret repeated her question. She spoke more gently now because, despite her impatience with him, she could see his suffering. "What happened, Adrian?"

"You know," he answered dully. "You knew him so you know the rest."

Margaret clasped his face between her palms. She said, "No. I can't believe . . ." She tightened her hold on him. "You were his son. He would have drawn the line at that. *Because* of that. You were his son."

"As if that mattered." Adrian jerked away from her. "Just like you were his wife. That didn't matter a whole hell of a lot either."

"But Guy and *Carmel*? Carmel Fitzgerald? Carmel who never had ten remotely amusing words to say to anyone and probably wouldn't have known a clever comment from—" Margaret brought herself up short. She looked away.

"Right. So she was perfect for me," Adrian said.

"She wasn't used to anyone clever so she was easy pickings."

"That's not what I meant. That's not what I was thinking. She's a lovely girl. You and she together—"

"What difference does it make what you were thinking? It's the truth. He saw it. She was going to be easy. Dad saw that and he had to make his move. Because if he ever left one patch of ground unploughed when it was right in front of him just begging for it, Mother—" His voice cracked.

Beyond them in the dining room, the clink of plates and cutlery suggested that the caterers were beginning to clear away the food as the reception drew to a close. Margaret glanced at the door behind her son and knew that it was only a matter of moments before they were interrupted. She couldn't bear the thought that he should be seen like this, with his face gone greasy and his chapped lips trembling. He was reduced to childhood in an instant and *she* was reduced to the woman she'd always been as his mother, caught between telling him to get a grip on himself before someone saw him as a puling sniveler and crushing him to her bosom to comfort him while vowing to be avenged on his adversaries.

But it was the thought of vengeance that brought Margaret quickly round to seeing Adrian as the man he was today, not as the child he once had been. And the chill on her neck turned to frost in her blood as she considered the ways that vengeance might have played out here on Guernsey.

The door handle rattled behind her son and the

door swung open, hitting him in the back. A grey-haired woman popped her head inside, saw Margaret's rigid face, said, "Oh! Sorry," and disappeared. But her intrusion was sign enough. Margaret hustled her son out of the room.

She led him upstairs and into her bedroom, thankful that Ruth had placed her in the western half of the house, away from her own room and away from Guy's. She and her son would have privacy here, and privacy was what they needed.

She sat Adrian down on the dressing table's stool and she fetched a bottle of single malt from her suitcase. Ruth was notoriously niggardly with the drink, and Margaret thanked God for this as otherwise she wouldn't have thought to come supplied. She poured a full two fingers and shot them down, then poured again and handed the glass to her son.

"I don't—"

"You do. This will steady your nerves." She waited until he had obeyed her, draining the glass and then holding it loosely between his palms. Then she said to him, "Are you certain, Adrian? He liked to flirt. You know that. It may have been nothing more. Did you see them together? Did you—" She hated to ask for the grisly details but she needed the facts.

"I didn't need to see them. She was different with me afterwards. I guessed."

"Did you speak to him? Accuse him?"

"Of course I did. What do you take me for?"

"And what did he say?"

"He denied it. But I forced him to—"

"*Forced* him?" She could scarcely breathe.

"I lied. I told him she'd confessed. So he did as well."

"And then?"

"Nothing. We went back to England, Carmel and I. You know the rest."

"My God, then why did you come *back* here again?" she asked him. "He'd had your fiancée right under your nose. Why did you—"

"I was badgered into coming back, as you might recall," Adrian said. "What did you tell me? He'd be so *pleased* to see me?"

"But if I'd known, I never would have even suggested, let alone insisted . . . Adrian, for the love of God. Why didn't you tell me this happened?"

"Because I decided to use it," he said. "If reason couldn't get him to make me the loan I needed, then I thought guilt could. Only, I forgot Dad was immune to guilt. He was immune to everything." Then he smiled. And at the moment, the chill-turned-frost went to ice in Margaret's blood when her son next said, "Well, practically everything, as things turned out."

Chapter 9

DEBORAH ST. JAMES FOLLOWED the adolescent boy at a distance. She wasn't at her best striking up conversations with strangers, but she wasn't about to leave the scene without at least putting her fingers into the situation. She knew that her reluctance did nothing more than confirm her husband's earlier trepidation about her coming to Guernsey by herself to look into China's difficulties, Cherokee's presence apparently not counting with Simon. So she was doubly determined that her natural reticence wouldn't defeat her in the present circumstance.

The boy didn't know she was behind him. He didn't appear to have any particular destination in mind. He forced his way out of the crowd in the sculpture garden first and then headed across a crisp oval lawn that lay beyond an ornate conservatory at one end of the house. At the side of this lawn, he leaped between two tall rhododendrons and scooped up a thin bough from a chestnut tree growing near a group of three outbuildings. At these, he veered suddenly to the east where, in the distance and through the trees, Deborah could see a stone

wall giving on to fields and meadows. But instead of
heading in that direction—the surest way to leave
behind him the funeral and everything that went
with the funeral—he began to trudge along the pebbly road that led back towards the house again. As he
walked, he roughly used his bough like a switch
against the shrubbery that grew lushly along the
drive. This bordered a series of meticulously kept
gardens to the east of the house, but he didn't enter
any of these either. Instead, he forged off through
the trees beyond the shrubbery and picked up his
pace when he apparently heard someone approaching one of the cars that were parked in this area.

Deborah lost him momentarily there. It was
gloomy near the trees and he was wearing dark
brown from head to toe, so he was difficult to see.
But she hurried forward in the general direction
she'd seen him take, and she caught him up on a path
that dipped down to a meadow. In the middle of
this, the tiled roof of what looked like a Japanese teahouse rose behind both a stand of delicate maples
and an ornamental wooden fence that was oiled to
maintain its original rich colour and brightly ac-
cented in red and black. It was, she saw, yet another
garden on the estate.

The boy crossed a dainty wooden bridge which
curved above a depression in the land. He tossed his
branch aside, picked his way along some stepping
stones, and strode up to a scalloped gate in the fence.
He shoved this open and disappeared inside. The
gate swung silently shut behind him.

Deborah quickly followed, crossing over the

bridge that spanned a little gully in which grey stones had been placed with careful attention to what grew round them. She approached the gate and saw what she hadn't seen before: a bronze plaque set into the wood. *À la mémoire de Miriam et Benjamin Brouard, assassinés par les Nazis à Auschwitz. Nous n'oublierons jamais.* Deborah read the words and recognised enough of them to know that the garden was one of remembrance.

She pushed open the gate upon a world that was different to what she'd seen so far on the ground of *Le Reposoir.* The lush and exuberant growth of plants and trees had been disciplined here. An austere order had been imposed upon it with much of the foliage stripped away from the trees and the shrubbery trimmed into formal shapes. These were pleasing to the eye and they melded one into the other in a pattern that directed one's gaze round the perimeter of the garden to yet another arched bridge, this one extending over a large meandering pond on which lily pads grew. Just beyond this pond stood the teahouse whose roof Deborah had glimpsed from the other side of the fence. It had parchment doors in the manner of private Japanese buildings, and one of these doors had been slid open.

Deborah followed the path round the perimeter of the garden and crossed the bridge. Beneath her she saw large and colourful carp swimming while before her the interior of the teahouse lay revealed. The open door displayed a floor covered by traditional mats and a single room furnished with one low table of ebony round which six cushions lay.

A deep porch ran the width of the teahouse, two steps giving access to it from the swept gravel path that continued round the garden itself. Deborah mounted these steps but made no attempt to do so surreptitiously. Better that she be another funeral guest having a stroll, she thought, than someone on the trail of a boy who probably didn't wish to make conversation.

He was kneeling at a teak cabinet that was built into the wall at the far side of the teahouse. He had this open and was lugging a heavy bag from within it. While Deborah watched, he wrestled it out, opened it, and dug round inside. He brought forth a plastic container. Then he turned and saw Deborah watching him. He didn't start at the sight of an un-expected stranger. He looked at her openly and without the slightest qualm. Then he got to his feet and walked past her, out onto the porch and from there to the pond.

As he passed, she saw that his plastic container held small round pellets. He took these to the edge of the water, where he sat on a smooth grey boulder and scooped up a handful, which he threw to the fish. The water was at once a swarm of rainbow activity.

Deborah said, "D'you mind if I watch?"

The boy shook his head. He was, she saw, about seventeen years old, and his face was marred by seri-ous acne, which grew even redder as she joined him on the rock. She watched the fish for a moment, their greedy mouths pumping at the water, instinct making them snap at anything that moved on its surface. Lucky for them, she thought, to be in this safe, protected environment, where what moved on the surface was actually food and not a lure.

She said, "I don't much like funerals. I think it's because I started at them early. My mum died when I was seven and whenever I'm at a funeral, it all comes back to me."

The boy said nothing, but his process of throwing the food into the water slowed marginally. Deborah took heart from this and went on.

"Funny, though, because I didn't feel it very much when it actually happened. People would probably say that's because I didn't understand, but I did, you know. I knew exactly what it meant if someone died. They'd be gone and I'd never see them again. They might be with angels and God but in any case, they'd be in a place that I wouldn't be going to for a long, long time. So I knew what it meant. I just didn't understand what it implied. That didn't sink in until much later, when the mother-daughter sorts of things that might have happened between us didn't happen between me and . . . well, between me and anyone."

Still he said nothing. But he paused in his feeding of the fish and watched the water as they continued to scramble for the pellets. They reminded Deborah of people in a queue when a bus arrives and what once was orderly collapses into a mass of elbows, knees, and umbrellas all shoving at once.

She said, "She's been dead almost twenty years and I still wonder what it might've been like. My dad never remarried and there's no other family and there are times when it seems it would be so lovely to be part of something bigger than just the two of us. Then I wonder, as well, what it could've been like if they'd've had other children, my mum and dad. She was only thirty-two when she died, which seemed ancient to me when I was seven but which I now see meant that she had years ahead of her to have had more children. I wish she had."

The boy looked at her then. She pushed her hair back from her face. "Sorry. Am I going on? I do that sometimes."

"You want to try?" He extended the plastic container to her.

She said, "Lovely. I would. Thanks." She dipped her hand into the pellets. She moved to the edge of the rock and let the food dribble from her fingers into the water. The fish came at once, knocking one another aside in their anxiety to feed. "They make it look like the water's boiling. There must be hundreds of them."

"One hundred twenty-three." The boy's voice was low—Deborah found she had to strain to hear him—and he spoke with his gaze back upon the pond. "He keeps the stock up because the birds go after them. Big ones, the birds. Sometimes a gull but they're generally not strong enough or fast enough. And the fish are smart. They hide. That's why the rocks're laid out so far over the edges of the pond: to give them a place when the birds show up."

"One has to think of everything, I suppose,"

Deborah said. "It's brilliant, this place, though, isn't it? I was having a wander, needing to get away from the grave site, and suddenly I saw the roof of the tea-house and the fence and it looked like it might be quiet in here. Tranquil, you know. So I came in."

"Don't lie." He set the container of pellets down between them as if he were drawing a line in the sand. "I saw you."

"Saw . . . ?"

"You were following me. I saw you back by the stables."

"Ah." Deborah upbraided herself for being so careless as to give herself away, even more for proving her husband right. But she damn well *wasn't* out of her depth, as Simon would doubtless declare her, and she determined to prove it. "I saw what happened at the grave site," she admitted. "When you were given the shovel? You seemed . . . Well, as I've lost someone as well—years ago, I admit—I thought you might want to . . . terribly arrogant, I realise. But losing someone is difficult. Sometimes it helps to talk."

He grabbed up the plastic container and dumped half of it directly into the water, which burst into a frenzy of activity. He said, "I don't need to talk about anything. And especially not about him."

Deborah's ears pricked up at this. "Was Mr. Brouard . . . ? He would have been rather old to be your dad, but as you were with the family . . . ? Your granddad perhaps?" She waited for more. If she was patient enough, she believed it would come: whatever it was that was eating him up inside. She said helpfully, "I'm Deborah St. James, by the way. I've come over from London."

"For the funeral?"

"Yes. As I said, I don't much like funerals as a rule. But then, who does?"

He snorted. "My mum. She's good at funerals. She's had the practice."

Deborah was wise enough to say nothing to this. She waited for the boy to explain himself, which he did, although obliquely.

He told her his name was Stephen Abbott and he said, "I was seven as well. He got lost in a whiteout. You know what that is?"

Deborah shook her head.

"It's when a cloud comes down. Or the fog. Or whatever. But it's really bad and you can't tell which way the hill is going and you can't see the ski runs so you don't know how to get out. All you see is white everywhere: the snow and the air. So you get lost. And sometimes—" He turned his face away. "Sometimes you die."

"Your dad?" she said. "I'm sorry, Stephen. What a horrible way to lose someone you love."

"She said he'd find his way down. He's an expert, she said. He knows what to do. Expert skiers always find their way. But it lasted too long and then the snow started, a real blizzard, and he was miles from where he ought to have been. When they finally found him it'd been two days and he'd been trying to hike out and he'd broken his leg. And then they said . . . they said if they'd only got there six hours sooner—" He drove his fist into what remained of the pellets. They sprayed out of the container and onto the rock. "He might've lived. But *she* wouldn't've liked that much."

"Why not?"

"It would've kept her from collecting her boyfriends."

"Ah." Deborah saw how it fitted together. A child loses his beloved father and then watches his mother move from one man to the next, perhaps out of a grief she cannot bear to face, perhaps in a frantic effort to replace what she's lost. But Deborah also saw how it might appear to that child: as if the mother hadn't loved the father in the first place.

She said, "Mr. Brouard was one of those boyfriends, then? Is that why your mother was with the family this morning? That was your mother, wasn't it, then? The woman who wanted you to have the shovel?"

"Yeah," he said. "That was her, all right." He brushed at the pellets that he'd spilled round them. They flipped into the water one by one, like the discarded beliefs of a disillusioned child. "Stupid cow," he muttered. "Bloody stupid cow."

"To want you to be part of the—"

"She thinks she's so clever," he cut in. "She thinks she's *such* a bloody good lay . . . Just spread 'em, Mum, and they'll be your puppets. Hasn't worked so far, but if you do it long enough, it bloody well might." Stephen surged to his feet, grabbing up the container. He strode back to the teahouse and went inside. Again, Deborah followed him.

From the doorway she said, "Sometimes people

do things when they miss someone terribly, Stephen. On the surface what they do looks irrational. Unfeeling, you know. Or even sly. But if we can get past what it looks like to us, if we can try to understand the reason behind it—"

"She started right after he *died,* all right?" Stephen shoved the bag of fish food back into the cupboard. He slammed its door. "One of the ski patrol instructors, only I didn't know what was going on right then. I didn't figure it out till we were in Palm Beach and by then we'd lived in Milan already and Paris and there was always a man, do you see, there was *always* . . . That's why we're here now, d'you get it? Because the last was in London and she couldn't get him to marry her and she's getting desperate because if she runs out of money and there's no one, then what the hell is she going to *do?*"

The poor boy cried at that, wrenching, humiliating sobs. Deborah's heart went out to him and she crossed the teahouse to his side. She said, "Sit here. Please sit down, Stephen."

He said, "I hate her. I really hate her. Sodding bitch. She's so bloody stupid she can't even *see* . . ." He couldn't go on, so hard was he weeping.

Deborah urged him down to one of the pillows. He dropped onto it on his knees, his head lowered to his chest and his body heaving.

Deborah didn't touch him although she wanted to. Seventeen years old, abject despair. She knew what it felt like: The sunlight was gone, the night never ended, and the feeling of hopelessness descended like a shroud.

"It feels like hate because it's so strong," she said. "But it isn't hate. It's something quite different. The flip side of love, I suppose. Hate destroys. But this . . . ? This, what you're feeling . . . ? It wouldn't harm anyone. So it isn't hate. Really."

"But you saw her," he cried. "You saw what she's like."

"Just a woman, Stephen."

"No! More than that. You saw what she's done."

At this, Deborah's intellect went on the alert. "What she's done?" she repeated.

"She's too old now. She can't cope with that. And she won't see . . . And I can't tell her. *How* can I tell her?"

"Tell her what?"

"It's too late. For any of it. He doesn't love her. He doesn't even want her. She can do anything she *wants* to make it different. But nothing's going to work. Not sex. Not going under the knife. Nothing. She'd lost him, and she was too bloody stupid to see it. But she ought to have seen. Why *didn't* she see? Why'd she just keep on doing things to make herself seem better? To try to make him want her when he didn't any longer?"

Deborah absorbed this carefully. With it, she pondered all the boy had previously said. The implication behind his words was clear: Guy Brouard had moved on from this boy's mother. The logical conclusion was that he'd gone on to someone else. But the truth of the matter could also be that the man had gone on to some*thing* else. If he hadn't wanted

Mrs. Abbott any longer, they needed to discover what it was he *had* wanted.

Paul Fielder arrived at *Le Reposoir* sweating, dirty, and breathless, with his rucksack askew on his back. Although he'd reckoned that it was far too late, he'd pedaled his bicycle from the Bouet to the Town Church first, hurtling along the waterfront as if all four Horsemen of the Apocalypse were in hot pursuit. There was a chance, he'd thought, that Mr. Guy's funeral had been delayed for one reason or another. If that had occurred, he would have still been able to be present for at least part of it.

But the fact of no cars sitting along North Esplanade and none in the car parks on the pier told him that Billy's scheme had paid off. His older brother had managed to keep Paul from attending the funeral of his only friend.

Paul knew it was Billy who'd done the damage to his bike. As soon as he got outside and saw it—the back tyre knifed and the chain removed and slung into the mud—he recognised his brother's nasty fingerprints all over the prank. He'd given a strangled cry and charged back into the house, where his brother was eating fried bread at the kitchen table and drinking a mug of tea. He had a fag burning in an ashtray next to him and another forgotten and smoking from the draining board over the sink. He was pretending to watch a chat show on the telly while their toddler sister played with a bag of flour on the floor, but the truth was that he was waiting for Paul to storm into the house and confront him in some way so that the two of them could get into a brawl.

Paul saw this directly he entered. Billy's smirk gave him away.

There'd been a time when he might have appealed to their parents. There was even a time when he might have flung himself mindlessly at his brother without considering the differences in their size and their strength. But those times had passed. The longtime meat market—a fixture of the proud old complex of colonnaded buildings that comprised Market Square in St. Peter Port—had closed forever, destroying his family's means of support. His mother was now behind a Boots till on the High Street, ringing up purchases, while his father had joined a road-works crew where the days were long and the labour was brutal. Neither of them was in the house at the moment to help and even if one of them had been, Paul wasn't about to burden them further. As for taking on Billy himself, he knew he was slow at times, but he wasn't stupid. Taking Billy on was what Billy wanted. He'd wanted it for months and had done much to make it happen. He was itching to assault someone, and he didn't care who that someone was.

Paul barely cast him a look. Instead, he leaped to the cupboard beneath the kitchen sink and brought out their father's tool box.

Billy followed him outside, ignoring their sister who remained on the kitchen floor with her hands thrust into the flour bag. Two more of their siblings were squabbling upstairs. Billy was supposed to be getting them off to school. But Billy never did much of anything he was supposed to do. Instead, he spent his days in the weed-filled back garden, pitching pennies into the beer cans that he emptied from dawn to dusk.

"Ohhh," Billy said with mock concern when his eyes lit on the ruin of Paul's bike. "Wha' the hell happened here, Paulie? Someone do something to your bike, di' they?"

Paul ignored him and flung himself to the ground. He began by removing the tyre first. Taboo, who'd been standing guard at the bike, sniffed round it suspiciously, a whine deep in his throat. Paul stopped and took Taboo over to a nearby lamppost. He tied the dog to it and pointed to the ground where he wanted him to lie. Taboo obeyed but it was clear he didn't like it. He didn't trust Paul's brother one iota and Paul knew the dog would have vastly preferred to stick close to his side.

"Need to go somewheres, do you?" Billy asked. "And your bike got wrecked. Wicked, that. What people will do."

Paul didn't want to cry because he knew that tears would give his brother more roads to take in tormenting him. It was true that tears would give him less satisfaction than defeating Paul in a brutal dust-up, but they still would serve as a better-than-nothing and Paul vastly preferred to give Billy nothing. He'd long ago learned that his brother had no heart and even less conscience. He lived to make the lives of others a torment. It was the only contribution he could make to the family.

So Paul ignored him, which Billy didn't like. He took up a station leaning against the house, and he lit yet another cigarette.

Rot your lungs, Paul thought. But he didn't say it. He just set about patching the worn old tyre, taking up the bits of rubber and the glue and stretching them across the ragged incision.

"Now lemme see where lit'le bruvver might've been going this morning," Billy said reflectively, dragging in on his fag. "Going to pay a call on Mummy down 't Boots? Take Dad his lunch somewheres out on the road-works crew? Hmm. Don't think so. Clobber's too posh. Matter of fac', where'd he get that shirt? Outta *my* cupboard? Better hope not. 'Cause pinching from me would require some discipline. But p'rhaps I oughter have a closer look. Just to make sure."

Paul didn't react. Billy, he knew, was a coward's bully. The only time he had the bottle to attack was when he believed his victims were cowed. Like their parents were cowed, Paul thought dismally. Keeping him in the house like a nonpaying lodger month after month because they were afraid what he'd do if they chucked him out.

Paul had once been like them, watching his brother cart off family belongings to flog in car-boot sales to keep himself in beer and fags. But that had been before Mr. Guy had come along. Mr. Guy, who always seemed to know what was going on in Paul's heart and who always seemed able to talk about it without preaching or making demands or expecting anything at all in return but companionship.

You just keep your eyes focused on what's important, my Prince. As to the rest of it? Let it go if it's not in the way of your dreams.

This was why he could repair his bike while his brother mocked him, challenging him either to fight or to cry. Paul closed his ears and concentrated. One tyre to patch, one chain to clean.

He could have caught the bus into town, but he didn't think of that until he had the bike back together and was halfway to the church. At that point, though, he was beyond berating himself for dimwittedness. He'd wanted so fiercely to be there for Mr. Guy's farewell that the sole thought he was even capable of producing when a bus trundled by him on the northern Number Five route and reminded him of what might have been was how easy it would be to ride out in front of the vehicle and put an end to everything.

That was when he finally cried, in sheer frustration and in desperation. He cried for the present in which his every aim appeared to be thwarted, and he cried for the future, which looked bleak and empty.

Despite seeing that not a single car remained near the Town Church, he hiked his rucksack higher on his shoulders and went inside anyway. First, though, he scooped up Taboo. He took the dog with him inside although he knew he was out of order in a very big way for this. But he didn't care. Mr. Guy had been Taboo's friend as well and anyway, he wasn't about to leave the animal out on the square not understanding what was going on. So he carried him inside where the scent of flowers and burnt candles was still in the air and a banner saying *Requiescat in Pace* still stood to the right of the pulpit. But those were the only signs that a funeral had taken place in St. Peter Port Church. After wandering the length of the centre aisle and trying to pretend he'd been one of the mourners, Paul left the building and returned to his bike. He headed south towards *Le Reposoir.*

He'd put on what went for his best clothes that morning, wishing he'd not run off from Valerie Duffy on the previous day when she'd made the offer of one of Kevin's old shirts. As a result, all he had was a pair of black trousers with bleach spots on them, his single pair of broken-down shoes, and a flannel shirt that his father used to wear on the colder days inside the meat market. Around the neck of this shirt, he'd looped a knitted tie that also belonged to his dad. And over it all he'd worn his mother's red anorak. He looked a wretched sight, and he knew it, but it was the best he could do.

Everything he had on was either grimy or sweated through when he got to the Brouard estate. For this reason, he pushed his bike behind an enormous camellia bush just inside the wall, and he ducked off the drive and walked up to the house beneath the trees instead of in the open, with Taboo trotting along beside him.

Ahead of him, Paul saw that people were coming out of the house in dribs and drabs, and as he paused to try to suss out what was happening, the hearse that had held Mr. Guy's coffin came his way, slowly passed by him where he stood half-hidden to the east of the drive, and turned out of the gates to make the journey back to town. Paul followed its route with his gaze before turning back to the house and understanding that he'd missed the burial as well. He'd missed everything.

He felt his whole body tightening and surging at once, as something tried to escape him as fiercely as he tried to keep it imprisoned. He took off his rucksack and clutched it to his chest, and he tried to believe that what he had shared with Mr. Guy had not been obliterated in the work of one moment but instead had been sanctified, blessed forever through the means of a message Mr. Guy left behind.

This, my Prince, is a special place, a you-and-I place. How good are you at keeping secrets, Paul?

Better than good, Paul Fielder vowed. Better than being able to hear his brother's taunts without listening to them. Better than being able to bear the searing fires of this loss without disintegrating completely. Better, in fact, than anything.

Ruth Brouard took St. James upstairs to her brother's study. This, he found, was in the northwest corner, and it overlooked an oval lawn and the conservatory in one direction and a semicircle of outbuildings that appeared to be old stables in the other direction. Beyond each of these, the estate spread out: more gardens, distant paddocks, fields, and woodland. St. James saw that the theme of sculpture beginning in the walled garden in which the murdered man had been buried extended to the rest of his estate as well. Here and there, a geometric form done in marble or bronze or granite or wood appeared among the trees and the plants that grew unrestrained across the land.

"Your brother was a patron of the arts." St. James turned from the window as Ruth Brouard quietly shut the door behind them.

"My brother," she replied, "was a patron of everything."

She didn't appear well, St. James decided. Her movements were studied and her voice sounded drained. She walked to an armchair and lowered herself into it. Behind her glasses, her eyes narrowed in what might have developed into a wince had she not been so careful to keep her face like a mask.

In the centre of the room, a walnut table stood, upon it the detailed model of a building set into a landscape that comprised the passing roadway in front of it, the garden behind it, even the miniature trees and shrubbery that the gardens would grow. The model was so detailed that it included both doors and windows and along the front of it what would eventually be carved into the facing stonework had been neatly applied by a skilled hand. *Graham Ouseley Wartime Museum* was incised into the frieze.

"Graham Ouseley." St. James stepped back from the model. It was low to the ground in the manner of a bunker, save for its entrance, which swept up dramatically like something designed by Le Corbusier.

"Yes," Ruth murmured. "He's a Guernseyman. Quite old. In his nineties. A local hero from the Occupation." She offered nothing more, but it was clear she was waiting. She'd read St. James's name and profession on the card he'd handed her and she'd immediately agreed to talk to him. But she obviously was going to wait to see what he wanted before volunteering any more information.

"Is this the local architect's version?" St. James asked. "I understand he built a model for your brother."

"Yes," Ruth told him. "This was done by a man from St. Peter Port, but his plan wasn't the one Guy finally chose."

"I wonder why. It looks suitable, doesn't it?"

"I've no idea. My brother didn't tell me."

"Must have been a disappointment to the local man. He appears to have gone to a lot of work." St. James bent to the model again.

Ruth Brouard stirred on her seat, shifting her torso as if seeking a more comfortable position, adjusting her glasses, and folding her small hands into her lap. "Mr. St. James," she said, "how may I help you? You said you've come about Guy's death. As your business is forensics . . . Have you news to give me? Is that why you're here? I was told that further studies of his organs were going to be made." She faltered, apparently over the difficulty of referring to her brother in parts instead of as a whole. She lowered her head and after a moment, she went on with "I was told there would be studies of my brother's organs and tissues. Other things as well. In England, I was told. As you're from London, perhaps you've come to give me information. Although if something's been uncovered—something unexpected—surely Mr. Le Gallez would have come to tell me himself, wouldn't he?"

"He knows I'm here but he hasn't sent me," St. James told her. Then he carefully explained the mission that had brought him to Guernsey in the first place. He concluded with "Miss River's advocate told me that you were the witness whose evidence DCI Le Gallez is building his case on. I've come to ask you about that evidence."

She looked away from him. "Miss River," she said.

"She and her brother were guests here for several days prior to the murder, I understand."

"And she's asked you to help her escape blame for what's happened to Guy?"

"I've not met her yet," St. James said. "I've not spoken to her."

"Then, why . . . ?"

"My wife and she are old friends."

"And your wife can't believe that her old friend has murdered my brother."

"There's the question of motive," St. James said. "How well did Miss River come to know your brother? Is there a chance she could have known him prior to this visit? Her brother doesn't give any indication of that, but he himself might not know. Do you?"

"If she's ever been to England, possibly. She could have known Guy. But only there. Guy's never been to America. That I know of."

"That you know of?"

"He might have gone at one time or another and not told me, but I can't think why. Or when, even. If he did, it would have been long ago. Since we've been here, on Guernsey, no. He would have told me. When he traveled in the past nine years, which was rarely once he retired, he always let me know where he could be reached. He was good that way. He was good in many ways, in fact."

"Giving no person a reason to kill him? No person other than China River, who also appears to have had no reason?"

"I can't explain it."

St. James moved away from the model of the museum and joined Ruth Brouard, sitting in the second armchair with a small round table between them. A picture stood on this table and he picked it up: an extended Jewish family gathered round a dining table, the men in yarmulkes, their women standing behind them, open booklets in their hands. Two children were among them, a young girl and boy. The girl wore spectacles, the boy striped braces. A patriarch stood at the head of the group, poised to break a large matzo into pieces. Behind him, a sideboard held a silver epergne and burning candles each of which shed an elongated glow on a painting on the wall, while next to him stood the woman who was obviously his wife, her head cocked towards his.

"Your family?" he said to Ruth Brouard.

"We lived in Paris," she replied. "Before Auschwitz."

"I'm sorry."

"Believe me. You can't be sorry enough."

St. James agreed with that. "No one can."

This admission on his part seemed to satisfy Ruth Brouard in some way, as perhaps did the gentleness with which he replaced the picture on the table. For she looked to the model in the centre of the room and she spoke quietly and without any rancour.

"I can tell you only what I saw that morning, Mr. St. James. I can tell you only what I did. I went to my bedroom window and watched Guy leave the house. When he reached the trees and passed onto the drive, she followed him. I saw her."

"You're certain it was China River?"

"I wasn't at first," she replied. "Come. I'll show you."

She took him back along a shadowy passage that was hung with early prints of the manor house. Not far from the stairway, she opened a door and led St. James into what was obviously her bedroom: simply furnished but furnished well with heavy antiques and an enormous needlepoint tapestry. A series of scenes comprised it, all of them combining to tell a single story in the fashion of tapestries predating books. This particular story was one of flight: an escape in the night as a foreign army approached, a hurried journey to the coast, a crossing made on heavy seas, a landing among strangers. Only two of the characters depicted were the same in every scene: a young girl and boy.

Ruth Brouard stepped into the shallow embrasure of a window and drew back sheer panels that hung over the glass. "Come," she said to St. James. "Look."

St. James joined her and saw that the window overlooked the front of the house. Below them, the drive circled round a plot of land planted with grass and shrubbery. Beyond this, the lawn rolled across to a distant cottage. A thick stand of trees grew round this building and extended up along the drive and back again to the main house.

Her brother had come out of the front door as was his habit, Ruth Brouard told St. James. As she watched, he crossed the lawn towards the cottage and disappeared into the trees. China River came out of those trees and followed him. She was in full sight. She was dressed in black. She was wearing her cloak with its hood drawn up, but Ruth knew it was China.

Why? St. James wanted to know. It seemed clear that anyone could have put his hands on China's cloak. Its very nature made it suitable for either a man or a woman to wear. And didn't the hood suggest to Miss Brouard—

"I didn't depend on that alone, Mr. St. James," Ruth Brouard told him. "I thought it odd that she would follow Guy at that hour of the morning because there seemed to be no reason for it. I found it unsettling. I thought I might be mistaken about what I'd seen, so I went to her room. She wasn't there."

"Perhaps elsewhere in the house?"

"I checked. The bathroom. The kitchen. Guy's study. The drawing room. The upstairs gallery. She wasn't anywhere inside, Mr. St. James, because she was following my brother."

"Did you have your glasses on when you saw her outside in the trees?"

"That's why I checked the house," Ruth said. "Because I didn't have them on when I first looked out of the window. It seemed to be her—I've learned to become good with sizes and shapes—but I wanted to be sure."

"Why? Did you suspect something of her? Or of someone else?"

Ruth put the sheer curtains back in place. She smoothed her hand over the thin material. She said as she did this, "Someone else? No. No. Of course not," but the fact that she spoke as she saw to the curtains prompted St. James to go on.

He said, "Who else was in the house at the time, Miss Brouard?"

"Her brother. Myself. And Adrian, Guy's son."

"What was his relationship with his father?"

"Good. Fine. They didn't see each other often.

His mother long ago put that into effect. But when they did see each other, they were terribly fond. Naturally, they had their differences. What father and son don't? But they weren't serious, the differences. They were nothing that couldn't be repaired."

"You're sure of that?"

"Of course I'm sure. Adrian is . . . He's a good boy but he's had a difficult life. His parents' divorce was bitter and he was caught in the middle. He loved both of them but he was made to choose. That sort of thing causes misunderstanding. It causes estrangement. And it isn't fair." She seemed to hear an undercurrent in her own voice and she took a deep breath as if to control it. "They loved each other in the way fathers and sons love each other when neither of them can ever get a grasp on what the other one is like."

"Where do you suppose that kind of love can lead?"

"Not to murder. I assure you of that."

"You love your nephew," St. James observed.

"Blood relatives mean more to me than they do to most people," she said, "for obvious reasons."

St. James nodded. He saw the truth in this. He also saw a further reality, but he didn't need to explore it with her at that moment. He said, "I'd like to see the route your brother took to the bay where he swam that morning, Miss Brouard."

She said, "You'll find it just east of the caretaker's cottage. I'll phone the Duffys and tell them I've given you permission to be there."

"It's a private bay?"

"No, not the bay. But if you pass by the cottage, Kevin will wonder what you're up to. He's protective of us. So is his wife."

But not protective enough, St. James thought.

Chapter 10

ST. JAMES CONNECTED WITH Deborah once again as she was emerging from beneath the chestnuts that lined the drive. In very short order, she related her encounter in the Japanese garden, indicating where it was with a gesture towards the southeast and a thicket of trees. Her earlier irritation with him seemed to be forgotten, for which he was grateful, and in this fact he was reminded once again of his father-in-law's words describing Deborah when St. James had—with amusing and what he had hoped was endearing antique formality—asked for permission to marry her. "Deb's a red-'ead and make no mistake about it, my lad," Joseph Cotter had said. "She'll give you aggro like you've never 'ad, but at least it'll be over in a wink."

She'd done a good job with the boy, he discovered. Despite her reticence, her compassionate nature gave her a way with people that he himself had never possessed. It had long suited her choice of profession—subjects far more willingly posed for their pictures if they knew the person behind the camera shared a common humanity with them—just as his even temperament and analytical mind had long suited his. And Deborah's success with Stephen Abbott underscored the fact that more than technique and skill in a laboratory were going to be needed in this situation.

"So that other woman who came forward for the shovel," Deborah concluded, "the one with the enormous hat? She was the current girlfriend, apparently, not a relation. Although it sounds as if she was hoping to be one."

" 'You saw what she's done,' " St. James murmured. "What did you make of his saying that, my love?"

"What she's done to make herself appealing, I expect," Deborah said. "I did notice . . . well, it was difficult not to, wasn't it? And you don't see them often here, not like in the States, where large breasts seem to be something of a . . . a national fixation, I suppose."

"Not that she's 'done' something else?" St. James asked. "Like eliminated her lover when he favoured another woman?"

"Why would she do that if she hoped to marry him?"

"Perhaps she needed to be rid of him."

"Why?"

"Obsession. Jealousy. Rage that can only be quelled in one way. Or perhaps something simpler altogether: Perhaps she was remembered in his will and she needed to eliminate him before he had a chance to change it in favour of someone else."

"But that doesn't take into consideration the

problem we've already faced," Deborah noted. "How could a woman actually have forced a stone into Guy Brouard's throat, Simon? Any woman."

"We go back to DCI Le Gallez's kiss," St. James said, "as unlikely as it is. 'She'd lost him.' Is there another woman?"

"Not China," Deborah asserted.

St. James heard his wife's determination. "You're quite certain, then."

"She told me she's recently broken off from Matt. She's loved him for years, since she was seventeen. I can't see how she'd get involved with another man so soon after that."

This, St. James knew, took them into tender territory, one that was occupied by Deborah herself as well as by China River. Not so many years had passed since Deborah had parted from him and found another lover. That they had never discussed the alacrity of her involvement with Tommy Lynley did not mean it wasn't the result of her sorrow and increased vulnerability. He said, "But she'd be more vulnerable now than ever, wouldn't she? Couldn't she possibly need to have a fling—something Brouard might have taken more seriously than she herself took it—to bolster herself up?"

"That's not really what she's like."

"But supposing—"

"All right. Supposing. But she certainly didn't *kill* him, Simon. You have to agree she'd need a motive."

He did agree. But he also believed that a preconceived notion of innocence was just as dangerous as a preconceived notion of guilt. So when he related what he'd learned from Ruth Brouard, he concluded carefully with "She did check for China in the rest of the house. She was nowhere to be found."

"So Ruth Brouard *says*," Deborah pointed out reasonably. "She could be lying."

"She could indeed. The Rivers weren't the only guests in the house. Adrian Brouard was also there."

"With reason to kill his dad?"

"It's something we can't ignore."

"She *is* his blood relative," Deborah said. "And given her history—her parents, the Holocaust?—I'd say it's likely she'd do anything to protect a blood relative first and foremost, wouldn't you?"

"I would."

They were walking down the drive in the direction of the lane and St. James guided them through the trees towards the path that Ruth Brouard had told him would lead to the bay where her brother had taken his daily swim. Their way passed by the stone cottage he'd observed earlier, and he noted that two of the building's windows looked directly onto the path. This was where the caretakers lived, he'd been told, and the Duffys, St. James concluded, might well have something to add to what Ruth Brouard had already told him.

The path grew cooler and more damp as it dipped into the trees. Either the land's natural fecundity or a man's determination had created an impressive array of foliage that screened the trail from the rest of the estate. Nearest to the path, rhododendrons flourished. Among them half a dozen varieties of ferns unfurled their fronds. The ground was spongy with the fall of autumn leaves left to decompose, and overhead the winter-bare branches of chestnuts spoke of the green tunnel they'd create in summer. It was silent here, save for the sound of their footsteps.

That silence didn't last, however. St. James was extending his hand to his wife to help her across a puddle, when a scruffy little dog bounded out of the bushes, yapping at both of them.

"Lord!" Deborah started and then laughed. "Oh, he's awfully sweet, isn't he? Here, little doggie. We won't hurt you."

She held her hand out to him. As she did so, a red-jacketed boy darted out the way the dog had come and scooped the animal up into his arms.

"Sorry," St. James said with a smile. "We appear to have startled your dog."

The boy said nothing. He looked from Deborah to St. James as his dog continued to bark protectively.

"Miss Brouard said this is the way to the bay," St. James said. "Have we made a wrong turn somewhere?"

Still the boy didn't speak. He looked fairly the worse for wear, with oleaginous hair clinging to his skull and his face streaked with dirt. The hands that held the dog were grimy and the black trousers he wore had grease crusted on one knee. He took several steps backwards.

"We haven't startled you as well, have we?" Deborah asked. "We didn't think anyone would be . . ."

Her voice faded as the boy turned on his heel and

crashed back in the direction he'd come. He wore a tattered rucksack on his back, and it pounded against him like a bag of potatoes.

"Who on earth . . . ?" Deborah murmured.

St. James wondered himself. "We'll want to look into that."

They reached the lane through a gate in the wall some distance from the drive. There they saw that the overflow of cars from the burial had departed, leaving the way unobstructed so that they easily found the descent to the bay, some one hundred yards from the entrance to the Brouard estate.

This descent was somewhere between a track and a lane—wider than one and too narrow to actually be considered the other—and it switched back on itself numerous times as it steeply dropped to the water. Rock walls and woodland sided it, along with a stream that chattered along the rough stones of the wall's base. There were no houses or cottages here, just a single hotel that was closed for the season, surrounded by trees, tucked into a depression in the hillside, and shuttered at every window.

In the distance below St. James and his wife, the English Channel appeared, speckled by what little sun was able to break through the heavy cover of clouds. With the sight of it came the sound of gulls. They soared among the granite outcroppings at the top of the cliffs, which formed the deep horseshoe that was the bay itself. Gorse and English stonecrop grew in undisturbed abundance here, and where the soil was deeper, tangled thickets of bony branches marked the spots where blackthorn and bramble would prosper in spring.

At the base of the lane a small car park made a thumbprint on the landscape. No cars stood in it, nor would any be likely to do so at this time of year. It was the perfect spot for a private swim or for anything that called for activity without witnesses.

A bulwark fashioned from stone protected the car park from tidal erosion, and to one side of this a slipway slanted down to the water. Dead and dying seaweed knotted thickly across this, just the sort of decaying vegetation that at another time of year would be infested with flies and gnats. Nothing moved or crawled within it in the middle of December, however, and St. James and Deborah were able to pick their way through it and thus gain access to the beach. The water lapped against this rhythmically, marking a gentle pulse against the coarse sand and the stones.

"No wind," St. James noted as he observed the mouth of the bay some distance from where they stood. "That makes it very good for swimming."

"But terribly cold," Deborah said. "I can't understand how he did it. In December? It's extraordinary, don't you think?"

"Some people like extremity," St. James said. "Let's have a look around."

"What are we looking for, exactly?"

"Something the police may have missed."

The actual spot of the murder was easy enough to find: The signs of a crime scene were still upon it in the form of a strip of yellow police tape, two discarded film canisters from the police photographer, and a globule of white plaster that had spilled when someone took a cast of a footprint. St. James and Deborah started at this spot and began working side by side in an ever-widening circumference round it.

The going was slow. Eyes fixed to the ground, they wheeled round and round, turning over the larger stones that they came upon, gently moving aside seaweed, sifting through sand with their fingertips. In this manner, an hour passed as they examined the small beach, uncovering a top to a jar of baby food, a faded ribbon, an empty Evian bottle, and seventy-eight pence in loose change.

When they came to the bulwark, St. James suggested that they begin at opposite ends and work their way towards each other. At the point at which they would meet, he said, they would just continue onwards so each of them would have separately inspected the entire length of the wall.

They had to go carefully, for there were heavier stones here and more crevices in which items could fall. But although each of them moved at earthworm pace, they met at the middle empty-handed.

"This isn't looking very hopeful," Deborah noted.

"It isn't," St. James agreed. "But it was always just a chance." He rested for a moment against the wall, his arms crossed on his chest and his gaze on the Channel. He gave consideration to the idea of lies: those people tell and those people believe. Sometimes, he knew, the people in both cases were the same. Telling something long enough resulted in belief.

"You're worried, aren't you?" Deborah said. "If we don't find something—"

He put his arm round her and kissed the side of her head. "Let's keep going," he told her but said nothing of what was obvious to him: Finding something could be even more damning than having the misfortune of finding nothing at all.

They continued like crabs along the wall, St. James slightly more inhibited by his leg brace, which made moving among the larger stones more difficult for him than it was for his wife. Perhaps this was the reason the cry of exultation—marking the discovery of something hitherto unnoticed—was given by Deborah some fifteen minutes into the final part of their search.

"Here!" she called. "Simon, look here."

He turned and saw that she'd reached the far end of the bulwark at the point where the slipway dipped down to the water. She was gesturing to the corner where the bulwark and the slipway met, and when St. James moved in her direction, she squatted to have a better look at what she'd found.

"What is it?" he asked as he came alongside her.

"Something metallic," she said. "I didn't want to pick it up."

"How far down?" he asked.

"Less than a foot, I dare say," she replied. "If you want me to—"

"Here." He handed her a handkerchief.

To reach the object, she had to wedge her leg

into a ragged opening, which she did enthusiastically. She crammed herself down far enough to grasp and then rescue what she'd seen from above.

This turned out to be a ring. Deborah brought it forth and laid it cushioned by the handkerchief on the palm of her hand for St. James's inspection.

It looked made of bronze, sized for a man. And its decoration was man-sized as well. This comprised a skull and crossed bones. On the top of the skull were the numbers 39/40 and below them four words engraved in German. St. James squinted to make them out: *Die Festung im Westen.*

"Something from the war," Deborah murmured as she scrutinised the ring herself. "But it can't have been here all these years."

"No. Its condition doesn't suggest that."

"Then what . . . ?"

St. James folded the handkerchief round it, but he left the ring resting in Deborah's hand. "It needs to be checked," he said. "Le Gallez will want to have it fingerprinted. There won't be much on it, but even a partial could help."

"How could they have not seen it?" Deborah asked, and St. James could tell she expected no answer.

Nonetheless he said, "DCI Le Gallez considers the evidence of an ageing woman not wearing her spectacles sufficient unto the day. I think it's a safe bet to conclude he isn't looking as hard as he could for anything that might refute what she's told him."

Deborah examined the small white bundle in her hand and then looked at her husband. "This could be evidence," she said. "Beyond the hair they found, beyond the footprint they have, beyond witnesses who might be lying about what they saw in the first place. This could change everything, couldn't it, Simon?"

"It could indeed," he said.

Margaret Chamberlain congratulated herself for insisting upon the reading of the will directly after the funeral reception. She'd earlier said, "Call the solicitor, Ruth. Get him over here after the burial," and when Ruth had told her Guy's advocate would be present anyway—yet *another* of the man's tedious island associates who had to be accommodated at the funeral—she thought this was far more than just as well. It was decidedly meant. Just in case her sister-in-law intended to thwart her, Margaret had cornered the man himself as he stuffed a crab sandwich into his face. Miss Brouard, she informed him, wanted to go over the will immediately after the last of the guests left the reception. He did have the appropriate paperwork with him, didn't he? Yes? Good. And would it present any difficulty to go over the details as soon as they had the privacy to do so? No? Fine.

So now they were gathered. But Margaret wasn't happy about who constituted the group.

Ruth had evidently done more than merely contact the solicitor upon Margaret's insistence. She'd also made sure that an ominous collection of individuals were present to take in the man's remarks.

This could mean only one thing: that Ruth was privy to the details of the will and that the details of the will favoured individuals other than family members. Why else would she have taken it upon herself to invite an assembly of virtual strangers to join the family for this serious occasion? And no matter how fondly Ruth greeted and seated them in the drawing room, they *were* strangers, defined—according to Margaret's thinking—as anyone not directly related by blood or marriage to the deceased.

Anaïs Abbott and her daughter were among them, the former as heavily made up as she'd been on the previous day and the latter as gawky and slump-shouldered as she'd been as well. The only thing different about them was their clothing. Anaïs had managed to pour herself into a black suit whose skirt curved round her little bum like cling film on melons, while Jemima had donned a bolero jacket that she wore with all the grace of a dustman in morning dress. The surly son had apparently disappeared, because as the company assembled in the upstairs drawing room beneath yet another of Ruth's tedious needlepoint depictions of Life As A Displaced Person—this one apparently having to do with growing up in care . . . as if she'd been the *only* child who'd had to endure it in the years following the war—Anaïs kept wringing her hands and telling anyone who'd listen that "Stephen's gone off somewhere . . . He's been inconsolable . . ." and then her eyes would fill yet again in an irksome display of eternal devotion to the deceased.

Along with the Abbotts, the Duffys were present.

Kevin—estate manager, groundsman, caretaker of *Le Reposoir,* and apparently whatever else that Guy had needed him to be at a moment's notice—hung back from everyone and stood at a window where he made a study of the gardens below him, adhering to what was evidently his policy of never doing more than grunting at anyone. His wife Valerie sat by herself with her hands gripped together in her lap. She alternated between watching her husband, watching Ruth, and watching the lawyer unpack his briefcase. If anything, she looked utterly bewildered to be included in this ceremony.

And then there was Frank. Margaret had been introduced to him after the burial. Frank Ouseley, she'd been told, longtime bachelor and Guy's very good friend. His virtual soul mate, if the truth be told. They'd discovered a mutual passion for things relating to the war and they'd bonded over that, which was enough to make Margaret observe the man with suspicion. He was behind the whole benighted museum project, she had learned. This made him the reason that God only knew how many of Guy's millions might well be diverted in a direction that was not her son's. Margaret found him particularly repugnant with his ill-fitting tweeds and badly capped front teeth. He was heavy as well, which was another mark against him. Paunches spoke of gluttony which spoke of greed.

And he was speaking to Adrian at the moment, Adrian who obviously didn't have the sense to recognise an adversary when he was standing in front of him breathing the same air. If things worked out the way Margaret was beginning to fear they might work out in the next thirty minutes or so, she and her son could very well be at legal loggerheads with this dumpy man. Adrian *might* be wise enough to realise that, if nothing else, and to keep his distance as a result.

Margaret sighed. She observed her son and noted for the first time how much he actually resembled his father. She also noted how much he did to play down that resemblance, cropping his hair drastically so Guy's curls weren't visible, dressing badly, shaving close to his skin to avoid anything that remotely resembled Guy's neatly trimmed beard. But he could do nothing about his eyes, which were so like his father's. Bedroom eyes, they'd been called, heavy-lidded and sensual. And he could do nothing about his complexion, swarthier than the average Englishman's.

She went to him where he stood near the fireplace with his father's friend. She linked her arm through his. "Sit with me, darling," she said to her son. "May I steal him from you, Mr. Ouseley?"

There was no need for Frank Ouseley to respond because Ruth had closed the drawing room door, indicating that all relevant parties were present. Margaret led Adrian to a sofa that formed part of a seating group near the table on which Guy's solicitor—a reedy-looking man called Dominic Forrest—had set out his papers.

Margaret didn't fail to notice that everyone was attempting to look as unanticipatory as possible. This included her own son upon whom she'd had to prevail to attend this meeting at all. He sat slumped, his face expressionless and his body a declaration of how little he cared to hear what his father had intended with his money.

This made no difference to Margaret because *she* cared. So when Dominic Forrest put on his half-moon spectacles and cleared his throat, she was all attention. He'd made sure that Margaret knew this formal reading-of-the-will situation was extremely irregular. Far better for beneficiaries to be made aware of inheritances in a setting that allowed them the privacy to absorb the information and to ask any questions they might have without the delicacy of their situation being revealed to parties who might have no vested interest in their individual welfare.

Which, Margaret knew, was legalese for how much Mr. Forrest would have preferred to be able to make arrangements to see each beneficiary separately in order to bill each one individually later. Nasty little man.

Ruth perched birdlike on the edge of a Queen Anne chair not far from Valerie. Kevin Duffy remained at the window, Frank at the fireplace. Anaïs Abbott and her daughter came to sit on a love seat where the one wrung her hands and the other tried to tuck her giraffe legs somewhere where they wouldn't seem so obtrusive.

Mr. Forrest took a seat and shook his papers with a flick of his wrist. The last will and testament of Mr. Brouard, he began, was written, signed, and witnessed on the second of October in this current year. It was a simple document.

Margaret didn't much like the way things were developing. She steeled herself to hear news that was potentially less than good. This was wise on her part, as things turned out, because in extremely short order Mr. Forrest revealed that Guy's entire fortune consisted of a single bank account and an investment portfolio. The account and portfolio, in accordance with the laws of inheritance in the States of Guernsey—whatever that meant—were to be divided equally into two parts. The first part, once again in accordance with the laws of inheritance in the States of Guernsey, was to be distributed evenly among Guy's three children. The second part was to be given half to one Paul Fielder and half to one Cynthia Moullin.

Of Ruth, beloved sister and lifelong companion of the deceased, there was no mention made at all. But considering the properties Guy owned in England, in France, in Spain, in the Seychelles, considering his international holdings, considering his stocks, his bonds, his works of art—not to mention *Le Reposoir* itself—none of which had even been *mentioned* in his will, it was no difficult feat to work out how Guy Brouard had made his feelings about his children crystal clear while simultaneously taking care of his sister. God in heaven, Margaret thought weakly. He must have given Ruth everything while he was still alive.

Silence, which was stunned at first and which only slowly turned to outrage on Margaret's part, greeted the conclusion of Mr. Forrest's recitation. The first thing she thought was that Ruth had orchestrated this entire event to humiliate her. Ruth had never liked her. Never, never, never, never *once* had she liked her. And during the years in which Margaret had kept Guy from his son, Ruth had no doubt brewed a real hatred of her. So what true pleasure she would be getting from this moment when she was able to witness Margaret Chamberlain get her deserved comeuppance: not only being sandbagged by learning that Guy's estate was not as it had seemed but also having to witness her son receiving even less of that estate than two complete strangers called Fielder and Moullin.

Margaret swung on her sister-in-law, ready to do battle. But she saw on Ruth's face a truth she didn't want to believe. Ruth had gone so pale that her lips were rendered in chalk, and her expression illustrated better than anything could that her brother's will was not what she had expected it to be. But there was more information than *that* contained in the combination of Ruth's expression and her invitation to the others to hear the will's reading. Indeed, those two facts led Margaret to an ineluctable conclusion: Not only had Ruth known about the existence of an *earlier* will, but she had also been privy to that will's contents.

Why else invite Guy's most recent lover to be present? Why else Frank Ouseley? Why else the Duffys? There could be only one reason for this: Ruth had invited them all in good faith to be present because Guy had at one time left each of them a legacy.

A legacy, Margaret thought. Adrian's legacy. Her

own *son's* legacy. Her vision seemed occluded by a thin red veil at the realisation of what had actually occurred. That her son Adrian should be *denied* what was rightfully his . . . That he should be in effect cut out of his own father's will, despite the fancy dancing Guy may have done to make it seem otherwise . . . That he should be placed in the humiliating position of actually receiving *less* than two people—Fielder and Moullin, whoever the hell they were—who were no apparent relation of Guy's . . . That the vast majority of his father's possessions had obviously already been disposed of . . . That he should thus be literally set adrift with *nothing* by the very man who had given him life and then abandoned him without a fight and then apparently felt *nothing* in that abandonment and then sealed whatever rejection was *implied* in the abandonment by having his way with his only son's lover when that lover was on the verge—yes the *verge*—of the kind of commitment that could have changed his life forever and made him whole at last . . . It was inconceivable. The act itself was unconscionable. And someone was going to pay for it.

Margaret didn't know how and she didn't know who. But she was determined to set matters right.

Setting them right meant first wresting away the money her former husband had left to two utter strangers. Who were they, anyway? Where were they? More important, what had they to do with Guy?

Two people clearly knew the answer to these questions. Dominic Forrest was one of them, he who was returning his paperwork to his briefcase and making some sort of noises about forensic accountants and banking statements and investment brokers and the like. And Ruth was the other, she who was hustling over to Anaïs Abbott—of all bloody people—and murmuring something into her ear. Forrest, Margaret knew, was unlikely to part with any more information than he'd given them during the reading of the will. But Ruth as her own sister-in-law and—crucially—as Adrian's aunt, Adrian who'd been so badly used by his father . . . Yes, Ruth would be forthcoming with facts when approached correctly.

Next to her, Margaret became aware of Adrian trembling and she brought herself round abruptly. She'd been so caught up in thoughts of what-to-do-now that she'd not even considered the impact this moment was probably having on her son. God knew that Adrian's relationship with his father had been a difficult one, with Guy vastly preferring a long line of sexual liaisons to a close connection with his eldest child. But to be dealt with in this fashion was cruel, far more cruel than a life cut off from paternal influence ever could have been. And he was suffering for it now.

So she turned to him, ready to tell him that they hadn't reached the end of *anything* in this moment, ready to point out that there were legal channels, modes of recourse, ways of settling or manipulating or threatening but in any case ways of getting what one wanted so he wasn't to worry and more than that he wasn't ever to believe that the terms of his father's will meant *anything* other than his father's momentary lunacy inspired by God only knew what . . . She was ready to say this, ready to put her arm round his shoulders, ready to buck him up and send her steel through his body. But she saw that none of that would be necessary.

Adrian wasn't weeping. He wasn't even withdrawing into himself.

Margaret's son was silently laughing.

Valerie Duffy had gone into the reading of the will worried for more than one reason, and only one of her worries was assuaged by the conclusion of the event. This was the worry pertaining to losing her home and her livelihood, which she'd feared might happen once Guy Brouard died. But the fact that *Le Reposoir* hadn't been mentioned in the will suggested that the estate had already been disposed of elsewhere, and Valerie was fairly certain in whose care and possession it now resided. That meant she and Kevin wouldn't be immediately forced out onto the street without employment, which was a vast relief.

The rest of Valerie's worries remained, however. These pertained to Kevin's natural taciturnity, which she generally found untroubling but which she now found unnerving.

She and her husband walked across the grounds of *Le Reposoir,* leaving the manor house behind them, heading for their cottage. Valerie had seen the variety of reactions on the faces of those who'd been gathered in the drawing room, and she'd read in each of them the hopes they'd had dashed. Anaïs Abbott had been relying upon financial exhumation from the grave she'd dug herself attempting to hold on to her man. Frank Ouseley had been anticipating a bequest enormous enough to build a monument to his father. Margaret Chamberlain had expected more than enough money to move her adult son permanently out from under her roof. And Kevin . . . ? Well, it was clear enough that Kevin had a lot on his mind, most of it having nothing to do with wills and bequests, so Kevin had walked into the drawing room without the handicap of a crowded canvas on which he'd painted his aspirations.

She looked at him now, just a quick glance as he walked beside her. She knew he would think it unnatural if she made no comment, but she wanted to be careful with how much she said. Some things didn't bear talking about.

"D'you think we ought to ring Henry, then?" she finally asked her husband.

Kevin loosened his tie and undid the top button of his shirt, unused to the type of clothes most other men wore with ease. He said, "I expect he'll know soon enough. Doubtless, half the island will know by supper."

Valerie waited for him to say more, but he didn't. She wanted to be relieved at this, but the fact that he didn't look at her told her his thoughts were on the run.

"Makes me wonder how he'll react, though," Valerie said.

"Does it, love?" Kevin asked her.

He said it low so that Valerie nearly couldn't hear him at all, but his tone alone would have conveyed enough to make her shiver. She said, "Why do you ask that, Kev?" in the hope that she could force his hand.

He said, "What people say they'll do and what they actually do are different sometimes, aren't they?" He moved his gaze to her.

Valerie's shiver altered to a permanent chill. She felt it sweep up her legs and shoot into her stomach, where it curled round like a hairless cat and just lay there, asking her to do something about it. She waited for her husband to introduce the obvious topic that everyone who'd been sitting in the drawing room was at that moment probably either thinking of or speaking of to someone else. When he didn't, she said, "Henry was at the funeral, Kev. Did you speak to him? He came to the burial as well. And to the reception. Did you see him there? I expect that means he and Mr. Brouard were friendly right to the end. Which is good, I think. Because it would be dreadful if Mr. Brouard died at odds with anyone, and especially with Henry. Henry wouldn't want a crack in their friendship to be troubling his conscience, would he?"

"No," Kevin said. "A troubled conscience is a nasty thing. Keeps you up at night. Makes it hard to think of anything else but what you did to get it in the first place." He stopped walking and Valerie did the same. They stood on the lawn. A sudden gust of wind from the Channel brought the salt air with it and with it as well the reminder of what had happened by the bay.

"Do you think, Val," Kevin said when a good thirty seconds had crawled by between them with Valerie making no reply to his comment, "that Henry's going to wonder about that will?"

She glanced away, knowing his gaze was still on her and still attempting to draw her out. He usually could cajole her into speaking, this husband of hers, because no matter the twenty-seven years of their marriage, she loved him the way she'd done from the first, when he'd stripped the clothes from her willing body and loved that body with his own. She knew the true value of having that kind of celebration with a man in your life and the fear of losing it pulled at her to speak and ask Kevin's pardon for what she'd done despite the promise she'd made never to do it because of the hell it might cause if she did.

But the pull of Kevin's look upon her wasn't enough. It drew her to the brink, but it couldn't shoot her over into certain destruction. She remained silent, which forced him to continue.

He said, "I can't see how he won't wonder, can you? The whole oddity of it begs for questions to be asked and answered. And if he doesn't ask them . . ." Kevin looked over in the direction of the duck ponds, where the little duck graveyard held the broken bodies of those innocent birds. He said, "Too many things mean power to a man, and when his power's taken from him he doesn't deal with that lightly. Because there's no laughing it off, you see, no saying 'Ah, it didn't mean all that much in the first place, did it.' Not if a man's identified his power. And not if he's lost it."

Valerie started them walking again, determined not to be caught another time by the pin of her husband's stare, fixed onto a display board like a captured butterfly, with the label *female forsworn* beneath her. "Do you think that's what's happened, Kev? Someone's lost his power? Is that what you think this is all about?"

"I don't know," he replied. "Do you?"

A coy woman might have said "Why would I . . . ?" but the last attribute Valerie possessed was the one of being coy. She knew exactly why her husband was asking her that question and she knew where it would lead them if she answered him directly: to an examination of promises given and a discussion of rationalisations made.

But beyond those things that Valerie didn't want to have present in any conversation with her husband, there was the fact of her *own* feelings that she had to consider now as well. For it was no easy matter to live with the knowledge that you were probably responsible for a good man's death. Going through the motions of day-after-day with that on your mind was trying enough. Having to cope with someone other than yourself knowing about your responsibility would make the burden of it intolerable. So there was nothing to be done save to sidestep and obfuscate. Any move she might make appeared to Valerie to be a losing one, a short journey on the long path of covenants broken and responsibilities not faced.

She wanted more than anything to reverse the wheel of time. But she could not do it. So she kept walking steadily towards the cottage, where at least there was employment for both of them, something to take their minds off the chasm that fast was developing between them.

"Did you see that man talking to Miss Brouard?" Valerie asked her husband. "The man with the bad leg? She took him off upstairs. Just near the end of the reception this was. He's no one I've seen round here before, so I was wondering . . . Could he have been her doctor? She isn't well. You know that, Kev, don't you? She's tried to hide it, but now it's getting worse. I wish she'd say something about it, though. So I could help her more. I can understand why she wouldn't say a word while he was alive—she wouldn't want to worry him, would she?—but now that he's gone . . . We could do a lot for her, you and I, Kev. If she'd let us."

They left the lawn and crossed a section of the drive that swung by the front of their cottage. They approached the front door, Valerie in the lead. She would have strode straight through it and hung up her coat and got on with her day, but Kevin's next words stopped her.

"When're you going to stop lying to me, Val?"

The words comprised just the sort of question that she would have *had* to answer at some other time. They implied so much about the changing

nature of their relationship that in any other circumstances the only way to refute that implication
would have been to give her husband what he was
asking for. But in the current situation, Valerie
didn't have to do that because as Kevin spoke, the
very man she'd been talking about the moment before came through the bushes that marked the path
to the bay.

He was accompanied by a red-haired woman.
The two of them saw the Duffys and, after exchang-
ing a quick word, they walked immediately over.
The man said he was called Simon St. James and he
introduced the woman, who was his wife, Deborah.
They had come from London for the funeral, he explained, and he asked the Duffys if he could have a
word with them both.

The most recent of the analgesics—that which her
oncologist had called the "one last thing" they were
going to try—no longer possessed the strength to
kill the brutal pain in Ruth's bones. The time had
obviously come to bring on morphine in a very big
way, but that was the physical time. The mental
time, defined by the moment when she admitted defeat over her attempt to govern the way her life
would end, still had not arrived. Until it had, Ruth
was determined to carry on as if the disease were not
running amok in her body like invading Vikings
who'd lost their leader.

She'd awakened that morning in an exquisite
agony that hadn't diminished as the day continued.

In the early hours, she'd maintained such a fine focus on carrying out her duties to her brother, his family, his friends, and the community that she'd been able to ignore the stranglehold which the fire had on most of her body. But as people said their final good-byes, it became more and more difficult to ignore what was so earnestly trying to claim her. The reading of the will had provided Ruth a momentary diversion from the disease. What followed the reading of the will was continuing to do so.

Her exchange with Margaret had been blessedly and surprisingly brief. "I'll deal with the rest of this mess later on," her sister-in-law had asserted, wearing the expression of a woman in the presence of rancid meat, her body stiff with outrage. "As for now, I want to know who the hell they are."

Ruth knew Margaret was referring to the two beneficiaries of Guy's will other than his children. She gave Margaret the information she wanted and watched her sweep from the room to engage in what Ruth knew very well was going to be a most dubious battle.

This left Ruth with the others. Frank Ouseley had been surprisingly easy. When she approached him to stumble through an embarrassed explanation, saying surely something could be done about the situation because Guy had made his feelings quite clear with respect to the wartime museum, Frank had said in reply, "Don't trouble yourself about this, Ruth," and had bade her goodbye without the slightest degree of rancour. He would be disappointed enough, though, considering the time and effort that he and

Guy had put into the island project, so before he could leave she told him that he wasn't to think the situation was hopeless, that she herself felt sure that something could be done to bring his dreams to reality. Guy had known how much the project meant to Frank and he'd surely intended . . . But she couldn't say more. She couldn't betray her brother and his wishes because she didn't yet understand what he'd done or why he had done it.

Frank had taken her hand into both of his, saying, "There'll be time to think about all this later. Don't worry about it now."

Then he'd gone, leaving her to deal with Anaïs next.

Shell shocked popped into Ruth's mind when she was at last alone with her brother's lover. Anaïs sat numbly on the same love seat she'd taken during Dominic Forrest's explanation of the will, her posture unchanging and the only difference being that she sat there now alone. Poor Jemima had been so eager to be dismissed that when Ruth murmured, "Perhaps you might find Stephen somewhere in the grounds, dear . . . ?" she'd caught one of her great large feet on the edge of an ottoman and nearly knocked over a small table in her haste to be gone. This haste was understandable. Jemima knew her mother quite well and was probably foreseeing what was going to be asked of her in the way of filial devotion in the next few weeks. Anaïs would require both a confidante and a scapegoat. Time would tell which role she would decide her gangling daughter was going to play.

So now Ruth and Anaïs were alone and Anaïs sat plucking the edge of a small cushion from the love seat. Ruth didn't know what to say to her. Her brother had been a good and generous man despite his foibles, and he'd earlier remembered Anaïs Abbott and her children in his will in a fashion that would have relieved her anxiety enormously. Indeed, that had long been Guy's way with his women. Each time he took a new lover for any period longer than three months, he altered his will to reflect the extent to which he and she were devoted to each other. Ruth knew this because Guy had always of necessity shared the contents of his wills with her. With the exception of this most current and final document, Ruth had read each one of them in the presence of Guy and his advocate because Guy had always wanted to be certain that Ruth understood how he meant his money to be distributed.

The last will Ruth had read had been drawn up some six months into her brother's relationship with Anaïs Abbott, shortly after the two of them had returned from Sardinia, where they'd apparently done very little more than explore all the permutations of what a man and woman could do to each other with their respective body parts. Guy had returned glaze-eyed from that trip, saying, "She's the one, Ruth," and his will had reflected this optimistic belief. Ruth had asked Anaïs to be present for that reason and she could see by the expression on her face that Anaïs believed Ruth had done so out of malice.

Ruth didn't know which would be worse at the

moment: allowing Anaïs to believe that she harboured such a desire to wound her that she would allow all her hopes to be dashed in a public forum or telling her that there had been an earlier will in which the four hundred thousand pounds left to her would have been the answer to her current dilemma. It had to be the first alternative, Ruth decided. For although she didn't actually want to be the recipient of anyone's antipathy, telling Anaïs about the earlier will would likely result in having to talk about why it had been altered.

Ruth lowered herself to the seat. She murmured, "Anaïs, I'm terribly sorry. I don't know what else to say."

Anaïs turned her head like a woman slowly regaining consciousness. She said, "If he wanted to leave his money to teenagers, why not mine? Jemima. Stephen. Did he only pretend . . . ?" She clutched the cushion to her stomach. "Why did he do this to me, Ruth?"

Ruth didn't know how to explain. Anaïs was devastated enough at the moment. It seemed inhuman to devastate her more. She said, "I think it had to do with Guy's having lost his own children, my dear. To their mothers. Because of the divorces. I think he looked at these others as a way of being a father once again when he couldn't any longer be a father to his own."

"And mine weren't enough for him?" Anaïs demanded. "My own Jemima? My Stephen? They were less important? So inconsequential that two virtual strangers—"

"Not to Guy," Ruth corrected her. "He's known Paul Fielder and Cynthia Moullin for years." Longer than you, longer than your children, she wanted to add but did not because she needed this conversation to end before it reached ground she couldn't bear to cover. She said, "You know about GAYT, Anaïs. You know how committed Guy was to being a mentor."

"So they insinuated themselves into his life, didn't they? Always with the hope . . . They got introduced and they came here and had a good look round and knew if they played their cards just so, there was a chance he'd leave them something. That's it. That's what happened. That's it." She threw the cushion to one side.

Ruth listened and watched. She marveled at Anaïs's capacity for self-delusion. She felt inclined to say And that's not what you yourself were up to, my dear? Were you instead attaching yourself to a man nearly twenty-five years your senior out of blind devotion? I don't think so, Anaïs. Instead, she said, "I think he was confident that Jemima and Stephen would do well in life under your wing. But the other two . . . They didn't have the same advantages your children have been blessed with. He wanted to help them out."

"And me? What did he intend for me?"

Ah, Ruth thought. Now we've arrived at the real point. But she had no answer that she was willing to give to Anaïs's question. All she said was "I'm so sorry, my dear."

To which Anaïs replied, "Oh, I expect you are."

She glanced round her as if she'd come fully awake, taking in her environment as if seeing it for the very first time. She gathered her belongings and rose. She headed towards the door. But there she paused and turned back to Ruth. "He made promises," she said. "He told me things, Ruth. Did he lie to me?"

Ruth replied with the only fact that felt safe to give the other woman. "I never knew my brother to lie."

And he never had done, not once, not to her. *Sois forte,* he had told her. *Ne crains rien. Je reviendrai te chercher, petite soeur.* And he'd been as good as that simple promise: returning to find her in care, where she'd been deposited by a harried country to whom two refugee children from France meant only two more mouths to feed, two more homes to find, two more futures dependent upon the appearance of two grateful parents who would come to fetch them. When those parents hadn't shown up and the great enormity of what had occurred in the camps became widespread knowledge, Guy himself had come. He had sworn fiercely beyond his own terror that *cela n'a d'importance, d'ailleurs rien n'a d'importance* to mitigate her fears. He'd spent his life proving that they could survive parentless—even friendless if necessary—in a land they had not claimed for themselves but one that had been thrust upon them. So Ruth did not see and had never seen her brother as a liar, despite knowing that he had to have been one, had to have created a virtual web of deceit in order to betray two wives and a score of lovers as he'd moved from woman to woman.

When Anaïs left her, Ruth considered these points. She pondered them in light of Guy's activities in the last several months. She realised that if he'd lied to her even by omission—as was the case with a new will she'd known nothing about—he could have lied about other things as well.

She rose and went to Guy's study.

Chapter 11

"AND ARE YOU QUITE certain of what you saw that morning?" St. James asked. "What time was it when she passed the cottage?"

"Shortly before seven," Valerie Duffy replied.

"Not fully light, then."

"No. But I'd gone to the window."

"Why?"

She shrugged. "Cup of tea in the morning. Kevin not down yet. Radio on. I was just standing there, organising the day in my head, the way people do."

They were in the sitting room of the Duffys' cottage, where Valerie had ushered them as Kevin disappeared into the kitchen for a few minutes to put on the kettle for a cup of tea. There they sat beneath the low ceiling until his return, amid shelves of photo albums, oversize art books, and every video made by Sister Wendy. It would have put a strain on the room to contain four people in the best of circumstances. With additional books piled on the floor and several stacks of cardboard boxes along the walls—not to mention the scores of family pictures everywhere—the human presence was overwhelming. As was the proof—if any were required—of Kevin Duffy's surprising education. One wouldn't expect a groundskeeper-handyman to have an advanced degree in art history, and perhaps that was why in addition to family photos, the walls also held Kevin's framed university degrees and several portraits of the graduate much younger and sans wife.

"Kev had parents who believed the purpose of education is education," Valerie had said as if in answer to an obvious and unasked question. "They didn't believe it necessarily had to lead to a job."

Neither of the Duffys had questioned St. James's advent or his right to make enquiries about the death of Guy Brouard. After he'd explained his profession to them and handed over his card for their perusal, they'd been willing enough to talk to him. They also didn't question why he'd come with his wife, and St. James said nothing to indicate that the accused murderer was well known to Deborah.

Valerie told them that she generally rose at six-thirty in the morning in order to see to Kevin's breakfast before heading over to the manor house to prepare the Brouards' meal. Mr. Brouard, she explained, liked to have a hot breakfast when he got back from the bay, so on this particular morning, she was up as usual despite the late night that had preceded it. Mr. Brouard had indicated he'd be swimming as he always did, and as good as his word, he passed by the window while she stood there with her tea. Not a half minute later, she saw a dark-cloaked figure follow him.

Did this cloak possess a hood? St. James wanted to know.

It did.

And was the hood up or down?

It was up, Valerie Duffy told him. But that hadn't prevented her from seeing the face of the person who wore it, because she passed quite near to the shaft of light that came from the window and that made it easy to see her.

"It was the American lady," Valerie said. "I'm sure of that. I got a glimpse of her hair."

"No one else relatively the same size?" St. James asked.

No one else, Valerie asserted.

"No one else blonde?" Deborah put in.

Valerie assured them she'd seen China River. And this was no surprise, she told them. China River had been thick enough with Mr. Brouard during her stay at *Le Reposoir*. Mr. Brouard was always charming to the ladies, of course, but even by his standards things had developed rapidly with the American woman.

St. James saw his wife frown at this, and he himself felt wary about taking Valerie Duffy at her word. There was something about the ease of her answers that was discomfiting. There was something more that couldn't be ignored in the manner in which she avoided looking at her husband.

Deborah was the one to say politely, "Did you happen to see any of this, Mr. Duffy?"

Kevin Duffy was standing in silence in the shadows. He leaned against one of the bookshelves with his tie loosened and his swarthy face unreadable. "Val's generally up before I am in the morning," he said shortly.

By which, St. James supposed, they were to take it that he had seen nothing at all. Nonetheless, he said, "And on this particular day?"

"Same as always," Kevin Duffy replied.

Deborah said, "Thick enough in what way?" to Valerie, and when the other woman looked at her blankly, she clarified. "You said China River and Mr. Brouard were thick enough? I was wondering in what way."

"They went out and about. She quite liked the estate and wanted to photograph it. He wanted to watch. And then there was the rest of the island. He was keen to show her round."

"What about her brother?" Deborah asked. "Didn't he go with them?"

"Sometimes he did, other times he just hung about here. Or went off on his own. She seemed to like it that way, the American lady. It made things just the two of them. Her and Mr. Brouard. But that's no real surprise. He was good with women."

"Mr. Brouard was already involved, though, wasn't he?" Deborah asked. "With Mrs. Abbott?"

"He was always involved somewhere and not always for long. Mrs. Abbott was just his latest. Then the American came along."

"Anyone else?" St. James asked.

For some reason the very air seemed to stiffen momentarily at this question. Kevin Duffy shifted on his feet, and Valerie smoothed her skirt in a deliberate movement. She said, "No one as far as I know."

St. James and Deborah exchanged a look. St. James saw on his wife's face the recognition of another direction their enquiry needed to take, and he didn't disagree. However, the fact that here before them was yet another witness to China River's following Guy Brouard towards the Channel—and a far better witness than Ruth Brouard, considering the inconsequential distance between the cottage and the path to the bay—was something that couldn't be ignored.

He said to Valerie, "Have you told DCI Le Gallez about any of this?"

"I've told him all of it."

St. James wondered what, if anything, it meant that neither Le Gallez nor China River's advocate had passed the information on to him. He said, "We've come across something that you might be able to identify," and he removed from his pocket the handkerchief in which he'd wrapped the ring that Deborah had plucked from among the boulders. He unfolded the linen and offered the ring first to Valerie and then to Kevin Duffy. Neither reacted to the sight of it.

"It looks like something from the war, that," Kevin Duffy said. "From the Occupation. Some sort of Nazi ring, I expect. Skull and crossed bones. I've seen 'em before."

"Rings like this one?" Deborah asked.

"I meant the skull and crossed bones," Kevin

replied. He shot his wife a look. "D'you know anyone who has one, Val?"

She shook her head as she studied the ring where
it lay in St. James's palm. "It's a memento, isn't it,"
she said to her husband, and then to St. James or
Deborah, "There's ever so much of that sort of thing
round the island. It could've come from anywhere."

"Such as?" St. James asked.

"Military antiques shop, for one," Valerie said.
"Someone's private collection, perhaps."

"Or some yob's hand," Kevin Duffy pointed out.
"The skull and crossed bones? Just the bit a National
Front yobbo might like to show off to his mates.
Make him feel the real man, you know. But it's a bit
too big and when he's not aware, it falls off."

"Anywhere else it might have come from?" St.
James asked.

The Duffys considered this. Another look passed
between them. Valerie was the one to say slowly and
as if with some thought, "No place at all that I can
think of."

Frank Ouseley felt an asthma attack coming on the
moment he swung his car into Fort Road. This was
no great distance from *Le Reposoir*, and as he'd actually been exposed to nothing that might have bothered his bronchial tubes on the route, he had to
conclude he was reacting in advance to the conversation he was about to have.

This wasn't even a necessary dialogue. How Guy

Brouard had intended his money to be distributed in
the event of his death wasn't Frank's responsibility, as
Guy had never sought his advice in the matter. So he
didn't actually have to be the bearer of bad tidings to
anyone since in a few days the whole of the will
would undoubtedly become public knowledge, island gossip being island gossip. But he still felt a loyalty that had its roots in his years as a teacher. He
wasn't enthusiastic about doing what needed to be
done, however, which was what his tightening chest
was telling him.

When he pulled up to the house on Fort Road,
he took his inhaler from the glove compartment and
used it. He waited for a moment till the tightness
eased and during this moment he saw that on the
middle of the green across the street from where he
sat, a tall thin man and two small boys were kicking
a football round the grass. Not one of them was very
good at it.

Frank climbed out of the car into a light cold
wind. He struggled into his overcoat and then
crossed over to the green. The trees that edged its far
side were quite bare of leaves in this higher, more
exposed spot on the island. Against the grey sky
their branches moved like the arms of supplicants,
and birds huddled in them as if watching the ball
players down below.

Frank tried to prepare his opening remarks as he
approached Bertrand Debiere and his sons. Nobby
didn't see him at first, which was just as well, because
Frank knew that his face was probably communicating what his tongue was reluctant to reveal.

The two little boys were crowing with pleasure at having their father's undivided attention. Nobby's face, so often pinched with anxiety, was momentarily relaxed as he played with them, kicking the ball gently in their direction and calling out encouragement as they tried to kick it back. The elder boy, Frank knew, was six years old and would be tall like his father and probably as ungainly. The younger was only four and joyful, running about in circles and flapping his arms when the ball was directed towards his brother. They were called Bertrand Junior and Norman, probably not the best names for boys in this day and age, but they wouldn't be aware of that till they learned it at school and started praying for nicknames that signaled more acceptance than that which their father had received at the hands of his own schoolmates.

This was, Frank realised, a large part of why he'd come to call on his former pupil: Nobby's passage through adolescence had been rough. Frank hadn't done as much as he could have done to smooth the way.

Bertrand Junior was the first one to see him. He stopped in mid-kick and stared at Frank, his yellow knitted cap pulled low on his face so that his hair was covered and only his eyes were visible. For his part, Norman used the moment to drop to the grass and roll about like a dog off the lead. He shouted, "Rain, rain, rain," for some reason and danced his legs in the air.

Nobby turned in the direction his older boy was looking. Seeing Frank, he caught the ball that

Bertrand Junior finally managed to kick and he tossed it back to his son, saying, "Keep an eye on your little brother, Bert," and walked to join Frank as Bertrand Junior promptly fell upon Norman and began to tickle him round his neck.

Nobby nodded at Frank and said, "They're about as good at sport as I was. Norman shows some promise, but he's got the attention span of a gnat. They're good boys, though. Especially at school. Bert does his sums and reads like a whiz. It's too soon to know about Norman."

Frank knew this fact would mean much to Nobby, who'd been burdened equally by learning problems and by the fact that his parents had assumed these problems were the result of being the only son—and hence slower to develop—in a family of girls.

"They've inherited that from their mum," Nobby said. "Lucky little sods. Bert," he called, "don't be so rough with him."

"Right, Dad," the boy called back.

Frank saw how Nobby swelled with pride at the words, but mostly at *Dad,* which he knew meant everything to Nobby Debiere. Precisely because his family was the centre of his universe had Nobby got himself into the position he was squirming in at this moment. Their needs—real and imagined—had long been paramount to him.

Aside from his words about his sons, the architect didn't speak more to Frank as he joined him. Once he turned from the boys, his face grew hard, as if he were steeling himself for what he knew was coming, and an expectant animosity shone from his eyes. Frank found himself wanting to begin by saying that he himself couldn't possibly be held to account for decisions that Nobby had impulsively taken, but the fact was that he did feel a certain amount of responsibility for Nobby. He knew it grew from his failure to be more of a friend to the man when he'd been a mere boy sitting at a desk in his classroom and suffering the abuse of a child who was a little too slow and a little too odd.

He said, "I've come from *Le Reposoir,* Nobby. They've gone over the will."

Nobby waited, silent. A muscle moved in his cheek.

"I think it was Adrian's mother who insisted it be done," Frank continued. "She does seem to be taking part in a drama the rest of us know very little about."

Nobby said, "And?" He managed to look indifferent, which Frank knew he was not.

"It's a bit odd, I'm afraid. Not straightforward as one might expect, all things considered." Frank went on to explain the simple terms of the will: the bank account, the portfolio, Adrian Brouard and his sisters, the two island adolescents.

Nobby frowned. "But what's he done with . . . ? The estate must be vast. It's got to go far beyond one account and a stock portfolio. How's he got round that?"

"Ruth," Frank said.

"He can't have left *Le Reposoir* to her."

"No. Of course not. The law would have blocked him. So leaving it to her was out of the question."

"Then what?"

"I don't know. A legal manoeuvre of some sort. He would have found one. And she would have gone along with whatever he wanted."

At this, Nobby's spine seemed to melt marginally, and his eyelids relaxed. He said, "That's a good thing, then, isn't it? Ruth knows what his plans were, what he wanted done. She'll go forward with the project. When she begins, it'll be no small problem to sit with her and have a look at those drawings and plans from California. To make her see he's chosen the worst possible design. Completely inappropriate for the site, not to mention for this part of the world. Not the least cost effective with regard to maintenance. As to the expense of building, it—"

"Nobby," Frank cut in. "It's not that simple."

Behind him, one of the boys screeched, and Nobby swung round to see that Bertrand Junior had removed his knitted cap and was pulling it soundly over his younger brother's face. Nobby called sharply, "Bert, stop that at once. If you won't play nicely, you'll have to remain inside with Mummy."

"But I was only—"

"Bertrand!"

The boy whipped the cap from his brother and began kicking the ball across the lawn. Norman trundled after him in hot pursuit. Nobby watched them for a moment before returning his attention to

Frank. His expression, drained of its previous and all too brief relief, now looked wary.

"Not that simple?" he asked. "Why, Frank? What could be simpler? You're not saying you actually like the American's design, are you? Over mine?"

"I'm not. No."

"Then what?"

"It's what's implied in the will."

"But you just said Ruth . . ." Nobby's face returned to its hardness, a look Frank recognised from his adolescence, that anger he contained as one young bloke among many, the loner who wasn't shown the friendship that might have made his road easier or at least less solitary. "What's implied in the will, then?"

Frank had thought about this. He'd considered it from every angle on the drive from *Le Reposoir* to Fort Road. If Guy Brouard had intended the museum project to go forward, his will would have reflected that fact. No matter how or when he'd disposed of the rest of his property, he would have left an appropriate bequest earmarked for the wartime museum. He had not done so, which seemed to Frank to make his final wishes clear.

He explained all this to Nobby Debiere, who listened with an expression of growing incredulity.

"Are you quite mad?" Nobby asked when Frank had finished his remarks. "What was the point of the party, then? The big announcement? The champagne and fireworks? The momentous display of that bloody elevation drawing?"

"I can't explain that. I can only look at the facts we have."

"Part of those facts is what went on that night, Frank. And what he said. And how he acted."

"Yes, but what did he actually say?" Frank persisted. "Did he talk about laying the foundation? About dates of completion? Isn't it odd that he did neither? I think there's only one reason for that."

"Which is?"

"He didn't intend to build the museum."

Nobby stared at Frank while his children romped on the lawn behind him. In the distance, from the direction of Fort George, a figure in a blue track suit jogged onto the green with a dog on a lead. He released the animal and it bounded freely, ears flopping as it raced towards the trees. Nobby's boys cried out happily, but their father didn't turn as before. Instead, he looked beyond Frank to the houses along Fort Road, and particularly to his own: a large yellow building trimmed in white, with a garden behind it for the children to play in. Inside, Frank knew, Caroline Debiere was probably working on her novel, the long-dreamed-of novel Nobby had insisted his wife create, quitting her job as a staff writer for *Architectural Review,* which was what she'd been happily doing as a career before she and Nobby had met and had concocted for themselves a set of dreams that were now being dashed by the cold reality brought about by Guy Brouard's death.

Nobby's skin suffused with blood as he took in Frank's words and their implication. "N-no inten-inten-in*ten*tion . . . N-never? D-do you m-mean that b-*bastard* . . ." He stopped. He seemed to try forcing calm upon himself, but it didn't appear to want to come.

Frank helped him out. "I don't mean he was having us all on. But I do think he changed his mind. For some reason. I think that's what happened."

"Wh-wh-what about the party, then?"

"I don't know."

"Wh-wh . . ." Nobby squeezed his eyes shut. He screwed up his face. He said the word *just* three times, as if it were an incantation that would free him of his affliction, and when he next spoke, his stammer was under control. He said once again, "What about the big announcement, Frank? What about that drawing? He brought it out. You were there. He showed it to everyone. He . . . God. Why did he do it?"

"I don't know. I can't say. I don't understand."

Nobby examined him then. He took a step backwards as if to get a better look at Frank, his eyes narrowing and his features becoming more pinched than ever. "Joke's on me, then, isn't it?" he said. "Just like before."

"What joke?"

"You and Brouard. Having a laugh at my expense. Wasn't enough for you and the lads, then, was it? Don't put Nobby in *our* group, Mr. Ouseley. He'll get up in front of the class to recite and we'll all look bad."

"Don't be absurd. Have you been listening to me?"

"Sure. I can see how it was done. Set him up,

knock him down. Let him think he's got the commission, and then pull the rug. The rules're the same. Only the game is different."

"Nobby," Frank said, "hear what you're saying. Do you actually think Guy set this up—set *all* this up—for the limited pleasure of humiliating you?"

"I do," he said.

"Nonsense. Why?"

"Because he liked it. Because it provided him the kicks he'd lost when he sold his business. Because it gave him power."

"That doesn't make sense."

"No? Look at his son, then. Look at Anaïs, poor cow. And if it comes to it, Frank, just look at yourself."

We've got to do something about this, Frank. You see that, don't you?

Frank averted his gaze. He felt the tightening, the tightening, the tightening. Once again, though, the air carried nothing that could have restricted his breathing.

"He said 'I've helped you out as far as I can,' " Nobby said quietly. "He said 'I've given you a leg-up, son. You can't expect more than that, I'm afraid. And certainly not forever, my good man.' But he'd promised, you see. He'd made me *believe*..." Nobby blinked furiously and turned away. He shoved his hands dejectedly into his pockets. He said again, "He made me believe..."

"Yes," Frank murmured. "He was good at that."

• • •

St. James and his wife parted ways a short distance from the cottage. A phone call from Ruth Brouard had come near the end of their interview with the Duffys, and it resulted in St. James handing over to Deborah the ring they'd found on the beach. He would go back to the manor house to meet with Miss Brouard. For her part, Deborah would take the ring in its handkerchief to Detective Chief Inspector Le Gallez for possible identification. It was unlikely that a usable fingerprint would be found on it, considering the nature of its design. But there was always a chance. Since St. James had nothing with him to make an examination of it—not to mention the jurisdiction to do so—Le Gallez would need to carry things further.

"I'll make my own way back and meet you at the hotel later," St. James told his wife. Then he looked at her earnestly and said, "Are you quite all right with this, Deborah?"

He wasn't referring to the errand he'd assigned her but rather to what they'd learned from the Duffys, particularly from Valerie, who was unshakable in her conviction that she'd seen China River following Guy Brouard to the bay. Deborah said, "She might have a reason to want us to believe there was something between China and Guy. If he had a way with the ladies, why not with Valerie as well?"

"She's older than the others."

"Older than China. But surely not that much older than Anaïs Abbott. A few years, I should guess.

And that still makes her . . . what? Twenty years younger than Guy Brouard?"

He couldn't discount that, even if she sounded to his ears far too eager to convince herself. Nonetheless, he said, "Le Gallez's not telling us everything he has. He wouldn't do. I'm a stranger to him, and even if I weren't, it doesn't work that conveniently, with the investigating officer opening his files to someone who'd normally be part of another arm of a murder investigation. And I'm not even that. I'm a stranger come calling without appropriate credentials and no real place in what's going on."

"So you think there's more. A reason. A connection. Somewhere. Between Guy Brouard and China. Simon, I can't think that."

St. James regarded her fondly and thought of all the ways that he loved her and all the ways that he continually wanted to protect her. But he knew that he owed her the truth, so he said, "Yes, my love. I think there may be."

Deborah frowned. She looked beyond his shoulder, where the path to the bay disappeared into a thick growth of rhododendrons. "I can't believe it," she said. "Even if she was that vulnerable. Because of Matt. You know. When that sort of thing happens— that kind of break-up between men and women—it still does take time, Simon. A woman needs to feel that there's something more between herself and the man who's next. She doesn't want to believe it's just . . . well, just sex . . ." A fan of crimson spread open on her neck and sent its colour up and across her cheeks.

St. James wanted to say, That's how it was for you, Deborah. He knew that she was inadvertently paying their love the highest compliment there was: telling him that she had not moved easily from himself to Tommy Lynley when it came down to it. But not all women were like Deborah. Some, he knew, would have needed the immediate reassurance of seduction upon the end of a long affair. To know they were still desirable to a man would be more important than to know they were loved by him. But he could say none of this. Too much lay connected to Deborah's love for Lynley. Too much was involved in his own friendship with the man.

So he said, "We'll keep our own minds open. Till we know more."

She said, "Yes. We'll do that."

"I'll see you later?"

"At the hotel."

He kissed her briefly, then twice more. Her mouth was soft and her hand touched his cheek and he wanted to stay with her even as he knew he couldn't. "Ask for Le Gallez at the station," he told her. "Don't hand over the ring to anyone else."

"Of course," she replied.

He walked back towards the house.

Deborah watched him, the way the brace on his leg hampered what would have otherwise been a natural grace and beauty. She wanted to call him back and explain to him that she *knew* China River in ways that were born of a trouble he couldn't understand, ways in which a friendship is forged that makes the understanding between two women perfect. There are bits of history between women, she wanted to tell her husband, that establish a form of truth that can never be destroyed and never be denied, which never need a lengthy explanation. The truth just *is* and how each woman operates within that truth is fixed if the friendship is real. But how to explain this to a man? And not just to any man but to her husband who'd lived for more than a decade in an effort to move beyond the truth of his own disability—if not denying it altogether—treating it like a mere bagatelle when, she knew, it had wreaked havoc over the greater part of his youth.

There was no way. There was only doing what she could to show him that the China River she knew was not a China River who would have easily given herself to seduction, who would ever have murdered anyone.

She left the estate and drove back to St. Peter Port, winding into the town down the long wooded slope of *Le Val des Terres* and emerging just above Havelet Bay. Along the waterfront, few pedestrians walked. One street up the hillside, the banks for which the Channel Islands were famous would be bustling with business at any time of the year, but here there was virtually no sign of life: no tax exiles sunning themselves on their boats and no tourists snapping pictures of the castle or the town.

Deborah parked near their hotel in Ann's Place, less than a minute's walk from the police station behind its high stone wall on Hospital Lane. She sat in the car for a moment once she'd turned off the engine. She had at least an hour—probably more—be-

fore Simon returned from *Le Reposoir*. She decided
to use it with a slight alteration in what he'd designed
for her.

Nothing was very far from anything else in St.
Peter Port. One was less than twenty minutes' walk
from everything, and in the central part of the
town—which was roughly defined by a misshapen
oval of streets that began with Vauvert and curved
anticlockwise to end up on Grange Road—the time
to get from point A to point B was cut in half.
Nonetheless, since the town had existed long before
motorised transportation, the streets were barely the
width of a car and they curved round the side of the
hill upon which St. Peter Port had developed, un-
rolling without any rhyme or reason, expanding the
town upwards from the old port.

Deborah crisscrossed through these streets to
reach the Queen Margaret Apartments. But when
she arrived and knocked on the door, it was to find
China's flat frustratingly empty. She traced her steps
back to the front of the building and considered
what to do.

China could be anywhere, she realised. She could
be meeting with her advocate, reporting in to the
police station, taking some exercise, or wandering
the streets. Her brother was probably with her,
though, so Deborah decided to see if she could find
them. She would walk in the general direction of
the police station. She'd descend towards the High
Street and then follow it back along the route that
would ultimately take her back up to the hotel.

Across the way from the Queen Margaret Apartments, stairs carved a path down the hill towards the harbour. Deborah made for these and dipped between tall walls and stone buildings, finally emerging into one of the older parts of the town, where a once-grand building of reddish stone stretched along one side of the street and the other side featured a series of arched entries into shops selling flowers, gifts, and fruit.

The grand old building was high-windowed and dim inside, looking disused with no lights shining despite the gloom of the day. Part of it, however, was still active with what appeared to be stalls. They lay beyond a wide and worn blue door that stood open from Market Street into the cavernous interior of the building. Deborah crossed to this entrance.

The unmistakable smell assailed her first: the blood and flesh of a butchery. Glass-fronted cases displayed chops and joints and minced meats, but there were very few of these stalls left in what had obviously once been a thriving meat market. Although the building with its ironwork and its decorative plaster would have interested China as a photographer, Deborah knew that the scent of dead animal would have quickly driven both the Rivers off, so she was unsurprised when she didn't find them inside. Nonetheless, she checked round the rest of the building to make sure, tracing a route through what was a sadly abandoned warehouse of a place where once there had been dozens of thriving little businesses. In a central portion of the great hall, where the ceiling soared above her and caused her footsteps to echo eerily, a row of stalls stood shuttered and across one of them the words *Sod you, Safeway* had been rendered in marker pen, expressing the sentiments of at least one of the merchants who had lost his livelihood to the chain supermarket that had apparently come to the town.

At the far end from the meat market, Deborah found a fruit and veg stall that was still in business, and beyond this once again was the street. She stopped to buy some hot-house lilies before leaving the building and pausing to examine the other shops outside.

Within the arches across the way, she could see not only the little businesses but also everyone making transactions within them, as there were few enough people doing so. Neither China nor Cherokee was among these customers, so Deborah pondered where else they might likely be.

She saw her answer right next to the stairs she'd descended. A small grocery proclaimed itself as Channel Islands Cooperative Society Limited, which sounded like something that would appeal to the Rivers who, for all their joking about her, were still the children of their vegan mother.

Deborah crossed to this shop and entered. She heard them at once because the grocery was small, albeit crowded with tall shelves that hid shoppers from the windows.

"I don't want anything," China was saying impatiently. "I *can't* eat if I can't eat. Could you eat if you were in my position?"

"There's got to be something," Cherokee replied. "Here. What about soup?"

"I *hate* canned soup."

"But you used to make it for dinner."

"My point. Would you want something that reminded you? Motel trash, Cherokee. Which is *worse* than trailer."

Deborah went round the corner of the aisle and found them standing in front of a small display of Campbell's. Cherokee was holding a tin of tomato and rice soup in one hand and a bag of lentils in the other. China had a wire basket over her arm. At the moment nothing was in it save a loaf of bread, a packet of spaghetti, and a jar of tomato sauce.

"Debs!" Cherokee's smile was part greeting but larger part relief. "I need an ally. She's not eating."

"I *am*." China looked exhausted, more so than she had on the previous day, with great dark circles beneath her eyes. She'd tried to hide these with makeup but hadn't been able to bring it off. She said, "Channel Islands Cooperative. I thought it would be health food. But . . ." She made a hopeless gesture that indicated the shop round them.

The only fresh items that the cooperative appeared to contain were eggs, cheese, pre-pack meat, and bread. Everything else was either tinned or frozen. Disappointing for someone used to browsing through the organic food markets of California.

"Cherokee's right," Deborah said. "You need to eat."

"I rest my case." Cherokee began piling items into the wire basket without much regard for what he was choosing.

China looked too dispirited to argue. Within a few minutes, their purchases were complete.

Outside, Cherokee was eager to hear a report on what the day had revealed so far to the St. Jameses. Deborah suggested they return to the flat before they have their conversation, but China said, "God, no. I've just got out. Let's walk."

So they wandered down to the harbour and crossed over to the longest of the piers. This reached out into Havelet Bay and extended to the heel print of land on which Castle Cornet squatted, sentry to the port. They continued beyond this fortification, right to the end, tracing a modest curve into the Channel waters.

At the end of the pier, it was China who brought the real subject up. She said to Deborah, "It's bad, huh? I can see it on your face. You might as well spill it," and despite her words, she turned to look at the water, the great grey heaving mass beneath them. Not so very far away, another island—was it Sark? Alderney? Deborah wondered—rose like a resting leviathan in the mist.

"What've you got, Debs?" Cherokee set down the grocery bags and took his sister's arm.

China moved away from him. She looked like a woman preparing herself for the worst. Deborah very nearly decided to paint things in a positive light. But there was no positive light that she could find, and even if there had been, she knew she owed her friends the facts.

So she told the Rivers what she and Simon had

managed to discover from their conversations at *Le Reposoir*. No fool, China saw the logical direction that the thoughts of any reasonable person would take once it became clear that she had not only spent time alone with Guy Brouard but had also been seen—ostensibly and by more than one person—following him on the morning of his death.

She said, "You think I had something going with him, don't you, Deborah? Well. That's just great." Her voice contained a blend of animus and despair.

"Actually, I—"

"And why not, anyway? Everyone must think it. A few hours alone, a couple of days . . . And he was rich as hell. So sure. We were fucking like goats."

Deborah blinked at the crude term. It was greatly unlike the China she'd known, who'd always been the more romantic of the two of them, devoted to one man for years, content with a future painted out in pastels.

China continued. "It didn't matter to me that he was old enough to be my grandfather. Hell, there was money involved. It never matters who you're fucking when there's money to be had from the job, does it?"

"Chine!" Cherokee protested. "Jeez."

China seemed to realise what she'd just said even as her brother spoke. More, she seemed to understand in a flash how it could be applied to Deborah's life, because she said hastily, "God. Deborah. I'm sorry."

"It's all right," Deborah said.

"I didn't mean . . . I wasn't thinking of you and . . . you know."

Tommy, Deborah thought. China meant she hadn't been thinking of Tommy and Tommy's money. It had never mattered but it had always *been* there, just one of a thousand things that looked so good from the outside if one didn't know how the inside felt. She said, "It's all right. I know."

China said, "It's just that . . . Do you really believe that I . . . With him? Do you?"

"She was just telling you what she knows, Chine," Cherokee said. "We need to know what everyone's thinking, don't we?"

China swung on him. "Listen, Cherokee. Shut up. You don't know what you're . . . Oh God, forget it. Just shut up, okay?"

"I'm only trying—"

"Well, *stop* trying. Stop hovering, too. I can't even breathe. I can't take a step without you following me."

"Look. No one wants you to have to go through this," Cherokee said to her.

She gave a laugh that ruptured, but she stopped the sob by bringing a fist to her mouth. "Are you crazy or what?" she demanded. "Everyone wants me to go through this. A patsy is needed. I fill the bill."

"Yeah, well, that's why we've got friends here now." Cherokee shot a smile at Deborah and then nodded at the lilies she was holding. "Friends with flowers. Where'd you get those, Debs?"

"In the market." Impulsively, she extended them to China. "That flat needs a bit of cheering up, I think."

China looked at the flowers, then at Deborah's face. "I think you're the best friend I've ever had," she said.

"I'm glad of it."

China took the flowers. Her expression softened as she looked down at them. Then she said to her brother, "Cherokee, give us some time alone, okay?"

He glanced from his sister to Deborah, saying, "Sure. I'll put those in water." He scooped up the two grocery bags and hooked his arm round the flowers. He said to Deborah, "Later, then," and gave her a look that spoke the words *good luck* as clearly as if he'd said them.

He headed back along the pier. China watched him. "I know he means well. I know he's worried. But having him here makes it worse. Like I have to contend with him along with the whole situation." She clasped her arms round her body, which was the first moment that Deborah saw she was wearing only a sweater against the cold. Her cloak would still be with the police, of course. And that cloak was so much the crux of her problem.

Deborah said, "Where did you leave your cloak that night?"

China studied the water for a moment before saying, "The night of the party? It must have been in my room. I didn't keep track of it. I'd been in and out all day, but I must've taken it upstairs at some point because when we got ready to leave that morning it was . . . I'm pretty sure it was lying across a chair. Next to the window."

"You don't remember putting it there?"

China shook her head. "It would've been an automatic thing, though. Wear it, take it off, toss it down. I've never been a neat freak. You know that."

"So someone could have removed it, used it early that morning when Guy Brouard went to the bay, and then returned it?"

"I guess. But I don't see how. Or even when."

"Was it there when you went to bed?"

"It could have been." She frowned. "I just don't know."

"Valerie Duffy swears she saw you following him, China." Deborah said it as gently as she could. "Ruth Brouard claims she searched the house for you as well once she saw someone she thought was you from the window."

"You believe them?"

"It's not that," Deborah said. "It's whether there's something that might have happened earlier that would make what they say sound reasonable to the police."

"Something that happened?"

"Between you and Guy Brouard."

"We're back to that."

"It's not what I think. It's what the police—"

"Forget it," China interrupted. "Come with me."

She led the way back along the pier. At the Esplanade, she crossed over without even a glance for traffic. She wound through several waiting buses at the town station and traced a zigzagging route to Constitution Steps, which shaped an inverted question mark on the side of one of the hills. These steps—like those Deborah had earlier descended to the market—took them up to Clifton Street and the Queen Margaret Apartments. China led the way round the back to Flat B. She was inside and at the small kitchen table before she said another word.

Then it was "Here. Read this. If it's the only way to make you believe, then you can check each grisly detail if you like."

"China, I do believe you," Deborah said. "You don't need—"

"Don't tell me what I don't need," China said insistently. "You think there's a chance I'm lying."

"Not lying."

"All right. Something I might've misinterpreted. But I'm telling you, there's *nothing* I could have misinterpreted. And nothing anyone else could've misinterpreted because nothing happened. Not between me and Guy Brouard. Not between me and anyone. So I'm asking you to read this for yourself. So that you can be sure." Against her hand, she slapped the legal pad on which she'd made her account of the days she'd spent at *Le Reposoir.*

"I believe your story," Deborah said.

"Read" was China's reply.

Deborah saw that nothing would satisfy her friend other than reading what she'd written. She sat at the table and took up the pad as China moved to the work top where Cherokee had left the grocery

bags and the flowers before taking himself off somewhere else.

China had been very thorough, Deborah saw
when she began reading her friend's document. She
displayed an admirable memory as well. Every interaction she'd had with the Brouards seemed accounted for, and when she'd not been with either
Guy Brouard or his sister or both of them together,
she'd accounted for that time as well. This had apparently been spent with Cherokee or often by herself as she took her photographs of the estate.

She'd documented where every interaction had
occurred during her time at *Le Reposoir*. Thus, it was
possible to track her movements, which was all for
the good because surely someone would be able to
confirm them.

Living room, she'd written, *looking at historical pictures of L.R. Guy, Ruth, Cherokee, and Paul F. there.*
The time and day followed.

Dining room, she went on, *lunch with Guy, Ruth,
Cherokee, Frank O., and Paul F. AA comes in later,
dessert time, with Duck and Stephen. Daggers at me.
Many daggers at Paul F.*

Study, she continued, *with Guy, Frank O., and
Cherokee, discussion about the museum-to-be. Frank O.
leaves. Cherokee goes with him to meet his dad and see the
water mill. Guy and I stay. Talk. Ruth comes in with
AA. Duck outside with Stephen and Paul F.*

Gallery, she wrote, *top of the house with Guy. Guy
showing off pictures, posing for camera. Adrian shows up.
Just arrived. Introductions all around.*

Grounds, she continued, *Guy and me. Talk about taking pictures of the place. Talk about* Architectural Digest. *Explain about doing things on spec. See the buildings and the different gardens. Feed the koi.*

Cherokee's room, she continued, *him and me. Talk about whether to stay or go.*

On and on she had written, in what appeared to be a dogged and detailed account of what had gone on in the days leading up to Guy Brouard's death. Deborah read it all and tried to look for key moments that could have been spied upon by someone else who used them for an end that had brought China into her present situation.

"Who's Paul F.?" Deborah asked.

China explained: a protégé of Guy Brouard's. Sort of a Big Brother thing. Did the Brits have Big Brothers like they had in the States? An older man taking on a young kid without a decent role model? That was the deal between Guy Brouard and Paul Fielder. He never said more than ten words at a time. Just looked at Guy with goo-goo eyes and followed him around like a dog.

"How old a boy?"

"Teenager. Pretty poor by the looks of his clothes. And his bike. He showed up pretty much every day on this rattletrap thing, more rust than anything else. He was always welcome. His dog, too."

The boy, the clothes, and the dog. The description matched the teenager she and Simon had come upon on their way to the bay. Deborah said, "Was he at the party?"

"What, the night before?" When Deborah nodded, China said, "Sure. Everyone was there. It was sort of the social event of the season, from what we could figure."

"How many people?"

China considered this. "Three hundred? More or less."

"Contained in one place?"

"Not exactly. I mean, it wasn't an open house or anything, but there were people wandering around all night. Caterers were coming and going from the kitchen. There were four bars. It wasn't chaos, but I don't think anyone was keeping track of who went where."

"So your cloak could have been pinched," Deborah said.

"I suppose. But it was there when I needed it, Debs. When Cherokee and I were leaving the next morning."

"You didn't see anyone when you were leaving?"

"Not a soul."

They were silent then. China emptied the grocery bags into the tiny fridge and the single cupboard. She rooted round for something to place the flowers in and finally settled on a cooking pot. Deborah watched her and wondered how to ask what she needed to ask, how to put the question in a way that her friend wouldn't read as suspicious or unsupportive. She had difficulties enough already.

"Earlier," Deborah said, "on one of the previous days I mean, did you go with Guy Brouard for his morning swim? Perhaps just to watch?"

China shook her head. "I knew he went swimming in the bay. Everyone admired him for it. Cold water, early morning, the time of year. I think he liked how people would be in awe that he'd swim every day no matter what. But I never went to watch him."

"Did anyone else?"

"I think his girlfriend did, from the way people talked about it. Sort of 'Anaïs, can't you do *something* to talk reason into that man?' And, 'I do try to whenever I'm there.' "

"So she would've gone with him that morning?"

"If she'd stayed the night. But I don't know if she did. She hadn't stayed over while we were there, Cherokee and me."

"But she did stay sometimes?"

"She made it pretty obvious. I mean, she made sure I knew. So she *may* have stayed over on the night of the party, but I don't think so."

The fact that China refused to colour what little she knew in such a way that might guide suspicion onto someone else was something that Deborah found comforting. It spoke of a character much stronger than her own. She said, "China, I think there're lots of directions the police could have taken looking into this."

"Do you? Really?"

"I do."

At this, China seemed to let go of something big and unnamed that she'd been holding within since the moment Deborah had come upon her and her brother in the grocery. She said, "Thank you, Debs."

"You don't need to thank me."

"Yes, I do. For coming here. For being a friend. Without you and Simon, I'd be anyone's victim. Will I get to meet him? Simon? I'd like to."

"Of course you will," Deborah said. "He's looking forward to it."

China came back to the table and took up the legal pad. She studied it for a moment, as if thinking something over, then extended it to Deborah as impulsively as Deborah had earlier handed over the lilies.

She said, "Give this to him. Tell him to go over it with a fine-tooth comb. Ask him to grill me whenever he wants to and as many times as he thinks he needs to. Tell him to get to the truth."

Deborah took the document and promised to hand it over to her husband.

She left the flat feeling buoyed. Outside, she walked back round the building, where she found Cherokee lounging against a railing across the street and in front of a holiday hotel that was closed for the winter. The collar of his jacket was turned up against the chill and he was drinking from a take-away cup of something steaming as he watched the Queen Margaret Apartments like an undercover cop. He pushed himself away from the railing when he spied Deborah, and he came across to her.

"How was it?" he asked. "Things go okay? She's been on edge all day."

"She's all right," Deborah said. "Bit anxious, though."

"I want to do something, but she won't let me. I try, and she just flies off the handle. I don't think she should be in there alone, so I hang around and say we ought to go for a drive or take a walk or play cards or watch CNN and see what's happening at home. Or something. But she just freaks."

"She's scared. I don't think she wants you to know just how much."

"I'm her *brother*."

"That may be why."

He thought about this, emptying the rest of his cup and crushing it between his fingers. He said, "It was always her taking care of me. When we were kids. When Mom was . . . well, being Mom. The protests. The causes. Not all the time but when someone needed a body willing to tie herself to a redwood tree or carry a placard for something. Off she'd go. Weeks at a time. Chine was the strong one all through that. It wasn't me."

"You feel indebted to her."

"Big time. Yeah. I want to help."

Deborah considered this: his need balanced against the situation they faced. She glanced at her watch and decided there was time.

"Come with me," she said. "There's something you can do."

Chapter 12

THE MORNING ROOM OF the manor house was fitted out with an enormous frame, St. James saw, similar to that used for making tapestries. But instead of weaving, what apparently went on at this device was needlepoint on an unthinkable scale. Ruth Brouard said nothing while he observed this frame and the canvas-like material stretched upon it, looking from it to a finished piece that hung on one of the walls of the room, a piece not unlike the one he'd seen earlier in her bedroom.

The enormous needlepoint seemed to depict the fall of France during the Second World War, St. James noted, with the Maginot Line beginning the story and a woman packing suitcases ending it. Two children watched this woman—a boy and a girl—while behind them a bearded old man in a prayer shawl stood with a book open on his palm and a woman his own age wept and appeared to be comforting a man who might have been her adult son.

"This is remarkable," St. James said.

On a drop-front desk, Ruth Brouard placed a manila envelope she'd been holding when she answered the door. "I find it therapeutic," she said, "and far less expensive than psychoanalysis."

"How long did it take?"

"Eight years. But I wasn't as quick then. I didn't need to be."

St. James observed her. He could see the disease in her too-careful movements and in the strain on her face. But he was reluctant to name or even mention it to her, so intent did she seem upon maintaining the pretence of vitality.

"How many have you planned?" he asked, giving his attention next to the unfinished work stretched upon the frame.

"As many as it takes to tell the whole story," she replied. "This one"—with a nod at the wall—"this was the first. It's a bit crude, but I got better with practice."

"It tells an important story."

"I think so. What happened to you? I know it's rude to ask, but I'm quite beyond that sort of social nicety at this point. I hope you don't mind."

He certainly would have done had the question come from someone else. But from her, there seemed to be a capacity for understanding that superseded idle curiosity and made her a kindred spirit. Perhaps, St. James thought, because she was so clearly dying.

He said, "Car crash."

"When was this?"

"I was twenty-four."

"Ah. I'm sorry."

"That's completely unnecessary. We were both drunk."

"You and the lady?"

"No. An old school friend."

"Who was driving, I expect. Who walked away without a scratch."

St. James smiled. "Are you a witch, Miss Brouard?"

She returned his smile. "I only wish I were. I'd've cast more than one spell over the years."

"Upon a lucky man?"

"Upon my brother." She turned the desk's straight-backed chair to face the room, and lowered herself to it, one hand on its seat. She indicated an armchair nearby. St. James took it and waited for her to tell him why she wanted to see him a second time.

She made it clear within a moment. Did Mr. St. James, she asked, know anything about the laws of inheritance on the island of Guernsey? Or, for that matter, was he aware of the restrictions these laws placed upon the disposition of one's money and property after one's death? It was rather a byzantine system, she said, one that had its roots in Norman Customary Law. Its primary feature was the preservation of family assets within the family, and its distinguishing mark was that there was no such thing as disinheriting a child, wayward or otherwise. One's children had the right to inherit a certain amount of property, no matter the condition of their relationship with their parents.

"There were many things my brother loved about the Channel Islands," Ruth Brouard told St. James. "The weather, the atmosphere, the powerful sense of community. Of course, the tax laws and the access to good banking. But Guy didn't like being told by a legal system how he was meant to distribute his property after his death."

"Understandable," St. James said.

"So he looked for a way round it, a legal loophole. And he found it, as anyone who knew him would have predicted he would."

In advance of their move to the island, Ruth Brouard explained, her brother had deeded all of his property over to her. He kept for himself a single bank account, into which he deposited a substantial sum of money which he knew he could not only invest but also live on quite nicely. But otherwise his every possession—the properties, the stocks, the bonds, the other accounts, the businesses—had been placed into Ruth's name. There had been only one proviso: that once on Guernsey she herself should agree to signing a will that he and an advocate would draw up for her. Since she had no husband or children, she could do with her property whatever she wanted upon her death, and in this way her brother would be able to do with his property what he wanted since she would write a will guided by him. It was a clever way to get round the law.

"My brother had been estranged from his two younger children for years, you see," Ruth explained. "He couldn't see why he should be forced to leave both the girls a fortune simply because he'd fathered them, which is what the island's inheritance law required him to do. He'd supported them through into adulthood. He'd sent them to the best schools, pulled strings to get one into Cambridge and the other into the Sorbonne. In return he'd got nothing. Not even a thank-you. So he said enough is enough and he sought a way to give something to those other people in his life who'd given so much to him when his own children hadn't. Devotion, I mean. Friendship, acceptance, and love. He could give to them generously, those people—as he wished to—but only if he filtered everything through me. So that's what we did."

"What about his son?"

"Adrian?"

"Did your brother want to cut him off as well?"

"He didn't wish to cut any of them off completely. He just wanted to lower the amount he'd be required by law to give to them."

"Who knew about this?" St. James asked.

"As far as I know, just Guy, Dominic Forrest—that's the advocate—and me." She reached for the manila envelope then, but she didn't unfasten its metal tabs. Instead, she set it on her lap and smoothed her hands across it as she went on. "I agreed to it in part to give Guy peace of mind. He was terribly unhappy about the sort of relationships his wives allowed him to have with his children, so I thought, Well, why not? Why not allow him to remember those people who'd touched his life when his own family wouldn't come near him? You see, I didn't expect . . ." She hesitated, folding her hands with care, as if considering how much to reveal. Then she appeared to take resolve from a study of the envelope she held, for she went on. "I didn't expect to outlive my brother. I thought when I finally told him about my . . . my physical situation, he'd more than likely suggest that we rewrite my will and perhaps leave everything to him. He'd've been hobbled by the law again at that point with regards to his own will, but I do think he might have preferred that to being left with only a single bank account, some investments, and no way of replenishing either should he need to do so."

"Yes, I see," St. James said. "I see how it was intended to be. But I take it that it didn't quite work that way?"

"I hadn't got round to telling him about my . . . situation. Sometimes I'd catch him looking at me and I'd think, He knows. But he never said. And I never said. I'd tell myself, Tomorrow. Tomorrow I'll speak to him about it. But I just never did."

"So when he died suddenly—"

"There were expectations."

"And now?"

"There are understandable resentments."

St. James nodded. He looked to the great wall-hanging and its depiction of a vital part of their lives. He saw that the mother packing suitcases was weeping, that the children clung to each other in fear. Through a window, Nazi tanks rumbled across a distant meadow and a division of goose-stepping troops advanced down a narrow street.

"I don't expect you've asked me here to advise

you what to do next," he said. "Something tells me you already know."

"I owe my brother everything, and I'm a woman who pays her debts. So yes. I haven't asked you here to tell me what to do about my own will now that Guy's dead. Not at all."

"Then may I ask . . . ? How can I help you?"

"Until today," she said, "I'd always known exactly the terms of Guy's wills."

"In the plural?"

"He rewrote his will rather more often than most people do. Every time he had a new one drawn up, he'd arrange a meeting for me with his advocate so that I knew what the terms of that will were going to be. He was good that way and he was always consistent. On the day the will was meant to be signed and witnessed, we went to Mr. Forrest's office. We'd go over the paperwork, see if any changes were required in my own will as a result, sign and witness all the documents, and afterwards go to lunch."

"But I take it that didn't happen with this last will?"

"It didn't happen."

"Perhaps he hadn't got round to it yet," St. James suggested. "He clearly didn't expect to die."

"This last will was written in October, Mr. St. James. More than two months ago. I've gone nowhere off the island in that time. Neither has— had—Guy. For this last will to be legal, he had to have gone into St. Peter Port to sign the paperwork. The fact that he didn't take me with him suggests he didn't want me to know what he planned to do."

"Which was?"

"Cut out Anaïs Abbott, Frank Ouseley, and the Duffys. He kept that as a secret from me. When I realised that, I saw how it was possible he'd kept other things from me as well."

They'd come to it now, St. James saw: the reason she'd asked to see him again. Ruth Brouard unclasped the fasteners of the envelope on her lap. She brought forth its contents and St. James saw that among them was Guy Brouard's passport, which was the first thing the man's sister handed over.

"This was his first secret," she said. "Look at the last stamp, the most recent one."

St. James flipped through the little booklet and found the relevant immigration markings. He saw that, in contradiction to what Ruth Brouard had told him during their earlier conversation that day, her brother had entered the state of California in the month of March, through Los Angeles International Airport.

"He didn't tell you about this?" St. James asked her.

"Of course not. I would have told you otherwise." She next handed him a pile of documents. St. James saw that these comprised credit card bills as well as hotel bills and receipts from restaurants and car hire firms. Guy Brouard had stayed five nights in the Hilton in a town called Irvine. He'd eaten at a place called Il Fornaio there, as well as at Scott's Seafood in Costa Mesa, and the Citrus Grille in Orange. He'd met with someone called William Kiefer, attorney-at-law, in Tustin, to whom he'd paid just over one thousand dollars for three appointments in five days, and he'd kept that lawyer's business card along with a receipt from an architectural firm called Southby, Strange, Willows, and Ward. *Jim Ward* had been scrawled on the bottom of this credit slip along with *mobile* and the relevant phone number.

"He seems to have made his museum arrangements in person, then," St. James noted. "This fits in with what we know his plans were."

"It does," Ruth said. "But he didn't *tell* me. Not one word about this trip at all. Don't you see what that means?"

Ruth's question was fraught with a sinister undertone, but St. James saw only that the information meant her brother might well have wanted a bit of privacy. Indeed, he could possibly have taken a companion with him and not wished his sister to know about that. But when Ruth went on, he realised that the new facts she had come across were not so much disconcerting her as they were confirming what she already believed.

She said, "California, Mr. St. James. She *lives* in California. So he had to have known her before she got to Guernsey. She came here having planned it all."

"I see. Miss River. But she doesn't live in this part of California," St. James pointed out. "She's from Santa Barbara."

"How far from this can that be?"

St. James frowned. He didn't actually know, having never been to California and being completely unfamiliar with its towns other than Los Angeles and

San Francisco, which, he knew, were more or less at opposite ends of the state. He *did* know, however, that the place was vast, connected by an incomprehensible network of motorways that were generally glutted with cars. Deborah would be the one to offer an opinion on the feasibility of Guy Brouard's having made a journey to Santa Barbara during his time in California. When she'd lived there, she'd done a great deal of traveling, not only with Tommy but also with China.

China. This thought tweaked his mind into recalling his wife's telling him about the visits she'd made to China's mother, to China's brother as well. A town like a colour, she'd said: Orange. Home of the Citrus Grille, whose receipt Guy Brouard had tucked among his papers. And Cherokee River—not his sister China—lived somewhere in that area. So how unlikely was it that Cherokee River, not China, had known Guy Brouard before coming to Guernsey?

St. James thought about what this implied and said to Ruth, "Where were the Rivers staying in the house those nights they were with you?"

"On the second floor."

"Their rooms facing which direction?"

"The front, the south."

"A clear view to the drive? The trees along it? The Duffys' cottage?"

"Yes. Why?"

"What made you go to the window that morning, Miss Brouard? When you saw the figure following your brother, what was it that made you look out in the first place? Was that normally what you did?"

She considered his question, finally saying slowly, "I generally wasn't yet up when Guy left the house. So I think it must have been . . ." She looked pensive. She folded her thin hands together on top of the manila envelope and St. James saw how papery her skin was, stretched like tissue across her bones. She said, "I'd actually heard a noise, Mr. St. James. It woke me, frightened me a bit because I thought it was the middle of the night still, with someone creeping about. It was so dark. But when I looked at the clock, I saw it was nearly the time Guy swam. I listened for a few moments, then I heard him in his room. So I assumed he'd made the noise himself." She saw the direction St. James was heading and said, "But it could have been someone else, couldn't it? Not Guy at all, but someone already up and about. Someone about to head out to wait by the trees."

"It seems so," St. James said.

"And their rooms were above my own," she said. "The Rivers' rooms. On the floor above. So you see—"

"Possibly," St. James said. But he saw more than that. He saw how one could look at partial information and ignore the rest. So he said, "And where was Adrian staying?"

"He *couldn't* have—"

"Did he know the situation with the wills? Yours and your brother's?"

"Mr. St. James, I assure you. He couldn't . . . Believe me, he wouldn't . . ."

"Assuming he knew the laws of the island and assuming he *didn't* know what his father had done to effectively cut him off from a fortune, he would believe he stood to inherit . . . what?"

"Either half of Guy's entire estate divided into thirds with his sisters," Ruth said with clear reluctance.

"Or one-third of everything had his father simply left the lot only to his children?"

"Yes, but—"

"A considerable fortune," St. James pointed out.

"Yes, yes. But you must believe me, Adrian wouldn't have harmed a hair on his father's head. Not for anything. And certainly not for an inheritance."

"He has money of his own, then?"

She didn't reply. A clock was ticking on a mantelpiece and the sound grew loud, like a waiting bomb. Her silence was answer enough for St. James.

He said, "What about your own will, Miss Brouard? What was the agreement you had with your brother? How did he want you to distribute the property that was held in your name?"

She licked her lower lip. Her tongue was nearly as pale as the rest of her. She said, "Adrian is a troubled boy, Mr. St. James. Most of his life, he's been tugged between his parents like a rope in a game. Their marriage ended badly, and Margaret made Adrian the instrument of her revenge. It made no difference to her when she married again and married well—

Margaret always marries well, you see—there was still the fact of Guy's having betrayed her and of her not knowing soon enough, not being clever enough to catch him in the actual act, which I think is what she wanted more than anything: my brother and some woman in bed and Margaret coming upon them like one of the Furies. But it didn't happen that way. Just some sort of squalid discovery . . . I don't even know of what. And she couldn't get past it, couldn't live beyond it. Guy was made to suffer as much as possible for humiliating her. Adrian was the rack she used. And to be used like that . . . It doesn't make the tree grow strong if you keep messing about with its roots. But Adrian's not a killer."

"You've left him everything in recompense, then?"

She'd been examining her hands, but, at that, she looked up. "No. I've done what my brother wanted."

"Which was?"

Le Reposoir, she said, was being left to the people of Guernsey for their use and pleasure, with a trust fund set up to see to the maintenance of the grounds, the buildings, and the furnishings. The rest—the properties in Spain, France, and England—the stocks and the bonds, the bank accounts, and all personal belongings not used at the time of her death to furnish the manor house or to decorate the estate grounds—would be sold and the proceeds of such a sale would fund the trust itself into infinity.

"I agreed to this because it's what he wanted,"

Ruth Brouard said. "He promised me that his children would be remembered in his own will, and they have been. Not as generously as they would have been had things gone as normal, of course. But remembered nonetheless."

"How?"

"He used the option he had to divide his estate in half. His three children got the first half, divided equally among them. The second half went to two other young people, teenagers here on Guernsey."

"Leaving them effectively more than his own children will receive."

"I . . . Yes," she said. "I suppose that's right."

"Who are these teenagers?"

She told him they were called Paul Fielder and Cynthia Moullin. Her brother, she said, set himself up as their mentor. The boy came to his attention through a programme of sponsorship at the local secondary school. The girl came to his attention through her own father, Henry Moullin, a glazier who'd constructed the conservatory and replaced the windows at *Le Reposoir.*

"The families are quite poor, especially the Fielders," Ruth concluded. "Guy would have seen that and, liking the children, he would have wanted to do something for them, something their own parents would never be able to do."

"But why keep this a secret from you, if that's what he did?" St. James asked.

"I don't know," she said, "I don't understand."

"Would you have disapproved?"

"I might have told him how much trouble he could be causing."

"In his own family?"

"In theirs as well. Both Paul and Cynthia have other siblings."

"Who weren't remembered in your brother's will?"

"Who weren't remembered in my brother's will. So a legacy left to one and not the others . . . I would have told him it had the potential to rupture their families."

"Would he have listened to you, Miss Brouard?"

She shook her head. She looked infinitely sad. "That was my brother's weakness," she told him. "Guy never listened to anyone."

Margaret Chamberlain was hard pressed to recall a time when she'd been as furious or as driven to do something about her fury. She thought she *may* have been so caught up in rage the day her suspicions about Guy's philandering had ceased to be suspicions at all and had become instead a full-blown reality that had felt like a fist driven into her stomach. But that day had been long ago and so much had happened in the intervening years—three more marriages and three more children, to be specific—that that time had faded into a tarnished memory which she generally didn't run a silver cloth over because, just like a piece of old and unfashionable silver, she had no use for it any longer. Nonetheless, she reckoned that what was consuming her was akin to that earlier provocation. And how ironic was it that both then and now the seed for what consumed her came from the same source?

When she felt like this, she generally had a difficult time deciding in what area she wished to strike out first. She knew that Ruth had to be dealt with, the provisions of Guy's will being so utterly bizarre that there could be only one explanation for them and Margaret was willing to bet her life that that explanation was spelled R-u-t-h. Beyond Ruth, however, there were the two beneficiaries of *half* of what was pretending to be Guy's entire estate. There was no way on heaven, on earth, or in hell that Margaret Chamberlain intended to stand by and watch two nobodies—unrelated to Guy by even the tiniest speck of blood—walk away with more money than the bastard's own son.

Adrian was less than helpful with information. He'd retreated to his room and when she'd cornered him there, demanding to know more who, where, and why than Ruth had been willing to impart, he'd said only, "They're kids. Someone to look at Dad the way he thought the fruit of his loins were supposed to look at him. We wouldn't cooperate. They were happy to. That's Dad for you, isn't it? Always rewarding devotion."

"Where are they? Where can I find them?"

"He's in the Bouet," he replied. "I don't know where. It's like council housing. He could be anywhere."

"What about the other?"

That was easier by far. The Moullins lived in *La Corbière,* southwest of the airport, in a parish called Forest. They lived in the looniest house on the island. People called it the Shell House and once you were in the vicinity of *La Corbière,* you couldn't miss it.

"Fine. Let's go," Margaret told her son.

At which point Adrian made it perfectly clear that he wasn't going anywhere. "What d'you think you're going to achieve?"

"I'm going to let them know who they're dealing with. I'm going to make it clear that if they expect to rob you of what is rightfully yours—"

"Don't bother." He was smoking incessantly, pacing the room, back and forth across the Persian carpet as if determined to create a trough in it. "It's what Dad wanted. It's his final . . . you know . . . The big slap goodbye."

"Stop *wallowing* in all this, Adrian." She couldn't help herself. It was too much to have to consider the fact that her son might be perfectly willing to accept a humiliating defeat just because his father had decided he was to do so. "There's more involved in this than your father's wishes. There're your rights as his flesh and blood. If it comes down to it, there're your sisters' rights as well, and you can't tell me JoAnna Brouard will sit by and do nothing once she learns how your father dealt with her girls. This is something that has the potential to mire itself in court for *years* if we don't do something. So we tackle these two beneficiaries first. And then we tackle Ruth."

He walked to the chest of drawers, varying his route for once and thank God. He crushed out his cigarette in an ashtray that was providing the bedroom with ninety percent of its malodorous air. He immediately lit another. "I'm not going anywhere," he said to her. "I'm out of it, Mother."

Margaret refused to believe that, at least not as a permanent condition. She told herself he was just depressed. He was humiliated. He was mourning. Not Guy, of course. But Carmel whom he'd lost to Guy, God curse his soul for betraying his own and only son in that inimitable fashion of his, the consummate Judas. But this was the very same Carmel who would come scampering back begging to be forgiven once Adrian took his proper place at the head of his father's fortune. Margaret had little doubt about that.

Adrian made no enquiry as Margaret said, "Very well," and searched through his things. He made no protest as she rooted his car keys out from the jacket he'd left lying on the seat of a chair. She added, "All right. Be out of it for now," and she left him.

In the glove compartment of the Range Rover, she found a map of the island, the sort of map that car hire firms pass out, on which their locations are predominantly displayed and everything else fades into illegibility. But since the car hire firm was at the airport and since *La Corbière* wasn't far from either, she was able to pinpoint the hamlet near the south shore of the island, on a lane that looked to be the approximate width of a feline's whisker.

She gunned the engine as an expression of her

feelings and set off. How difficult could it be, she told herself, to trace a route back to the airport and then venture left at *La Rue de la Villiaze*? She wasn't an idiot. She could read the street signs. She wouldn't get lost.

Those beliefs, naturally, presupposed that there would actually *be* street signs. Margaret soon discovered that part of the whimsical nature of the island lay in the manner in which street markings were hidden: generally waist-high and behind a growth of ivy. She also quickly found that one needed to know towards which parish one wished to be headed in order not to end up in the middle of St. Peter Port which, like Rome, appeared to be where all roads led.

Four false starts had her damp with anxious perspiration, and when she finally found the airport, she drove right past *La Rue de la Villiaze* without noticing it, so tiny was the street when it appeared. Margaret was used to England, where main routes bore some resemblance to main routes. On the map, the street was coloured red, so in her mind it possessed at least two nicely marked lanes, not to mention a large sign indicating she'd found what she was looking for. She was, unfortunately, all the way to a triangular intersection in the middle of the island, one marked by a church half-hidden in a depression in the land, before she thought she may have gone too far. At which point, she pulled onto what went for the verge, studied the map, and saw—with her irritation intensifying—that she'd overshot her mark and would have to try it all again.

This was when she finally cursed her son. Had he not been such a *gormless* and *pathetic* excuse of a . . . But no, no. True, it would have been more convenient to have had him with her, to have had the ability to drive directly to her destination without half a dozen false starts. But Adrian needed to recover from the blow of his father's will—his bloody bloody *bloody* father's will—and if he wanted an hour or so to do that, so be it, Margaret thought. She could cope on her own.

This made her wonder, though, if that was in part what had happened to Carmel Fitzgerald: just one too many moments when she realised there would be times when she would have to cope on her own, times when Adrian took to his room, or worse. God knew Guy could drive anyone with a sensitive nature into the ground, not to mention into self-loathing, and if that had happened to Adrian while he and Carmel had been guests at *Le Reposoir,* what might have the young woman thought, how vulnerable might she have actually been to the advances of a man so clearly in his element, so virile, and so bloody *capable.* Vulnerable as hell, Margaret thought. Which Guy had no doubt seen and acted upon with absolutely no conscience.

But, by God, he would pay for what he'd done. He couldn't pay in life. But he would pay now.

So caught up was she in this resolution that Margaret very nearly missed *La Rue de la Villiaze* a second time. But at the last moment, she saw a narrow lane veering to the right in the vicinity of the airport. She took it blindly and found herself zipping past a pub and then a hotel and then out into the countryside, coursing between tall banks and hedges beyond which lay farmhouses and fallow fields. Secondary lanes that looked more like tractor tracks began to pop up round her, and just when she was deciding to try any one of them in the hope it might lead her somewhere identifiable, she came to a junction in the road she was traveling and found the miracle of a sign post, pointing to the right and *La Corbière.*

Margaret muttered her thanks to the driving deity that had seen her to this point and turned into a lane that was indistinguishable from any of the others. Had she encountered another car, one of them would have had to reverse back to the lane's starting point, but her luck held and along the route that passed a whitewashed farmhouse and two flesh-coloured stone cottages, she saw no other vehicle.

What she did see at a dogleg was the Shell House. As Adrian had suggested, only a blind man could have missed it. The building itself was of stucco painted yellow. The shells from which it took its name served as decoration along the drive, topping the boundary wall, and within the large front garden.

It was the most tasteless display Margaret could ever recall seeing, something that looked assembled by a madman. Conch shells, ormer shells, scallop shells, and the occasional abalone shell formed borders, first. They stood alongside flowerbeds in which more shells—glued onto twigs and branches and flexible metal—comprised the flowers. In the middle of the lawn a shallow shell-embedded pond raised its shell-embedded sides and provided an environment for—mercifully—non-shelled goldfish. But all round this pond stood shell-encrusted pedestals on which shell-formed idols posed for purposes of adoration. Two full-sized shell lawn tables and their appropriate shell chairs each held tea services of shell and shell food on their sandwich plates. And along the front wall ran a miniature firestation, a school, a barn, and a church, all of them glinting white from the molluscs that had given their lives to fashion them. It was, Margaret thought as she climbed out of the Range Rover, enough to put one off bouillabaisse forever.

She shuddered at such a monument to vulgarity. It brought back too many unpleasant memories: childhood summer holidays on the coast of Essex, all those aitches dropped, all those greasy chips consumed, all that doughy flesh so hideously reddened in order to proclaim to one and all that enough money had been saved for a holiday at the sea.

Margaret shoved aside the thought of it, the remembered sight of her parents on the steps of a hired beach hut, arms slung round each other, bottled beer in their hands. Their sloppy kisses and then her mother's giggles and what followed the giggles.

Enough, Margaret thought. She advanced determinedly up the drive. She called out a confident hello, then a second and a third. No one came out of the house. There were gardening tools arrayed on the front walk, however, although God only knew to what purpose anyone intended to put them in this environment. Nonetheless, they suggested someone was at home and at work in the garden, so she approached the front door. As she did so, a man came round the side of the house, carrying a shovel. He was grubbily clad in blue jeans so dirty that they might have stood up on their own had he not been wearing them. Despite the cold, no jacket protected him, just a faded blue work shirt on which someone had embroidered *Moullin Glass* in red. The theme of climatic indifference was one that the man carried down to his feet, on which he wore sandals only, although he also had on socks. These, however, displayed more than one hole and his right big toe protruded from one of them.

He saw Margaret and stopped, saying nothing. She was surprised to realise that she recognised him: the overnourished Heathcliff she'd seen at Guy's funeral reception. Close up, she saw that the darkness of his skin was due to his face being weathered to the condition of unsoaped leather. His eyes were hostile observing her, and his hands were covered with myriad healed and unhealed cuts. Margaret might have been intimidated by the level of animosity coming from him, but she already felt her own animosity, and even if that had not been the case, she was not a woman who was easily alarmed.

"I'm looking for Cynthia Moullin," she told the man as pleasantly as she could. "Can you tell me where I might find her, please?"

"Why?" He carried the shovel onto the lawn, where he began digging round the base of one of the trees.

Margaret bristled. She was used to people hearing her voice—God knew she'd spent years enough developing it—and jumping to at once. She said, "I believe it's either yes or no. You can or you can't help me find her. Have you a problem understanding me?"

"I've a problem caring one way or t'other." His accent was so thick with what Margaret assumed was island patois that he sounded like someone from a costume drama.

She said, "I need to speak to her. It's essential I speak to her. I've been told by my son that she lives in this place"—she tried to make *this place* not sound like *this rubbish tip,* but she decided she could be forgiven if she failed—"but if he's wrong, I'd appreciate your telling me. And then I'll be happy to get out of your hair." Not, Margaret thought, that she wanted to be *in* his hair which, albeit thick, looked unwashed and lousy.

He said, "Your son? Who mightee be?"

"Adrian Brouard. Guy Brouard was his father. I expect you know who he is, don't you? Guy Brouard? I saw you at his funeral reception."

These last remarks seemed to get his attention, for he looked up from his shoveling and inspected Margaret head to toe, after which he silently crossed the lawn to the porch, where he took up a bucket. This was filled with some sort of pellets which he carried to the tree and poured liberally into the trench he'd dug round its trunk. He set down the bucket and moved to the next tree, where he began more digging.

"See here," Margaret said, "I'm looking for Cynthia Moullin. I'd like to speak to her at once, so if you know where I can find her . . . She does live here, doesn't she? This is the Shell House?" Which was, Margaret thought, the most ridiculous question she could have asked. If this wasn't the Shell House, there was a bigger nightmare waiting for her somewhere, and she found that difficult to get her mind round.

"So you're th' first," the man said with a nod. "Always wondered wha' th' first 'as like. Says a lot 'bout a man, his first. Y'know? Tells you why he went the way he went in the afters."

Margaret strained to decipher his words through his accent. She caught every fourth or fifth utterance, and from that she was able to reach the conclusion that the creature was referring in some way that was less than flattering to her sexual partnership with Guy. This wasn't *about* to do. She was meant to have control over the conversation. Men always reduced things to poke-and-thrust if they could. They thought it was an efficacious manoeuvre guaranteed to fluster any woman with whom they spoke. But Margaret Chamberlain was not any woman. And she was gathering her wits to make this clear to the man when a mobile rang and he was forced to fish it out of his pocket, flip it open, and reveal himself as a fraud.

He said, "Henry Moullin," into the phone and listened for nearly a minute. And then in a voice perfectly different from that with which he'd been entertaining Margaret, he said, "I'd first have to do the measurements on the site, Madam. There's no real way I can tell you how long that sort of project would take until I see what I'd be working with." He listened again and in short order dug a black diary out of another pocket. Into this, he scheduled some sort of appointment with someone he called, "Certainly. Happy to do it, Mrs. Felix." He returned the phone to his pocket and looked at Margaret quite as if he hadn't been trying to bamboozle her into believing he was someone shearing sheep outside of Casterbridge.

"Ah," Margaret said with grim pleasantry, "now that we have that out of the way, perhaps you'll answer the question and tell me where I can find Cynthia Moullin. I take it you must be her father?"

He was as unrepentant as he was unembarrassed. He said, "Cyn's not here, Mrs. Brouard."

"Chamberlain," Margaret corrected him. "Where is she? It's essential I speak to her at once."

"Not possible," he said. "She's gone to Alderney. Helping out her gran."

"And this gran has no phone?"

"When it's working, she has one."

"I see. Well, perhaps that's just as well, Mr. Moullin. You and I can sort things out ourselves and she won't have to know a thing about it. Nor will she have to be disappointed."

Moullin removed from his pocket a tube of some sort of ointment, which he squeezed into his palm. He eyed her as he rubbed the mixture into the many cuts on his hands, as if he had not the slightest care that he was also rubbing garden soil into them.

"You'd best tell me what it is," he said, and there was a masculine directness to his manner that was simultaneously disconcerting and somewhat arousing. Margaret had an instant's bizarre vision of herself as woman-to-his-man, sheer animal stuff that she wouldn't have thought possible to entertain. He took a step in her direction and she took a step backwards in reflex. His lips moved in what might have been amusement. A frisson shot through her. She felt like a character in a bad romance novel, one moment away from ravishment.

Which was just enough to infuriate her, enabling her to wrest the upper hand back. "This is something that you and I can probably resolve ourselves, Mr. Moullin. I can't think you wish to be drawn into a protracted legal battle. Am I right?"

"Legal battle over what?"

"The terms of my former husband's will."

A glint in his eye indicated heightened interest. Margaret saw this and realised compromise was something that might work: settling on a lesser sum to avoid having to spend it all on solicitors—or whatever they called them over here—who would hash things out in court for years as if members of the Jarndyce clan had come calling.

She said, "I'm not going to lie to you, Mr. Moullin. Your daughter's been left a considerable fortune in my former husband's will. My son—Guy's oldest child and his only male heir, as you may know—has been left far less. I'm sure you'll agree there's a gross inequity here. So I'd like to set it right without legal recourse."

Margaret hadn't thought in advance about what the man's reaction might be to learning about his daughter's inheritance. In fact, she hadn't much cared what his reaction would be. All she'd thought of was sorting this situation out to Adrian's benefit in any way she could. A person of reason, she'd decided, would see things her way when she laid them out in terms that were tinged with allusions to future litigation.

Henry Moullin said nothing at first. He turned from her. He went back to his digging, but his breathing had altered. It was harsh and his pace was faster than it had been before. He jumped on the shovel and drove it into the ground. Once, twice, three times. As he did so, the back of his neck changed from unsoaped leather to so deep a red that Margaret feared he might have a seizure on the spot. Then he said, "My daughter, God *damn* it," and stopped his digging. He seized the bucket of pellets. He hurled them into the second trench with no regard for how they spilled up and over its sides. He said, "Does he think he can . . . Not for a single God damn *moment* . . ." And before Margaret could say another word, before she could sympathise, however factitiously, with his obvious distress over Guy's intrusion into his ability to support his own child, Henry Moullin grabbed up the shovel again. This time, though, he swung round on her. He raised it and advanced.

Margaret cried out, cringing, hating herself for cringing, hating him for making her cringe, and looking for a quick escape. But her only option for flight was to leap over the shell firestation, the shell chaise longue, the shell tea table, or—like a long-jumper—the shell-crusted pond. As she started to head for the chaise longue, however, Henry Moullin shoved past her and went after the shell firestation. He struck at it blindly, "God *damn*." Fragments flew everywhere. He reduced it to rubble in three brutal blows. He went on to the barn and then to the school while Margaret watched, awestruck by the power of his rage.

He said nothing more. He flung himself from one fanciful shell creation to the next: the schoolhouse, the tea table, the chairs, the pond, the garden of artificial shell flowers. Nothing seemed to spend him. He didn't stop till he'd worked all the way back to the path that led from the drive to the front door. And there he finally threw his shovel at the yellow house itself. It narrowly missed one of the grated front windows. It fell with a clatter onto the walk.

The man himself stood panting. Some of the cuts on his hands had reopened. Fresh cuts had been made by fragments of the shells and the concrete that had held the shells together. His filthy jeans were white with dust, and when he wiped the backs of his hands along them, blood stained that white in feathery streaks.

Margaret said, "Don't!" without even thinking. "Don't let him do this to you, Henry Moullin."

He stared at her, breathing hard, blinking as if this would somehow clear his head. All aggression seeped out of him. He looked round at the devastation he'd wrought in the front of his house and he said, "Bastard had two already."

JoAnna's girls, Margaret thought. Guy had his daughters. He'd had and lost the opportunity for fatherhood given to him. But he hadn't been a man to take such a loss lightly, so he'd replaced all of his abandoned children with others, others much more likely to turn a blind eye to the faults so apparent to his own flesh and blood. For they were poor, and he was rich. Money bought love and devotion where it could.

Margaret said, "You need to see to your hands. You've cut them. They're bleeding. No, don't wipe them—"

But he did so anyway, adding more streaks onto the dust and grime on his jeans and, when that didn't suffice, wiping them on his dust-caked work shirt as well. He said, "We don't want his damn money. We don't need it. You can set fire to it in Trinity Square for all it means to us."

Margaret thought he might have said that at first and saved them both from a frightening scene, not to mention saved the front garden as well. She said, "I'm very happy to hear that, Mr. Moullin. It's only fair to Adrian—"

"But it's Cyn's money, isn't it," Henry Moullin went on, dashing her hopes as effectively as he'd dashed to pieces the creations of shell and cement that surrounded them. "If Cyn wants the payoff . . ." He trudged to the shovel where it lay on the path to the door. He picked it up. He did the same to a rake and a dustpan. Once he had them, however, he gazed round, as if unsure what he'd been doing with them in the first place.

He looked at Margaret and she saw that his eyes were bloodlined with grief. He said, "He comes here. I go there. We work side by side for years. And it's: You're a real artist, Henry. You aren't meant to do greenhouse work all your life. It's: Break out and break away from it, man. I believe in you. I'll help you a bit. Let me take you on. Nothing ventured, nothing ever God damn gained. And I believed him, see. I wanted it. More than this life here. For my girls, I wanted it, yes, for my girls. But for me as well. Where's the sin in that?"

"No sin," Margaret said. "We all want the best for our children, don't we? I do, too. That's why I'm here, because of Adrian. My son and Guy's. Because of what was done to him. He was cheated out of his due, Mr. Moullin. You do see how wrong that is, don't you?"

"We were all cheated," Henry Moullin said. "Your ex-husband was good at that. He spent years setting every one of us up, biding his time with us all. Not a man to take, our Mr. Brouard, not a man to operate wrong side of the law. Wrong side of what was *moral,* see. Wrong side of what was dutiful and right. He had us lapping milk from his hands without our knowing he'd put poison in it."

"Don't you want to be part of making that right?" Margaret said. "You can, you know. You can talk to your daughter, you can explain. We wouldn't ask Cynthia to give up all the money he's left her. We'd only want to make things even, a reflection of who is Guy's blood and who isn't."

"That's what you want?" Henry Moullin said. "That's what you think will balance the scales? You're just like him, then, aren't you, Missus? Think money makes up for every sin. But it doesn't, and it never will."

"You won't talk to her, then? You won't explain? We're going to have to take this to another level?"

"You don't get it, do you?" Henry Moullin asked. "There *is* no talking to my girl any longer. There *is* no explaining left to be done."

He turned and carried his tools the way he'd come with the shovel just a few minutes earlier. He disappeared round the side of the house.

Margaret stood for a moment, unmoving on the path, and found herself for the first time in her life at a loss for words. She felt nearly overwhelmed by the strength of the hate that Henry Moullin left behind him. It was like a current that pulled her into a tide from which there was only the barest hope of escape.

Where she least expected to find it, she felt a kinship with this disheveled man. She understood what he was going through. One's children were one's own, belonging to no one else in quite the same way they belonged to you. They were not the same as one's spouse, one's parents, one's siblings, one's partners, or one's mates. One's children were *of* one's body and soul. No intruder easily broke the bond that was created from that kind of substance.

But if an intruder attempted or, God forbid, succeeded . . . ?

No one knew better than Margaret Chamberlain the extent someone might go to in order to preserve a relationship one had with his child.

Chapter 13

St. James stopped at the hotel first when he returned to St. Peter Port, but he found their room empty and no message at reception from his wife. So he went on to the police station, where he interrupted DCI Le Gallez in the midst of wolfing down a baguette crammed with prawn salad. The DCI took him to his office, offering a portion of his sandwich (which St. James refused) and a cup of coffee (which St. James accepted). He put chocolate digestives on offer as well, but since they looked as if their coating had melted and reconstituted itself one time too many, St. James declined and made do with the coffee alone.

He brought Le Gallez into the picture with regard to the wills of the Brouards, brother and sister. Le Gallez listened as he chewed, and he jotted notes on a legal pad that he snared from a plastic in-and-out box on his desk. As St. James spoke, he watched the DCI underline *Fielder* and *Moullin,* adding a question mark next to the second name. Le Gallez interrupted the flow of information to explain that he knew about the dead man's relationship with Paul Fielder, but Cynthia Moullin's was a new name to come up. He also jotted down the facts of the Brouard wills and listened politely as St. James posited a theory he'd considered on the way back to town.

The earlier will that Ruth Brouard knew about remembered individuals deleted from the more recent document: Anaïs Abbott, Frank Ouseley, Kevin and Valerie Duffy, along with Guy Brouard's children as required by law. This being the case, she had asked those individuals to be present when the will was read. If, St. James pointed out to Le Gallez, any of those beneficiaries had known about the earlier will, they had a clear motive to do away with Guy Brouard, hoping to collect sooner rather than later what was coming to them.

"Fielder and Moullin weren't in the earlier will?" Le Gallez enquired.

"She didn't mention them," St. James replied, "and as neither was present when the will was read this afternoon, I think it's safe to conclude that the legacies they were left came as a surprise to Miss Brouard."

"But to them?" Le Gallez asked. "They might have been told by Brouard himself. Which puts them in the frame with motives as well. Wouldn't you say?"

"I suppose it's possible." He didn't think it likely, considering the two were teenagers, but he welcomed any indication that Le Gallez's thinking was, at least for the moment, encompassing something more than China River's putative guilt.

Seeing the inspector's thoughts ranging wider

than they had been earlier, St. James hated to do anything that might remind Le Gallez of his previous mindset, but he knew that his conscience would never rest unless he was completely honest with the other man. "On the other hand . . ." St. James felt reluctant to do so—his loyalty to his wife seemed to call for a similar loyalty to her friends—and despite knowing how the inspector was likely to react to the information, he next handed over the material that Ruth Brouard had passed to him during their last conversation. The DCI flipped through Guy Brouard's passport first, then went on to the credit card bills and the receipts. He spent a moment studying the receipt from the Citrus Grille, tapping his pencil against it as he took another bite of his sandwich. After some thought, he swung his chair round and reached for a manila folder. He opened this to reveal a set of typed notes, which he fingered through till he found what he apparently wanted.

"Postal codes," he said to St. James. "They both begin with nine two. Nine two eight and nine two six."

"One of them is Cherokee River's, I take it?"

"You knew already?"

"I know he lives somewhere in the area Brouard visited."

"The second code's his," Le Gallez said. "The nine two six. The other is this restaurant's: the Citrus Grille. What does that suggest to you?"

"That Guy Brouard and Cherokee River passed some time in the same county."

"Nothing more, then?"

"How can it suggest more? California's a large state. Its counties are probably large as well. I'm not sure anyone can extrapolate from postal codes that Brouard and River met prior to River's coming to the island with his sister."

"You find nothing coincidental in this? Nothing suspiciously coincidental?"

"I would do, yes, if we had only the facts right in front of us at this moment: the passport, the receipts, and Cherokee River's home address. But a lawyer—no doubt with a similar postal code—hired River to deliver architectural plans to Guernsey. So it seems reasonable to assume that Guy Brouard was in California, meeting that lawyer—as well as the architect, who probably also has a similar postal code—and not with Cherokee River. I don't expect they knew each other till the moment River and his sister arrived at *Le Reposoir.*"

"But you'll agree that we can't discount it?"

"I'd say we can't discount anything."

Which, St. James knew, included the ring that he and Deborah had found at the bay. He asked DCI Le Gallez about this, about the possibility of there being fingerprints upon it, or at least a partial print that might be useful to the police. The ring's appearance suggested it hadn't been lying on the beach for any length of time, he pointed out. But no doubt the DCI had himself already reached that conclusion when he'd examined it.

Le Gallez set his sandwich aside and wiped his fingers on a paper napkin. He took up a cup of coffee that he'd been ignoring as he ate, and he cradled it in his palm before he spoke. The two words he said made St. James's heart sink.

"What ring?"

Bronze, brass, some baser metal, St. James told him. It was fashioned into a skull and crossed bones with the numbers thirty-nine-stroke-forty on the skull's forehead along with an inscription in German. He'd sent it into the station earlier with instructions that it be handed over to DCI Le Gallez personally.

He didn't add that his own wife had been the courier because he was in the process of steadying himself to hear the inevitable from the DCI. He was already asking himself what that inevitable meant, although he thought he knew the answer.

"Haven't seen it," Le Gallez told him, and he picked up the phone and rang reception to make sure the ring wasn't waiting for him below. He spoke to the duty officer in charge, describing the ring as St. James had done. He grunted when the officer made a reply and he eyed St. James as he listened at some length to a recitation on one subject or another. He finally said, "Well, bring it *up* here, man," which allowed St. James to breathe easily again. He went on with "For God's sake, Jerry, I'm not the person to grouse to about the bloody fax machine. Just sort it out and have done with it, will you?" and he slammed down the phone with a curse and dashed St. James's peace of mind a second time in three minutes when he next spoke.

"No ring in sight. Want to tell me more about it, then?"

"There may have been a misunderstanding." Or a traffic accident, St. James wanted to add, although he knew this was an impossibility since he'd taken the same route his wife would have taken to return from *Le Reposoir* and there hadn't been so much as a broken headlamp on the road to suggest a car crash had kept Deborah from fulfilling her duty. Not that anyone drove fast enough on the island for a car crash, anyway. A minor collision, perhaps, with bumpers crunching or wings denting. But that would be the extent of it. Even that wouldn't have kept her from bringing the ring to Le Gallez as he'd instructed her to do.

"A misunderstanding." Le Gallez spoke with far less affability now. "Yes. I do see, Mr. St. James. We've got ourselves a misunderstanding." He looked up as a figure appeared in his doorway, a uniformed officer bearing paperwork in his hand. Le Gallez waved him off for a moment. He got up from his seat and shut the door of his office. He faced St. James with his arms crossed over his chest. He said, "I don't much mind if you nose about, Mr. St. James. It's a free you-know-what, and if you want to talk to this bloke or that bloke and he doesn't mind, it's fine by me. But when you start messing about with evidence, we've got another situation entirely."

"I do understand. I—"

"I don't think so. You've come here with your mind made up, and if you think I'm not aware of that and where it can lead, you'd best think again. Now, I want that ring. I want it at once. We'll deal later with where it's been since you lifted it off the beach. *And* with why you lifted it, by the way. Because you know bloody damn well what you ought to've done. Have I made myself clear?"

St. James hadn't been reprimanded since adolescence, and the experience—so similar to being dressed down by an outraged schoolmaster—wasn't pleasant. His skin crawled with the mortification of the moment, made worse because he knew he richly deserved it. But that didn't make the ordeal any less chastening, nor did it go any length to soften the blow this moment could do to his reputation should he not be able to handle the situation expeditiously.

He said, "I'm not sure what happened. But you have my most profound apologies. The ring—"

"I don't *want* your bloody apologies," Le Gallez barked. "I want that ring."

"You'll have it directly."

"That, Mr. St. James, damn well better be the case." The DCI stepped away from the door and swung it open.

St. James couldn't remember a time he'd been dismissed with so little ceremony. He stepped out into the hall, where the uniformed officer stood waiting with his paperwork in hand. The man averted his eyes, as if with embarrassment, and hurried into the DCI's office.

Le Gallez slammed the door shut behind him. But not before he snapped, "Sodding little cripple," as a parting remark.

• • •

Virtually all the dealers in antiques on Guernsey were in St. Peter Port, Deborah found. As one might expect, they were in the oldest part of the town, not far from the harbour. Rather than visit them all, however, she suggested to Cherokee that they begin on the phone. So they retraced their steps down to the market and from there they crossed over to the Town Church. To one side of it stood the public telephone they needed, and while Cherokee waited and watched her earnestly, Deborah fed coins into the phone and rang up the antiques shops till she was able to isolate those that offered militaria. It seemed logical to begin there, broadening the investigation if they found it necessary.

As things turned out, only two shops in the town had military items among their merchandise. Both of them were in Mill Street, a cobbled pedestrian walkway snaking from the meat market up a hillside, wisely closed to traffic. Not, Deborah thought as they found it, that a car could have possibly passed along the street without running the risk of scraping the buildings on either side. It reminded her of the Shambles in York: slightly wider, but just as redolent of a past in which horse-drawn carts would have lurched along, acting the part of transport.

Small shops along Mill Street reflected a simpler period, defined by spare decoration and no-nonsense windows and doors. They were housed in buildings that might easily have served as homes, with three trim floors, dormer windows, and chimney pots lined up like waiting schoolboys on their roofs.

There were few people about in the area, which was some distance from the main shopping and banking precincts of the High Street and its extension, *Le Pollet*. Indeed, it seemed to Deborah as she and Cherokee looked for the first name and address which she'd scribbled upon the back of a blank cheque, that even the most optimistic of retailers stood a good chance of failure if he opened a shop here. Many of the buildings were vacant, with *to let* or *for sale* signs in their windows. When they located the first of the two shops they were seeking, its front window was hung with a droopy going-out-of-business banner that looked as if it had been passed round from shop owner to shop owner for quite some time.

John Steven Mitchell Antiques offered little in the way of military memorabilia. Perhaps owing to its imminent closure, the shop contained only a single display case whose contents had a military origin. These comprised mainly medals, although three dress daggers, five pistols, and two *Wehrmacht* hats accompanied them. While Deborah found this a disappointing show, she decided that since everything in the case was German in origin, matters might actually be more hopeful than they appeared.

She and Cherokee were bent over the case, studying its merchandise, when the shop owner—presumably John Steven Mitchell himself—joined them. They'd apparently interrupted his washing up after a meal, if his stained apron and damp hands were any indication. He offered his help pleasantly enough as he wiped his hands on an unappealingly dingy dishcloth.

Deborah brought forth the ring that she and Simon had found on the beach, careful not to touch it herself and asking John Steven Mitchell not to touch it either. Did he recognise this ring? she asked him. Could he tell them anything about it?

Mitchell fetched a pair of spectacles from the top of a till and bent over the ring where Deborah had placed it on the case of military items. He took up a magnifying glass as well, and he studied the inscription on the forehead of the skull.

"Western bulwark," he murmured. "Thirty-nine, forty." He paused as if considering his own words. "That's the translation of *die Festung im Westen*. And the year . . . Actually, it suggests a memento of some sort of defensive construction. But it could be a metaphorical reference to the assault on Denmark. On the other hand, the skull and crossed bones were specific to the *Waffen-SS,* so there's that connection as well."

"But it's not something from the Occupation?" Deborah asked.

"It would have been left then, when the Germans surrendered to the Allies. But it wouldn't have been directly connected to the Occupation. The dates aren't right for that. And the term *die Festung im Westen* doesn't have any meaning here."

"Why's that?" Cherokee had kept his eyes on the ring while Mitchell was examining it, but he raised them now.

"Because of the implication," Mitchell answered. "They built tunnels, of course. Fortifications, gun emplacements, observation towers, hospitals, the lot. Even a railway. But not an actual bulwark. And even if they had done, this is commemorating something from a year before the Occupation began." He bent to it a second time with his magnifying glass. "I've never actually seen anything like it. Are you considering selling?"

No, no, Deborah told him. They were only trying to find out where it had come from since from its condition it was obvious it hadn't been lying out in the open since 1945. Antiques shops had seemed the logical place for them to start looking for information.

"I see," Mitchell told them. Well, if information was what they wanted, they'd be wise to speak to the Potters just up the street. Potter and Potter Antiques, Jeanne and Mark, a mother and son, he clarified. She was a porcelain expert and wouldn't be much help. But there was very little about the German army in the Second World War that he didn't know.

In short order, Deborah and Cherokee were in Mill Street again, this time climbing higher, past a shadowy opening between two buildings that was called Back Lane. Just beyond this alley, they found Potter and Potter. Unlike the previous shop, this one looked like a viable enterprise.

Potter the mother was in attendance, they found as they went in. She sat in a rocking chair with her slippered feet on a tufted hassock, and she gave her attention to the screen of a television no bigger than a shoe box. On it she was watching a film: Audrey Hepburn and Albert Finney driving in the country-side in a vintage MG. A car not unlike Simon's, Deborah saw, and for the first time since making the decision to bypass the police station in favour of seeking out China River, she felt a twinge. It was like a string pulling at her conscience, a thread that might unravel if tugged upon too strongly. She couldn't call it guilt, exactly, because she knew she had nothing about which she ought to be feeling guilty. But it was definitely something unpleasant, a bad psychic taste that wanted getting rid of. She wondered why she felt it at all. How maddening, really, to be in the middle of something important and to have something else make an unreasonable attempt to claim one's attention.

Cherokee, she saw, had found the military section of the shop, and it was considerable. Unlike John Steven Mitchell Antiques, Potter and Potter offered everything from old gas masks to Nazi napkin rings. They even had an anti-aircraft gun for sale, along with an ancient cine projector and a film called *Eine gute Sache*. Cherokee had gone straight for a display case with electric shelves that rose and fell on a tumbler one after another upon the push of a button. In here the Potters kept medals, badges, and insignia from military uniforms. China's brother was scanning each shelf. One foot nervously tapping the floor told the tale of how intent he was on finding something that might prove useful to his sister's situation.

Potter the Mother roused herself from Audrey and Albert. She was plump, with thyroid-troubled eyes that were nonetheless friendly when she spoke to Deborah. "Can I help, love?"

"With something military?"

"It'll be my Mark you want." She padded to a half-closed door, which she opened to reveal a stairway. She walked like a woman who needed a hip replacement, one hand holding on to whatever she happened to pass. She called upstairs for her son, and his disembodied voice replied. She told him there were customers below and he'd have to leave off the computer for now. "Internet," she said to Deborah confidentially. "I think it's as bad as heroin, I do."

Mark Potter clattered down the stairs, looking very little like an addict of anything. Despite the time of year, he was very tanned, and his movements radiated vitality.

What could he do for them? he wanted to know. What were they looking for? He was getting in new items all the time—"People die, but their collections remain, all the better for the rest of us, if you ask me"—so if there was something they were looking for that he didn't have, chances were quite good he could get it for them.

Deborah brought forth the ring again. Mark Potter's face brightened when he saw it. "Another one!" he cried. "How extraordinary! I've seen only one of those in all the years I've been dealing. And now another. How'd you come upon it?"

Jeanne Potter joined her son on the other side of the cabinet, where Deborah had placed the ring with the same request she'd made at the other shop that they not touch it. She said, "That's just like the one you sold, love, isn't it?" And to Deborah, "We had it here ever so long. Bit grim, it was, just like that one. Never thought we'd sell it. Not everyone likes that sort of thing, do they?"

"Did you sell it recently?" Deborah asked.

The Potters looked at each other. She said, "When . . . ?"

He said, "Ten days? Perhaps two weeks?"

"Who bought it?" Cherokee asked. "D'you remember?"

"Definitely," Mark Potter said.

And his mother, with a smile, "You would, love. Always the eye, you have."

Potter grinned, said, "That's not it, and you know it. Stop teasing me, you silly old cow." Then he spoke to Deborah. "An American lady. I remember because we get few enough Americans on Guernsey and never any at this time of year. Well, why would we? They've got bigger places on their minds for travel than the Channel Islands, haven't they?"

Next to her, Deborah heard Cherokee's intake of breath. She said, "You're certain she was American?"

"California lady. I heard her accent and asked. Mum did as well."

Jeanne Potter nodded. "We talked about movie stars," she said. "I've never been myself, but I always thought if you lived in California you saw them walking about the streets. She said no, that wasn't the case."

"Harrison Ford," Mark Potter said. "Don't tell fibs, Mum."

She laughed and looked flustered. "Go *on* with you, then." And then to Deborah, "I quite like Harrison. That little scar on his chin? Something so manly about him."

"You're very naughty," Mark told her. "What would Dad've thought?"

Cherokee interposed, saying hopefully, "What did she look like? The American lady? Do you remember?"

They didn't see much of her, as things turned out. She had a head wrap on—Mark thought it was a scarf; his mother thought it was a hood—and it covered her hair and dropped over the top part of her face. As the light wasn't all that bright inside the shop, and as it was likely raining that day . . . They couldn't add much about what she looked like. She was all in black, though, if that was any help. And she was wearing leather trousers, Jeanne Potter recalled. She remembered them especially, those leather trousers. Just the sort of thing *she* would've liked to wear at that age had they existed then and had she ever had the figure for them, which she had not.

Deborah didn't look at Cherokee, but she didn't have to. She'd told him where she and Simon had found the ring, so she knew he was despairing at this new bit of information. He did try to make the best of it, though, because he asked the Potters if there was any place else on the island where a ring like this—*another* ring like this, he emphasised—might have come from.

Both of the Potters considered the question, and ultimately Mark was the one to answer. There was only one place, he informed them, that another ring like this might have come from. He named the place, and when he did so, his mother seconded the notion at once.

Out in the Talbot Valley, Mark said, lived a serious collector of wartime lumber. He had more items than the rest of the island put together.

He was called Frank Ouseley, Jeanne Potter added, and he lived with his father in a place called *Moulin des Niaux*.

Speaking to Nobby Debiere about the potential demise of the plans to build a museum hadn't been easy for Frank. He'd done it, though, out of a sense of obligation to the man whom he'd failed in so many ways as a youth. Next he was going to have to speak to his father. He owed Graham Ouseley much as well, but it was lunacy to think that he could forever pretend their dreams were being incarnated just down the lane from St. Saviour's Church, as his father expected.

He could, of course, still approach Ruth about the project. Or, for that matter, he could speak with Adrian Brouard, his sisters—providing he could find them—and Paul Fielder and Cynthia Moullin as well. The advocate hadn't named any actual sum of money these individuals stood to inherit since that would be in the hands of bankers, brokers, and forensic accountants. But there had to be a huge amount involved because it was impossible to believe that Guy might have disposed of *Le Reposoir,* its contents, and his other properties in whatever way he'd disposed of them, without assuring his own future with an enormous bank account and a portfolio of investments with which to replenish that account if necessary. He was far too clever for that.

Speaking to Ruth would be the most efficacious method of moving the project forward. She was the likeliest candidate to be the legal owner of *Le Reposoir*—however this manoeuvre had been effected—and if that was the case, she might be manipulated into feeling a duty to fulfill her brother's promises to people, perhaps agreeing to build a humbler version of the Graham Ouseley Wartime Museum in the grounds of *Le Reposoir* itself, which would allow the sale of the land they'd acquired for the museum near St. Saviour's, which would in turn help to fund the building. On the other hand, he could speak to Guy's heirs and try to wring the funding from them, persuading them to construct what would in effect be a memorial to their benefactor.

He could do that, Frank knew, and he should do that. Indeed, had he been another sort of man altogether, he *would* do that. But there were other considerations beyond the creation of a structure to house more than half a century's amassment of military goods. No matter how much such a structure might have enlightened the people of Guernsey, no matter what such a structure could have done to establish Nobby Debiere as an architect in the public arena, the truth of the matter was that Frank's personal world was going to be a far better place without a wartime museum in it.

So he wouldn't be speaking to Ruth about carrying on her brother's noble work. Nor would he corral any of the others with the hope of squeezing funds from them. As far as Frank was concerned, the matter was over. The museum was as dead as Guy Brouard.

Frank squeezed his old Peugeot into the track that led to *Moulin des Niaux*. As he jolted the fifty yards to the water mill, he noted how overgrown the way had become. The brambles were fast overtaking the asphalt. There would be plenty of blackberries in the coming summer, but no road to get to the mill or its cottages if he didn't do something to cut back the branches, ivy, holly, and ferns.

He knew he *could* do something about the undergrowth now. Having made his decision, having drawn the metaphorical line in the nonexistent sand at long last, he had bought himself a degree of freedom that he hadn't even realised he'd been missing. That freedom opened up his world, even to thinking about something as ordinary as trimming bushes. How odd it was, he thought, to be obsessed. The rest of the world simply faded away when one submitted oneself to the constricting embrace of single fixation.

He turned in the gate just beyond the water

wheel and crunched over the gravel on the drive. He parked at the end of the cottages, the Peugeot's bonnet pointing towards the stream that he could hear but not see through a thicket of elms long since overgrown with ivy. This trailed from branches nearly to the ground like an invitation from Rapunzel. It provided a useful screen from the main road through the Talbot Valley, but at the same time it hid a pleasant burbling stream from the garden where deck chairs in spring and summer could have allowed one to enjoy it. More work needing done round the cottages, Frank realised. Yet another indication of how much he'd let everything go.

In the house, he found his father nodding in his chair with pages of the *Guernsey Press* scattered like overlarge playing cards round him on the floor. Frank realised as he saw the paper that he hadn't told Mrs. Petit to keep it from his father, so he had an uneasy few moments as he gathered the pages up and scanned them for a mention of Guy's death. He breathed more easily when he saw there was none today. Tomorrow would be different with coverage of the funeral. For today, he was safe.

He went on to the kitchen where he put the newspaper back into order and set about making their tea. On her final visit to Graham, Mrs. Petit had thoughtfully brought a pie along with her, and she'd affixed a jaunty label to its tin. *Chicken & leek, enjoy!* was written on a from-Betty's-kitchen card woven through the plastic tines of a miniature pitchfork upended and driven through the crust.

This would do nicely, Frank thought. He filled

the kettle and rooted out the tea tin. He spooned English Breakfast into the pot.

He was setting the plates and the cutlery on the table mats when his father stirred in the sitting room. Frank heard him give an awakening snort first, followed by the startled gasp of someone who hadn't intended to fall asleep.

"Time's it?" Graham Ouseley called out. "That you, Frank?"

Frank went to the door. He saw that his father's chin was wet and that a string of saliva had followed a groove from his mouth to form a stalactite of phlegm on his jaw.

"Getting our tea," he said.

"How long you been home?"

"A few minutes. You were asleep. I didn't like to wake you. How'd you get on with Mrs. Petit?"

"She helped me to the toilet. I don't like women in the toilet with me, Frank." Graham plucked at the blanket that was covering his knees. "Where you been all these hours? What time's it gone?"

Frank looked at the old alarm clock on the cooker. He was surprised to see it was after four. "Let me ring Mrs. Petit so she doesn't think she's meant to pop round any longer," he said. After he'd done that, he went back to answer his father's question, only to find him nodding off again. The blanket had slipped, so Frank adjusted it, tucking it in round Graham's spindly legs and easing back the old man's chair to keep his head from flopping onto his bony chest. With a handkerchief, he wiped his father's chin and removed the stringy saliva from his jaw. Old age, he thought, was a real bugger. Once a man's three-score-and-ten was exceeded, he was on the slippery slope to complete incapacity.

He got their tea ready: high tea in the old manner of labourers. He heated the pie and sliced wedges from it. He put out a salad and buttered the bread. When the food was laid out and the tea was brewed, he went to fetch Graham and brought him into the kitchen. He could have served him on a tray in his chair, but he wanted them to be face-to-face for the conversation that they needed to have. Face-to-face implied man-to-man: two men speaking, not a father and his son.

Graham ate the chicken-and-leek pie appreciatively, the affront at having been taken to the toilet by Mrs. Petit forgotten in the pleasure of her cooking. He even had a second helping, a rare occurrence for a man who normally consumed less food than an adolescent girl.

Frank decided to allow him to enjoy the meal before he broke the news. So they dined mostly in silence, with Frank meditating on the best approach into their conversation and Graham commenting only sporadically on the food, mostly on the gravy, which was the best he'd had, he declared, since Frank's mum passed on. That was how he always referred to Grace Ouseley's drowning. The tragedy at the reservoir—Graham and Grace thrashing in the water and only one of them emerging alive—had been lost to time.

The food spurred Graham's thoughts from his wife to wartime and specifically to the Red Cross parcels the islanders had at long last received when the lack of supplies on Guernsey had reduced the populace to parsnip coffee and sugar beet syrup. From Canada had come an unthinkable largesse, Graham informed his son: chocolate biscuits, my lad, and didn't they go a treat with real tea? sardines and milk powder, tins of salmon and prunes and ham and corned beef. Ah, it was a fine, *fine* day when the Red Cross parcels proved to the people of Guernsey that, small though the island was, it was not forgotten by the rest of the world.

"An' we needed to see that, we did," Graham declared. "The Jerrys might've wanted us to think their bloody sod of a Führer was going to walk on water and multiply the loaves once the world was his, but we'd've died, Frankie, before he passed as much as a sausage in *our* direction."

A smear of gravy was on Graham's chin, and Frank leaned forward and wiped it off. He said, "Those times were tough."

"But people don't know it like they ought, do they? Oh, they think of the Jews and the gypsies, they do. They think of places like Holland and France. And the Blitz. Bloody hell, how they think of the Blitz, which the *noble* English—those very same English whose bloody king *abandoned* us to the Jerrys, mind you, with a farewell-for-now-and-I-know-you'll-get-on-with-the-enemy-lads-and-lasses . . ." Graham had a gobbet of chicken pie on his fork and he held it shakily in the air, where it hung suspended like an example of those German bombers and just as likely to drop its load.

Frank leaned forward again and gently guided the fork to his father's mouth. Graham accepted the chicken, chewing and talking at once. "They still live it, those English, Frank. London gets bombed and the world is meant never to forget it for fifteen seconds, while here . . . ? Hell. We may's well've just been minor *inconvenienced,* for all the memories the world has of what happened. Never you mind the port getting bombed—twenty-nine dead in that, Frankie, and never a weapon we even had to defend ourselves—and those poor Jew ladies sent to the camps and the executions of whoever they chose to call a spy. It might've not happened for all the world knows. But we shall soon fix that up right and proper. Won't we, boy?"

So here was the moment at last, Frank thought. He wouldn't have to manufacture an entrée to the conversation he needed to have with his father. All he had to do was to seize the day, so he made the decision before he could talk himself out of it and said, "Dad, there's something come up, I'm afraid. I haven't wanted to tell you about it. I know what the museum means to you, and I guess I didn't have the nerve to put a spanner in the dream."

Graham cocked his head and presented to his son what he always claimed was his better ear. "Say again?" he said.

Frank knew for a fact that there was nothing wrong with his father's hearing unless something was being said that he preferred not to hear. So he just went on. Guy Brouard, he told his father, had passed away a week ago. His death was quite sudden and unexpected and clearly he'd been fit as a fiddle and unthinking of his own demise since he'd not considered what his passing might do to their plans for the wartime museum.

"Wha's this?" Graham shook his head as if trying to clear it. "You say Guy's *dead*? That's not what you're saying, is it, my boy?"

Unfortunately, Frank said, that's exactly what he was saying. And the fact of the matter was that, for some reason, Guy Brouard hadn't provided for every eventuality in the fashion one might have expected of him. His will left no money for the wartime museum, so the plan to build it was going to be shelved.

Graham said, "Doing what?" as he swallowed his food and with a trembling hand took up his milky tea. "Set out mines, they did. *Schrapnellemine* Thirty-fives. Demolition charges, too. *Riegel* mines. Put up warning flags but think what it was like. Little yellow banners telling us not to set foot on what was ours. The world's got to know this, laddie. Got to know we used carageen moss for our jelly."

"I know, Dad. It's important that no one forgets." Frank had little appetite for the rest of his pie. He pushed the plate towards the centre of the table and scooted his chair so that he was speaking directly into his father's ear. No mistaking what I'm telling you, his actions said. Listen up, Dad. Things have changed for good. He said, "Dad, there's not going to be a museum. We don't have the money. We were depending on Guy to finance the building and he's not left funds in his will to do that. Now, I know you can hear me, Dad, and I'm sorry to say it, *that* sorry, believe me. I wouldn't have told you at all—I didn't actually plan to tell you Guy had passed away—but once I heard his will read, I felt I didn't have the choice. I'm sorry." And he told himself that he *was* sorry although that was only part of his tale.

Graham's hand splashed hot tea onto his chest as he tried to raise the cup to his lips. Frank reached forward to steady his movement, but Graham jerked away from him, spilling more. He wore a thick waistcoat fully buttoned over his flannel shirt, so the liquid didn't scald him. And it seemed more important to him to avoid contact with his son than to dampen his clothes. "Me and you," Graham muttered, his eyes looking dim. "We had our plan, Frankie."

Frank wouldn't have thought he could feel so wretchedly wounded as he watched his father's defences fall. The sensation, he thought, was akin to seeing a Goliath drop to his knees in front of him. He said, "Dad, I wouldn't hurt you for the world. If I knew of a way to build your museum without Guy's help, I'd do it. But there is no way. The cost's too high. We've got no course left but to let the idea go."

"People need to know," Graham Ouseley protested, but his voice was weak and neither tea nor food was of interest to him any longer. "No one's meant to forget."

"I agree." Frank sorted through his thoughts to find a way to ease the blow's pain. "Perhaps, in time, we'll find a way to make that happen."

Graham's shoulders drooped and he looked round the kitchen, like a sleepwalker awakened and confused. His hands fell to his lap and began to crumple his table napkin convulsively. His mouth worked upon words that he didn't say. His glance took in familiar objects and he seemed to cling to them for what they afforded him of comfort. He pushed away from the table and Frank rose as well, thinking his father wanted the toilet, his bed, or his chair in the sitting room. But as he took Graham's elbow, the old man resisted. What he wanted, it turned out, was on the work top where Frank had placed it, neatly refolded to its tabloid size with the shield of two crosses offset between the word *Guernsey* and its fellow, *Press.*

Graham snatched up the newspaper and clutched it to his chest. "So be it," he said to Frank. "The way's different, but the outcome's the same. That's what counts."

Frank tried to suss out the connection his father was making between the dissolution of their plans and the island's newspaper. He said doubtfully, "I expect the paper will run the story. From that we might interest a tax exile or two in making donations. But as to whether we'd be able to bring in enough cash from just an article in the paper . . . I don't think we can depend on it, Dad. Even if we could, this sort of thing takes years." He didn't add the rest: that at ninety-two his father hardly possessed those years.

Graham said, "I'll ring 'em up myself. They'll come. They'll be interested, they will. Once they know, they'll come running." He even took three doddering steps towards the telephone, and he lifted the receiver as if he meant to make the call forthwith.

Frank said, "I don't think we can expect the paper to see the story with the same sort of urgency, Dad. They'll probably cover it. It's got human interest value, for certain. But I don't think you ought to get your hopes—"

"It's time," Graham persisted, as if Frank had not spoken. "I promised myself. Before I die, I'll do it, I told myself. There's those who kept the faith and those who didn't. And the time has come. Before I die, Frank." He rustled through some magazines that lay on the work top beneath a collection of a few days' post. He said, "Where's that directory gone to? What's the number, boy? Let's make the call."

But Frank was fixated on keeping the faith and breaking the faith and what his father actually meant. There were a thousand different ways to do each in life—keep or break faith—but in wartime when a land was occupied, there was only one. He said carefully, "Dad, I don't think . . ." God, he thought, how to stop his father from so reckless a course? "Listen, this isn't a good way to go about it. And it's far too soon—"

"Time's going," Graham said. "Time's almost gone. I swore to myself. I swore on their graves. They died for *G.I.F.T.* and no one paid. But now they shall. That's the way it is." He unearthed the directory from a drawer of tea towels and table mats, and although it was no thick volume, he heaved it

with a grunt to the work top. He began to leaf
through it and his breath came fast, like a runner
near the end of the race.

Frank said in a final effort to stop him, "Dad,
we've got to assemble the proof."

"We've *got* the bloody proof. It's all up here." He
pointed to his skull with a crooked finger, badly
healed during wartime in his futile flight from discovery: the Gestapo coming for the men behind
G.I.F.T., betrayed by someone on the island in
whom they'd put their trust. Two of the four men
responsible for the news-sheet had died in prison.
Another had died attempting to escape. Only Graham had survived, but not unscathed. And not
without the memory of three good lives lost in the
cause of freedom and at the hands of a whisperer
too long unidentified. The tacit agreement between
politicians in England and politicians on the island
precluded investigation and punishment once the
war was over. Bygones were supposed to be bygones, and since evidence was deemed to be insufficient "to warrant the institution of criminal
proceedings," those whose self-interest had brought
about the death of their fellows lived on untouched
by their pasts, into a future their own acts had denied men far better than they themselves were. Part
of the museum project would have set that record
straight. Without the museum's collaboration section, the record into eternity would be as it was:
the fact of betrayal locked in the minds of those
who committed it and those who were affected
by it. Everyone else would be allowed to live on

without the knowledge of who had paid the price for the freedoms they now enjoyed and who had forced that fate upon them.

"But, Dad," Frank said although he knew he spoke in vain, "you're going to be asked for more proof than your word alone. You must know that."

"Well, see about getting it out of all that clobber," Graham said with a nod towards the wall to indicate the cottages next door, where their collection was housed. "We'll have it ready for them when they come. Get on with it, boy."

"But, Dad—"

"No!" Graham slammed his frail fist down onto the directory and he shook the telephone receiver at his son. "You get on with it and you do it now. No nonsense, Frank. I'm naming names."

Chapter 14

DEBORAH AND CHEROKEE SAID very little on their way back to the Queen Margaret Apartments. The wind had come up and a light rain was falling, which gave them the excuse for silence, Deborah sheltering herself beneath an umbrella and Cherokee hunching his shoulders and turning up the collar of his coat. They retraced their route back down Mill Street and crossed the small square. The area was completely deserted, save for a yellow van parked in the middle of Market Street, into which an empty display case was being loaded from one of the vacant butcher's stalls. It was a dismal indication of the market's demise, and as if making a comment on the proceedings, one of the removal men stumbled and dropped his end of the case. Its glass shattered; its side dented. His partner cursed him for a bloody clumsy fool.

"Tha's gonna cost us big!" he shouted.

What the other man said was lost as Deborah and Cherokee turned the corner and began ascending Constitution Steps. But the thought was there, hanging between them: that which they'd done was costing them big.

Cherokee was the one to break their silence. Midway up the hill, where the steps turned, he paused and said Deborah's name. She stopped in her climb and looked at him. The rain, she saw, had beaded his curly hair with a net of tiny drops that caught the light and his eyelashes spiked childlike with the damp. He was shivering. They were protected here from the wind, but even if that hadn't been the case, he wore a heavy jacket, so Deborah knew he wasn't reacting to the cold.

His words affirmed this. "It's got to be nothing."

She didn't pretend to need clarification. She knew how unlikely it was that anything else was on his mind. She said, "We still have to ask her about it."

"They said there could be others on the island. And that guy they mentioned—the one in Talbot Valley?—he's got a collection from the war that you wouldn't believe. I've seen it myself."

"When?"

"One of the days . . . He was there for lunch and he was talking about it with Guy. He offered to show it to me, and Guy talked it up, so I thought, What the hell? and I went. Two of us went."

"Who else?"

"Guy's kid friend. Paul Fielder."

"Did you see another of these rings then?"

"No. But that doesn't mean there wasn't one. This guy had stuff everywhere. Boxes and bags of it. File cabinets. Shelves. It's all inside a couple of duplexes, and it's completely unorganized. If he had a ring and the ring ended up missing for one reason or another . . . Hell, he wouldn't even *know*. He can't have everything catalogued."

"Are you saying Paul Fielder may have pinched a ring while you were there?"

"I'm not saying anything. Just that there's got to be another ring, because no way did China . . ." Awkwardly he drove his hands into his pockets and looked away from Deborah, up the hill in the direction of Clifton Street, the Queen Margaret Apartments, and the sister who waited for him in Flat B. "No way did China hurt anyone. You know it. I know it. This ring . . . It's someone else's."

His voice was determined, but what the determination was all about was a question that Deborah didn't want to ask. She knew there was no real way round the confrontation that they needed to have with China. No matter what either one of them believed, there was still the matter of the ring to be dealt with.

She said, "Let's get to the flat. I think it's going to pour in another minute or two."

They found China watching a boxing match on the television. One of the boxers was taking a particularly nasty beating, and it was obvious that the match needed to be ended. But the howling crowd clearly was not about to allow that. Blood, their screams declared, would definitely have blood. China seemed oblivious to all this. Her face was a blank.

Cherokee went to the television and changed the

channel. He found a cycle race being covered in a sun-drenched land that looked like Greece but could have been anywhere that was not this wintry place. He muted the sound and left the picture. He went to his sister, saying, "You okay? Need anything?" He touched China's shoulder tentatively.

She stirred then. "I'm okay," she told her brother. She offered him a small half-smile. "Just thinking."

He returned her smile. "Got to stay away from that. Look where it's got me. I'm always thinking. If I hadn't been, we wouldn't be in the mess we're in now."

She shrugged. "Yeah. Well."

"You eat anything?"

"Cherokee . . ."

"Okay. All right. Forget I asked."

China seemed to realise that Deborah was also there. She turned her head and said, "I thought you'd gone to Simon, to give him that list of what I've done on the island."

Here was a simple way to address the issue of the ring, so Deborah took it. She said, "It's not quite complete, though. That list doesn't actually have everything on it."

"What d'you mean?"

Deborah set her umbrella in a stand near the door and came to the sofa, where she sat by her friend. Cherokee pulled a chair over and joined them.

"You didn't mention Potter and Potter Antiques," Deborah pointed out. "In Mill Street. You were there and you bought a ring from the son. Did you forget?"

China cast a look at her brother as if for a further explanation, but Cherokee said nothing. She turned back to Deborah. "I didn't list any of the stores I've been in. I didn't think . . . Why would I? I was in Boots several times, I was in a couple of shoe stores. I bought a newspaper once or twice, and I got some breath mints. The battery went out in my camera, so I replaced it with one I got down in the arcade . . . the one off the High Street? But I didn't write down any of that and there're probably more stores I've forgotten. Why?" Then to her brother, "What's this all about?"

Deborah answered her by bringing out the ring. She unfolded the handkerchief that enclosed it and extended her hand so that China could see it in its linen nest. "This was on the beach," she said, "at the bay where Guy Brouard died."

China didn't attempt to touch the ring, as if she knew what it meant that Deborah had it wrapped in a handkerchief and that it had been found in the vicinity of a homicide. She looked at it, though. She looked long and hard. She was so pale already that Deborah couldn't tell if any colour left her cheeks. But her teeth caught her lips within her closed mouth, and when she next looked at Deborah, her eyes were unmistakably frightened.

"What're you asking me?" she said. "Did I kill him? D'you want to ask that straight out?"

Deborah said, "The man at the shop—Mr. Potter?—he said an American woman bought a ring like this from him. An American woman from California. A woman wearing leather trousers and perhaps a cloak, I suppose, because a hood was over her head. She and this man's mother—Mrs. Potter?—talked about movie stars. They remembered that she—this woman from America?—told them that one generally doesn't see movie stars in—"

"All right," China said. "You've made your point. I bought the ring. A ring. That ring. I don't know. I bought a ring from them, okay?"

"Like this one?"

"Well, obviously," China snapped.

"Look, Chine, we've got to find out—"

"I'm cooperating!" China shrieked at her brother. "All right? I'm cooperating like a good little girl. I came into town and I saw that ring and I thought it was perfect so I bought it."

"Perfect?" Deborah asked. "For what?"

"For Matt. Okay? I got it for Matt." China looked embarrassed at her own admission, a gift for a man she'd declared herself done with. As if she knew how this appeared to the others, she went on. "It was nasty, and I liked that about it. It was like sending him a voodoo doll. Skull and crossed bones. Poison. Death. It felt like a good way to tell him how I feel."

Cherokee got up at this and walked over to the television, where riders were spinning along the edge of a cliff. The sea lay beyond them and the sun glittered off it. He killed the picture and returned to his seat. He didn't look at his sister. He didn't look at Deborah.

As if his actions made the comment his silence implied, China responded, saying, "Okay, so it's a stupid thing to do. So it makes things go on between us when they shouldn't. So it asks for a reply of some sort from him. I *know* that, okay? I know it's stupid. I wanted to do it anyway. That's just how it is. How it was when I saw it. I bought it and that's it."

"What did you do with it?" Deborah said. "The day that you bought it?"

"What d'you mean?"

"Did they put it in a bag for you? Did you put the bag inside another? Did you put it in your pocket? What happened next?"

China considered these questions; Cherokee looked up from examining his shoes. He appeared to realise where Deborah was heading, because he said, "Try to remember, Chine."

"I don't know. I probably shoved it in my purse," she said. "That's what I usually do when I buy something small."

"And afterwards? When you got it back to *Le Reposoir*? What would you have done with it then?"

"Probably . . . I don't know. If it was in my purse, I would've left it there and forgotten about it. Otherwise, I might've put it in my suitcase. Or on the dressing table till we packed to leave."

"Where someone could have seen it," Deborah murmured.

"If that's even the same ring," Cherokee said.

There *was* that, Deborah thought. For if the ring she held was merely a duplicate of the ring that China had purchased from the Potters, they had a startling coincidence on their hands. However unlikely that coincidence was, the slate needed to be cleared of it before they went any further. She said,

"Did you pack the ring when you left? Is it among your things now? Perhaps tucked away where you've forgotten about it?"

China smiled, as if aware of an irony she was about to disclose. "I wouldn't know, Debs. Right now the cops have everything I own. At least everything I brought with me. If I packed the ring or put it in my suitcase when I got it back to *Le Reposoir*, it'll be with all the rest of my stuff."

"So that will need to be checked into," Deborah said.

Cherokee nodded at the ring in Deborah's palm. "What happens with that?"

"It goes to the police."

"What'll they do with it?"

"I expect they'll try to get latent fingerprints off it. They might manage a partial."

"If they do, what then? I mean, if the print's Chine's . . . if the ring's the same . . . Won't they know it's been planted? The ring, I mean."

"They might suspect that," Deborah said. She didn't add what she also knew to be the situation: The interest of the police always lay in assessing guilt and closing the case. The rest they put into other hands. If China had no ring in her possession identical to this one and if her prints were upon the one that Deborah had found at the bay, the police weren't required to do anything more than document those two facts and pass them along to the prosecutors. It would be up to China's own advocate to argue another interpretation of the ring in court during her trial for murder.

Certainly, Deborah thought, both China and Cherokee had to know this. They weren't babes in the woods. The troubles China's father had had with the law in California must have given them both an education in what went on when a crime occurred.

Cherokee said, "Debs" in a thoughtful tone that elongated the nickname, making it sound like an appeal. "Is there any way . . ." He looked at his sister as if gauging a reaction to something he hadn't yet said. "This is a tough one to ask. Is there any way you could lose that ring?"

"Lose . . . ?"

China said, "Cherokee, don't."

"I have to," he said to her. "Debs, if that ring *is* the one China bought . . . And we know there's a chance it is, right? . . . I mean, why do the cops have to know you found it? Can't you just toss it down a storm drain or something?" He seemed to comprehend the magnitude of what he was asking Deborah to do, because he rushed on, saying, "Look. The cops already think she did it. Her prints on this, they'll just use it as another way to nail her. But if you lose it . . . it falls out of your pocket on the way to your hotel, let's say . . . ?" He watched her hopefully, one hand extended, as if he wished her to deposit the offending ring on his palm.

Deborah felt held by his gaze, its frankness and hope. She felt held by what his gaze implied about the history she shared with China River.

"Sometimes," Cherokee said to her quietly, "right and wrong get twisted. What looks right turns out to be wrong and what looks wrong—"

"Forget it," China interrupted. "Cherokee, forget it."

"But it would be no big deal."

"*Forget* it, I said." China reached for Deborah's hand and curved her fingers closed round the linen-covered ring. "You do what you have to do, Deborah." And to her brother, "She's not like you. It's not as easy as that for her."

"They're fighting dirty. We've got to do the same."

"*No,*" China said, and then to Deborah, "You've come to help me out. I'm grateful for that. You just do what you have to do."

Deborah nodded but felt the difficulty of saying "I'm sorry."

She couldn't escape the sensation of having let them down.

St. James wouldn't have thought himself the kind of man who let agitation get the better of him. Since the day he'd awakened in a hospital bed—remembering nothing but a final shot of tequila that he shouldn't have drunk—and gazed up into the face of his mother and had seen there the news he himself had confirmed not an hour later by a neurologist, he'd governed himself and his reactions with a discipline that would have done a military man proud. He'd considered himself an unshakeable survivor: The worst had happened and he had not broken on the wheel of personal disaster. He'd been maimed, left crippled, and abandoned by the woman he loved, and he'd emerged from it all with his core intact. *If I can cope with that, I can cope with anything.*

So he was unprepared for the disquiet he began to feel the moment he learned that his wife had not delivered the ring to DCI Le Gallez. And he was ultimately undone by the level that disquiet reached when the minutes passed without Deborah's return to the hotel.

He paced at first: across their room and along the small balcony outside their room. Then he flung himself into a chair for five minutes and contemplated what Deborah's actions might mean. This only heightened his anxiety, however, so he grabbed up his coat and finally left the building altogether. He would set out after her, he decided. He crossed the street without a clear idea of what direction he needed to take, thankful only that the rain had eased, which made the going easier.

Downhill seemed good, so he started off, skirting the rock wall that ran along a bear-pit sort of garden sunk into the landscape across from the hotel. At its far end stood the island's war memorial, and St. James had reached this when he saw his wife coming round the corner where the dignified grey façade of the Royal Court House stretched the length of *Rue du Manoir.*

Deborah raised her hand in greeting. As she approached him, he did what he could to calm himself.

"You made it back," she said with a smile as she came up to him.

"That's fairly obvious," he replied.

Her smile faded. She heard it all in his voice. She

would. She'd known him for most of her life, and he'd thought he knew her. But he was fast discovering that the gap between what he thought and what was was beginning to develop the dimensions of a chasm.

"What is it?" she asked. "Simon, what's wrong?"

He took her arm in a grip that he knew was far too tight, but he couldn't seem to loosen it. He led her to the bear-pit garden and forcibly guided her down the steps.

"What've you done with that ring?" he demanded.

"Done with it? Nothing. I've got it right—"

"You were to take it straight to Le Gallez."

"That's what I'm doing. I was going there now. Simon, what on earth . . . ?"

"Now? You were taking it there now? Where's it been in the meantime? It's hours since we found it."

"You never said . . . Simon, why're you acting like this? Stop it. Let me go. You're hurting me." She wrenched away and stood before him, her cheeks burning colour. There was a path in the garden along its perimeter and she set off down this, although it actually went nowhere but along the wall. Rainwater pooled here blackly, reflecting a sky that was fast growing dark. Deborah strode right through it without hesitation, uncaring of the soaking she was giving her legs.

St. James followed her. It maddened him that she'd walk away from him in this manner. She seemed like another Deborah entirely, and he wasn't about to have that. If it was to come to a chase between them, she would win, naturally. If it was to come to anything other than words and intellect between them, she would also win. That was the curse of his handicap, which left him weaker and slower than his own wife. This, too, angered him as he pictured what the two of them must look like to any watcher from the street above the sunken park: her sure stride carrying her ever farther from him, his pathetic mendicant's plea of a hobble in pursuit.

She reached the far end of the little park, the deepest end. She stood in the corner, where a pyracantha, heavy with red berries, leaned its burdened branches forward to touch the back of a wooden bench. She didn't sit. Instead, she remained at the arm of the bench and she ripped a handful of berries from the bush and began to fling them mindlessly back into the greenery.

This angered him further, the childishness of it. He felt swept back in time to being twenty-three to her twelve, confronted with a fit of incomprehensible pre-adolescent hysteria about a hair cut she'd hated, wrestling scissors from her before she had a chance to do what she wanted to do, which was to make the hair worse, make herself look worse, punish herself for thinking a hair cut might make a difference in how she was feeling about the spots on her chin that had appeared overnight and marked her as forever changing. "Ah, she's a handful, she is, our Deb," her father had said. "Needs a woman's touch," which he never gave her.

How convenient it would be, St. James thought, to blame Joseph Cotter for all of it, to decide that he

and Deborah had come to this moment in their marriage because her father had remained a widower.
That would make things easier, wouldn't it. He'd
have to look no further for an explanation of why
Deborah had acted in such an inconceivable manner.

He reached her. Foolishly, he said the first thing
that came into his head. "Don't ever run from me
again, Deborah."

She swung round with a handful of berries in her
fist. "Don't you *dare* . . . Don't you *ever* talk to me
like that!"

He tried to steady himself. He knew that an esca-
lating argument would be the only outcome of this
encounter unless one of them did something to calm
down. He also knew how unlikely it was that Deborah would be the one to rein in. He said as mildly as
he could which, admittedly, was only marginally less
combative than before, "I want an explanation."

"Oh, you *want* that, do you? Well, pardon me if I
don't feel like giving you one." She slung the berries
onto the path.

Just like a gauntlet, he thought. If he picked it up,
he knew quite well there would be an all-out war
between them. He was angry, but he didn't want
that war. He was still sane enough to see that any
sort of battle would be useless. He said, "That ring
constitutes evidence. Evidence is meant to go to the
police. If it doesn't go directly to them—"

"As if *every* piece of evidence goes directly," she
retorted. "You know that it doesn't. You know that
half the time police dig up evidence that no one
even *knew* was evidence in the first place. So it's

been through half a dozen way stations before it comes to them. You know that, Simon."

"That doesn't give anyone the right to create way stations," he countered. "Where have you been with that ring?"

"Are you interrogating me? Have you any idea what that *sounds* like? Do you care?"

"What I care about at the moment is the fact that a piece of evidence that I assumed was in the hands of Le Gallez was not in his hands when I mentioned it to him. Do *you* care what that means?"

"Oh, I see." She raised her chin. She sounded triumphant, the way a woman tends to sound when a man walks into a mine field she's laid. "This is all about you. *You* looked bad. Egg on your face without a napkin to be had."

"Obstructing a police investigation isn't egg on anyone's face," he said tersely. "It's a crime."

"I *wasn't* obstructing. I've *got* the damn ring." She thrust her hand into her shoulder bag, brought out the ring wrapped in his handkerchief, grabbed his arm in a grip that was as tight as his own had been on hers, and slammed the shrouded ring into his palm. "There. Happy? Take it to your precious DCI Le Gallez. God knows what he might think of you if you don't run it over there straightaway, Simon."

"Why are you acting like this?"

"Me? Why are you?"

"Because I told you what to do. Because we have evidence. Because we know it's evidence. Because we knew it then and—"

"No," she said. "Wrong. We did *not* know that.

We suspected. And based upon that suspicion, you asked me to take the ring. But if it was so crucial that the police get their hands on it in the next breath—if the ring was so *obviously* critical—you damn well might've brought it into town yourself instead of swanning round wherever you decided to swan, which was obviously more important to you than the ring in the first place."

St. James heard all this with rising irritation. "And *you* know damn well I was talking to Ruth Brouard. Considering she's the sister of the murder victim, considering that she *asked* to see me, as you well know, I'd say we have something that was marginally important for me to attend to at *Le Reposoir.*"

"Right. Of course. While what *I* was attending to has the value of dust motes."

"What you were *supposed* to be attending to—"

"Don't harp on about that!" Her voice rose to a screech. She seemed to hear it herself, for when she went on, she spoke more quietly although with no less anger. "What I was *attending* to"—she gave the verb the auditory equivalent of a sneer—"was this. China wrote it. She thought you might find it useful." She rooted through her shoulder bag a second time and brought forth a legal pad folded in half. "I also found out about the ring," she went on with a studied courtesy that was as meaningful as the sneer. "Which I'll tell you about if you think the information might be important enough, Simon."

St. James took the legal pad from her. He ran his gaze over it to see the dates, the times, the places, and the descriptions, all written in what he presumed was China River's hand.

Deborah said, "She wanted you to have it. As a matter of fact, she asked that you have it. She also bought the ring."

He looked up from the document. "What?"

"I think you heard me. The ring or one like it . . . China bought it in a shop in Mill Street. Cherokee and I tracked it down. Then we asked her about it. She admitted she bought it to send to her boyfriend. Her ex. Matt."

Deborah told him the rest. She delivered the information formally: the antiques shops, the Potters, what China had done with the ring, the possibility of another like it having come from the Talbot Valley. She concluded with "Cherokee says he saw the collection himself. And a boy called Paul Fielder was with him."

"Cherokee?" St. James asked sharply. "He was there when you tracked down the ring?"

"I believe I said that."

"So he knows everything about it?"

"I think he has the right."

St. James cursed in silence: himself, her, the whole situation, the fact that he'd involved himself in it for reasons he didn't want to consider. Deborah wasn't stupid, but she was clearly in over her head. To tell her this would escalate the difficulty between them. Not to tell her—in some way, diplomatically or otherwise—ran the risk of jeopardising the entire investigation. He had no choice.

"That wasn't wise, Deborah."

She heard his tone. Her reply was sharp. "Why?"

"I wish you'd told me in advance."

"Told you what?"

"That you intended to reveal—"

"I *didn't* reveal—"

"You said he was there when you tracked the source of the ring, didn't you?"

"He wanted to help. He's worried. He feels responsible because he was the one who wanted to make this trip and now his sister's likely to stand trial for murder. When I left China, he looked like . . . He's *suffering* with her. *For* her. He wanted to help, and I didn't see the harm in letting him."

"He's a suspect, Deborah, as well as his sister. If she didn't kill Brouard, someone else did. He's one of the people who were on the property."

"You *can't* be thinking . . . He *didn't* . . . Oh, for God's sake! He came to London. He came to see us. He went to the embassy. He agreed to see Tommy. He's desperate for someone to prove China innocent. Do you honestly think he'd do all that—do *any* of that—if he was the killer? Why?"

"I have no answer for that."

"Ah. Yes. But you still insist—"

"I do have this, though," he interrupted. He hated himself even as he allowed the bitter rush of pleasure to wash through him: He'd cornered her and now he had the blow to defeat her, to establish exactly who was in the right and who in the wrong. He told her about the paperwork he'd delivered to Le Gallez and what that paperwork revealed about where Guy Brouard had been on a trip to America that his own sister hadn't known he'd taken. It didn't matter to St. James that, during his discussion with Le Gallez, he'd argued the very opposite of what he was now telling his wife about the potential connection between Brouard's trip to California and Cherokee River. What did matter was that he impress upon her his own supremacy in matters that touched upon murder. Hers was the world of photography, his words suggested: celluloid images manipulated in a darkroom. His, on the other hand, was the world of science, the world of fact. Photography, however, was another word for fiction. She needed to keep all that in mind the next time she decided to forge a path he knew nothing about.

At the conclusion of his remarks, she said, "I see," and her posture was stiff. "Then I'm sorry about the ring."

"I'm sure you did what you thought was right," St. James told her, feeling all the magnanimity of a husband who's reestablished his rightful place in his marriage. "I'll take it over to Le Gallez right now and explain what happened."

"Fine," she said. "I'll go with you if you like. I'm happy to make the explanation, Simon."

He was gratified by the offer and what it revealed about her realisation of wrongdoing. "That's really not necessary," he told her kindly. "I'll handle it, my love."

"Are you sure you want to?" The question was arch.

He should have known what her tone meant, but

he failed miserably, saying, instead, like the fool who thinks he can ever better a woman at anything, "I'm happy to do it, Deborah."

"Funny, that. I wouldn't have thought."

"What?"

"That you'd forgo the opportunity to see Le Gallez put the thumbscrews on me. Such a fun sight. I'm surprised you want to miss it."

She gave a bitter smile and pushed past him abruptly. She hurried back up the path in the direction of the street.

DCI Le Gallez was climbing into his car in the police station's courtyard when St. James came through the gates. The rain had begun to fall once again as Deborah left him in the sunken garden, and although in his haste he'd departed the hotel without an umbrella, he didn't follow Deborah in order to pick one up from reception. Following Deborah at that point seemed like an act of importuning her. As he had nothing to importune her for, he didn't want to give the appearance of doing so.

She was behaving outrageously. It was true that she'd managed to collect some information that could prove valuable: Discovering where the ring had come from saved everyone time, and managing to uncover a potential secondary origin of the ring provided ammunition that *could* shake the local police from their belief in China River's guilt. But that didn't excuse the stealthy and dishonest manner in which she'd gone about her private investigation. If she was going to set off on a path of her own devising, she needed to tell him first so that he didn't end up looking every which way the perfect fool in front of the lead officer in the case. And no matter what she'd done, what she'd discovered, and what she'd gathered from China River, there remained the fact that she'd shared with the woman's brother a score of valuable details. She'd *had* to be made to see the utter foolishness of such an action.

End of story, St. James thought. He'd done what he had the right and the obligation to do. Still, he didn't want to follow in her wake. He told himself he'd give her time to cool off and to reflect. A little rain wouldn't hurt him in the cause of her education.

In the grounds of the police station, Le Gallez saw him and paused, the door of his Escort hanging open. Two identical infant safety seats were strapped in the back seat of the car, empty. "Twins," Le Gallez said abruptly when St. James glanced at them. "Eight months old." As if these admissions accidentally indicated a fellowship with St. James that he did not feel, he went on. "Where is it?"

"I have it." St. James added everything that Deborah had told him about the ring and finished with "China River doesn't recall where she last put it. She says if this ring isn't actually the one she bought, you'll have hers already among the rest of her belongings."

Le Gallez didn't ask to see the ring at once. Instead, he slammed the door of his car, said "Come with me, then," and went back inside the station.

St. James followed. Le Gallez led the way upstairs

to a cramped room that appeared to do service as the forensic laboratory. Black-and-white photographs of footprints hung on drooping strings against one wall, and the simple equipment to lift latent finger-prints with cyanoacrylate fuming stood beneath them. Beyond this, a door marked *darkroom* burned a red light, indicating it was in use. Le Gallez pounded three times upon this, barked "Prints, McQuinn," and "Let's have it," to St. James.

St. James handed over the ring. Le Gallez did the necessary paperwork on it. McQuinn emerged from the darkroom as the DCI signed his name, adding a flourish of dots beneath it. In short order, what went for the full strength of the island's forensic depart-ment was applied to the evidence from the bay where Guy Brouard had perished.

Le Gallez left McQuinn to his glue fumes. He next led the way to the evidence room. From the officer in charge there, he demanded the documents listing China River's belongings. He looked through them and reported what St. James had already begun to suspect would be the case: There was no ring among anything the police had already taken from China River.

Le Gallez, St. James thought, should have been greatly satisfied by this. The information, after all, put yet another nail into China River's fast-closing coffin. But instead of gratification, the DCI's face appeared to reflect annoyance. He looked as if a piece to the puzzle that he'd thought would take one shape had taken another.

Le Gallez eyed him. He examined the list of evidence another time. The evidence officer said, "It's just not there, Lou. Wasn't earlier, isn't now. I had a second look through everything. It's all straightforward. Nothing applies."

St. James understood from this that Le Gallez wasn't looking for a ring alone in his examination of the paperwork. The DCI obviously had come up with something else, something he hadn't revealed at their earlier meeting. He studied St. James as if considering how much he wished to tell him. He breathed the word "Damn," and then said, "Come with me."

They went to his office, where he swung the door shut and indicated a chair he wanted St. James to use. He himself pulled out his own desk chair and plopped into it, rubbing his forehead and reaching for a phone. He punched in a few numbers, and when someone on the other end answered, he said, "Le Gallez. Anything? . . . Hell. Keep looking, then. Perimeter. Fingertip. Whatever it takes . . . I bloody well *know* how many people've had the chance to mess things about there, Rosumek. Believe it or not, being able to count is one of the qualifications for my rank. Get on with it." He dropped the phone.

"You're doing a search?" St. James asked. "Where? At *Le Reposoir*?" He didn't wait for confirmation. "But you would've been calling it off just now if that ring was what you were looking for." He pondered this point, saw there was only one conclusion he could draw from it, and said, "You've had a report from England, I expect. Do the post-mortem details prompt a search?"

"You're nobody's fool, are you?" Le Gallez reached for a folder and took out several sheets that were stapled together. He didn't refer to them as he brought St. James into the picture. "Toxicology," he said.

"Something unexpected in the blood?"

"Opiate."

"At the time of death? So what are they saying? He was unconscious when he choked?"

"Looks that way."

"But that can only mean—"

"That the over isn't over." Le Gallez didn't sound pleased. There was little wonder in that. Because of this new information, in order to tie things together, either the victim himself or the police's number-one suspect in his murder now needed to be linked to opium or to any of its derivatives. If that couldn't be made to happen, Le Gallez's case against China River shattered like an egg dropped on stone.

"What are your sources of it?" St. James asked. "Any chance he was a user?"

"Shooting up before he went for a swim? Making early-morning visits to the local dope den? Not likely unless he wanted to drown."

"No track marks on his arms?"

Le Gallez shot him a do-you-think-we-are-complete-fools look.

"What about residue in the blood from the previous night? You're right—it doesn't make sense he'd use a narcotic before swimming."

"It doesn't make sense he'd use at all."

"Then someone drugged him that morning? How?"

Le Gallez looked uncomfortable. He thrust the paperwork back onto his desk. He said, "The man choked on that stone. No matter what was in his blood, he died the same bloody way. He choked on that stone. Let's not forget it."

"But at least we can see how the stone came to be lodged in his throat. If he'd been drugged, if he'd lost consciousness, how difficult would it be to shove a stone down his throat and allow him to suffocate? The only question would be how he came to be drugged. He wouldn't have sat by and allowed an injection. Was he diabetic? A substitution made for his insulin? No? Then he had to have . . . what? Drunk it in a solution?" St. James saw Le Gallez's eyes tighten marginally. He said to the DCI, "You think he did drink it, then," and he realised why the detective was suddenly being so amenable to St. James's having new information despite the difficulty caused by Deborah's failure to bring the ring immediately to the station. It was a form of quid pro quo: an unspoken apology for insult and loss of temper given in exchange for St. James's willingness to refrain from dragging Le Gallez's investigation over the metaphorical coals. Considering this, St. James said slowly as he reflected on what he knew of the case, "You must have ignored something at the scene, something innocent looking."

"We didn't ignore it," Le Gallez said. "It got tested along with everything else."

"What?"

"Brouard's Thermos. His daily dose of ginkgo and green tea. He drank it every morning after his swim."

"On the beach, you mean?"

"On the bloody effing beach. Quite the fanatic about his daily dose of ginkgo and green, matter of fact. The drug has to've been mixed with it."

"But there was no trace when you tested it?"

"Salt water. We reckoned Brouard rinsed it out."

"Someone certainly did. Who found the body?"

"Duffy. He goes down to the bay because Brouard's not returned to the house and the sister's phoned to see if he's stopped at the cottage for a cuppa. He finds him laid out cold as a fish and he comes back on the run to phone emergency because it looks like a heart attack to him and why wouldn't it? Brouard's nearly seventy years old."

"So in the coming and going, Duffy could have rinsed the Thermos."

"Could have done, yes. But if he killed Brouard, he either did it with his wife as an accomplice or with her knowledge, and in either case that makes her the best liar I've come across. She says he was upstairs and she was in the kitchen when Brouard went for his swim. He—Duffy—never left the house, she says, till he went searching for Brouard down the bay. I believe her."

St. James glanced at the phone then, and considered the call Le Gallez had made with its allusions of an ongoing search. "So if you're not looking for how he was drugged that morning—if you've decided the drug came from the Thermos—you must be looking for what held the opiate till it was used, something it might have been put in to convey it onto the estate."

"If it was in the tea," Le Gallez said, "and I can't think where else it could have been, that suggests a liquid form. Or a soluble powder."

"Which in turn suggests a bottle, a vial, a container of some sort . . . with fingerprints on it, one would hope."

"Which could be anywhere," Le Gallez acknowledged.

St. James saw the difficulty that the DCI was in: not only an enormous estate to search but also a cast of hundreds to suspect now, since the night before Guy Brouard's death *Le Reposoir* had been peopled by partygoers, any one of whom might have come to the celebration with murder in mind. For despite the presence of China River's hair on Guy Brouard's body, despite the image of an early-morning stalker in China River's cape, and despite the misplaced skull-and-crossed-bones ring on the beach—a ring purchased by China River herself—the opiate ingested by Guy Brouard shouted a tale that Le Gallez would now be forced to hear.

He wouldn't much like the predicament he was in, though: Until this moment, his evidence suggested China River was the killer, but the presence of the narcotic in Brouard's blood showed a premeditation that was in direct conflict with the fact that she'd met Brouard only upon coming to the island.

"If the River woman did it," St. James said, "she would have had to bring the narcotic with her from the States, wouldn't she? She couldn't have hoped to find it here on Guernsey. She wouldn't have known what the place was like: how big the town, where to make the score. And even if it *was* her hope to get a drug here and she brought it off by asking round St. Peter Port till she found it, the question still remains, doesn't it? *Why* did she do it?"

"There's nothing among her belongings that she could have used to transport it in," Le Gallez said as if St. James had not just brought up an extremely cogent point. "No bottle, jar, vial. Nothing. That suggests she tossed it out. If we find it—when we find it—there'll be residue. Or fingerprints. Even one. No one allows for every possibility when they kill. They think they will. But killing doesn't come naturally to people if they're not psychopaths, so they get unhinged when they bring it off and they forget. One detail. Somewhere."

"But you're back to the why of it," St. James argued. "China River has no motive. She gains nothing by his death."

"I find the container with her prints on it, and that's not my problem," Le Gallez returned.

That remark reflected police work at its worst: that damnable predisposition of investigators to assign guilt first and interpret the facts to fit it second. True, the Guernsey police had a cloak, hair on the body, and eyewitness reports of someone following Guy Brouard in the direction of the bay. And now they had a ring purchased by their principal suspect and found at the scene. But they *also* had an element that should have thrown a spanner directly into their case. The fact that the toxicology report wasn't doing that explained why innocent people ended up serving prison terms and why the public's faith in due process had long ago altered to cynicism.

"Inspector Le Gallez," St. James began carefully, "on one hand we have a multimillionaire who dies and a suspect who gained nothing from his death. On the other hand, we have people in his life who might well have had expectations of an inheritance. We have a disenfranchised son, a small fortune left to two adolescents unrelated to the deceased, and a number of individuals with disappointed dreams that appear to be related to plans Brouard made to build a museum. It seems to me that motives for murder are falling out of the trees. To ignore them in favour of—"

"He was in California. He would have met her there. The motive comes from that time."

"But you've checked into the others' movements, haven't you?"

"None of them went to—"

"I'm not talking about their going to California," St. James said. "I'm talking about the morning of the murder. Have you checked to verify where the rest of them were? Adrian Brouard, the people connected to the museum, the teenagers, relatives of the teenagers eager for some cash, Brouard's other associates, his mistress, her children?"

Le Gallez was silent, which was answer enough.

St. James pressed on. "China River was there in

the house, it's true. It's also true that she may have met Brouard in California, which remains to be seen. Or her brother may have met him and introduced them to each other. But other than that connection—which may not even exist—is China River *acting* like a murderer? Has she ever acted like one? She made no attempt to flee the scene. She left as scheduled with her brother that morning and didn't bother to disguise her trail. She gained absolutely nothing by Brouard's death. She possessed no reason to want him dead."

"As far as we know," Le Gallez inserted.

"As far as we know," St. James agreed. "But to pin this on her based on evidence that *anyone* could have planted . . . If nothing else, you've got to see that China River's advocate is going to tear your case to pieces."

"I don't think so," Le Gallez said simply. "In my experience, Mr. St. James, if you follow the smoke, you find the fire."

Chapter 15

PAUL FIELDER USUALLY AWOKE to the sound of his alarm clock, an old, chipped black tin affair that he religiously wound every night and set with some care, always mindful that one of his younger brothers may have messed it about sometime during the day. But the next morning it was the phone that awakened him, followed by the sound of feet clumping up the stairs. He recognised the heavy tread and closed his eyes tightly on the off chance Billy came into the room. Why his brother would be up at all in the early morning was a mystery to Paul, unless he'd never gone to bed last night. That wouldn't be unusual. Sometimes Billy stayed up watching the telly till there was nothing more to watch and then he sat and smoked in the sitting room, playing records on their parents' old stereo. He played them loud, but no one told him to lower the sound so that the rest of the family could sleep. The days when anyone said anything to Billy that might set him off had long since passed.

The door of the bedroom crashed open, and Paul kept his eyes squeezed shut. Across the small room from his own bed, his youngest brother gave a startled cry, and for a moment Paul felt the guilty relief of one who believes he's going to escape torture in favour of some other victim. But as things turned out, that cry was only one of surprise at the sudden noise, because a slap on Paul's shoulder followed hard on the heels of the door's abrupt opening. Then Billy's voice said, "Hey. Stupid git. Y'think I don' know you're faking? Ge' up. Gonna have a visitor, you are."

Paul stubbornly kept his eyes closed, which may or may not have prompted Billy to grab him by the hair and lift his head. He breathed the rank breath of early morning into Paul's face and said, "Want some tongue, little wanker? Help you wake up? Like it better from blokes, don' you?" He gave Paul's head a shake and then dropped it to the pillow. "You're lame, you are. Bet you even have a stiffie with nowhere to put it. Le's check that out."

Paul felt his brother's hands on the covers and he reacted to that. Truth was, he did have a stiffie. He always had one in the morning, and from conversations he'd overheard during games at school, he'd reckoned it was normal, which had been a big relief to him, because he'd begun to wonder what it meant that he woke up daily with his prong at the perpendicular.

He gave a cry not unlike his little brother's and clutched on to the blanket. When it became obvious that Billy was going to have his way, he leaped out of bed and raced to the bathroom. He slammed the door shut and locked it. Billy pounded against the wood.

"Now he's pulling the pud," he laughed. "Not so much fun without help, though, is it? One of those you-'n'-me wank jobs you like so much."

Paul ran the water in the bathtub and flushed the toilet. Anything to drown his brother out.

Over the rush of water, he heard other voices shouting outside the door, followed by Billy's crazed laughter, followed by knocking that was gentler but insistent. Paul turned off the water and stood next to the tub. He heard his father's voice.

"Open up, Paulie. Need to talk to you."

When Paul had the door open, his father was standing there, dressed for his day with the road-works crew. He wore crusty blue jeans and dirt-smeared boots and a thick flannel shirt that was foetid with the scent of heavy sweat. He should have had his butcher's clothes on, Paul thought, and the sadness of it felt like a grip on his throat. He should have been wearing the smart white coat and the smart white apron covering trousers that were clean every day. He should have been setting off to work where he'd worked from the earliest time Paul could remember. He should have been ready to set out the meat on his very own stall at the far end of the market, where no one now worked because everything that had once been there was as gone as death made everything in the end.

Paul wanted to slam the door on his father: on the dirty clothes his father never would have worn, on his face unshaven as it never would have been. But before he had the chance to do that, his mother appeared in the doorway as well, carrying with her the scent of frying bacon, part of the breakfast she insisted that Paul's father eat every day to keep up his strength.

"Get dressed, Paulie," she said over her husband's shoulder. "You got an advocate coming to call on you."

"Know what this is all about, Paul?" his father asked.

Paul shook his head. An advocate? To see him? He wondered and thought there was some mistake.

"You been going to school like you ought?" his father said.

Paul nodded, unrepentant of the lie. He'd been going to school like he *thought* he ought, which was when other things didn't get in the way. Things like Mr. Guy and what had happened. Which brought grief back to Paul in a rush.

His mum appeared to read this. She reached in the pocket of her quilted dressing gown and brought out a tissue that she pressed into Paul's hand. She said, "You be quick, luv," and "Ol, let's see to your breakfast," to her husband. She added, "He's gone below," over her shoulder as they left Paul to prepare himself for his visitor. As if in unnecessary explanation, the booming of the television sounded. Billy had gone on to another interest.

Alone, Paul did what he could to get ready to meet an advocate. He washed his face and his armpits. He dressed in the clothes he'd worn a day earlier. He brushed his teeth, and he combed his hair. He looked at himself in the mirror and he wondered. What did it actually mean? The woman, the book, the church, and the labourers. She held a quill pen and it pointed to something: the tip to the book and the feathers to the sky. But what did that mean? Perhaps nothing at all but he couldn't believe that.

How are you at keeping secrets, my Prince?

He went below, where his father was eating and Billy—the television forgotten—was smoking, slouched in his chair with his feet propped on the kitchen rubbish bin. He had a cup of tea at his elbow and he hoisted it when Paul entered the room, saluting him with a smirk. "Good wank, Paulie? Cleaned the toilet seat, I hope."

"Watch your mouth," Ol Fielder said to his older son.

"Oooh, tha' scared, I am" was Billy's reply.

"Eggs, Paulie?" his mother asked. "I c'n do you fried. Or boiled if you like."

"Las' meal before he gets taken away," Billy said. "You wank in the nick and all the boys'll want some of it, Paulie."

The sound of the youngest Fielder squalling from the stairway interrupted this conversation. Paul's mum handed the frying pan to his dad, asked him to mind how the eggs were cooking, and went in search of her only daughter. When she was brought into the kitchen on her mother's hip, there was much to do to settle her crying.

The door bell buzzed as the two younger Fielder boys clattered down the stairs and took their places at the table. Ol Fielder went to answer it, and in short enough order he called out for Paul to come to the sitting room. "You, too, Mave," he called to his wife, which was invitation enough for Billy to join them uninvited.

Paul hung back at the doorway. He didn't know very much about advocates, and what he *did* know didn't make him eager to meet one. They got involved in trials, and trials meant people in trouble. No matter which way the bread was sliced, people in trouble might well mean Paul.

The advocate proved to be a man called Mr. Forrest, who looked from Billy to Paul in some confusion, obviously wondering which young man was which. Billy solved that problem by shoving Paul forward. He said, "Here's wha' you want, then. Wha's he done?"

Ol Fielder introduced everyone. Mr. Forrest looked round for a place to sit. Mave Fielder swept a pile of washed laundry from the biggest armchair and said, "Please do sit," although she herself remained standing. No one, in fact, seemed to know what to do. Feet shifted, a stomach growled, and the little one squirmed in her mother's arms.

Mr. Forrest had a briefcase with him, which he placed on a PVC-covered ottoman. He didn't sit because no one else did. He rooted through some papers and cleared his throat.

Paul, he informed the parents and the older brother, had been named one of the principal beneficiaries in the will of the late Guy Brouard. Did the

Fielders know about the laws of inheritance on Guernsey? No? Well, he would explain them, then.

Paul listened along, but he didn't understand much. It was only by watching his parents' expressions and listening to Billy say "Wha'? *Wha'*? Shit!" that he realised something extraordinary was happening. But he didn't know it was happening to *him* until his mother cried, "Our Paulie? He's going to be *rich*?"

Billy said, "Fucking shit!" and swung to Paul. He might have said more, but Mr. Forrest began to use the expression "our young Mr. Paul" in reference to the beneficiary upon whom he'd come to call, and this seemed to do something profound to Billy, something that made him shove Paul to one side and hulk out of the room. He left the house altogether, slamming the front door so hard that it felt as if the air pressure had changed in the room.

His dad was smiling at him and saying, "This is good news, this is. Best to you, son."

His mum was murmuring, "Good Jesus, good God."

Mr. Forrest was saying something about accountants and sorting out exact amounts and who got how much and how it was determined. He was naming Mr. Guy's children and Henry Moullin's girl Cyn as well. He was talking about how Mr. Guy had disposed of his property and why, and he was saying that if Paul was going to need advice when it came to investments, savings, insurance, bank loans, and the like, he could phone up Mr. Forrest straightaway, and Mr. Forrest would be only too happy to give all the assistance that he could. He fished out his business cards and pressed one into Paul's hand and one into his dad's hand. They were to ring him once they sorted out the questions they wanted to ask, he told them. Because, he smiled, there *would* be questions. There always were in situations like these.

Mave Fielder asked the first one. She licked dry lips, glanced at her husband nervously, and readjusted the baby on her hip. She said, "How much . . . ?"

Ah, Mr. Forrest said. Well, they didn't quite know yet. There were bank statements, brokerage statements, and outstanding bills to be gone through—a forensic accountant was already at it—and when that was done, they would have the correct figure. But he was willing to hazard a guess . . . although he wouldn't want them to depend upon it or to do anything in expectation of it, he added hastily.

"D'you want to know, Paulie?" his father asked him. "Or would you rather wait till they have the exact amount?"

"I expect he wants to know straightaway," Mave Fielder said. "I'd want to know, wouldn't you, Ol?"

"It's Paulie's to say. What about it, son?"

Paul looked at their faces, all shining and smiling. He knew the answer he was meant to give. He wanted to give it because of what it would mean to them to hear good news. So he nodded then, a quick bob of his head, an acknowledgement of a future that had suddenly expanded beyond anything any of them had dreamed.

They couldn't be absolutely certain till all the accounting was done, Mr. Forrest told them, but as Mr. Brouard had been a shrewd-as-the-dickens businessman, it was safe to say that Paul Fielder's share of the estate would likely be in the vicinity of seven hundred thousand pounds.

"Jesus died on the cross," Mave Fielder breathed.

"Seven hundred . . ." Ol Fielder shook his head as if clearing it. Then his face—so sad for so long with a failed man's sadness—lit with an unshakable smile. "Seven hundred thousand pounds? Seven hundred . . . ! Think of it! Paulie, son. Think of what you can *do*."

Paul mouthed the words *seven hundred thousand*, but they were incomprehensible to him. He felt rooted to the spot and quite overcome by the sense of duty that now fell upon him.

Think of what you can do.

This reminded him of Mr. Guy, of words spoken as they stood on the very top of the manor house at *Le Reposoir*, gazing out upon trees unfurling in springtime April splendour and garden after garden coming back to life.

To whom much is given, even more is expected, my Prince. Knowing this keeps one's life in balance. But living by it is the real test. Could you do that, son, if you were in that position? How would you begin to go about it?

Paul didn't know. He hadn't known then and he

didn't know now. But he had the glimmer of an idea because Mr. Guy had given him that. Not directly, because Mr. Guy didn't do things directly, as Paul had discovered. But he had it all the same.

He left his parents and Mr. Forrest talking about the whens and the splendid wherefores of his miraculous inheritance. He returned to his bedroom, where, under the bed, he'd shoved his rucksack for safekeeping. He knelt—bum in the air and hands on the floor—to root it out, and as he did so, he heard the scrabble of Taboo's claws on the lino in the hallway. The dog came snuffling in to join him.

This reminded Paul to close the door, and for good measure he shoved one of the room's two bureaus in front of it. Taboo leaped up on his bed, circling for a spot to lie on that smelled most of Paul, and when he'd found it, he sank down contentedly and watched his master bring forth the rucksack, wipe the slut's wool from it, and unfasten its plastic buckles.

Paul sat next to the dog. Taboo placed his head on Paul's leg. Paul knew he was meant to scratch the dog's ears, and he did so, but he gave the duty short shrift. There were other concerns that had to take precedence over loving his animal this morning.

He didn't know what to make of what he had. When he'd first unrolled it, he'd seen it wasn't exactly the kind of pirate's treasure map he'd expected, but still, he'd known it was a map of some kind because Mr. Guy wouldn't have put it there for him to find had it been anything else. He'd recalled then, as he'd studied his find, that Mr. Guy had often spoken in riddles: where a duck rejected by the rest of the flock stood for Paul and his mates at school, or a car sending out plumes of nasty black exhaust stood for a body hopelessly polluted with bad food, cigarettes, and lack of exercise. That was Mr. Guy's way because he didn't like to preach at anyone. What Paul hadn't anticipated, however, was that Mr. Guy's approach to helpful conversation might bleed over to messages he'd left behind as well.

The woman before him held a quill. *Wasn't* it a quill? It *looked* like a quill. She had a book open upon her lap. Behind her rose a building tall and vast and beneath it labourers worked on its construction. It looked like a cathedral to Paul. And she looked like . . . He couldn't say. Downcast, perhaps. Infinitely sad. She was writing in the book as if documenting . . . What? Her thoughts? The work? What was being done behind her? What *was* being done? A building being raised. A woman with a book and a quill and a building being raised, all of it comprising a final message to Paul from Mr. Guy.

You know many things you think you don't know, son. You can do anything you want.

But with this? What *was* there to be done? The only buildings associated with Mr. Guy that Paul knew about were his hotels, his home at *Le Reposoir,* and the museum he and Mr. Ouseley talked of constructing. The only women associated with Mr. Guy that Paul knew about were Anaïs Abbott and Mr. Guy's sister. It seemed unlikely that the message Mr. Guy wanted Paul to have had anything to do with Anaïs Abbott. And it seemed even more unlikely that Mr. Guy would send him a hidden message about one of his hotels or even his house. Which left Mr. Guy's sister and Mr. Ouseley's museum as the core of the message. Which had to be what the message itself meant.

Perhaps the book on the woman's lap was an account she was keeping of the museum's construction. And the fact that Mr. Guy had left this message for Paul to find—when he clearly could have given it to anyone else—comprised Mr. Guy's instructions for the future. And the inheritance Paul had been left by Mr. Guy fit in with the message he had been sent: Ruth Brouard would keep the project going forward, but Paul's was the money that would build it.

That had to be it. Paul knew it. But more, he could feel it. And Mr. Guy had talked to him more than once about feelings.

Trust what's inside, my boy. There lies the truth.

Paul saw, with a jolt of pleasure, that *inside* had meant more than just inside one's heart and soul. It also had meant inside the dolmen. He was to trust what he found inside that dark chamber. Well, he would do so.

He hugged Taboo and felt as if a mantle of lead had been lifted from his shoulders. He'd been wandering in the dark since he'd learned of Mr. Guy's death. Now he had a light. But more than that, really. He had far more. Now he had a good sense of direction.

• • •

Ruth didn't need to hear the oncologist's verdict. She saw it on his face, especially on his forehead, which looked even more lined than usual. She understood from this that he was fending off the feelings that invariably went with imminent failure. She wondered what it must be like to choose as one's life work bearing witness to the passing of countless patients. Doctors, after all, were meant to heal and then to celebrate victory in the battle against illness, accident, or disease. But cancer doctors went to war with weapons that were often insufficient against an enemy that knew no restrictions and was governed by no rules. Cancer, Ruth thought, was like a terrorist. No subtle signs, just instant devastation. The word alone was enough to destroy.

"We've gone as far as we can with what we've been using," the doctor said. "But there comes a time when a stronger opioid analgesic is called for. I think you know we've reached that time, Ruth. Hydromorphone isn't enough now. We can't increase the dosage. We have to make the change."

"I'd like another alternative." Ruth knew her voice was faint, and she hated what that revealed about her affliction. She was meant to be able to hide from the fire, and if she couldn't do that, she was meant to be able to hide the fire from the world. She forced a smile. "It wouldn't be so bad if it simply throbbed. There'd be that respite between the pulsing, if you know what I mean. I'd have the memory of what it was like . . . in those brief pauses . . . what it was like before."

"Another round of chemo, then."

Ruth stood firm. "No more of that."

"Then we must move to morphine. It's the only answer." He observed her from the other side of his desk, the veil in his eyes that had been shielding him from her seemed to drop for an instant. The man himself appeared as if naked before her, a creature who felt too many other creatures' pain. "What are you afraid of, exactly?" His voice was kind. "Is it the chemo itself? The side effects from it?"

She shook her head.

"The morphine, then? The idea of addiction? Heroin users, opium dens, addicts nodding off in back alleyways?"

Again, she shook her head.

"Then the fact that morphine comes at the end? And what that means?"

"No. Not at all. I know I'm dying. I'm not afraid of that." To see *Maman* and Papa after such a long time, to see Guy and be able to say I'm so sorry . . . What, Ruth thought, was there to fear in this? But she wanted to be in control of the *means* and she knew about morphine: how at the end it robbed you of the very thing you yourself were gallantly attempting to release on a sigh.

"But it's not necessary to die in such agony, Ruth. The morphine—"

"I want to go knowing I'm going," Ruth said. "I don't want to be a breathing corpse in a bed."

"Ah." The doctor placed his hands on his desk, folded them neatly so that his signet ring caught the light. "You've an image of it, haven't you? The patient comatose and the family gathered round the bedside watching her at her most defenceless. She lies immobile and not even conscious, unable to communicate no matter what's in her mind."

Ruth felt the call of tears but she didn't reply to it. Fearful that she might, she simply nodded.

"That's an image from a long time ago," the doctor told her. "Of course, we can make it a present-day image if that's what the patient wants: a carefully orchestrated slide into a coma, with death waiting at the end of the descent. Or we can control the dosage so that the pain gets dulled and the patient remains alert."

"But if the pain's too great, the dosage has to be equal to it. And I know what morphine does. You can't pretend it doesn't debilitate."

"If you have trouble with it, if it makes you too sleepy, we'll balance it with something else. Methylphenidate, a stimulant."

"More drugs." The bitterness Ruth heard in her voice was a match for the pain in her bones.

"What's the alternative, Ruth, beyond what you already have?"

That was the question, with no easy answer that she could accept and embrace. There was death at her own hand, there was welcoming torture like a Christian martyr, or there was the drug. She would have to decide.

She thought about this over a cup of coffee, which she sipped at the Admiral de Saumarez Inn. A fire was blazing there, just a few steps off Berthelot Street, and Ruth found a tiny nearby table that was empty. She eased herself down into a chair and ordered her coffee. She drank it slowly, savouring its bitter flavour as she watched the flames lick greedily at the logs.

She wasn't supposed to be in the position she was in, Ruth thought wearily. As a young girl, she'd thought she would one day marry and have a family as other girls did. As a woman who moved into first her thirties and then her forties without that happening, she'd thought she could be of service to the brother who'd been everything to her throughout her life. She was not meant for other pursuits, she told herself. So be it. She would live for Guy.

But living for Guy brought her face-to-face over time with how Guy lived, and that had been difficult for her to accept. She had managed it eventually, telling herself that what he did was just a reaction to the early loss he had endured and to the endless responsibilities that had been foisted upon him because of that loss. She had been one of those responsibilities. He'd met it wholeheartedly. She owed him much. This had allowed her to turn a blind eye until the time she'd felt she could no longer do so.

She wondered why people reacted as they did to the difficulties they'd encountered in childhood. One person's challenge became another person's excuse, but in either case their childhood was still the reason behind what they did. This simple precept had long been evident to her whenever she'd evaluated her brother's life: his drive to succeed and to prove his worth determined by early persecution and loss, his restless endless pursuit of women merely a reflection of a boyhood starved of a mother's love, his failed attempts in the role of father only an indication of a paternal relationship terminated before it had a chance to bloom. She knew all this. She'd pondered it. But in all her pondering, she'd never considered how the precepts governing the role of childhood worked in lives other than Guy's.

In her own, for example: an entire existence dominated by fear. People said they would return and they never did—that was the backdrop against which she'd acted her part in the unfolding drama that became her life. One could not function in such an anxious climate, however, so one sought ways to pretend the fear didn't exist. A man might leave, so cling to the man who could not do so. A child might grow, change, and flee the nest, so obviate that possibility in the simplest way: have no children. The future might bring challenges that could thrust one into the unknown, so exist in the past. Indeed, make one's life a tribute to the past, become a documentarist of the past, a celebrant of it, a diarist of it. In this way, live outside of fear which, as it turned out, was just another way of living outside of life.

But was that so wrong? Ruth couldn't think so, especially when she considered what her attempts to live inside life had led to.

"I want to know what you intend to do," Margaret had demanded this morning. "Adrian's been robbed of what's rightfully his—on more than one front and you know it—and I want to know what you intend to do. I don't care how he managed it, frankly, what sort of legal fancy-dancing he did. I'm beyond all that. I just want to know how you mean to put it right. Not if, Ruth. How. Because you know where this is going to lead if you don't do something."

"Guy wanted—"

"I don't bloody care what you think Guy wanted because I *know* what he wanted: what he always wanted." Margaret advanced on Ruth where she'd been sitting, at her dressing table, trying to put some artificial colour on her face. "Young enough to be his daughter, Ruth. Younger than his own daughters, even, if it comes down to it. Someone who by no stretch of the imagination was meant to be available to him. That's what he was up to this last time. And you know it, don't you?"

Ruth's hand trembled so she couldn't twirl her lipstick up from the tube. Margaret saw this and she leaped upon it, interpreting it as the reply Ruth had no intention of speaking outright.

"My God, you *did* know." Margaret's voice was hoarse. "You knew he meant to seduce her, and you did nothing to stop it. As far as you were concerned—as far as you've *always* been concerned—bloody little Guy could do no wrong, no matter who got hurt in the process."

Ruth, I want it. She wants it as well.

"What did it matter, after all, that she was merely the latest in a *very* long line of women he just had to have? What did it matter that in taking her he was acting out a betrayal that *no* one would recover from? With him, there was always the pretence that he was doing them some kind of gentlemanly favour. Enlarging their world, taking them under his wing, saving them from a bad situation, and we both know what that situation was. When all along what he was really doing was bucking himself up in the easiest way he could find. You knew it. You saw it. And you let it happen. As if you had no responsibility to anyone other than yourself."

Ruth lowered her hand, which was by now shaking far too much to be useful. Guy *had* done wrong. She would admit that. But he hadn't set out to do so. He hadn't planned in advance . . . or even thought about . . . No. He wasn't that sort of monster. It was just a case of her being there one day and the blinkers falling from Guy's eyes in the way they fell when he suddenly saw and just as suddenly wanted and thought that he had to have, because *She's the one, Ruth.* And she was always "the one" to Guy, which was how he justified whatever he did. So Margaret was right. Ruth had known the peril.

"Did you watch?" Margaret asked her. She'd been gazing at Ruth from behind, at her reflection in the mirror, but now she came round and stood so that Ruth had to look at her and even if she hoped to do otherwise, Margaret removed the lipstick from her hand. "Is that what it was? Were you part of it? No longer in the background, Guy's little Boswell of the needlepoint, but an active participant in the drama this time. Or maybe a Peeping Thomasina? A female Polonius behind the arras?"

"No!" Ruth cried.

"Oh. Then just someone who didn't get involved. No matter what he did."

"That *isn't* true." There was too much to bear: her own physical pain, the grief of her brother's murder, bearing witness to the destruction of dreams before her eyes, loving too many people in conflict with each other, seeing the wheel of Guy's misplaced passion keep turning in revolutions that never once changed. Not even at the end. Not even after *She's truly the one, Ruth,* one last time. Because she hadn't been, but he had to tell himself that she was, because if he hadn't done that, he'd have had to face what he himself really was, an old man who'd tried and failed to recover from a lifelong grief he'd never allowed himself to feel. There'd been no luxury for that with *Prends soin de ta petite soeur,* the injunction that became the motto on a family escutcheon that existed only in her brother's mind. So how could she have called him to account? What demands could she have made? What threats?

None. She could only try to reason with him. When that failed, because it was doomed to failure the moment he said *She's the one* yet again as if he'd never made that declaration three dozen times before, she knew that she would have to take another route to stop him. This would be a new route, representing frightening and uncharted territory for her. But she had to take it.

So Margaret was wrong, at least in this. She hadn't played the part of Polonius, lurking and listening, having her suspicions confirmed and at the same time getting a vicarious satisfaction from something she herself never had. She'd known. She'd tried to reason with her brother. When that had failed, she'd acted.

And now . . . ? She was left with the aftermath of what she'd done.

Ruth knew she had to make reparation for this somehow. Margaret would have her think that wresting Adrian's rightful inheritance from the legal quagmire Guy had created to keep the young man from it would be an appropriate form of restitution. But that was because Margaret wanted a quick solution to a problem that had been years in the making. As if, Ruth thought, an infusion of money into Adrian's veins would ever be the answer to what had long ailed him.

In the Admiral de Saumarez Inn, Ruth finished the last of her coffee and dropped the necessary money onto the table. She worked her way back into her coat with some difficulty and fumbled with the buttons and her scarf. Outside, the rain was falling softly, but a streak of light sky in the direction of France made a promise that the weather might improve as the day wore on. Ruth hoped that would be the case. She'd come to town without her umbrella.

She had to ascend the incline of Berthelot Street, and she found this difficult. She wondered how long she'd be able to manage and how many months or even weeks she had before she would be forced to her bed for the final countdown. Not long, she hoped.

Near the top of her climb, New Street veered off

to the right in the general direction of the Royal Court House. In this vicinity, Dominic Forrest had his office.

Ruth entered to find that the advocate had just returned from making a few morning calls. He could see her if she didn't mind waiting for fifteen minutes or so. He had to return two phone calls that were most important. Would she like a coffee?

Ruth demurred. She didn't sit because she wasn't sure if she would be able to rise again without assistance. Instead, she found a copy of *Country Life,* and she looked at the photos without actually seeing them.

Mr. Forrest came to fetch her within the promised fifteen minutes. He looked grave when he called her name, and she wondered if he'd been standing at the doorway to his office, watching her and making an assessment of how much longer she'd be able to go on. It seemed to Ruth that a greater part of her world observed her that way now. The more she did to appear normal and unaffected by disease, the more people seemed to watch her as if waiting for the lie to be flushed out.

Ruth took a seat in Forrest's office, knowing how odd it would look if she remained standing throughout their meeting. The advocate asked if she would mind if he had a coffee . . . ? He'd been up for hours, getting an early start on the day, and he found he needed a jolt of caffeine right now. Would she take a slice of gâche at least?

Ruth said no, she was really quite fine, as she'd

just come from her own cup of coffee at Admiral de Saumarez. She waited till Mr. Forrest had his cup and his slice of the island bread, though, before she launched into the reason for her visit.

She told the advocate of her confusion regarding Guy's will. She'd been witness to his previous wills, as Mr. Forrest knew, and it had been something of a shock to her to hear the changes he'd made in the legacies: nothing for Anaïs Abbott and her children, the wartime museum forgotten, the Duffys ignored. And to see less money left to Guy's own children than to his two . . . She struggled for words and settled on *local protégés* . . . It was a most bewildering situation.

Dominic Forrest nodded solemnly. He *had* wondered what was going on, he admitted, when he'd been asked to go over the will in front of individuals who were not beneficiaries of it. That was irregular—Well, the whole reading of the will in such a meeting in this day and age was a bit irregular, wasn't it?—but he'd thought perhaps Ruth was surrounding herself with friends and loved ones during a troubling time. Now he saw that Ruth herself had been left in the dark as to her brother's final testament. That explained much about the oddity of the formal reading. "I did wonder when you didn't come with him the day he signed the documents. You'd always done before. I thought perhaps you weren't feeling well, but I didn't ask at the time. Because . . ." He shrugged, looking both sympathetic and embarrassed. He, too, knew, Ruth realised. So

Guy had probably known as well. But like most people, he didn't know what to say. *I'm sorry you're dying* seemed too vulgar.

"But you see, he always told me before," Ruth said. "Every will. Every time. I'm trying to understand why he kept this final version a secret."

"Perhaps he believed it would upset you," Forrest said. "Perhaps he knew you'd disagree with the changes in the bequests. Moving part of the money out of the family."

"No. It can't be that," Ruth said. "The other wills did the same."

"But not a fifty-fifty split. And in earlier versions his children each inherited more than the other beneficiaries. Perhaps Guy thought you might pounce on this. He knew you'd understand what the terms of his will meant the moment you heard them."

"I *would* have protested," Ruth admitted. "But that wouldn't have changed things. My protests never counted with Guy."

"Yes, but that was before . . ." Forrest made a little gesture with his hands. Ruth took it to mean the cancer.

Yes. It made sense if Guy knew she was dying. He'd listen to the wishes of a sister not long for this world. Even Guy would do that. And to listen to her would have meant to leave his three children a legacy that at least equaled—if it did not exceed—that which he'd left to the two island adolescents, which was exactly what Guy had not wanted to do. His daughters had long made themselves nothing to him; his son had been a lifelong disappointment. He wanted to remember the people who had returned his love in the manner he'd decided love ought to be returned. So he'd cooperated with the laws of inheritance and left his children the fifty percent they were owed, freeing him to do whatever he wanted with the rest.

But not to tell her . . . Ruth felt as if she'd been set adrift into space, but it was a storm-tossed space in which she had nothing to grasp on to any longer. For Guy had kept her in the dark, her brother and her rock. In less than twenty-four hours she had uncovered a trip to California that had gone unmentioned and now a deliberate ruse to mete out punishment and reward to the young people who had disappointed him and the young people who had not.

"He was quite intent upon this final will," Mr. Forrest said, as if to reassure her. "And the manner in which it was written would have left his children a substantial amount of money no matter what the other beneficiaries received. He started with two million pounds nearly ten years ago, as you recall. Invested wisely, this could have developed into enough of a fortune to make anyone happy even if they were left only part of it."

Past the wrenching knowledge of what her brother had done to hurt so many people, Ruth heard the *would have* and *could have* of Mr. Forrest's remarks. He seemed suddenly at a great distance from her, the space into which she'd been thrust whipping her ever farther away from the rest of humanity. She said, "Is there something more I need to know, Mr. Forrest?"

Dominic Forrest appeared to consider this question. "Need to know? I wouldn't say you need to. But on the other hand, considering Guy's children and how they're going to react . . . I think it's wise to be prepared."

"For what?"

The advocate took up a piece of paper that lay next to the telephone on his desk. "I had a message from the forensic accountant. The phone calls I needed to make? Returning his was one of them."

"And?" Ruth could see his hesitation in the way Forrest looked at the paper, the same sort of hesitation her doctor employed when marshaling his forces to relay bad news. So she knew enough to prepare herself, although that didn't go far towards keeping her from wanting to run from the room.

"Ruth, there's very little money left. Just under two hundred and fifty thousand pounds. A considerable amount in the normal scheme of things, yes. But when you consider he began with two million . . . He was a shrewd businessman, no one shrewder. He knew when, where, and how to invest. There should be far more than what there is right now in his accounts."

"What happened . . . ?"

"To the rest of that money?" Forrest finished. "I don't know. When the forensic accountant gave his report, I told him there had to be some kind of mistake. He's looking into things, but he's said it was a straightforward affair as far as he could tell."

"What does that mean?"

"Evidently ten months ago, Guy sold off a significant portion of his holdings. Over three and a half million pounds at the time."

"To put in the bank? In his savings, perhaps?"

"It's not there."

"To make a purchase?"

"There's no record of that."

"Then what?"

"I don't know. I've only just found out ten minutes ago that the money is missing, and all I can tell you is what's left: a quarter of a million pounds."

"But as his advocate, you *must* have known—"

"Ruth, I just spent part of the morning letting his beneficiaries know they were each to inherit something in the vicinity of seven hundred thousand pounds, perhaps more. Believe me, I didn't know the money was gone."

"Could someone have stolen it?"

"I don't see how."

"Embezzled it at the bank or the stockbroker's?"

"Again, how?"

"Could he have given it away?"

"He could have. Yes. Right now the accountant is looking for paper trails. The logical person to have been slipped a fortune on the side is his son. But at the moment?" He shrugged. "We don't know."

"If Guy did give Adrian money," Ruth said, more to herself than to the advocate, "he kept quiet about it. They both kept quiet. And his mother doesn't know. Margaret, his mother?"—this to the advocate—"she doesn't know."

"Until we find out more, we can only assume everyone has a legacy much reduced from what it might otherwise be," Mr. Forrest said. "And you should prepare yourself for a fair amount of animosity."

"Reduced. Yes. I hadn't thought of that."

"Start thinking of it, then," Mr. Forrest told her. "As things stand now, Guy's children are inheriting less than sixty thousand pounds apiece, the other two have been left round eighty-seven thousand pounds, and you are sitting on property and belongings worth millions. When all this becomes clear, there's going to be enormous pressure on you to make things right in the eyes of other people. Till we get everything sorted out, I suggest you hold firm to what we know of Guy's wishes about the estate."

"There may be more to know," Ruth murmured.

Forrest dropped his notes from the forensic accountant onto his desk. "Believe me, there's definitely more to know," he agreed.

Chapter 16

AT HER END OF the line, Valerie Duffy listened to the phone ring on and on. She whispered, "Answer it, answer it, *answer* it," but the ringing continued. Although she didn't want to break the connection, she finally forced herself to do so. A moment later, she had herself convinced she'd misdialed the number, so she began again. The call went through; the ringing commenced. The result was the same.

Outside, she could see the police carrying on with their search. They'd been dogged but thorough in the manor house and they'd moved on to the outbuildings and the gardens. Soon, Valerie reckoned, they would decide to search the cottage as well. It was part of *Le Reposoir* and their orders had been—according to the sergeant in charge—to conduct a thorough and painstaking search of the premises, Madam.

She didn't want to consider what they were looking for, but she had a fairly good idea. An officer had descended the stairs with Ruth's medicines in an evidence bag and it was only through stressing how essential the medicines were to Ruth's well-being that Valerie had been able to persuade the constable not to remove every single one of the pills from the house. They didn't need all of them, surely, she'd argued. Miss Brouard had terrible pain and without her medicine—

Pain? the constable had interrupted. So we've got painkillers here? and he shook the bag for emphasis, as if any were needed.

Well, certainly. All they had to do was to read the labels and take note of the words *for pain,* which surely they had seen when they picked the drugs out of her medicine cabinet.

We've had our instructions, Madam, were the words the constable used in reply. By which declaration Valerie assumed they were to remove all drugs that they found, no matter their purpose.

She asked if they would leave the majority of the pills behind. Take a sample from each bottle and leave the rest, she suggested. Surely you can do that for Miss Brouard's sake. She'll do very badly without them.

The constable agreed to do so, but he wasn't pleased. As Valerie left him to return to her work in the kitchen, she felt his eyes boring into her back and knew she'd made herself the object of his suspicion. For this reason, she didn't want to make her phone call from the manor house. So she'd crossed to the cottage and rather than place the call from the kitchen where she wouldn't be able to see what was going on in the grounds of *Le Reposoir,* she made it instead from the upstairs bedroom. She sat on Kevin's side of the bed, closer to the window, and because of this, as she watched the police separate and head into the gardens and the individual buildings on the estate, she was able to breathe in the scent of Kev from a work shirt he'd left over the arm of a chair.

Answer, she thought. Answer. *Answer.* The ringing went on.

She turned from the window and hunched over the phone, concentrating on sending the force of her will through the receiver. If she let the connection go on long enough, surely the irritating noise alone would force an answer.

Kevin wouldn't like this. He'd say, "Why're you doing this, Val?" And she wouldn't be able to make a reply that was direct and honest, because for too long there had simply been too much at stake to be direct and honest about anything.

Answer, answer, *answer,* she thought.

He'd left quite early. The weather was getting rougher every day, he'd said, and he needed to see to that leak in the front windows of Mary Beth's house. With the exposure she had—looking directly west onto Portelet Bay—when the rains came, she was going to have a real problem on her hands. The lower windows affected the sitting room and the water would destroy her carpet, not to mention encourage mould to grow, and Val knew how Mary Beth's girls both had allergies to damp. Upstairs, even worse, the windows belonged to the two girls' bedrooms. He couldn't have his nieces sleeping in their beds while the rain seeped in and ran down the wallpaper, now, could he? He had responsibilities as a brother-in-law, and he didn't like to disregard them.

So off he'd gone to see to his sister-in-law's windows. Helpless, helpless Mary Beth Duffy, Valerie thought, thrust into an untimely widowhood by a defect of heart that had killed her husband, walking from a taxi to the door of a hotel in Kuwait. All over for Corey in less than one minute. Kev shared that defect of heart with his twin, but none of them had known that till Corey died on that street, in that endless sunshine, in that heat of Kuwait. Thus Kevin owed his life to Corey's death. A congenital defect in one twin suggested the possibility of such a defect in the other. Kevin had magic planted in his chest now, a device that would have saved Corey had anyone ever suspected that there was something wrong with his heart.

Valerie knew her husband felt doubly responsible for his brother's wife and his brother's children as a result. While she tried to remind herself that he was only living up to a sense of obligation that wouldn't have even existed had Corey not died, she couldn't help looking at the bedside clock and asking herself how long it really did take to seal four or five windows.

The girls would be at school—Kev's two nieces—and Mary Beth would be grateful. Her gratitude in conjunction with her grief could combine to make an intoxicating brew.

Make me forget, Kev. Help me forget.

The phone kept ringing, ringing, ringing. Valerie

listened, head bent to the task. She pressed her fingers against her eyes.

She knew quite well how seduction worked. She'd seen it happen before her eyes. A world history between a man and a woman grew from sidelong glances and knowing looks. It gained definition from those moments of casual contact for which existed an easy explanation: Fingers touch when a plate is passed; a hand on the arm merely emphasises an amusing remark. After that, a flush on the skin presaged a hunger within the eyes. In the end came the reasons to hang about, to see the beloved, to be seen and desired.

How had all of them come to this? she wondered. Where would everything lead if no one spoke?

She'd never been able to lie convincingly. Put to the question, she either had to ignore it, walk away from it, pretend to misunderstand it, or tell the truth. Looking someone in the eye and deliberately misleading them was beyond her meagre acting abilities. When asked "What do you know about this, Val?" her only options were to run or to speak.

She'd been absolutely certain of what she'd seen from the window on the morning of Guy Brouard's death. She was certain still, even now. She'd been certain then because it had all seemed so much in keeping with how Guy Brouard lived: the early-morning passage on his way to the bay where every day he reenacted a swim that was less exercise to him than it was reassurance of a prowess and virility that time was finally draining away, and then moments later, the figure who followed him. Valerie was certain now about who that figure had been because she'd seen the way Guy Brouard had been with the American woman—charming and charmed in that manner he had, part old world courtesy, part new world familiarity—and she knew how his ways could make a woman feel and what his ways could cause a woman to do.

But to kill? That was the problem. She could believe China River had followed him to the bay, probably for a tryst that had been prearranged. She could believe that a great deal—if not everything and then some—had passed between them before that morning as well. But she could not bring herself to think the American woman had killed Guy Brouard. Killing a man—and especially killing a man as this man had been killed—was not the work of a woman. Women killed their rivals for a man's affections; they didn't kill the man.

With this in mind, it stood to reason that China River herself had been the one in danger. Anaïs Abbott couldn't have been pleased to witness her lover giving his attention to someone besides herself. And were there others, Valerie wondered, who'd watched the two of them—China River and Guy Brouard—and put down the quick understanding that had developed between them as the budding of a relationship? Not just a stranger come to stay a few days at *Le Reposoir* and then to move on but a threat to someone's plans for the future, plans that had, until China River's advent upon Guernsey, seemed breathlessly close to fruition. But if that was the case, why kill Guy Brouard?

Answer, *answer*, Valerie told the phone.

And then, "Val, what're the police doing here?"

Valerie dropped the receiver into her lap. She whirled round to find Kevin standing in the doorway of their bedroom, his half-unbuttoned shirt suggesting he'd planned to change his clothes. She gave a fleeting moment to wonder why—her scent upon them, Kev?—but then saw that he was choosing from the wardrobe something heavier against the cold: a thick wool fisherman's sweater that he'd be able to work in outside.

Kevin looked at the phone in her lap, then at her. Faintly, the ear piece emitted the sound of continued ringing at the other end of the line. Valerie grabbed it up and replaced it in the cradle. She became aware of what she hadn't noticed before: sharp pain in the joints of her hands. She moved her fingers but winced with the shock of dull soreness. She wondered she hadn't noticed it before.

Kevin said, "Bad, is it?"

"Comes and goes."

"Ringing the doctor, were you?"

"As if that would change things. There's nothing wrong is what he keeps saying. You don't have arthritis, Mrs. Duffy. And those pills of his . . . I expect they're nothing but sugar, Kev. Humouring me. But the pain is *real*. Days I can't even make my fingers work."

"Another doctor, then?"

"It's so hard for me to find someone I trust." How true, she thought. At whose knee had she learned such suspicion and doubt?

"I meant the phone," Kevin said as he pulled the grey wool sweater over his head. "Are you trying another doctor? If the pain's got worse, you need to do something."

"Oh." Valerie looked at the phone on the bedside table so as to avert her eyes from her husband's. "Yes. Yes. I was trying . . . I couldn't get through." She produced a quick smile. "Don't know what the world's coming to when doctors' phones don't get answered, not even in their surgeries." She slapped her hands on her thighs in a gesture of finality, and she rose from the bed. "I'll fetch those pills, then. If it's all in my head like the doctor thinks, p'rhaps the pills'll fool my body into believing."

Taking her pills gave her time to collect herself. She fetched them from the bathroom and carried them down to the kitchen so that she could take them as she always took medicine: with orange juice. There was nothing out of the ordinary in that for Kevin to notice.

When he descended the stairs and joined her, she was ready for him. She said brightly, "All's well with Mary Beth? Get her windows done up?"

"She's worried about Christmas coming. This first one without Corey."

"Rough, that is. She's going to miss him for a long long time. Like I'd miss you, Kev." Valerie dug a fresh dishcloth out of the linen drawer and set to wiping down the work tops with it. They didn't need it, but she wanted to be doing something to stop the truth spilling out. Keeping occupied went hand in glove with making sure her voice, her body, and her expressions did nothing to betray her, and she wanted that: the comfort of knowing that she was safe, with her feelings guarded. "It's trying as well, I expect, when she sees you. She looks at you, sees Corey."

Kevin didn't reply. She was forced to look at him. He said, "It's the girls she's worried over. They're asking Father Christmas to bring their daddy back. Mary Beth's worried what'll happen with them when he doesn't."

Valerie rubbed at the work top, where a too-hot pot had burnt a black smudge into its old surface. Rubbing wouldn't alleviate the problem, though. It had been created too long ago and should have been seen to then.

Kevin said again, "What're the police doing here, Val?"

"Searching."

"For?"

"They're not saying."

"It's to do with . . . ?"

"Yes. What else? They've taken Ruth's pills—"

"They're not thinking *Ruth*—"

"No. I don't know. I don't think so." Valerie stopped her rubbing and folded the dishcloth. The spot remained, unchanged.

"Not like you to be here this time of day," Kevin said. "Work to be done in the big house? Meals to prepare?"

"Had to stay out of the way of that lot," she said, meaning the police.

"They ask that of you?"

"Just the way it seemed."

"They'll search here if they've searched there." He gazed towards the window as if he could see the manor house from the kitchen, which he could not. "I wonder what they're looking for."

"I don't know," she told him again, but her throat felt tight.

From the front of the cottage, a dog began to bark. The barking changed to yelping. Someone shouted. Valerie and her husband went to the sitting room, where the windows looked out onto a lawn and beyond it the drive, at the point where it circled round the bronze sculpture of the swimmers and the dolphins. There, they saw, Paul Fielder and Taboo were having a run-in with the local police in the person of a single constable, backed against a tree as the dog snapped at his trousers. Paul dropped his bicycle and began to pull the dog away. The constable advanced, red of face and loud of voice.

"I'd better see to that," Valerie said. "I don't want our Paul ending up in trouble."

She grabbed her coat, which she'd left on the back of an armchair when she'd come into the cottage. She headed for the door.

Kevin said nothing till her hand was on the knob, at which point he merely spoke her name.

She looked back at him: the rugged face, the work-hardened hands, the unreadable eyes. When he next spoke, she heard his question but could not bring herself to reply:

"Is there anything you want to tell me?" he asked her.

She smiled at him brightly and shook her head.

Deborah sat beneath the silver sky not far from the looming statue of Victor Hugo, whose granite cloak and granite scarf billowed back forever in the wind that blew from his native France. She was alone on the gentle slope of Candie Gardens, having walked up the hill from Ann's Place directly after leaving the hotel. She'd slept badly, far too aware of the proximity of her husband's body, and determined not to roll next to him unconsciously during the night. This frame of mind didn't welcome Morpheus: She rose before dawn and went out for a walk.

After her angry encounter with Simon on the previous evening, she'd returned to the hotel. But there she felt like a guilt-stricken child. Furious at herself for welcoming the smallest sense of remorse into her consciousness when she knew she had done nothing wrong, she soon left again and she didn't return till after midnight, when she could be reasonably assured that Simon would be asleep.

She'd gone to China. "Simon," she told her, "is being completely impossible."

"Ain't that the definition of m-a-n." China drew Deborah inside and they made pasta together, with China at the cooker and Deborah leaning against the sink. "Tell all," China said affably. "Auntie is here to apply the Band-Aids."

"That stupid ring," Deborah said. "He's worked himself into a state about it." She explained the entire story as China poured a jar of tomato sauce into a pan and commenced stirring. "You'd think I'd committed a crime," she concluded.

"It was stupid anyway," China said when Deborah was finished. "I mean even buying it in the first place. It was an impulse thing." She cocked her head in Deborah's direction. "Just the kind of thing you'd never do."

"Simon seems to feel that bringing the ring round here was impulsive enough."

"He does?" China stared at the cooking pasta for a moment before replying matter-of-factly. "Well. I c'n see why he hasn't been exactly desperate to meet me, then."

"That isn't it," Deborah protested quickly. "You mustn't . . . You'll meet him. He's eager to . . . He's heard so much about you over the years."

"Yeah?" China looked up from the sauce to regard her evenly. Deborah felt herself growing sticky under her gaze. China said, "It's okay. You were going on with your life. There's nothing wrong with that. California wasn't your best three years. I can see why you wouldn't want to remember if you could help it. And keeping in touch . . . It would have been a form of remembering, huh? Anyway, sometimes that happens with friendships. People are close for a while and then they're not. Things change. Needs change. People move on. That's just how it is. I've missed you, though."

"We should have stayed close," Deborah said.

"Tough to manage when someone doesn't write. Or call. Or anything." China shot her a smile. It was sad, though, and Deborah could feel it.

"I'm sorry, China. I don't know why I didn't write. I meant to, but time starting passing and then . . . I should have written. E-mailed. Phoned."

"Beat a tom-tom."

"Anything. You must have felt . . . I don't know . . . You probably thought I forgot you. But I didn't. How could I? After everything?"

"I did get the wedding announcement." *But no invitation to the wedding itself* was unsaid.

Deborah heard it, nonetheless. She sought a way to explain. "I suppose I thought you'd find it odd. After Tommy. All of a sudden after everything that happened, I'm marrying someone else. I suppose I didn't know how to explain."

"You thought you had to? Why?"

"Because it looked . . ." Deborah wanted a good word to describe how her shift from Tommy Lynley to Simon St. James might have appeared to someone who hadn't known the whole story of her love for Simon and her estrangement from him. It had all been too painful to speak of to anyone while she was in America. And then Tommy had been there, stepping into a void that even he had not known at the time existed. It was all too complicated. It always had been. Perhaps that was why she'd kept China as part of an American experience that included Tommy and thus had to be relegated to the past when her time with Tommy ended. She said, "I never did speak much about Simon, did I?"

"Never mentioned his name. You watched for the mail a whole lot and you looked like a puppy whenever the phone rang. When the letter you were waiting for never came and the phone call didn't either, you'd disappear for a couple of hours. I figured there was someone back home you were putting behind you, but I didn't want to ask. I figured you would tell me when you were ready. You never did." China emptied the cooked pasta into a colander. She turned from the sink, steam rising behind her. "It was something we could have shared," she said. "I'm sorry you didn't trust me enough."

"That's not how it was. Think of everything that happened, all the things that show I trusted you completely."

"The abortion, sure. But that was physical. The emotional part you never trusted with anyone. Even when you married Simon. Even now when you've been hassling with him. Girlfriends are for sharing, Debs. They're not just conveniences, like Kleenex when you need to blow."

"Is that what you think you were to me? What you are to me now?"

China shrugged. "I guess I'm not sure."

In Candie Gardens now, Deborah reflected upon her evening with China. Cherokee had put in no appearance while she was there—"He said he was going to a movie, but he's probably scamming on some woman in a bar"—so there was no distraction and no way to avoid looking at what had happened to their friendship.

On Guernsey they were in an odd reversal of roles, and that created an uncertainty between them. China, long the nurturing partner in their relationship, ever caring for a foreigner who'd come to California wounded by a love unacknowledged, had been forced by her current circumstances to become China the supplicant dependent upon the kindness of others. Deborah, always at the receiving end of China's ministrations, had taken up the mantle of Samaritan. This alteration in the way they interacted with each other put them out of sorts, further out of sorts than they might have been had there existed between them only the hurt caused by the years during which they had not communicated. So neither quite knew the right thing to do or say. But both of them, Deborah believed, did actually feel the same at heart, no matter how inarticulate was her effort to express it: Each was concerned for the other's welfare, and each was a bit defensive about herself. They were in the process of finding their way with each other, a way forward that was also a way out of the past.

Deborah rose from her bench as milky sunlight struck the cinder path leading to the garden's gate. She followed this path between lawn and shrubbery and skirted a pond where goldfish swam, delicate miniatures of the fish in *Le Reposoir*'s Japanese garden.

Outside in the street, morning traffic was building, and pedestrians were hurrying on their way into the centre of town. Most of them crossed over the road into Ann's Place. Deborah followed them round the gentle curve that exposed the hotel.

Outside, she saw, Cherokee was leaning his hips against the low wall that marked the boundary of the sunken garden. He was eating something wrapped in a paper napkin and drinking from a steaming take-away cup. All the time, he kept his attention on the hotel façade.

She went up to him. So intent was he upon his observation of the building across the street that he didn't notice her, and he started when she said his name. Then he grinned. "It actually works," he said. "I was sending you a telepathic message to come outside."

"Telephonic generally works better," she replied. "What're you eating?"

"Chocolate croissant. Want some?" He extended it to her.

She covered his hand with hers and held it steady. "Fresh, as well. How lovely." She munched.

He extended the cup from which the fragrance of hot coffee plumed. She sipped. He smiled. "Excellent."

"What?"

"What just happened right here."

"Which was?"

"Our marriage. In some of the most primitive Amazon tribes, you would've just become my woman."

"What would that entail?"

"Come to the Amazon with me and find out." He took a bite of croissant and observed her closely. "I don't know what was going on with me back then. I never realised how hot you are. It must've been because you were taken."

"I'm still taken," Deborah pointed out.

"Married women don't count."

"Why?"

"It's pretty tough to explain."

She joined him in leaning against the wall, took his coffee from him, and indulged in another sip. "Try."

"It's a guy thing. Pretty basic rules. You can make a move on a woman if she's single or married. Single because she's available and, let's face it, she's generally looking for someone to give her a thumbs-up about how she looks, so she'll accept a move. Married because her husband's probably ignored her one time too many, and if he hasn't, she'll let you know right up front so you don't have to waste your time. But the woman who's *attached* to some guy but not married to him is totally off limits. She's immune to your moves, and if you try one on her, you're going to hear from her man eventually."

"That sounds like the voice of experience," Deborah observed.

He gave a quirky grin.

"China thought you were out scamming after women last night."

"She said you came over. I wondered why."

"Things were touchy over here last evening."

"Which makes you available for a move. Touchy

is very good news for moves. Have some more croissant. Have some more coffee."

"To seal our Amazon marriage?"

"See? You're thinking like a South American already."

They laughed together companionably.

Cherokee said, "You should've come to Orange County more often. It would've been nice."

"So you could have scammed on me?"

"Nah. That's what I'm doing now."

Deborah chuckled. He was teasing, of course. He no more wanted her than he wanted his own sister. But the undercurrent between them—that man-woman charge—was pleasurable, she had to admit. She wondered how long it had been missing from her marriage. She wondered *if* it was missing. She merely wondered.

Cherokee said, "I wanted your advice. I couldn't sleep worth horse dung last night trying to decide what to do."

"About?"

"Calling Mom. China doesn't want her involved. She doesn't want her to know anything about it. But I'm thinking she has the right. This *is* our mom we're talking about. China says there's nothing she can do here and that's true. But she could *be* here, couldn't she? Anyway, I was thinking I'd call her. What d'you say?"

Deborah considered this. At its best, China's relationship with her mother had been more like an armed truce between armies engaged in an internecine struggle. At its worst, it had been a pitched battle. China's loathing of her mother had deep roots in a childhood of deprivation, which itself had grown from Andromeda River's passionate devotion to social and environmental issues that had caused her to disregard the social and environmental issues directly affecting her own children. As a result, she'd had very little time for Cherokee and China, whose formative years had been spent in thin-walled motels where the only luxury was an ice maker next to the proprietor's office. As long as Deborah had known China, she'd possessed a deep reservoir of anger against her mother for the conditions in which she'd raised her children while all the time waving placards of protest for endangered animals, endangered plants, and children endangered by conditions not unlike those her own two children endured.

"Perhaps you ought to wait a few days," Deborah suggested. "China's on edge . . . well, who wouldn't be? If she doesn't want her here, it might be best to respect her wishes. For now, at least."

"You think it's going to get worse, don't you?"

She sighed. "There *is* this business with the ring. I wish she hadn't bought it."

"You and me both."

"Cherokee, what happened between her and Matt Whitecomb?"

Cherokee looked at the hotel and appeared to be studying the windows on the first floor, where curtains were still drawn against the morning. "It was going nowhere. She couldn't see that. It was what it was, which wasn't much, and she wanted it to be more so that's how she made herself see it."

"It wasn't much after thirteen years?" Deborah asked. "How can that be?"

"It can be because men are assholes." Cherokee drank down the rest of his coffee and went on. "I'd better get back to her, okay?"

"Of course."

"And you and I, Debs? . . . We've got to work harder to get her out of this mess. You know that, right?" He reached out, and it seemed for a moment as if he intended to caress her hair or her face. But he dropped his hand to her shoulder and squeezed. Then he strode off in the direction of Clifton Street, some distance from the Royal Court House, where China would stand trial if they didn't do something soon to prevent it.

Deborah returned to her hotel room. There, she discovered that Simon was in the midst of one of his morning rituals. He generally had either her or her father's assistance, however, and using the electrodes by himself was an awkward business for him. Still, he seemed to have managed their placement with a fair degree of precision. He lay on the bed with a copy of yesterday's *Guardian,* and he read its front section as electricity stimulated the useless muscles in his leg to prevent them from atrophying.

This was, she knew, his primary vanity. But it also represented a remnant of hope that someday a way would be found that he could walk normally again. When that day arrived, he wanted his leg to be capable of doing the job.

Her heart went out to Simon whenever she caught him at a moment like this. He knew it, though, and because he hated anything that smacked of pity, she always made the effort to pretend his activity was as normal as brushing his teeth.

He said, "When I woke and you weren't here, I had a bad moment. I thought you'd been gone all night."

She took off her coat and went to the electric kettle, which she filled with water and plugged in. She put two bags into the teapot. "I was furious with you. But not enough to sleep on the street."

"I didn't actually think the street was where you'd end up."

She glanced over her shoulder at him, but he was examining an inside page of the broadsheet. "We talked about old times. You were asleep when I got back. And then I couldn't sleep. One of those toss-and-turn nights. I was up early, so I had a walk."

"Nice day out there?"

"Cold and grey. We might as well be in London."

"December," he said.

"Hmm," she replied. Inside, however, she was shouting, "Why in God's name are we talking about the *weather.* Is this what it comes to in every marriage?"

As if reading her mind and wishing to prove her wrong, Simon said, "It's apparently her ring, Deborah. There was no other among her belongings in the evidence room at the station. They can't be certain, of course, till they—"

"Are her fingerprints on it?"

"I don't know yet."

"Then . . ."

"We have to wait and see."

"You think she's guilty, don't you?" Deborah heard the bitterness in her voice, and although she tried to sound like him—rational, thoughtful, dealing with the facts and not allowing them to colour the feelings—she failed in the effort. "Some incredible help we're turning out to be."

"Deborah," Simon said quietly, "come here. Sit on the bed."

"*God,* I hate it when you talk to me like that."

"You're angry about yesterday. My approach with you was . . . I know it was wrong. Harsh. Unkind. I admit it. I apologise. Can we move past it? Because I'd like to tell you what I've learned. I wanted to tell you last night. I would have told you. But things were difficult. I was foul and you were within your rights to make yourself scarce."

This was as far as Simon had ever gone in admitting he had taken a misstep in their marriage. Deborah recognised this and approached the bed, where his leg muscles twitched with electrical activity. She sat on the edge of the mattress. "The ring might be hers, but that doesn't mean she was there, Simon."

"Agreed." He went on to explain how he'd spent the hours after they'd parted at the sunken garden.

The difference in time between Guernsey and California had made it possible to contact the attorney who had hired Cherokee River to carry the architectural plans across the ocean. William Kiefer began their conversation by citing attorney-client privilege, but he was cooperative once he learned that the client in question had been murdered on a beach in Guernsey.

Guy Brouard, Kiefer explained to Simon, had hired him to set in motion a rather unusual series of tasks. He wished Kiefer to locate someone perfectly trustworthy who would be willing to courier a set of important architectural plans from Orange County to Guernsey.

At first, Kiefer told Simon, the assignment seemed idiotic to him, although he hadn't mentioned that particular word to Mr. Brouard during their brief meeting. Why not use one of the conventional courier services that were set up to do exactly what Brouard wanted and at minimal cost? FedEx? DHL? Even UPS? But Mr. Brouard, as things turned out, was an intriguing combination of authority, eccentricity, and paranoia. He had the money to do things his way, he told Kiefer, and his way was to ensure he got what he wanted when he wanted it. He'd carry the plans himself, but he was in Orange County only to make arrangements for them to be drawn up. He couldn't stay as long as necessary to have them ready.

He wanted someone responsible to do the couriering, he said. He was willing to pay whatever it took to get just that sort of person. He didn't trust a man alone to do the job—apparently, Kiefer explained, he had a loser son who made him think no youngish man was worth anyone's faith—and he didn't want a woman traveling alone to Europe because he didn't like the idea of women on their own and he didn't want to feel responsible should something happen to her. He was old-fashioned that way. So they settled on a man and woman together. They would look for a married couple of any age to fill the bill.

Brouard, Kiefer said, was eccentric enough to offer five thousand dollars for the job. He was tight enough to offer only tourist-level travel. Because the couple in question had to be able to leave whenever the plans were ready, it seemed the best source of potential couriers might be the local University of California. So Kiefer posted the job there and waited to see what would happen.

In the meantime, Brouard paid him his fee and added the five thousand dollars which would be promised to the courier. Neither cheque bounced, and while Kiefer thought the scenario was bizarre, he made certain it wasn't illegal by checking out the architect to make sure he *was* an architect and not some arms manufacturer, a plutonium source, a drug dealer, or a supplier of substances for biological warfare.

Because obviously, Kiefer said, none of those types were about to send anything by a legitimate courier service.

But the architect turned out to be a man called Jim Ward, who'd even attended high school with Kiefer. He confirmed every part of the story: He was assembling a set of architectural plans and elevation drawings for Mr. Guy Brouard, *Le Reposoir,* St. Martin, Island of Guernsey. Brouard wanted those plans and those drawings ASAP.

So Kiefer set about making everything happen on his end of things. A slew of applicants lined up to do the job, and from them he chose a man called Cherokee River. He was older than the others, Kiefer explained, and he was married.

"Essentially," Simon concluded, "William Kiefer confirmed the Rivers' story down to the last comma, question mark, and full stop. It was a strange way of doing things, but I'm getting the impression that Brouard liked doing things strangely. Keeping people off balance kept him in control. That's important to rich men. It's generally how they got rich to begin with."

"Do the police know all this?"

He shook his head. "Le Gallez's got all the paperwork, though. I expect he's one step from finding out."

"Will he release her, then?"

"Because the basic story she told checks out?" Simon reached for the case that was the source of the electrodes. He switched the unit off and began detaching himself from the wires. "I don't think so, Deborah. Not unless he comes up with something that points definitively to someone else." He grabbed his crutches from the floor and swung himself off the bed.

"And is there something else? Pointing to someone else?"

He didn't reply. Instead, he took his time with his leg brace, which lay next to the armchair beneath the window. To Deborah, there seemed to be countless adjustments he made to it this morning and an endless procedure to be gone through before he was dressed, standing on his feet, and willing to continue their conversation.

Then he said, "You sound worried."

"China wondered why you . . . Well, you haven't seemed to want to meet her. It looks to her as if you've got a reason to keep your distance. Do you?"

"Superficially, she's the logical person for someone to frame for this crime: She and Brouard evidently spent some time together alone, her cloak appears to have been fairly easy for someone to get their hands on, and anyone with access to her bedroom would also have access to her hair and her shoes. But premeditation in murder demands a motive. And any way you look at it, motive is something she didn't have."

"Still, the police may think—"

"No. They know they've got no motive. That clears the way for us."

"To find one for someone else?"

"Yes. Why do people premeditate murder? Revenge, jealousy, blackmail, or material gain. That's where we need to direct our energies now, I dare say."

"But that ring . . . Simon, if it's definitely China's?"

"We'd better be damn quick about our work."

Chapter 17

MARGARET CHAMBERLAIN MAINTAINED A death grip on the steering wheel as she drove back to *Le Reposoir*. The death grip kept her in focus, aware only of the effort required to keep the appropriate degree of pressure in her grasp. This, in turn, allowed her to stay present in the Range Rover so that she could course south along *Belle Greve* Bay without thinking about her encounter with what went for the Fielder family.

Finding them had been a simple matter: There were only two Fielder listings in the telephone directory and one of them lived on Alderney. The other was domiciled in *Rue des Lierres* in an area between St. Peter Port and St. Sampson. Finding this on the map had presented little difficulty. Finding it in reality had, however, been another matter, as this part of town—called the Bouet—was as ill-marked as it was ill-featured.

The Bouet turned out to be an area that reminded Margaret a little too much of her distant past as one of six children in a family where ends not only didn't meet, they didn't even acknowledge the existence of each other. In the Bouet lived the fringe dwellers of the island's society, and their homes looked like the homes of such people in every town in England. Here were hideous terraced houses with narrow front doors, aluminium windows, and siding stained by rust. Overfilled rubbish bags took the place of shrubbery, and instead of flowerbeds, what few lawns there were had their patchy expanses broken up by debris.

As Margaret got out of her car along the street, two cats hissed at each other over possession of a half-eaten pork pie that lay in the gutter. A dog rooted in an overturned dustbin. Gulls fed upon the remains of a loaf of bread on a lawn. She shuddered at the sight of all this even as she knew it suggested she would have a distinct advantage in the coming conversation. The Fielders were clearly not in a position to hire a solicitor to explain their rights to them. It should not, she thought, prove a difficult matter to wrest from them Adrian's rightful due.

She hadn't counted on the creature who answered her knock on the door. He was a hulking mass of unkempt unwashed unseemly male antagonism. To her pleasant enquiry of "Good morning. Do the parents of Paul Fielder live here?" he replied, "Could be they do, could be they don't," and he fastened his eyes upon her breasts with the deliberate intention of unnerving her.

She said, "You aren't Mr. Fielder, are you? Not the father . . ." But, of course, he couldn't have been. For all his deliberate sexual precocity, he looked no more than twenty years old. "You must be a brother? I'd like to speak to your parents, if they're here. You might tell them this is about your brother. Paul Fielder is your brother, I take it?"

He lifted his eyes from her chest momentarily. "Little git," he said, and stepped away from the door.

Margaret took this as invitation to enter, and when the lout disappeared to the rear of the house, she took this as further invitation to follow. She found herself in a cramped kitchen smelling of rancid bacon, alone with him, where he lit a cigarette on the gas burner of the hob and turned to face her as he inhaled.

"Wha's he done now?" Brother Fielder asked.

"He's inherited a fair sum of money from my husband, from my former husband, to be exact. He's inherited it away from my son, to whom it is owed. I'd like to avoid a lengthy court battle over this matter, and I thought it best to see if your parents felt likewise."

"Did you?" Brother Fielder asked. He adjusted his filthy blue jeans round his hips, shifted his legs, and broke wind loudly. "Pardon," he said. "Must mind my manners with a lady. I forget."

"Your parents aren't here, I take it?" Margaret settled her bag on her arm in an indication that their encounter was quickly drawing to a close. "If you'll tell them—"

"Could be they're just 'bove stairs. They like to go at it in the morning, they do. What 'bout you? When d'you like it?"

Margaret decided her conversation with this yob had gone on long enough. She said, "If you'll tell them Margaret Chamberlain—formerly Brouard—stopped by . . . I'll phone them later." She turned to go the way she'd come.

"Margaret Chamberlain Formerly Brouard," Brother Fielder repeated. "Don't know if I c'n remember that much. I'll need some help with all that. Real mouthful, it is."

Margaret stopped in her progress to the front door. "If you have a piece of paper, I'll write it down."

She was in the passage between front door and kitchen and the young man joined her there. His proximity in the narrow corridor made him seem more threatening than he otherwise might have been, and the silence in the house round and above them seemed amplified suddenly. He said, "I di'n't have a paper in mind. I don't ever remember any good with papers."

"Well, then. That's that, isn't it? I'll just have to phone and introduce myself to them." Margaret turned—although she was loath to put him out of her sight—and made for the door.

He caught her up in two steps and trapped her hand on the knob. She felt his breath hot on her neck. He moved against her so she was pressed into the door. When he had her there, he released her hand and groped downward till he'd found her crotch. He grabbed hard and jerked her back against him. With his other hand he reached for and squeezed her left breast. It all happened in a second. "This'll help me remember good enough," he muttered.

All Margaret could think, ludicrously, was what

had he done with the cigarette he'd lit? Was it in his hand? Did he mean to burn her?

The lunacy of those thoughts in circumstances in which burning was *clearly* the last thing on the creature's mind acted as a spur to free her from fear. She drove her elbow backwards into his ribs. She drove the heel of her boot into the centre of his foot. In the moment his grip loosened upon her, she shoved him back and got herself out of the door. She wanted to stay and drive her knee into his bollocks—God, how she was *itching* to do that—but although she was a tigress when enraged, she had never been a fool. She made for her car.

As she drove in the direction of *Le Reposoir*, she found that her body was shot through with adrenaline and her response to the adrenaline was rage. She directed it at the loathsome excuse of a human being she'd found in the Bouet. How *dared* he . . . Who the *hell* did he think . . . What did he *intend* . . . She could bloody well have *killed* . . . But that lasted only so long. It spent itself as the realisation of what might have happened grew in her mind, and *this* redirected her fury onto a more appropriate recipient: her son.

He hadn't gone with her. He'd left her to deal with Henry Moullin herself on the previous day, and he'd done exactly the same this morning.

She was finished with it, Margaret decided. By God, she was finished. She was finished with orchestrating Adrian's life without the slightest assistance or even any thanks. She'd been fighting his battles since the day he was born, and that was *over.*

At *Le Reposoir,* she slammed the door of the Range Rover and stalked to the house, where she opened and slammed *its* door as well. The slams punctuated the monologue going on in her head. She was *finished.* Slam. He was bloody well on his *own.* Slam again.

No sound came in response to her ministrations upon the heavy front door. This infuriated her in ways she wouldn't have expected, and she charged across the old stone hall with her boot heels marking an enraged tattoo. She fairly flew up the stairs to Adrian's room. The only things keeping her from bursting in on him were concern that some sign of what she'd just gone through might be apparent on her person and fear that she'd find Adrian engaged in some disgusting personal activity.

And perhaps, she thought, *that's* what had driven Carmel Fitzgerald into the all-too-willing arms of Adrian's own father. She'd had a first-hand experience of one or another of Adrian's odious methods of self-soothing when under pressure and she'd run to Guy in confusion, seeking solace and an explanation, both of which Guy had been all too willing to give her.

He's rather odd, my son, not quite what one expects from a real man, my dear.

Oh yes, oh too right, Margaret thought. Adrian's one chance for normalcy ripped from his hands. And at his own fault, which was maddening to Margaret in the extreme. When—good God *when*— would her son transform himself into the man she meant him to be?

In the upstairs corridor, a gilt mirror hung over a mahogany chest, and Margaret paused here to check her appearance. She dropped her gaze to her bosom, where she half-expected the imprint of Brother Fielder's filthy fingers to be all over her yellow cashmere sweater. She could still feel his hands. She could still smell his breath. Monster. Cretin. Psychopath. Thug.

At Adrian's door she knocked twice, not gently. She said his name, turned the knob, and entered. He was in bed. He wasn't asleep, however. He was lying with his gaze fixed on the window, where the curtains were drawn back to expose the grey day outside, and the casement was fully open.

Margaret's stomach lurched and the anger drained out of her. No one normal, she thought, would have been in bed under these conditions.

Margaret shivered. She strode to the window and inspected the ledge along it and the ground beneath it. She turned back to the bed. The duvet was drawn up to Adrian's chin, the lumps beneath it marking the position of his limbs. She followed this topography till her glance reached his feet. She would look, she told herself. She would know the worst.

He made no sound of protest as she lifted the duvet round his legs. He didn't move as she studied the bottoms of his feet for signs that he'd been outside in the night. The curtains and the window both suggested he'd had an episode. He'd never before climbed onto a ledge or a roof in the middle of the night, but his subconscious mind was not always governed by what rational people did and didn't do.

"Sleepwalkers don't generally put themselves in danger," Margaret had been told. "They do at night what they'd do in the day."

That, Margaret thought grimly, was exactly the point.

But if Adrian had wandered out of the room instead of just round it, there was no sign of that on his feet. She crossed a bout of sleepwalking off the list of potential blips on her son's psychological screen and next checked the bed. She made no effort to be gentle with him as she dug her hands round his hips, feeling for wet spots on the sheets and mattress. She was relieved to find that there were none. The waking coma—which was what she called his periodic descents into daylight trances—could thus be dealt with.

At one time she'd done it gently. He was her poor boy, her dearest darling, so different from her other strapping, successful sons, so sensitive to everything that went on round him. She'd roused him from this twilight state with gentle caresses on his cheeks. She'd massaged his head into wakefulness and murmured him back to earth.

But not now. Brother Fielder had squeezed the milk of maternal kindness and concern right out of her. Had Adrian been with her in the Bouet, none of what had gone on there would have occurred. No matter how utterly ineffectual he was as a male, his presence as another human being—as a *witness,* mind you—in the Fielder home surely would have done something to halt the progress of Brother Fielder's assault upon her.

Margaret grabbed the duvet and whipped it off her son's body. She threw it on the floor and snapped the pillow out from beneath Adrian's head. When he blinked, she said, "Enough is enough. Take charge of your life."

Adrian looked at his mother, then at the window, then back at his mother, then at the duvet on the floor. He didn't shiver in the cold. He didn't move. "Get out of bed!" Margaret shouted.

He came fully awake at that. He said, "Did I . . . ?" in reference to the window.

Margaret said, "What do you think? Yes and no," in reference both to the window and to the bed. "We're hiring a solicitor."

"They're called—"

"I don't bloody *care* what they're called. I'm hiring one and I want you with me." She went to the wardrobe and found his dressing gown. She threw it at him and shut the window as he finally got out of bed.

When she turned, he was watching her, and she could tell from his expression that he was completely conscious and finally reacting to her invasion of his room. It was as if an awareness of her examination of his body and his environment seeped slowly into his mind, and she saw it happening: that dawning understanding and what accompanied it. This would make him more difficult to deal with, but Margaret had always known she was more than a match for her son.

"Did you knock?" he asked.

"Don't be ridiculous. What do you think?"

"Answer me."

"Don't you *dare* talk to your mother like that. Do you know what I've been through this morning? Do you know where I've been? Do you know why?"

"I want to know if you knocked."

"Listen to yourself. Have you any idea what you sound like?"

"Don't change the subject. I've a right—"

"Yes. You have a right. And that's what I've been doing since dawn. Seeing to your rights. Trying to get them for you. Trying—for all the thanks I'm getting—to talk some sense into the very people who've ripped your rights out of your hands."

"I want to know—"

"You sound like a sniveling two-year-old. Stop it. Yes, I knocked. I banged. I shouted. And if you think I intended to walk away and wait for you to come out of whatever little fantasy world you'd taken yourself to, then you can have another good think about things. I'm tired of working for you when you have no interest in working for yourself. Get dressed. You're taking some action. Now. Or I'm finished with all of this."

"Be finished, then."

Margaret advanced on her son, grateful for the fact that he'd inherited his father's height and not her own. She had two inches over him, nearly three. She used them now. "You're impossible. You defeat yourself. Do you have any idea how unappealing that is? How it makes a woman feel?"

He went to the chest of drawers, where he'd laid a packet of Benson and Hedges. He shook one out and lit it. He drew in on it deeply and said nothing for a moment. The indolence of his movements was aggravation incarnate.

"Adrian!" Margaret heard herself shriek and knew the horror of sounding like her mother: that charwoman's voice tinctured with the tones of hopelessness and fear, both of which had to be hidden by calling them rage. "Answer me, damn you. I *won't* accept this. I've come to Guernsey to ensure your future and I have no intention of standing here and allowing you to treat me like—"

"What?" He swung round to her. "Like what? Like a piece of furniture? Moved this way and that. Like you treat me?"

"I do *not*—"

"D'you think I don't know what this is all about? What it's always been about? What *you* want. What *you* have planned."

"How can you say that? I've worked. I've slaved. I've organised. I've arranged. More than half my life, I've lived to make yours into something you can be proud of. To make you the equal of your brothers and your sisters. To make you a *man*."

"Don't make me laugh. You've worked to make me good for nothing, and now that I am, you're working to get me out of your hair. You think I can't see it? You think I don't know it? That's what this is all about. Has been since you stepped off the plane."

"That's not true. Worse, it's vicious, ungrateful, and designed to—"

"No. Let's make sure we're on the same page in all of this if you want me to be part of *acquiring* what

I'm intended to acquire. You want me to have that money so you can be rid of me. 'No more excuses, Adrian. You're on your own.' "

"That isn't true."

"Don't you think I know what a loser I am? What an embarrassment to have around?"

"Don't you say that about yourself. Don't you *ever* say it!"

"With a fortune in my hands, the excuses are gone. I'm out of your house and out of your life. I even have enough money to put myself away in the mad house if it comes down to that."

"I want you to have what you deserve. God in heaven, can't you see that?"

"I see it," he replied. "Believe me. I see. But what makes you think I don't have what I deserve? Already, Mother. Now. Already."

"You're his son."

"Yes. That's the point. His son."

Adrian stared at her long and hard. It came to Margaret that he was sending her a message, and she could feel its intensity in the gaze if not in the words. It seemed to her all at once as if they'd become strangers to each other, two people having pasts that were unrelated to this present moment in which their lives had intersected by chance.

But there was safety in feeling that strangeness and distance. Anything else ran the risk of encouraging the unthinkable to invade her thoughts.

Margaret said calmly, "Get dressed, Adrian. We're going to town. We've a solicitor to hire and little time to waste."

"I sleepwalk," he said, and at last he sounded at least marginally broken. "I do all sorts of things."

"That's certainly not something we need discuss now."

St. James and Deborah separated after their conversation in the hotel room. She would seek out the possible existence of another German ring like the one they'd found on the beach. He would seek out the beneficiaries of Guy Brouard's will. Their objectives were essentially the same—an attempt to uncover a motive behind the murder—but their approaches would be different.

Having admitted to himself that the clear signs of premeditation strongly pointed to anyone *but* the River siblings as complicit in the murder, St. James offered his blessing on Cherokee's accompanying Deborah to talk to Frank Ouseley about his collection of wartime memorabilia. When it came down to it, she was safer with a man if she found herself interviewing a murderer. For his part, he would go alone, seeking out the individuals most affected by Guy Brouard's will.

He began with a trip to *La Corbière,* where he found the Moullin household on a bend in one of the narrow lanes that snaked across the island between skeletal hedgerows and tall earthen banks knotted with ivy and thick sea grasses. He knew only the general area that the Moullins lived in— *La Corbière* itself—but it was no difficult matter to locate them exactly. He stopped at a large yellow farmhouse just outside the tiny hamlet and made an enquiry of a woman optimistically hanging laundry in the misty air. She said, "Oh, it's the Shell House you're wanting, dearie," and she pointed vaguely towards the east. Follow the road past the turn to the sea, she informed him. He couldn't miss it.

That proved to be the case.

St. James stood on the drive and surveyed the grounds of the Moullin residence for a moment before proceeding farther. He frowned at the curious sight of it: a wreckage of shells and wire and concrete where apparently had once existed a fanciful garden. A few objects remained to illustrate what the place had been like. A shell-formed wishing well stood untouched beneath an enormous sweet chestnut, and a whimsical shell-and-concrete chaise longue held a shell pillow on which the words *Daddy Says* . . . had been fashioned in bits of broken indigo glass. Everything else had been reduced to rubble. It looked as if a hurricane of sledgehammers had slammed into the grounds surrounding the small, squat house.

To one side of this building stood a barn, and music issued from inside: Frank Sinatra by the sound of it, crooning a pop tune in Italian. St. James headed in this direction. The barn door hung partially open, and he could see that its interior was whitewashed and lit by rows of fluorescent tubes that dangled from the ceiling.

He called out a hello that went unacknowledged. He stepped inside and found himself in a glassmaker's workshop. It appeared to be the manufacturing place for two entirely different kinds of objects. One half of it was given to the precise fashioning of greenhouse and conservatory glass. The other half appeared devoted to glass as art. In this section large sacks of chemicals had been piled not far from an unlit furnace. Against this leaned long pipelike tubes for blowing, and on shelves what had been blown was arranged, decorative pieces that were richly coloured: huge plates on stands, stylised vases, modern sculptures. The objects were all more suited to a Conran restaurant in London than to a barn on Guernsey. St. James took them in with some surprise. Their condition—lovingly dustless and pristine—was a contrast to the condition of the furnace, the pipes, and the chemical sacks, all of which wore a thick coating of grime.

The glassmaker himself was oblivious of the presence of anyone. He was working at a wide bench on the greenhouse-and-conservatory side of the barn. Above him hung the plans for a complicated conservatory. To either side of these and beneath them hung drawings of other projects even more elaborate. As he made a swift cut in the transparent sheet that lay across his bench, the man didn't refer to any of these plans or drawings but rather to a simple paper napkin on which some dimensions looked to be scrawled.

This had to be Moullin, St. James thought, the father of one of Brouard's beneficiaries. He called the man's name, speaking louder this time. Moullin looked up. He removed wax earplugs from his ears, which explained why he hadn't heard St. James's approach but did little to explain why Sinatra had been serenading him.

He next went to the source of the music—a CD player—where Frank had gone on to *Luck Be a Lady Tonight.* Moullin cut him off mid-phrase. He reached for a large towel with whales spouting water upon it and covered the CD player, saying, "I use it so people know where to find me out here. But he gets on my nerves, so I use the plugs as well."

"Instead of a different kind of music?"

"I hate it all, so it doesn't matter. What can I do for you?"

St. James introduced himself and handed over his card. Moullin read it and flipped it onto the work-bench, where it landed next to his napkin calculations. His face became immediately wary. He'd noted St. James's occupation, obviously, and would have little inclination to believe that a forensic scientist from London had come calling with building a conservatory in mind.

St. James said, "You appear to have had some damage to your garden. I wouldn't think vandalism is a common problem here."

"You come to inspect it?" Moullin asked. "Is that a job for the likes of you?"

"Have you phoned the police?"

"Didn't need to." Moullin took a metal tape measure from his pocket and used it against the sheet of glass he'd cut. He made a tick next to one of his calculations and carefully leaned the pane against a stack of a dozen or more others that he'd already seen to. "I did it myself," he said. "It was time."

"I see. Home improvement."

"Life improvement. My girls started it when the wife left us."

"You've more than one daughter?" St. James asked.

Moullin seemed to weigh the question before answering. "I've three." He turned and took up another sheet of glass. He put it on the bench and bent over it: a man not to be disturbed from his work. St. James took the opportunity to approach. He glanced at the plans and the drawings above the bench. The words *Yates, Dobree Lodge, Le Vallon* identified the site of the complicated conservatory. The other drawings, he saw, were for stylised windows. They belonged to *G. O. Wartime Museum.*

St. James examined Henry Moullin at work before he said anything else. He was a thick-boned man who looked strong and fit. His hands were muscled, which was evident even beneath the plasters that at the moment were crosshatching them haphazardly.

"You've cut yourself, I see," St. James said. "That must be an occupational hazard."

"True enough." Moullin sliced through the glass and then repeated the action, with an expertise that gave the lie to his remark.

"You make windows as well as conservatories?"

"The plans would indicate that." He raised his head and tilted it towards the wall of drawings. "If it's glass, I do it, Mr. St. James."

"Would that be how you came to the attention of Guy Brouard?"

"It would."

"You were intended to do the museum windows?" St. James gestured towards the drawings posted on the wall. "Or were these just on spec?"

"I did all the glasswork for the Brouards," Moullin answered. "Took down the original greenhouses on the property, built the conservatory, replaced windows in the house. Like I said, if it's glass, I do it. So that would be the case for the museum as well."

"But you can't be the only glazier on the island. Not with all the greenhouses I've seen. It wouldn't be possible."

"Not the only one," Moullin acknowledged. "Just the best. Brouards knew that."

"Which made you the logical one to employ for the wartime museum?"

"You might say that."

"As I understand it, though, no one knew what the exact architecture was going to be on the building. Until the night of the party. So for you to make drawings in advance . . . Did you fit them to the local man's plans? I've seen his model, by the way. Your drawings look suitable for his design."

Moullin ticked off another item on his paper-napkin list and said, "Did you come here to talk about windows?"

"Why only one?" St. James asked.

"One what?"

"Daughter. You've three but Brouard remembered only one in his will. Cynthia Moullin. Your . . . what? Is she your oldest?"

Moullin got another sheet of glass and made two more cuts. He used the tape measure to confirm his result and said, "Cyn's my oldest."

"Any thoughts why he singled her out? How old is she, by the way?"

"Seventeen."

"Finished school yet?"

"She's doing Further Education in St. Peter Port. University's what he suggested for her. She's clever enough, but there's nothing like that here. She'd need England for it. England costs money."

"Which you didn't have, I take it. Nor did she."

Till he died hung between them like smoke from an unseen cigarette.

"Right. It was all about money. Yeah. Lucky us." Moullin turned from the workbench to face St. James. " 'S that all you want to know, or is there more?"

"Any thoughts about why only one of your daughters was remembered in the will?"

"None."

"Surely the other two girls would benefit from higher education as well."

"True."

"Then . . . ?"

"They weren't the right age. Not set to go to university yet. All in good time."

This remark pointed the way to an overall illogic in what Moullin was suggesting, and St. James seized upon it.

"But Mr. Brouard couldn't have expected to die, could he? At sixty-nine, he wasn't a young man, but to all reports, he was fit. Isn't that the case?" He didn't wait for Moullin to answer. "So if Brouard meant your oldest daughter to be educated with the money he left her . . . When was she supposed to be educated, by his account? He might not have died for twenty years. Or more."

"Unless we killed him, of course," Moullin said. "Or isn't that where you're heading?"

"Where is your daughter, Mr. Moullin?"

"Oh, come on, man. She's seventeen years old."

"She's here, then? May I speak with—"

"She's on Alderney."

"Doing what?"

"She's caring for her gran. Or hiding out from the coppers. Have it which way you will. It's no matter to me." He went back to his work, but St. James saw that the vein in his temple throbbed, and when he made his next cut on the sheet of glass, it went off the mark. He muttered a curse and flung the resulting ruined pieces in a rubbish bin.

"Can't afford to make too many errors in your line of work," St. James noted. "I suppose that could get expensive."

"Well, you're something of a distraction, aren't you?" Moullin rejoined. "So if there's nothing else, I've work to do and not a hell of a lot of time to do it."

"I understand why Mr. Brouard left money to a boy called Paul Fielder," St. James said. "Brouard was a mentor to him, through an established organisation on the island. GAYT. Have you heard of it?

So they had a formal arrangement for their relationship. Is that how your daughter met him as well?"

"Cyn had no relationship with him," Henry
Moullin said, "GAYT or otherwise." And despite his
earlier words, he apparently decided to work no
more. He began returning his cutting tools and
measures to their appropriate storage places, and he
grabbed up a whiskbroom and swept the workbench
clear of minuscule fragments of glass. "He had his
fancies, and that's what it was with Cyn. One fancy
today, another tomorrow. A bit of I can do this, I can
do that, and I can do whatever I want because I've
the funds to play Father Christmas Come to
Guernsey if I decide to do it. Cyn just got lucky.
Like musical chairs with her in the right spot when
the tune dried up. Another day, it might've been one
of her sisters. Another month and it probably
would've been. That was it. He knew her better
than the other girls because she'd be on the grounds
when I was working. Or she'd stop by to visit her
aunt."

"Her aunt?"

"Val Duffy. My sister. She helps out with the
girls."

"How?"

"What do you mean, how?" Moullin demanded,
and it was clear that the man was reaching his limit.
"Girls need a woman in their lives. Do you want the
ABC's on why, or can you figure it out for yourself?
Cyn'd go over there and the two of them would
talk. *Girl* business this was, all right?"

"Changes in her body? Problems with boys?"

"I don't know. I kept my nose where it's meant to be, which is on my face and not in their affairs. I just blessed my stars that Cyn had a woman she could talk to and that woman was my sister."

"A sister who'd let you know if there was something amiss?"

"There was nothing amiss."

"But he had his fancies."

"What?"

"Brouard. You said he had his fancies. Was Cynthia one of them?"

Moullin's face purpled. He took a step towards St. James. "God *damn.* I ought to—" He stopped himself. It looked like an effort. "We're speaking of a *girl,*" he said. "Not a full-grown woman. A girl."

"Old men have fancied young girls before."

"You're twisting my words."

"Then untwist them for me."

Moullin took a moment. He stepped away. He looked across the room to his creative glass pieces. "Like I said. He had fancies. Something caught his eye, he shook fairy dust on it. He made it feel special. Then something else caught his eye and he moved the fairy dust over to that. It's the way he was."

"Fairy dust being money?"

Moullin shook his head. "Not always."

"Then what?"

"Belief," he said.

"What sort of belief?"

"Belief in yourself. He was good that way. Prob-

lem was, you started thinking there might be something to his belief if you got lucky."

"Like money."

"A promise. Like someone was saying, Here's
how I can help you if you work hard enough but
you've got to do that first—the hard work itself—
and then we'll see what we will see. Only no one
ever *said* it, did they, not exactly. But somehow the
thought got planted in your mind."

"In yours as well?"

On a sigh, Moullin said, "In mine as well."

St. James considered what he'd learned about
Guy Brouard, about the secrets he kept, about his
plans for the future, about what each individual had
apparently believed about the man himself and about
those plans. Perhaps, St. James thought, these aspects
of the dead man—which might otherwise have
been merely reflections of a wealthy entrepreneur's
caprice—were instead symptoms of larger and more
injurious behaviour: a bizarre power game. In this
game, an influential man no longer at the helm of a
successful business retained a form of control over
individuals, with the exercise of that control being
the ultimate objective of the game. People became
chess pieces and the board was their lives. And the
principal player was Guy Brouard.

Would that be enough to drive someone to kill?

St. James supposed that the answer to that question lay in what each person actually did as a result of
Brouard's professed belief in him. He glanced round
the barn once more and saw some of the answer in
the glass pieces that were diligently cared for and the

furnace and blowing pipes that were not. "I expect he made you believe in yourself as an artist," he noted. "Is that what happened? Did he encourage you to live your dream?"

Moullin abruptly began walking towards the door of the barn, where he snapped off the lights and stood silhouetted by the day outside. He was a hulking figure there, described not only by the bulky clothes he wore but also by his bull-like strength. St. James reckoned that he'd had little trouble destroying his daughters' handiwork in the garden.

He followed him. Outside, Moullin shoved the barn door closed and padlocked it through a thick metal hasp. He said, "Making people think larger than what they were was what he did. If they chose to take steps they might've not taken without him coaxing them . . . Well, I s'pose that's just their own affair. No skin off anyone else's arse, is it, if someone extends himself and takes a risk."

"People generally don't extend themselves without some idea of the venture's success," St. James said.

Henry Moullin looked over to the garden where the smashed shells dusted the lawn like snow. "He was good at ideas. Having them and giving them. The rest of us . . . we were good at belief."

"Did you know about the terms of Mr. Brouard's will?" St. James asked. "Did your daughter know?"

"Did we kill him, you mean? Quick to douse his lights before he changed his mind?" Moullin dug his hand into his pocket. He brought out a heavy-looking set of keys. He began to walk along the drive towards the house, crunching through the gravel and the shells. James walked at his side, not because he expected Moullin to expatiate on the topic he himself had brought up but because he'd caught a glimpse of something among the man's keys and he wanted to make sure it was what he thought it was.

"The will," he said. "Did you know about its terms?"

Moullin didn't reply till he'd reached the front porch and had inserted his key in the door's deadbolt lock. He turned to reply.

"We didn't know a thing about anyone's will," Moullin said. "Good day to you."

He turned back to the door and let himself inside, and the lock on the door snapped smartly behind him. But St. James had seen what he wanted to see. A small pierced stone hung from the ring holding Henry Moullin's keys.

St. James stepped away from the house. He wasn't such a fool as to think he'd heard all there was to hear from Henry Moullin, but he knew he'd taken matters as far as he could just then. Still, he stood for a moment on his way back down the drive and considered the Shell House: its curtains drawn against the daylight, its door locked, its garden ruined. He pondered what it meant to have fancies. He dwelled on the influence it gave one person to be privy to another person's dreams.

As he stood there, not particularly focused on anything, movement from the house caught his eye. He sought it out and saw it at a small window.

Inside the house, a figure at the glass flicked the curtains into place. But not before St. James caught a glimpse of fair hair and saw a gauzy shape fade from view. In other circumstances he might have thought he was looking at a ghost. But the unmistakable body of a female very much corporeal was backlit briefly by a light within the room.

Chapter 18

PAUL FIELDER WAS MIGHTILY relieved to see Valerie Duffy charging across the lawn. Her black coat flapped open as she ran, and the fact that she hadn't buttoned it told him she was on his side.

"See here," she cried as the police constable seized Paul by the shoulder and Taboo seized the policeman by the leg. "What are you doing to him? This's our Paul. He belongs here."

"Why's he not identifying himself, then?" The constable had a walrus moustache, Paul observed, and a bit of his breakfast cereal still hung from it, quivering when he talked. Paul watched this flake in some fascination as it swayed to and fro like a climber dangling from a perilous cliff.

"I'm *telling* you who he is," Valerie Duffy said. "He's called Paul Fielder and he belongs here. Taboo, stop that. Let the nasty man go." She found the dog's collar and dragged him off the constable's leg.

"I ought to have you both in for assault." The man released Paul with a shove that thrust him towards Valerie. This set Taboo barking again.

Paul flung himself to his knees by the dog and buried his face in the smelly fur of his neck. Taboo gave off barking at this. He continued to growl, however.

"Next time," the walrus moustache said, "you identify yourself when you're spoken to, boy. You don't, I'll have you in the nick so fast . . . That dog'll be put down as well. Should be anyway for what he did. Just look at these trousers. He's ripped a damn hole. You see that? Might've been my *leg*. Flesh, boy. Blood. He had his shots? Where're his documents? I'll have them off you right now."

"Don't be a mad fool, Trev Addison," Valerie said, and her voice was sharp. "Yes, I know who you are. I was at school with your brother. And you know well's I, you do, that no one walks round with their dog's papers on them. Now, you've had a fright and so has the boy. The dog as well. Let's leave it at that and not make things worse."

The use of his name seemed to do something to settle the constable, Paul saw, because he looked from Paul to the dog and to Valerie, and then he adjusted his uniform and brushed his trousers. He said, "We've got our orders."

"You do," Valerie said, "and we mean to let you follow them. Come with me, though, and let's get those trousers repaired. I can do it for you in a wink and we can let the rest go."

Trev Addison glanced along the edge of the drive where one of his colleagues was thrusting back shrubbery, bent over to the task. It looked like tiresome work that anyone might have wanted to take ten minutes away from. He said reluctantly, "I don't know as I ought . . ."

"Come on with you," Valerie said. "You can have a cup of tea."

"In a wink, you say?"

"I've two grown sons, Trev. I can make repairs faster than you can drink that tea."

He said, "All right, then," and to Paul, "Mind you stay out of the way, hear? Police business's going on in these grounds."

Valerie told Paul, "You go to the kitchen in the big house, love. Make yourself a cocoa. There're fresh ginger biscuits, as well." She gave him a nod and set off back across the lawn with Trev Addison following behind her.

Paul waited, rooted to the spot, till they disappeared back inside the Duffys' cottage. He found that his heart had been pounding like thunderbolts, and he rested his forehead against Taboo's back. The musty, damp dog scent of him was as welcome and familiar as the touch of his mother's hand on his cheek whenever he'd been feverish as a child.

When his heart at last slowed, he raised his head and scrubbed at his face. When the policeman had grabbed him, his rucksack had been shaken loose from his shoulders and it now lay on the ground in a heap. He scooped it up and trotted towards the house.

He went round the back, as usual. There was much activity going on. Paul had never seen so many policemen in one location before—aside from on the telly—and he paused just beyond the conservatory and tried to sort out what they were doing. Searching, yes. He could tell that much. But he couldn't imagine what for. It seemed to him that someone must have lost something valuable the day of the funeral, when everyone returned to *Le Reposoir* for the burial service and the reception afterwards. Yet while that seemed likely, it *didn't* seem likely that half the police force would be looking for that something. It would have had to belong to someone awfully important, and the most important person on the island was the one who had died. So who else . . . ? Paul didn't know and couldn't reckon. He went into the house.

He used the conservatory door, which was unlocked as always. Taboo pattered along behind him, his nails *snick*ing against the bricks that comprised the conservatory's floor. It was pleasantly warm and humid inside, and the dripping of water from the irrigation system made a hypnotising rhythm that Paul would have liked to sit and listen to for a while. But he couldn't do that because he'd been told to make himself cocoa. And above all else when it came to *Le Reposoir,* Paul liked to do exactly as he'd been told. That was how he kept the privilege of coming to the estate just that: a treasured privilege.

Do right by me, I'll do right by you. That's the basis of what's important, my Prince.

Which was another reason Paul knew what he was supposed to do. Not only with regard to the cocoa and the ginger biscuits, but with regard to the inheritance as well. His parents had come up to his room when the advocate left them and had knocked on his door. His dad had said, "Paulie, we're going to need to talk about this, son," and his mother had said, "You're a rich lad, love. Just think what you can do with all that money." He'd let them in and they'd spoken to him and to each other, but although he'd seen their lips moving well enough and had heard the occasional word or phrase, he'd already worked out what he was meant to do. He'd come directly to *Le Reposoir* to set about doing it.

He wondered if Miss Ruth was in the house. He hadn't thought to see if her car was outside. She was the person he'd come calling upon. If she wasn't there, he intended to wait.

He took himself to the kitchen: along the stone hall, through the doorway, and down another corridor. The house was silent, although a creaking of the floor above his head told him Miss Ruth was probably at home. Still, he was wise enough to know that he oughtn't to creep round someone else's house looking for them, even if he'd come to see them especially. So when he got to the kitchen, he ducked inside. He'd have his cocoa and biscuits and by the time he was done, Valerie would be there and she would usher him upstairs to see Miss Ruth.

Paul had been in the kitchen of *Le Reposoir* enough times to know where everything was. He settled Taboo beneath the work table in the centre of the room, put the rucksack next to him for his head, and went to the pantry.

Like the rest of *Le Reposoir*, it was a magical place, filled with smells he wasn't able to identify, as well as boxes and tins of foodstuffs he'd never heard of. He always loved it when Valerie sent him into the pantry to fetch something for her in the midst of her cooking if he was hanging about. He always liked to prolong the experience as much as possible, breathing in the mixture of extracts, spices, herbs, and other cooking ingredients. That took him to a spot in the universe that was utterly unlike the one he knew.

He lingered there now. He uncapped a row of bottles and lifted them to smell one by one. *Vanilla,* he read on one label. *Orange, almond, lemon.* The fragrances were so heady that when he inhaled, he could feel the scent take up residence behind his eyes.

From the extracts he went on to the spices, taking in the cinnamon first. When he got to the ginger, he took a pinch no bigger than the edge of his littlest fingernail. He placed it on his tongue and felt his mouth water. He smiled and went on to the nutmeg, the cumin, the curry, the cloves. Afterwards came the herbs, then the vinegars, then the oils. And from there he mingled with the flour, the sugar, the rice, and the beans. He picked up boxes and read their backs. He held packets of pastas against his cheek and rubbed their cellophane wrappers on his skin. He'd never seen such abundance as he saw here. It was a wonder to him.

He sighed at last with satiated pleasure and rooted out the cocoa tin. He carried it to the work top and fetched milk from the fridge. From above the cooker, he took down a pan and he carefully measured out one mug of milk and no more, which he even more carefully poured into the pan to heat. This moment represented the first time ever he'd been allowed to use the kitchen, and he meant to make Valerie Duffy proud of the diligence he employed to enact the rare privilege.

He lit the burner and sought out a spoon to measure the cocoa. The ginger biscuits were on the work table, still fresh from the oven on their cooling racks. He pinched one for Taboo and fed it to the dog. He took two for himself and stuffed one into his mouth. The other he wanted to savour with his cocoa.

A clock bonged somewhere within the house. As if accompanying it, footsteps moved along a corridor directly above him. A door opened, a light snapped on, and someone began descending the back staircase into the kitchen.

Paul smiled. Miss Ruth. With Valerie not there, she'd need to get her own mid-morning coffee if she wanted it. And it was there, steaming in the glass carafe. Paul fetched another mug, a spoon, and the sugar for her, making everything ready. He imagined the conversation to come: her eyes widening in surprise, her lips rounding to an O, her murmured "Paul, my *dearest* boy" when she understood exactly what he meant to do.

He bent down and eased the rucksack from beneath Taboo's head. The dog looked up, tilting his ears towards the staircase. A low growl rumbled deep within his throat. A yip followed this, then a full-fledged bark. Someone said, "What on earth . . . ?" from the stairs.

That voice didn't belong to Miss Ruth. A Viking-sized woman came round the corner. She saw Paul and demanded, "Who the *hell* are you? How'd you get in? What are you doing here? Where's Mrs. Duffy?"

Far too many questions at once, and Paul was caught with a ginger biscuit in his hand. He felt his eyes go as round as Miss Ruth's lips would have done, and his eyebrows shot up in the direction of his hairline. At that same instant, Taboo darted out from beneath the table, barking like a Doberman and baring his teeth. His legs were splayed out and his ears were back. He didn't ever like people talking harsh.

Viking Woman backed away. Taboo advanced on her before Paul had a chance to catch him by his collar. She started shrieking, "Get him away, get him, God damn it, *get* him!" as if she thought the dog actually meant to do her harm.

Her shouting only made Taboo bark louder. And just at that moment, the milk that was heating on the stove boiled over.

It was too much at once—the dog, the woman, the milk, the biscuit in his hand that *looked* like he'd pinched it, only he hadn't, because Valerie had told him to have one, and even if he had taken *three*, which was two more than she'd said he could take, that was fine, really, that was all right, that wasn't a crime.

Fsssshhhhh. The milk frothed onto the burner beneath the pan. The smell of it as it hit the direct heat burst into the air like a covey of birds. Taboo barked. The woman shouted. Paul was a pillar of concrete.

"You stupid boy!" Viking Woman's voice sounded like metal on metal. "Don't just stand there, for God's sake," and the milk burned behind him. She backed towards the wall. She turned her head as if she didn't want to see her own destruction at the teeth of an animal who was in truth more terrified than she was, but instead of fainting or trying to get away, she began shouting "Adrian! Adrian! For God's sake, Adrian!" and because her attention was no longer on him or on the dog, Paul felt his limbs unfreeze and move on their own.

He darted forward and grabbed Taboo, dropping his rucksack to the floor. He pulled the dog over to the cooker and fumbled for the controls that would douse the heat beneath the milk. In the meantime, the dog still barked, the woman still shouted, and someone came clattering down the back stairs.

Paul lifted the pan from the cooker to take it to the sink, but with one hand on the dog who was trying to escape, he didn't have the right balance. He lost the proper grip. The scalded mess ended up on the floor, and Taboo ended up where he'd been at first: inches away from the Viking woman, looking like he meant to have her for elevenses. Paul dived after him and dragged him off. Taboo continued to bark like a demon.

Adrian Brouard crashed into the room. He said into the uproar, "What the *devil* . . . ?" and then, "Taboo! That's enough! Shut up!"

Viking Woman cried, "You *know* this creature?" and Paul wasn't sure if she meant himself or the dog.

Not that it mattered, because Adrian Brouard

knew them both. He said, "This is Paul Fielder, Dad's—"

"*This?*" The woman turned her gaze on Paul. "This filthy little . . ." She seemed to be at a loss for a term that would suit the interloper in the kitchen.

Adrian said, "This." He'd come downstairs in only the bottoms of his pyjamas and his slippers, as if he'd been caught in the act of finally dressing for the day. Paul couldn't imagine not being up and about and busy with something at this hour.

Seize the day, my Prince. One never knows if there'll be another.

Paul's eyes smarted with tears. He could *hear* the voice. He could feel his presence as strongly as if he'd strode into the room. He would have solved this problem in an instant: one hand out to Taboo and the other to Paul and What have we here? in his soothing voice.

"Shut that animal up," Adrian said to Paul, although Taboo's barking had subsided to a growl. "If he bites my mother, you'll be in trouble."

"More trouble than you're already in," Adrian's mother snapped. "Which is plenty, let me tell you. Where's Mrs. Duffy? Did she let you in?" And then a shout of "Valerie! Valerie Duffy! Come here at once."

Taboo *didn't* like shouting, but the foolish woman hadn't sorted this yet. Once she raised her voice, he began to bark anew. There was nothing for it but to hustle him from the room, but Paul couldn't do that, clean up the mess, and fetch his rucksack simultaneously. He felt his bowels loosen with anxiety. He felt his brain expanding. In another moment, he knew that he would explode from both ends, and this knowledge was enough to spur him to decide.

Past the Brouards a corridor extended to a door that gave onto the vegetable garden. Paul began to pull Taboo in this direction as the Viking woman said, "Don't even *think* of leaving without cleaning up the mess you've made, you little toad."

Taboo snarled. The Brouards backed away. Paul managed to get him down the passage without another outburst—despite Viking Woman's shriek of "Come back here at once!"—and he pushed the dog outside and into the fallow garden. He shut the door on him, steeling his heart when Taboo yelped in protest.

Paul knew the dog was only trying to protect him. He also knew that anyone with a grain of common sense would have understood that. But the world was not a place where one could depend upon people having common sense, was it? This fact made them dangerous because it made them afraid and sly.

So he had to get away from them. Because she hadn't come to see what the ruckus was all about, Paul knew that Miss Ruth couldn't possibly be home. He would have to return when it was safe to do so. But he couldn't leave the remains of this disastrous encounter with the other Brouards behind him. That, of all things, would not be right.

He went back to the kitchen and paused in the doorway. He saw that despite the Viking woman's words, she and Adrian were already in the process of wiping up the floor and cleaning off the top of the cooker. The air in the room still hung with the odour of scalded milk, however.

". . . an end to this nonsense," Adrian's mother was saying. "I'll have him sorted out straightaway and make *no* mistake about it. If he thinks he can just walk in here without a by-your-leave . . . as if he owns the place . . . as if he's not what he *patently* is, which is a useless little piece of common—"

"Mother." Adrian, Paul saw, had spied him by the door and with that single word, so did Viking Woman. She'd been wiping off the cook top but now she was standing with the dishcloth in her hand and she balled it up with her large, ringed fingers. She gave him such a scrutiny from head to toe with *such* a look of disgust on her face that Paul felt a shiver come over him and knew he had to be gone at once. But he wasn't about to leave without the rucksack and the message it contained about the plan and the dream.

"You may inform your parents that we're hiring a solicitor about this business of the will," Viking Woman told him. "If your imagination has led you to believe you're walking off with one penny of Adrian's money, you're very much mistaken. I intend to battle you in every court I can find, and by the time I'm finished, whatever money you schemed to have off Adrian's father will be gone. Do you understand? You will *not* win. Now, get out of here. I don't want to see your face again. If I do, I'll have the police after you. And that bloody mongrel of yours I'll have put down."

Paul didn't move. He wouldn't leave without his rucksack, but he wasn't sure how to get to it. It lay where he'd kicked it, by the leg of the table at the centre of the room. But between him and it stood both the Brouards. And nearness to them spelled certain danger to himself.

"Did you hear me?" Viking Woman demanded. "I said get out. You've no friends here despite what you apparently think. You are not welcome in this house."

Paul saw that one way he could get to the rucksack was to scramble beneath the table for it, so that was what he did. Before Adrian's mother finished what she was saying, he was on his hands and knees and scuttling across the floor like a crab.

"Where's he going?" she demanded. "What's he doing now?"

Adrian seemed to realise Paul's intention. He snatched the rucksack at the same moment Paul's own fingers closed about it.

"My God, the little beast's stolen something!" Viking Woman cried. "This *is* the limit. Stop him, Adrian."

Adrian attempted to do so. But all the images that the word *stolen* planted within Paul's brain—the rucksack gone through, the discovery, the questions, the police, a cell, the worry, the shame—gave him a strength he otherwise would not have possessed. He yanked so hard that he pulled Adrian Brouard off balance. The man crashed forward into the table, fell to his knees, and smacked his chin against the wood. His mother cried out, and that gave Paul the opening he needed. He jerked the rucksack away and leaped to his feet.

He charged in the direction of the corridor. The vegetable garden was walled but its gate gave onto the estate grounds. There were places to hide at *Le Reposoir* that he wagered neither of the Brouards were aware of, so he knew that if he made it to the fallow garden, he'd be completely safe.

He dashed down the corridor to the sound of Viking Woman crying out, "Darling, are you all right?" And then, "Chase him, for God's sake. Adrian! Get him." But Paul was faster than both mother and son. The last thing he heard was "He's got something in that pack!" before the door closed behind him and he fled with Taboo towards the garden gate.

Deborah was surprised by the Talbot Valley. It looked like a miniature dale transported from Yorkshire, where she and Simon had honeymooned. A river had carved it eons in the past, and one side consisted of rolling green slopes where the fawn-coloured cattle of the island grazed, sheltered from sunlight and the occasional harsh weather by stands of oaks. The road coursed along its other side, a steep hill held back by granite walls. Along them grew ashes and elms and beyond them, the land rose to hilltop pastures. The area was as different to the rest of the island as Yorkshire was to the South Downs.

They were looking for a little lane called *Les Niaux*. Cherokee was relatively certain where it would be, having already paid a visit there. Nonetheless, he had a map spread out on his knees, and he acted as navigator for their journey. They nearly overshot the mark on their approach, but he said, "Here! Turn," when they came upon an opening in a hedgerow. He added, "I swear. These streets look like our driveways at home."

Calling the stretch of paved trail a street was certainly giving it more than its due. It dipped off the main road like the entrance to another dimension, one that was defined by thick vegetation, damp air, and the sight of water passing through the cracks in boulders nearby. Not fifty yards along this lane, an old water mill appeared to their right. It stood less than five yards off the road, topped by an old sluice from which greenery draped.

"This is it," Cherokee said, folding the map and storing it in the glove compartment. "They live in the cottage at the end of the row. The rest . . ."—he gestured to the dwellings they passed as Deborah pulled the car into the wide yard in front of the water mill—"this is where he keeps all his war stuff."

"He must have a lot of it," Deborah said, for there were two other cottages besides the one which Cherokee indicated that Frank Ouseley used as his home.

"That's putting it mildly," Cherokee replied. "That's Ouseley's car. We could be in luck."

Deborah knew they would need it. The presence of a ring on the beach where Guy Brouard had died—one identical to the ring China River had purchased, one that was also identical to the ring that was apparently now missing from her belongings—didn't help the cause of her proclaimed innocence. She and Cherokee needed Frank Ouseley to recognise a description of that ring. Moreover, they needed him to realise that one just like it had been nicked from his collection.

A log fire burned somewhere nearby. Deborah and Cherokee took in its scent as they approached the front door of Ouseley's cottage. "Makes me think of the canyon," Cherokee said. "Middle of winter there, you never even know you're in Orange County. All the cabins and the fires. Snow on Saddleback Mountain sometimes. It's the best." He looked around. "I don't think I knew that till now."

"Second thoughts about living on a fishing boat, then?" Deborah said.

"Hell," he said ruefully, "I had second thoughts about *that* after fifteen minutes in St. Peter Port gaol." He paused at the square of concrete that served as the cottage's front porch. "I know I'm to blame for all of this. I've put China where she is because it's always been the fast and easy buck for me, and I know it. So I need to get her out of this mess. If I can't do that . . ." He sighed, and his breath was a puff of fog in the air. "She's scared, Debs. So am I. I guess that's why I wanted to call Mom. She wouldn't have helped much—she might even have made things worse—but still . . ."

"She's still Mum," Deborah finished for him. She squeezed his arm. "It's going to work out. It will. You'll see."

He covered her hand. "Thanks," he said. "You're . . ." He smiled. "Never mind."

She raised an eyebrow. "Were you thinking of making one of your moves on me, Cherokee?"

He laughed. "You betcha."

They knocked on the door and then rang the bell. Despite the chatter of a television inside and the presence of a Peugeot outside, no one answered. Cherokee pointed out that Frank might be working among his immense collection, and he went to check the other two cottages as Deborah knocked on the door again. She heard a quavering voice call out, "Hold your damn horses," and she said to Cherokee, "Someone's coming." He rejoined her at the step and as he did so, keys and bolts operated on the other side of the door.

An old man swung it open. A very old man. His thick eyeglasses glinted at them, and with one frail hand he held himself upright against the wall. He seemed to keep himself steady through a combination of that wall and willpower, but it looked as if it cost him a tremendous effort. He should have been using a Zimmer frame or at least a cane, but he had neither with him.

"Well, here you be," he said expansively. "Day early, aren't you? Well, no matter, that. All to the good. Come in. Come in."

Clearly, he was expecting someone else. Deborah herself had been expecting a much younger man. But Cherokee cleared that up for her when he said, "Is Frank here, Mr. Ouseley? We saw his car outside," and made it evident that the old pensioner was Frank Ouseley's father.

"It's not Frank you're wanting," the man said. "It's me. Graham. Frank's gone to take that pie tin back to the Petit farm. 'F we're lucky, she'll do us another chicken and leek before the week's over. Got my fingers crossed on that one, I have."

"Will Frank return soon?" Deborah asked.

"Oh, we've time enough for our business 'fore he gets here," Graham Ouseley declared. "Don't you worry about that. Frankie doesn't like what I'm up to, I got to tell you. But I promised myself I'd do the right thing 'fore I died. And I mean to do it, with or without the boy's blessing."

He doddered into an overheated sitting room, where he scooped a remote from the arm of a chair, pointed it to the television where a chef was expertly slicing bananas, and doused the picture. He said, "Let's have at this in the kitchen. There's coffee."

"Actually, we've come—"

"No trouble." The old man interrupted what he clearly thought was going to be Deborah's protest. "Like to be hospitable."

There was nothing for it but to follow him to the kitchen. It was a small room made smaller by the clutter it held: Stacks of newspapers, letters, and documents shared space with cooking utensils, crockery, cutlery, and the occasional misplaced gardening tool. "Sit yourselfs down," Graham Ouseley told them as he eased his way over to a coffee press that held four inches of some greasy-looking liquid that he unceremoniously dumped with its sodden grounds into the sink. From a bowing shelf he took down a canister, and with a shaking hand he spooned up fresh grounds: both into the cafetiere and onto the floor. He shuffled across this and captured the kettle from the cook top. At the tap he filled it with water, setting it to boil. When he'd managed all this, he beamed with pride. "That's *that*," he announced, rubbing his hands together and then frowning, said, "Why the hell're you two still on your feet?"

They were on their feet because, obviously, they were not the guests the old man meant to receive into his home. But as his son wasn't there—although due to return soon if his errand and the presence of his car were any indication—Deborah and Cherokee exchanged a glance that said "Well, why not?" They would enjoy a coffee with the old man and simply wait.

Nonetheless, Deborah felt it only fair to say, "Frank's due back soon, Mr. Ouseley?"

To which he replied rather peevishly, "Listen up. You're not to *worry* about Frank. Sit down. Gotcher notepad ready? No? Good God. You must have memories like elephants, the two of you." He lowered himself to one of the chairs and loosened his tie. Deborah noticed for the first time that he was nattily dressed in tweeds and a waistcoat, and his shoes had been polished. "Frank," Graham Ouseley informed them, "is born to worry. He doesn't like to think what might come of this business between you and me. But I'm not concerned. What c'n they do to me that they haven't done ten times over, eh? I owe it to

the dead, I do, to hold the living accountable. We all
have it as our duty, that, and I mean to do mine before I die. Ninety-two I am. Four score and more'n
ten, it is. What d'you make of that?"

Deborah and Cherokee murmured their amaze-
ment. On the stove the kettle whistled.

"Let me," Cherokee said, and before Graham
Ouseley could voice a protest, he got to his feet.
"You tell your story, Mr. Ouseley. I'll make the cof-
fee." He gave the old man an appealing smile.

This appeared to be enough to mollify him, because Graham remained where he was as Cherokee
saw to the coffee, moving round the kitchen to find
cups, spoons, and sugar. As he brought things to the
table, Graham Ouseley rested back in his chair. He
said, "It's quite a tale, you two. Let me tell you about
it," and he proceeded to do so.

His story took them back more than fifty years, to
the German occupation of the Channel Islands. Five
years living under the bleeding jackboot, he called it,
five years of trying to outwit the damn Krauts and to
live with dignity despite degradation. Vehicles con-
fiscated right down to bicycles, wireless sets declared
verboten, deportation of longtime residents, executions of those deemed "spies." Slave camps where
Russian and Ukrainian prisoners worked to build
fortifications for the Nazis. Deaths in European
labour camps, where those who defied German rule
were sent. Documents studied into the time of one's
grandparents to ascertain whether there was Jewish
blood to be purged from the populace. And quislings
aplenty among the honest people of Guernsey: those

devils willing to sell their souls—and their fellow islanders—for whatever the Germans promised them.

"Jealousy and spite," Graham Ouseley declared.
"They sold us out for that as well. Old scores settled
by whispering a name to the devil Nazis."

He was glad to tell them that most of the time it
was a foreigner betraying someone: a Dutchman living in St. Peter Port who became wise to someone's
hidden wireless, an Irish fisherman from St. Sampson who witnessed a midnight landing of a British
boat down near Petit Port Bay. While there was no
excusing that and even less forgiving it, the fact that
the quisling was foreign born made the betrayal less
of an evil than when a native islander did it. But that
happened as well: a Guernseyman betraying his fellows. That was what had happened to gift.

"Gift?" Deborah asked. "What sort of gift?"

Not gift, *G.I.F.T.*, Graham Ouseley informed
them, an acronym for Guernsey Independent From
Terror. It was the island's underground news-sheet
and the people's only source of truth about Allied
activities during the war. This news was meticulously gleaned at night from contraband radio receivers that were tuned to pick up the BBC. The
facts of the war were typed up on single sheets of paper in the wee hours by candlelight behind the
shrouded windows of the vestry of *St. Pierre-du-Bois,*
and then distributed by hand to trusted souls who
were hungry enough for word of the outside world
that they were willing to risk Nazi interrogation and
the aftermath of Nazi interrogation in order to
have it.

"Quislings among them," Graham Ouseley declared. "Should've known, the rest of us. Should've taken more care. Should never've trusted. But they were of *us*." He thumped his chest with his fist. "You understand me? They were of *us*."

The four men responsible for *G.I.F.T.* were arrested upon the word of one of these quislings, he explained. Three of those men died as a result of that arrest—two in prison and the other attempting escape. Only one of the men—Graham Ouseley himself—survived two hellish years incarcerated before being freed, one hundred pounds of skin, bones, lice, and tuberculosis.

But they destroyed more than just the creators of *G.I.F.T.,* those quislings who betrayed them, Ouseley said. They informed on those who sheltered British spies, on those who hid escaped Russian prisoners, on those whose only "crime" was to chalk a V for victory on the cycle-seats of Nazi soldiers as they drank at night in hotel bars. But the quislings were never forced to pay for their misdeeds, and that's what rankled with those who'd suffered at their hands. People died, people were executed, people went to prison and some never returned. For more than fifty years, no one spoke up publicly to name the names of those responsible.

"Blood on their hands," Graham Ouseley declared. "I mean to make them *pay*. Oh, they'll fight against it, won't they? They'll deny it hot and loud. But when we spread out the proof . . . And tha's how I want to do it, you two. Names first in the paper, and let 'em deny the whole thing and get themselves advocates to set things right. Then the proof comes, and we watch them squirm like they damn well should've squirmed when Jerry finally surrendered to the Allies. *That's* when all of this should've come out. The quislings, the bloody profiteers, the Jerrybags, and their bastard Kraut babies."

The old man was working himself into a lather, his lips wet with spittle. Deborah began to fear for his heart as his skin took on a bluish tinge. She knew it was time to make him understand that they were not who he thought they were, which was apparently reporters come to hear his story and to print it in the local newspaper.

She said, "Mr. Ouseley, I'm terribly afraid—"

"No!" He shoved his chair back from the table with a surprising strength that sloshed the coffee from their mugs and the milk from its jug. "You come with me if you don't believe the story. My boy Frank and I, we've got us the proof, you hear that?" He struggled to his feet, and Cherokee surged up to help him. Graham shook the assistance off, however, and trundled unsteadily towards the front door. Once again, there seemed nothing for it but to follow him, to mollify him, and to hope that his son arrived back at the water mill before the old man suffered from his exertions.

St. James stopped at the Duffys' cottage first. He was unsurprised when no one was there. In the middle of the day, both Valerie and Kevin would doubtless be at work: he somewhere in the grounds of *Le Re-*

posoir and she in the manor house itself. She was the person he wanted to talk to. The undercurrent that he'd felt during his previous conversation with her needed clarifying now that he knew she was the sister of Henry Moullin.

He found her, as he expected, in the big house, which he was allowed to approach once he identified himself to the police who were still searching the grounds. She answered the door with a bundle of sheets crumpled under her arm.

St. James didn't waste time with social niceties. They would rob him of the advantage of surprise and allow her to marshal her thoughts. Instead, he said, "Why didn't you mention when we spoke earlier that there's another fair-haired woman involved?"

Valerie Duffy made no reply, but he could see the confusion in her eyes, followed by the calculation going on inside her head. She shifted her gaze from him as if she wished to seek out her husband. She would have liked his support, St. James surmised, and he was determined that she should not have it.

She said faintly, "I don't understand." She set the sheets on the floor inside the doorway and retreated to the interior of the house.

He followed her into the stone hall, where the air was icy and tinctured with the smell of dead fires. She stopped by the enormous refectory table in the room's centre, and began to gather up dried leaves and fallen berries from an autumnal floral arrangement that was offset with tall white candles.

St. James said, "You claimed that you saw a fair-haired woman following Guy Brouard to the bay on the morning of his death."

"The American—"

"As you'd like us to believe."

She looked up from the flowers. "I saw her."

"You saw someone. But there are other possibilities, aren't there? You merely failed to mention them."

"Mrs. Abbott's fair."

"And so, I suspect, is your niece. Cynthia."

To her credit, Valerie didn't move her gaze from his face. Also to her credit, she said nothing till she made certain she knew how much he himself knew. She was nobody's fool.

"I've spoken to Henry Moullin," St. James said. "I believe I've seen your niece. He'd like me to think she's on Alderney with her grandmother, but something tells me that if there's a grandmother living, Alderney isn't where I'd find her. Why does your brother have Cynthia hidden away in the house, Mrs. Duffy? Does he have her locked in her room as well?"

"She's going through a difficult stage," Valerie Duffy finally said, and she went back to the flowers, the leaves, and the berries as she spoke. "Girls her age go through them all the time."

"What sort of stage requires imprisonment?"

"The sort where there's no talking to them. No talking sense, that is. They don't want to hear it."

"Talking sense about what?"

"Whatever their current fancy is."

"And hers is . . . ?"

"I wouldn't know."

"Not according to your brother," St. James pointed out. "He says she confided in you. He gave me the impression the two of you are close."

"Not close enough." She took a handful of the leaves over to the fireplace and tossed them in. From a pocket in the apron she wore, she drew out a rag and used it to dust off the top of the table.

"So you approve of his locking her in the house? While she's in this stage of hers?"

"I didn't say that. I *wish* Henry wouldn't . . ." She paused, stopped her dusting, and seemed to be trying to gather her thoughts once again.

St. James said, "Why did Mr. Brouard leave her money? Her and not the other girls? A seventeen-year-old being left a small fortune at the expense of her benefactor's children and her own siblings? What was the purpose of that?"

"She wasn't the only one. If you know about Cyn, you've been told about Paul. They both have siblings. He has even more than Cyn. None of them were remembered. I don't know why Mr. Brouard did it like that. Perhaps he fancied the thought of the disruption a load of money could cause among young people in a family."

"That's not what Cynthia's father claims. He says the money was meant for her education."

Valerie dusted a spotless area on the table.

"He also says Guy Brouard had other fancies. I'm wondering if one of them led to his death. Do you know what a fairy wheel is, Mrs. Duffy?"

Her dusting hand slowed. "Folklore."

"Island folklore, I expect," St. James said. "You were born here, weren't you? Both you and your brother?"

She raised her head. "Henry isn't the one, Mr. St. James." She said it quite calmly. A pulse fluttered in her throat, but she gave no other indication of being bothered by the direction St. James's words were taking.

"I wasn't actually thinking of Henry," St. James said. "Has he a reason to want Guy Brouard dead?"

She flushed completely at that and bent back to her needless task of dusting.

"I noticed that he was involved in Mr. Brouard's museum project. In the original project, by the look of the drawings in his barn. I'm wondering if he was supposed to be involved in the revised project as well? Do you know?"

"Henry's good with glass" was her reply. "That brought them together in the first place. Mr. Brouard needed someone to do the conservatory here. It's large, complicated. An off-the-peg conservatory wouldn't do. He needed someone for the greenhouses as well. And the windows when it came down to it. I told him about Henry. They spoke to each other and found common ground. Henry's worked for him ever since."

"Is that how Cynthia came to Mr. Brouard's attention?"

"Lots of people came to Mr. Brouard's attention," Valerie said patiently. "Paul Fielder. Frank Ouseley.

Nobby Debiere. Henry and Cynthia. He even sent Jemima Abbott to modeling school in London and gave her mum a helping hand when she needed it. He took an interest. He invested in people. That was his way."

"People usually expect a return on their investments," St. James pointed out. "And not always a financial one."

"Then you'd be wise to ask each of them what Mr. Brouard was expecting in return," she said pointedly. "And p'rhaps you can start with Nobby Debiere." She balled up her duster and returned it to the pocket of her apron. She moved back in the direction of the front door. There she scooped up the linen she'd deposited on the floor, and she balanced it on her hip and faced St. James. "If there's nothing else . . ."

"Why Nobby Debiere?" St. James asked her. "That's the architect, isn't it? Did Mr. Brouard ask something special from him?"

"If he did, Nobby wasn't looking too inclined to give it to him on the night before he died," Valerie announced. "They were arguing by the duck pond after the fireworks. 'I won't let you ruin me,' Nobby was saying. Now, I wonder what he meant by that?"

This was too obvious an effort to direct him away from her own relations. St. James wasn't about to let matters go so easily. He said, "How long have you and your husband worked for the Brouards, Mrs. Duffy?"

"Since the first." She shifted the bed linen from

one arm to the other and looked at her watch meaningfully.

"So you were familiar with their habits."

She made no immediate reply to this, but her eyes
narrowed a millimetre as she sorted through the
possibilities that were implied by this statement.
"Habits," she said.

"Like Mr. Brouard's morning swim, for example."

"Everyone knew about his swim."

"About his ritual drink as well? The ginkgo and
green tea? Where was that kept, by the way?"

"In the kitchen."

"Where?"

"In the pantry cupboard."

"And you work in the kitchen."

"Are you suggesting that I . . . ?"

"Where your niece came to chat? Where your
brother—at work on the conservatory, perhaps—
came to chat as well?"

"Everyone friendly with Mr. Brouard would've
been in and out of the kitchen. This isn't a formal
house. We don't make pretty distinctions between
those who work behind the green baize door and
those who loll round in front of it. We don't have a
green baize door or anything that could possibly sig-
nify one. The Brouards aren't like that, and they
never were. Which was why—" She stopped herself. She gripped the sheets more firmly.

"Which was why . . . ?" St. James repeated
quietly.

"I've work to do," she said. "But if you wouldn't mind a suggestion?" She didn't wait for him to welcome whatever thoughts she wished to share. "Our family matters have no bearing on Mr. Brouard's death, Mr. St. James. But I expect if you dig around a bit more, you'll find someone else's family matters do."

Chapter 19

FRANK HADN'T BEEN ABLE to take the pie tin to Betty Petit and effect a return to *Moulin des Niaux* with anything close to the alacrity he'd been hoping for. The childless and widowed farmwife had few visitors and when one dropped by, coffee and fresh brioches were called for. The one factor that enabled Frank to make his escape in under an hour was his father. *Can't leave Dad alone for long* served him well when he needed it to do so.

When he made his turn into the mill yard, the first thing he saw was the Escort parked next to his Peugeot, a large Harlequin sticker plastered across its rear window identifying it as an island rental. He looked immediately to the cottage, where the front door hung open. He frowned at this and began to hurry towards it. At the threshold, he called out, "Dad?" and "Hullo?" but a moment sufficed to tell him no one was there.

Only one place, then, was the alternative. Frank beat a hasty path to the first of the cottages where their war memorabilia were stored. As he passed the small sitting room window what he saw within made his head fill with the sound of rushing water. The River woman's brother was standing at one side of the filing cabinet with a red-headed woman at his side. The top drawer gaped open and Frank's father stood before it. Graham Ouseley clutched onto the side of this drawer with one hand to keep himself upright. With the other hand he wrestled with a batch of documents that he was trying to prise out.

Frank moved without pause. Three strides took him to the cottage door, and he threw it open. Its swollen wood shrieked against the old floor. "What the hell," he said sharply. "What the *hell*'re you doing? Dad! Stop it! Those documents are fragile!" Which asked the question in the mind of anyone reasonable, of course, of what they were doing crammed into the filing cabinet higgledy-piggledy. But this was not the moment for worrying about that.

As Frank plunged across the room, Graham looked up. "It's time, boy," he said. "I've said it and said it. You know what we've got to do."

"Are you mad?" Frank demanded. "Get out of that stuff!" He took his father's arm and tried to ease him a step backwards.

His father jerked away. "No! Those men're owed. There're debts to be paid and I mean to pay them. I *survived*, Frank. Three of them dead and me still alive. All these years later when *they* could have been. Granddads, Frank. Great-granddads by now. But all of that come to nothing because of a God damn quisling who needs to face the music. You got that, son? Time for people to pay."

He fought Frank like a teenager being disciplined, but without a teenager's youthful agility. His frailty made Frank reluctant to get rough with him. At the same time, however, it served the purpose of making the effort to control him so much more difficult.

The red-head said, "I think he believes we're journalists. We did try to tell him . . . We've actually come to talk to you."

"Just get out," Frank said over his shoulder to her, and he tempered the order with "For a minute. Please."

River and the red-head left the cottage. Frank waited till they were safely outside. Then he pulled his father away from the filing cabinet and slammed the drawer home, saying, "You God damn fool," between his teeth.

This curse got Graham's attention. Frank rarely swore, and never at his father. His devotion to the man, the passions they shared, the history that bound them, and the lifetime they'd spent together had always obviated any inclination he might have had towards either anger or impatience when it came to his father's stubborn will. But this circumstance constituted the absolute limit of what Frank was willing to endure. A dam burst inside him—despite having been so meticulously constructed in the last two months—and he let forth a stream of invective that he hadn't known was part of his vocabulary.

Graham shrank back from the sound of it. His shoulders fell, his arms dropped to his sides, and behind his thick spectacles, his vague eyes filled with frustrated and frightened tears.

"I meant . . ." His stubbled chin dimpled. "I meant to do good."

Frank hardened his heart. "Listen to me, Dad," he said. "Those two are not journalists. Do you understand me? They are not journalists. That man . . . He's . . ." God. How to explain? And what would be the point of explaining? "And the woman . . ." He didn't even know who she was. He thought he'd seen her at Guy's funeral, but as to what she was doing at the water mill . . . and with the River woman's brother . . . He needed to have the answer to that question at once.

Graham was watching him in utter confusion. "They said . . . They've come to . . ." And then dismissing this entire line of thinking, he grabbed Frank's shoulder and cried, "It's *time,* Frank. I could die any day, I could. I'm the only one left. You see that, don't you? Tell me you see. Tell me you know. An' if we're not to have our museum . . ." His grip was tighter than Frank would have thought possible. "Frankie, I can't let them die in vain."

Frank felt pierced by this remark, as if it lanced his spirit as well as his flesh. He said, "Dad, for God's sake," but he couldn't finish. He pulled his father to him and hugged the old man hard. Graham let a sob escape against his son's shoulder.

Frank wanted to cry with him but he didn't have the tears. And even if a well of them had been stored within him, he could not have let that well overflow.

"I got to do it, Frankie," his father whimpered. "It's important, it is."

"I know that," Frank said.

"Then . . ." Graham stepped away from his son and wiped his cheeks on the sleeve of his tweed jacket.

Frank put his arm round his father's shoulders and said, "We'll talk about it later, Dad. We'll find a way." He urged him towards the door and, the "journalists" being gone from his sight, Graham co-operated as if they were completely forgotten as, indeed, they probably were to him. Frank took him back to their own cottage where the door still stood open. He assisted his father inside and to his chair.

Graham leaned fully against him as Frank turned him towards the chair's comfortable seat. His head drooped as if it had grown too heavy, and his spectacles slid to the end of his nose. "Feeling a bit queer, lad," he said in a murmur. "P'rhaps best to have a bit of a kip."

"You've overdone it," Frank told his father. "I mustn't leave you alone any more."

" 'M *not* a dirty-arsed infant, Frank."

"But you get up to no good if I'm not here to watch you. You're as stubborn as gum on a shoe sole, Dad."

Graham smiled at the image, and Frank handed him the remote for the television. "Can you keep yourself out of trouble for five minutes?" Frank asked his father kindly. "I want to see what's what out there." He indicated the sitting room window, and hence the out-of-doors, with a tilt of his head.

When his father was absorbed once again by the television, Frank tracked down River and the red-head. They were standing near the tattered deck chairs on the overgrown lawn behind the cottages. They appeared to be in deep discussion. As Frank approached them, their conversation ceased.

River introduced his companion as a friend of his sister's. She was called Deborah St. James, he said, and she and her husband had come over from London to help China. "He deals with this kind of thing all the time," River said.

Frank's main concern was his father and not leaving him alone to get up to further mischief, so he replied to the introduction with as much courtesy as he could muster. "How may I help you?"

They answered him in concert. Their visit apparently had to do with a ring that was associated with the Occupation. It was identified by an inscription in German, by a date, and by its unusual design of skull and crossed bones.

"D'you have anything like that in your collection?" River sounded eager.

Frank looked at him curiously, then at the woman, who was watching him with an earnestness that told him how important the information was to them both. He thought about this fact and about every possible implication of every possible answer he might give. He finally said, "I don't believe I've ever seen anything like that."

To which River said, "But you can't be sure, can you?" When Frank didn't affirm this, he went on, gesturing to the two additional cottages that grew out from the water mill. "You've got a hell of a lot of stuff in there. I remember your saying not all of it's even catalogued yet. That's what you guys were doing, right? You and Guy were getting it ready to show, but first you had to have lists of what you have and where it is right now and where to put it in the museum, right?"

"That's what we were doing, yes."

"And the kid helped out. Paul Fielder. Guy brought him along now and then."

"As well as his son once and the Abbott boy as well," Frank said. "But what's this got to do with—"

River turned to the red-head. "See? There're other ways to go. Paul. Adrian. The Abbott kid. The cops want to think every road leads to China, but it damn well doesn't, and here's our proof."

The woman said gently, "Not necessarily. Not unless . . ." She looked pensive and directed her next remarks to Frank. "Is there a chance you've catalogued a ring like the one we've described and merely forgotten it? Or a chance that someone besides yourself catalogued it? Or even that you had one among your things and have forgotten you have it?"

Frank admitted that there was that possibility, but he allowed himself to sound doubtful because he knew the request she was likely to make and he didn't want to grant it. She made it straightaway, nonetheless. Could they have a look among his wartime artifacts, then? Oh, she knew there was no realistic way they were going to be able to go through everything, but there was always a slim chance that they could get lucky . . .

"Let's have a look through the catalogues at least," Frank said. "If there was a ring, one of us would have documented it as long as we'd already come across it."

He took them the way his father had taken them and pulled out the first of the notebooks. There were four of them and counting, each of them set up to log possession of a particular type of wartime article. So far he had a notebook for wearing apparel, one for medals and insignia, one for ammunition and arms, one for documents and papers. A perusal of the notebook for medals and insignia showed River and the St. James woman that no ring like the one they were describing had yet come to light. This did not, however, mean that no ring lay somewhere among the vast assortment of material still to be gone through. Within a minute it was quite clear that both of his visitors knew that.

Were the rest of the medals and the other insignia kept in one place, Deborah St. James wanted to know, or were they spread throughout the collection? She meant the medals and the insignia not catalogued already. Frank recognised that.

He told her that they weren't kept in one place. He explained that the only items that were stored with like items were those that had already been handled, sorted through, and catalogued. Those things, he explained, were in organised containers that had been carefully labeled for convenient access when the time came to set up exhibits in the wartime museum. Each article was logged into the designated notebook, where it was given an item number and a container number against the day it would be called for.

"Since there was no ring mentioned in the catalogue," Frank said regretfully, and he let an eloquent silence fill in the rest of his remark: There was probably no ring at all, unless it was hidden somewhere among the Gordian knot of articles still to be dealt with.

"But there *were* rings catalogued," River pointed out.

His companion added, "So during a sorting period, someone could even have pinched a skull-and-crossed-bones ring without your knowing, isn't that right?"

"And that person could have been anyone who came with Guy at one time or another," River added. "Paul Fielder. Adrian Brouard. The Abbott kid."

"Perhaps," Frank said, "but I don't know why someone would."

"Or the ring could have been stolen from you at another time, couldn't it?" Deborah St. James said. "Because if something got pinched from your uncatalogued material, would you even know it was missing?"

"I suppose that depends on what it is that was taken," Frank answered. "Something large, something dangerous . . . I'd probably know. Something small—"

"Like a ring," River persisted.

"—I might overlook." Frank saw the glances of satisfaction they exchanged. He said, "But see here, why is this important?"

"Fielder, Brouard, and Abbott." Cherokee River

spoke to the red-head and not to Frank, and within a brief span of time, the two of them took their leave. They thanked Frank for his help and hurried to their car. He overheard River saying in reply to something the woman pointed out to him, "They all could have wanted it for different reasons. But China didn't. Not at all."

At first Frank thought River was referring to the skull-and-crossed-bones ring. But he soon came to realise they were talking about the murder: wanting Guy dead and, perhaps, needing him dead. And beyond that, knowing that death might well be the only answer to imminent peril.

He shuddered and wished he had a religion that would give him the answers he needed and the route to walk. He closed the door of the cottage on the very thought of death—untimely, unnecessary, or otherwise—and he gave his gaze to the mishmash of wartime belongings that had defined his own life and the life of his father over the years.

It had long been *Look what I've got here, Frankie!*

And *Happy Christmas, Dad. You'll never guess where I found that one.*

Or *Think of whose hands fired this pistol, son. Think of the hate that pressed the trigger.*

Everything he now had had been amassed as a way to have an unbreakable bond with a giant of a man, a colossus of spirit, dignity, courage, and strength. One couldn't be like him—couldn't even hope to be like him, to have lived as he lived, to have survived all that he had survived—so one shared what he loved and in that way, one made a tiny mark on the ledger on which one's own father's mark was and would always be larger than life, bold and proud.

That had begun it, that need to be *like*, so basic and ingrained that Frank often wondered if sons were somehow programmed from conception to strive for perfect paternal emulation. If that wasn't possible—Dad too much a Herculean figure, never diminished by infirmity or age—then something else needed to be created, to serve as a son's irrefutable proof of a worthiness that matched his father's.

Inside the cottage, Frank observed the concrete testimony of his personal worth. The idea of the wartime collection and the years of searching out everything from bullets to bandages had grown like the abundant vegetation that surrounded the water mill: undisciplined, exuberant, and unrestrained. The seed had been planted in the form of a trunk of goods preserved by Graham's own mother: ration books, air raid precautions, licences to purchase candles. Seen and fingered through, those belongings had served as inspiration for the great project that had circumscribed Frank Ouseley's life and exemplified his love for his father. He'd used the amassment of goods as a means of speaking all the words of devotion, admiration, and sheer delight that he had long found impossible to say.

The past is always with us, Frankie. It behooves those of us who were part of it to pass the experience on to them that follows. Else how d'we keep the bad from extending itself? Else how d'we tip our hats to the good?

And what better way to preserve that past and to acknowledge it fully than to educate others not only in the classroom, as he'd done for years, but also through exposure to the relics that defined a time long gone? His father had sheets of *G.I.F.T.*, the occasional pronouncement from the Nazis, a *Luftwaffe* cap, a party membership pin, a rusty pistol, a gas mask, and a carbide lamp. Frank the boy had held these artifacts in his hands and had pledged himself to the cause of amassment at the age of seven.

Let's start a collection, Dad. D'you want to? It'd be such fun, wouldn't it? There's got to be lots of stuff on the island.

It wasn't a game, boy. You're not meant to think it was ever a game. You understand me?

And he did. He *did*. That was his torment. He understood. It had never been a game.

Frank drove from his head the sound of his father's voice, but in its place came another sound, an explanation of both the past and the future that arose from nowhere, comprising words whose source he felt he knew well but could not have named: *It is the cause, it is the cause, my soul.* He whimpered like a child caught in a bad dream, and he forced himself to move into the nightmare.

The filing cabinet, he saw, hadn't shut completely when he'd shoved it home. He approached it tentatively, like an untried soldier crossing a mine field. When he reached it unscathed, he curled his fingers round the handle of the drawer, half-expecting it to singe his flesh as he pulled.

He was finally part of the war he'd longed to

serve in with distinguished valour. He finally knew what it was to want to run wildly away from the enemy, to a small safe place he could hide, a place that did not actually exist.

By the time she returned to *Le Reposoir*, Ruth Brouard saw that a batch of police constables had moved from the estate grounds to the lane and were progressing along towards the cut-off that would take them down to the bay. Their work, it seemed, was finished at *Le Reposoir* itself. Now they would be searching the earthen bank and the hedgerows—and perhaps, even, both the wooded areas and the fields beyond—to locate whatever it was that would prove whatever needed proving about whatever they knew or thought they knew or fancied about the death of her brother.

She ignored them. Her time in St. Peter Port had drained her of nearly every ounce of her strength and was threatening to rob her of that which had long sustained her in a life marked by flight and fear and loss. Throughout everything that might have demolished the core of another child—that foundation carefully laid by two loving parents, by grandparents and doting aunts and uncles—she had been able to hold on to who she was. The reason had been Guy and what Guy represented: family and a sense of having *come* from some place even if that place was gone forever. But now it seemed to Ruth as if the *fact* of Guy himself as a living, breathing human whom she had known and loved was inches away from being obliterated. If that happened, she didn't know how or if she could recover. More, she didn't think she would want to.

She eased along the drive beneath the line of chestnuts and thought how good it would be to sleep. Every movement was an effort and had been so for weeks, and she knew that the immediate future held no palliative for what she suffered. Morphine carefully administered might mitigate the misery that ceaselessly occupied her bones, but only complete oblivion would remove from her mind the suspicions that were beginning to plague her.

She told herself that what she'd learned had a thousand and one explanations. But knowing that didn't alter the fact that some of those explanations might well have cost her brother his life. It didn't matter that what she'd uncovered about Guy's final months could have actually alleviated the guilt she felt for her part in the heretofore unexplained circumstances that surrounded his murder. What possessed importance was the fact that she hadn't known what her brother had been doing, and the existence of that very simple *not knowing* was enough to begin the process of emptying her of her long-held beliefs. To allow that would bring horror upon horror into Ruth's life, however. Thus, she knew she had to build bulwarks against the possibility of losing what had given her world its definition. But she didn't know how to do it.

From Dominic Forrest's office she'd gone to Guy's broker and then to his banker. From them, she'd seen the journey that her brother had been on in the ten months that preceded his death. Selling enormous lumps of securities, he'd moved cash into and out of his bank account in such a way that the fingerprints of illegality seemed to be smudged across everything he'd done. The impassive faces of Guy's monetary advisors had suggested much, but all they would present her with was facts so bare as to beg to be clothed with the garments of her darkest suspicions.

Fifty thousand pounds here, seventy-five thousand pounds there, building ever building to an immense two hundred and fifty thousand pounds in early November. There would be some sort of paper trail, of course, but she didn't want to try to follow it just yet. All she wanted to do was to confirm what Dominic Forrest had told her were the results of the forensic accountant's exploration into Guy's monetary situation. He'd invested and reinvested carefully and wisely, as was his wont throughout the nine years since they had come to the island, but suddenly in his final months, money had slipped through his fingers like sand . . . or had been drawn from him like blood . . . or had been required . . . or had been donated . . . or . . . what?

She didn't know. For a risible moment, she told herself that she didn't care. It wasn't important—the money itself—and that was true enough. But what the money represented, what the *absence* of money suggested in a situation in which Guy's will had seemed to indicate there was plenty to be spread among his children and his two other beneficiaries . . . This Ruth could not so easily dismiss.

Because the thought of all this led her ineluctably to her brother's murder and how and if it was connected to that money.

Her head ached. There were too many pieces of information swimming round up there, and they seemed to press against her skull, each one of them jockeying for a position in which it would receive the most attention. But she didn't want to attend to any of them. She wanted only to sleep.

She pulled her car round the side of the house, past the rose garden where the leafless bushes had already been pruned for winter. Just beyond this garden, the drive curved again and led the way to the old stable where she kept her car. When she braked in front of it, she knew she didn't have the strength to draw the doors open. So she merely turned the key, stilled the engine, and rested her head on the steering wheel.

She felt the cold seep into the Rover, but she remained where she was, her eyes closed as she listened to the comforting silence. It soothed her as nothing else could have done. In silence there was nothing else to be learned.

But she knew she couldn't stay there long. She needed her medicine. And rest. God, how she needed rest.

She had to use her shoulder to open the car door. When she was on her feet, she was surprised to find herself feeling unequal to the task of walking across the gravel in the direction of the conservatory, where she would be able to let herself into the house. So instead, she leaned against the car, which was how she came to notice movement in the area of the duck pond.

She thought at once of Paul Fielder and that thought led her in the direction of someone's having to break the news to him that his inheritance wasn't going to be as immense as Dominic Forrest had earlier led him to believe. Not that it would matter greatly. His family was impoverished, his father's business ruined by the relentless pressures of modernisation and convenience on the island. Anything that came into his hands was going to be a vast amount more than he could ever have hoped to have . . . if he'd known about Guy's will in the first place. But that was another speculation that Ruth didn't wish to entertain.

The walk to the duck pond took an effort of will. But when Ruth got there, emerging between two rhododendrons so that the pond spread out in front of her like a pewter platter that took its colour from the sky, she found that she hadn't seen Paul Fielder at all, busy building duck shelters to replace those that had been destroyed. Instead, it was the man from London who stood at the pond's edge. He'd taken a position a yard from some discarded tools. But the focus of his attention appeared to be the duck graveyard across the water.

Ruth would have turned to go back to the house in the hope of escaping his notice. But he glanced her way and then back at the graves. He said, "What happened?"

"Someone didn't like ducks," she replied.

"Who wouldn't like ducks? They're harmless enough."

"One would think so." She didn't say more, but when he looked at her, she felt as if he read the truth on her face.

He said, "The shelters were destroyed as well? Who was rebuilding them?"

"Guy and Paul. They'd built the originals. The whole pond was one of their projects."

"Perhaps someone didn't like that." He directed his gaze at the house.

"I can't think who," she said, although she herself could hear how artificial her words sounded, and she knew—and feared—that he didn't believe her for a moment. "As you said, who could dislike ducks?"

"Someone who disliked Paul? Or the relationship Paul had with your brother?"

"You're thinking of Adrian."

"Is he likely to have been jealous?"

Adrian was likely, Ruth thought, to be anything. But she didn't intend to talk about her nephew to this man or to anyone else. So she said, "It's damp here. I'll leave you to your contemplation, Mr. St. James. I'm going inside."

He accompanied her, unbidden. He limped next to her in silence and there was nothing for it but to allow him to follow her back through the shrubbery and into the conservatory whose door, as ever, remained unlocked.

He took note of this. Was it always so? he asked her.

Yes. It was. Living in Guernsey was not like living in London. People felt more secure here. Locks were unnecessary.

She felt him gazing at her as she spoke, felt his grey-blue eyes boring into the back of her head as she moved before him along the brick path in the humid air beneath the glass. She knew what he was thinking about an unlocked door: access and egress for anyone wishing to harm her brother.

At least this was a better direction for his thoughts to be taking than where they'd been heading when he spoke about the deaths of the innocent ducks. She didn't believe for a moment that an unknown intruder had anything to do with her brother's death. But she would allow this speculation if it kept the Londoner from considering Adrian.

He said, "I spoke to Mrs. Duffy earlier. You've been to town?"

Ruth said, "I saw Guy's advocate. His bankers and his brokers as well." She took them into the morning room. Valerie, she saw, had already been there. The windows were uncovered to let in the milky December daylight and the gas fire burned to cut the chill. A carafe of coffee stood on a table next to the sofa, with a single cup and saucer at its side. Her needlepoint box was open in anticipation of her working upon the new tapestry, and the post lay stacked upon her drop-front desk.

Everything about the room declared this a normal day. But it wasn't. Nor would any day be normal again.

This thought spurred Ruth to speak. She told St.

James exactly what she had learned in St. Peter Port. She lowered herself to the sofa as she spoke and gestured him to one of the chairs. He listened in silence and when she was done, he offered her an array of explanations. She'd considered most of them on the drive from town. How could she not when murder sprawled at the end of the trail they appeared to lay?

"It suggests blackmail, of course," St. James said. "That sort of depletion of funds, with the amounts increasing over time—"

"There was nothing in his life he could have been blackmailed over."

"So it might seem at first. But he apparently had secrets, Miss Brouard. We know that much from his trip to America when you thought he was elsewhere, don't we?"

"He had no secret to call for this. There's a simple explanation for what Guy did with the money, one that's completely aboveboard. We just don't know what it is yet." Even as she spoke, she didn't believe herself, and she could see by the sceptical expression on his face that St. James didn't believe her either.

He said—and she could tell he was trying to be gentle with her—"I expect you know at heart that the way he was moving money about probably wasn't legitimate."

"No, I *don't* know—"

"And if you want to find his killer—which I think you do—you know we have to consider possibilities."

She made no reply. But the misery she felt was compounded by the compassion in his face. She *hated* that: people's sympathy. She always had done. Poor dear child having lost her family to the maw of the Nazis. We must be charitable. We must allow her her little moments of terror and grief.

"We have his killer." Ruth made the declaration stonily. "I saw her that morning. We know who she is."

St. James went his own direction, as if she'd said nothing. "He might have been making a payoff of some kind. Or an enormous purchase. Perhaps even an illegal purchase. Weapons? Drugs? Explosives?"

"Preposterous," she said.

"If he sympathised with a cause—"

"Arabs? Algerians? Palestinians? The Irish?" she scoffed. "My brother was as politically inclined as a garden gnome, Mr. St. James."

"Then the only conclusion is that he willingly gave the money to someone over time. And if that's the case, we need to look at the potential recipients of a glut of cash." He looked towards the doorway, as if considering what lay beyond it. "Where's your nephew this morning, Miss Brouard?"

"This has nothing to do with Adrian."

"Nonetheless . . ."

"I expect he's driving his mother somewhere. She's not familiar with the island. The roads are poorly marked. She'd need his help."

"He's been a frequent visitor to his father, then? Throughout the years? Familiar with—"

"This is *not* about Adrian!" She sounded shrill even to her own ears. Her bones felt pierced by a hundred spikes. She needed to be rid of this man, no matter his intentions towards her and her family. She needed to get to her medicine and to douse herself with enough to render her body unconscious, if that was even possible. She said, "Mr. St. James, you've come for some reason, I expect. I know this isn't a social call."

"I've been to see Henry Moullin," he told her.

Caution swept over her. "Yes?"

"I didn't know Mrs. Duffy is his sister."

"There wouldn't be a reason for anyone to tell you."

He smiled briefly in acknowledgement of this point. He went on to tell her that he'd seen Henry's drawings of the museum windows. He said they put him in mind of the architectural plans in Mr. Brouard's possession. He wondered if he might have a look at them.

Ruth was so relieved that the request was simple that she granted it at once without considering all the directions her doing so might actually take them. The plans were upstairs in Guy's study, she told him. She would fetch them at once.

St. James told her he'd accompany her if she didn't mind. He wanted to have another look at the model Bertrand Debiere had constructed for Mr. Brouard. He wouldn't take long, he assured her.

There was nothing for it but to agree. They were on the stairs before the Londoner spoke again.

"Henry Moullin," he said, "appears to have his daughter Cynthia locked up inside the house. Have you any idea how long that's been going on, Miss Brouard?"

Ruth continued climbing, pretending she hadn't heard the question.

St. James was unrelenting, however. He said, "Miss Brouard . . . ?"

She answered quickly as she headed down the corridor towards her brother's study, grateful for the muted day outside and the darkness of the passage, which would hide her expression. "I have no idea whatsoever," she replied. "I make it a habit to stay out of the business of my fellow islanders, Mr. St. James."

"So there wasn't a ring logged in with the rest of his collection," Cherokee River said to his sister. "But that doesn't mean someone didn't snatch it sometime without him knowing. He says Adrian, Steve Abbott, and the Fielder kid all have been there at one time or another."

China shook her head. "The ring from the beach's mine. I know it. I can feel it. Can't you?"

"Don't say that," Cherokee said. "There's going to be another explanation."

They were in the flat at the Queen Margaret Apartments, gathered in the bedroom where Deborah and Cherokee had found China sitting at the window in a ladderback chair she'd brought from the kitchen. The room was extraordinarily cold, made so by the fact that the window was open, framing a view of Castle Cornet in the distance.

"Thought I'd better get used to looking at the world from a small square room with a single window," China had explained wryly when they came upon her.

She hadn't donned a coat or even a sweater. The goose-pimples on her skin had their own goose-pimples, but she didn't seem to be aware of this.

Deborah took off her own coat. She wanted to reassure her friend with a fervency identical to Cherokee's, but she also didn't want to give her false hope. The open window provided an excuse to avoid a discussion of the growing blackness of China's situation. She said, "You're freezing. Put this on," and she draped her coat round China's shoulders.

Cherokee leaned past them and shut the window. He said to Deborah, "Let's get her out of here," and he nodded in the direction of the sitting room, where the temperature was marginally higher.

When they had China seated and Deborah had found a blanket to wrap round her legs, Cherokee said to his sister, "You know, you need to take better care of yourself. We can do some things for you, but we can't do that."

China said to Deborah, "He thinks I've done it, doesn't he? He hasn't come because he thinks I've done it."

Cherokee said, "What're you—"

Understanding, Deborah cut him off. "Simon doesn't work that way. He examines evidence all the time. He's got to have an open mind to do it. That's how it is just now for him. His mind is open."

"Why hasn't he come over here, then? I wish that he would. If he did—if we could meet and I could talk to him . . . I'd be able to explain if things need explaining."

"Nothing," Cherokee said, "needs explaining because you didn't do anything to anyone."

"That ring . . ."

"It got there. On the beach. It just got there somehow. If it's yours and you can't remember having it in your pocket when you went down to check out the bay sometime, then you're being framed. End of story."

"I wish I'd never bought it."

"Hell, yes. Damn right. Jesus. I thought you'd closed the book on Matt. You said you made it over between you."

China looked at her brother evenly and for so long a time that he looked away. "I'm not like you," she finally said.

Deborah saw that a secondary communication had passed between brother and sister with this. Cherokee grew restless and shifted on his feet. He shoved his fingers through his hair and said, "Hell. China. Come on."

China said to Deborah, "Cherokee still surfs. Did you know that, Debs?"

Deborah said, "He mentioned surfing but I don't think he actually said . . ." She let her voice drift off. Surfing was so patently not what her old friend was talking about.

"Matt taught him. That's how they first became friends. Cherokee didn't have a surfboard but Matt was willing to teach him on his own. How old were you then?" China asked her brother. "Fourteen?"

"Fifteen." He mumbled his answer.

"Fifteen. Right. But you didn't have a board." She said to Deborah, "To get good, you need a board of your own. You can't keep borrowing someone else's because you need to practise all the time."

Cherokee went to the television and picked up the remote. He examined it, pointed it at the set. He turned the set on and just as quickly turned it off. He said, "Chine, come on."

"Matt was Cherokee's friend first, but they grew apart when he and I got together. I thought this was sad, and I asked Matt once why it happened that way. He said things change between people sometimes and he never said anything else. I thought it was because their interests were different. Matt went into film making, and Cherokee just did his Cherokee thing: played music, brewed beer, did his swap-meet number with the phony Indian stuff. Matt was a grown-up, I decided, while Cherokee wanted to be nineteen forever. But friendships are never that simple, are they?"

"You want me to leave?" Cherokee asked his sister. "I can go, you know. Back to California. Mom can come over. She can be with you instead."

"Mom?" China gave a strangled laugh. "That would be perfect. I can see her now, going through this apartment—not to mention through my clothes—removing anything vaguely related to animals. Making sure I have my daily allotment of vitamins and tofu. Checking to be certain the rice is brown and the bread whole grain. That would be sweet. A great distraction, if nothing else."

"Then what?" Cherokee asked. He sounded despairing. "Tell me. What?"

They faced each other, Cherokee still standing and his sister still sitting, but he seemed much smaller in comparison with her. Perhaps, Deborah thought, it was a reflection of their personalities that made China seem so relatively large a figure. "You'll do what you have to do," China told him.

He was the one to break the gaze they each held steadily on the other. During their silence, Deborah thought fleetingly of the entire nature of sibling relationships. She was in water without gills when it came to understanding what went on between brothers and sisters.

With her gaze still on her brother, China said, "D'you ever wish you could turn back time, Debs?"

"I think everyone wishes that now and then."

"What time would you choose?"

Deborah pondered this. "There was an Easter before my mum died . . . A fête on one of the village greens. There were pony rides available for fifty p and I had just that much money. I knew if I spent it, it would be all gone, up in smoke for three minutes in the pony ring and I'd have nothing to spend on anything else. I couldn't decide what to do. I got all hot and bothered because I was afraid that whatever I *did* decide would be the wrong decision and I'd regret it and be miserable. So we talked about it, Mum and I. There's no wrong decision, she told me.

There's just what we decide and what we learn from deciding." Deborah smiled at the memory. "I'd go back to that moment and live onward from there all over again if I could. Except she wouldn't die this time."

"So what did you do?" Cherokee asked her. "Ride the pony? Or not?"

Deborah considered the question. "Isn't that odd? I can't remember. I suppose the pony wasn't all that important to me, even then. It was what she said to me that made a difference. It was how she was."

"Lucky," China said.

"Yes," Deborah replied.

A knock sounded on the door at that, followed by a ringing of the buzzer that seemed insistent. Cherokee went to see who'd come calling.

He opened the door to reveal two uniformed constables standing on the front step, one of them looking round anxiously as if checking the potential for ambush and the other having removed a baton which he was slapping lightly against his palm.

"Mr. Cherokee River?" Baton Constable said. He didn't wait for a reply, as he clearly knew to whom he was speaking. "You'll need to come with us, sir."

Cherokee said, "What? Where?"

China rose. "Cherokee? What . . . ?" but she didn't apparently need to finish her question.

Deborah went to her. She slid her arm round her old friend's waist.

Deborah said, "Please. What's going on?"

Whereupon Cherokee River was given the formal caution by the States of Guernsey Police.

They'd brought handcuffs with them, but they didn't use them. One of them said, "If you'll come with us, sir."

The other took Cherokee by the arm and led him briskly away.

Chapter 20

THE SECONDARY COTTAGES AT the water mill were poorly provided with light because generally Frank didn't work inside either of them in the late afternoons or evenings. But he didn't need a lot of light to find what he was looking for among the papers in the filing cabinet. He knew where the single document was, and his personal hell comprised the fact that he also knew what the document said.

He drew it forth. A crisp manila folder held it like a layer of smooth skin. Its skeleton, however, was a tattered envelope with crumpled corners, long missing its little metal clasp.

During the final days of the war, the occupying forces on the island had suffered from a degree of hubris that was most surprising, considering the defeats piling upon the German military everywhere else. On Guernsey, they had even refused to surrender at first, so determined were they to disbelieve that their plan for European domination and eugenic perfection would come to nothing. When Major-General Heine finally climbed aboard HMS *Bulldog* to negotiate the terms of his surrender of the island, it was a full day after victory had been declared and was being celebrated in the rest of Europe.

Holding on to what little they had left in those final days, and perhaps wanting to leave their mark on the island as every successive presence on Guernsey had done throughout time, the Germans had not destroyed all that they had produced. Some creations—like gun emplacements—were impervious to easy demolition. Others—like that which Frank held in his hands—acted as an unspoken message that there were islanders whose self-interest had superseded their feelings of brotherhood and whose actions as a result wore the guise of espousing the German cause. That this guise was inaccurate wouldn't have meant anything to the Occupiers. What counted was the shock value attached to having betrayal writ large and bold: in spiky handwriting, in black and white.

Frank's curse was the respect for history that had sent him first to read it at university, then to teach it to largely indifferent adolescents for nearly thirty years. It was the same respect that had been inculcated in him by his father. It was the same respect that had encouraged him to amass a collection which, he had hoped, would serve the purpose of remembrance long after he was gone.

He'd always believed the truth in the aphorism about remembering the past or being doomed to repeat it. He'd long seen in the armed struggles round the world man's failure to acknowledge the futility of aggression. Invasion and domination resulted in oppression and rancour. What grew from that was violence in all of its forms. What didn't grow from that was inherent good. Frank knew this, and he believed it fervently. He was a missionary attempting to win his small world to the knowledge he had been taught to hold dear, and his pulpit was constructed from the wartime properties that he'd collected over the years. Let these objects speak for themselves, he'd decided. Let people see them. Let them never forget.

So like the Germans before him, he'd destroyed nothing. He'd compiled so vast an array of goods that he'd long ago lost track of all that he had. If it was related to the war or the Occupation, he had wanted it.

He hadn't really even known what he had among his collection. For the longest time, he merely thought of everything only in the most generic terms. Guns. Uniforms. Daggers. Documents. Bullets. Tools. Hats. Only the advent of Guy Brouard made him start thinking differently.

It could actually be a monument of sorts, Frank. Something that will serve to distinguish the island and the people who suffered. Not to mention those who died.

That was the irony. That was the cause.

Frank carried the flimsy old envelope over to a rotting cane-bottomed chair. A floor lamp stood next to this, its shade discoloured and its tassel disengaged, and he switched it on and sat. It poured yellow light on his lap, which was where he placed the envelope, and he studied it for a minute before he opened it, drawing out a batch of fourteen fragile pieces of paper.

From halfway down the stack, he slid one out. He smoothed it against his thighs; he set the others onto the floor. He examined the remaining one with an intensity that would have suggested to an uninformed onlooker that he had never pondered it before. And why would he have done so, really? It was such an innocuous piece of paper.

6 Würstchen, he read. *1 Dutzend Eier, 2 kg. Mehl, 6 kg. Kartoffeln, 1 kg. Bohnen, 200 gr. Tabak.*

It was a simple list, really, shoved in among the records of purchases of everything from petrol to paint. It was an unimportant document in the overall scheme of things, the sort of slip that might have gone misplaced without anyone ever being the wiser. Yet it spoke to Frank of many things, not the least of which was the arrogance of the Occupiers, who documented every move they made and then saved those documents against the time of a victory whose advocates they would want to identify.

Had Frank not spent every one of his formative years right on into his solitary adulthood being taught the inestimable value of everything remotely related to Guernsey's time of trial, he might have deliberately misplaced this single piece of paper, and no one would have been the wiser. But *he* would still have known that it had once existed, and nothing would ever obliterate that knowledge.

Indeed, had the museum remained unconsidered by the Ouseleys, this paper probably would have remained undiscovered, even by Frank himself. But once he and his father had grasped on to Guy Brouard's offer to build the Graham Ouseley Wartime

Museum for the education and betterment of the present and future citizens of Guernsey, the sorting, sifting, and organising essential to such an enterprise had begun. In the process, this list had come to light. *6 Würstchen*, in 1943. *1 Dutzend Eier, 2 kg. Mehl, 6 kg. Kartoffeln, 1 kg. Bohnen, 200 gr. Tabak.*

Guy had been the one to find it, the one to say, "Frank, what d'you make of this?" as he spoke no German.

Frank himself had supplied the translation, doing it mindlessly and automatically, without pausing to read every line of it, without pausing to consider the ramifications. The meaning sank in as the last word—*Tabak*—drifted between his lips. As he'd become conscious of the implications, he'd lifted his gaze to the top of the paper and then shifted it to Guy, who'd already read it. Guy, who had lost both parents to the Germans, lost an entire family, lost a heritage.

Guy said, "How will you deal with this?"

Frank made no reply.

Guy said, "You're going to have to. You can't let it go. Holy God, Frank. You don't intend to let it go, do you?"

That had been the colour and the flavour of their days ever after. *Have you dealt with it, Frank? Have you brought it up?*

Frank had thought he wouldn't need to now, with Guy dead and buried and the only one who knew. Indeed, he'd thought he would never need to. But the past day had taught him otherwise.

Who forgets the past repeats it.

He got to his feet. He replaced the other papers in their envelope and returned the envelope to its folder. He shut the filing cabinet on it, and he turned out the light. He pulled the cottage door closed behind him.

Inside his own cottage, he found his father asleep in his armchair. An American detective show was playing on the television, two policemen with NYPD on the back of their windbreakers poised—handguns at the ready—to burst through a closed door and do violence behind it. At another time, Frank would have roused his father and taken him upstairs. But now he passed him and climbed upwards himself, seeking the solitude of his room.

On the top of his chest of drawers stood two framed photographs. One depicted his parents on their wedding day after the war. In the other, Frank and his father posed at the base of the German observation tower not far from the end of *Rue de la Prevote*. Frank couldn't remember who had taken the picture, but he did remember the day itself. They'd been pelted by rain but had hiked along the cliff path anyway, and when they'd arrived, the sun had burst upon them. God's approval for their pilgrimage, Graham had said.

Frank leaned the list from the filing cabinet against this second picture. He backed away from it like a priest unwilling to turn his back on the consecrated bread. He felt behind him for the end of his bed, and he lowered himself to it. He gazed on the insubstantial document and tried not to hear the challenge of that voice.

You can't let this go.

And he knew he couldn't. Because *It is the cause, my soul.*

Frank had limited experience in the world, but he wasn't an ignorant man. He knew that the human mind is a curious creature that can frequently act like a funhouse mirror when it comes to details too painful to recall. The mind can deny, refashion, or forget. It can create a parallel universe if necessary. It can devise a separate reality for any situation it finds too difficult to bear. In doing this, Frank knew, the mind did not lie. It simply came up with the strategy to cope.

The trouble arose when the coping strategy obliterated the truth instead of merely shielding one from it temporarily. When that occurred, desperation resulted. Confusion reigned. Chaos followed.

Frank knew they were on the cusp of chaos. The time had come to act, but he felt immobilised. He'd given his life to the service of a chimera, and despite knowing this fact for two months, he found that he was still reeling from it.

Exposure now would render meaningless more than half a century of devotion, admiration, and belief. It would make a miscreant out of a hero. It would end a life in public disgrace.

Frank knew that he could prevent all this. Only a single piece of paper, after all, stood between an old man's fantasy and the truth.

• • •

On Fort Road, an attractive albeit heavily pregnant woman answered the door of the Bertrand Debiere household. She was the architect's wife, Caroline, she informed St. James. Bertrand was working in the back garden with the boys. He was taking them off her hands for a few hours while she got some writing done. He was good that way, a model husband. She didn't know how or why she'd managed to be so lucky as to end up his wife.

Caroline Debiere noted the collection of large sheets of paper that St. James carried rolled up under his arm. Was this about business? she inquired. Her voice gave a fair indication of how eager she was for that to be the case. He was a fine architect, her husband, she told St. James. Anyone wanting a new building, a renovation of an old one, or an extension of an existing structure would not go wrong hiring Bertrand Debiere to design it.

St. James told her that he was interested in having Mr. Debiere examine some pre-existing plans. He'd called in at his office, but a secretary had told him Mr. Debiere had left for the day. He'd looked in the phone directory and taken the liberty of tracking the architect down at home. He hoped this wasn't an inconvenient time . . . ?

Not at all. Caroline would fetch Bertrand from the garden if Mr. St. James wouldn't mind waiting in the sitting room.

A happy shout rose from outside, at the back of the house. Pounding followed it: the sound of hammer striking nail and wood. Hearing this, St. James said he didn't want to take Mr. Debiere from what he was doing, so if the architect's wife didn't mind, he'd join him and his children in the garden.

Caroline Debiere looked relieved at this, doubtless happy that she would be able to continue her work without having her sons handed over to her. She showed St. James the way to the back door and left him to his meeting with her husband.

Bertrand Debiere turned out to be one of the two men St. James had seen duck out of the procession to Guy Brouard's grave site and engage in intense conversation in the grounds of *Le Reposoir* on the previous day. He was a crane of a man, so tall and gangly that he looked like a character from a Dickens novel, and at the moment he was in the lowest branches of a sycamore tree, pounding together the foundation of what was clearly going to be a tree house for his sons. There were two of them, and they were helping in the way of small children: The elder was passing nails to his father from a leather waist pouch that he wore round his shoulders while the younger was employing a plastic hammer against a piece of wood at the base of the tree, on his haunches and chanting, "I am pounding, I am nailing," and being no use to his father whatsoever.

Debiere saw St. James crossing the lawn, but he finished pounding his nail before he acknowledged him. St. James noticed that the architect's gaze took in his limp and fixed on its cause—the leg brace whose cross piece ran through the heel of his shoe—but then it traveled upwards and fixed, like his wife's, on the roll of papers beneath St. James's arm.

Debiere lowered himself from the tree limbs and said to the older boy, "Bert, take your brother inside please. Mum'll have those biscuits for you now. Mind you have only one each, though. You don't want to ruin your tea."

"The lemony ones?" the elder boy asked. "Has she done the lemony ones, Dad?"

"I expect so. Those are what you asked for, aren't they?"

"The lemony ones!" Bert breathed the words to his little brother.

The promise of those biscuits prompted both boys to drop what they were doing and scamper to the house, shouting, "Mummy! Mum! We want our biscuits!" and bringing an end to their mother's solitude. Debiere watched them fondly, then scooped up the nail pouch that Bert had haphazardly discarded, spilling half of its contents onto the grass.

As the other man collected the nails, St. James introduced himself and explained his connection to China River. He was on Guernsey at the request of the accused woman's brother, he told Debiere, and the police were aware that he was making independent enquiries.

"What sort of enquiries?" Debiere asked. "The police already have their killer."

St. James didn't want to go in the direction of China River's guilt or innocence. Instead, he indicated the roll of plans beneath his arm and asked the architect if he wouldn't mind having a look at them.

"What are they?"

"The plans for the design Mr. Brouard selected

for the wartime museum. You've not seen them yet, have you?"

He'd seen only what the rest of the islanders at Brouard's party had seen, Debiere informed him: the detailed, three-dimensional drawing that was the American architect's rendering of the building.

"A total piece of crap," Debiere said. "I don't know what Guy was thinking about when he decided on it. It's about as suitable as the space shuttle for a museum on Guernsey. Huge windows in the front. Cathedral ceilings. The place would be impossible to heat for less than a fortune, not to mention the fact that the entire structure looks like something designed to sit on a cliff and take in the view."

"Whereas the museum's actual location . . . ?"

"Down the lane from St. Saviour's Church, right next door to the underground tunnels. Which is about as far inland and away from any cliff as you can get on an island this size."

"The view?"

"Sod all. Unless you consider the car park for the tunnels a worthy view."

"You shared your concerns with Mr. Brouard?"

Debiere's expression became cautious. "I talked to him." He weighed the nail pouch in his hand as if considering whether he would put it on and resume his work on the tree house. A quick glance at the sky, taking in what little remained of daylight, apparently prompted him to forgo further building. He began to gather the pieces of timber he'd assembled on the lawn at the base of the tree. He carried them to a large blue polythene tarpaulin at one side of the garden, where he neatly stacked them.

"I was told that things between you went a bit further than talking," St. James said. "You argued with him, apparently. Directly after the fireworks."

Debiere didn't reply. He merely continued carrying timber to the pile, a patient log man like Ferdinand doing the magician's bidding. When he had this task completed, he said quietly, "I was m-m-meant to get the bloody commission. Everyone knew it. So when it w-w-w-went to someone else . . ." He returned to the sycamore where St. James waited and he put one hand on its mottled trunk. He took a minute during which it seemed that he worked to be the master of his sudden stammer. "A tree house," he finally said in derision of his own efforts. "Here I am. A bloody tree house."

"Had Mr. Brouard told you you'd have the commission?" St. James asked.

"Told me directly? No. That w-w-" He looked pained. When he was ready, he tried again. "That wasn't Guy's way. He never promised. He merely suggested. He made you think of possibilities. Do *this,* my man, and the next thing you know, *that* will happen."

"In your case, what did that mean?"

"Independence. My own firm. Not a minion or a drone, working for someone else's glory, but my own ideas in my own space. He knew that's what I wanted and he encouraged it. He was an entrepreneur, after all. Why shouldn't the rest of us be?" Debiere examined the bark of the sycamore tree and gave a bitter laugh. "So I left my job and forged out on my own, started my own firm. He'd taken risks in his life. I would, too. Of course, it was easier for me, thinking I was secure with an enormous commission."

"You said you wouldn't let him ruin you," St. James reminded him.

"Words overheard at a party?" Debiere said. "I don't remember what I said. I just remember having a look at that drawing instead of drooling over it like everyone else. I could see how wrong it was and I couldn't understand why he'd chosen it when he'd said . . . when he'd . . . he'd as much as promised. And I remember f-f-*feeling*—" He stopped. His hand was white at the knuckles from the grip he had upon the tree.

"What happens with his death?" St. James asked. "Does the museum get built anyway?"

"I don't know," he said. "Frank Ouseley told me the will didn't allow for the museum. I can't imagine Adrian would care enough to fund it, so I expect it's going to be up to Ruth, if she wants to go forward."

"I dare say she might be amenable to suggestions at this point."

"Guy made it clear that the museum was important to him. She's going to know that without anyone telling her, believe me."

"I didn't mean amenable to building the museum," St. James said. "I meant amenable to changes in the design. Amenable in ways her brother wasn't, perhaps. Have you spoken to her? Do you intend to?"

"I intend to," Debiere said. "I've not much choice."

"Why is that?"

"Look around, Mr. St. James. I've two boys and a baby on the way. A wife I talked into leaving her job to write her novel. A mortgage here and a new office in Trinity Square, where my secretary expects to be paid now and then. I need the commission and if I don't get it . . . So I'll talk to Ruth. Yes. I'll argue my case. I'll do anything it takes."

He apparently recognised the wealth of meaning in his final statement because he moved away from the tree abruptly and returned to the pile of timber at the edge of the lawn. He pulled the sides of the blue tarpaulin up round the neat stack of boards, revealing rope precisely coiled on the ground. This he took up and used to tie the polythene sheet protectively over the wood, whereupon he began to gather up his tools.

St. James followed him when he took his hammer, nails, level, tape measure, and saw into a handsome shed at the bottom of the garden. Debiere replaced these items above a workbench, and it was on this bench that St. James set the plans he'd taken from *Le Reposoir*. His main intention had been to learn whether Henry Moullin's elaborate windows could be used on the building design that Guy Brouard had chosen, but now he saw that Moullin wasn't the only person whose participation in the construction of the wartime museum might have been crucial to him.

He said, "These are what the American architect

sent over to Mr. Brouard. I'm afraid I know nothing about architectural drawings. Will you look at them and tell me what you think? There appear to be several different kinds."

"I've already told you."

"You might want to add more when you see them."

The papers were large, well over a yard long and nearly as wide. Debiere sighed his agreement to inspect them and reached for a hammer to weigh the edges down.

They were not blueprints. Debiere informed him that blueprints had gone the way of carbon paper and manual typewriters. These were black-and-white documents that looked as if they'd come off an elephantine copying machine, and as he sorted through them, Debiere identified each for what it was: the schematic of every floor of the building; the construction documents with labels indicating the ceiling plan, the electrical plan, the plumbing plan, the building sections; the site plan showing where the building would sit at its chosen location; the elevation drawings.

Debiere shook his head as he fingered through them. He murmured, "Ridiculous" and "What's the idiot *thinking?*" and he pointed out the ludicrous size of the individual rooms that the structure would contain. "How," he demanded, indicating one of the rooms with a screwdriver, "is *this* supposed to be set up as a gallery? Or a viewing room? Or whatever the hell it's designed to be? Look at it. You could comfortably fit three people into a room that size, but that's the limit. It's no bigger than a cell. And they're all like that."

St. James examined the schematic that the architect was indicating. He noted that nothing on the drawing was identified and he asked Debiere if this was normal. "Wouldn't you generally label what each room is meant to be?" he asked. "Why's that missing from these drawings?"

"Who the hell knows," Debiere said dismissively. "Shoddy work's my guess. Not surprising considering he submitted his design without even bothering to walk the site. And look at this—" He'd pulled one of the sheets out and placed it on top of the stack. He tapped his screwdriver against it. "Is this a courtyard with a *pool,* for God's sake? I'd love to have a talk with this idiot. Probably designs homes in Hollywood and thinks no place's complete unless twenty-year-olds in bikinis have a spot to lie in the sun. What a waste of space. The whole thing's a disaster. I can't believe that Guy—" He frowned. Suddenly, he bent over the drawing and looked at it more closely. He appeared to be searching for something but whatever it was, it wasn't part of the building itself because Debiere looked at all four corners of the paper and then directed his gaze along the edges. He said, "This is damn odd," and shifted the first paper to one side so that he could see the one under it. Then he went to the next, then the one after that. He finally looked up.

"What?" St. James asked.

"These should be wet-signed," Debiere said. "Every one of them. But not one is."

"What d'you mean?"

Debiere pointed to the plans. "When these're complete, the architect stamps them. Then he signs his name over that stamp."

"Is that a formality?"

"No. It's essential. It's how you tell the plans are legitimate. You can't get them approved by planning or building commissions if they're not stamped, and you sure as hell can't find a contractor willing to take on the job, either."

"So if they aren't legitimate, what else might they be?" St. James asked the architect.

Debiere looked from St. James to the plans. And then back to St. James once again. "Stolen," he replied.

They were silent, each of them contemplating the documents, the schematics, and the drawings that lay across the workbench. Outside the shed, a door slammed and a voice cried out, "Daddy! Mum's made you short bread as well."

Debiere roused himself at this. His forehead creased as he apparently tried to comprehend what seemed so patently incomprehensible: a large gathering of islanders and others at *Le Reposoir,* a gala event, a surprising announcement, a mass of fireworks to mark the occasion, the presence of everyone important on Guernsey, the coverage in the paper and on island television.

His sons were shouting "Daddy! Daddy! Come in for tea!" but Debiere didn't seem to hear them. He murmured, "What did he *intend* to do, then?"

The answer to that question, St. James thought, might go far to shedding more light on the murder.

Finding a solicitor—Margaret Chamberlain refused to think of or call them *advocates* because she didn't intend to employ one for longer than it took to strong-arm her former husband's beneficiaries out of their inheritances—turned out to be a simple matter. After leaving the Range Rover in the car park of a hotel on Ann's Place, she and her son walked down one slope and up another. Their route took them past the Royal Court House, which assured Margaret that lawyers were going to be quite easy to come by in this part of town. At *least* Adrian had known that much. On her own, she would have been reduced to the telephone directory and a street map of St. Peter Port. She would have had to ring and do her importuning without having seen the situation into which her phone call was received. This way, however, she had no need to ring at all. She could storm the citadel of her choosing, satisfactorily on the controlling end of employing a legal mind to do her bidding.

The offices of Gibbs, Grierson, and Godfrey ended up as her selection. The alliteration was an annoyance, but the front door was imposing and the lettering on the brass plate outside was of a stark nature that suggested a ruthlessness which Margaret's mission required. Without an appointment, then, she entered with her son and requested to see one of the eponymous members of the organisation. As she made her request, she stifled her desire to tell Adrian to stand up straight, assuring herself it was enough that he had—for her benefit and protection—earlier arm-wrestled that little hooligan Paul Fielder into submission.

As luck would have it, none of the founders were in their offices on this afternoon. One of them had apparently died four years earlier and the other two were out on some sort of quasi-important lawyerly business, according to their clerk. But one of the junior advocates would be able to see Mrs. Chamberlain and Mr. Brouard.

How junior? Margaret wanted to know.

It was a loose term only, she was assured.

The junior advocate turned out to be junior in title alone. She was otherwise a middle-aged woman called Juditha Crown—"Ms. Crown," she told them—with a fat mole beneath her left eye and a mild case of halitosis that appeared to have been brought on by a half-eaten salami sandwich which sat on a paper plate on her desk.

As Adrian slouched nearby, Margaret disclosed the reason for their call: a son cheated out of his inheritance and an inheritance that was absent at least three-quarters of the property it should have comprised.

That, Ms. Crown informed them with an archness that Margaret found a little too condescending for her liking, was highly unlikely, Mrs. Chamberlain. Had Mr. Chamberlain—

Mr. Brouard, Margaret interrupted. Mr. Guy

Brouard of *Le Réposoir,* Parish of St. Martin's. She was his former wife, and this was their son, Adrian Brouard, she announced to Ms. Crown and added pointedly, Mr. Guy Brouard's eldest and his only male heir.

Margaret was gratified to see Juditha Crown sit up and take notice of this, if only metaphorically. The lawyer's eyelashes quivered behind her gold-framed spectacles. She gazed upon Adrian with heightened interest. It was a moment during which Margaret found she could finally feel grateful for Guy's relentless pursuit of personal accomplishment. If nothing else, he had name recognition and, by association, so did his son.

Margaret laid out the situation for Ms. Crown: an estate divided in half, with two daughters and a son sharing the first half of it and two relative strangers—*strangers,* mind you, in the person of two local *teenagers* practically unknown to the family—sharing the other half equally between them. Something needed to be done about this.

Ms. Crown nodded sagely and waited for Margaret to continue. When Margaret didn't, Ms. Crown asked if there was a current wife involved. No? Well, then—and here she folded her hands on the desk top and formed her lips into a glacially polite smile—there didn't seem to be anything irregular about the will. The laws of Guernsey dictated the manner in which property could be bequeathed. Half of it had to go by law to the legal progeny of the testator. In cases where there was no surviving spouse, the other half could be dispersed according to the whimsy of the deceased. This was apparently what the gentleman in question had done.

Margaret was aware of Adrian next to her, of the restlessness that prompted him to dig through his pocket at this point and bring out a matchbook. She thought he intended to smoke despite there being no ashtray evident anywhere in the room, but instead he used the edge to clean beneath his fingernails. Seeing this, Ms. Crown made a moue of distaste.

Margaret wanted to rail at her son, but she settled on nudging his foot with hers. He moved his away. She cleared her throat.

The division of inheritance prescribed by the will was only part of what concerned her, she told the lawyer. There was the more pressing matter of all that was missing from what should have legally been the inheritance, no matter who received it. The will made no mention of the estate itself—the house, the furnishings, and the land that comprised *Le Reposoir.* It made no mention of Guy's properties in Spain, in England, in France, in the Seychelles and God only knew where else. It mentioned no personal possessions like cars, boats, an aeroplane, a helicopter, nor did it detail the significant number of miniatures, antiques, silver, art, coins, and the like that Guy had collected over the years. Surely all this belonged in the will of a man who was after all a successful entrepreneur to the tune of several significant multimillions. Yet his will had consisted of one savings account, one chequing account, and one investment account. How, Margaret inquired with a deliberate play on the words, did Ms. Crown *account* for that?

Ms. Crown looked thoughtful but only for the space of some three seconds, after which she asked Margaret if she was certain of her facts. Margaret told her huffily that of course she was certain. She didn't run about attempting to employ solicitors—

Advocates, Ms. Crown murmured.

—without first making sure she had her facts straight. As she'd said in the beginning, at least three-quarters of the estate of Guy Brouard was missing, and she meant to do something about it for Adrian Brouard, the scion, the eldest child, the only son of his father.

Here Margaret looked to Adrian for some sort of murmur of assent or enthusiasm. He balanced his right ankle on his left knee, displayed an unappealing expanse of fish-white leg, and said nothing. He hadn't, his mother noticed, put on socks.

Juditha Crown gazed at the lifeless-looking leg-flesh of her potential client and had the grace to keep from shuddering. She returned her attention to Margaret and said that if Mrs. Chamberlain would wait for a moment, she thought she might have something that would help.

What would help was backbone, Margaret thought. Backbone to infuse along the cooked noodle that currently went for Adrian's spine. But she said to the lawyer, Yes, yes, anything that could help them was more than welcome and if Ms. Crown was too busy to take their case, perhaps she'd be willing to recommend . . . ?

Ms. Crown left them as Margaret was making this appeal. She closed her door delicately behind her, and as she did so, Margaret could hear her speaking to the clerk in the anteroom. "Edward, where've we got that explanation of *Retrait Linager* you send out to clients?" The clerk's reply was muted.

Margaret used this intermezzo in the proceedings to say to her son fiercely, "You might participate. You *might* make things easier." For a moment, there in the kitchen of *Le Reposoir,* she'd actually thought her son had turned a corner. He'd wrestled with Paul Fielder like a man who meant business, and she'd felt a real blossoming of hope . . . prematurely, however. It had withered on the vine. "You might even seem interested in your future," she added.

"I can't possibly top your interest, Mother," Adrian replied laconically.

"You're maddening. No wonder your father—" She stopped herself.

He cocked his head and offered her a sardonic smile. But he said nothing as Juditha Crown rejoined them. She had a few typed sheets of paper in her hand. These, she told them, explained the laws of *Retrait Linager.*

Margaret wasn't interested in anything but garnering either the lawyer's consent or her refusal to work on their behalf so she could be about the rest of her business. There was much to do, and sitting round a solicitor's office reading explanations of arcane statutes was not high on her list of priorities. Still, she took the papers from the other woman and rustled round in her bag for her spectacles. While she did so, Ms. Crown informed both Margaret and her son of the legal ramifications of either owning or disposing of a large estate while a resident of Guernsey.

The law didn't take lightly to someone disinheriting his offspring on this particular Channel Island, she told them. Not only could one not leave money willy-nilly irrespective of one's having reproduced, but one also could not simply sell off one's entire estate in *advance* of one's demise and hope to get round the law in that way. Your children, she explained, had the first right to purchase your estate for the same amount you had it on offer should you decide to sell it. Of course, if they couldn't afford it, you were off the hook and you could then proceed with selling it and giving away every penny or spending it in advance of your death. But in either case, your children had to be informed *first* that you intended to dispose of what would otherwise be their inheritance. This safeguarded the possession of property within a single family as long as that family could afford to keep it.

"I take it your father didn't inform you of an intention to sell anytime prior to his death," Ms. Crown said directly to Adrian.

"Of course he didn't!" Margaret said.

Ms. Crown waited for Adrian to confirm this statement. She said that if that was indeed the case before them, there was only one explanation for what appeared to be a large chunk of missing inheritance. There was only one very *simple* explanation, as a matter of fact.

And that was? Margaret asked politely.

That Mr. Brouard had never owned any of the property he was suspected to have owned, she replied.

Margaret stared at the woman. "That's absurd," she said. "Of course he owned it. He owned it for years. That and everything else. He's *owned* . . . See here. He wasn't someone's tenant."

"I'm not suggesting that he was," Ms. Crown replied. "I'm merely suggesting that what appeared to belong to him—indeed, what he himself no doubt purchased throughout the years or at least throughout the years that he lived on this island— was in fact purchased by him for someone else. Or purchased by someone else at his direction."

Hearing this, Margaret felt the dawning of a horror she didn't want to acknowledge, let alone face. She heard herself say hoarsely, "That's impossible!" and she felt her body surge upwards as if her legs and her feet had declared war on her ability to control them. Before she knew it, she was bending over Juditha Crown's desk, breathing directly into her face. "That's utter lunacy, d'you hear me? It's idiocy. D'you *know* who he was? Have you any idea of the fortune he amassed? Have you ever heard of Chateaux Brouard? England, Scotland, Wales, France, and God only knows how many hotels. What was all that if not Guy's empire? Who else could have owned it if not Guy Brouard?"

"Mother . . ." Adrian, too, was on his feet. Margaret turned to see that he was donning his leather jacket, preparatory to leaving. "We've found out what we—"

"We've found out nothing!" Margaret cried. "Your father cheated you all your life and I'm not about to let him cheat you in his death. He's got bank accounts hidden and property unmentioned and I mean to find them. I mean you to have them, and *nothing*—d'you hear me?—is going to prevent that from happening."

"He outsmarted you, Mother. He knew—"

"Nothing. He knew *nothing*." She swung on the lawyer as if Juditha Crown were the person who had foiled her plans. "Who, then?" she demanded. "*Who?* One of his little tarts? Is that what you're suggesting?"

Ms. Crown appeared to know what Margaret was talking about without being told, because she said, "It would have been someone he could trust, I dare say. Someone he could trust implicitly. Someone who would do what he wanted done with the property, no matter whose name it was in."

There was only one person, naturally. Margaret knew this without that person being identified, and she supposed she'd known from the moment she'd heard the reading of that will in the upstairs drawing room. There was only one soul on the face of the earth whom Guy could have relied upon to have *everything* gifted to her upon his purchase of it and to have done nothing with it but to hold on to it and disperse it according to his wishes at the time of her own death . . . or sooner, if that was asked of her.

Why hadn't she thought of this? Margaret demanded of herself.

But the answer to that was simple enough. She

hadn't thought of it because she hadn't known the law.

She swept out of the office and into the street, burning up from head to toe. But she was not defeated. She was nowhere close to being defeated, and she wanted to make this clear to her son. She swung round on him.

"We're going to talk to her at once. She's your aunt. She knows what's right. If she hasn't yet had the injustice of all this spread out in front of her . . . She could never see *anything* in him but godlike . . . His mind was unbalanced and he hid that from her. He hid it from everyone, but we shall prove—"

"Aunt Ruth knew," Adrian said bluntly. "She understood what he wanted. She cooperated with him."

"She can't have." Margaret clutched his arm with a strength designed to make him see and understand. It was time for him to gird for battle whatever loins he had and if he couldn't do that, she bloody well intended to do it for him. "He must have told her . . ." What? she asked herself. What had Guy said to his sister to make her believe that what he intended to do was for the best: his good, her good, the good of his children, the good of everyone? *What* had he said?

"It's done," Adrian said. "We can't change the will. We can't change the way he worked all this out. We can't do anything except let it be." He shoved his hand into his leather jacket and brought out the matchbook once again, along with a packet of cigarettes. He lit up and chuckled, although his expression was far from amused. "Good old Dad," he said as he shook his head. "He buggered us all."

Margaret shivered at his emotionless tone. She took another tack. "Adrian, Ruth's a good soul. She's completely fair-hearted. If she knows how much this has hurt you—"

"It hasn't." Adrian picked a piece of tobacco from his tongue, inspected it on the end of his thumb, and flicked it into the street.

"Don't say that. Why must you always pretend that your father's—"

"I'm not pretending. I'm not hurt. What would be the point? And even if I *were* wounded by this, it wouldn't matter. It wouldn't change a thing."

"How can you say . . . ? She's your aunt. She loves you."

"She was there," Adrian said. "She knows what his intentions were. And, believe me, she won't veer an inch from them. Not when she already knows what he wanted from the situation."

Margaret frowned. " 'She was there.' Where? When? What situation?"

Adrian stepped away from the building. He turned up the collar of his jacket against the chill, moving off in the direction of the Royal Court House. Margaret saw all this as a way to avoid replying to her questions, and her antennae went up. As did a pernicious sense of dread. She stopped her son at the foot of the war memorial and she accosted him beneath the sombre gaze of that melancholy soldier.

"Don't walk away from me like that. We're not

finished here. What situation? What haven't you told me?"

Adrian tossed his cigarette towards a score of motor scooters that stood in disorganised ranks not far from the memorial. "Dad didn't intend me to have money," he said. "Not now. Not ever. Aunt Ruth knew that. So even if we appeal to her—to her sense of loyalty or fair play or whatever else you want to call it—she's going to remember what he wanted and that's what she's going to do."

"How could she possibly know what Guy intended at the time of his death?" Margaret scoffed. "Oh, I see how she could have known what he intended when this mess was set up. She would have had to know then in order to cooperate with him then. But that's just it. Then. It's what he wanted *then*. People change. Their wishes change. Believe me, your aunt Ruth will see that when it's put to her."

"No. It was more than just then," Adrian said, and he began to push past her, to move towards the car park where they'd left the Range Rover.

Margaret said, "Damn it. Stay where you are, Adrian," and she heard the trepidation in her voice, which annoyed her, which in turn directed her annoyance onto him. "We've plans to lay and an approach to map out. We're not about to accept this situation as your father created it: like good little Christians with our cheeks averted. For all we know, he made his arrangements with Ruth in a fit of pique one day and he regretted it afterwards but never expected to die before he had a chance to put it all right." Margaret drew a breath and considered

the implication behind what she was saying. "Someone knew that," she said. "That has to be it. Someone knew that he intended to change everything, to
favour you the way you were meant to be favoured.
Because of that, Guy had to be eliminated."

"He wasn't going to change a thing," Adrian said.

"Stop it! How can you know—"

"Because I asked him, all right?" Adrian shoved
his hands into his pockets and looked generally miserable. "I *asked* him," he repeated. "And she was
there. Aunt Ruth. In the room. She heard us talking. She heard me ask him."

"To change his will?"

"To give me money. She heard the whole thing. I
asked. He said he didn't have it. Not what I needed.
Not that much. I didn't believe him. We rowed. I
left him in a rage and she stayed behind." He looked
back at her then, his expression resigned. "You can't
think they didn't talk everything through afterwards.
She'd've said, What should we do about Adrian?
And he would've said, We let things be."

Margaret heard all this like a cold wind calling.
She said, "You asked your father again . . . ? After
September? You'd asked him for money again since
September?"

"I asked. He turned me down."

"When?"

"The evening before the party."

"But you told me you hadn't . . . since last September . . ." Margaret saw him turn away from her
again, his head lowered as it had lowered so many
times in childhood over a legion of disappointments

and defeats. She wanted to rage against them all, but particularly against whatever fate it was that made Adrian's life so difficult for him. Beyond that maternal reaction, however, Margaret felt something else that she didn't want to feel. Nor could she risk identifying it. She said, "Adrian, you *told* me . . ." Mentally, she went back through the chronology of events. What had he said? that Guy had died before his son had had the opportunity to ask him a second time for the money he needed to bankroll his business. Internet access, it was, the wave of the future. A wave he could ride to make his father proud to have produced such a visionary son. "You said you'd had no chance to ask him for money on this visit."

"I lied," Adrian replied flatly. He lit another cigarette and he didn't look her way.

Margaret felt her throat go dry. "Why?"

He made no reply.

She wanted to shake him. She needed to force an answer from him because only with an answer could she possibly discover the rest of the truth so that she would know what she was dealing with so that she could move quickly and plan for whatever might come next. But beneath that need to scheme, to excuse, to do anything it took to keep her son safe, Margaret was aware of a deeper feeling.

If he'd lied to her about having spoken to his father, he'd lied about other things as well.

After his conversation with Bertrand Debiere, St. James arrived back at the hotel in a pensive frame of mind. The young receptionist in the lobby handed him a message, but he didn't open it as he climbed the stairs to his room. Instead, he wondered what it meant that Guy Brouard had gone to considerable trouble and expense to obtain a set of architectural documents which apparently weren't legitimate. Had he known this or had he been the dupe of an unscrupulous businessman in America who took his money and handed over a design for a building that no one would be able to build because it wasn't an official design in the first place? And what did it mean that it wasn't an official design? Was it thus plagiarised? *Could* one plagiarise an architectural design?

In the room, he went for the telephone, digging out of his pocket the information he'd gleaned earlier from Ruth Brouard and DCI Le Gallez. He found the number for Jim Ward and punched it into the phone while he organised his thoughts.

It was morning still in California, and the architect had apparently just arrived at his office. The woman who answered the phone said, "He's just walking in . . ." and then "Mr. W., someone with a way cool accent is asking for you . . ." and then into the phone, "Where're you calling from anyway? What'd you say your name was?"

St. James repeated it. He was phoning from St. Peter Port on the island of Guernsey in the English Channel, he explained.

She said, "Wow. Hang on a sec, okay?" And just before she sent him into limbo, St. James heard her say, "Hey. Where's the English Channel, you guys?"

Forty-five seconds passed, during which time St. James was entertained by lively reggae music through the ear piece of the phone. Then the music clicked off abruptly and a man's pleasant voice said, "Jim Ward. How can I help you? Is this more about Guy Brouard?"

"You've spoken to DCI Le Gallez, then," St. James said. He went on to explain who he was and what he was doing involved in the situation on Guernsey.

"I don't think there's much I can do to help you," Ward said. "As I told that detective when he called, I had only one meeting with Mr. Brouard. His project sounded interesting, but I hadn't gotten further than arranging to have those samples sent over. I was waiting to hear if he wanted something else. I'd dropped a few new pictures in the mail so he could look over several other buildings I have going up in north San Diego. But that was it."

"What do you mean by samples?" St. James asked. "What we have here—and I've been looking at them today—appear to be an extensive set of drawings. I've gone over them with a local architect—"

"They are. Extensive, that is. I gathered up one project's paperwork from start to finish for him: a big spa that's going up here on the coast. I put together everything but the eight-and-a-half-by-elevens, the bound book. I told him they would give him an idea of how I work, which was what he wanted before he'd ask me to do anything more. It was a strange way of going at it, if you ask me. But it wasn't any real problem to accommodate him, and it saved me time to—"

St. James cut in. "Are you saying that what was couriered over here *wasn't* the set of plans for a museum?"

Ward laughed. "Museum? No. It's a high-end spa: head-to-foot pampering for the cosmetic-surgery crowd. When he asked me for a sample of my work—for as complete a set of plans as I could get to him—that was the easiest to lay my hands on. I told him that. I said that what I'd send wouldn't reflect what I'd do for a museum. But he said that was fine by him. Anything would do, just as long as it was complete and he'd be able to understand what he was looking at."

"So that's why these aren't official plans," St. James said, more to himself than to Ward.

"Right. Those are just copies from the office here."

St. James thanked the architect and rang off. Then he sat on the edge of the bed and stared at the tops of his shoes.

He was experiencing a decidedly down-the-rabbit-hole sort of moment. It was appearing more and more that the museum had been something Brouard was using as a blind. But as a blind for what? And in any case the nagging question was: Had it been a blind from the very beginning? And if that turned out to be the case, had one of the principals involved in its development—someone, perhaps, depending upon its creation and having invested in it in any number of ways—discovered this fact and struck out in an act of revenge for having been ill-used by Brouard?

St. James pressed his fingers to his forehead and demanded of his brain that it sort out everything. But as appeared to be the case for everyone associated with the murder victim, Guy Brouard stayed one step ahead of him. It was a maddening feeling.

He'd placed the folded note from reception on the dressing table, and he caught a glimpse of it as he rose from the bed. It was, he saw, a message from Deborah and it appeared to have been written in a furious hurry.

Cherokee's been arrested! she'd scrawled. *Please come as soon as you get this.* The word *please* had been underlined twice, and she had added a hastily sketched map to the Queen Margaret Apartments on Clifton Street, which St. James took himself to at once.

His knuckles barely touched the door of Flat B before Deborah answered it. She said, "Thank God. I'm so glad you're here. Come in, my love. Meet China at last."

China River was sitting tailor-fashion on the sofa, round her shoulders a blanket that she held to her like a shawl. She said to St. James, "I never thought I'd actually meet you. I never thought . . ." Her face crumpled. She raised a fist to her mouth.

"What's happened?" St. James asked Deborah.

"We don't know," she replied. "The police wouldn't say when they took him. China's solicitor . . . China's advocate . . . he set off to talk to them as soon as we phoned him, but we haven't yet heard back from him. But, Simon"—and here she

lowered her voice—"I think they've got something . . . something they've found. What else could
it be?"

"His prints on that ring?"

"Cherokee didn't know about the ring. He'd
never seen it. He was as surprised as I when we took
it to the antiques shop and were told—"

"Deborah," China cut in from the sofa. They
turned to her. She looked markedly hesitant. And
then just as remarkably regretful. "I . . ." She seemed
to reach inside herself for the resolve to continue.
"Deborah, I showed that ring to Cherokee right
when I bought it."

St. James said to his wife, "Are you sure he
didn't—"

"Debs didn't know. I didn't say. I didn't want to
because when she showed me the ring—here in the
apartment—Cherokee didn't say a word. He didn't
act like he even recognised it. I couldn't figure
out . . . you know, why he . . ." Nervously, she bit at
the cuticle of her thumbnail. "He didn't say . . . And
I didn't think . . ."

"They took his belongings as well," Deborah said
to St. James. "He had a duffel and a rucksack. They
wanted them especially. There were two of them—
two constables, I mean—and they said, 'This is it?
This is everything you've brought with you?' After
they took him, they came back and had a look
through all the cupboards. Under the furniture as
well. And through the rubbish."

St. James nodded. He said to China, "I'll have a
word with DCI Le Gallez directly."

China said, "Someone had it planned from the beginning. Find two dumb Americans, two who've never been out of the country, who'll probably *never* have enough money to even get out of California unless they hitchhike. Offer them a once-in-a-life-time opportunity. It'll sound so good, too good to be true, and they'll jump at the chance. And then we'll have them." Her voice quavered. "We've been set up. First me. Now him. They're going to say we planned it together before we ever left home. And how can we prove that we didn't? That we didn't even *know* these people. Not one of them. How can we prove it?"

St. James was loath to say what needed to be said to Deborah's friend. There was, indeed, a bizarre comfort for her in thinking that she and her brother were now in the quicksand together. But the truth of the matter lay in what two witnesses had seen on the morning of the murder and in what signs had been left at the crime scene. The additional truth lay in who had now been arrested and why.

He said, "I'm afraid it's fairly clear there was only one killer, China. One person was seen following Brouard to the bay and one set of footprints was next to his body."

The lights were dim in the room, but he saw China swallow. "Then it didn't matter which one of us got accused. Me or him. But they definitely needed two of us here to double the chance that one of us would be fingered. It was all planned out, set up from the first. You see that, don't you?"

St. James was silent. He did see that someone had

thought everything through. He did see that the crime had not been the work of a single moment. But he also saw that, as far as he knew right now, only four people had possessed the information that two Americans—two potential fall-guys for a murder—would be traveling to Guernsey to make a delivery to Guy Brouard: Brouard himself, the lawyer he'd employed in California, and the River siblings. With Brouard dead and the lawyer accounted for, that left only the Rivers to have planned out the murder. One of the Rivers.

He said carefully, "The difficulty is that apparently no one knew you were coming."

"Someone must have. Because the party was arranged . . . the museum party . . ."

"Yes. I see that. But Brouard appears to have led a number of people to believe that the design he'd chosen was going to be Bertrand Debiere's. That tells us that your arrival—your presence at *Le Reposoir*—was something of a surprise to everyone but Brouard himself."

"He must have told someone. *Everyone* confides in someone else. What about Frank Ouseley? They were good friends. Or Ruth? Wouldn't he have told his own sister?"

"It doesn't appear that way. And even if he had done, she had no reason to—"

"Like we *did*?" China's voice raised. "Come *on*. He told someone we were coming. If not Frank or Ruth . . . Someone knew. I'm telling you. Someone knew."

Deborah said to St. James, "He might have told

Mrs. Abbott. Anaïs. The woman he was involved with."

"And she could have passed the word along," China said. "Anyone could have known from that point."

St. James had to admit that this was possible. He had to admit it was even likely. The problem was, of course, that Brouard's having told *anyone* about the eventual arrival of the Rivers begged the question of a crucial detail that still needed sorting out: the apocryphal nature of the architectural plans. Brouard had presented the elevation water colour as the genuine article, the future wartime museum, when he'd known all along that it was nothing of the sort. So if he'd told someone else that the Rivers were bringing plans from California, had he also told that person the plans were phony?

"We do need to speak with Anaïs, my love," Deborah urged. "Her son as well. He was . . . He was definitely in a state, Simon."

"You see?" China said. "There're others, and one of them knew we were coming. One of them planned things from there. And we've got to find that person, Simon. Because no way are the cops about to do it."

Outside, they found a soft rain had begun to fall, and Deborah took Simon's arm, tucking herself into his side. She liked to think he might interpret her gesture as one made by a woman seeking shelter in the strength of her man, but she knew it wasn't in his nature to flatter himself in that way. He would know it was what she did to assure herself that he didn't slip on a cobblestone made slick by water and, depending upon his mood, he would humour her or not.

Humouring her for whatever reason appeared to be his choice. He ignored her motives and said, "The fact that he said nothing to you about the ring . . . Not even that his sister had bought it or had mentioned buying it or had mentioned seeing it or anything of that nature . . . It doesn't look good, my love."

"I don't want to consider what it means," she admitted. "Especially if her fingerprints are clearly all over it."

"Hmm. I did think you were heading in that direction towards the end. Despite the remark about Mrs. Abbott. You looked . . ." Deborah felt him glance at her. "You looked . . . stricken, I suppose."

"He's her *brother,*" Deborah said. "I just can't stand to think her own brother . . ." She wished to dismiss the very idea, but she couldn't. There it resided, as it had done from the moment her husband had pointed out that no one had known the River siblings were coming to Guernsey. From that instant, all she'd been able to think of was the countless times throughout the years when she'd heard of Cherokee River's exploits just this side of the law. He'd been the original Man with a Plan, and the Plan had always involved the easy acquisition of cash. That had been the case when Deborah had lived with China in Santa Barbara and listened to tales of Cherokee's exploits: from the rent-a-bed operation of his teens in which he allowed his room to be used on an hourly basis for adolescent assignations, to the thriving cannabis farm of his early twenties. Cherokee River as Deborah knew him had been an opportunist from the first. The only question was how one defined the opportunity he may have seen and jumped upon in Guy Brouard's death.

"What I can't stand to think of is what it means about China," Deborah said. "About what he intended to happen to her . . . I mean, that she should be the one . . . Of all people . . . It's horrible, Simon. Her own brother. How could he ever . . . ? I mean, *if* he's done this in the first place. Because, really, there has to be another explanation. I don't want to believe this one."

"We can look for another," Simon said. "We can talk to the Abbotts. To everyone else as well. But, Deborah . . ."

She looked up to see the concern on his face. "You do need to prepare yourself for the worst," he said.

"The worst would be China standing trial," Deborah responded. "The worst would have been China's going to prison. Taking the fall for . . . taking the fall for . . . for someone . . ." Her words died out as she realised how right her husband was. Without warning, with no time to adjust, she felt as if she were caught between two alternatives named *bad* and *worse*. Her first loyalty was to her old friend. So she knew she should have been experiencing a fair degree of joy from the fact that a false arrest and a faulty prosecution that could have resulted in China's imprisonment appeared—at this eleventh hour—to have been obviated altogether. But if the cost of China's rescue came at the expense of knowing that her own brother had orchestrated the events that had led to her arrest . . . How could anyone celebrate China's deliverance after being presented with that sort of information? And how could China herself ever recover from such a betrayal? "She's not going to believe he's done this to her," Deborah finally said.

Simon asked quietly, "What about you?"

"Me?" Deborah stopped walking. They had reached the corner of Berthelot Street, which sloped steeply down to the High Street and the quay beyond it. The narrow lane was slick, and the rain snaking towards the bay was beginning to form serious rivulets that promised to grow in the coming hours. It was no wise spot for a man uncertain of his footing to walk, yet Simon turned towards it resolutely while Deborah thought about his question.

She saw that midway down the slope, the windows of the Admiral de Saumarez Inn winked brightly in the gloom, suggesting both shelter and comfort. But she knew these were specious offerings even at the best of times, no more permanent than the rain that fell on the town. Nonetheless, her husband headed towards them. She didn't answer his question till they were safely within the shelter of the inn's front door.

Then she said to him, "I hadn't considered it, Simon. I'm not exactly sure what you mean, anyway."

"Just what I said. Can you believe?" he asked her. "Will you be able to believe? When it comes down to it—if it comes down to it—are you willing to believe Cherokee River has framed his own sister? Because that will likely mean he came to London expressly to fetch you. Or me. Or both of us, for that matter. But he didn't come only to go to the embassy."

"Why?"

"Did he fetch us, you mean? To have his sister believe he was helping her. To make sure she didn't dwell on anything that could have caused her to look on him with suspicion or, worse, turn the spotlight on him in the eyes of the police. I'd suggest that he was applying salve to his conscience as well by at least having someone here for China, but if he intended her to take the fall for a murder, I don't actually believe he has a conscience in the first place."

"You don't like him, do you?" Deborah asked.

"It's not a matter of liking or disliking. It's a matter of looking at the facts, seeing them for what they are, and spelling them out."

Deborah saw the truth in this. She understood that Simon's dispassionate assessment of Cherokee River came from two sources: his background in a science that was drawn upon regularly during criminal investigations and the brief time in which he'd known China's brother. Simon, in short, had nothing whatsoever invested in Cherokee's innocence or his guilt. But that was not the case for her. She said, "No, I can't believe he's done this. I just can't believe it."

Simon nodded. Deborah thought his face looked unaccountably bleak, but she told herself it could have been the light. He said, "Yes. That's what I'm worried about," and he preceded her farther into the inn.

You know what this means, don't you, Frank? You do know what this means.

Frank couldn't recall if Guy Brouard had said those exact words or if they'd merely appeared on his face. He knew, in either case, that they had definitely existed in some manner between them. They were as real as the name G. H. Ouseley and the address *Moulin des Niaux* that an arrogant Aryan hand had written on the top of the receipt for food: sausages, flour, eggs, potatoes, and beans. And tobacco so that the Judas among them would no longer have to smoke whatever leaves could be culled from roadside bushes, dried, and rolled within flimsy tissue.

Without asking, Frank knew the price that had been paid for these goods. He knew because three of those foolhardy men who'd typed up *G.I.F.T.* in the dim and dangerous candlelight of the vestry of *St. Pierre du Bois* had gone to labour camps for their efforts while a fourth had been merely shipped to a gaol in France. The three had died in or because of those labour camps. The fourth had served only a year. When he had spoken of that year at all, he'd spoken of that time in French gaol as cruel, as disease-ridden and grossly inhuman, but that, Frank realised, was how he needed that time to be seen. He probably even remembered it that way because remembering it as a logical and necessary removal from Guernsey for his own protection once his colleagues stood betrayed . . . remembering it as a way to safeguard himself as a spy owing much to the Nazis upon his return . . . remembering it as recompense for an act committed because he was *hungry,* for the love of God, and not because he particularly believed in anything at all . . . How could a man face having brought about the deaths of his associates in order to fill his belly with decent food?

Over time the lie that Graham Ouseley had been one of those betrayed by a quisling had become his reality. He could not afford it to be otherwise, and the fact that he himself was the quisling—with the deaths of three good men on his conscience—would no doubt spin his troubled mind into utter confusion were it laid in front of him. Yet laying it in front of him was exactly what would happen once the press started leafing through the documents they would ask for in support of his naming of names.

Frank could only imagine what life would be like when the story first broke. The press would play it out over days, and the island's television and radio stations would pick up the tale forthwith. To the howls of protests from the descendants of the collaborators—as well as those collaborators who, like Graham, were still alive—the press would then supply the relevant proof. The story wouldn't run without that proof being offered in advance, so among those quis-lings named by the paper, Graham Ouseley's name would appear. And what a delicious irony for the various media to dwell upon: that the man determined to name the scoundrels who'd caused detentions, de-portations, and deaths was himself a villain of the highest order, a leper needing to be driven from their midst.

Guy had asked Frank what he intended to do with this knowledge of his father's perfidy, and Frank had not known. As Graham Ouseley could not face the truth of his actions during the Occupation, Frank had found he could not face the responsibility for setting the record straight. Instead, he'd cursed the evening he'd first met Guy Brouard at the lecture in town, and he bitterly regretted the moment when he'd seen in the other man an interest in the war that matched his own. Had he not seen that and acted impulsively upon it, everything would be different. That receipt, long kept among others by the Nazis to identify those who aided and abetted, would have remained buried among the vast accumulation of documents that were part of a collection amassed but not thoughtfully sorted, labeled, or identified in any way.

Guy Brouard's advent into their lives had changed all that. Guy's enthusiastic suggestion that a proper storage facility be arranged for the collection—coupled with his love for the island that had become his home—had mated to produce a monster. That monster was knowledge, and that knowledge de-manded recognition and action. This was the

quagmire across which Frank had been fruitlessly attempting to find a way.

Time was short. With Guy's death, Frank had
thought they'd bought silence. But this day had
shown him otherwise. Graham was determined to
set off on the course of his own destruction. Although he'd managed to hide himself away for more
than fifty years, his refuge was gone, and there was
no sanctuary now from what would befall him.

Frank's legs felt as if he were dragging irons as he
approached the chest of drawers in his bedroom. He
picked up the list from where he'd placed it and as he
descended the stairs he carried it in front of him like
a sacrificial offering.

In the sitting room, the television was showing
two doctors in scrubs, hovering over a patient in an
operating theatre. Frank switched this off and turned
to his father. He was still asleep, with his jaw agape, a
dribble of saliva pooling in the cavity of his lower lip.

Frank bent to him and put his hand on Graham's
shoulder. He said, "Dad, wake up. We've got to
talk," and he gave him a gentle shake.

Graham's eyes opened behind the thick glass of
his spectacles. He blinked in confusion, then said,
"Must've dropped off, Frankie. Wha's the time?"

"Late," Frank said. "Time to go to sleep
properly."

Graham said, "Oh. Righ', lad," and he made a
move to rise.

Frank said, "Not yet, though. Look at this first,
Dad," and he held the food receipt out before him,
level with his father's failing vision.

Graham knitted his brows as his gaze swept over the piece of paper. He said, "Wha's this, then?"

"You tell me. It's got your name on it. See? Right here. There's a date as well. Eighteenth of August, nineteen forty-three. It's mostly written in German. What d'you make of it, Dad?"

His father shook his head. "Nothing. Don't know a thing about it." His assertion seemed genuine, as it no doubt was to him.

"D'you know what it says? The German, I mean. Can you translate it?"

"Don't speak Kraut, do I? Never did. Never will." Graham rustled round in his chair, moved forward, and put his hands on its arms.

"Not yet, Dad," Frank said to stop him. "Let me read this to you."

"Time for bed, you said." Graham's voice sounded wary.

"Time for this first. It says six sausages. One dozen eggs. Two kilos flour. Six kilos potatoes. One kilo beans. And tobacco, Dad. Real tobacco. Two hundred grams of it. This is what the Germans gave to you."

"The Krauts?" Graham said. "Rubbish. Where'd you get . . . Lemme see." He made a weak grab for it.

Frank moved it out of his reach and said, "Here's what happened, Dad. You were sick of it, I think. The scrabbling just to stay alive. Thin rations. Then no rations at all. Brambles for tea. Potato peels for cake. You were hungry and tired and sick to death of eating roots and weeds. So you gave them names—"

"I *never*—"

"You gave them the ones they wanted because what *you* wanted was a decent smoke. And meat. God, how you wanted meat. And you knew the way to get it. That's what happened. Three lives in exchange for six sausages. A fair bargain when you've been reduced to eating the household cat."

"Tha's not true!" Graham protested. "You gone mad, or what?"

"This is your name, isn't it? This is the signature of the *Feldkommandant* on the bottom of the page. Heine. Right there. Look at it, Dad. You were approved from on high for special treatment. Slipped a little sustenance now and then to see you through the war. If I have a look through the rest of the documents, how many more of these am I going to find?"

"I don' know what you're talking about."

"No. You don't. You've made yourself forget. What else could you do when the lot of them died? You didn't expect that, did you? You thought they'd just do time and come home. I'll give you that much."

"You've gone mad, boy. Let me out of this chair. Back away with you. Back away, I say, or I'll know the reason why."

That paternal threat he'd heard as a child, so infrequently as to be nearly forgotten, worked on Frank now. He took a step back. He watched his father struggle out of the chair.

"I'm going to bed, I am," Graham said to his son.

" 'Nough of this twaddle. Things to do tomorrow and I mean to be rested 'n order to do 'em. And mind you, Frank"—with a trembling finger pointed at Frank's chest—"don't you plan to stand in my way. You *hear* me? There's tales to be told and I mean to tell 'em."

"Aren't you listening to me?" Frank asked in anguish. "You were *one* of them. You turned in your mates. You went to the Nazis. You struck a deal. And you've spent the last sixty years denying it."

"I *never* . . . !" Graham took a step towards him, his hands balled into determined fists. "People *died,* you bastard. Good men—better than you could ever be—went to their deaths 'cause they wouldn't submit. Oh, they were told to, weren't they? Cooperate, keep the upper lip stiff, soldier through it somehow. King's deserted you but he *cares,* he does, and someday when this's all over, you'll get to see him doff his hat your way. Meantime, act like you're doing what Jerry says to do."

"Is that what you told yourself? You were just *acting* like a bloke who's cooperating? Turning in your friends, watching their arrests, going through the charade of your own deportation when you knew all along it was just a sham? Where did they actually send you, Dad? Where did they hide you for your 'prison term'? Didn't anyone notice when you got back that you looked just a little too well for a gent who's spent a year in gaol during wartime?"

"I had TB! I had to take the cure."

"Who diagnosed it? Not a Guernsey doctor, I

expect. And if we ask for tests now—the sort of tests that show you once had TB—how will they turn out? Positive? I doubt it."

"That's rubbish, that is," Graham shrieked. "It's rubbish, rubbish, rubbish. You give me that paper. You hear me, Frank? You hand it over."

"I'll not," Frank said. "And you'll not speak to the press. Because if you do . . . Dad, if you do . . ." He finally felt the full horror of it all descend upon him: the life that was a lie and the part that he'd inadvertently but nonetheless enthusiastically played in creating it. He'd worshipped at the shrine of his father's bravery for all of his fifty-three years, only to learn that his religion of one knelt before even less than a golden calf. The grief of this piece of unwanted wisdom was unbearable. The rage that went with it was enough to engulf and fracture his mind. He said brokenly, "I was a little boy. I believed . . ." and his voice cracked on the declaration.

Graham hitched up his trousers. "Wha's this, then? Tears? Tha's all you got inside you? We had plenty to cry about, we did, back then. Five long years of hell on earth, Frankie. *Five* years, boy. Did you hear us crying? Did you see us wringing our hands and wondering what to do? Did you watch us waiting like patient saints for someone to drive the Jerrys from this island? It wasn't like that. We resisted, we did. We painted the V. We hid our radio receivers in the muck. We clipped telephone lines and took down our street signs and hid slave labourers when they escaped. We took in British soldiers when they landed as spies and we could've been shot at a moment's notice for doing it. But cry like babies? Did we ever cry? Did we snivel and pule? No such thing. We took it like men. 'Cause that's what we were." He headed for the stairs.

Frank watched him in wonder. He saw that Graham's version of history was so firmly rooted in his mind that there was going to be no simple way to extirpate it. The proof Frank held in his hands did not exist for his father. Indeed, he could not afford to let it exist. Admitting he had betrayed good men would be tantamount to admitting he was a homicide. And he would not do that. He would never do that. Why, Frank thought, had he ever believed Graham would?

On the stairs, his father grasped on to the handrail. Frank very nearly moved forward to assist Graham as he always did, but he found that he couldn't bring himself to touch the old man in his usual manner. He would have had to place his right hand on Graham's arm and to wind his left arm round Graham's waist, and he couldn't bear the thought of that contact. So he stood immobile and watched the old man struggle with seven of the steps.

"They're coming," Graham said, more to himself than to his son this time. "I rang 'em, I did. It's time the truth was told right and proper and I mean to tell it. Names're being named round here. There's going to be punishment meted out."

Frank's was the voice of powerless childhood as he said, "But, Dad, you can't—"

"Don't you tell me what I can and I can't!" his

father roared from the stairs. "Don't you bloody dare *ever* tell your dad what his business is. We suffered, we did. Some of us died. And there's them that're going to pay for it, Frank. That's the end of it. You hear me? That is the *end*."

He turned. He gripped the rail more firmly. He wobbled as he lifted his foot to climb another step. He began to cough.

Frank moved then, because the answer was simple, at the heart of things. His father spoke the only truth he knew. But the truth they shared—father and son—was the truth that said someone had to pay.

He reached the stairs and sprinted up them. He stopped when Graham was within his reach. He said, "Dad. Oh, Dad," as he grasped his father by the turn-ups of his trousers. He jerked on them once, swiftly and hard. He stepped out of the way as Graham crashed forward.

The crack of his head against the top step was loud. Graham gave a startled cry as he fell. But after that he was completely soundless as his body slid quickly down the stairs.

Chapter 21

ST. JAMES AND DEBORAH had their breakfast the next morning by a window that overlooked the small hotel garden, where undisciplined knots of pansies formed a colourful border round a patch of lawn. They were in the midst of laying out their plans for the day when China joined them, the black she wore from head to toe heightening her spectral appearance.

She gave them a quick smile that telegraphed her apology for descending on them so early. She said, "I need to do something. I can't just sit around. I had to before, but I don't have to now, and my nerves are shot. There's got to be something . . ." She seemed to notice the tumbling quality of what she was saying because she stopped herself and then said wryly, "Sorry. I'm operating on something like fifty cups of coffee. I've been awake since three."

"Have some orange juice," St. James offered. "Have you had breakfast?"

"Can't eat," she answered. "But thanks. I didn't say that yesterday. I meant to. Without you two here . . . Just thanks." She sat on a chair at an adjoining table, scooting it over to join St. James and his wife. She looked round at the other occupants of the dining room: men in business suits with mobile phones next to their cutlery, briefcases on the floor by their chairs, and newspapers unfolded. The atmosphere was as hushed as a gentleman's club in London. She said in a low voice, "Like a library in here."

St. James said, "Bankers. A lot on their minds."

Deborah said, "Stuffy." She offered China an affectionate smile.

China took the juice that St. James poured for her. "My mind won't stop the stream of if-onlys. I didn't want to come to Europe and if only I'd stayed firm . . . If only I'd refused to talk about it again . . . If only I'd had enough work going on to keep me at home . . . He might not have come either. None of this would have happened."

"It doesn't do any good, thinking that," Deborah said. "Things happen because they happen. That's all. Our job isn't to un-happen them"—she smiled at her neologism—"but just to move forward."

China returned her smile. "I think I've heard that before."

"You gave good advice."

"You didn't like it at the time."

"No. I suppose it seemed . . . well, heartless, really. Which is how things always seem when you want your friends to join you in a long-term wallow."

China wrinkled her nose. "Don't be so rough on yourself."

"You do the same, then."

"Okay. A deal."

The two women gazed fondly at each other. St. James looked from one to the other and recognised that a feminine communication was going on, one that he couldn't comprehend. It concluded with Deborah saying to China River, "I've missed you," and China returning with a soft laugh, a cock of her head, and a "Boy, that'll teach you." At which point, their conversation closed.

The exchange served as a reminder to St. James that Deborah had more of a life than was expressed by the stretch of years he had known her. Coming into his conscious world when she was seven years old, his wife had always seemed a permanent part of the map of his particular universe. While the fact that she had a universe of her own did not come as a shock to him, he found it disconcerting to be forced to accept that she'd had a wealth of experiences in which he was not a participant. That he *could* have been a participant was a thought for another morning when far less was at stake.

He said, "Have you spoken to the advocate yet?"

China shook her head. "He's not in. He would've stayed at the station as long as they were questioning him, though. Since he didn't call me . . ." She fingered a piece of toast from the rack as if she meant to eat it, but she pushed it away instead. "I figured it went on into the night. That's how it was when they talked to me."

"I'll begin there, then," St. James told her. "And you two . . . I think you need to pay a call on Stephen Abbott. He spoke to you the other day, my love," to Deborah, "so I expect he'll be willing to speak to you again."

He led the two women outside and round to the car park. There they spread out a map of the island on the Escort's bonnet and traced a route to *Le Grand Havre,* a wide gouge into the north coast of the island comprising three bays and a harbour, above which a network of footpaths gave access to military towers and disused forts. Acting as navigator, China would guide Deborah to that location, where Anaïs Abbott had a house in *La Garenne.* In the meantime, St. James would pay a call at the police station and glean from DCI Le Gallez whatever information he could regarding Cherokee's arrest.

He watched his wife and her friend drive off, their route established. They dipped down Hospital Lane and followed the road in the direction of the harbour. He could see the curve of Deborah's cheek as the car made its turn towards St. Julian's Avenue. She was smiling at something her friend had just said.

He stood for a moment and thought about the myriad ways he might caution his wife had she been willing and able to hear him. It's not what I *think,* he would have told her in explanation. It's everything that I do not yet know.

Le Gallez, he hoped, would fill in the gaps in his knowledge. St. James sought him out.

The DCI had just arrived at the police station. He still had on his overcoat when he came to fetch St. James. He shed this on a chair in the incident room and directed St. James to a china board, at the top of which a uniformed constable was attaching a line of colour photographs.

"Check them," Le Gallez said with a nod. He looked quite pleased with himself.

The pictures, St. James saw, featured a medium-size brown bottle, the sort that often contained prescription cough syrup. It lay cradled in what looked like dead grass and weeds, with a burrow rising on either side of it. One of the pictures showed its size in comparison with a plastic ruler. Others showed its location with respect to the nearest live flora, to the apparent field in which it lay, to the hedgerow shielding the field from the road, and to wood-shrouded road itself which St. James recognised since he'd walked it himself.

"The lane that leads to the bay," he said.

"That's the spot, all right," Le Gallez acknowledged.

"What is it, then?"

"The bottle?" The DCI went to a desk and picked up a piece of paper that he read from, saying, "*Eschscholzia californica.*"

"Which is?"

"Oil of poppy."

"You've got your opiate, then."

Le Gallez grinned. "That we do."

"And *californica* means . . ."

"Just what you'd expect. His prints are on the bottle. Big as life. Clear and lovely. A sight for work-sore eyes, let me tell you."

"Damn," St. James murmured, more to himself than to the DCI.

"We've got our man." Le Gallez sounded completely confident of his facts, every bit as if he hadn't been equally confident that they'd got their woman twenty-four hours earlier.

"How've you got it sorted, then?"

Le Gallez used a pencil to gesture to the pictures as he spoke. "How'd it get there, you mean? I figure it like this: He wouldn't have put the opiate in the Thermos the night before or even earlier that morning. Always the chance that Brouard might rinse it out before he used it for his tea. So he followed him down to the bay. He put the oil in the Thermos while Brouard was swimming."

"Taking the risk of being seen?"

"What sort of risk was it? It's not even dawn, so he doesn't expect anyone to be out and about. In case anyone is, he's wearing his sister's cloak. For his part, Brouard's swimming out in the bay and he's not paying attention to the beach. No big deal for River to wait till he's swimming. Then he slips down to the Thermos—he was following Brouard, so he would've seen where he left it—and he pours the oil inside. Then he slips away wherever: into the trees, behind a rock, near the snack hut. He waits for Brouard to come out of the water and drink the tea like he does every morning and everyone knows it. Ginkgo and green tea. Puts hair on the chest and more important puts fire in the bollocks, which is what Brouard wants in order to keep the girlfriend happy. River waits for the opiate to do the trick. When it does, he's on him."

"And if it hadn't done the trick on the beach?"

"No matter to him, was it?" Le Gallez shrugged eloquently. "It was still before dawn, and the opiate would take effect somewhere on Brouard's route home. He'd be able to get to him no matter where it happened. When it happened on the beach, he shoved the stone down his throat and that was it. He reckoned the cause of death would be labeled as choking on a foreign object, and indeed it was. He got rid of the poppy-oil bottle by tossing it into the bushes as he trotted home. Didn't realise that toxicology tests would be run on the body no matter what the cause of death looked like."

There was sense to this. Killers invariably made some sort of miscalculation somewhere along the line, which was largely how killers got themselves caught. With Cherokee River's fingerprints on the bottle that had contained the opiate, it made sense that Le Gallez would turn his sights on him. But all the other details in the case remained to be explained. St. James chose one of them.

"How do you account for the ring? Are his prints on it as well?"

Le Gallez shook his head. "Couldn't get a decent print from it. A partial of a partial, but that was it."

"Then?"

"He would've taken it with him. He may even have intended to shove it down Brouard's throat instead of the stone. The stone muddied the waters for us for a bit, and that would've been nice, to his way of thinking. How blatant would he want it to be that his sister was the killer after all? He wouldn't've wanted to hand it to us. He would've wanted us to work a little to reach the conclusion."

St. James considered all this. It was reasonable enough—despite his wife's loyalties to the River siblings—but there was something else that Le Gallez wasn't talking about in his haste to close the case without pinning the crime on a fellow islander. He said, "You do see, I expect, that what applies to Cherokee River applies to others as well. And there are others who at least have motives for wanting Brouard dead." He didn't wait for Le Gallez to argue, hastening on to say, "Henry Moullin has a fairy wheel hanging among his keys and a dream to be a glass artist—at Brouard's urging—that apparently came to nothing. Bertrand Debiere's apparently in debt because he assumed he'd get the commission for Brouard's museum. And as to the museum itself—"

Le Gallez cut in with a flick of his hand. "Moullin and Brouard were fast friends. Had been for years. Worked together to change the old Thibeault Manor to *Le Reposoir.* No doubt Henry gave him the stone at one time or another as a token of friendship. Way of saying, 'You're one of us now, my man.' As for Debiere, I can't see Nobby killing the very man whose mind he hoped to change, can you?"

"Nobby?"

"Bertrand." Le Gallez had the grace to look embarrassed. "Nickname. We were at school together."

Which likely made Debiere even less a potential candidate for murderer in the eye of the DCI than

he would have been merely as a Guernseyman. St.
James sought a way to prise open the inspector's
mind, if only a crack. "But why? What motive could
Cherokee River have? What motive could his sister
have had when *she* was your principal suspect?"

"Brouard's trip to California. Those months ago.
River laid his plan then."

"Why?"

Le Gallez lost patience. "Look, man, I don't
know," he said hotly. "I don't *need* to know. I just
need to find Brouard's killer and I've done it. Right,
I fingered the sister first, but I fingered her on the
evidence he planted. Just like I'm fingering him on
the evidence now."

"Yet someone else could have planted all of it."

"Who? Why?" Le Gallez hopped off his desk and
advanced on St. James rather more aggressively than
the moment warranted, and St. James knew he was
inches away from being tossed unceremoniously
from the station.

He said quietly, "There's money missing from
Brouard's account, Inspector. A great deal of money.
Did you know that?"

Le Gallez's expression altered. St. James seized the
advantage.

"Ruth Brouard told me about it. It was evidently
paid out over time."

Le Gallez considered this. He said with less conviction than before, "River could have—"

St. James interrupted. "If you want to think
River was involved in that—in a blackmail scheme
of some sort, let's say—why would he kill the goose

when the golden eggs are still coming? But *if* that's the case, if River was indeed blackmailing Brouard, why would Brouard accept him—of all people—as a courier selected by his lawyer in America? He would have *had* to be told the name by Kiefer prior to River's coming, else how would he have known who to fetch from the airport? When he was told and if the name was River, he would have put a stop to that at once."

"He didn't know in time," Le Gallez countered, but he was beginning to sound far less sure of himself.

St. James pressed forward. "Inspector, Ruth Brouard didn't know her brother was running through his fortune. My guess is that no one else knew, either. At least not at first. So doesn't it make sense that someone may have killed him to stop him from depleting his funds? If it doesn't suggest that, doesn't it suggest he was involved in something illegal? And doesn't *that* suggest a motive for murder far more ironclad than anything either of the Rivers have?"

Le Gallez was silent. St. James could see by his expression that the DCI was abashed by being presented with a piece of information about his murder victim that he himself should have had. He looked to the china board where the pictures of the bottle that had contained the opiate declared that his killer had been found. He looked back to St. James and seemed to ponder the challenge with which the other man had presented him. He finally said,

"Right. Come with me, then. We've got phone calls to make."

"To?" St. James asked.

"The only people who can make a banker talk."

China was an excellent navigator. Where there were signs, she called out the names of the streets they were passing as they rolled north along the esplanade, and she got them without a wrong turn to Vale Road at the northern end of *Belle Greve* Bay.

They passed through a little neighbourhood with its grocer, hairdresser, and car repair shop, and at a traffic light—one of the few on the island—they coursed to the northwest. In the way Guernsey had of continually changing its landscape, they found themselves in an agricultural area less than a half mile along the road. This was defined by a few acres of greenhouses that winked in the morning sunlight and, beyond them, a stretch of fields. Perhaps a quarter of a mile into this area, Deborah recognised it and wondered that she hadn't done so before. She glanced warily at her friend in the passenger seat, and she saw from China's expression that she, too, realised where they were.

China said abruptly, "Pull in here, okay?" when they came to the turn for the States Prison. When Deborah braked in a lay-by some twenty yards along the lane, China climbed out of the car and walked over to a tangle of hawthorn and blackthorn that served as a hedge. Above this and in the distance rose two of the buildings that comprised the prison. With its pale yellow exterior and red-tiled roof, it might have been a school or a hospital. Only its windows—iron-barred—declared it for what it was.

Deborah joined her friend. China looked closed off, and Deborah was hesitant to break into her thoughts. So she stood next to her in silence and felt the frustration of her own inadequacy, especially when she compared it to the tender kinship she'd received from this woman when she herself had been in need.

China was the one to speak. "He couldn't handle it. No way in hell."

"I don't see how anyone could." Deborah thought of prison doors closing and keys being turned and the stretch of time: days which melted into weeks and months until years had passed.

"It'd be worse for Cherokee," China said. "It's always worse for men."

Deborah glanced at her. She recalled China's description—years ago—of the single time she'd visited her father in prison. "His eyes," she'd said. "He couldn't keep them still. We were sitting at this table, and when someone passed too close behind him, he flew around like he expected to be knifed. Or worse."

He'd been in for five years that particular time. The California prison system, China told her, kept its arms permanently open for her father.

Now China said, "He doesn't know what to expect inside."

"It's not going to come to that," Deborah told her. "We'll sort this out soon enough and you can both go home."

"You know, I used to gripe about being so poor. Rubbing two pennies together in the hope they would make a quarter someday. I hated that. Working in high school just to buy a pair of shoes at a place like Kmart. Waiting on tables for years to get enough money to go to Brooks. And then that apartment in Santa Barbara. That dump we had, Debs. God, I hated all of it. But I'd take it all back this second just to be out of here. He drives me crazy most of the time. I used to dread picking up the telephone when it rang because I was always afraid it'd be Cherokee and he'd be saying, 'Chine! Wait'll you hear the plan,' and I'd know it was going to mean something shady or something he wanted me to help finance. But right now . . . at this very instant . . . I'd give just about anything to have my brother standing next to me and to have both of us standing on the pier in Santa Barbara with him telling me about his latest scam."

Impulsively Deborah put her arms round her friend. China's body was unyielding at first, but Deborah held on till she felt her soften. She said, "We'll get him out of this. We'll get you both out of it. You *will* go home."

They returned to the car. As Deborah reversed it out of the lay-by and made the turn back onto the

main road, China said, "If I'd known they were going to come for him next . . . This sounds like a martyr thing. I don't mean it that way. But I think I'd
rather do the time myself."

"No one's going to prison," Deborah said. "Simon is going to see to that."

China held the map open on her lap and looked
at it as if checking their route. But she said tentatively, "He's nothing like . . . He's very different . . .
I wouldn't ever have thought . . ." She stopped altogether. Then, "He seems very nice, Deborah."

Deborah glanced at her and completed her
thought. "But he's nothing like Tommy, is he?"

"Not in any way. You seem . . . I don't know . . .
less free with him? Less free, anyway, than you were
with Tommy. I remember how you laughed with
Tommy. And had adventures together. And acted
wild. Somehow I don't see you doing that with
Simon."

"No?" Deborah smiled, but it was forced. There
was plain truth in what her friend was saying—her
relationship with Simon couldn't have been more
different to her time with Tommy—but somehow
China's observation felt like a criticism of her husband, and that criticism put her in the position of
wanting to defend him, a sensation she didn't like.
"Perhaps that's because you're seeing us in the midst
of something serious just now."

"I don't think that's it," China said. "Like you
said, he's different from Tommy. Maybe it's because
he's . . . you know. His leg? He's more serious about
life because of that?"

"Perhaps it's just that he has more to be serious about." Deborah knew this wasn't necessarily true: As a homicide detective, Tommy had professional concerns that far outweighed Simon's. But she sought a way to explain her husband to her friend, a way to allow her to see that loving a man who dwelt almost entirely within his own head wasn't that terribly different to loving a man who was outspoken, passionate, and thoroughly involved in life. It's because Tommy can afford to be those things, Deborah wanted to tell her in defence of her husband. Not because he's wealthy but because he's simply who he is. And who he is is sure, in ways that other men aren't.

"His handicap, you mean?" China said after a moment.

"What?"

"What Simon has to be more serious about."

"I never actually think about his handicap," Deborah told her. She kept her gaze on the road so her friend couldn't read her face for the message that said this was a lie.

"Ah. Well. Are you happy with him?"

"Very."

"Well then, lucky you." China gave her attention back to the map. "Straight across at the intersection," she said abruptly. "Then right at the one after that."

She guided them to the north end of the island, an area completely unlike the parishes that held *Le Reposoir* and St. Peter Port. The granite cliffs of the south end of Guernsey gave way on the north to dunes. A sandy coast replaced the steep and wooded descent to bays, and where vegetation protected the land from the wind, it was marram grass and bindweed that grew on the mobile dunes, red fescue and sea spurge where the dunes were fixed.

Their route took them along the south end of *Le Grand Havre*, a vast open bay where small boats lay protected on the shore for the winter. On one side of this section of the water, the humble white cottages of *Le Picquerel* lined a road that veered west to the collection of bays that defined the low-lying part of Guernsey. On the other side, *La Garenne* forked to the left, a route named for the rabbit warrens that had at one time housed the island's chief delicacy. It was a thin strip of pavement that followed the eastern swoop of *Le Grand Havre*.

Where *La Garenne* curved with the coastline, they found Anaïs Abbott's house. It stood on a large piece of land walled off from the road by the same grey granodiorite blocks that had been used in the construction of the building itself. An expansive garden had been planted in front and a path wound through it to the house's front door. Anaïs Abbott was standing there, arms crossed beneath her breasts. She was in conversation with a briefcase-carrying balding man who appeared to be having difficulty keeping his eyes focused above the level of her neck.

As Deborah parked on the verge across the lane from the house, the man extended his hand to Anaïs. They shook in conclusion of some sort of deal, and he came down the stone path between the hebe and the lavender. Anaïs watched him from the step and, as his car was parked just in front of Deborah's, she saw her next two visitors as they alighted from the Escort. Her body stiffened visibly and her expression—which had been soft and earnest in the presence of the man—altered, her eyes narrowing with swift calculation as Deborah and China came up the path towards her.

Her hand went to her throat in a protective gesture. She said, "Who are you?" to Deborah and "Why are you out of gaol? What does this mean?" to China. And "What are you doing here?" to them both.

"China's been released," Deborah said, and introduced herself, explaining her presence in vague terms of "trying to sort matters out."

Anaïs said, "Released? What does that mean?"

"It means that China's innocent, Mrs. Abbott," Deborah said. "She didn't harm Mr. Brouard."

At the mention of his name, Anaïs's lower lids reddened. She said, "I can't *talk* to you. I don't know what you want. Leave me alone." She made a move for the door.

China said, "Anaïs, wait. We need to talk—"

She swung round. "I *won't* talk to you. I don't want to see you. Haven't you done enough? Aren't you satisfied yet?"

"We—"

"No! I saw how you were with him. You thought I didn't? Well, I did. I *did*. I *know* what you wanted."

"Anaïs, he just showed me his house. He showed me the estate. He wanted me to see—"

"He wanted, he wanted," Anaïs scoffed, but her voice quavered, and the tears that filled her eyes spilled over. "You knew he was mine. You knew it, you saw it, you were *told* it by everyone, and you went ahead anyway. You decided to seduce him and you spent every minute—"

"I was just taking pictures," China said. "I saw the chance to take pictures for a magazine at home. I told him about that and he liked the idea. We didn't—"

"Don't you dare deny it!" Her voice rose to a cry. "He turned away from me. He said he couldn't but I know he didn't want . . . I've lost everything now. *Everything.*"

Her reaction was suddenly so extreme that Deborah began to wonder if they had stepped out of the Escort into another dimension and she sought to intervene. "We need to talk to Stephen, Mrs. Abbott. Is he here?"

Anaïs backed into the door. "What do you want with my son?"

"He went to see Frank Ouseley's Occupation collection with Mr. Brouard. We want to ask him about that."

"Why?"

Deborah wasn't about to tell her anything more, and certainly not anything that might make her think her son could bear some responsibility for Guy Brouard's murder. That would likely push her over the edge on which she was obviously teetering. She said, walking a thin line between truth, manipulation, and prevarication, "We need to know what he recalls seeing."

"Why?"

"Is he at home, Mrs. Abbott?"

"Stephen didn't harm anyone. How dare you even suggest . . ." Anaïs opened the door. "Get off my property. If you want to talk to anyone, you can talk to my advocate. Stephen isn't here. He isn't going to talk to you now or ever."

She went inside and slammed the door, but before she did so, her glance betrayed her. She looked back in the direction they had come, where a church steeple rose on a slope of land not a half mile away.

That was the direction they took. They retraced their route up *La Garenne* and used the steeple as their guide. They found themselves in short order at a walled graveyard that rose along a little hillside on the top of which was the church of *St. Michel de Vale,* whose pointed steeple bore a blue-faced clock with no minute hand and an hour hand pointing—permanently, it seemed—to the number six. Thinking that Stephen Abbott might be inside, they tried the church door.

Inside, however, all was silence. Bell ropes hung motionless near a marble baptismal font, and a stained glass window of Christ crucified gazed down on an altar with its decorative spray of holly and berries. There was no one in the nave and no one in the Chapel of Archangels to one side of the main altar, where a flickering candle indicated the presence of the Sacrament.

They returned to the graveyard. China was saying, "She was probably trying to fake us out. I bet he's at the house," when Deborah caught sight of a pond across the street. It had been hidden from the road by reeds, but from the vantage point of the little hilltop, they could see it spread out not far from a red-roofed house. A figure was throwing sticks into the water, an indifferent dog at his side. As they watched, the boy gave the dog a shove towards the pond.

"Stephen Abbott," Deborah said grimly. "No doubt entertaining himself."

"Nice guy" was China's reply as they followed the path back to the car and crossed the road.

He was throwing yet another stick into the water when they emerged from the heavy growth round the pond. He was saying, "Come *on*," to the dog, who hunkered not far away, staring dismally at the water with the forbearance of an early Christian martyr. "Come on!" Stephen Abbott cried. "Can't you do *anything?*" He threw another stick and then another, as if determined to prove himself the master of a creature who no longer cared about submission or the rewards therein.

"I expect he doesn't want to get wet," Deborah said. Then, "Hullo, Stephen. D'you remember me?"

Stephen glanced over his shoulder at her. Then his gaze slid to China. It widened but only momentarily before his face became closed and his eyes hard. "Stupid dog," he said. "Just like this stupid island. Just like everything. Bloody stupid."

"He looks cold," China said. "He's shivering."

"He thinks I'm going to wallop him. Which I am if he doesn't get his arse in the water. Biscuit!" he shouted. "Come on. Get out there and get that fucking stick."

The dog turned his back.

"Pile of shit's deaf anyway," Stephen said. "But he knows what I mean. He knows what I want him to do. And *if* he knows what's good for him, he's going to do it." He looked round and found a stone, which he weighed in his hand to see its potential for harm.

"Hey!" China said. "Leave him alone."

Stephen looked at her, lip curled. Then he flung the stone, shouting, "Biscuit! You useless piece of crap! Get out of here!"

The rock hit the dog squarely on the side of the head. He yelped, leaped to his feet, and bounded into the reeds, where they could hear him thrashing round and whimpering.

"My sister's dog anyway," Stephen said dismissively. He turned away to throw stones in the water, but not before Deborah saw that his eyes were filling.

China took a step towards him, her expression furious, saying, "Look, you little creep," but Deborah put out a hand to stop her. She said, "Stephen—" gently, but he interrupted her before she could go on.

" 'Take the dog out of here,' she tells me," he said bitterly. " 'Just take him for a walk, darling.' *I* say tell Jemima to take him. Her stupid dog anyway. But no. She can't do that. Duck's too busy bawling in her room 'cause she doesn't want to leave this shit hole, if you can believe it."

"Leave?" Deborah said.

"We're out of here. The estate agent's sitting in the living room just trying to keep his greasy hands off Mum's milkers. He's talking about coming to 'some sort of mutually beneficial arrangement' like he doesn't really mean he wants to stuff her ASAP. The dog's barking at him and Duck's in hysterics 'cause just about the last place she wants to live is with Gran in Liverpool, but I don't care, do I? Anything, let me tell you, to get out of this slag heap. So I bring that stupid dog out here but I'm not Duck, am I, and she's the only person he ever wants."

"Why're you moving?" Deborah could hear in China's voice the leaps her friend was making. She was making a few of them herself, not the least of which grew from the sequence of events that had brought the Abbott family to this moment.

"That's pretty obvious," Stephen replied. Then before they could delve further into this subject, he said, "What d'you want, anyway?" and he glanced towards the rushes and reeds where Biscuit had gone quiet, as if he'd found shelter.

Deborah asked him about *Moulin des Niaux*. Had he ever been there with Mr. Brouard?

He'd gone once. "Mum made a big deal of it, but the only reason he asked me to go was that *she* insisted." He sputtered a laugh. "We were supposed to *bond*. Stupid cow. Like he ever meant . . . It was completely stupid. Me, Guy, Frank, Frank's dad, who's about two million years old, and all this junk. Piles and piles of it. Boxes. Bags. Cabinets. Buckets of it. Everywhere. Bloody waste of time."

"What did you do there?"

"Do? They were going through hats. Hats, caps, helmets, whatever. Who wore what when, why, and how. It was so stupid—such a stupid waste of time. I went for a walk along the valley instead."

"So you didn't go through the war stuff yourself?" China asked.

Stephen seemed to hear something in her voice, because he said, "Why d'you want to know? What're you doing here anyway? Aren't you supposed to be locked up?"

Deborah once again intervened. "Was anyone else there with you? The day that you went to see the war collection?"

He said, "No. Just Guy and me." He gave his attention back to Deborah and to the topic—it seemed—that dominated his thoughts. "Like I said, it was supposed to be our big bonding experience. I was supposed to fall all over myself with joy because he wanted to act like a dad for fifteen minutes. He was supposed to decide I'd do much better as a son than Adrian since *he's* such a pathetic twit and in comparison at least I have a chance of going to university without falling apart because my mummy's not there to hold my hand. It was all so stupid, stupid, *bloody* stupid. As if he was ever going to marry her."

"Well, it's over now," Deborah told him. "You're going back to England."

"Only," he said, "because she didn't get what she wanted from Brouard." He cast a scornful look in the direction of *La Garenne*. "As if she ever would have. To think she was ever going to get *anything* off him. I tried to tell her, but she never listens. Anyone with brains could see what he intended."

"What?" China and Deborah spoke simultaneously.

Stephen looked at them with the same degree of scorn he'd directed at his home and his mother within it. "He was having it elsewhere," he said succinctly. "I kept trying to tell her that, but she wouldn't listen. She just couldn't think that she'd gone to such trouble to snare him—under the knife and everything, even if he was the one to pay for it—while all the time he was shagging someone else. 'It's your imagination,' she told me. 'Darling, you aren't making this up because you've been a little unsuccessful, are you? You'll have your own girlfriend someday. Just see if you won't. Big, handsome, *strapping* lad like you.' God. *God*. What a stupid cow."

Deborah sifted through all this for a clear understanding: the man, the woman, the boy, the mother, and all the reasons for an accusation. She said, "D'you know the other woman, Stephen?" as China took another anxious step towards him. They were getting somewhere at last, and Deborah gestured to her to keep her from frightening the boy into silence through her desire to get to the bottom of the matter quickly.

" 'Course I know her. Cynthia Moullin."

Deborah glanced at China, who shook her head. Deborah said to Stephen, "Cynthia Moullin? Who is she?"

A schoolmate, it turned out. A teenage girl from the College of Further Education.

"But how do you know this?" Deborah asked, and when he rolled his eyes expressively, she saw the truth. "You lost her to Mr. Brouard? Is that it?"

He said, "Where's that stupid dog?" in answer.

When her brother didn't pick up the phone on this third successive morning that she'd rung him, Valerie Duffy couldn't take it any longer. She got in her car and drove to *La Corbière* once Kevin had set about his work on the estate, once Ruth had finished her breakfast, and once she herself had an hour to spare from her duties in the house. She knew she would not be missed.

The first thing Valerie noticed at the Shell House was the ruin of the front garden, and this frightened her instantly, speaking eloquently as it did of her brother's temper. Henry was a good man—a supportive brother, a loyal friend, and a loving father to his girls—but he had a fuse that, when lit, burned to the explosive in a matter of seconds. As an adult, she'd never seen his temper in action, but she'd seen the devastation of its display. He'd yet to direct it at a human being, though, and that was what she'd been counting on on the day she'd dropped in, when she'd found him in the house baking the scones his youngest girl loved and told him that her employer and his dear friend Guy Brouard was having regular intercourse with Henry's oldest daughter.

It had been the only way she knew to put a stop

to the affair. Talking to Cynthia hadn't put even a dent in the machine of their mating. "We're in love, Aunt Val," the girl had told her with all the wide-eyed innocence of a virgin recently and pleasurably deflowered. "Haven't you ever been in love?"

Nothing could convince the girl that men like Guy Brouard didn't fall in love. Even the knowledge that he was having it off with Anaïs Abbott at the same time as he was enjoying Cynthia made not the slightest difference to the girl. "Oh, we talked about that. He's got to do it," Cynthia said. "Else people might think he was having me."

"But he *is* having you! He's sixty-eight years old! My God, he could be arrested for this."

"Oh no, Auntie Val. We waited till I was of age."

"Waited . . . ?" Valerie had seen in an instant the years that her brother had worked for Guy Brouard at *Le Reposoir,* bringing along one of his girls occasionally because it was important to Henry that he spend time with each of them individually, to make up for the fact that their mother had deserted them for life with a rock star whose celestial glow had long since been extinguished.

Cynthia had been the most frequent of her father's companions. Valerie had thought nothing of this till she'd first seen the looks pass between the girl and Guy Brouard, till she'd noted the casual contact between them—just a hand brushing against an arm—till she'd followed them once and watched and waited and then confronted the girl to learn the worst.

She'd had to tell Henry. There was no other choice when Cynthia couldn't be talked out of the road she was traveling. And now there were the consequences of telling him, hanging over her like the blade of a guillotine that waits for the signal to be released.

She picked her way through the sad debris of the fanciful front garden. Henry's car was parked to one side of the house, not far from the barn where he made his glass, but the barn itself was shut and locked, so she went to the front door. There she steadied herself for a moment before she knocked.

This was her brother, she told herself. She had nothing to worry about and even less to fear from him. They'd weathered a difficult childhood together in the home of a bitter mother who—like Henry himself in a repetition of history—had been deserted by a faithless spouse. They shared more than blood because of this. They shared memories so powerful that nothing could ever be more important than the way they'd learned to lean upon each other, to parent each other in the physical absence of one genitor and the emotional disappearance of the other. They had made it not matter. They had sworn it would not colour their lives. That they had failed at this was nobody's fault, and it certainly wasn't for want of determination and effort.

The front door swung open before she could knock, and her brother stood before her with a basket of laundry balanced on his hip. His expression was as black as she'd ever seen it. He said, "Val. What the hell do you want?" after which he stalked to the kitchen, where he'd built a lean-to that served as a laundry room.

She couldn't help noticing when she followed him that Henry was doing the washing as she herself had taught him. Whites, darks, and bright colours all carefully separated, towels comprising an individual load.

He saw her observing him and a look of self-loathing flitted across his face. "Some lessons die hard," he told her.

She said, "I've been phoning. Why haven't you answered? You've been home, haven't you?"

"Didn't want to." He opened the washing machine, where a load was done, and he began shoving this into the dryer. Nearby in a sink, water dripped rhythmically into something that was soaking. Henry inspected this, dumped a splash of bleach in it, and stirred it vigorously with a long wooden spoon.

"Not good for business, that," Valerie said. "People might be wanting you for work."

"Answered the mobile," he told her. "Business calls come there."

Valerie swore silently at this piece of news. She hadn't thought of his mobile. Why? Because she'd been too frightened and worried and guilt-ridden to think about anything but calming her own ragged nerves. She said, "Oh. The mobile. I hadn't thought of the mobile."

He said, "Right," and began tossing his next load of laundry into the washer. These were the girls' clothes: jeans, jumpers, and socks. "You hadn't thought, Val."

The contempt in his voice stung, but she refused to let him intimidate her into leaving the house. She said, "Where're the girls, Harry?"

He glanced at her when she used the nickname. For an instant she could see past the loathing he wore as his mask and he was again the little boy whose hand she'd held when they'd crossed the Esplanade to bathe at the pools below Havelet Bay. You can't hide from me, Harry, she wanted to tell him. But instead she waited for his answer.

"School. Where else would they be?"

"I suppose I meant Cyn," she admitted.

He made no reply.

She said, "Harry, you can't keep her locked—"

He pointed his finger at her and said, "No one's locked anywhere. You hear me? *No* one is locked."

"You've let her out, then. I did see you've taken the grille off the window."

Instead of answering, he reached for the detergent and poured it onto the clothes. He didn't measure it and he looked at her as he poured and poured, as if challenging her to offer advice. But she'd done that once, only once, God forgive her. And she'd come to assure herself that nothing had resulted from her saying, "Henry, you've got to take action."

She said, "Has she gone off somewhere, then?"

"Won't come out of her room."

"You've taken the lock off the door?"

"No need for it now."

"No need?" She felt a shudder run through her.

She clasped her arms round her body although the house was not the least bit cold.

"No need," Henry repeated, and as if he wanted to illustrate a point, he went to the sink where the water was dripping and he used the wooden spoon to fish something out.

It was a pair of woman's knickers that he held up, and he allowed the water to run off them and pool on the floor. Valerie could see the faint stain that was still upon them despite the soaking and despite the bleach. She felt a wave of nausea as she understood exactly why her brother had kept his daughter in her room.

"So she's not," Valerie said.

"One breeze in hell." He jerked his head in the direction of the bedrooms. "So she won't come out. You can talk to her if you have a mind to. But she's got the door locked from the inside now and she's been wailing like a cat when you drown its kittens. Bloody little fool." He slammed down the lid of the washing machine, pushed a few buttons, and set it to its business.

Valerie went to her niece's bedroom door. She tapped on it and said her name, adding, "It's Auntie Val, darling. Will you open the door?" but Cynthia was utterly silent within. At this, Valerie thought about the worst. She cried, "Cynthia? Cynthia! I'd like to speak to you. Open the door please." Again, silence was the only reply. Deathly silence. Inhuman silence. There seemed to Valerie to be only one way that a seventeen-year-old girl went from wailing like a cat to perfect stillness. She hurried back to her brother.

"We need to get into that bedroom," she said. "She may have harmed—"

"Rubbish. She'll come out when she's ready." He barked a bitter laugh. "Maybe she's grown to like it in there."

"Henry, you can't just let her—"

"Don't *tell* me what I can and can't!" he shouted. "Don't you *sodding* ever tell me one bloody thing more. You've told me enough. You've done your part. I'll cope with the rest the way I want to."

This was her biggest fear: her brother's coping. Because what he was coping with was something far larger than a daughter's sexual activity. Had it been some boy from town, from the college, Henry might have warned Cynthia of the dangers, might have seen to it that every precaution was taken to safeguard her from the fallout of sex that was casual but nonetheless highly charged because it was all so new to her. But this had been more than the budding of a daughter's sexual awareness. This had been a seduction and a betrayal so profound that when Valerie had first revealed it to her brother, he had not believed her. He could not *bring* himself to believe her. He'd retreated from the information like an animal stunned by a blow to the head. She'd said, "Listen to me, Henry. It's the truth, and if you don't do something, God only knows what will happen to the girl."

Those were the fateful words: *if you don't do some-*

thing. The affair was now over, and she was desperate to know what that *something* had been.

Henry looked at her long after he had spoken, with *the way I want to* ringing between them like the bells of St. Martin's Church. Valerie raised her hand to her lips and pressed them back against her teeth as if this gesture could stop her from saying what she was thinking, what she most feared.

Henry read her as easily as he'd always done. He gave her a look from head to toe. He said, "Got the guilts, Val? Not to worry, girl."

Her relieved, "Oh Harry, thank God, because I—" was cut short when her brother completed his confession.

"You weren't the only one to tell me about them."

Chapter 22

RUTH ENTERED HER BROTHER'S bedroom for the first time since his death. The moment had come, she decided, to sort through his clothes. Not so much because anything made this an immediate necessity, but because sorting through his clothes afforded her employment, which was what she wanted. She wanted to do something *related* to Guy, something that would put her close enough to feel his comforting presence but at the same time keep her distant enough to prevent her from learning anything more about the many ways in which he'd deceived her.

She went to the wardrobe and removed his favourite tweed jacket from its hanger. Taking a moment to absorb the familiar scent of his shaving lotion, she slid her hand into each pocket in turn, emptying them of a handkerchief, a roll of breath mints, a biro, and a piece of paper torn from a small spiral notebook, its ragged edges still intact. This last was folded into a tiny square, which Ruth unfolded. $C + G = $ ♥ *4ever!* had been written upon it in an unmistakably adolescent hand. Ruth hastily crumpled the paper in her fist and found herself looking left and right as if someone might have been watching her, some avenging angel seeking the sort of proof she herself had just stumbled upon.

Not that she required proof at this point. Not that she had ever required it. One didn't need proof for what one knew was a monstrous fact because one had actually *seen* the truth of it before one's eyes . . .

Ruth experienced the same kind of sickness that had hit her on the day she'd returned unexpectedly early from her Samaritans meeting. She'd not yet had a diagnosis for her pain. Calling it arthritis, she'd been dosing herself with aspirin and hoping for the best. But on this day, the intensity of the aching made her useless for anything other than getting herself home and getting herself supine on her bed. So she'd left the meeting long before its conclusion and she'd driven back to *Le Reposoir.*

Climbing the stairs took an effort: her will against the reality of her weakness. She won that battle and staggered along the corridor to her bedroom, next to Guy's. She had her hand on the doorknob when she heard the laughter. Then a girl's voice cried out, "Guy, don't! That tickles!"

Ruth stood like salt because she knew that voice and *because* she knew it, she didn't move from her door. She couldn't move because she couldn't believe. For that reason, she told herself there was probably a very simple explanation for what her brother was doing in his bedroom with a teenager.

Had she quickly removed herself from the corridor, she might have been able to cling to that belief.

But before she could even think about making herself scarce, her brother's bedroom door opened. Guy came out, shrugging a dressing gown over his naked body as he said into the room, "I'll use one of Ruth's scarves, then. You'll love it."

He turned and saw his sister. To his credit—to his one and only credit—his cheeks went from flushed to waxen in an instant. Ruth took a step towards him, but he grabbed the knob of the door and pulled it shut. Behind it, Cynthia Moullin called out, "What's going on? Guy?" while Guy and his sister faced each other.

Ruth said, "Step away, *frère*," as Guy said hoarsely, "Good God, Ruth. Why are you home?"

She said, "To see, I suppose," and she shouldered past him to reach the door.

He didn't try to stop her, and she wondered at that now. It was almost as if he'd wanted her to see everything: the girl on the bed—slender, beautiful, naked, fresh, and so unused—and the tassel he'd been teasing her with, left on her thigh, where he'd last been applying it.

She'd said, "Get dressed," to Cynthia Moullin.

"I don't think I will" was the girl's reply.

They'd stayed there, the three of them, actors waiting for a cue that did not come: Guy by the door, Ruth near the wardrobe, the girl on the bed. Cynthia looked at Guy and raised an eyebrow, and Ruth had wondered how *any* adolescent caught in this kind of situation could possibly look so sure of what would happen next.

Guy said, "Ruth."

Ruth said, "No." And to the girl, "Get dressed and get out of this house. If your father could see you—"

Which was as far as she got because Guy came to her then and put his arm round her shoulders. He said her name again. Then quietly—and incredibly—into her ear, "We want to be alone right now, Ruthie, if you don't mind. Obviously, we didn't know you'd come home."

It was the absolute rationality of Guy's statement in circumstances where rationality was least expected that propelled Ruth out of the room. She went into the corridor, and Guy murmured, "We'll talk later" as he shut the door. Before it closed completely, Ruth heard him say to the girl, "I suppose we'll do without the scarf for now," and then the old floor creaked under him as he crossed to her and the old bed creaked as he joined her on it.

Afterwards—hours, it seemed, although it was probably twenty-five minutes—water ran for a while and a hair dryer blew. Ruth lay on her bed and listened to the sounds, so domestic and natural that she could almost pretend she'd been mistaken in what she'd seen.

But Guy did not allow that. He came to her once Cynthia had departed. It was dark by then, and Ruth hadn't yet turned on a light. She would have preferred to remain in the darkness indefinitely, but he didn't allow that. He made his way over to her bedside table and switched on the lamp. "I knew you wouldn't be sleeping," he said.

He looked at her long, murmured, *"Ma soeur*

chérie," and sounded so deeply troubled that at first Ruth thought he meant to apologise. She was wrong.

He went to the small overstuffed armchair and sank into it. He looked somehow *transported,* Ruth thought.

"She's the one," he said in a tone that a man might use to identify a sacred relic. "She's come to me at last. Can you credit that, Ruth? After all these years? She's definitely the one." He rose as if the emotion within him couldn't be contained. He began to move about the room. As he spoke, he touched the curtains at the window, the edge of Ruth's earliest needlepoint, the corner of the chest of drawers, the lace that fretted the edge of a mat. "We mean to marry," he said. "I'm not telling you that because you found us . . . like that today. I meant to tell you after her birthday. We both meant to tell you. Together."

Her birthday. Ruth gazed at her brother. She felt caught in a world she didn't recognise, one ruled by the maxim If it feels good, do it; explain yourself later but only if you're caught.

Guy said, "She'll be eighteen in three months. We thought a birthday dinner . . . You, her father, and her sisters. Perhaps Adrian will come over from England as well. We thought I'd put the ring in among her gifts and when she opens it . . ." He grinned. He looked, Ruth had to admit, rather like a boy. "What a surprise it'll be. Can you keep mum till then?"

Ruth said, "This is—" but could go no further with words. She could only imagine and *what* she imagined was too terrible to face, so she turned her head away.

Guy said, "Ruth, you've nothing to fear from this. Your home is with me as it always has been. Cyn knows that and she wants it as well. She loves you like . . ." But he didn't complete the thought.

This allowed her to complete it. "A grandmother," she said. "And what does that make you?"

"Age isn't important in love."

"My God. You're fifty years—"

"I know how much older I am," he snapped. He came back to the bed and stood looking down at her. His face was perplexed. "I thought you'd actually celebrate this. The two of us. Loving each other. Wanting a life together."

"How long?" she asked.

"No one knows how long anyone's going to live."

"I meant how long. Today . . . This couldn't have been . . . She was too familiar."

Guy didn't answer at first and Ruth's palms dampened as she realised exactly what his reluctance implied. She said, "Tell me. If you don't, she will."

He said, "Her sixteenth birthday, Ruth."

It was worse than she'd thought because she knew what it meant: that her brother had taken the girl on the very day it had become completely legal to do so. This would mean he'd had his eye on her for God only knew how long. He'd laid his plans, and he'd carefully orchestrated her seduction. My God, she thought, when Henry found out . . . when he worked it all out as she herself had just done . . .

She said numbly, "But what about Anaïs?"

"What about Anaïs?"

"You said the same about her. Don't you remember? You said, 'She's the one.' And you believed it then. So what makes you think—"

"This is different."

"Guy, it's always different. In your mind, it's different. But that's only because it's new."

"You don't understand. How could you? Our lives have taken such different paths."

"I've seen you walk every step of yours," Ruth said, "and this is—"

"Bigger," he cut in. "Profound. Transforming. If I'm mad enough to walk away from her and from what we have, then I deserve to be alone forever."

"But what about Henry?"

Guy looked away.

Ruth saw, then, that Guy knew very well that in order to get to Cynthia, he'd engaged in a calculated use of his friend Henry Moullin. She saw that Guy's "Let's get Henry to take a look at the problem" about this or that round the estate had been his way of gaining access to Henry's daughter. And just as he would doubtless rationalise this machination with regard to Henry if she challenged him about it, so would he continue to rationalise what she knew was in effect yet another delusion about a woman who'd ostensibly won his heart. Oh, he *believed* that Cynthia Moullin was the one. But so had he believed about Margaret and then JoAnna and all the Margarets and JoAnnas since them, up to and including Anaïs Abbott. He was talking about marrying this latest Margaret-and-JoAnna only because she was eighteen years old and she wanted him and he liked what this did for his old man's ego. In time, though, his eye would stray. Or hers would. But in either case, people were going to be hurt. They were going to be devastated. Ruth had to do something to prevent all that.

So she'd spoken to Henry. Ruth told herself this action was to save Cynthia from getting her heart broken, and she needed to believe that even now. A thousand different things had made the affair between her brother and the teenager more than just morally and ethically wrong. If Guy lacked the wisdom and the courage to end it gently and to set the girl free to have a full and real life—a life with a future—then she must take steps to make it impossible for him to do anything else.

Her decision had been to tell Henry Moullin only a partial truth: that Cynthia was, perhaps, getting too fond of Guy. Hanging about *Le Reposoir* a bit too much instead of spending time with her friends or upon her studies, making excuses to drop in at the estate and visit her aunt, using far too many of her free hours following Guy about. Ruth called it calf love and said that Henry might want to speak to the girl . . .

He'd done so. Cynthia responded with a frankness Ruth had not expected. It wasn't a school-girl crush and it wasn't calf love, she told her father placidly. There was really nothing to worry about, Daddy. They meant to marry, for she and her father's friend were lovers and had been for nearly two years.

So Henry stormed to *Le Reposoir* and found Guy feeding the ducks at the edge of the tropical garden. Stephen Abbott had been with him, but that hadn't mattered a whit to Henry. He shouted, "You filthy piece of rot!" and advanced upon Guy. "I'm going to kill you, you bastard. I'll cut off your prick and shove it down your throat. God damn you to hell. You *touched* my daughter!"

Stephen had come on the run to fetch Ruth, babbling. She caught the name Henry Moullin and the words "yelling about Cyn" and she dropped what she was doing and followed the boy outside. Hurrying across the croquet lawn, she could hear the raging for herself. She looked round frantically for someone who could intervene, but Kevin and Valerie's car was gone and only she and Stephen were there to stop the violence.

For it would be violence, Ruth had realised. How stupid she'd been to think a father would face the man who'd seduced his daughter and not want to throttle him, not want to kill him.

Even as she approached the tropical garden, she could hear the blows. Henry was grunting and raging, the ducks were squawking, but Guy was utterly silent. As the grave. She gave a cry and rushed through the shrubbery.

The bodies were everywhere. Blood, feathers, and death. Henry stood amid the ducks he'd beaten with the board he still carried. His chest heaved, and his face was twisted with his tears.

He'd lifted a shaking arm and pointed to Guy, who stood transfixed near a palm, a bag of feed spilling out at his feet. "You stay *away*," Henry hissed at him. "I'll kill you next if you touch her again."

Now in Guy's bedroom, Ruth relived it all. She felt the tremendous weight of her own responsibility for what had happened. Meaning well had not been enough. It had not spared Cynthia. It had not saved Guy.

She folded her brother's coat slowly. She turned as slowly and went back to the wardrobe to pull out the next garment.

As she was removing trousers from a hanger, the bedroom door swung open and Margaret Chamberlain said, "I want to talk to you, Ruth. You managed to avoid me at dinner last night—the long day, the arthritis, the necessary rest . . . how convenient for you. But you aren't going to avoid me now."

Ruth stopped what she was doing. "I haven't been avoiding you."

Margaret sputtered derisively and came into the room. She looked, Ruth saw, much the worse for wear. Her French twist was askew, with locks of hair slipping from its generally careful roll. Her jewellery didn't complement her day's clothing as it always did, and she'd forgotten the sunglasses that, rain or shine, habitually perched on the top of her head.

"We've been to see a solicitor," she announced. "Adrian and I. You knew we would, of course."

Ruth laid the trousers gently on Guy's bed. "Yes," she said.

"So did he, obviously. Which was why he made sure we'd be cut off at the pass before we got to it."

Ruth said nothing.

Margaret's lips became thin. She said, "Isn't that the case, Ruth?" with a malignant smile. "Didn't Guy know exactly how I'd react when he disinherited his only son?"

"Margaret, he didn't disinherit—"

"Don't let's pretend otherwise. He investigated the laws on this contemptible little pimple of an island and he discovered what would happen to his property if he didn't hand every bit of it over to you upon purchase. He couldn't even *sell* it without telling Adrian first, so he made sure he never owned it in the first place. What a plan it was, Ruthie. I hope you enjoyed destroying the dreams of your only nephew. Because that's what's happened as a result of this."

"It had nothing to do with destroying anyone," Ruth told her quietly. "Guy didn't arrange things this way because he didn't love his children, and he didn't do it because he wanted to hurt them."

"Well, that's not how things turned out, is it?"

"Please listen, Margaret. Guy didn't . . ." Ruth hesitated, trying to decide how to explain her brother to his former wife, how to tell her that nothing was ever as simple as it looked, how to make her understand that part of who Guy was was who Guy wanted his children to be. "He didn't believe in entitlement. That's all it was. He created himself from nothing, and he wanted his children to have that same experience. The richness of it. The sort of confidence that only—"

"What utter nonsense," Margaret scoffed. "That absolutely *flies* in the face of everything that . . . You know it does, Ruth. You damn well *know* it." She stopped as if to steady herself and to marshal her thoughts, as if she believed there was something she could actually base a case upon, one that would force change upon a circumstance that was fixed in concrete. "Ruth," she said with an obvious effort at calm, "the whole *point* of building a life is to give your children more than you yourself had. It's not to place them in the same position you had to struggle up from. Why would anyone try to have a future better than his present if he knew it was all to be for nothing?"

"It's not for nothing. It's learning. It's growing. It's facing challenges and getting through them. Guy believed it builds character to build your own life. He did that and was the better man for it. And that's what he wanted for his children. He didn't want them to be in a position where they would never have to work again. He didn't want them to contend with the temptation to do nothing with their lives."

"Ah. But that didn't apply to the other two. It's fine to tempt *them,* because for some reason they aren't supposed to struggle. Is that it?"

"JoAnna's girls are in the same position that Adrian's in."

"I'm not talking about Guy's daughters, and you know it," Margaret said. "I'm talking about the other two. Fielder and Moullin. Considering their circumstances, they're being left a fortune. Each of them. What've you to say about that?"

"They're special cases. They're different. They haven't had the advantages—"

"Oh no. They haven't. But they're snatching at them now, aren't they, Ruthie?" Margaret laughed and walked over to the open wardrobe. She fingered a pile of the cashmere sweaters Guy favoured in lieu of shirts and ties.

"They were special to him," Ruth said. "Foster grandchildren, I suppose you could call them. He was something of a mentor to them and they were—"

"Little thieves," Margaret said. "But let's make sure they have their rewards despite their sticky fingers."

Ruth frowned. "Thieves? What're you talking about?"

"This: I caught Guy's protégé—or shall I continue to think of him as his grandchild, Ruth?—stealing from this house. Yesterday morning, this was. In the kitchen."

"Paul was probably hungry. Valerie sometimes feeds him. He'll have taken a biscuit."

"And shoved it into his rucksack? And set his mongrel on me when I tried to see what he'd squirreled away? You go ahead and let him walk off with the silver, Ruth. Or one of Guy's little antiques. Or a piece of jewellery. Or whatever the hell it was that he had. He ran off when he saw us—Adrian and I—and if you don't think he's guilty of something, then you might ask him why he grabbed that rucksack and fought us both when we tried to get it away."

"I don't believe you," Ruth said. "Paul wouldn't take a thing from us."

"Wouldn't he? Then I suggest we ask the police to have a rummage round his rucksack themselves."

Margaret walked to the bedside table and picked up the telephone receiver. She held it provocatively to her sister-in-law. "Shall I ring them or will you do it, Ruth? If that boy's innocent, he's got nothing to fear."

Guy Brouard's bank was in *Le Pollet,* a narrow extension of the High Street that paralleled the lower North Esplanade. A relatively short thoroughfare largely cast in shadow, it was nonetheless faced on either side with buildings that spanned nearly three hundred years. It served as a reminder of the changeable nature of towns everywhere: A former grand townhouse of the eighteenth century—replete with dressed granite and quoined corners—had been refashioned during the twentieth century into a hotel while nearby a pair of nineteenth-century houses of random stone now served as clothing shops. The curved glass windows of Edwardian shop fronts so short a distance from the townhouse spoke of the life of trade that had burgeoned in this area in the days preceding World War I, while behind them loomed a completely modern extension to a London financial institution.

The bank that Le Gallez and St. James were seeking stood at the end of *Le Pollet,* not far from a taxi rank that gave way to the quayside. They walked there in the company of DS Marsh of the Fraud Department, a youngish man with antiquated mutton-chop sideburns, who commented, "Bit of overkill here, wouldn't you say, sir?" to the DCI.

Le Gallez responded acerbically. "Dick, I like to give 'em a reason to cooperate from the start. Saves time that way."

"I'd say a call from the FIS'd do that, sir," Marsh pointed out.

"Hedging my bets is a habit, lad. And I'm not a man to ignore my habits. Financial Intelligence might loosen their tongues, to be sure. But a visit from Fraud . . . ? That'll loosen their bowels."

DS Marsh smiled and rolled his eyes. He said, "You blokes in Homicide don't get enough entertainment."

"We take it where we can find it, Dick." He drew open the heavy glass door of the bank and ushered St. James inside.

The managing director was a man called Robilliard, and as it turned out, Le Gallez was already well known to him. When they walked into his office, the managing director rose from his chair, said, "Louis, how are you?" and extended his hand to the DCI. He went on with "We've missed you at football. How's the ankle?"

"Recovered."

"We'll expect you on the pitch at the weekend, then. From the looks of you, you could use the exercise."

"Croissants in the morning. They're killing me," Le Gallez admitted.

Robilliard laughed. "Only the fat die young."

Le Gallez introduced his companions to the managing director, saying, "We've come for a chat about Guy Brouard."

"Ah."

"He did his banking here, yes?"

"His sister as well. Is there something dodgy about his accounts?"

"It's looking that way, David. Sorry." Le Gallez went on to explain what they knew: the divesting of a significant portfolio of stocks and bonds followed by a series of withdrawals from this bank, made over a relatively short period of time. Ultimately, he concluded, they appeared to have seriously depleted his account. Now the man was dead—as Robilliard probably knew if he'd been conscious in recent weeks—and as his death was a homicide . . . "We've got to take a look at everything," Le Gallez concluded.

Robilliard looked thoughtful. "Of course you do," he said. "But to use anything from the bank as evidence . . . You'll need an order from the Bailiff. I expect you know that."

"That I do," Le Gallez said. "But all we want is information at the moment. Where'd that money go, for instance, and how did it go there?"

Robilliard considered this request. The others waited. Le Gallez had earlier explained to St. James that a phone call from the Financial Intelligence Service would be enough to prise general information from the bank but that he preferred the personal touch. It would not only be more effective, he said, but it would also be more expeditious. Financial institutions were required by law to disclose suspicious transactions to the FIS when the FIS asked them to do so. But they didn't exactly have to jump to do it. There were dozens of ways they could drag their feet. For this reason, he'd requested the attendance of the Fraud Department in the person of DS Marsh. Guy Brouard had been dead for too many days for them to have time to cool their heels while the bank did the two-step round what the law quite plainly required it to do.

Robilliard finally said, "As long as you understand the situation with regard to evidence . . ."

Le Gallez tapped himself on the temple. "Got it up here, David. Give us what you can."

The managing director went to do so personally, leaving them to enjoy the view of the harbour and St. Julian's pier that unfolded from his window. "Decent telescope, you see France from here," Le Gallez commented.

To which Marsh replied, "But who would want to," and both men chuckled like locals whose hospitality towards tourists had long ago worn thin.

When Robilliard returned to them some five minutes later, he carried a computer print-out. He gestured to a small conference table, where they sat. He laid the print-out on the table in front of him.

He said, "Guy Brouard held a large account. Not as large as his sister's, but large. There's been little movement in and out of hers in the last few months, but when you consider who Mr. Brouard was—Chateaux Brouard . . . the extent of that business when he was directing it?—there was no real reason to red-flag movement in or out of his account."

"Message received," Le Gallez said, and to Marsh, "Got it, Dick?"

"We're cooperating so far," Marsh acknowledged.

St. James had to admire the small-town deal-making that was going on among the men. He could only imagine how convoluted the entire procedure could become if parties began demanding legal counsel, orders from the head of the judiciary, or an injunction from the FIS. He waited for further developments among them, and they were immediate.

"He's made a collection of wire transfers to London," Robilliard told them. "They've gone to the same bank, to the same account. They began"—he referred to the print-out—"just over eight months ago. They continued through the spring and the summer in increasing amounts, culminating in a final transfer on the first of October. The initial transfer is five thousand pounds. The final is two hundred and fifty thousand pounds."

"Two hundred and fifty thousand? All this to the same account each time?" Le Gallez said. "Good Christ, David. Who's watching the bloody store round here?"

Robilliard coloured faintly. "As I said. The Brouards are major account holders. He ran a business with holdings all over the world."

"He was God damn *retired*."

"There's that, yes. But you see, had the transfers been made by someone we didn't know quite so well—an in-and-out situation set up by a foreign national, for example—we would have red-flagged it at once. But there was nothing to suggest an irregularity. There's still nothing to suggest that." He detached a yellow Post-it from the top of the print-out. He went on to say, "The name on the receiving account is International Access. It has an address in Bracknell. Frankly, I expect it was a start-up company in which Brouard was investing. If you look into it, I'll wager that's exactly what you'll find out."

"What you'd *like* us to find out," Le Gallez said.

"That's all I know," Robilliard countered.

Le Gallez didn't let up. "All you know or all you want to tell us, David?"

To which question, Robilliard slapped his hand on the print-out and said, "See here, Louis. Not a damn thing tells me this is anything other than what it looks like."

Le Gallez reached for the paper. "Right. We'll see about that."

Outside, the three men paused in front of a bakery, where Le Gallez looked longingly at a display of chocolate croissants in the window. DS Marsh said, "It's something to look into, sir, but as Brouard's dead, I wouldn't bet anyone over in London's going to break a sweat getting to the bottom of this."

"It could be a legitimate transaction," St. James pointed out. "The son—Adrian Brouard—I understand he lives in England. And there're other children as well. There's a possibility that one of them owns International Access, and Brouard was doing what he could to prop it up."

"Investment capital," DS Marsh said. "We'll need to get someone in London to deal with the bank over there. I'll phone FSA and give them the word, but my guess's at this point, they're going to want a court order. The bank, that is. If you phone Scotland Yard—"

"I have someone in London," St. James cut in. "Someone at the Yard. He might be able to help. I'll ring him. But in the meantime . . ." He considered all that he'd learned over the past several days. He followed the likely trails that each piece of information had been laying down. "Let me deal with the London end of things, if you will," he said to Le Gallez. "After that, I'd say it's time to speak frankly with Adrian Brouard."

Chapter 23

"So that's the fact of it, lad," Paul's dad said to him. He clasped Paul's ankle and smiled fondly, but Paul could see the regret in his eyes. He'd seen it even before his father had asked him to come upstairs to his bedroom for "a bit of a heart-to-heart, Paulie." The telephone had rung, Ol Fielder had answered it, had said, "Yessir, Mr. Forrest. Boy's sitting right here," and had listened long, his face going through a slow alteration from pleasure to concern to veiled disappointment. "Ah well," he'd said at the conclusion of Dominic Forrest's comments, "it's still a good sum, and you won't see our Paul turning his nose up at it, I can tell you that."

Afterwards, he'd asked Paul to follow him upstairs, ignoring Billy's "Wha's this about, then? Our Paulie not turning into the next Richard Branson af'er all?"

They'd gone to Paul's room, where Paul had sat with his back to the headboard of his bed. His father sat on the edge of it, explaining to him that what Mr. Forrest had previously thought would be an inheritance of some seven hundred thousand pounds had in reality turned out to be an amount in the vicinity of sixty thousand. A good deal less than Mr. Forrest had led them to expect, to be sure, but still a sum not to sniff at. Paul could use it in any number of ways, couldn't he: technical college, university, travel. He could buy himself a car so he wouldn't have to rely on that old bike any longer. He could set himself up in a little business if he liked. He might even purchase a cottage somewhere. Not a nice one, true, not even a big one, but one he could work on, fixing it up, making it real sweet over time so when he married someday . . . Ah well, it was all dreams, wasn't it? But dreams were good. We all have them, don't we?

"Hadn't got that money all spent in your head, had you, lad?" Ol Fielder asked Paul kindly when he'd concluded his explanation. He gave Paul a pat on the leg. "No? I didn't think so, son. You've got some wisdom about these things. Good it was left to you, Paulie, and not to . . . Well, you know what I mean."

"So, tha's the news, is it? What a bloody good laugh."

Paul looked to see his brother had joined them, uninvited as usual. Billy lolled in the doorway, against the jamb. He was licking the frosting from an untoasted Pop-Tart. "Sounds like our Paulie's not going somewheres else to live the high life after all. Well, all's I c'n say is I like that, I do. Can't think what it'd be like round here without Paulie wanking off in his bed every night."

"That'll do, Bill." Ol Fielder rose and stretched

his back. "I expect you've some sort of business to see to this morning, like the rest of us."

"You expect that, do you?" Billy said. "No. I don't have no business to *see* to. Guess I'm different to you lot, huh? Not so easy for me to get employment."

"You could try," Ol Fielder said to Billy. "Tha's the only difference between us, Bill."

Paul shifted his gaze between his brother and his father. Then he lowered it to observe his trouser knees. He saw they were thin to the point of shredding at a touch. Too much wear, he thought, with nothing else to choose from.

"Oh, tha's the case, is it?" Billy asked. Paul flinched at the tone because he knew that his father's declaration, while completely well meaning, was the invitation Billy wanted to spar. He'd been carrying his anger round for months, just waiting for an excuse to let it fly. It had only got worse when their dad had got himself taken on by the road crew, leaving Billy behind to pick at his wounds. "Tha's the *only* difference, is it, Dad? Nothing else, is there?"

"You know the fact of it, Bill."

Billy took a step into the bedroom. Paul shrank into the bed. Billy was of a height with their father and although Ol outweighed him, he was far too mild. Besides, he couldn't waste the energy to spar. He needed all the resources he had to hold his part with the road crew every day, and even if that hadn't been the case, he wasn't ever a man to brawl.

That, of course, had been the problem in Billy's eyes: the fact that there was no fight in their father.

All of the stalls in the St. Peter Port market had got the word that their leases would not be renewed because the whole place was going to be shut down, to make way for a redevelopment scheme that meant trendy boutiques, antiques dealers, cappuccino stalls, and tourist shops. They would be displaced—the whole lot of butchers, fishmongers, and green grocers—and they could take it in the neck one at a time as their leases came up, or they could go at once. It hadn't mattered to the Powers That Be, as long as they were gone when they were ordered to be gone.

"We'll fight 'em," Billy had vowed at the dinner table. Night after night, he'd laid his plans. If they couldn't win, they'd burn the place down because *no one* took away the Fielder family business without paying the price.

He'd reckoned without his dad, though. Ol Fielder had long been a man of peace.

As he was at this moment, with Billy in front of him, itching to get into it and looking for an opening.

He said, "Got to get to work, Bill. You'd do best to find yourself a job."

"I had a job," Billy told him. "Just like you. Just like my granddad and great-granddad as well."

Ol shook his head. "That time's past, son." He made a move towards the door.

Billy took him by the arm. "You," Billy said to his father, "are a useless piece of shit," and as Paul gave a strangled cry of protest, Billy snarled at him, "And *you* stay out of it, you wanking little twit."

"I'm off to work, Bill," their father said.

"You're off to nowhere. We're talking about this, we are. Right now. And *you* are looking at what you done."

"Things change," Ol Fielder said to his son.

"You let them change," Billy said. "That was ours. Our work. Our money. Our *business.* Grand-dad left it to you. *His* dad built it up and he left it to him. But did you fight for it? Did you try to save it?"

"Had no grounds for saving it. You know that, Bill."

"It was meant to be *mine* like it was yours. It was what I was s'posed to bloody do."

"I'm sorry," Ol said.

"*Sorry?*" Billy jerked his father's arm. "Sorry won't do shit. Won't change what is."

"And what'll change that?" Ol Fielder asked. "Let go m' arm."

"Why? You scared of a little pain? That why you didn't want to take them on? Scared you might've got messed with, Dad? Little bunged up, maybe? Little bruised?"

"I got work to go to, lad. Let me go. Don't push at this, Billy."

"I'll push when I push. And you'll go when I say you c'n go. Right now we're talking this out."

"No purpose to that. It is what it is."

"Don't you *say* that!" Billy's voice rose. "Don't you sodding tell me. I worked the meat since I was ten years old. I learned the trade. I did it good. For all them years, Dad. Blood on my hands and on my clothes, the smell of it so strong that they called me

Roadkill. You know that, Dad? But I di'n't mind 'cause it was a life. That's what I was building, a life. That stall was mine and now it's nothing and that's what I'm left with. You let it all get snatched away 'cause you di'n't want to get your hair mussed. So what've I got left? You tell me, Dad."

"It happens, Bill."

"Not to me!" Billy shouted. He released his father's arm and shoved him. He shoved him once, then twice, then a third time, and Ol Fielder did nothing to stop him. "Fight me, you fuck." Billy cried with each shove. "Fight me. *Fight* me."

On the bed Paul watched this through a blur. Dimly somewhere else in the house, he heard Taboo barking and voices going on. Telly, he thought. And, Where's Mum? Can't she *hear*? Won't she come to stop him?

Not that she could. Not that anyone could, now or ever. Billy had liked the violence of butchering, implied though it had been. He had liked the cleavers and the blows to the meat that severed flesh from bone or bone itself into pieces. That being gone from his life, he'd had an itch for months to feel the power once again of decimating something, of slicing it down till there was nothing left. It was all pent up inside him—this need to do harm—and he was about to gratify it.

"Won't fight with you, Billy," Ol Fielder said as his son shoved him a final time. The backs of his legs were against the side of the bed, and he sank down onto it. "Won't fight you, son."

"Too afraid you'd lose? Come on. Get up." And

Billy used the heel of his hand sharply against his father's shoulder. Ol Fielder winced. Billy grinned without humour. "Yeah. Tha's it. Have a taste of it now? Get up, you sod. Get up. Get *up*."

Paul reached for his father, to pull him to a safety that didn't exist. Billy turned on him next. "You keep away, wanker. Out of this. Hear? We got business, him and me." He grabbed his father's jaw and squeezed it, twisting his head to one side so Paul could clearly see his father's face. "Check this mug out," Billy told him. "Pathetic worm. Won't fight no one."

Taboo's barking got louder. Voices came near.

Bill brought his father's face back around. He pinched his nose and grabbed both of his ears. "Wha's it going to take?" he mocked him. "What makes you into a real man, Dad?"

Ol shoved his son's hands away from his head. "Enough!" His voice was loud.

"Already?" Billy laughed. "Dad, Dad. We're just starting up."

"I said enough!" Ol Fielder shouted.

This was what Billy wanted and he danced away in delight. His hands made fists and he laughed, punching triumphantly at the air. He turned back to his father and mimicked the fancy footwork of a boxer. He said, "Where d'you want it, then? In here or outside?"

He advanced on the bed, throwing jabs and thrusts. But only one of them connected with their father's body—a blow to the temple—before the room seemed full of people. Blue-uniformed men

came crashing through the door, followed by Mave
Fielder carrying Paul's youngest sibling. Right behind her were the two middle boys, jam on their
faces and toast in their hands.

Paul thought they'd come to separate his father
and his oldest brother. Somehow someone had rung
the police and they'd been nearby, so close as to be
able to get here in record time. They would take
care of matters and drag Billy away. They'd lock him
up, and there'd be peace in the house at last.

But what happened was something far different.
One said, "Paul Fielder?" to Billy. "You Paul
Fielder?" as the other advanced on Paul's brother.
That one said, "What's going on here, sir?" to Paul's
father. "Is there some sort of trouble?"

Ol Fielder said no. No, there was no trouble here,
just a family squabble that was being sorted out.

This your boy Paul, the constable wanted to
know.

"They want our Paulie," Mave Fielder said to her
husband. "They won't say why, Ol."

Billy crowed. "Caught you at last, you tosser," he
said to Paul. "Been making a real spectacle of yourself at the public loo? Warned you about hanging
about down there, di'n't I?"

Paul quivered against the headboard of his bed.
He saw that one of his younger brothers was holding
on to Taboo's collar. The dog was continuing to
bark, and one of the constables said, "Will you shut
that thing up?"

"Got a gun?" Billy asked with a laugh.

"Bill!" Mave cried. Then, "Ol? Ol? What's this about?"

But, of course, Ol Fielder knew no more than anyone else.

Taboo continued to bark. He squirmed, trying to get away from Paul's youngest brother.

The constable ordered, "Do something about that bloody animal!"

Taboo just wanted to be released, Paul knew. He just wanted to reassure himself that Paul wasn't hurt.

The other constable said, "Here. Let me . . ." And he grabbed Taboo's collar to drag him away.

The dog bared his teeth. He snapped at him. The constable gave a cry and kicked him soundly. Paul flew off the bed to go to his dog, but Taboo ran yelping down the stairs.

Paul tried to follow, but he found himself held back. His mother was crying, "What's he done? What's he done?" as Billy laughed wildly. Paul's feet scrabbled for purchase on the floor, one of them accidentally kicking a constable's leg. That man grunted and his grip on Paul loosened. Which gave Paul time to grab his rucksack and make for the door.

"Stop him!" someone yelled.

It was a small matter to do so. The room was so crowded that there was nowhere to go and certainly no place to hide. In short order Paul was being marched down the stairs and out of the house.

He existed within a whirlwind of images and sounds from that moment forward. He could hear his mum continuing to ask what they wanted with her little Paulie, he could hear his dad saying, "Mave. Girl, try to be calm." He could hear Billy laughing and, somewhere, Taboo barking, and outside he could see the neighbours lined up. Above them, he could see the sky was blue for the first time in days, and against it the trees that edged the lumpy car park looked like impressions rendered in charcoal.

Before he knew what was happening to him, he was in the back of a police car with his rucksack clutched to his chest. His feet were cold and he looked down at them to realise he had on no shoes. He was still in his tattered bedroom slippers, and no one had thought to give him time to put on a jacket.

The car door slammed and the engine roared. Paul heard his mother continue her shouting. He screwed his head round as the car began to move. He watched his family fade away.

Then from round the side of the crowd, Taboo came running after them. He was barking furiously and his ears were flapping.

"Damn fool dog," the constable who was driving murmured. " 'F he doesn't go back home—"

"Not our problem," the other said.

They pulled out of the Bouet into Pitronnerie Road. When they reached *Le Grand Bouet* and picked up speed, Taboo was still frantically running behind them.

Deborah and China had a bit of trouble finding Cynthia Moullin's home in *La Corbière*. They'd been told that it was commonly called the Shell House and that they wouldn't be able to miss it despite its being on a lane the approximate width of a bicycle tyre, which was itself the offshoot of another lane that wound between banks and hedges. It was on their third try when they finally saw a post box done up in oyster shells that they decided they might well have found the spot they were looking for. So Deborah pulled their car into the drive, which allowed them to note a vast wreckage of more shells in the garden.

"The house formerly known as Shell," Deborah murmured. "No wonder we didn't see it at first."

The place looked deserted: no other car in the drive, a closed-up barn, curtains drawn tight against diamond-paned windows. But as they climbed out of the car onto the shell-strewn driveway, they noted a young woman crouched at the far side of what was left of a fanciful garden. She embraced the top of a small shell-crusted concrete wishing well, with her blonde head resting upon its rim. She looked rather like a statue of Viola after the shipwreck, and she didn't move as Deborah and China approached her.

She did speak, however, saying, "Go away. I don't want to see you. I've phoned Gran and she says I can come to Alderney. She *wants* me there, and I mean to go."

"Are you Cynthia Moullin?" Deborah asked the girl.

She raised her head, startled. She looked from China to Deborah as if attempting to make out who they were. Then she looked beyond them, perhaps to see if they were accompanied by anyone else. There being no one with them, her body slumped. Her face settled back to its expression of despair.

"I thought you were Dad," she said dully, and lowered her head to the rim of the wishing well again. "I want to be dead." She went back to clutching the sides of the well as if she could force her will upon her body.

"I know the feeling," China said.

"No one knows the feeling," Cynthia rejoined. "No one knows because it's mine. *He's* glad. He says, 'You can go about your business now. The milk's been spilt and what's over is over.' But that's not how it is. He just thinks it's over. But it never will be. Not for me. I will *never* forget."

"D'you mean you and Mr. Brouard being over?" Deborah asked her. "Because he's dead?"

The girl looked up again at the mention of Brouard. "Who are you?"

Deborah explained. On their drive from *Le Grand Havre* China had told her that she'd not heard a whisper about Guy Brouard and anyone called Cynthia Moullin while she herself had been at *Le Reposoir.* As far as she'd known, Anaïs Abbott was Guy Brouard's only lover. "They both sure acted like it," China had said. So it was clear that this girl had been out of the picture prior to the Rivers' arrival on Guernsey. It remained to be seen why she was out of the picture and at whose instigation.

Cynthia's lips began trembling, curving down-

wards as Deborah introduced China and herself and
laid out the reasons for their visit to the Shell House.
By the time everything had been explained to her,
the first tears were snaking down her cheeks. She
did nothing to stop them. They dripped onto the
grey sweatshirt she was wearing, marking it with
miniature ovals of her grief.

"I wanted it," she wept. "He wanted it, too. He
never said and I never said but we both *knew.* He just
looked at me this one time before we did it and I
knew everything had changed between us. I could
see it all in his face—what it would mean to him and
everything—and I said to him, 'Don't use anything.'
And he smiled that smile which meant he knew
what I was thinking and it was okay. It would've
made everything easier in the end. It would've made
it logical for us to get married."

Deborah looked at China. China mouthed her
reaction: *wow.* Deborah said to Cynthia, "You were
engaged to Guy Brouard?"

"Would've been," she said. "And now . . . Guy.
Oh Guy." She wept without embarrassment, like a
little girl. "There's nothing left. If there'd been a
baby, I'd've had something. But now he's truly, really
dead and I can't bear it and I hate him. I hate him. I
hate him. He says, 'Go on, now. Get on with your
life. You're free to go about like before,' and he acts
like he didn't *pray* for this to happen, like he didn't
think I'd run off if I could and hide till I'd had the
baby and it was too late for him to do *anything* to
stop it. He talks about how it would've ruined my

life, when my life's ruined *now*. And he's glad about that. He's glad. He's *glad*." She threw her arms round the wishing well, weeping against its granular rim.

They definitely had their question answered, Deborah thought. There could hardly be a cloud in the sky of certainty about Cynthia Moullin's relationship with Guy Brouard. And the *he* that she hated had to be her father. Deborah couldn't imagine who else would have had the concerns she was attributing to the *he* she so despised.

She said, "Cynthia, may we help you into the house? It's cold out here and as you've only that sweatshirt . . ."

"No! I will *never* go back in there! I'll stay out here till I die. I *want* to."

"I don't expect your dad's going to let that happen."

"He wants it as much as I do," she said. " 'Hand over the wheel,' he says to me. 'You're not deserving of its protection, girl.' Like I was supposed to be hurt by that. Like I was supposed to get his *meaning*. He's saying 'You're no daughter of mine,' and I'm supposed to hear that without his saying it. But I don't care a bloody whit, see. I do not care."

Deborah looked at China in some confusion. China shrugged her own mystification. These were waters far too deep just to wade in. Obviously, some sort of life belt was needed.

"I'd already given it to Guy anyway," Cynthia said. "Months ago. I told him to carry it with him always. It was stupid, I know. It wasn't anything but a stupid stone. But I told him it would keep him safe, and I expect he believed . . . because I told him . . . I told him . . ." Her sobbing renewed. "But it didn't, did it? It was only a bloody stupid *stone.*"

The girl was a fascinating mix of innocence, sensuality, naivete, and vulnerability. Deborah could see her appeal to a man who might want to educate her in the ways of the world, to protect her from it simultaneously, and to initiate her into some of its delights. Cynthia Moullin offered something of a full-service relationship, a definite temptation for a man with a need to maintain an aura of superiority at all times. In fact, Deborah could see herself in the younger girl before her: the person she might have been had she not struck out on her own in America for three years.

It was this realisation that prompted her to kneel by the girl and put her hand gently on the back of her neck. She said, "Cynthia, I'm terribly sorry for what you're going through. But please. Let us take you into the house. You want to die now, but you won't want that always. Believe me. I know it."

"So do I," China said. "Really, Cynthia. She's telling you the truth."

The idea of sisterhood implied in their statements seemed to reach the girl. She allowed herself to be helped to her feet and once upon them, she wiped her eyes on the sleeves of her sweatshirt and said pathetically, "Got to blow my nose."

Deborah said, "There'll be something you can use in the house."

Thus, they got her from the wishing well to the front door. She stiffened there, and for a moment

Deborah thought she might not enter, but when Deborah called out a hello and asked if anyone was at home and no answer came, Cynthia became willing to go inside. There, she used a tea towel as a handkerchief. Afterwards, she wandered into the sitting room and curled into an old overstuffed chair, putting her head on its arm and pulling down a knitted blanket from its back to cover her.

"He said I'd have to have an abortion." She spoke numbly now. "He said he'd keep me locked up till he knew if I'd need one. No way was he going to have me running off somewhere to have that bastard's bastard, he said. I said it wasn't going to be anyone's bastard because we'd marry long before it was born, and he went quite mad at that. 'You'll stay till I see the blood,' he said. 'As for Brouard, we'll see about him.' " Cynthia's gaze was fixed on the wall opposite her chair, where a collection of family pictures hung. Central to them was a large shot of a seated man—presumably her dad—surrounded by three girls. He looked earnest and well-meaning. They looked serious and in need of fun. Cynthia said, "He couldn't see what *I* wanted. It didn't matter to him. And now there's nothing. If I at least had the baby from it all . . ."

"Believe me, I understand," Deborah said.

"We were in love but he didn't get it. He said he seduced me but that's not how it was."

"No," Deborah said. "It doesn't happen like that, does it?"

"It doesn't. It *didn't*." Cynthia crumpled the blanket in her fists and brought it up to her chin. "I could see that he liked me from the first and I liked him back. That's what it was. Just us liking each other. He talked to me. I talked to him. And he really *saw* me. I wasn't just there in the room for him, like a chair or something. I was real. He told me that himself. And it happened over time, the rest of it. But not one single thing that I wasn't ready for. Not one thing that I didn't want to happen. Then Dad found out. I don't know how. He ruined it for both of us. Made it ugly and foul. Made it sound like something Guy did for a laugh. Like he had a bet with someone that he could be my first and he needed the bedsheets to prove it."

"Dads are protective that way," Deborah said. "He probably didn't mean—"

"Oh, he meant it. And that's what Guy was like anyway."

"Getting you to bed on a *bet?*" China exchanged an unreadable look with Deborah.

Cynthia hastened to correct her. "Wanting to show me what it could be like. He knew I'd never . . . I told him. He talked about how important it was for a woman's first time to be . . . he said . . . exultant. *Exultant*. And it was. Like that. Every time. It was."

"So you felt bound to him," Deborah said.

"I wanted him to live forever, with me. I didn't care he was older. What difference did it make? We weren't just two bodies on a bed shagging. We were two souls that found each other and meant to stay together, no matter what. And that's how it would've been if he hadn't . . . he hadn't . . ." Cynthia put her head back on the arm of the chair and began to weep again. "I want to die, too."

Deborah went to her. She stroked her head and said, "I'm so sorry. To lose him and then not to have his baby either . . . You must feel crushed."

"I feel destroyed," she sobbed.

China remained where she was, a few feet away. She crossed her arms as if to protect herself from the onslaught of Cynthia's emotion. She said, "It probably doesn't help to know it right now, but you *will* get through this. You'll actually even feel better someday. In the future. You'll feel completely different."

"I don't *want* to."

"Nope. We never do. We love like crazy and it seems like if we lose that love, we'll shrivel up and die, which would be a blessing. But no man's worth us ending up dead, no matter who he is. And anyway, things don't happen that way in the real world. We just muddle on. We finally get through it. Then we're whole again."

"I don't *want* to be whole!"

"Not right now," Deborah said. "Right now you want to grieve. The strength of your grieving marks the strength of your love. And letting grief go when the time comes to do it honours that love."

"Really?" The girl's voice was a child's, and she looked so childlike that Deborah found herself wanting to fly to her protection. All at once, she understood completely how this girl's father must have felt when he learned Guy Brouard had taken her.

"That's what I believe," Deborah said.

They left Cynthia Moullin with that final thought, curled beneath her blanket, her head pillowed on one arm. Her weeping had left her exhausted but calm. She would sleep now, she told them. Perhaps she'd be able to dream of Guy.

Outside on the shell-strewn path to the car, China and Deborah said nothing at first. They paused and surveyed the garden, which looked like something a careless giant had trampled upon, and China stated flatly, "What a godawful mess."

Deborah glanced at her. She knew that her friend wasn't talking about the decimation of whatever crusty ornaments had once decorated the lawn and the flowerbeds. "We do plant landmines in our lives," she commented.

"More like nuclear bombs, you ask me. He was something like seventy years old. And she's . . . what? Seventeen? That ought to be God damned child abuse. But oh no, he was careful about that one, wasn't he?" She drove her hand through her short hair in a gesture that was rough, abrupt, and so like her brother's. She said, "Men are pigs. If there's a decent one out there, I'd sure as hell like to meet him sometime. Just to shake his hand. Just to say howdy-fucking-do. Just to know they aren't all out for the great big screw. All this you're-the-one and I-love-you bullshit. Why the hell do women keep going for it?" She glanced at Deborah, and before Deborah could reply, she went on with "Oh. Forget it. Never mind. I always forget. Getting trampled by men doesn't apply to you."

"China, that's—"

China waved her off. "Sorry. *Sorry.* I shouldn't have . . . It's just that seeing her . . . listening to that . . . Never mind." She hurried towards the car.

Deborah followed. "We all get handed pain that we have to deal with. That's just what happens, like a by-product of being alive."

"It doesn't have to be that way." China opened her door and slumped into the car. "Women don't have to be so stupid."

"We're groomed to believe in fairy tales," Deborah said. "A tormented man saved by the love of one good woman? We're fed that idea from the cradle."

"But we didn't exactly have the man-in-torment in *this* scenario," China pointed out with a gesture towards the house. "So why'd she fall for him? Oh, he was charming. Decent-looking. He was in good shape, so he didn't *seem* like seventy. But to be talked into it . . . I mean as your first . . . Any way you cut it, he could've been her grandfather. Her great-grandfather, even."

"She seems to have loved him all the same."

"I bet his bank account had something to do with that. Nice house, nice estate, nice car, nice whatever. The promise of being lady of the manor. Great vacations all around the world for the asking. All the clothes you want. Y' like diamonds? They're yours. Fifty thousand pairs of shoes? We can manage that. Want a Ferrari? No problem. *That,* I bet, made Guy Brouard sexy as hell to her. I mean, look at this place. Look at where she comes from. She was easy pickings. *Any* girl from a place like this would've been easy pickings. Sure, women have always gone for the tormented idiot. But make them the promise of heavy money, and they're going to go for *that* big time."

Deborah heard all this, her heart beating light and fast in her throat. She said, "Do you really believe that, China?"

"Damn right I believe it. And men know the score. Flash the cash around and see what happens. Chances are it'll be just like flypaper. Money means more to most women than whether the man can even stand upright. If he's breathing and he's loaded, say no more. Let's sign the deal. But we'll call it love, first. We'll say we're happy as hell when we're with him. We'll claim that when we're together, the birds sing right in our ears and the earth starts trembling and the seasons shift. But scrape away all that and it comes down to the cash. We can love a man with bad breath, one leg, and no dick, just as long as he can support us in the manner we'd like to become accustomed to."

Deborah couldn't reply. There were too many ways in which China's declarations could be applied to herself, not only to her relationship with Tommy that had come so hard upon the heels of her broken-hearted abandoning of London for California all those years ago, but also to her marriage, which fell some eighteen months after the affair with Tommy had ended. On the surface it all looked like something that was the very image of what China was describing: Tommy's considerable fortune wore the guise of initial lure; Simon's much lesser wealth still served to allow her freedoms most women her age never had. The fact that none of it was what it seemed . . . that money and the security it offered sometimes felt like a web that had been spun round her to keep her entrapped . . . not her own woman . . . having nothing to contribute anywhere at all . . . How could that be said to matter when it was placed beside the great good fortune of having once had a wealthy lover and now a husband who was able to support her?

Deborah swallowed all of this down. Her life, she knew, was of her own making. Her life, she knew, was something China had little knowledge of. She said, "Yes. Well. One woman's true love is another's meal ticket. Let's get back to town. Simon should have spoken to the police by now."

Chapter 24

ONE BENEFIT OF BEING the close friend of an Acting Superintendent in CID was having immediate access to him. St. James waited only a moment before Tommy's voice came over the line, saying with some amusement, "Deb managed to get you to Guernsey, didn't she? I thought she would."

"She actually didn't want me to come," St. James replied. "I managed to convince her that playing Miss-Marple-Goes-to-St.-Peter-Port was not in the best interests of anyone."

Lynley chuckled. "And it goes . . . ?"

"Forward but not as smoothly as I'd like." St. James brought his friend up-to-date with the independent investigation that he and Deborah were attempting to effect while simultaneously staying out of the way of the local police. "I don't know how much longer I'll be able to carry on on the dubious strength of my reputation," he concluded.

"Hence the phone call?" Lynley said. "I spoke to Le Gallez when Deborah came to the Yard. He was perfectly clear: He doesn't want the Met messing about with his case."

"It's not that," St. James hastened to reassure him. "Just a phone call or two you might make for me."

"What sort of phone call?" Lynley sounded wary.

St. James explained. When he was done, Lynley told him that the Financial Services Authority was the UK body that truly ought to be involved in any questions about English banking. He would do what he could to wrest information from the bank that had received the wire transfers from Guernsey, but it might come down to a court order, which could take a bit more time.

"This all may be perfectly legitimate," St. James told him. "We know the money went to a group called International Access in Bracknell. Can you go at it from that end?"

"We may have to. I'll see what I can do."

The call concluded, St. James descended to the hotel lobby, where he privately admitted to himself that he was long overdue for a mobile phone as he attempted to impress upon the receptionist the importance of her tracking him down should any phone calls come to him from London. She took down the information and she was none-too-happily assuring him that she'd pass any messages along when Deborah and China returned from their trip to *Le Grand Havre*.

The three of them went to the hotel lounge, where they ordered morning coffee and exchanged information. Deborah, St. James saw, had made a number of not unrealistic leaps with what she'd gathered. For her part, China did not use these facts to try to mould his thinking about the case, and for that St. James had to admire her. In the same position, he wasn't sure he could have been so circumspect.

"Cynthia Moullin talked about a stone," Deborah said in conclusion. "She said she'd *given* Guy Brouard this stone. To protect him, she said. And her dad wanted it back from her. Which made me wonder if this was the same stone that was used to choke him. He has a loud-and-clear motive, her dad. He even had her locked up until her period started so he could see she wasn't pregnant by Guy Brouard."

St. James nodded. "Le Gallez's conjecture is that someone may have intended to use the skull-and-crossed-bones ring to choke Brouard but changed course when it turned out that Brouard was carrying that stone."

"With that someone being Cherokee?" China didn't wait for an answer. "There's no *why* to that any more than there was a why to it when they pinned it on me. And don't they need a why, Simon? To make it stick?"

"In the best of all worlds, yes." He wanted to add the rest of what he knew—that the police had found something that would be as important to them as a motive—but he wasn't willing to share that information with anyone. It wasn't so much that he suspected China River or her brother of the crime. It was more that he suspected *everyone* and the way of caution was to hold one's cards close.

Before he could go on—choosing between temporising and outright prevaricating—Deborah spoke. "Cherokee wouldn't have known Guy Brouard had that stone."

"Unless he saw him with it," St. James said.

"How could he?" Deborah countered. "Cynthia said Brouard carried it with him. Doesn't that suggest he'd have it in a pocket rather than in the palm of his hand?"

"It could do, yes," St. James said.

"Yet Henry Moullin *did* know he had it. He'd explicitly asked his daughter to hand it over, which's what she told us. If she told him she'd given her good-luck charm or protection from the evil eye or *whatever* it is to the very man her father was up in arms about, why wouldn't he march right over there and demand it back?"

"There's nothing to say he didn't do that," St. James pointed out. "But until we know for sure—"

"We pin the tail on Cherokee," China finished flatly. She looked at Deborah as if to say *See?*

St. James didn't like the suggestion of girls-versus-boys that this look implied. He said, "We keep our minds open. That's all."

"My brother didn't do this," China said insistently. "Look: We've got Anaïs Abbott with a motive. We've got Henry Moullin with a motive, too. We've even got Stephen Abbott with a motive if *he* wanted into Cynthia's pants or wanted to separate his mom from Brouard. So *where* does Cherokee fit? Nowhere. And why? Because he didn't do it. He didn't know these people any more than I did."

Deborah added, "You can't discount everything that points to Henry Moullin, not in favour of

Cherokee, can you? Not when there's nothing that even indicates he might've been involved in Guy Brouard's death." She appeared to read something on St. James's face as she made the final remark, though, because she went on to say, "Unless there *is* something. And there must be, because why else would they have arrested him. So of course there's something. What've I been thinking? You went to the police. What did they tell you? Is it about the ring?"

St. James glanced at China—who leaned towards him attentively—and then back at his wife. He shook his head and said, "Deborah," and then concluded with a sigh that breathed his apology. "I'm sorry, my love."

Deborah's eyes widened as she seemed to realise what her husband was saying and doing. She looked away from him and St. James could see her pressing her hands into her lap as if this gesture would contain her temper. Evidently, China read her as well because she stood, despite her coffee going undrunk. She said, "I think I'll go see if they'll let me talk to my brother. Or I can find Holberry and send a message in with him. Or . . ." She hesitated, her gaze going to the door of the lounge, where two women loaded with Marks & Spencer bags were coming in for a break in their morning shopping. Watching them get settled, listening to their easy laughter and chatter, China looked bleak. She said to Deborah, "I'll catch you later, okay?" She nodded to St. James and grabbed her coat.

Deborah called out her name as she hurried from

the room, but China didn't turn. Deborah did, on her husband. "Was that completely necessary?" she demanded. "You as much as called him a murderer. And you think she's in on it as well, don't you? Which is why you wouldn't say what you have, not in front of her. You think they did it. Together. Or one of them. That's what you think, isn't it?"

"We don't know they didn't do it," St. James replied, although this wasn't really what he wanted to say to Deborah. Instead of responding, he knew he was reacting to his wife's tone of accusation despite realising that this reaction came from irritation and was a first step on the path of arguing with her.

"*How* can you say that?" Deborah demanded.

"Deborah, how can you not?"

"Because I've just *told* you what we've come up with, and none of it has to do with Cherokee. *Or* with China."

"No," he agreed. "What you've come up with doesn't have to do with them."

"But what you have does. That's what you're saying. And like a good little detective, you're keeping it to yourself. Well, that's just fine. I may as well go home. I may as well just let you—"

"Deborah."

"—handle it all on your own since you're so intent on doing that." Like China, she began to put on her coat. She struggled with it, though, and was unable to make the dramatic exit she no doubt wished to make.

He said, "Deborah. Sit down and listen."

"Don't *talk* to me like that. I'm not a child."

"Then don't act like—" He stopped himself at the edge and raised his hands, palms towards her in a gesture that said *Let's call this to a halt.* He forced himself to be calm and forced his voice to be reasonable. "What I believe isn't important."

"Then you *do*—"

"And," he cut in determinedly, "what you believe isn't important either. The only thing that *is* important is the facts. Feelings can't intrude in a situation like this."

"Good God, you've made your decision, haven't you? Based on what?"

"I haven't made any decision at all. It's not my place to do that, and even if it were, no one's asking for my decision."

"Then?"

"Things don't look good. That's what it is."

"What d'you know? What do they have?" When he didn't answer at once, she said, "God in heaven, you don't *trust* me? What d'you think I'm going to do with the information?"

"What *would* you do if it implicates your friend's brother?"

"What sort of question is that? What d'you think I'd do: tell him?"

"The ring . . ." St. James hated to say it, but it had to be said. "And as it turned out, he recognised it from the first but still said nothing at all. How do you explain that, Deborah?"

"I'm not meant to explain it. He is. He will."

"You believe in him that much?"

"He's not a killer."

But the facts suggested otherwise, although St. James couldn't take the risk of revealing them to her. *Eschscholzia californica,* a bottle in a field, fingerprints on the bottle. And everything that had gone on in Orange County, California.

He pondered for a moment. Everything pointed to River. But there was one detail that still did not: the movement of money from Guernsey to London.

Margaret stood at the window and made a sharp exclamation each time a bird so much as flew by the house. She'd made two more phone calls to the States police, demanding to know when they could expect something to be done about that "miserable little thief," and she was anticipating the arrival of someone who would listen to her story and take the appropriate action. For her part, Ruth tried to concentrate on her needlepoint.

Margaret, however, was a profound distraction. It was "You'll be protesting out of the other side of your mouth about his innocence in another hour" and "I'll show you what truth and honesty are" and other editorial remarks as they waited. What they waited for Ruth didn't know, for all her sister-in-law had said was "They're dealing with it at once," after her first call to the police.

As *at once* stretched on, Margaret became more agitated. She was well on her way to talking herself into yet another phone call to demand action from the authorities, when a panda car rolled up in front of the house and she crowed, "They've got him!"

She hurried to the door, and Ruth did her best to follow, getting up stiffly from her chair and finding herself limping along in Margaret's wake. Her sister-in-law charged outside, where one of two uniformed constables was opening the back door of the car. She thrust herself between the policeman and the back seat's occupant. When Ruth finally got there, Margaret had reached inside to grab Paul Fielder by the collar, and she was in the act of pulling him roughly from the car.

"Thought you got away with it, didn't you?" she demanded.

"See here, Madam," the constable said.

"Let me have that rucksack, you little thief!"

Paul struggled in her grasp and clutched his rucksack to his chest. He kicked at her ankles. She cried, "He's trying to escape," and to the police, "*Do* something, damn you. Get that rucksack from him. He's got it in there."

The second constable came round the side of the car. He said, "You're interfering with—"

"Well, I damn well *wouldn't* be if either of you would do your jobs!"

"Stand away, Madam," Constable One said.

Ruth said, "Margaret, you're only frightening him. Paul dear, would you come into the house? Constables, will you help him inside, please?"

Margaret reluctantly released the boy and Paul raced to Ruth. His arms were extended and his meaning was clear. She, and no other, was to have his rucksack.

Ruth ushered the boy and the constables into the

house, the rucksack in one hand and her arm through Paul's. She made it a companionable gesture. He was trembling like a shaken duster, and she wanted to say he had nothing to fear. The idea that this boy would have stolen a single thing from *Le Reposoir* was ludicrous.

She was sorry for the anxiety he was going through, and she knew that her sister-in-law's presence would only serve to aggravate it. She should have done something to keep Margaret from making her phone call to the police, Ruth realised. But short of locking her in the attic or cutting the phone lines, she didn't know what that something was.

Now that the damage was done, though, she could at least prevent Margaret from attending what was no doubt going to be a terrifying interview for the poor boy. So when they got into the stone hall, she said, "Come this way. Paul, constables? If you'll go into the morning room. You'll find it down those two steps just beyond the fireplace." And when she saw Paul's gaze fix on the rucksack, she patted it and said to him gently, "I'll bring it in a moment. You go with them, dear. You'll be quite safe."

When the constables had taken Paul to the morning room and closed the door behind them, Ruth turned to her sister-in-law. She said, "I've given you your way in this, Margaret. Now you'll give me mine."

Margaret was nobody's fool. She recognised the way the wind was blowing her plans to confront the boy who'd stolen money that was meant for her son. She said, "Open that rucksack and see the truth."

"I'll do that with the police," Ruth said. "If he's taken something—"

"You'll make excuses for him," Margaret said bitterly. "Of *course* you will. You make excuses for everyone. It's a way of life for you, Ruth."

"We can talk later. If there's more to say."

"You're not keeping me out of there. You can't."

"That's true. But the police can. And they will."

Margaret's back stiffened. Ruth could see that she knew she was defeated in this but was searching for a final comment that would illustrate everything she had suffered and was continuing to suffer at the hands of the contemptible Brouards. Not finding it, however, she turned abruptly. Ruth waited till she heard her sister-in-law's footsteps on the stairs.

When she joined the two constables and Paul Fielder in the morning room, she gave the boy a tender smile. She said, "Sit down, dear," and to the constables, "Please," and she indicated two chairs and the sofa. Paul chose the sofa, and she joined him on it. She patted his hand and murmured, "I'm terribly sorry. She gets over-excited, I'm afraid."

"See here. This boy's been accused of stealing—"

Ruth held up her hand to stop the constable. She said, "I expect that's a figment of my sister-in-law's feverish imagination. If something's missing, I don't know what it is. I'd trust this boy anywhere in my house at any time. With *all* my possessions." To prove her point, she returned the rucksack unopened to the boy, saying, "I'm only sorry for the inconvenience to everyone. Margaret's terribly upset by my brother's death. She's not acting rationally just now."

She thought that would put an end to everything, but she was wrong. Paul pushed the rucksack back at her, and when she said "Why, Paul, I don't quite understand," he unfastened its clasps and pulled out a cylindrical object: something that rolled into itself.

Ruth looked from it to him, puzzled. Both of the constables got to their feet. Paul pressed the offering into Ruth's hands and when she didn't quite know what to do with it, he did it for her. He unrolled what he had and spread it upon her knees.

She looked at it. She said, "Oh my dear God," and suddenly understood.

Her vision blurred, and in an instant she forgave her brother everything: the secrets he'd kept and the lies he'd told. The uses to which he'd put other people. The need to be virile. The compulsion to seduce. Once again she was that little girl whose hand had been clutched in her elder brother's. *"N'aie pas peur,"* he had said. *"N'aie jamais peur. On rentrera à la maison."*

One of the constables was speaking, and only dimly was Ruth aware of his voice. She dismissed a thousand memories from her mind and managed to say, "Paul didn't steal this. He was keeping it for me. He meant me to have it all along. I dare say he was holding it till my birthday. Guy would have wanted to keep it safe. He would've known Paul would do that for him. I expect that's what happened."

More than that, she couldn't say. She found she was overcome by emotion, staggered by the significance of what her brother had done—and the unimaginable trouble he had gone to—to honour her, their family, and its heritage. She murmured to the constables, "We've caused you great trouble. I apologise for that." It was enough to encourage them to take their leave.

She remained on the sofa with Paul. He eased over next to her. He pointed to the building that the painter had depicted, to the tiny workmen who were labouring on it, to the ethereal woman who sat in the foreground, her eyes lowered to the enormous book in her lap. Her gown spread round her in folds of blue. Her hair swept back as if touched by a breeze. She was every bit as lovely as she'd been when Ruth had last seen her more than sixty years ago: ageless and untouched, frozen in time.

Ruth felt for Paul and took his hand in hers. *She* was shaking now, and she couldn't speak. But she could act, and that was what she did. She brought his hand to her lips and then got to her feet.

She motioned for him to come with her. She would take him upstairs so that he might see for himself and completely understand the nature of the extraordinary gift he'd just given her.

Valerie found the note upon her return from *La Corbière*. It was two words long, rendered in Kevin's disciplined hand: *Cherie's recital*. The fact that he'd written nothing more spoke of his displeasure.

She felt a tiny stab. She'd forgotten about the little girl's Christmas concert at the school. She'd been meant to go along with her husband to applaud the vocal efforts of their six-year-old niece, but in the apprehension of needing to know how far her responsibility went in the death of Guy Brouard, she'd been unaware of anything else. Kevin might even have reminded her about the concert at breakfast, but she wouldn't have heard him. She was already laying her plans for the day: how and when she could slip down to the Shell House without being missed, what she would say to Henry when she got there.

When Kevin arrived home, she was making chicken stock, skimming fat from the top of a boiling pot. A new recipe for soup lay on the work top next to her. She'd cut it from a magazine in the hope that it might tempt Ruth to eat.

Kevin came in the door and stood watching her, his tie loosened and his waistcoat undone. He was overdressed for a Christmas pageant presented by the under-ten set, Valerie saw, and she felt a secondary stab at the sight of him: He looked good; she should have been with him.

Kevin's glance went to the note he'd left stuck upon the refrigerator. Valerie said, "I'm sorry. I forgot. Cherie did well?"

He nodded. He removed his tie and wrapped it round his hand, setting it on the table next to a bowl of unshelled walnuts. He took off his jacket and then his waistcoat. He pulled out a chair and sat.

"Mary Beth all right?" Valerie asked.

"Well as you'd expect, first Christmas without him."

"Your first Christmas without him as well."

"It's different for me."

"I suppose. Good the girls have you, though."

A silence came between them. The chicken stock burbled. Tyres crunched on the gravel drive a short distance from the kitchen window. Valerie looked out and saw a police car leaving the grounds of the estate. She frowned at this, returned to the stock pot and added chopped celery. She threw in a handful of salt and waited for her husband to speak.

"Car was gone when I needed it to get into town," he said. "I had to use Guy's Mercedes."

"That must've fit you like a picture, all dressed up like you were. Did Mary Beth like the fancy ride?"

"I went on my own. Too late to fetch her. I wasn't on time for the concert as it was. I was waiting for you. Thought for sure you'd just run out somewhere. Picking up medicine at the chemist for the big house or something."

She made another pass across the top of the stock, removing a nonexistent slick of fat. Ruth wouldn't eat soup with too much fat in it. She'd see the delicate ovals of it, and she'd push the bowl away. So Valerie had to be vigilant. She had to give the chicken stock all her attention.

"Cherie missed you," Kevin persisted. "You were meant to go."

"Mary Beth didn't ask where I was, though, did she?"

Kevin didn't answer.

"So . . ." Valerie said as pleasantly as she could. "Those windows of hers sealed up nicely in her house now, Kev? No more leaking?"

"Where were you?"

She went to the fridge and looked inside, trying to think what she could tell him. She pretended a survey of the fridge's contents, but all the time her thoughts swarmed like gnats round overripe fruit.

Kevin's chair scraped on the floor as he got to his feet. He came to the fridge and shut its door. Valerie returned to the cooker and he followed her there. When she picked up the spoon to see to the stock, he took the spoon from her. He set it with care on the utensil holder. "It's time to talk."

"What about?"

"I think you know."

She wouldn't admit to that or to anything. She couldn't afford to. So she directed them elsewhere. She did it knowing the terrible risk involved, the risk that put her in the position of repeating her mother's misery: that curse of desertion that seemed to haunt her family. She'd lived her childhood and her girlhood in its shadow and she'd done everything in her power to ensure that she would never have to see the back of a spouse walking away. It had happened to her mother. It had happened to her brother. But she'd sworn it would never happen to her. When we work and strive and sacrifice and love, we are owed devotion in return, she'd believed. She'd had it for years and had it without question. Still, she had to risk losing it in order to give protection where it was now most needed.

She readied herself and said, "You miss our boys, don't you? That's part of what happened. We did a good job with them, but they're gone to their own lives and you miss the fathering. That started it. I saw the longing in you the first time those girls of Mary Beth's were sitting here having their tea."

She didn't look at her husband and he didn't say anything. In any other situation, she could have interpreted his silence as assent and let the rest of the conversation go. But in this situation she could not do so when letting one conversation go ran the risk of another conversation beginning. There were too few safe subjects to choose from at this point, so she chose this one, telling herself they would have come to it eventually.

She said, "Isn't it true, Kev? Isn't that how everything started?" Despite her deliberate choice of subject, despite the fact that she was making the choice cold-bloodedly as a way to keep that other more terrible knowledge safeguarded forever, she remembered her mother and how it had been for her: the begging and the tears and the do not leave me I will do anything I will be anything I will be her if that's what you ask of me. She promised herself if it came to that, she would not go the way of her mother.

"Valerie." Kevin's voice sounded hoarse. "What's happened to us?"

"You don't know?"

"Tell me."

She looked at him. "Is there an us?"

He appeared so perplexed that for an instant she wanted to stop where they were, as far as they'd gone, so close to the border but still not crossing it. But she could not do that. "What're you talking about?" he asked.

"Choices," she said. "Walking away from them

when they're yours to make. Or making them and walking away from others. That's what's happened. I've been watching it happen. I've been looking round it, looking past it, trying not to see it. But it's there all the same, and you're right. It's time we talked."

"Val, did you tell—"

She stopped him from going in that direction. She said, "Men don't stray unless there's a barrenness, Kev."

"Stray?"

"Somewhere, a barrenness. In what they already have. First I thought, Well he can act like their dad without becoming their dad, can't he? He can give them what a dad gives his girls and we'll be all right with that, Kev and me. He can stand in Corey's place in their lives. He can do that much. It'll be fine if he does." She swallowed and wished she didn't have to say it. But she knew that, like her husband, she had no real choice in the matter. "I thought," she said, "when I thought about it, Kev: He doesn't need to do the same for Corey's wife."

Kevin said, "Hang on. You've been thinking . . . Mary Beth . . . me?"

He looked appalled. She would have felt relieved had she not needed to press forward to make sure every other thought was obliterated from his mind save the thought that she had suspected him of falling in love with his brother's widow. "Isn't that how it was?" she asked him. "Isn't that how it is? I want the truth here, Kev. I think I'm owed it."

"Truth's what we all want," Kevin said. "I'm not sure we're owed it."

"In a marriage?" she said. "Tell me, Kevin. I want to know what's going on."

"Nothing," he said. "I don't see how you came to believe something ever was going on."

"Her girls. Her phoning. Her needing you to do this and that. You being there for her and missing our boys and wanting . . . I can tell you miss our boys, Kev."

"Of course I do. I'm their dad. Why wouldn't I miss them? But that doesn't mean . . . Val, I owe Mary Beth what a brother owes to his sister. Nothing more, nothing less. I'd expect you of all people would have understood that. Has that been what this is all about?"

"What?"

"The silence. The secrets. Like you've been hiding something from me. You have, haven't you? Hiding something? You always talk but you've stopped lately. When I asked . . ." He gestured with his hand and then dropped it to his side. "You wouldn't say. So I thought . . ." He looked away from her, studying the chicken stock as if it were a potion.

"Thought what?" she asked, because in the end she had to know and he had to speak so that she could deny and in denying put the subject at rest between them.

"First," he said, "I decided you'd told Henry despite the promise to hold your tongue. I thought

Jesus God she's told her brother about Cyn and she thinks he's given Brouard the chop and she won't tell me because I warned her off the idea in the first place. But then I decided it was something else, something worse. Worse for me, that is."

"What?"

"Val, I knew his ways. He had the Abbott woman, but she wasn't for him. He had Cyn, but Cyn's just a girl. He was wanting a woman with a woman's ways and a woman's knowledge, one who'd be as necessary to him as he was to her. And you're that kind of woman, Val. He knew that. I saw that he knew it."

"So you thought Mr. Brouard and I . . . ?" Valerie could hardly credit it: not only the belief itself that he held—as irrational as it was—but also her luck in his holding it. He looked so miserable that her heart swelled. She wanted to laugh at the lunacy of the idea that Guy Brouard might have wanted her of all people, with her work-roughened hands and her children-borne body, unaltered by the plastic surgeon's knife. You fool, he was after youth and beauty to replace his own, she wanted to tell her husband. But instead she said, "Why on earth would you ever have thought that, love?"

"It's not your nature to be secretive," he said. "If it wasn't about Henry—"

"Which it wasn't," she said as she smiled at her husband and allowed the lie to own her in whatever way it would.

"Then what else could it have possibly been?"

"But to think that Mr. Brouard and me . . . How'd you think I'd ever be interested in him?"

"I didn't think. I only saw. He was who he was and you were keeping secrets from me. He was rich and God knows we'll never be and that might've counted for something with you. While you . . . That was the easy part."

"Why?"

He held out his hands. His face told her that what he was about to say was the most reasonable part of the fantasy he'd been living with. "Who wouldn't have made a move on you if he stood the slightest chance of success?"

She felt her whole body soften towards him: at the question he'd asked, the expression on his face, the movement of his arms. She felt the softness come into her eyes and upon her features. She went to him. She said, "There's been only one in my life, Kevin. Few enough women can say that. Fewer still can be proud to say it. I can say it and I'm proud to be able to. There's always and only been you."

She felt his arms come round her. He pulled her to him without gentleness. He held on to her without desire. It was reassurance that he was seeking, and she knew it since she sought reassurance herself.

Blessedly, he asked nothing further of her.

So she said nothing more at all.

Margaret opened her second suitcase on the bed and began to remove more of her clothing from the chest of drawers. She'd folded it all carefully when she'd arrived, but now she had no concern about how it got itself repacked. She was finished with this place and finished with the Brouards. God only knew when the next flight to England was, but she meant to be on it.

She'd done what she could: for her son, for her former sister-in-law, for bloody everyone. But Ruth's dismissal of her was the final straw, more final than had been the straw of her last conversation with Adrian.

"Here's what she thinks," she'd announced. She'd gone to his bedroom looking for him and not finding him there. She'd finally unearthed him on the top floor of the house, in the gallery where Guy had kept some of the antiques he'd collected over the years along with most of the artworks. The fact that all of this could have been Adrian's—*should* have been Adrian's . . . No matter that the canvases were all of that modern nonsense stuff—smears of paint and figures looking like something sliced up by a food processor—they were probably valuable, they should have been her son's, and the thought that Guy had structured his final years to deliberately deny his son what he was *owed* . . . Margaret burned. She vowed she would be avenged.

Adrian wasn't doing anything in the gallery. He was merely in the act of being Adrian, slumped in an armchair. The room was cold and against its chill, Adrian had donned his leather jacket. His legs were stretched out in front of him and his hands were in his pockets. His might have been the posture of someone watching a favourite football team get thoroughly humiliated on the pitch, but Adrian's eyes were not fixed on a television. Instead, they were fastened onto the mantel. Half a dozen family pictures stood there, among them Adrian with his father. Adrian with his half-sisters. Adrian with his aunt.

Margaret said his name and "Did you hear me? She thinks you've no right to his money. He thought that as well, according to her. She says he didn't believe in *entitlements*. That's the way she put it. As if we're supposed to actually believe that story. If your father had had the great good fortune of having someone leave *him* an inheritance, d'you think he would have turned up his nose at it? Would he have said 'Oh dear. No thanks. It's not good for me. Better leave it to someone whose purity wouldn't be spoiled by unexpected money.' Not very likely. They're hypocrites, both of them. What he did, he did to punish me through you, and she's happy as a slug on a lettuce leaf just to carry on with his plan. Adrian! Are you listening? Have you heard a single word I've said?"

She'd wondered if he'd escaped to one of his twilight states, which would be so bloody typical of him. Just sink into the self for an extended period of faux catatonia, my fine young man. Leave Mummy to handle the difficult details in your life.

Finally, it was all too much for Margaret: the history of phone calls from the schools that Adrian couldn't succeed in, with the San sisters telling her confidentially that there was "really nothing wrong with the boy, Madam"; the psychologists with their sympathetic expressions informing her that those apron strings simply *had* to be cut if her son was to improve; the husbands who'd found their protective wings not large enough to shelter a stepson with so many problems; the siblings punished for tormenting him; the teachers lectured for misunderstanding him; the doctors disagreed with for failing to help him; the pets dispensed with for failing to please him; the employers begged for third and fourth chances; the landlords interceded with; the potential girlfriends importuned and manipulated . . . And all of it done to bring her to this moment when he was meant to *listen* at least, to murmur a single word of acknowledgement, to say to her, "You did your best, Mum," or perhaps even to grunt but, no, that asked too much of him, didn't it, that asked him to put out a little effort, that asked him to have some gumption, to care about having a life that *was* a life and not just an extension of hers because God *God* a mother was guaranteed something, wasn't she? Wasn't she at least guaranteed the knowledge that her children had the will to survive if left on their own?

But motherhood had guaranteed her absolutely nothing from her oldest son. Seeing this, Margaret felt her resolve finally crack.

She said "Adrian!" and when he didn't reply, she smacked him hard across the cheek. She shrieked, "I'm not a piece of furniture! Answer me at once! Adrian, if you don't—" She raised her hand again.

He caught it as she began to bring it down on his

face. He held it hard and kept it in his grasp as he stood. Then he tossed it to one side like so much rubbish and said, "You always make things worse. I don't want you here. Go home."

She said, "My God. How *dare* you . . ." But that was all she managed to utter.

He said, "Enough," and left her in the gallery.

So she'd come to her room, where she'd taken her suitcases from beneath the bed. She'd packed the first and she was on the second. She *would* go home now. She would leave him to his fate. She would give him the opportunity he apparently wanted to see how he liked coping with life on his own.

Two car doors slammed in quick succession on the drive, and Margaret went to her window. She'd heard the police leave not five minutes earlier, and she'd seen they hadn't taken the Fielder boy with them. She hoped they'd returned for him, having come up with a reason to lock the little beast away. But she saw below her a navy Ford Escort, its driver and passenger engaged in conversation over its bonnet.

The passenger she recognised from the reception that had followed Guy's funeral: the disabled, ascetic-looking man she'd seen lurking near the fireplace. His companion, the driver, was a red-headed woman. Margaret wondered what they wanted, who they'd come to see.

She was answered soon enough. For along the drive from the direction of the bay, Adrian came walking. The fact that the newcomers were turned his way told Margaret they'd probably seen him on the lane as they'd driven in and were in fact waiting for him to join them.

All her antennae went up. No matter her previous resolve to leave her son to his fate, Adrian talking to strangers while his father's murder went unsolved was Adrian in jeopardy.

Margaret was holding a nightdress preparatory to placing it in her suitcase. She tossed it on the bed and hurried from the room.

She heard the murmur of Ruth's voice from Guy's study as she headed for the stairs. She made a mental note to deal later with her sister-in-law's refusal to let her confront that little yobbo-in-training while the police were in attendance. Now there was a more pressing situation to handle.

Once outside, she saw that the man and his red-headed companion were walking to join her son. She called out, "Hello? Hello, there. May I help you with something? I'm Margaret Chamberlain."

She saw the brief flicker on Adrian's face and registered it as mild contempt. She almost left him to them—God knew he deserved to have to thrash round on his own—but she found she couldn't do it without knowing exactly what they wanted.

She caught up with the visitors and introduced herself again. The man said that he was called Simon Allcourt-St. James, that his companion was his wife, Deborah, and that the two of them had come to see Adrian Brouard. He nodded at Margaret's son as he imparted this bit, one of those I-know-that's-you nods that precluded Adrian's escape should he think about effecting one.

"What's this about?" Margaret said pleasantly. "I'm Adrian's mother, by the way."

"Do you have a few minutes?" Allcourt-St. James asked Adrian as if Margaret hadn't made her meaning clear.

She felt a bristling inside her but she tried to keep her voice as pleasant as before. "I'm sorry. We haven't time for a chat. I'm due to leave for England and as Adrian's going to need to drive me to—"

"Come inside," Adrian said. "We can talk in there."

"Adrian, darling," Margaret said. She looked at him long and hard, telegraphing her message: Stop being a fool. We have no idea who these people are.

He ignored her and led the way to the door. She had little choice but to follow, saying, "Well, yes. I suppose we do have a few minutes, don't we?" in an effort to portray a unified front.

Margaret would have forced them to conduct their chat on their feet in the stone hall where the air was cold and there were only hard chairs against the walls to sit on: the better to make their visit brief. Adrian, however, took them up to the drawing room. There, he had the good sense not to ask her to leave, and she ensconced herself in the middle of one of the sofas to make sure they felt her presence.

St. James—for so he asked to be called when she used his double-barreled surname—didn't seem to mind that she was going to witness whatever he had to say to her son. Neither did his wife, who joined Margaret on the sofa unbidden, and maintained a watchful presence as if she'd been told to make a study of the participants in their discussion. For his part, Adrian seemed unconcerned that two strangers had come to call upon him. His concern didn't alter when St. James began to talk about money—large sums of it—that was missing from his father's estate.

It took Margaret a moment to digest the implications behind what St. James was revealing and to realise the extent to which Adrian's inheritance had just been decimated. As paltry as it had been, considering what it *should* have been had Guy not cleverly prevented his son from benefiting from his fortune, it now appeared that the sum was far *less* than she had even supposed it would be.

Margaret cried out, "Are you actually telling us—"

"Mother," Adrian interrupted her. "Go on," he then said to St. James.

Apparently, the Londoner had come for more than just revealing the change in Adrian's expectations. Guy had been wiring his money out of Guernsey for the last eight or nine months, he told them, and St. James had come to see if Adrian knew anything about why his father had been sending large sums to an account in London with an address in Bracknell. He had someone working on this information in England, he informed Adrian, but if Mr. Brouard could make their job easier by giving them any details he himself might have . . . ?

That meaning was as clear as Swiss air, and before

Adrian could speak, Margaret said, "Precisely what is your job, Mr. St. James? Frankly—and please do understand that I don't intend to be rude—I don't see why my son should answer any of your questions, whatever they might be." This should have been enough to warn Adrian to keep his mouth shut, but naturally, it wasn't.

Adrian said, "I don't know why my father would have been wiring money anywhere."

"He wasn't sending it to you? For personal reasons? A business venture? Or any other reason? Debt of some kind?"

Adrian brought a crumpled packet of cigarettes from the pocket of his jeans. He dug one out and lit it. "My father didn't support my business ventures," he said. "Or anything else I did. I wanted him to. He didn't. That's it."

Margaret winced inwardly. He couldn't hear how he sounded. He didn't know what he looked like. And he *would* offer them more than they were asking. Whyever not when he had such a wonderful chance to spite her? They'd had words, and here was an opportunity to even the score, which he would take without bothering to think of the ramifications of what he said. He was maddening, her son.

St. James said to him, "So you've no connection with International Access, Mr. Brouard?"

"What's that?" Margaret asked cautiously.

"The recipient of all the wire transfers from Mr. Brouard's father. Over two million pounds in wire transfers, as it turns out."

Margaret tried to look interested rather than

aghast, but she felt as if a steel band were closing over her intestines. She forced herself to keep her gaze off her son. If Guy had actually sent him money, she thought, if Adrian had lied to her about this as well . . . Because *hadn't* International Access been the name Adrian had been contemplating for the company he'd wished to start? So typical of him to title the scheme before he had it up and running. But wasn't that it? His brainchild and the brilliant idea that would make him millions if only his father would act the part of venture capitalist? Yet Adrian had claimed his father had invested nothing in his idea, not so much as fifty pence. If that wasn't the case, if Guy had given him the money all along . . .

Anything that made Adrian look guilty of anything had to be dealt with at once. Margaret said, "Mr. St. James, I can assure you that if Guy sent money to England, he didn't send it to Adrian."

"No?" St. James sounded as pleasant as she herself was attempting to sound, but she didn't miss the look he exchanged with his wife, nor did she misinterpret what it meant. At the least, they thought it curious that she was speaking for an adult son who appeared perfectly capable of speaking for himself. At worst, they thought her an interfering bitch. Well, let them think what they would. She had more important concerns than how she appeared to two strangers.

"I expect my son would have told me about it. He tells me everything," she said. "Since he didn't tell me about his father sending him money, Guy didn't send him money. There you have it."

St. James said, "Indeed," and looked at Adrian. "Mr. Brouard? Perhaps for reasons other than business?"

"You've already asked that," Margaret pointed out.

"I don't think he's actually answered," St. James's wife said politely. "Not completely, that is."

And *she* was exactly the sort of woman Margaret particularly loathed: sitting there so placidly, all tumbling hair and perfect skin. She was probably delighted to be seen and not heard, like a Victorian wife who'd learned to lie back and contemplate England.

Margaret said, "See here," and Adrian interrupted. "I didn't have money off my dad," he said. "For any reason."

Margaret said, "There. Now, if there's nothing else, we have a great deal to do before I leave." She started to rise.

St. James's next question stopped her. "Is there anyone else, then, Mr. Brouard? Anyone else you know of in England whom he might have wanted to help out in some way? Someone who might be associated with a group called International Access?"

This was the limit. They'd given the bloody man what he wanted. Now what they wanted was his departure. "If Guy was sending his money anywhere," Margaret said archly, "there was probably a woman involved. I, for one, suggest you look into that. Adrian? Darling? Will you help me with my suitcases? Surely it's time we left."

"Any woman in particular?" St. James asked.

"I'm aware of his relationship with Mrs. Abbott, but as she's here on Guernsey . . . Is there someone in England we should be talking to?"

They would, Margaret saw, have to give him the name if they were to be rid of him. And far better that the name should come from them than that this man should dig it up for himself and use it later to tar her son. From them it could still sound innocent. From anyone else it would sound as if they had something to hide. She said to Adrian, attempting to make her tone casual if not *slightly* impatient in order to let the interlopers know they were imposing upon her time, "Oh . . . There was that young woman who came with you to visit your father last year. Your little chess-playing friend. What was her name? Carol? Carmen? No. Carmel. That was it. Carmel Fitzgerald. Guy was quite taken with her, wasn't he? They even had something of a fling to-gether, as I recall. Once your father knew you and she weren't . . . well, you know. Wasn't that her name, Adrian?"

"Dad and Carmel—"

Margaret kept going, to make certain the St. Jameses understood. "Guy liked the ladies, and as Carmel and Adrian weren't a couple . . . Darling, perhaps he was even more taken with Carmel than you thought. You were amused by it; I remember that. 'Dad's picked Carmel as his Flavour of the Month' you called it. I remember we laughed at the pun. But *is* there a chance that your father might have been fonder of her than you thought? You did tell me she spoke of it as something of a lark, but perhaps to Guy there was something more significant . . . ? It wouldn't have been exactly like him to buy someone's affection, but that's because he'd never had to. And in her case . . . Darling, what do you think?"

Margaret held her breath. She knew she'd spoken at too great a length, but there was no help for it. He had to be given the clues to how he was to portray the relationship between his father and the woman he himself had been meant to marry. All he had to do now was pick up the thread, say "Oh yes, Dad and Carmel. What a laugh that was. You need to talk to her if you're looking for where his money went," but he said none of it.

Instead, he said to the man from London, "It wouldn't be Carmel. They hardly knew each other. Dad wasn't interested. She wasn't his type."

In spite of herself, Margaret said, "But you told me . . ."

He glanced at her. "I don't think I did. You assumed. And why not? It was so logical, wasn't it?"

Margaret could see that the other two had no idea what Mother and son were talking about, but they were definitely interested in finding out. She was so flummoxed by the news her son was giving her, however, that she couldn't sift through it quickly enough to decide how much damage would come from having in front of them the conversation she needed to have with Adrian. God. How much *more* had he lied about? And if she so much as breathed the word *lie* in the presence of these Londoners, what on earth would they do with it? Where would they take it?

She said, "I jumped to conclusions. Your father always . . . Well, you know how he was round women. I assumed . . . I must have misunderstood . . . You did say she took it as a lark, though, didn't you? Perhaps you were talking about someone else and I merely thought you meant Carmel . . . ?"

He smiled sardonically, actually enjoying the spectacle of his mother back-pedaling from what she'd only just claimed. He let her dangle in the wind of her declarations for a moment longer before he interceded.

He said to the others, "I don't know about anyone in England, but Dad was having it off with someone on the island. I don't know who it was, but my aunt knows."

"She told you?"

"I heard them arguing about it. All I can tell you is it's someone young, because Ruth threatened to tell her father. She said if that's the only way she could stop Dad from carrying on with a girl, she'd do it." He smiled without humour and added, "He was a piece of work, my dad. I'm not surprised someone finally killed him."

Margaret closed her eyes, fervently wished something would transport her from the room, and cursed her son.

Chapter 25

ST. JAMES AND HIS wife didn't have to go in search of Ruth Brouard. She found them herself. She came to the drawing room, fairly glowing excitement. She said, "Mr. St. James, what very good fortune. I phoned your hotel, and they said you'd come here." She ignored her sister-in-law and her nephew, asking St. James to come with her, please, because everything was suddenly crystal clear and she meant him to know all about it straightaway.

"Shall I . . . ?" Deborah asked with a nod towards the outside of the house.

She was to come as well, Ruth told her when she learned her identity.

Margaret Chamberlain protested, saying, "What's this all about, Ruth? If it's to do with Adrian's inheritance—"

But Ruth continued to ignore her, going so far as to shut the door as she was speaking and then saying to St. James, "You'll have to forgive Margaret. She's rather . . ." She shrugged meaningfully, going on to add, "Do come with me. I'm in Guy's study."

Once there, she wasted no time with preambles.

"I know what he did with the money," she told them. "Here. Look. See for yourself."

Across her brother's desk, St. James saw, an oil painting lay. It was some twenty-four inches high and eighteen inches wide, and it was weighted on its ends by volumes from the bookshelves. Ruth touched it tentatively, as if it were a devotional object. She said, "Guy finally brought it home."

"What is it?" Deborah asked, standing near to Ruth and gazing down at the picture.

"The pretty lady with the book and the quill," Ruth said. "She belonged to my grandfather. To his father before him, to his father as well, and to every father before that as far as I know. She was meant to be Guy's eventually. And I expect he spent all that money to find her. There's nothing else . . ." Her voice altered, and St. James raised his head from the painting to see that behind her round-framed spectacles Ruth Brouard's eyes were full. "It's all there's left now, of them. You see."

She removed her glasses and, wiping her eyes on the sleeve of her heavy sweater, she went to a table that stood between two armchairs at one end of the room. There, she picked up a photograph and returned to them with it. "Here it is," she said. "You can see it in the picture. *Maman* gave this to us the night we left because everyone was in it. You can see them there. *Grandpère*, *Grandmère*, *Tante* Esther, *Tante* Becca, their brand-new husbands, our parents, us. She said, '*Gardez-la . . .*'" Ruth seemed to realise she'd gone to another place and time. She switched back to English. "I beg your pardon. She said, 'Keep this till we meet again, so you'll know us when you see us.' We didn't know that would never happen. And look. In the photo. There she is above the sideboard. The pretty lady with the book and the quill, where she always was. See the little figures behind her in the distance . . . all of them busy building that church. Some huge gothic thing that took one hundred years to complete and there she is, sitting there so . . . well, so serenely. As if she knows something about that church that the rest of us will never be privy to." Ruth smiled down at the painting fondly although her eyes glistened. *"Très cher frère,"* she murmured. *"Tu n'as jamais oublié."*

St. James had joined Deborah in looking at the photograph as Ruth Brouard spoke. He saw that, indeed, the painting before them on the desk was the same painting that was in the picture, and the photograph itself was the one he'd noticed the last time he was in this room. In it, an extended family gathered round a table for Passover dinner. They all smiled happily at the camera, at peace with a world that would soon destroy them.

"What happened to the painting?"

"We never knew," Ruth said. "We could only surmise. When the war ended, we waited. We thought for a time that they'd come for us, our parents. We didn't know, you see. Not at first. Not for quite some time because we kept hoping . . . Well, children do that, don't they? It was only later that we found out."

"That they'd died," Deborah murmured.

"That they'd died," Ruth said. "They'd remained

in Paris too long. They fled to the south thinking they'd be safe there, and that was the last we heard from them. They'd gone to Lavaurette. But there was no protection from the Vichy, was there? They betrayed the Jews when it was asked of them. They were worse than the Nazis, actually, because after all the Jews were French, the Vichy's own people." She reached for the photograph that St. James still held, and she gazed at it as she continued to talk. "At the end of the war, Guy was twelve, I was nine. It was years before he could go to France and find out what had happened to our family. We knew from the last letter we had that they'd left everything behind but the clothing they could fit into one suitcase each. So the pretty lady with the book and the quill remained, along with the rest of their belongings, in the safekeeping of a neighbour, Didier Bombard. He told Guy that the Nazis came for it all, as property of Jews. But of course he might have been lying. We knew that."

"How on earth would your brother have found it, then?" Deborah asked. "After all these years?"

"He was a very determined man, my brother. He would have hired as many people as he needed: first to search for it and then to acquire it."

"International Access," St. James noted.

Ruth said, "What's that?"

"It's where his money went, the money he had transferred out of his account here on Guernsey. It's a company in England."

"Ah. So that's it." She reached for a small lamp that lit the top of her brother's desk, and she moved it over, the better to shine more brightly upon the painting. "I expect that's who found it. It makes sense, doesn't it, when you think about the enormous collections of art that are bought and sold every day in England. When you talk to them, I imagine they'll tell you how they tracked this down and who was involved in getting it back for us. Private investigators, most likely. Perhaps a gallery as well. He would have had to *buy* it back, of course. They wouldn't have just handed it over to him."

"But if it's yours . . ." Deborah said.

"How could we prove it? We had only that one family photo as proof, and who would look at a photo of a family dinner and decide the picture hanging on the wall in the background is the same as this one?" She gestured to the painting before them on the desk. "We had no other documents. There *were* no other documents. This had always been in the family—the pretty lady with the book and the quill—and other than this one photo, there was no way to prove it."

"Testimony of people who'd seen it in your grandfather's house?"

"They're all dead now, I presume," Ruth said. "And besides Monsieur Bombard, I wouldn't have known who they were anyway. So Guy had no other way to retrieve this but to buy it from whoever had it, and that's what he did, depend upon it. I expect it was his birthday gift to me: to bring back to the family the only thing left of the family. Before I died."

In silence, they looked down upon the canvas stretched across the desk. That the painting was old there could be no doubt. It looked Dutch or Flemish to St. James, and it was a mesmerising work, a thing of timeless beauty that had no doubt at one time been an allegory both for the artist and for the artist's patron.

"I wonder who she is," Deborah said. "A gentlewoman of some sort, because look at her robes. They're very fine, aren't they? And the book. It's so large. To have had a book like that . . . even to have been able to read at that time . . . She must have been quite rich. Perhaps she's a queen."

"She's just the lady with the book and the quill," Ruth said. "That's enough for me."

St. James stirred himself from his contemplation of the picture, saying to Ruth Brouard, "How did you happen upon this this morning? Was it here in the house? Among your brother's things?"

"Paul Fielder had it."

"The boy your brother mentored?"

"He gave it to me. Margaret thought he'd stolen something from the house because he wouldn't let anyone near his rucksack. But this is what he had in it, and he handed it over to me straightaway."

"When was this?"

"This morning. The police brought him over from the Bouet."

"Is he still here?"

"I expect he's on the grounds somewhere. Why?" Ruth's face grew grave. "You're not thinking he stole this, are you? Because really, he wouldn't have. It's not in his nature."

"May I take this with me, Miss Brouard?" St.

James touched the edge of the painting. "For a while. I'll keep it quite safe."

"Why?"

He said only, "If you wouldn't mind," by way of answer. "You needn't worry. I'll get it back to you quickly."

She looked at the painting as if loath to part with it, as she no doubt was. After a moment, though, she nodded and then removed the books from either end of the canvas. She said, "It needs to go into a frame. It needs to be properly hung."

She handed the canvas over to St. James. He took it from her and said, "I expect you knew your brother was involved with Cynthia Moullin, didn't you, Miss Brouard?"

Ruth switched off the light that was on the desk and moved it back to its original position. For a moment, he thought she might not answer, but she finally said, "I discovered them together. He said he would have told me eventually. He said he meant to marry her."

"You didn't believe him?"

"Too many times, Mr. St. James, my brother claimed he'd finally found her. 'She's the one,' he would say. 'This woman, Ruth, is definitely the one.' He always believed it at the moment . . . because he always mistook that frisson of sexual attraction for love, the way many people do. Guy's trouble was that he couldn't seem ever to rise above that. And when the feeling faded—as these things do—he always assumed it was the death of love and not merely a chance to *begin* to love."

"Did you tell the girl's father?" St. James asked.

Ruth walked from the desk to the model of the wartime museum on its central table. She brushed nonexistent dust from its roof. "He left me no choice. He wouldn't end it. And it was wrong."

"Because?"

"She's a girl, scarcely more than a child. She's had no experience. I was willing to turn a blind eye when he played round with older women *because* they were older. They knew what they were doing, no matter what they thought he was doing. But Cynthia . . . This was too much. He took things too far. He left me no choice but to go to Henry. It was the only way I could think of to save them both. Her from heartbreak and him from censure."

"That didn't work, did it?"

She turned from the museum model. "Henry didn't kill my brother, Mr. St. James. He didn't lay a hand on him. When he had the chance to, he couldn't bring himself to do it. Believe me. He's not that sort of man."

St. James saw how necessary it was for Ruth Brouard to believe in this fact. If she allowed her thoughts to go in any other direction, the responsibility she'd face would be excruciating. And what she had to bear already was excruciating enough.

He said, "Are you certain of what you saw from your window the morning your brother died, Miss Brouard?"

"I saw her," she said. "Following him. I saw her."

"You saw someone," Deborah corrected her gently. "Someone in black. From a distance."

"She wasn't in the house. She followed him. I know this."

"Her brother's been arrested," St. James said. "The police seem to think they made a mistake earlier. Is there a chance you could have seen her brother instead of China River? He would have had access to her cloak, and if someone who'd earlier seen her wearing it and then saw him in it . . . It would be logical to assume you were looking at China." St. James avoided Deborah's gaze as he spoke, knowing how she would react to the intimation that either of the Rivers was involved in this case. But there were still issues that had to be dealt with, no matter Deborah's feelings. "Did you search the house for Cherokee River as well?" he asked her. "Did you check his bedroom as you said you checked China's?"

"I *did* check hers," Ruth Brouard protested.

"Adrian's room? Did you check there? What about your brother's room? Did you look for China there?"

"Adrian didn't . . . Guy and that woman never . . . Guy *didn't* . . ." Ruth's words died off.

Which was all the answer that St. James needed.

When the drawing room door closed upon their visitors, Margaret wasted no time in getting to the bottom of matters with her son. He'd started to follow their lead and leave the room himself, but she got to the door ahead of him and blocked his way. She said, "Sit down, Adrian. We have things to talk about."

She heard the menace in her voice and she wished she could remove it, but she was too damn tired of having to draw upon her decidedly finite reserves of maternal devotion, and there was nothing for it now but to face the facts: Adrian had been a difficult child from the day of his birth, and difficult children often turned into difficult adolescents who in their turn became difficult adults.

She'd long seen her son as a victim of circumstances, and she'd used those circumstances to explain away his every oddity. Insecurity brought about by the presence of men in his life who clearly didn't understand him was how she had rationalised years of sleepwalking and fugue states from which only a tornado could have roused her son. Fear of being abandoned by a mother who'd remarried not once but three times was how she excused his failure to make a life on his own. Early childhood trauma clarified that single terrible incident of public defecation that had resulted in his expulsion from university. There had always been a reason for everything in Margaret's eyes. But she could not come up with a reason for his lying to the very woman who'd given her life to make his more livable. She wanted something in exchange for that. If she couldn't have the revenge she yearned for, an explanation would do.

She said again, "Sit down. You're not going anywhere. We have something to discuss."

He said, "What?" and Margaret was infuriated that he sounded not wary but actually irritated, as if she were presuming on his valuable time.

"Carmel Fitzgerald," she said. "I intend to get to the bottom of this."

He met her eyes with his own, and she saw he had the temerity actually to look insolent, like an adolescent blatantly caught in an act that has been forbidden him, an act he very much *wanted* to be caught in as a mark of a defiance he refused to verbalise. Margaret felt her palms itch with the desire to slap that expression from Adrian's face: that slightly raised upper lip and those flaring nostrils. She contained herself and walked to a chair.

He remained by the door but he didn't leave the room. He said, "Carmel. All right. What about her?"

"You told me that she and your father—"

"You assumed. I told you sod all."

"Don't you dare use that sort of—"

"Sod all," he repeated. "Jack shit, Mother. Bum-fucking nothing."

"Adrian!"

"You *assumed*. You've spent your whole life comparing me with him. And that being the case, why would anyone prefer the son to the father?"

"That isn't true!"

"Funnily enough, though, she did prefer me. Even with him there. You could say it was because she wasn't his type and she knew it—not blonde, not submissive the way he liked them, not appropriately awed by his money and his power. But the fact is she wasn't impressed by him, no matter the charm he poured on. She knew it was just a game, and it was, wasn't it: the clever talk, the anecdotes, the probing questions while giving a woman all of his attention. He didn't want her, not really, but if she'd been willing, he would've gone for it because that's what he always did. Second nature. You know. Who better than you? Only she wasn't willing."

"Then why on earth did you tell me . . . did you imply . . . And you can't deny it. You *did* imply. Why?"

"You'd already worked it out in your head. Carmel and I ended things after we came here to see him, and what other reason could there possibly have been? I'd caught him with his hands down her knickers—"

"Stop that!"

"And I'd been forced to end it. Or she'd ended it, liking him better than me. That was the only thing you could work out, wasn't it? Because if it wasn't that, if I hadn't lost her to Dad, then it would have to be something else, and you didn't want to think what that was because you'd been hoping all of it was finally passed."

"You're talking nonsense."

"So here's what it was, Mother. Carmel was willing to take just about anything. She wasn't a looker and she didn't have much spark to her either. She wasn't likely to hook up with more than one bloke in her life, so she was willing to settle. And having settled, she wasn't likely to go after other men. In short, she was perfect. You saw it. I saw it. Everybody saw it. Carmel saw it, too. We were made for each other. But there was only one problem: a compromise she wasn't able to make."

"What sort of compromise? What are you talking about?"

"A nocturnal compromise."

"Nocturnal? You sleepwalked? She was frightened? She didn't understand that these things—"

"I peed the bed," he cut in. His face blazed humiliation. "All right? Happy? I peed the bed."

Margaret attempted to keep the aversion from her voice as she said, "That could have happened to anyone. A night of too much drink . . . A nightmare, even . . . The confusion of being in a house not your own . . ."

"Every night we were here," he said. "Every night. She was sympathetic, but who can blame her for calling things off? Even a mousy little chess player without a hope in hell of *ever* having another man draws the line somewhere. She'd been willing to put up with the sleepwalking. The night sweats. The bad dreams. Even my occasional descent into the fog. But she drew the line at having to sleep in my piss, and I can hardly blame her. I've been sleeping in it myself for thirty-seven years, and it gets unpleasant."

"No! You were past that. I *know* you were past that. Whatever happened here in your father's house, it was an aberration. It won't happen again because your father is dead. So I'll phone her. I'll tell her."

"That eager, are you?"

"You deserve—"

"Let's not lie. Carmel was your best chance of being rid of me, Mother. It just didn't work out the way you hoped."

"That isn't true!"

"Isn't it?" He shook his head in amused derision. "And here I was thinking you wanted no more lies." He turned back to the door, no mother there any longer to stop him leaving the room. He opened it. He said over his shoulder as he stepped from the drawing room, "I'm finished with this."

"With what? Adrian, you can't—"

"I can," he said. "And I do. I am what I am, which is, let's face it, exactly what you wanted me to be. Look where that's brought us both, Mother. Right to this moment: the two of us stuck with each other."

"Are you blaming me?" she asked him, aghast at how he was deciding to interpret her every loving gesture. No thanks for protecting him, no gratitude for guiding him, no acknowledgement for interceding for him. My God, if nothing else, she was at *least* owed a nod of his head in the direction of her tireless interest in his affairs. "Adrian, are you blaming me?" she demanded again when he didn't reply.

But all the answer she received was a bark of laughter. He closed the door upon her and went on his way.

"China said she wasn't involved with him," Deborah said to her husband once they were out on the drive. She weighed every word. "But she could be . . . perhaps not wanting to tell me. Embarrassed to have had a fling with him because she's on the rebound from Matt. She can't actually've been proud of that.

Not for moral reasons, but because . . . well, it's rather sad. It's . . . it's quite needy in a way. And she'd hate that about herself: being needy. She'd hate what that says about her."

"It would explain why she wasn't in her own room," Simon agreed.

"And it gives someone else a chance—someone who knew where she was—to pick up her cloak, that ring, a few of her hairs, her shoes . . . It would have been easy."

"Only one person could have done it, though," Simon pointed out. "You see that, don't you?"

Deborah glanced away. "I can't believe that of Cherokee. Simon, there *are* others, others with opportunity and, better yet, with motive. Adrian for one. Henry Moullin for another."

Simon was silent, watching a small bird darting among the bare branches of one of the chestnut trees. He said her name on a breath—much like a sigh—and Deborah felt the difference in their positions acutely. He had information. She had none. Clearly, he attached it to Cherokee.

Because of all this, Deborah felt herself harden under his tender gaze. She said, "What's next, then?" with some formality.

He accepted the shift in her tone and her mood without protest, saying, "Kevin Duffy, I think."

Her heart leaped at this alteration in direction. "So you *do* think there's someone else."

"I think he bears talking to." Simon was holding the canvas he'd taken from Ruth Brouard and glanced down at it now. "In the meantime, will you track down Paul Fielder, Deborah? He's somewhere nearby, I expect."

"Paul Fielder? Why?"

"I'd like to know where he got this painting. Did Guy Brouard give it to him for safekeeping or did the boy see it, take it, and give it to Ruth only when he was caught with it in his rucksack?"

"I can't imagine he stole it. What would he have wanted with it? It's not the sort of thing one expects a teenager to steal, is it?"

"It's not. But on the other hand, he doesn't seem to be an ordinary teenager. And I've got the impression the family's struggling. He might have thought the painting was something he could sell to one of the antiques shops in the town. It bears looking into."

"D'you think he'll tell me if I ask him?" Deborah said doubtfully. "I can't exactly accuse him of taking the painting."

"I think you can manage to get people to talk about anything," her husband replied. "Paul Fielder included."

They parted then, Simon heading for the Duffys' cottage and Deborah remaining at the car, trying to decide which direction to go in her search for Paul Fielder. Considering what he'd been through already that day, she reckoned he'd want a bit of peace and quiet. He'd be in one of the gardens, she suspected. She would have to check them one by one.

She began with the tropical garden since it was nearest to the house. There, a few ducks swam placidly in a pond, and a chorus of larks chattered in an elm, but no one was either watching or listening, so she checked the sculpture garden next. This held the burial spot of Guy Brouard, and when Deborah found its weather-worn gate standing open, she was fairly certain she would find the boy inside.

This turned out to be the case. Paul Fielder sat on the cold ground next to his mentor's grave site. He was gently patting round the bases of a score of pansies that had been planted along the edge of the grave.

Deborah wove her way through the garden to join him. Her footsteps crunched along the gravel and she did nothing to mute the sound of her approach. But the boy didn't raise his head from the flowers.

Deborah saw that his feet were sockless, that he wore slippers instead of shoes. A smudge of earth was on one of his thin ankles, and the bottoms of his blue jeans were dirty and frayed. He was inadequately dressed for the coolness of the day. Deborah couldn't believe he wasn't shivering.

She mounted the few moss-edged steps to the grave. Instead of joining the boy, however, she went to the arbor just beyond him, where a stone bench stood beneath winter jasmine. The yellow flowers cast a mild fragrance in the air. She breathed it in and watched the boy minister to the pansies.

"I expect you miss him awfully," she finally said. "It's a terrible thing to lose someone you love. A friend, especially. We never seem to have enough of them. At least, that's how it's always seemed to me."

He bent over a pansy and pinched off a wilted

blossom. He rolled it between his thumb and his index finger.

Deborah saw from a flicker of his eyelids that he was listening, though. She continued. "I think the most important thing about friendship is the freedom it gives you to be who you are. Real friends just accept you, with all of your warts. They're there in good times. They're there in bad times. You can always trust them to speak the truth."

Paul tossed the pansy away. He pulled at nonexistent weeds among the rest of the plants.

"They want the best for us," Deborah said. "Even when we don't know what's best for ourselves. I expect that's the sort of friend Mr. Brouard was to you. You're lucky to have had him. It must be awful with him gone."

Paul got to his feet at this. He wiped his palms down the sides of his jeans. Afraid he might run off, Deborah plunged ahead speaking, trying to find a way into the silent boy's confidence.

"When someone's gone like that—especially like . . . I mean the terrible way he left . . . the way he died—we'd do just about anything to bring them back to us. And when we can't and when we *know* that we can't, then we want to have something of theirs, as a means of holding on to them for just a while longer. Till we can let them go."

Paul shuffled his slippered feet in the gravel. He wiped his nose on the sleeve of his flannel shirt and shot Deborah a wary look. He turned his head hastily and fixed his eyes on the gate some thirty yards away. Deborah had shut it behind her and she silently berated herself for having done so. He would feel trapped by her. As a result, he wouldn't be very likely to speak.

She said, "The Victorians had the right idea. They made jewellery from dead people's hair. Did you know that? It sounds macabre, but when you think about it, there was probably great comfort in having a brooch or a locket that contained a small part of someone they loved. It's sad that we don't do that any longer, because we still want something, and if a person dies and doesn't leave us a part of them . . . what can we do but take what we can find?"

Paul stopped the movement of his feet. He stood perfectly still, like one of the sculptures, but a smudge of colour appeared on his cheek like a thumbprint against his fair skin.

Deborah said, "I'm wondering if that's what happened with the painting you gave to Miss Brouard. I'm wondering if Mr. Brouard showed it to you because he meant to surprise his sister with it. Perhaps he said it was a secret that only the two of you would keep. So you knew that no one else was aware he had it."

The smudges of colour flamed unevenly towards the boy's ears. He glanced at Deborah, then away. His fingers clutched at the tail of his shirt, which hung limply out of his blue jeans at one side and which was just as worn.

Deborah said, "Then when Mr. Brouard died so suddenly, perhaps you thought you'd have that picture as a memento. Only he and you knew about it, after all. What would it hurt? Is that what happened?"

The boy flinched as if struck. He gave an inarticulate cry.

Deborah said, "It's all right. We've got the painting back. But what I wonder—"

He spun on his toe and fled. He shot down the steps and along the gravel path as Deborah rose from the stone bench and called his name. She thought she'd lost him, but midway across the garden he stopped next to a huge bronze nude of a squatting, heavily pregnant woman with a melancholy expression and great, pendulous breasts. He turned back to Deborah, and she saw him chew on his lower lip and watch her. She took a step forward. He didn't move. She began to walk towards him the way one would approach a frightened fawn. When she was some ten yards from him, he took off again. But then he stopped at the garden gate and looked back at her another time. He pulled the gate open and left it open. He struck off to the east, but he didn't run.

Deborah understood that she was meant to follow.

Chapter 26

ST. JAMES FOUND KEVIN Duffy round the side of
the cottage, labouring in what appeared to be a dor-
mant vegetable garden. He worked the earth with a
heavy pitchfork but stopped what he was doing
when he saw St. James.

He said, "Val's gone to the big house. You'll find
her in the kitchen."

"It's you I'd like to talk to, actually," St. James said.
"Do you have a moment?"

Kevin's gaze went to the canvas St. James was
holding, but if he recognised it, he gave no sign.
"Take your moment, then," he said.

"Did you know Guy Brouard was your niece's
lover?"

"My nieces are six and eight years old, Mr. St.
James. Guy Brouard was many things to many people. But pedophilia wasn't among his interests."

"Your wife's niece, I mean. Cynthia Moullin," St.
James said. "Did you know Cynthia was having a relationship with Brouard?"

He didn't answer, but his glance moved over to
the manor house, which was answer enough.

"Did you speak to Brouard about it?" St. James asked.

No answer again.

"What about the girl's father?"

"I can't help you with any of this," Duffy said. "Is that all you've come to ask me?"

"No, actually," St. James said. "I've come to ask you about this." Carefully, he unrolled the old canvas.

Kevin Duffy drove the tines of the pitchfork into the ground, but he left the implement standing upright in the soil. He approached St. James, wiping his hands on the seat of his jeans. He looked at the painting, and a deep breath whistled between his lips.

"Mr. Brouard apparently went to a great deal of trouble to get this back," St. James said. "His sister tells me it's been missing from the family since the nineteen-forties. She doesn't know where it came from originally, she doesn't know where it's been since the war, and she doesn't know how her brother got it back. I'm wondering if you can shed light on any of this."

"Why would I—"

"You've two shelves of art books and videos in your sitting room, Mr. Duffy, and a degree in art history hanging on your wall. That suggests you might know more about this painting than the average groundskeeper."

"I don't know where it's been," he replied. "And I don't know how he got it back."

"That leaves the last," St. James pointed out. "So you do know where it came from originally?"

Kevin Duffy hadn't stopped looking at the painting. After a moment he said, "Come with me," and he went into the cottage.

By the door, he kicked off his muddy boots and took St. James through to the sitting room. He flipped on a set of overhead lights that shone directly upon his books and he reached for a pair of spectacles that lay on the arm of a threadbare chair. He moved along his collection of art volumes until he had the one he wanted. He pulled this from the shelf, sat, and turned to its index. Finding what he was looking for, he riffled through pages till he had the appropriate one. He looked at it long before he turned the volume round on his lap to face St. James. He said, "See for yourself."

What St. James saw was not a photo of the painting—as he'd thought he'd be seeing, considering Duffy's reaction to it—but instead it was a drawing, a mere study for a future painting. It was partially coloured, as if the artist had intended to check which hues would work best together in the final piece. He'd done only her gown, though, and the blue he'd chosen for it was the same as that which had ended up on the painting. Perhaps, having made a quick decision about the rest of the work and finding it unnecessary to colour the drawing in further, the artist had simply gone on to the actual canvas itself, the canvas St. James now held in his hands.

The composition and figures in the drawing in

the book were identical to the painting that Paul Fielder had given to Ruth Brouard. In them both, the pretty lady with the book and the quill sat placidly in the foreground while in the background a score of workers heaved round the stones that formed a massive Gothic cathedral. The only thing different between the study and the finished work was that someone along the line had given the former a title: It was called *St. Barbara* and anyone wishing to see it would find it among the Dutch masters in Antwerp's Royal Museum of Fine Art.

"Ah," St. James said slowly. "Yes. When I saw it, I thought it was significant."

"Significant?" Kevin Duffy's tone blended reverence with incredulity. "That's a Pieter de Hooch you've got in your hands. Seventeenth century. One of the three Delft masters. Until this moment, I don't expect anyone knew that painting even existed."

St. James looked down at what he held. He said, "Good God."

"Look at every art history volume you can get your hands on and you'll never find that painting," Kevin Duffy said. "Just the drawing, the study. That's all. Far's anyone knew, de Hooch never made the painting itself. Religious subjects weren't his thing, so it's always been assumed he was just dabbling and then put the effort aside."

"As far as anyone knew." St. James saw how Kevin Duffy's assertion corroborated Ruth's claim. The painting, she had said, had always been in her family, as long as anyone could remember. Generation after generation, each father had passed it on to his children: a family heirloom. Because of this fact, probably no one had thought of taking the painting to an expert to learn exactly what it was. It was simply, as Ruth herself had said, the family's picture of the pretty lady with the book and the quill. St. James told Kevin Duffy what Ruth Brouard had called it.

"Not a quill," Kevin Duffy said. "She's holding a palm. It's the symbol of a martyr. You see it in religious paintings."

St. James examined the painting more closely and saw that indeed it appeared to be a palm frond, but he also saw how a child, uneducated in the symbols that were used in paintings of this period and looking upon the picture over time, could have interpreted it as a long and elegant quill pen. He said, "Ruth told me her brother went to Paris when he was old enough, after the war. He went to collect the family's belongings but everything they'd owned was gone. I assume that would have included the painting."

"That would have gone first," Duffy agreed. "The Nazis were intent on grabbing up what they deemed Aryan art. 'Repatriating' was what they called it. Truth was the bastards were taking everything they could get their hands on."

"Ruth seems to think the family's neighbour—a Monsieur Didier Bombard—had access to their belongings. As he wasn't Jewish, if he was the one who had the painting, why would it have ended up in German hands?"

"Lots of ways art ended up with the Nazis. Not

just outright theft. There were French go-betweens, art dealers who acquired for them. And German dealers who put adverts in Paris newspapers, asking for art to be brought round for prospective buyers in this or that hotel. Your Monsieur Bombard could have sold the painting that way. If he didn't know what it was, he might have taken it along to one of them and been grateful to get two hundred francs in exchange."

"From there, though? Where would it have gone?"

"Who's to know?" Duffy said. "At the end of the war, the Allies set up investigation units to get art back to their owners. But it was everywhere. Göring alone had trainloads of it. But millions of people were dead—entire families wiped out with no one left to claim their possessions. And if you *were* left alive but you couldn't prove something belonged to you, you were out of luck." He shook his head. "That's what happened to this, I expect. Or someone with sticky fingers from one of the Allied armies stashed it in his duffel and took it home as a souvenir. Or someone in Germany—a single owner perhaps—bought this from a French dealer during the war and managed to keep it hidden when the Allies invaded. The point is if the family was dead, who was to know who owned what? And how old was Guy Brouard at the time? Twelve? Fourteen? At the end of the war he wouldn't have been thinking of getting back his family's belongings. He would have thought of that years later, but by then this would have been long gone."

"And it would have taken years more to find it," St. James said. "Not to mention an army of art historians, conservationists, museums, auction houses, and investigators." Plus a small fortune, he added to himself.

"He was lucky to find it at all," Duffy said. "Some pieces went missing during the war and never turned up again. Others are still being argued over. I can't think how Mr. Brouard proved this was his."

"He appears to have bought it back rather than attempted to prove anything," St. James explained. "There's an enormous amount of money that's gone missing from his accounts. It's been wired to London."

Duffy raised an eyebrow. "That's the case?" He sounded doubtful. "I suppose he could have picked it up through an estate auction. Or it could have turned up in an antiques shop in a country village or in a street market. Hard to believe no one would have known what it was, though."

"But how many people are experts in art history?"

"Not so much that," Duffy said. "But anyone can see it's old. You'd think they'd've taken it to be valued somewhere along the line."

"But if someone actually nicked it at the end of the war...? A soldier picks it up... where? Berlin? Munich?"

"Berchtesgaden?" Duffy offered. "Nazi bigwigs all had homes there. And it was crawling with Allied soldiers at the end of the war. Everyone went for the pickings."

"All right. Berchtesgaden," St. James agreed. "A

soldier picks this up there when the plundering's going on. He takes it home to Hackney and hangs it up above the sofa in the semidetached and never thinks another thing of it. There it stays till he dies and it gets handed on to his kids. They've never thought much about anything their parents own, so they sell up. Auction. Car boot sale. Whatever. This gets bought at that point. It ends up in a stall. On Portobello Road, for example. Or Bermondsey. Or a shop in Camden Passage. Or even in the country, as you suggested. Brouard's had people looking for it for years, and when they see it, they snatch it up."

"I suppose it could have happened that way," Duffy said. "No. Truth is, it *has* to have happened that way."

St. James was intrigued by the decisive quality of Duffy's statement. He said, "Why?"

"Because it's the only way Mr. Brouard could have ever got this back. He had no way to prove it was his. That meant he had to buy it back. He couldn't've have got it from a Christie's or Sotheby's, could he, so it would have had to be—"

"Hang on," St. James said. "Why not a Christie's or Sotheby's?"

"He would have been outbid. Some place like the Getty with bottomless pockets. An Arab oil magnate. Who knows who else."

"But Brouard had money . . ."

"Not money like this. Not money enough. Not with Christie's or Sotheby's knowing exactly what they had their hands on and the whole art world bidding to get it."

St. James looked at the painting: eighteen inches by twenty-four inches of canvas, oil paint, and undeniable genius. He said slowly, "Exactly how much money are we talking about, Mr. Duffy? What d'you reckon this painting's worth?"

"At least ten million pounds, I'd say," Kevin Duffy told him. "And that's before the bidding opens."

Paul took Deborah round the back of the manor house, and at first she thought he was heading for the stables. But he didn't give these a second glance. Instead, he continued across the yard that separated the stables from the house and gave way to some shrubbery, which he plunged through as well.

Following him, she found herself on a wide expanse of lawn beyond which a woodland of elms stood. Paul ducked into these and Deborah increased her pace so as not to lose him. When she got to the trees, she saw there was an easy path to follow, the ground made spongy by the heavy fall of leaves that lay upon it. She wound along this until ahead of her in the distance she caught a glimpse of a rough stone wall. She saw Paul clambering up. She thought she might lose him for good at this point, but when he reached the top, he paused. He glanced back as if to see if she was still following him, and he waited until she'd reached the bottom of the wall herself, at which point he extended his hand to her and helped her over to the other side.

There Deborah saw that the careful forms and details of *Le Reposoir* gave way to a large but disused paddock, where weeds, bushes, and brambles grew rampant nearly to waist height and a path beaten through them led to a curious mound of earth. She wasn't surprised when Paul dropped from the wall and scurried along this path. At the mound of earth, he headed right and skirted its base. She hastened to follow.

She was wondering how an odd lump of land could hide a painting, when she saw the carefully placed stones that ran along the bottom of the mound. She realised then that she was looking at no natural hillock, but, rather, something that had been built by man in prehistory.

The path to the right was as beaten down as had been the access from the wall, and a short distance round the perimeter of the mound, she found Paul Fielder working the combination on a lock that held closed a worn and crooked oak door, which would allow them inside. He appeared to hear her, for he used his shoulder to shelter the lock's combination from her view. With a click and a snap he had it off, and he used his foot to shove the door open while he carefully put the lock in his pocket. The resulting opening into the mound was no more than three and a half feet high. Paul crouched, crab-walked through it, and quickly disappeared into the darkness.

There was nothing for it but to run off and report back to Simon like a dutiful little wife or to follow the boy. Deborah did the latter.

Inside the door, a narrow and musty passage pressed down on her, less than five feet from stone floor to stone ceiling. But after some six yards the passage opened and heightened to a central vault, dimly illuminated from the daylight outside. Deborah stood upright, blinked, and waited for her eyes to adjust. When they did, she realised she was within a large chamber. It was tightly constructed entirely of granite—floor, walls, and ceiling—with what looked like a sentry stone at one side in which one's imagination could almost see the ancient carving of a warrior with his weapon ready to ward off interlopers. An additional piece of granite raised off the floor some four inches seemed to serve as a form of altar. A candle stood near it, but this was not lit. Nor was the boy anywhere inside.

Deborah had a bad moment. She pictured herself locked up in this place with no one knowing exactly where she was. She allowed herself a fervent curse for having blithely followed Paul Fielder, but then she stilled her nerves and she called Paul's name. In reply she heard the scratch of a match. Light flared from a fissure to her right in a misshapen stone wall. She saw that it indicated the presence of yet another chamber, and she went in this direction.

The aperture that she found was not more than ten inches wide. She slid through it, brushing close to the damp coolness of the exterior stone wall, and saw that this secondary chamber had been fitted out with plenty of candles and a small folding camp bed. At its head was a pillow; at its foot was a carved wooden box; in the middle Paul Fielder was sitting with a book of matches in one hand and a lit candle in the other. This he set about fixing into a niche

formed by two of the stones in the external wall.
When he'd managed this, he lit a second candle and
dripped wax from it to fix it to the floor.

"Is this your secret place?" Deborah asked him
quietly. "Is this where you found the picture, Paul?"

She thought it unlikely. It seemed more reasonable to assume this was a hiding place for something
else entirely, and she was fairly certain what that
something else was. The camp bed gave mute testimony to that, and when Deborah reached for the
wooden box at the foot of this bed and opened its
top, she had affirmation for what she'd assumed.

The box contained condoms of various types:
ribbed, smooth, coloured, and flavoured. There
were enough to suggest that regular use was made of
this place for sex. Indeed, it was the perfect spot for
assignations: hidden from view, probably forgotten,
and suitably fanciful for a girl who thought of herself
and her man as potentially star-crossed. This, then,
would be where Guy Brouard had brought Cynthia
Moullin for their trysts. The only question was why
he had apparently brought Paul Fielder here as well.

Deborah glanced at the boy. In the candlelight she
couldn't help noticing the cherubic quality to his
smooth-skinned face and the way his fair hair curled
round his head like something from a Renaissance
painting. There was a decidedly feminine quality to
him, one that was emphasised by his delicate features
and fine-boned body. While it had seemed true that
Guy Brouard was a man whose interests appeared to
confine itself to the ladies, Deborah knew she

couldn't discount the possibility that Paul Fielder, too, had been the object of Brouard's fancy.

The boy was looking at the open box on Deborah's lap. Slowly, he took up a handful of the little foil packages and looked at them as they lay in his palm. Then as Deborah said gently, "Paul, were you and Mr. Brouard lovers?" he shoved the condoms down into the box and slammed its carved top home.

Deborah looked at him and repeated her question.

The boy turned away abruptly, blew out the candles, and disappeared through the fissure through which they'd both just come.

Paul told himself that he wouldn't cry because it didn't mean anything. Not really. He was a man and, from what he'd learned from Billy, his own dad, the telly, the occasional nicked *Playboy,* and the lads at school—when he actually went to school—a man did these things all the time. That he'd done it here in their special place . . . Because he had to have done it here, hadn't he? What else could those shiny little packets mean if not that he'd brought someone else here, brought a woman here, brought another person here who was important enough to him to share his secret place?

Can you keep this our special secret, Paul? If I take you inside, can you promise me never to tell anyone that this place is here? I expect it's been completely forgotten over time. I'd like to keep it that way as long as I can. Are you willing . . . ? Can you promise?

Of course he could. He could and he did.

He'd seen the camp bed, but he'd thought Mr. Guy had used it for naps, for camp-outs, maybe meditating or praying. He'd seen the wooden box as well, but he'd not opened it because he'd been taught from childhood and from rough experience never to put his mitts on something that wasn't his. Indeed, he'd nearly stopped the red-headed lady from opening it herself just now. But she'd had it on her lap and had its lid lifted before he could snatch it from her. When he'd seen what was in it . . .

Paul wasn't stupid. He knew what they meant. He'd reached for them anyway because he'd actually thought they might disappear like something one would reach for in a dream. But they remained decidedly real, concrete little declarations of what this place had really meant to Mr. Guy.

The lady had spoken but he'd not heard the words, just the sound of her voice as the room spun round him. He had to get away and not be seen, so he'd blown out the candles and fled.

But of course, he couldn't leave. He had the lock and if nothing else, he *was* responsible. He couldn't leave the door hanging open. He had to lock up because he'd promised Mr. Guy . . .

And he wouldn't cry because it was bloody *stupid* to cry. Mr. Guy was a man and a man had needs and he got them filled somewhere and that was the end of it. This had nothing to do with Paul or with his friendship with the man. They were mates from the first and mates to the end, and even the fact that he'd shared this place with someone else didn't change that, did it? *Did* it?

After all, what had Mr. Guy said? It shall be our secret, then.

Had he said no one else would ever share that secret? Had he indicated that no one else would ever have enough importance to be included in the knowledge of this place? He hadn't, had he? He hadn't lied. So to be upset now . . . to be in a tizzy . . .

How d'you like it, arse bandit? How's he give it to you, then?

That's what Billy thought. But that had never been the case. If Paul had ever longed to be closer, it was a longing that sprang from wanting to be *like,* not wanting to be *one.* And being *like* came from sharing, which was what they'd done here.

Secret places, secret thoughts. A place to talk and a place to be. That's what this is for, my Prince. That's how I use it.

He'd used it for more than that, apparently. But that didn't have to make it less sacred unless Paul allowed that to happen.

"Paul? Paul?"

He heard her coming round the end of the inner chamber. She was feeling her way as she would have to do with the candles suddenly extinguished. She'd be all right once she got into the main chamber, though. There were no candles lit here, but the daylight outside filtered in, creating a shaft of illumination down the main passage that eased within like an encroaching fog bank when it reached the interior of the mound.

"Are you here?" she asked. "Ah. There you are. You gave me a real fright. I thought . . ." She laughed quietly, but Paul could tell she was nervous and ashamed of being nervous. He knew how that felt.

"Why did you bring me here?" she asked him. "Is it . . . well, *is* it about that picture?"

He'd nearly forgotten. The sight of that box, open and displaying and telling him things . . . He'd nearly forgotten. He'd wanted her to know and to understand because someone had to. Miss Ruth didn't think he'd stolen anything from *Le Reposoir*, but there would always be suspicion in everyone else's eyes if he didn't somehow explain where he'd got the painting. He couldn't bear seeing it among them—that suspicion—because *Le Reposoir* was his sole refuge on the island and he didn't want to lose it, couldn't bear to lose it, couldn't face having to be home with Billy or at school listening to taunts and jeers with no hope of escape and nothing on earth ever to look forward to again. But to tell someone from the estate itself about this place would be to betray the secret he'd sworn to keep forever: where this dolmen was. He couldn't do that so all he could do was to tell a stranger who wouldn't care and wouldn't ever come here again.

Only now . . . He couldn't show her the *exact* spot. He had his own secret to protect. Yet he needed to show her something, so he went to the low altar stone and he knelt just in front of the crevice at its base behind it, which ran along its length. He brought the candle out from that crevice and lit it. He gestured downward so the lady could see.

"Here?" she said. "The painting was here?" She looked from the shallow depression to him and it felt like she was studying his face, so Paul nodded solemnly. He showed her how it might have lain in the depression and how, if it had done so, it would not have been visible to anyone who did not come to the far side of the altar stone and kneel as Paul himself was kneeling.

"How odd," the lady said quietly. She offered him a kind smile, however. She said, "Thank you, Paul. You know, I don't think you were ever going to keep that painting for yourself, were you? I've a feeling you're not that type of person at all."

"Mr. Ouseley, it's our job to make this transition as easy for you as we can," the girl said to Frank. She sounded more sympathetic than he would have thought possible in someone her age. "We're here to help you through your loss. So anything you'd *like* us to handle from the mortuary, we *can* handle from the mortuary. We're here for your convenience. I encourage you to take advantage of that."

What Frank thought of all this was that she was far too young to be the person who did the meeting and greeting, the arrangement making, and the selling of talents provided by Markham & Swift Funeral Services. She looked about sixteen, although she was probably somewhere in her twenties, and she had introduced herself as Arabella Agnes Swift, oldest great-granddaughter of the founder. She'd clasped his hand warmly and had taken him into her office which, with consideration for the grief-stricken people with whom she generally met, was as unofficelike as possible. It was fitted out like a grandmother's sitting room with a three-piece suite and a coffee table and family pictures on the mantel of a faux fireplace in which an electric fire glowed. Arabella's picture was among them. In it, she wore the robes of a university graduate. Hence, Frank's conclusion about her real age.

She was waiting politely for him to reply. She'd discreetly positioned a leather volume on the coffee table, within which were doubtless photographs of the coffins from which the bereaved could choose. She held a flip-up spiral notebook on her lap, but she didn't pick up the pen that she'd laid neatly across it when she'd joined him on the sofa. She was every inch the modern professional and not a single inch the lugubrious Dickensian character that Frank had expected to find behind the doors of Markham & Swift Funeral Services.

"We can also do the ceremony here in our chapel, if that's what you prefer," she said, her tone quite kind. "Some people aren't regular churchgoers. Some prefer a more agnostic approach to a funeral."

"No," Frank finally said.

"So you will be holding the service in a church? If I could make a note of the name? The minister as well?"

"No ceremony," Frank said. "No funeral. He wouldn't want that. I want him . . ." Frank stopped himself. *I want* was not the way to put it. "He preferred cremation. You handle that, don't you?"

"Oh yes. We can do, of course," Arabella assured him. "We'll make all the arrangements and transport the body to the States Crematorium. You'll just need to pick out the urn. Let me show you . . ." She leaned forward and he caught the scent of her perfume, a pleasant fragrance that he knew was probably a comfort to those who needed comfort. Even he, who didn't need her condolences, was reminded from it of being held close to his mother's breast. How did scent-makers know what odour would produce that quick trip backwards in memory? he wondered.

"There are different sorts," Arabella went on. "Your choice can be governed by what you want to do with the ashes. Some people find it a comfort to keep them, while others—"

"No urn," Frank interrupted. "I'll just take the ashes as they come. In a box. In a bag. However they come."

"Oh. Well, of course." Her face was utterly dispassionate. It was not for her to comment upon what the loved ones of the departed did with the departed's remains, and she'd been trained well enough to know that. Frank's decision would not bring Markham & Swift the business they were probably used to, but that was not Frank's problem.

So the arrangements were made quickly and with a minimum of fuss. In very little time, Frank found himself climbing behind the wheel of the Peugeot, negotiating his way down Brock Road and afterwards up towards St. Sampson's harbour.

It had been an easier process than he had expected. He'd left the cottage first, going to the other two adjoining cottages to check on their contents and to lock their doors for the night. Returning then, he'd gone to his father, who sprawled unmoving at the base of the stairs. He'd cried out, "Dad! God! I told you *never* to climb . . ." as he rushed to his side. He found his father's breathing was shallow, nearly nonexistent. He paced the floor and looked at his watch. After ten minutes, he went to the phone and punched in emergency. He made his report. Then he waited.

Graham Ouseley died before the ambulance got to *Moulin des Niaux*. As his soul passed from earth to judgement, Frank found himself weeping for both of them and for what they had lost, which was how the paramedics came upon him: crying like a child and cradling his father's head, where a single bruise marked the spot where his forehead had struck the stairs.

Graham's personal physician was in quick attendance, clamping a heavy paw on Frank's shoulder. He would have gone quickly, Dr. Langlois informed him. He probably had a heart attack trying to get up the stairs. Too much strain, you know. But considering how little bruising there was on the face . . . Chances were very good that he was unconscious when he hit the wooden step and dead shortly thereafter with no knowledge even of what had suddenly happened to him.

"I'd just gone to lock up the cottages for the night," Frank explained, feeling the tears on his cheeks drying to burn the cracked skin round his eyes. "When I came back . . . I'd always told him *never* to try . . ."

"They're independent, these old blokes," Langlois said. "I see this all the time. They know they're not spry but they're not about to be a burden to anyone, so they just don't ask for what they need when they need it." He squeezed Frank's shoulder. "Very little you could have done to change that, Frank."

He'd stayed while the 'medics brought in their trolley and he'd lingered even after the body was borne away. Frank had felt compelled to offer him tea, and when the doctor confided, "Wouldn't say no to a whisky," he brought forth and poured two fingers of Oban single malt and watched the other man down it appreciatively.

Before he left, Langlois said, "The suddenness of it all when a parent goes is a shock, no matter how much we prepare ourselves. But he was . . . what? Ninety?"

"Ninety-two."

"Ninety-two. He would have been prepared. They are, you know. That lot, that age. They had to be prepared half a century ago. I expect he thought any day he lived after nineteen-forty was a gift from God."

Frank desperately wanted the man to be gone, but

Langlois prattled on, telling him what he least wanted to hear: that the mould into which such men as Graham Ouseley had been poured at birth had long since been broken; that Frank should rejoice at having had such a father and for so many years, indeed into his own senior age; that Graham had been proud of having such a son with whom he could live in peace and harmony even unto death; that Frank's tender and unceasing devotion had meant much to Graham . . .

"Treasure that," Langlois told him solemnly. Then he'd gone, leaving Frank to climb the stairs to his room, to sit on the bed, to lie on it eventually, and to wait dry-eyed for the future to arrive.

Now, having reached South Quay, he found himself trapped in St. Sampson. Behind him traffic from The Bridge was backing up as shoppers left the commercial precinct of the town and headed for their homes while in front of him, a tailback extended all the way to Bulwer Avenue. There, at the junction, an articulated lorry had apparently made too sharp a turn into South Quay and was jackknifed in an impossible position with too many vehicles trying to get past it, too little space in which to manoeuvre, and too many people hanging about offering advice. Seeing this, Frank jerked the Peugeot's wheel to the left. He eased out of the traffic and onto the edge of the quay, where he parked facing the water.

He got out of the car. The dressed granite of the harbour walls enclosed few boats at this time of year, and the December water that lapped against the stones had the advantage of being free from the petrol slicks of high summer left by careless casual boaters who were the constant bane of local fishermen. Across the water at the north end of The Bridge, the shipping yard sent forth its cacophony of pounding, welding, scraping, and cursing as craft brought out of the water for the winter were overhauled for the future season. While Frank knew what each sound was and how each related to the work being done on the boats in the yard, he let it stand in place of something else altogether, transforming the pounding to the steady march of jackboots on cobblestones, the scraping to the rasp of a slide arm as a rifle was cocked, the cursing to the orders given—understandable in any language—when it was time to fire.

He couldn't rid his head of the stories, even now, when he most needed to: fifty-three years of them, told over and over but never worn out and never unwelcome until this moment. Yet still, they came on, whether he wanted them or not: 28 June 1940, 6:55 P.M. The steady drone of approaching aircraft and the steadier rise of dread and confusion in those gathered at the harbour in St. Peter Port to see the mail steamer off, as was their simple custom, and in those whose lorries were queued up to deposit their loads of tomatoes into the holds of the cargo vessels . . . There were too many people in the area and when the six planes came, they left the dead and the wounded behind them. Incendiary bombs dropped upon the lorries and high explosives blew them into the sky, while machine guns strafed the crowd without regard. Men, women, and children.

Deportations, interrogations, executions, and enslavements all came after that. As did the immediate winnowing out of drops of Jewish blood and the countless proclamations and mandates. Hard labour for this and death by firing squad for that. Control of the press, control of the cinema, control of information, control of minds.

Black marketeers rose up to make a profit from the misery of their fellows. Unlikely heroes developed from farmers with radio receivers hidden in their barns. A people, reduced to scavenging for food and scavenging for fuel, marked time in circumstances that seemed forgotten by the rest of the world as the Gestapo moved among them, watching, listening, and waiting to pounce on anyone who made a single wrong move.

People died, Frankie. Right here on this island, people suffered and died because of the Hun. And some people fought him only way that they could. So don't you ever forget that, lad. You walk proud. You come from stock that knew the worst of times and lived to tell about them. Isn't just any lad on this island can say that about what happened here, Frank.

The voice and the memories. The voice continually *instilling* the memories. Frank could shake neither one, even now. He felt he'd be haunted the rest of his life. He could drown himself in the Lethe, but that would not suffice to wipe clean his brain.

Fathers were not supposed to lie to their sons. If

they chose to become fathers in the first place, it should be to pass along the life's truths that they'd learned at the knee of experience. Whom else could the son of a man trust if not the man himself?

That was what it came down to for Frank as he stood alone on the quayside, observing the water but seeing instead a reflection of the history that had ruthlessly moulded a generation of islanders. It came down to trust. He'd given it as the only gift a child can ever give to the distant and awesome figure of his parent. Graham had taken this trust happily and then abused it mightily. What then remained was the frail latticework of a relationship built of straw and glue. The rough wind of revelation had destroyed it. The insubstantial structure itself might never have been.

To have lived more than half a century pretending he was not responsible for the deaths of good men . . . Frank did not know how he would ever scrape together a fond feeling for his father from the foul detritus which that single fact left in Graham Ouseley's wake. He *did* know he could not do it now. Perhaps someday . . . If he reached the same age . . . If he looked on life differently at that point in time . . .

Behind him, he heard the line of traffic begin to move at last. He turned and saw that the lorry at the junction had finally managed to disentangle itself from its situation. He climbed back into his own car then and eased into the stream of vehicles leaving St. Sampson. He headed with them towards St. Peter Port, picking up speed at last when he cleared the industrial area in Bulwer Avenue and burst from it onto the road that followed the elongated crescent of *Belle Greve* Bay.

He had another stop to make before returning to the Talbot Valley, so he kept on south with the water on his left and St. Peter Port rising like a grey terraced fortress on his right. He wound up through the trees in *Le Val des Terres* and pulled into Fort Road not fifteen minutes after the time he'd agreed to appear at the Debieres' house.

He would have preferred to avoid another conversation with Nobby. But when the architect had phoned him and had been so insistent, habitual guilt produced sufficient motivation for Frank to say, "Very well, I'll call in" and to name the time he'd most likely turn up.

Nobby answered the door himself and took Frank into the kitchen, where in the apparent absence of his wife, he was getting the boys' tea. The room was unbearably hot, and Nobby was greasy-faced with sweat. The air was heavily laden with the odour of a batch of fish fingers previously burnt. From the sitting room came the noise of a computer game in operation, with suitable explosions rhythmically sounding as the player skilfully obliterated bad guys.

"Caroline's in town." Nobby bent to inspect a baking sheet that he eased out of the oven. The current set of fish fingers steamed upon it, producing a further malevolent odour. He grimaced. "How can they stand these things?"

"Anything their parents hate," Frank noted.

Nobby shoved them onto the work top and used

a wooden spoon to push them onto a plate. He grabbed a bag of frozen chips from the fridge and dumped these onto the baking sheet, which he returned to the oven. In the meantime, on the hob a pan boiled enthusiastically. It sent a cloud of steam to hover like the ghost of Mrs. Beeton above them.

Nobby stirred this and lifted out a spoonful of peas. They were unnaturally green, as if dyed. He looked at them doubtfully, then dropped them back into the boiling water. He said, "She should be here for this. She's better at it. I'm hopeless."

Frank knew that his former pupil had not phoned him for a cooking lesson, but he also knew he wouldn't be able to stand it much longer in the overheated kitchen. So he took over, seeking out a colander into which he dumped the peas, then covering them and the odious fish fingers with foil while the chips were cooking. This done, he opened the kitchen window and said, "What did you want to see me about, Nobby?" to the other man, who'd gone to set the table for his sons.

"She's in town," he said.

"You mentioned that."

"She's applying for a job. Ask me where."

"All right. Where?"

Nobby gave a laugh, utterly devoid of humour. "Citizens Advice Bureau. Ask me doing what."

"Nobby . . ." Frank was tired.

"Writing their bloody pamphlets," Nobby said with another laugh, this one high and sounding wild. "She's gone from *Architectural Review* to Citizens Advice. Credit that to me. I told her to resign.

Write your novel, I told her. Go after your dream. Just like I did."

"I'm sorry it happened," Frank said. "You can't possibly know how sorry."

"I don't expect I can. But here's the real kick in the arse: It was all for nothing. Right from the first. Have you realised that? Or did you know it all along?"

Frank frowned. "How? What was . . . ?"

Nobby had been wearing one of his wife's aprons, and he took this off and laid it on the back of a kitchen chair. He looked crazily as if he were enjoying their conversation, and his enjoyment increased with what he next revealed. The plans that Guy had arranged to have delivered from America were false, he said. He'd seen them himself, and they weren't legitimate. From what he could tell, they weren't even plans for a museum. So what did Frank Ouseley think of that?

"He didn't intend to build a museum," Nobby informed him. "It was all a game of build-'em-up-knock-'em-down. And we were the nine pins. You, me, Henry Moullin, and anyone else who would've been involved. Puff up our expectations with his big plans and then watch us squirm and beg as we get deflated: That was the story. The game went only as far as me, though. Then Guy got chopped and the rest of you were left hanging and wondering how to get the project up and running without him here to give his 'blessing.' But I wanted you to know. No sense in my being the only one to have reaped the benefit of Guy's unusual sense of humour."

Frank struggled to digest this information. It ran contrary to everything he'd known about Guy and everything he'd experienced as the man's friend. Guy's death and the terms of his will had put paid to the museum. But that there had never been the intention of building it . . . Frank couldn't afford to think that now. Or ever, for that matter. The cost was too great.

He said, "The plans . . . The plans that the Americans delivered . . . ?"

"Phony as hell," Nobby said pleasantly. "I saw them. A bloke from London brought them here. I don't know who drew them or what they're for, but what they aren't for is a museum down the lane from St. Saviour's Church."

"But he had to have . . ." What? Frank wondered. He had to have what? Known that someone would look closely at the plans? When? That night? He'd unveiled a skilled drawing of a building which he'd declared was the selected design, but no one had thought to ask him about the plans themselves. "He must have been duped," Frank said. "Because he did intend to build that museum."

"With what money?" Nobby asked. "As you pointed out, his will didn't leave a penny towards building anything, Frank, and he didn't give Ruth the high sign that she was to fund it if something happened to him. No. Guy wasn't anyone's dupe. But we were. The lot of us. We played right along."

"There's got to be some sort of mistake. A misunderstanding. Perhaps he'd made a bad investment recently and lost the funds he intended to build with.

He wouldn't have wanted to admit to that . . . He wouldn't have wanted to lose face in the community, so he carried on as if nothing had changed so no one would know . . ."

"You think so?" Nobby made no effort to hide the incredulity in his voice. "You actually think so?"

"How else can you explain . . . ? Wheels had already been set in motion, Nobby. He would have felt responsible. You'd left your job and set yourself up. Henry had invested in his glassmaking. There were stories in the paper and expectations in people's minds. He would have to confess or pretend to carry on if he'd lost that money, hoping that people would lose interest over time if he dragged his feet long enough."

At the table, Nobby crossed his arms. "That's what you actually think?" His tone suggested that the former student had become the present master. "Yes. Indeed. I can see how you might need to hold on to that belief."

Frank thought he saw the sudden realisation flash on Nobby's face: the fact that he himself—possessor of thousands of items of ostensibly beloved wartime memorabilia—did not want that material ever to see the light of day. And while that was indeed the truth of the matter, there was no way Nobby Debiere could have known it. The matter was too complicated for him to be able to suss out. As far as he knew, Frank Ouseley was just another disappointed member of the group who'd hung their hats on a scheme that had come to nothing.

Frank said, "I suppose I'm reeling from all this. I

just can't believe . . . There has to be an explanation somewhere."

"I've just given it to you. I only wish Guy were here so he could enjoy the result of his machinations. Look. Let me show you." Nobby went to a corner of the work top, where it appeared that the family kept the day's post. Unlike the rest of the house, it was a messy area, with stacks of letters, magazines, catalogues, and telephone directories all piled together. From the bottom of this pile, Nobby brought out a single sheet and handed it over.

Frank saw that it was the copy and the artwork for an advertisement. In it, a cartoon Nobby Debiere stood at a draughtsman's table on which was spread out some sort of drawing. Around his cartoon feet lay partially unrolled scrolls on which other drawings appeared. The copy introduced his new enterprise as Bertrand Debiere's Repairs, Refurbishments, and Renovations and the address of the establishment was right there on Fort Road.

"I've had to let my secretary go, of course," Nobby said with a forced cheer that was chilling to hear. "So she's out of work as well, which I'm sure would have delighted Guy no end had he only lived to see it happen."

"Nobby . . ."

"And I'll be working from home, as you see, which is excellent, of course, since Caroline might be spending most of her time in town. I burned my bridges with the firm when I resigned, but no doubt in time I'll be able to get taken on by another if I haven't been blackballed altogether. Yes. It's wonderful, isn't it, to see how everything's turning out?" He took the advert from Frank's hand and shoved it, crumpled, beneath the telephone directory.

"I'm sorry," Frank said. "The way it all turned out . . ."

"It's for the best, no doubt," Nobby said. "For someone."

Chapter 27

ST. JAMES FOUND RUTH Brouard in her conservatory. It was larger than it had appeared when he'd
first seen it on the day of the funeral, and the air was
humid and warm. As a result, the glass of the conservatory dripped condensation. Water from the windows and from an irrigation system made a constant
pattern of splatters as drops fell upon the broad
leaves of tropical plants and upon the brick path that
wound among them.

Ruth Brouard was in the centre of the glass
house, where the bricks widened out to form a circular seating area large enough to accommodate a
chaise longue, one white wicker chair, a similar
table, and a small pond in which lily pads floated.
She was on the couch with her legs resting on a tapestry cushion. A tray of tea sat on the table next to
her. A photograph album lay open upon her lap.

Ruth said to him, "Forgive the heat," with a nod
to the electric fire that was set up on the bricks,
adding to the conservatory's warmth. "I find it a
comfort. It actually doesn't do much to alter the
course of things, but it feels like it does." Her glance

went to the painting he held loosely rolled, but she said nothing about it. Instead, she invited him to pull a chair near so that she could show him "who we were."

The album, he saw, served as a document of the Brouards' years in care in England. In it, pictures depicted a boy and girl in wartime and in postwar London, always together, always staring seriously into the camera's lens. They grew older but their solemn expressions barely altered, posing in front of this door, or that gate, in this garden, before that fireplace.

"He never forgot me," Ruth Brouard said as she turned the pages. "We weren't ever with the same family together and I was terrified every time he left: that he wouldn't return, that something might happen to him and I wouldn't be told. He'd just stop appearing one day. But he said that couldn't happen and even if it did, I would know. I would sense it, he said. I would feel a shift in the universe, so *unless* I felt that, I wasn't to worry." She closed the album and set it to one side. "I didn't feel it, though, did I? When he went to the bay, Mr. St. James, I didn't sense it at all."

St. James handed her the painting. "But what good fortune to have found this," she said quietly as she took it. "In a small measure, it brings my family back." She laid the painting on top of the album and looked at him. "What else?" she asked.

He smiled. "You're certain you're not a witch, Miss Brouard?"

"Perfectly," she replied. "You do need something more from me, don't you?"

He admitted that he did. It was clear to him from her words and her actions that she had no idea of the value of the painting that her brother had managed to find for her. He didn't do anything to change that for the moment. Somehow, he knew its importance to her wouldn't be altered by learning it was the work of a master.

He said, "You may be right about your brother having spent most of his money to locate this. But I'd like to check through his accounts to be sure. You've records here, haven't you?"

She said she had, that Guy kept his accounts in his study. If Mr. St. James wanted to follow her, she'd be happy to show him where. They took the painting and the photo album with them, although it was fairly obvious that Ruth Brouard would have innocently left both in the conservatory till she returned to fetch them.

In her brother's study, she went round switching on lamps against the fading daylight. Surprisingly, from a cabinet next to his desk, she brought out a leather account book of the sort one would expect to find a Bob Cratchit using. She saw St. James's reaction to this, and she smiled.

"We ran the hotel business on computers," she said. "But Guy was old-fashioned when it came to his personal finances."

"It does seem . . ." St. James searched for a euphemism.

She supplied it. "Antiquated. Not like Guy at all. But he never caught on to computers. Push-button phones and microwave ovens were as far as he went before technology got away from him. But this is easy enough to follow, you'll see. Guy kept good records."

As St. James sat at the desk and opened the ledger, Ruth brought out two more. Each of them, she explained, covered three years of her brother's expenses. These were not great, since the vast majority of the money was in her name, and it was from her own accounts that the estate had always been maintained.

In possession of the most recent ledger, St. James scanned it to see what the last three years had been like for Guy Brouard. It didn't take long to note a pattern in how he spent his money during that time, and that pattern was spelled A-n-a-ï-s A-b-b-o-t-t. Brouard had put out funds for his lover time and again, paying for everything from cosmetic surgery to property taxes to the mortgage on her house to holidays in Switzerland and Belize to her daughter's tuition at modeling school. Beyond that, he'd listed expenses for a Mercedes-Benz, for ten sculptures identified by artist and title, for a loan to Henry Moullin that he'd described as "furnace," and for what appeared to be additional loans or gifts to his son. More recently, he'd apparently purchased a plot of land in St. Saviour, and he'd made payments to Bertrand Debiere as well as to De Carteret Cabinet Design, Tissier Electric, and Burton-Terry Plumbing.

From those, St. James concluded that Brouard had indeed intended to build the wartime museum initially, even to employ Debiere as its designer. But all of the payments that could have been even remotely related to producing a public building had ceased nine months ago. Then, in place of the careful accounting Brouard had been making, a list of numbers finished off the page and began another, ultimately being bracketed off together but without the single recipient being identified. Nonetheless, St. James had a fairly good idea of what that identification was: International Access. The figures corresponded to those the bank had provided Le Gallez. He noted that the final payment—the largest of all—had apparently been wired out of Guernsey on the very day that the River siblings had come to the island.

St. James asked Ruth Brouard for a calculator, which she handed over from a drawer in her brother's desk. He added up the list of those debits that had been applied to the unnamed recipient. They totaled over two million pounds.

"How much money did your brother begin with when you two settled here?" he asked Ruth. "You told me he put nearly everything into your name but he did hold something back for his own expenses, didn't he? Have you any idea how much?"

"Several million pounds," she said. "He thought he could live quite well off the interest once the money was invested properly. Why? Is there something . . . ?"

She didn't add the word *wrong* since it was hardly

necessary. From the very first, there had been little enough right about her brother's post-mortem finances.

The telephone ringing saved St. James from having to make an immediate reply. Ruth answered it from the extension on the desk and handed the receiver over to St. James.

"You've not endeared yourself to your hotel's receptionist," Thomas Lynley said to him from London. "She's encouraging you to purchase a mobile. I'm passing along that message."

"Received. Have you unearthed something?"

"I have indeed. It's an intriguing situation, although I don't expect you're going to be pleased to hear about it. It's going to throw a spanner."

"Let me guess. There's no International Access in Bracknell."

"Dead on. I rang an old mate of mine from Hendon. He works Vice in that area. He went round to the address that's listed as International Access and found a tanning salon. They'd been in that location for eight years—the tanning business being evidently quite good in Bracknell—"

"I'll note that for future reference."

"—and they claimed to have not the slightest idea what my man was talking about. This prompted further discussion with the bank. I mentioned FSA to them and they became willing to part with some information about the International Access account. Apparently, money wired to that account from Guernsey was then wired onward some forty-eight hours later to a place called Jackson Heights in Queens, New York."

"Jackson Heights? Is that—"

"The location, not the name on the account."

"Did you get a name out of them?"

"Vallera and Son."

"Some sort of business?"

"Apparently so. But we don't know what sort. Neither does the bank. Theirs is not to question why, et cetera. But it's looking like . . . well, you know what it's looking like: something to whet the American government's appetite for investigation."

St. James studied the pattern on the rug beneath his feet. He became aware of Ruth Brouard next to him, and he looked up to see her watching him. Her expression was earnest but beyond that, he could read nothing from her face.

He rang off on Lynley's assurance that wheels were in motion to try to get someone from Vallera & Son on the telephone, although he cautioned St. James not to expect any cooperation from the other side of the Atlantic. "If this is what it appears to be, we may be at a dead end unless we involve a strong-arming agency over there. Internal Revenue. FBI. New York City Police."

"*That* should do it," St. James commented acerbically.

Lynley chuckled. "I'll be in touch." Then he was gone.

When he'd replaced the receiver, St. James took a moment to consider everything that Lynley's information implied. He set it next to everything else he knew, and he didn't much like the result he came up with.

"What is it?" Ruth Brouard finally asked him.

He stirred himself. "I'm wondering if you still have the package that the museum plans came in, Miss Brouard."

At first, Deborah St. James didn't see her husband when she came through the shrubbery. It was dusk and she was thinking about what she'd seen inside the prehistoric mound that Paul Fielder had taken her to. More than that, she was thinking what it meant that the boy had known the combination to the lock and had been so determined to keep that combination shielded from her view.

So she didn't see Simon until she was nearly upon him. He was engaged with a rake on the far side of the three outbuildings closest to the manor house. He was going through the estate's rubbish, having apparently upended four bins.

He stopped when she called his name. To her question, "Career change to Bennie the Binman?" he smiled and said, "It's a thought, although I'd confine myself to the rubbish of pop stars and politicians. What have you discovered?"

"All you need to know and more."

"Paul spoke to you about the painting? Well done, my love."

"I'm not sure Paul ever actually speaks," she admitted. "But he took me to the place where he'd found it, although I thought he meant to lock me inside at first." She went on to explain the location and nature of the mound Paul had taken her to, including the information about the combination lock and the contents of the two stone chambers. She concluded with "The condoms . . . the camp bed . . . It was obvious what Guy Brouard used it for, Simon. Although, to be honest, I don't quite understand why he just didn't have his flings in the house."

"His sister was there most of the time," St. James reminded her. "And as the flings involved a teenager . . ."

"In the plural, if Paul Fielder was one of them. I suppose that's it. It's all so unsavoury, isn't it?" She glanced back towards the shrubbery, the lawn, the trail through the woods. "Well, believe me, they were out of sight there. You'd have to know exactly where the dolmen is on the property to be able to find it."

"Did he show you where in the dolmen?"

"Where he'd found the painting?" When Simon nodded, Deborah explained.

Her husband listened, his arm balancing his weight against the rake like a resting farmhand. When she'd completed her description of the altar stone and the crevice behind it and he'd clarified that the crevice was indeed in the floor itself, he shook his head. "That can't be right, Deborah. The painting's worth a fortune." He told her everything he'd learned from Kevin Duffy. He ended by saying, "And Brouard would have known it."

"He would have known it was a de Hooch? But how? If the painting was in his family for generations, if it had been handed down from father to son as a family heirloom . . . How would he have known? Would *you* have known?"

"Never. But if nothing else, he would have known what he spent to get the painting back, which was something in the vicinity of two million pounds. I can't believe after having gone to that expense and to whatever trouble it entailed to find the canvas that he would have deposited it even for five minutes inside a dolmen."

"But if it was locked . . . ?"

"That's not the point, my love. We're talking about a seventeenth-century painting. He wasn't going to put it in a hiding place where either the cold or the damp could have harmed it."

"So you think Paul's lying?"

"I'm not saying that. I'm just saying it's unlikely that Brouard put the painting in a prehistoric chamber. If he wanted to hide it—in anticipation of his sister's birthday, as she claims, or for any other reason—there are dozens of places inside his own house where he could have stowed it with far less danger of its being damaged."

"Then someone else . . . ?" Deborah said.

"I'm afraid that's the only thing making any sense." He went back to work with the rake.

"What are you looking for, then?" She heard the trepidation in her voice, and she knew he heard it as well, because when he looked at her, his eyes had grown darker, the way they always did when he was worried.

He said, "The way it came to Guernsey."

He turned back to the rubbish and continued to spread it out till he'd found what he was apparently looking for. It was a tube some thirty-six inches in length with an eight-inch diameter. At both ends its circumference was ringed by a serious-looking metal washer whose sides lapped down to fasten snugly and immovably against the tube itself.

Simon rolled it from the rubbish and bent awkwardly to pick it up. Turned on its side, it revealed a slice from the top to the bottom in the surface of the tube. The slice had been widened to a gaping incision with frayed edges where the external skin of the tube had been forced open to reveal its real structure. What they had was a tube secreted within another tube, and it didn't take a nuclear scientist to deduce what the resulting hidden inner space had been used for.

"Ah," Simon murmured. He looked at Deborah.

She knew what he was thinking because she was thinking it herself and she didn't want to think it. She said, "May I have a look . . . ?" and she took it from him gratefully when he handed the tube over without comment.

Inspected, the tube revealed what Deborah thought was a most important detail: The only way into the inner compartment was clearly through the outer shell. For the rings on each end of the tube had been fixed so immovably in place that prising them off would have damaged the entire structure irreversibly. It would also have told anyone else who looked at the tube—namely, the recipient of it if not customs officials—that someone had tampered with it. Yet there was not a single mark round the metal rings on either end. Deborah pointed this out to her husband.

"I see that," he said. "But you understand what that means, don't you?"

Deborah felt flustered by the intensity of his scrutiny and the intensity of his question. She said, "What? That whoever brought this to Guernsey didn't know—"

"Didn't open it in advance," he interrupted. "But that doesn't mean that person didn't know what was in it, Deborah."

"How can you say that?" She felt wretched. Her inner voice and all of her instincts were shouting *no*.

"Because of the dolmen. Its presence in the dolmen. Guy Brouard was killed for that painting, Deborah. It's the only motive that explains everything else."

"That's too convenient," she countered. "It's also what we're meant to believe. No"—as he started to speak—"do listen, Simon. You're saying they knew in advance what was in it."

"I'm saying one of them knew, not both."

"All right. One. But if that's the case—if they wanted—"

"He. I'm saying *he* wanted," her husband put in quietly.

"Yes. Fine. But you're being single-minded in this. If he—"

"Cherokee River, Deborah."

"Yes. Cherokee. If he wanted the painting, if he knew it was in the tube, why on earth bring it here to Guernsey? Why not just disappear with it? It doesn't make sense that he'd bring it all this way and *then* steal it. There's another explanation altogether."

"Which is?"

"I think you know. Guy Brouard opened this package and showed that painting to someone else. And that was the person who killed him."

Adrian was driving too fast and far too close to the centre of the road. He was passing other cars indiscriminately and slowing for nothing. In short, he was driving with the deliberate intent to unnerve her, but Margaret was determined not to be provoked. Her son was so lacking in subtlety. He wanted her to demand that he drive differently so that he could continue to drive exactly as he pleased and thus prove to her once and for all that she had no suzerainty over him. It was just the sort of thing one would expect of a ten-year-old engaged in a game of I'll-show-you.

Adrian had infuriated her enough already. It took every ounce of self-control Margaret had not to lash out at him. She knew him well enough to understand that he wasn't about to part with any information which he'd decided to withhold because at this point he would believe that parting with anything was an indication that she had won. Won what, she didn't know and could not have said. All she had *ever* wanted for her eldest son was a normal life with a successful career, a wife, and children.

Was that too much to hope and plan for? Margaret certainly didn't think so. But the last few days had shown her that her every attempt to smooth the way for Adrian, her every intercession on his behalf, the excuses she'd made for everything from sleepwalking to inadequate bowel control were just so many pearls in a food trough frequented by swine.

Very well, she thought. So be it. But she would not leave Guernsey till she'd sorted him out about one thing. Evasions were fine. Looked at one way, they could even be construed as a pleasing sign of a long-delayed adulthood. But outright lies were unacceptable, now and always. For lies were the stuff of the terminally weak-minded.

She saw now that Adrian had probably been lying to her most of his life, both by action and by implication. But she'd been so caught up in her efforts to keep him away from the malign influence of his father that she'd accepted his version of every event in which he'd got caught up: from the supposedly accidental drowning of his puppy the night before her second marriage to the recent reason for his engagement's termination.

That he was still lying to her was something about which Margaret had little doubt. And this International Access business spoke of the greatest untruth he'd yet delivered.

So she said, "He sent you that money, didn't he? Months ago. What I'm wondering is what you spent it on."

Unsurprisingly, Adrian replied with "What are you talking about?" He sounded indifferent. No. He actually sounded *bored*.

"Betting, was it? Card playing? Idiotic stock market gambles? I know there's no International Access because you haven't left the house in more than a year for anything other than visiting your father or seeing Carmel. But perhaps that's it. Did you spend it on Carmel? Did you buy her a car? Jewellery? A house?"

He rolled his eyes. "Of course. That's exactly what I did. She agreed to marry me, and it must have been because I laid on the dosh like jelly on toast."

"I'm not joking about this," Margaret said. "You've lied about asking your father for money, you've lied about Carmel and her involvement with your father, you've allowed me to believe that your engagement ended because you wanted 'different things' from the woman who'd previously agreed to marry you . . . Exactly when haven't you lied?"

He glanced her way. "What difference does it make?"

"What difference does *what* make?"

"Truth or lies. You see only what you want to see. I just make that easier for you." He barreled past a minivan that was trundling along ahead of them. He sat on the horn as they overtook it and regained their own lane mere inches—it seemed—from an oncoming bus.

"How on earth can you say that?" Margaret demanded. "I've spent the better part of my life—"

"Living mine."

"That is *not* the case. I've been involved, as any mother would be. I've been concerned."

"To make sure things went your way."

"*And,*" Margaret ventured onward, determined that Adrian would *not* direct the course of their conversation, "the gratitude I've received for my effort has all come in the form of outright falsehoods. Which is unacceptable. I deserve and demand nothing less than the truth. I mean to have it this instant."

"Because you're owed it?"

"That's right."

"Of course. But not because you're naturally interested."

"How *dare* you say that! I came here for you. I exposed myself to the absolute agony of my memories of that marriage—"

"Oh please," he scoffed.

"—because of you. To make sure you got what you deserved from your father's will because I *knew* he'd do anything he could to keep it from you. That was the only way he had left to punish me."

"And why would he be interested in punishing you?"

"Because he believed that I'd won. Because he couldn't cope with losing."

"Won what?"

"Won you. I kept you from him for your own good, but he couldn't see that. He could see it only as my act of vengeance because to see it any other way would have meant that he'd have to look at his life and assess the effect it might have had on his only son had I allowed you to be exposed to it. And he didn't want to do that. He didn't want to look. So he blamed me for keeping you apart."

"Which you never intended to do, of course," Adrian pointed out sardonically.

"Of course I intended it. What would you have had me do? A string of lovers. A string of mistresses when he was married to JoAnna. God only knows what else. Orgies, probably. Drugs. Drinking. Necrophilia and bestiality for all I know. Yes, I protected you from that. I'd do it all again. I was right to do it."

"Which is why I owe you," Adrian said. "I get the picture. So tell me"—he glanced at her as they paused to filter into the traffic at an intersection which would direct them towards the airport— "what is it exactly that you want to know?"

"What happened to his money? Not the money that bought all the things that were put into Ruth's name, but the other money, the money he kept, because he *must* have kept a mountain of it. He couldn't have had his little flings and kept a woman as high-maintenance as Anaïs Abbott on cash that Ruth doled out to him. She's far too censorious to be financing his mistress's lifestyle anyway. So what in God's name happened to his money? He either gave it to you already or it's hidden somewhere and the *only* way I will know whether I ought to continue to pursue this is if you tell me the truth. Did he give you money?"

"Don't pursue it" was his laconic reply. They were coming up to the airport, where a plane was making its approach to touch down, presumably the same plane that would fuel up and, within the hour, take Margaret back to England. Adrian turned in along the lane to the terminal and came to stop in front of it rather than parking in one of the bays across the way. "Let it go," he said.

She tried to read his face. "Does that mean . . . ?"

"It means what it means," he said. "The money's gone. You won't find it. Don't try."

"How do you . . . He gave it to you, then? You've had it all along? But if that's the case, why haven't you said . . . ? Adrian, I want the truth for once."

"You're wasting your time," he said. "And that's the truth."

He shoved open his car door and went to the back of the Range Rover. He opened the back of it and the cold air rushed in as he pulled her suitcases out and dumped them with no notable ceremony on the kerb. He came round to her door. It seemed their conversation was finished.

Margaret got out, drawing her coat more closely round her. Here in this exposed area of the island, a chill wind was gusting. It would ease her flight back to England, she hoped. In time, it would do the same for her son. She did know that about Adrian despite what he seemed to think about the situation and despite how he was acting at the moment. He would be back. It was the way of the world in which they lived, the world she had created for both of them.

She said, "When are you coming home?"

"That's not your concern, Mother." He fished out his cigarettes and took five tries to light one in the wind. Anyone else would have given up after the second match went out, but not her son. He was, in at least this way, so like his mother.

She said, "Adrian, I'm fast running out of patience with you."

"Go home," he told her. "You shouldn't have come."

"What exactly are you planning to do, then? If you're not coming home with me."

He smiled without pleasure before striding round to his side of the car. He spoke to her over its bonnet. "Believe me, I'll think of something," he said.

St. James parted with Deborah as they climbed the slope from the car park towards the hotel. She'd been thoughtful all the way back from *Le Reposoir*. She'd driven the route with her usual care, but he could tell that her mind wasn't on the traffic or even on the direction they were traveling. He knew she was thinking about her proffered explanation to a priceless painting's being cached in a prehistoric, stone-lined mound of earth. He certainly couldn't fault her for that. He was thinking of her explanation as well, simply because he couldn't discount it. He knew that just as her predilection for seeing the good in all people might lead her to ignore basic truths about them, so could his penchant for distrusting everyone lead him to see things as they were not. So neither of them spoke on the drive back to St. Peter Port. It was only as they approached the hotel's front steps that Deborah turned to him as if she'd reached some sort of decision.

"I won't come in just yet. I'll have a walk first."

He hesitated before replying. He knew the peril of saying the wrong thing. But he also knew the greater peril of not saying anything in a situation in which Deborah knew more than she ought to know as a party who was not disinterested.

He said, "Where are you going? Wouldn't you rather have a drink? A cup of tea or something?"

Her expression altered round the eyes. She knew what he was really saying despite his efforts to pretend otherwise. She said, "Perhaps I need an armed guard, Simon."

"Deborah . . ."

She said, "I'll be back soon enough," and headed off, not in the direction they had come but down towards Smith Street, which led to the High Street and the harbour beyond.

He could do nothing but let her go, admitting as he did so that he knew no better than she at this moment what the truth was about the death of Guy Brouard. All he had were suspicions, which she appeared to be bound and determined not to share.

Upon entering the hotel, he heard his name called and saw the receptionist standing behind the counter with a slip of paper extended towards him. "Message from London," she told him as she gave him the paper as well as his room key. He saw that she'd written "Super Linley" on a message chit in apparent reference to his friend's position at New Scotland Yard but nonetheless looking like a characterisation that would no doubt have amused the acting superintendent, despite the misspelling of his name. "He says to get a mobile phone," she added meaningfully.

Up in the room, St. James didn't return Lynley's call at once. Instead, he went to the desk beneath the window and punched in a different number.

In California, Jim Ward was engaged in a "meeting of the partners," St. James was told when the call went through. Alas, the meeting was being held not in the office but at the Ritz Carlton hotel. "On the coast," he was told with some importance by a woman who'd identified herself as "Southby, Strange, Willow, and Ward. Crystal speaking."

"They're all uncommunico," she added. "But I could take a message."

St. James didn't have time to wait for a message to get through to the architect, so he asked the young woman—who seemed to be munching on celery sticks—if she could help him.

"Do what I can," she said cheerfully. "I'm studying to be an architect myself."

Good fortune looked down on him when he asked her about the plans which Jim Ward had sent to Guernsey. It hadn't been that long ago that the documents had left the offices of Southby, Strange,

Willow, and Ward, and as it so happened, Crystal herself was in charge of all post, UPS, FedEx, DHL, and even Internet transmittals of drawings. Since this particular situation had differed so radically from their usual procedure, she remembered it all and would be only too happy to explain it to him . . . if he could wait just a moment " 'cause the other line is ringing."

He waited, and in due course her cheerful voice came back on the line. In the normal way things were done, she told him, the plans would have gone overseas via the Net to another architect, who'd carry the project on from there. But in this case, the plans were just samples of Mr. Ward's work and there was no rush to get them there. So she packaged them "like always" and handed them over to an attorney who showed up to claim them. That, she'd discovered, was an arrangement that had been made between Mr. Ward and the client overseas.

"A Mr. Kiefer?" St. James asked. "Mr. William Kiefer? Was that who came for them?"

She couldn't remember the name, Crystal said. But she didn't think it was Kiefer. Although . . . wait. Come to think of it, she didn't recall the guy's giving a name at all. He just said he was there to pick up the plans that were going to Guernsey so she'd handed them over.

"They got there, di'n't they?" she asked with some concern.

They certainly had.

How had they been packaged? St. James asked.

Regular way, she told him. Oversize mailing tube

of heavy cardboard. "It didn't get wrecked on the way, did it?" she asked with equal concern.

Not in the way she was thinking, St. James said. He thanked Crystal and rang off thoughtfully. He punched in the next number and had immediate success when he asked for William Kiefer: In less than thirty seconds, the California attorney came on the line.

He disputed Crystal's version of events. He hadn't sent someone to pick up the architectural drawings at all, he said. Mr. Brouard had told him explicitly that the plans would be delivered to his office by someone from the architectural firm when they were ready. At that point, he was to make arrangements for the couriers to carry the plans from California to Guernsey. That's what happened and that's what he did.

"Do you recall the person who delivered the plans from the architect, then?" St. James asked.

"I didn't see him. Or her. Or whoever it was," Kiefer answered. "The person just left the plans with our secretary. I got them when I came back from lunch. They were packed up, labeled, and ready to go. But she might remember . . . Hold on a minute, will you?"

It was more than a minute during which St. James was entertained by piped music: Neil Diamond misusing the English language in the cause of maintaining a dreadful rhyme scheme. When the phone line crackled to life again, St. James found himself talking to one Cheryl Bennett.

The person who brought the architectural plans

to Mr. Kiefer's office was a man, she told St. James. And to the question of whether she remembered anything particular about him, she giggled. "Definitely. You hardly ever see them in Orange County."

"Them?"

"Rastas." The man who brought the plans was a Caribbean type, she revealed. "Dreads down to his you-know-what. Sandals, cut-offs, and a Hawaiian shirt. Pretty odd-looking for an architect, I thought. But maybe he just did their deliveries or something."

She hadn't gotten his name, she concluded. They didn't talk. He had headphones on and was listening to music. He reminded her of Bob Marley.

St. James thanked Cheryl Bennett and soon rang off.

He walked to the window and studied its view of St. Peter Port. He thought about what she had said and what it all might mean. Upon reflection, there was only one possible conclusion to be reached: Nothing they'd learned so far was anything like what it appeared to be.

Chapter 28

SIMON'S DISTRUST WAS A spur to Deborah, and an additional spur was the fact that he would probably justify that distrust by telling himself it was owing to her not delivering that Nazi ring to the local police on his timeline. Yet his current doubts were not a reflection of the real situation. The truth was that Simon distrusted her because he *always* distrusted her. This was his reflex reaction to anything that came up which asked her for a bout of adult thinking, of which he seemed to believe her incapable. And that reaction was itself the bane of their entire relationship, the outcome of her having married a man who'd once acted in the role of second parent. He didn't always return to that role in moments of conflict. But the galling fact that he fell back upon it at all—ever—was enough to encourage her to take whatever action he most didn't want her to take.

This was why she went to the Queen Margaret Apartments when she could have window-shopped on the High Street, climbed the slope to Candie Gardens, walked out to Castle Cornet, or browsed in the jewellery shops tucked away in the Commercial Arcade. But she got no results from her visit to Clifton Street. So she dropped down the steps that rose from the market precinct below and told herself that she *wasn't* searching for China, and even if she was, what did it matter? They were old friends and China would be waiting to be reassured that the situation in which she and her brother found themselves was well on its way to being resolved.

Deborah did want to offer her that reassurance. It was the least she could do.

China wasn't in the old market at the base of the steps, and she wasn't in the food shop where Deborah had come upon both of the Rivers earlier. It was only when Deborah gave up entirely on the thought of finding her friend that she located her as she herself was turning the corner from the High Street into Smith Street.

She began ascending the slope, resigned to returning to the hotel. She paused to buy a newspaper from a vendor, and as she was tucking her purse back into her shoulder bag, she caught a glimpse of China halfway up the hill, stepping out of a shop and heading farther upwards, towards the point where Smith Street fanned out at its apex, creating a plaza that accommodated the World War I memorial.

Deborah called out her friend's name. China turned and scanned the pedestrians who were also heading upwards, well-dressed businessmen and -women at the end of their working day in the many banks below. She lifted her hand in greeting and waited for Deborah to join her.

"How's it going?" she asked when Deborah got close enough to hear her speak. "Anything?"

Deborah said, "We don't quite know." And then to direct their conversation into another area, one which didn't put her at risk of wanting to offer specifics in the cause of reassurance, she said, "What're you doing?"

"Candy," she said.

Deborah thought at first of the gardens, which made little sense since China was nowhere near them. But then her mind did the little sidestep that she'd learned to do while she was in America, making a quick translation of China's version of English into her own. She said, "Oh. *Candy.*"

"I was looking for Baby Ruths or Butterfingers." China patted her capacious shoulder bag in which she'd apparently stowed the sweets. "Those're his favourites. But they don't have them anywhere, so I got him what I could. I'm hoping they'll let me see him."

They hadn't done on her first visit to Hospital Lane, China told her. She'd gone directly to the police station when she'd left Deborah and her husband earlier, but she'd been refused access to her brother. During a suspect's interrogation period, she'd been told, they allowed only his advocate inside to see him. She should have known this, naturally, having been held for questioning herself. She'd phoned Holberry. He'd said he would do what he could to make arrangements for her to see her brother, which was what had led her to go out and about looking for the chocolate bars. She was on her way to deliver them. She glanced towards the plaza and the junction of streets a short distance above them. "Want to come with?"

Deborah said that she did. So they walked together to the police station, a mere two minutes from the point at which they'd met.

At the reception counter, they learned from an unfriendly special constable that Miss River would not be allowed to see her brother. When China said that Roger Holberry had made specific arrangements for her to be admitted, the special informed her that he personally knew nothing about anything from Roger Holberry, so if the ladies didn't mind, he'd be getting on with his work.

"Call the guy in charge," China told him. "The investigator. Le Gallez. Holberry probably got in touch with him. He said he'd make arrangements . . . Look. I'd just like to see my brother, okay?"

The man was immovable. If arrangements *had* been made, he informed China, by Roger Holberry via anyone, then that person—be it DCI Le Gallez or the Queen of Sheba—would have made certain that reception had access to that information. Barring that occurrence, no one save the suspect's advocate was allowed inside to see him.

"But Holberry *is* his advocate," China protested.

The man smiled in perfect unfriendliness. "I don't see him with you," he replied, making much of looking over her shoulder.

China began to make a hot remark which started

with "Listen, you little—" when Deborah intervened. She said calmly to the special, "Perhaps you can just take some sweets to Mr. River . . . ?" at which point China said abruptly, "Forget it," and stalked out of the station, her delivery unmade.

In the courtyard that served as the car park, Deborah found her sitting on the edge of a planter, savagely tearing at the shrubbery it held. As Deborah approached, China said, "Bastards. What d'they think I'm going to do? Break him out?"

"Perhaps we can get through to Le Gallez ourselves."

"I'm sure he'd be thrilled to give us a break." China threw her handful of leaves to the ground.

"Did you ask the advocate how he's coping?"

" 'As well as can be expected, considering the circumstances,' " China replied. "Which was supposed to make me feel better but which could mean anything, and don't I know it. There's jack shit in those cells, Deborah. Bare walls, bare floor, a wooden bench that they'll only too cooperatively make up into a bed if you're forced to be there overnight. A stainless steel toilet. A stainless steel sink. And that big blue immovable door. Not a magazine in sight, not a book, not a poster, not a radio, not a crossword puzzle, not a deck of cards. It'll make him nuts. He's not prepared . . . he isn't the type . . . God. I was so glad to get out. I couldn't breathe in there. Even the prison was better. And no way can he . . ." She seemed to force herself to slow down. "I need to get Mom over here. He'd want her here, and if I do that much, I can feel less guilty about being relieved that someone else is inside and I'm not. Jesus. What does *that* make me?"

"Feeling relieved to be out is human nature," Deborah said.

"If I could just get in to see him, to find out he's okay."

She stirred on the planter's edge and Deborah thought she intended to attack the fortress of the police station another time. But Deborah knew it would be useless, so she stood. "Let's walk."

She headed back the way they'd come, dipping to the far side of the war memorial and taking the direct route to the Queen Margaret Apartments. Too late Deborah realised that this route would curve directly in front of the Royal Court House, at whose steps China hesitated, gazing up at the imposing front of the building that housed all the legal machinery of the island. High above it flew Guernsey's flag, three lions on red, snapping in the breeze.

Before Deborah could suggest that they move on, China was climbing the steps to the front doors of the building. She went inside, so there was nothing for Deborah to do but to follow, which she hurriedly did.

She found China in the lobby, consulting a directory. When joined, she said, "You don't have to stay with me. I'll be okay. Simon's probably waiting for you anyway."

"I want to stay with you," Deborah said. "China, it's going to be all right."

China said, "Is it." She strode across the lobby, past the doors of wood and translucent glass on which were printed the various departments to be found within. She headed for a dramatic stairway that climbed past an oak wall holding the gilt-painted names of old island families, and on the floor above the entry she found what she was apparently looking for: the chamber in which trials were held.

This didn't seem the best place for China to go to lighten her spirits, and her choice of it served to underscore the differences between her and her brother. In the same position, with a sibling innocent of a crime but still under arrest, Cherokee had been all action in keeping with his restless nature: the ultimate man with the ultimate plan. Deborah could see that despite its being the despair of his sister, Cherokee's scheming character had its advantages, one of which was never to give in to disheartenment.

"This isn't a good place for you to be right now," Deborah said to her friend as China sat at the end of the room farthest from the judge's bench.

As if Deborah hadn't spoken, China said, "Holberry told me about the way they do trials here. When I figured I was going to be the one, I wanted to know how things would play out, so I asked him." She looked straight ahead, as if she could see the scene in front of them as she described it. "Here's the deal: They don't use juries. Not like we do. I mean, not like at home. There's no putting people in the jury box and asking them questions to make sure they haven't already decided to send someone to the chair. What they use here are professional jurors. It's their job, like. But I don't see how you can get a fair trial out of that. Doesn't it mean anyone can talk to them in advance? And they can read about the case if they want to, can't they? They can probably even conduct their own investigations, for all I know. But it's different than at home."

"That makes it scary," Deborah admitted.

"At home I'd have an idea what to do right now because I'd know how things work. We could find someone who knows how to scope out jurors and choose the best ones. We could give interviews to the press. We could talk to TV reporters or something. We could mould public opinion in some way so that if it came to a trial—"

"Which it won't," Deborah said firmly. "Which it *won't*. You do believe that, don't you?"

"—we'd at least have made some kind of inroad into how people feel and what they think. He's not without friends. I'm here. You're here. Simon's here. We could do something. Couldn't we? If things were the same, like at home . . . ?"

Home, Deborah thought. She knew her friend was right. What she was having to face would be so much less excruciating if she were at home, where the people were familiar, the objects all round were familiar, and where, most important, the procedure itself—or at least what led up to it—was also familiar.

Deborah realised that she couldn't offer China the sense of ease that came with familiarity, not in this place that spoke of a frightening future. She could only suggest a marginally less awful environment in which she might be able to comfort the woman who'd been such a comfort to her.

She said softly into the silence that followed China's remarks, "Hey, girlfriend . . ."

China looked at her.

Deborah smiled and chose what China herself might have said and what China's brother definitely would have said. "It's a downer here. Let's blow this joint."

Despite her present frame of mind, Deborah's old friend smiled in turn. "Yeah. All right. Cool," she said.

When Deborah rose and offered China her hand, she took it. And she didn't let go till they were out of the courtroom, down the stairs, and out of the building.

In a thoughtful state, St. James rang off from his second conversation of the day with Lynley. Vallera & Son hadn't been difficult to extract information from, according to what the New Scotland Yard superintendent had told him. Whoever had been at the receiving end of Lynley's call had apparently not been playing with a full deck of the intelligence cards: Not only had the individual yelled to someone "Dad! Hey! Got a call from Scotland here! D'you believe it?" when Lynley had identified himself after tracking down the business in Jackson Heights, New York, but he had also been cooperatively voluble when Lynley inquired as to the exact nature of Vallera & Son's professional pursuit.

In an accent worthy of *The Godfather*, the man—Danny Vallera he said he was called—informed

Lynley that Vallera & Son was an enterprise that cashed paycheques, offered loans, and wired money "all around the world if you want. Why? You looking to send some bucks over here? We c'n do that for you. We c'n change stuff to dollars. What you got over there in Scotland, anyway? You guys use francs? Crowns? You on the euro? We c'n do it all. 'Course, it's gonna cost you."

Affable to the end and clearly without a grain of sense—much less suspicion—he'd explained that he and his dad wired money in increments of nine thousand nine hundred and ninety-nine dollars— "And you can add the ninety-nine cents if you want to"—with a chuckle—"but that seems like stretching things, don't it?"—for discriminating individuals who didn't want the Feds to come knocking upon their doors, which they probably would do if over time Vallera & Son reported wire transfers of ten thousand dollars or more as required by "Uncle Samuel and the Washington jerk-offs." So if someone from Scotland wanted to send someone in the U.S. of A. anything less than ten thousand buckos, Vallera & Son would be happy to play the middleman in the operation, for a fee of course. In the U.S. of A., centre of politicians on the take, lobbyists on the give, elections fixed, and capitalism gone mad, there was always a fee.

And if the amount to be wired was more than nine thousand nine hundred ninety-nine dollars and ninety-nine cents, what happened then? Lynley had inquired.

Oh, then Vallera & Son had to report the amount to the Feds.

And what did the Feds do?

Got interested when they got around to getting interested. If your name was Gotti they got interested pronto. If you were Joe Schmo Recently in the Dough, it might take them longer.

"It was all quite illuminating," Lynley had said to St. James at the conclusion of his report. "Mr. Vallera might have gone on indefinitely because he seemed to be delighted to have a call from Scotland."

St. James chuckled. "But he didn't go on?"

"Apparently Mr. Vallera Senior came on the scene. There was some background noise suggesting someone's displeasure and the line went dead shortly thereafter."

"You're owed, Tommy," St. James said.

"Not by Mr. Vallera Senior, I hope."

Now in his hotel room, St. James contemplated his next move. Without getting one agency or another of the United States government involved, he reached the ineluctable conclusion that he was on his own, that he would have to ferret out more facts in one way or another and use those facts to smoke out Guy Brouard's killer. He considered several ways of going at the problem, made his decision, and descended to the lobby.

There he inquired about using the hotel's computer. The receptionist, to whom he had not endeared himself earlier by having her track him round the island, didn't meet his request with unbridled enthusiasm. She drew her lower lip in under her protruding upper teeth and informed him she would have to check with Mr. Alyar, the hotel's manager. "We don't usually give residents access . . . People generally bring their own. You don't have a laptop?" She didn't add "*or* a mobile?" but the implication was there. *Get with it* her expression told him just before she went in search of Mr. Alyar.

St. James cooled his heels in the lobby for nearly ten minutes before a barrel-shaped man in a double-breasted suit approached him from beyond a door that led into the inner reaches of the hotel. He introduced himself as Mr. Alyar—Felix Alyar, he said—and asked if he could be of help.

St. James explained his request more fully. He handed over his business card as he spoke, and he offered DCI Le Gallez's name in an effort to seem as legitimate a part of the ongoing investigation as possible.

With far more good grace than the receptionist had possessed, Mr. Alyar agreed to allow St. James access to the hotel's computer system. He welcomed him behind the reception counter and into a business office behind it. There, two additional employees of the establishment sat at work at terminals and a third fed documents into a fax machine.

Felix Alyar directed St. James to a third terminal and said to the faxer, "Penelope, this gentleman will be using your station," before he left "with the hotel's compliments" and a smile that bordered on the flagrantly insincere. St. James thanked him and made short work of accessing the Internet.

He began with the *International Herald Tribune*, logging on to their Web site, where he discovered that any story over two weeks old could be accessed only from the site at which the story itself had originated. He was unsurprised, considering the nature of what he was looking for and the limited scope of the paper. So he went on to *USA Today,* but there the news had to cover too wide an area and was thus confined to the Big Story in nearly every case: governmental issues, international incidents, sensational murders, bold heroics.

His next choice was the *New York Times,* where he typed in PIETER DE HOOCH first and, when that brought him nothing, ST. BARBARA second. But here again, he achieved no useful result, and he began to doubt the hypothesis he'd developed upon first hearing about Vallera & Son of Jackson Heights, New York, and upon then hearing the exact nature of Vallera & Son's business.

The only option left, considering what he knew, was the *Los Angeles Times,* so he moved on to that broadsheet's Web site and began a search of their archives. As before, he entered the time period he'd been using all along—the last twelve months—and he followed that with the name Pieter de Hooch. In less than five seconds, the monitor's screen altered and a list of relevant articles appeared, five of them on one page and an indication that more followed.

He chose the first article and waited as the computer downloaded it. What appeared first on the screen was the headline *A Dad Remembers.*

St. James scanned the article. Phrases leaped out at

him as if rendered in a script bolder than the rest. It was when he saw the words *decorated World War II veteran* that he slowed down his reading of the story. This covered a long-ago, heretofore unheard of triple-transplant operation—heart, lungs, and kidneys—that had been performed at one St. Clare's Hospital in Santa Ana, California. The recipient had been a fifteen-year-old boy called Jerry Ferguson. His father, Stuart, was the decorated veteran mentioned in the article.

Car salesman Stuart Ferguson—for so he was—had apparently spent the remainder of his days seeking ways to repay St. Clare's for having saved his boy's life. A charity hospital whose policy it was to turn away no one, St. Clare's had required no payment for what had amounted to a hospital bill well over two hundred thousand dollars. A car salesman with four children had little hope of amassing that kind of money, so upon his death Stuart Ferguson had willed St. Clare's the only thing of potential value that he possessed: a painting.

"We had no idea . . ." his widow was quoted as saying. "Stu certainly never knew . . . He got it during the war, he said . . . A souvenir . . . That's all I ever learned about it."

"I just thought it was some old picture," Jerry Ferguson commented after the painting had been evaluated by experts at the Getty Museum. "Dad and Mom had it in their bedroom. You know, I never thought much about it."

Thus, it seemed that the delighted Sisters of Mercy, who ran St. Clare's Hospital on a shoestring budget and spent most of their time raising the funds just to keep it afloat, had found themselves the recipients of a priceless work of art. A photograph accompanying the story featured the adult Jerry Ferguson and his mother presenting Pieter de Hooch's painting of St. Barbara to a dour-looking Sister Monica Casey, who, at the time of presentation, had absolutely no idea what she was laying her pious hands upon.

When later asked if they had regrets about parting with something so valuable, Ferguson's mother and son said, "It gave us a surprise to think of what was hanging in the house all those years" and "Heck, it was what Dad wanted and that's good enough for me." For her part, Sister Monica Casey admitted to "heart flutters aplenty" and she explained that they would sell the de Hooch at auction once they had it properly cleaned and restored. In the meantime, she'd told the newspaper reporter, the Sisters of Mercy would keep the de Hooch "some place quite safe."

But not safe enough, St. James thought. That fact had put the ball in motion.

He clicked on the succeeding stories and he felt little surprise at the manner in which events had unfolded in Santa Ana, California. He read them quickly—for that was all the time it took to ascertain how Pieter de Hooch's *St. Barbara* had made the journey from St. Clare's Hospital to Guy Brouard's home—and he printed up the relevant ones.

He gathered them together with a paper clip. He went upstairs.

• • •

Deborah made tea as China alternately picked up the telephone receiver and dropped it back into its cradle, sometimes punching in a few numbers, sometimes not even getting that far. On their walk back to the Queen Margaret Apartments, she had finally decided to phone her mother. She had to be informed what was going on with Cherokee, China said. But now that she faced the Moment of Truth, as she called it, she couldn't quite bring herself to do it. So she'd punch in the numbers for the international line. She'd punch in the number one for the United States. She'd even get as far as punching in the area code for Orange, California. But then she'd lose her nerve.

As Deborah measured out the tea, China explained her hesitation. This turned out to be the child of her superstition. "It's like I'll jinx things for him if I call."

Deborah recalled her using this expression before. Think you'll do well on a photographic assignment or perhaps an exam and you'd fail completely, having jinxed yourself in advance. Say that you expect a phone call from your boyfriend and you'd jinx the possibility of his calling. Remark upon the ease with which traffic was flowing on one of California's massive motorways, and you were sure to hit an accident and a four-mile tailback in the next ten minutes. Deborah had named this kind of skewed thinking "The Law of Chinaland," and she had grown quite used to being careful not to jinx a situation while she lived with China in Santa Barbara.

She said, "How would it jinx things, though?"

"I don't know for sure. It just feels like that. Like I'll call her and tell her what's going on, and she'll come over, and then everything will just get worse."

"But that seems to violate the basic law of China-land," Deborah observed. "At least the way I remember it." She set the electric kettle to boil.

At Deborah's use of the old term, China smiled, it seemed in spite of herself. "How?" she asked.

"Well, as I recall how things work in Chinaland, you aim for the direct opposite of what you truly want. You don't let Fate know what you have in mind so that Fate can't get in there and cock things up. You go round the back way. You sneak up on what you want."

"Fake the bastard out," China murmured.

"Right." Deborah took mugs from the cupboard. "In this particular case, it seems to me that you have to ring your mum. You have no choice. If you ring her and insist that she come to Guernsey—"

"She doesn't even have a passport, Debs."

"Which is all the better. It will cause enormous trouble for her to get here."

"Not to mention the expense."

"Mmmm. Yes. That practically guarantees success." Deborah leaned against the work top. "She must get a passport quickly. That means a trip to . . . where?"

"Los Angeles. Federal Building. Off the San Diego Freeway."

"Past the airport?"

"Way past. Past Santa Monica even."

"Wonderful. All that ghastly traffic. All that difficulty. So she must go there first and get her passport. She must make all her travel arrangements. She must fly to London and then to Guernsey. And having gone to all that trouble—herself in a state of tearing anxiety—"

"She gets here to find that it's all been resolved."

"Probably one hour before she arrives." Deborah smiled. "And *voilà*. The Law of Chinaland in action. All that trouble and all that expense. For nothing, as things turn out." Behind her, the kettle clicked off. She poured water into a stout green teapot, took that to the table, and gestured for China to join her there. "But if you don't ring her . . ."

China left the phone and came into the kitchen. Deborah waited for her to conclude the thought. Instead of doing so, however, China sat and fingered one of the tea mugs, turning it slowly between her palms. She said, "I gave up that kind of thinking a while back. It was always only a game anyway. But it stopped working. Or maybe I stopped working. I don't know." She pushed the mug to one side. "It started with Matt. Did I ever tell you? When we were teenagers. I walk past his house and if I don't look to see if he's in the garage or mowing the lawn for his mom or something, if I don't even *think* about him when I pass by, he'll be there. But if I look or if I think about him—even think his name—then he won't be. It always worked. So I went on with it. If I act indifferent, he'll be interested in me. If I don't want to date him, he'll want to date me. If I think he'll never even want to kiss me goodnight, he'll do it. He'll have to. He'll be desperate to. At one level I always knew that wasn't how things really work in the world—thinking and saying the exact opposite of what you truly want—but once I started seeing the world that way—playing that game—I just kept going. It ended up with: Plan out a life with Matt and it'll never happen. Forge ahead on my own, and there he'll be, panting to hook up permanently."

Deborah poured the tea and gently eased a mug back over to China. She said, "I'm sorry how things turned out. I know how you felt about him. What you wanted. Hoped for. Expected. Whatever."

"Yeah. Whatever. That's the word, all right." The sugar stood in a dispenser in the centre of the table. China upended this so that the white granules poured like snowfall into her cup. When it looked to Deborah as if the brew would be completely undrinkable, China finished with the dispenser.

"I wish it had worked out the way you wanted," Deborah said. "But perhaps it still will."

"The way your life worked out? No. I'm not like you. I don't land on my feet. I never have. I never will."

"You don't know—"

"I ended it with one man, Deborah," China cut in impatiently. "Believe me, okay? In my case there wasn't another man—crippled or not—just waiting for things to go bust so he could step in and take over where the other left off."

Deborah flinched from the sting behind her old friend's words. "Is that how you see my life . . . how things turned out? Is that . . . China, that's not fair."

"Isn't it? There I was, struggling with Matt from the get-go. On again, off again. Great sex one day, big break-up the next. Get back together with the promise it'll be 'different this time.' Fall into bed and screw our brains out. Break up three weeks later over something really stupid: He says he'll be there at eight and he doesn't show up till eleven-thirty and he doesn't bother to call and let me know he'll be late and I can't *deal* with it a second longer so I say that's it, get out, that's it, I've had it. Then ten days later, he calls. He says, Look, baby, give me another chance, I need you. And I believe him because I'm so incredibly stupid or desperate, and we begin the process all over again. And all the time, there you are with a fucking duke, of all things—or *whatever* he was. And when he's out of the picture permanently, ten minutes later Simon steps in. Like I said. You always land on your feet."

"But it wasn't *like* that," Deborah protested.

"No? Tell me how it was. Make it sound like my situation with Matt." China reached for her tea but she didn't drink. Instead, she said, "You can't do that, can you? Because your situation has never been like mine."

"Men aren't—"

"I'm not *talking* about men. I'm talking about life. How it is for me. How it's God damn always been for you."

"You're seeing only the outside of it," Deborah argued. "You're comparing that—the superficial part of it—to how you feel inside. And that doesn't make sense. China, I didn't even have a mother. You know that. I grew up in someone else's house. I spent the first part of my life frightened to death of my own shadow, bullied at school for having red hair and freckles, too shy to make a single request of anyone, even of my father. I was pathetically grateful if someone so much as patted me on the head like a dog. The only companions I had till I was fourteen were books and a third-hand camera. I lived in someone else's house, where my father was little more than a servant, and I always thought Why couldn't he have *been* someone? Why doesn't he have a career, like a doctor or a dentist or a banker or something? Why doesn't he go out to a proper job like other kids' dads? Why—"

"Jesus. My dad was in *prison*," China cried. "That's where he is now. That's where he was then. He's a dope dealer, Deborah. Do you hear me? Do you get it? He's a fucking dope dealer. And my mom . . . How'd you like Miss USA Redwood Tree for a mother? Save the spotted owl or the three-legged ground squirrel. Stop a dam being built or a road going in or an oil well being drilled but don't ever—*ever*—remember a birthday, pack a school lunch, make sure your kids have a decent pair of shoes. And for God's sake don't ever be around for a Little League game or a Brownie meeting or a teacher conference or anything as a matter of fact because God knows the loss of endangered dandelions might upset the whole fucking ecosystem. So don't—*don't*—try to compare your poor life in some mansion—sniveling daughter of a servant—with mine."

Deborah drew a shaky breath. There seemed nothing more to say.

China took a gulp of her tea, her face averted.

Deborah wanted to argue that no one on earth ever got to put in a request for the hand of cards they were dealt in life, that it was how one played the hand that counted, not what the hand was. But she didn't say this. Nor did she remark that she'd learned long ago with the death of her mother that good things *could* arise from bad. For saying that would smack of self-satisfaction and supercilious preaching. It would also lead them inevitably to her marriage to Simon, which would never have come about had his family not believed it necessary to get her grieving father away from Southampton. Had they not put Joseph Cotter in charge of renovating a run-down family house in Chelsea, she would never have come to live with, to grow to love, and ultimately to marry the man with whom she now shared her life. But that was dangerous ground for her to tread on in conversation with China. She had far too much to deal with right now.

Deborah knew she possessed information that could alleviate some of China's concerns—the dolmen, the combination lock on its door, the painting inside it, the state of the mailing tube in which that painting had been unwittingly smuggled into the UK and onwards onto Guernsey by Cherokee River, what the state of that mailing tube implied—but she knew she owed it to her husband not to mention any of this. So instead, she said, "I know you're frightened, China. He'll be okay, though. You've got to believe that."

China turned her head away further. Deborah saw the trouble she had in swallowing. She said, "The moment we set foot on this island, we were someone's patsies. I wish we'd handed over those stupid plans and just taken off. But no. I thought it would be so cool to do a story on that house. And I wouldn't have been able to sell it anyway. It was dumb. It was stupid. It was a just-so-typical China screw-up. And now . . . I did this to us both, Deborah. He would have left. He would've been happy to leave. That's what he wanted to do. But I thought here's a chance to get some pictures, do a story on spec. Which was even stupider than anything else, because when the hell have I ever been able to do a story on spec and sell it? Never. Jesus. I am *such* a loser."

This was too much. Deborah got to her feet and went to her friend's chair. She stood behind it and dropped her arms round China. She pressed her cheek against the top of her head and said, "Stop it. *Stop* it. I swear to you—"

Before she could finish, the door of the flat popped open behind them and the cold evening December air *whoosh*ed into the room. They turned and Deborah took a step to hurry over to shut it. But she stopped when she saw who was standing there.

"Cherokee!" she cried.

He looked utterly done in—unshaven and rumpled—but he grinned nonetheless. He held up a hand to stifle their exclamations and questions, and he disappeared for a moment back outside. Next to Deborah, China got up slowly.

Cherokee reappeared. In each hand was a duffel bag, which he threw inside the flat. Then, from within his jacket he brought out two small dark blue booklets, each of which was embossed in gold upon its cover. He tossed one to his sister and he kissed the other. "Our ticket to ride," he said. "Let's blow this joint, Chine."

She stared at him and then looked down at the passport in her hands. She said, "What . . . ?" And then as she dashed across the room to hug him, "What happened? *Cherokee.* What *happened?*"

"I don't know and I didn't ask," her brother replied. "A cop came to my cell with our stuff about twenty minutes ago. Said, 'That'll be all, Mr. River. Just get your ass off this island by tomorrow morning.' Or words to that effect. He even gave us tickets back to Rome, if that's our pleasure, he said. With the States of Guernsey's apologies for the inconvenience, of course."

"That's what he said? The *inconvenience?* We ought to sue these bastards to hell and back, and—"

"Whoa," Cherokee said. "I'm not interested in doing anything but getting out of this place. If there was a flight tonight, believe me, I'd be on it. Only question is, do you want to do Rome?"

"I want to do *home,*" China replied.

Cherokee nodded and kissed her forehead. "Got

to admit it. My shack in the canyon never sounded so good."

Deborah watched this scene between brother and sister, and her own heart lightened. She knew who was responsible for Cherokee River's release, and she blessed him. Simon had come to her aid more than once in her life, but never more rewardingly than at this moment. He'd actually listened to her interpretation of the facts. But not only that. He'd finally heard her speaking.

Ruth Brouard completed her meditation, feeling more at peace than she'd felt in months. Since Guy's death, she'd skipped her daily thirty minutes of quiet contemplation, and she'd seen the result in a mind that careened from one subject to another and in a body that panicked against each new onslaught of pain. Thus she'd been running off to meet advocates, bankers, and brokers when she wasn't combing through her brother's papers for some indication of how and why he'd altered his will. When she wasn't doing that, she'd been off to the doctor to try to alter her medication so as to manage her pain more efficiently. Yet all along, the answers and the solutions she required had been contained in simply going within.

This session proved she was still capable of sustained contemplation. Alone in her room with a single candle burning on the table next to her, she'd sat and concentrated on the flow of her breath. She'd willed away the anxiety that had been plaguing her. For half an hour she'd managed to let go of grief.

Daylight had faded to darkness, she saw as she rose from her chair. Utter stillness pervaded the house. The companionable noises she'd known so long, living with her brother, left with his death a vacuum in which she felt like a creature thrust unexpectedly into space.

This was how it would be till her own death. She could only wish that it might come soon. She'd held herself together quite well while she'd shared the house with guests, making Guy's funeral arrangements and carrying them out. But the cost to her had been a high one, and the payment declared itself in pain and fatigue. The solitude she had now provided her with the opportunity to recover from what she'd been through. It also provided her with a chance to let go.

No one to pretend health for any longer, she thought. Guy was dead and Valerie already knew despite Ruth's never having told her. But that was all right, because Valerie had held her tongue from the first. Ruth didn't acknowledge it, so Valerie didn't mention it. One couldn't ask for more from a woman who spent so much time in one's own home.

From her chest of drawers, Ruth took up the bottle and shook two of the pills into her palm. She downed them with water from the carafe by her bed. They would make her drowsy, but there was no one in the house for whom she had to be sprightly now. She could nod over her dinner if she desired. She could nod over a television programme. She could, if she wished, nod off right here in her bed-room and stay nodded off till dawn. A few more pills would accomplish that. It was a tempting thought.

Below her, however, she heard a car crunch in the gravel as it moved along the drive. She went to the window in time to see the rear end of a vehicle disappear round the side of the house. She frowned at this. She expected no one.

She went to her brother's study, to the window. Across the yard, she could see, someone had pulled a large vehicle into one of the old stables. The brake lights were still on, as if the driver was considering what to do next.

She watched and waited, but nothing changed. It seemed that whoever was inside the car was waiting for her to make the next move. She did so.

She left Guy's study and went to the stairs. She was stiff from sitting for her lengthy meditation, so she took them slowly. She could smell her dinner, which Valerie had left on the hob in the kitchen. She headed there, not because she was hungry but because it seemed the reasonable thing to do.

Like Guy's study, the kitchen was at the back of the house. She could use the dishing up of her meal as an excuse to see who'd come to *Le Reposoir*.

She had her answer when she finally negotiated the last of the stairs. She followed the corridor to the back, where a door was ajar and a shaft of light cre-ated a diagonal slice on the carpet. There she pushed against the panels and saw her nephew standing at the hob, energetically stirring whatever it was that Valerie had left simmering on its back burner.

She said, "Adrian! I thought . . ."

He swung round.

Ruth said, "I thought . . . You're here. But when your mother said she was leaving . . ."

"You thought I'd be going as well. That makes sense. Wherever she goes, I generally follow. But not this time, Aunt Ruth." He held out a long wooden spoon for her to taste what appeared to be beef bourguignon. He said, "Are you ready for this? D'you want to eat in the dining room or in here?"

"Thank you, but I'm not very hungry." What she was was light-headed, perhaps the result of pain medication on an empty stomach.

"That's been obvious," Adrian told her. "You've lost a lot of weight. Doesn't anyone mention it?" He went to the dresser and took down a serving bowl. "But tonight, you're going to eat."

He began scooping the beef into the bowl. When he had it filled, he covered it and took from the fridge a green salad that Valerie had also prepared. From inside the oven, he brought out another bowl—this one of rice—and he began setting all of this on the table in the centre of the kitchen. He followed up with a water goblet, crockery, and cutlery for one.

Ruth said, "Adrian, why have you come back? Your mother . . . Well, she didn't say *exactly,* I suppose, but when she told me she was leaving, I assumed . . . My dear, I know how disappointed you are about your father's will, but he was quite adamant. And no matter what, I feel I must respect—"

"I don't expect you to do anything about the situation," Adrian told her. "Dad made his point. Sit down, Aunt Ruth. I'll fetch you some wine."

Ruth felt some concern and confusion. She waited where he left her and sought out the larder which Guy had long ago turned into his wine cellar. There she could hear Adrian making his selection from among his father's expensive bottles. One of them clinked on the old marble shelf on which meats and cheeses had once been kept. In a moment, she heard the sound of pouring.

She considered his actions, wondering what he was up to. When he returned moments later, he bore an opened burgundy in one hand and a single glass of wine in the other. The bottle was old, she saw, and its label was dusty. Guy wouldn't have used it for so unimportant a meal.

She said, "I don't think . . ." but Adrian swept past her and pulled out a chair from beneath the table with much ceremony.

"Sit, Madam," he said. "Dinner is served."

"Aren't you eating?"

"I had something on the way back from the airport. Mum got off, by the way. She's probably already landed by now. We've washed our hands of each other at last, which William—that's her current husband, in case you've forgotten—will no doubt deeply appreciate. Well, what else can you expect? He didn't plan on taking in a permanent lodger in the person of his stepson when he married her, did he?"

If Ruth hadn't known otherwise about her nephew, she would have seen both his behaviour and his conversation as evidence of a manic state. But in the thirty-seven years of his life, she'd never witnessed anything in him that could be remotely described as manic. This, then, was something else she was seeing. She just didn't know how to label it. Or what it meant. Or how, indeed, she should feel about it.

"Isn't it odd?" Ruth murmured. "I quite thought you'd packed. I didn't *see* the suitcases, but I . . . It's odd, isn't it, how things appear to us when we have our minds made up about them?"

"How right you are." He dished out rice for her and topped it with the beef. He set the plate in front of her. "That's the trouble we bring on ourselves: looking at life with preconceived notions. Looking at people with preconceived notions. You're not eating, Aunt Ruth."

"My appetite . . . It's difficult."

"I'm going to make things easier, then."

"I don't see how you can."

"I know," he said. "But I'm not actually as useless as I look."

"I didn't mean . . ."

"It's okay." He lifted her glass. "Have a sip of wine. One thing—probably the only thing—I learned from Dad was how to pick out a wine. This little selection"—he held the wine to the light and gazed at it—"I'm pleased to say has outstanding legs, magnificent length, excellent bouquet, a little bite at the finish . . . Fifty quid a bottle, perhaps? More? Well, no matter. It's perfect for what you're eating. Have a taste."

She smiled at him. "If I didn't know better, I'd think you were hoping to get me drunk."

"Poison you more likely," Adrian said. "And inherit the fortune that doesn't exist. I trust I'm not your beneficiary either."

"I *am* sorry about that, my dear," Ruth told him. And then as he urged the wine upon her, "I can't. My medicine . . . The mixture wouldn't be good for me, I'm afraid."

"Ah." He set the glass down. "Not willing to live a little dangerously, then?"

"I left that to your father."

"And look where it got him," Adrian said.

Ruth dropped her gaze and fingered her cutlery. "I'm going to miss him."

"I expect you are. Have some of the beef. It's very good."

She looked up. "Have you tasted it?"

"No one cooks like Valerie. Eat up, Aunt Ruth. I won't let you leave the kitchen till you have at least half of your dinner."

Ruth didn't miss the fact that he didn't answer the question. In conjunction with his return to *Le Reposoir* when she'd expected him to leave with his mother, this gave her pause. She could see no real reason to be leery of her nephew, though. He knew about his father's will, and she'd just told him about her own. Still, she said, "All this concern about me. I'm quite . . . quite flattered, I suppose."

They observed each other over the table, over the steaming bowls of beef and rice. The silence between them was different from the silence Ruth had enjoyed earlier, however, and she found herself glad when the telephone rang, fracturing the moment with its insistent double *brring*.

She began to rise to answer it.

Adrian intercepted her. He said, "No. I mean you to eat, Aunt Ruth. You've spent at least a week not taking care of yourself. Whoever it is will phone back eventually. In the meantime, you'll get some food inside you."

She lifted her fork although its weight seemed enormous. She said, "Yes. Well. If you insist, my dear . . ." because she realised it didn't really matter one way or another. The end was going to be just the same. "But if I might ask . . . Why are you doing this, Adrian?"

"The one thing no one ever understood was that I actually loved him," Adrian replied. "In spite of everything. And he'd want me here, Aunt Ruth. You know that as well as I. He'd want me to see things through to the end because that's what he would have done himself."

He spoke a truth that Ruth could not deny. That was the reason she lifted her fork to her mouth.

Chapter 29

When Deborah left the Queen Margaret Apartments, Cherokee and China were going through their belongings to make certain everything was accounted for in advance of their removal from the island. Cherokee first demanded China's shoulder bag, however, and rustled through it noisily in search of her wallet. He was looking for funds so that they might all go out to dinner and carouse for the night, he announced. However, he ended up saying, "*Forty* pounds, Chine?" when he saw the paucity of his sister's cash position. He went on to declare, "Jesus. I'll have to spring for the meal myself, I guess."

"Now, *that* makes a change," China remarked.

"But wait." Cherokee held up one finger in the manner of a man hit by sudden inspiration. "I bet there's an ATM you can use on the High Street."

"And if there isn't," China added, "by sheer coincidence I happen to have my credit card."

"God. Today is my lucky day."

Brother and sister laughed together companionably. They opened their duffel bags to sort through everything. At this point, Deborah said her good-nights. Cherokee was the one who saw her to the door. Outside, he stopped her in the dim light on the step.

In the shadows, he looked much like the young boy he would probably always be at heart. He said, "Debs. Thanks. Without you here . . . without Simon . . . Just . . . thanks."

"I don't think we actually did much."

"You did a lot. And anyway, you were here. In friendship." He gave a brief laugh. "I wish it could have been more. Damn. Married lady. I was never lucky when it came to you."

Deborah blinked. She grew hot but said nothing.

"Wrong time, wrong place," Cherokee continued. "But if things had been different, either then or now . . ." He looked past her to the tiny courtyard and beyond that to the lights of the street. "I just wanted you to know. And it's not because of this, because of what you've done for us. It's the way it always was."

Deborah said, "Thank you. I'll remember, Cherokee."

"If there's ever a time . . ."

She put a hand on his arm. "There won't be," she said. "But thank you."

He said, "Yeah. Well," and he kissed her on the cheek. Then, before she could move away, he held her chin and kissed her full on the mouth as well. His tongue touched her lips, parted them, lingered, and withdrew. "I wanted to do that the first time I saw you," he said. "How the hell did these English guys get so lucky?"

Deborah stepped away but still tasted him. She felt her heart beat lightly, fast and pure. But that would not be the case if she stood in the semi-darkness with Cherokee River a moment longer. So she said, "The English are always lucky," and she left him by the door.

She wanted to think about that kiss and all that had preceded it as she walked back to the hotel. So she didn't walk directly there. Instead, she descended Constitution Steps and wended her way over to the High Street.

Very few people were out. The shops were closed, and what restaurants there were sat farther along, towards *Le Pollet.* Three people waited in a queue at Cherokee's cash machine in front of a Nat West and a group of five adolescent boys were sharing a loud mobile phone conversation that echoed off the buildings which lined the narrow street. A skinny cat ascended the steps from the quay and slunk along, hugging the front of a shoe shop while somewhere nearby a dog barked frantically and a man's voice shouted to silence it.

Where the High Street veered right and became *Le Pollet,* descending to the harbour in a slope of neatly set cobblestones, Smith Street marked a passage up the hill. Deborah turned here and began the climb, thinking about the way in which twelve brief hours had managed to turn the day on its ear. What had begun in concern and growing desperation had ended in revelry. In revelation as well. But that was something she quickly dismissed. Cherokee's words, she knew, came from the exuberant pleasure of the moment, of experiencing a freedom he had so nearly lost. One couldn't take seriously anything that was said in the height of such jubilation.

But the kiss . . . She could take that seriously. For what it was, only, which was simply a kiss. She'd liked the feel of it. More, she'd liked the excitement of it. But she was wise enough not to confuse excitement with anything more. And she felt neither disloyalty to Simon nor guilt. It had, after all, been only a kiss.

She smiled as she relived the moments that had led up to it. Such childlike joy had always been a characteristic of China's brother. This interlude on Guernsey had been the exception in his thirty-three years, not the rule.

They could resume their travels now or return to their homes. In either case, they took part of Deborah with them, the part that had grown from girl to woman in three brief years in California. No doubt Cherokee would continue to exasperate his sister. China would continue to frustrate her brother. They would continue to spar as any two complex personalities might. But they would always come together in the end. Such was the way of siblings.

Thinking about their relationship, Deborah passed the shops in Smith Street, barely aware of her surroundings. It was only when she reached the midpoint that she stopped, some thirty yards from the news vendor where she'd bought a paper earlier. She gazed at the buildings on either side of the street: Citizens Advice Bureau, Marks & Spencer, Davies Travel, Fillers Bakery, St. James's Gallery,

Buttons Bookshop . . . Seeing all of them and more, she frowned. She retraced her steps to the bottom of the street and then walked more slowly—more conscientiously—once again to the top. She stopped when she got to the war memorial. *I'll have to spring for the meal myself.*

She hurried to the hotel.

She found Simon not in their room but in the bar. He was reading a copy of the *Guardian* as he enjoyed a whisky, which sat at his elbow. A contingent of businessmen were sharing the bar with him, noisily tossing back their gin-and-tonics as they dipped into bowls of crisps. The air was acrid with their cigarette smoke and with the sweat of too many unwashed bodies soaked through at the end of a long day of offshore finance.

Deborah worked her way through them to join her husband. She saw that Simon was dressed for dinner. She said hastily, "I'll go up and change."

He said, "No need. Shall we go on in? Or would you like a drink first?"

She wondered why he didn't ask where she'd been. He folded the newspaper and picked up his whisky, waiting for her reply. She said, "I . . . perhaps a sherry?"

He said, "I'll fetch it," and he went to do so, weaving his way through the others in the bar.

When he returned with her drink, she said, "I've been with China. Cherokee was released. They were told they could go. They were told they *had* to go, in fact, as soon as there's a flight available off the island. What's happened?"

He seemed to study her, and he did so for a moment that went on and on and brought new heat to her cheeks. He said, "You quite like Cherokee River, don't you?"

"I quite like them both. Simon, what's happened? Tell me. Please."

"The painting was stolen, not purchased," he said, and added evenly, "In Southern California."

"Southern California?" Deborah knew she sounded immediately worried but could not help it despite the events of the last two hours.

"Yes. Southern California." Simon told her the story of the painting. All the time he gazed at her, a long look that began to vex her, making her feel like a child who has in some way disappointed her parent. She *hated* that look of his—she always had—but she said nothing, waiting for him to complete his explanation. "The good nuns of St. Clare's Hospital took precautions with the painting when they knew what they had, but they didn't take enough. Someone inside either learned or already knew the route, the means, and the destination. The van was armoured and the guards had weapons coming and going, but this is America we're talking about, land of the free and the easy purchase of everything from AK-47s to explosives."

"The van was waylaid, then?"

"Bringing the picture back from being restored. As easy as that. And waylaid by something they would never have suspicions about on a California motorway."

"A tailback. Road-works."

"Both."

"But how was it done? How could someone get away?"

"The van overheated in the crush of cars, assisted by a slow leak in the radiator, as was discovered later. The driver pulled onto the verge. He had to get out to see to the motor. A motorcyclist took care of the rest."

"In front of all those witnesses? In all the other cars and lorries?"

"Yes. But what did they actually see? A cyclist stopping to offer help to a disabled vehicle, first, and then later that same cyclist skimming along between the traffic lanes where the cars are idling—"

"Unable to follow him. Yes. I see how it happened. But where . . . How would Guy Brouard have known . . . All the way in Southern California?"

"He'd been looking for the painting for years, Deborah. If I found the story about it on the Internet, how difficult would it have been for him to do the same? And once he had the information, his money and one visit to California did the rest."

"But if he didn't know how important a piece it was . . . who the artist was . . . anything, really . . . Simon, that means he would have had to follow every story about art that he could get his hands on. For years."

"He had the time to do it. And this particular story was extraordinary. A World War Two veteran makes a deathbed gift of his wartime 'souvenir' to the hospital that saved his son's life in childhood. The gift turns out to be a priceless work of art that no one even knew the artist had painted. It's worth millions upon millions and the nuns are going to sell it at auction to bolster their hospital's funds. It's a big story, Deborah. It was only a matter of time before Guy Brouard saw it and did something about it."

"So he went there personally . . ."

"To make the arrangements, yes. That's all. To make the arrangements."

"So . . ." Deborah knew how he might interpret her next question, but she asked it anyway because she needed to know, because something wasn't right and she could *sense* it. She'd sensed it in Smith Street. She sensed it now. "If all this happened in California, why has DCI Le Gallez released Cherokee? Why is he telling them both—Cherokee and China—to leave the island?"

"I expect he's got new evidence," Simon answered. "Something pointing to someone else."

"You didn't tell him . . . ?"

"About the painting? No, I didn't tell him."

"Why?"

"The person who delivered the painting to the Tustin attorney for transport to Guernsey wasn't Cherokee River, Deborah. He bore no resemblance to Cherokee River. Cherokee River was not involved."

Before Paul Fielder could even put his hand on the knob, Billy opened the front door of their terraced house in the Bouet. Obviously, he'd been waiting for Paul's return, no doubt sitting in the lounge with the television blaring, smoking his fags and drinking his lager, shouting to be left alone if one of the younger kids happened too near. He'd've been watching through the window for the moment Paul came up the uneven path. When he saw Paul trudging in the direction of the door, he'd stationed himself where he would be the first to have contact with him.

Paul wasn't inside the house before Billy said, "Well, lookit here. The cat's furball's finally come home. Police done with you, wanker? They show you a good time up the gaol? I hear that's what they do best, the cops."

Paul pushed past him. He heard his dad calling out, "That our Paulie?" from somewhere upstairs and his mum said, "Paulie? That you, dear?" from the kitchen.

Paul looked towards the stairs and then the kitchen and wondered what his parents were both doing home. When darkness fell, his dad always returned from the road crew, but his mum worked long hours at the till at Boots and she always worked overtime if she could get it, which was most days. As a result, evening meals were pretty much a catch-as-catch-can affair. You took a tin of soup or one of baked beans. You might make toast. You did for yourself, except for the little ones. Paul generally did for them.

He went towards the stairs, but Billy stopped him. He said, "Hey. Where's the dog, wanker? Where's your constant con-pan-yon?"

Paul hesitated. At once, he felt fear grip his insides. He hadn't seen Taboo since the morning, when the police had come. In the back of the panda car, he'd squirmed round in his seat because Taboo was following. The dog was barking. He was running behind them, determined to catch them up.

Paul looked round. Where was Taboo?

He put his lips together to whistle, but his mouth was too dry. He heard his father's tread on the stairs. At the same moment, his mum came from the kitchen. She wore an apron with a ketchup stain on it. She wiped her hands on a towel.

"Paulie," his dad said in a sombre voice.

"Dear," his mum said.

Billy laughed. "He got hit. Stupid dog got hit. First a car then a lorry and he just kept on going. Ended up barking like a wild hyena on the side of the road and waiting for someone to come along an' shoot him."

Ol Fielder snapped, "That's enough, Bill. Get out to the pub or wherever you're going."

Billy said, "I don't aim to—"

Mave Fielder cried, "You'll mind your dad this instant!" in a shriek that was so out of character in Paul's mild-mannered mother that her firstborn child gaped at her like a feeding fish before he shuffled to the door, where he picked up his denim jacket.

"Dumb shit," he said to Paul. "Can't even take care of nothing, can you? Not even a stupid dog." He pushed out into the night and slammed the door behind him. Paul could hear him laugh foully and say, "Sod all of you losers."

But nothing Billy said or did could touch him.

He stumbled into the lounge but saw nothing in front of him except the vision of Taboo. Taboo racing behind the police car. Taboo on the side of the road, fatally injured but barking and snarling frantically so that no one would come near for fear of his teeth. It was all his fault for not shouting out for the police to stop long enough for his dog to leap into the car. Or at least long enough for him to take the mongrel back home and tie him up.

He felt his knees against the worn old sofa and he sank onto it with his vision gone blurry. Someone hurried across the room to join him there, and he felt an arm go round his shoulders. It was meant to be a comfort to him, but it felt like a band of hot metal. He cried out and tried to jerk away.

"I know you're cut up about this, son," his father's voice said, into his ear so he couldn't miss the words. "They got the poor thing down the vet's. They phoned right up. Got your mum at work because someone down there knew whose dog it was and—"

It. His dad was calling Taboo *it*. Paul couldn't bear the sound of such a *nothing* word to refer to his friend, the only person who knew him through and through. Because he *was* a person, that mangy dog. He was no more an *it* than Paul was himself.

". . . so we'll go right over. They're waiting," his father finished.

Paul looked up at him, confused, frightened. What had he said?

Mave Fielder seemed to know what Paul was thinking. She said, "They haven't put him down yet,

love. I told them no. I said to wait. I said Our
Paulie's got to be there to say goodbye so you do
what you can to make that poor dog comfortable
and you stop right there till Paul's by his side. Dad'll
take you now. Kids and I . . ." She gestured back towards the kitchen, where doubtless Paul's brothers
and sister were having tea, a special treat with their
mother home to cook it for once. "We'll wait here
for you, dear." And as Paul and his father rose, she
added, "I'm that sorry, Paul," as he passed her.

Outside, Paul's dad said nothing more. They
shambled over to his old van with *Fielder's Butchery,
The Meat Market* still visible in faded red on the side.
They clambered inside in silence and Ol Fielder
started up the engine.

It took far too long to get there from the Bouet,
for the twenty-four-hour surgery was all the way
over on Route Isabelle and there was no direct way
to it. So they had to negotiate the journey to and
through St. Peter Port at the worst time of day, and
all along Paul was in the clutch of an illness that
turned his stomach liquid. His palms became wet and
his face became icy. He could see the dog but he
could see nothing else: just the image of him running
along and barking barking behind that police car because the only person he loved in the world was being taken from him. They'd never been parted, Paul
and Taboo. Even when Paul was at school, the dog
was there, patient as a nun and never far away.

"Here, lad. Come inside, all right?"

His dad's voice was gentle, and Paul allowed himself to be led to the door of the surgery. Everything

was a blur. He could smell the mix of animals and medicines. He could hear the voices of his dad and the veterinary assistant. But he couldn't really see and it wasn't until he'd been drawn to the back, to the quiet dim corner spot where an electric heater kept a shrouded form warm and a drip sent something soothing into that small form's veins.

"He's got no pain," Paul's father murmured into his ear just before Paul reached out to the dog. "We told 'em that, son. Keep him comfortable. Don't put him out 'cause we want him to know his Paulie's with him. That's just what they've done."

Another voice joined them. "This is the owner? You're Paul?"

"This is him," Ol Fielder said.

They talked over Paul's head as he bent to the dog, easing back the blanket to see Taboo with his eyes half-closed, lightly panting, a needle inserted into a shaved strip along his leg. Paul lowered his face to the dog's. He breathed into Taboo's licorice nose. The dog whimpered, and his eyes fluttered wearily. His tongue came out—so weak the movement was—and he touched it to Paul's cheek in a faint hello.

Who could know what they shared, what they were, and what they knew together? No one. Because what they had, were, and knew was between them alone. When people thought of a dog, they thought of an animal. But Paul had never thought of Taboo like that. Dog, he knew, was God spelled backwards. Being with a doG was being with love and hope.

Stupid, stupid, stupid, his brother would have said.

Stupid, stupid, stupid, the whole world would have said.

But that made no difference to Paul and Taboo. They shared a soul together. They were part of one being.

". . . surgical procedures," the vet was saying. Paul couldn't tell if he spoke to his dad or to someone else. ". . . spleen, but that doesn't have to be fatal . . . the biggest challenge . . . those back legs . . . could be a fruitless endeavour at the end of it all . . . difficult to know . . . it's a very tough call."

"Out of the question, 'm afraid," Ol Fielder said regretfully. "The cost . . . Don't mean to put too fine a point on it."

". . . understand . . . of course."

"I mean, this today . . . what you've done . . ." He sighed gustily. "This'll take some . . ."

"Yes. I see . . . Of course . . . Long shot anyway, what with the hips crushed . . . extensive orthopaedic . . ."

Paul looked up from Taboo as he realised what they were talking about, his father and the vet. From his position, bent to the dog, both of them looked like giants: the vet in his long white coat and Ol Fielder in his dusty work clothes. But they were giants of sudden promise to Paul. They held out hope, and that was all he needed.

He straightened and took his father's arm. Ol Fielder looked at him, then shook his head. "It's more than we can pay, my boy, more than your mum and me can afford. And even if they did all of it to him, poor Taboo'd likely never be the same."

Paul turned his anxious gaze upon the vet. He wore a plastic tag that called him Alistair Knight, D.V.M., MRCVS. The vet said, "He'd be slower, that's the truth of it. Over time, he'd be arthritic as well. And as I said, there's a chance none of it would keep him alive in the first place. Even if it did, his convalescence would take months on end."

"Too much," Ol Fielder said. "You see that, don't you, Paulie? Me and your mum . . . We can't manage it, lad . . . A fortune, we're talking about. We haven't got . . . I'm that sorry, Paul."

Mr. Knight squatted and ran his hand along Taboo's tousled fur. He said, "He's a good dog, though. Aren't you, boy?" And as if he understood, Taboo sent his pale tongue forth again. He shivered and wheezed. His front paws twitched. "We'll need to put him down, then," Mr. Knight said, rising. "I'll fetch the jab." And to Paul, "It'll be a comfort to both of you if you hold him."

Paul bent to the dog again, but he didn't lift Taboo in his arms as he otherwise might have done. Lifting him would do him more damage, and Paul meant no more damage to be done.

Ol Fielder shuffled on his feet as they waited for the vet to return. Paul gently drew the cover up over his hurt Taboo. He reached out and moved the electric fire closer, and when the vet rejoined them with two hypodermics in his hand, Paul was finally ready.

Ol Fielder squatted. So did the vet. Paul reached out and stayed the doctor's hand. "I got the money," he said to Mr. Knight so clearly, he might have been speaking the first words ever spoken between two people. "I don't care what it costs me. Save my dog."

Deborah and her husband were just tucking into their first course at dinner when the maître d' approached them deferentially and spoke to Simon. There was a gentleman, he said—he seemed to be using the word loosely—who wanted to speak to Mr. St. James. He was waiting just outside the restaurant door. Did Mr. St. James wish to send him a message? To speak with him now?

Simon turned in his chair to look in the direction the maître d' had come from. Deborah did the same and saw a lumpy man in a dark green anorak lurking beyond the doorway, watching them, watching *her,* it seemed. When her eyes met his, he shifted them to Simon.

Simon said, "It's DCI Le Gallez. Excuse me, my love," and he went to speak to the man.

Both of them turned their backs to the doorway. They spoke for less than a minute and Deborah watched, trying to interpret the unexpected appearance of the police at their hotel as she also tried to gauge the intensity—or lack thereof—of their conversation. In short order, Simon returned to her, but he did not sit.

"I've got to leave you." His face looked grave. He picked up the napkin he'd left on the chair and folded it precisely, as was his habit.

"Why?" she asked.

"It seems I was right. Le Gallez has new evidence. He'd like me to have a look at it."

"That can't wait? Till after . . . ?"

"He's champing at the bit. Apparently he wants to make an arrest tonight."

"Arrest? Of whom? With your approval or something? Simon, that doesn't—"

"I must go, Deborah. Continue with your meal. I shouldn't be gone long. It's only the police station. I'll just pop round the corner and be back directly." He bent and kissed her.

She said, "Why did he come personally to get you? He could have . . . Simon!" But he was walking off.

Deborah sat for a moment, staring at the single candle that flickered on their table. She had that uneasy sensation that tends to fall upon a listener when she hears a bald-faced lie. She didn't want to race after her husband and demand an explanation, but at the same time she knew that she couldn't just sit there docilely like a doe in the forest. So she found the middle ground, and she left the restaurant in favour of the bar, where a window overlooked the front of the hotel.

There she saw Simon shrugging into his coat. Le Gallez was speaking to a uniformed constable. Out in the street, a police car stood idling with a driver behind the wheel. Behind that car waited a white police van through whose windows Deborah could see the silhouettes of other policemen.

She gave a little cry. She could feel the pain of it and knew that pain for what it was. But she had no time to assess the damage. She hurried from the bar.

She'd left her bag and her coat in their room. At Simon's suggestion, she realised now. He'd said, "You won't be needing any of that, will you, my love," and she'd cooperated as she *always* cooperated . . . with him so wise, so concerned, so . . . *what?* So determined to keep her from following him. While he, of course, had his own coat somewhere quite close to the restaurant because he'd known all along that Le Gallez was going to come calling in the midst of their meal.

But Deborah wasn't the fool her husband apparently thought she was. She had the advantage of intuition. She also had the greater advantage of having already been where she believed they were going. Where they *had* to be going, despite everything Simon had said to her earlier to make her think otherwise.

With her coat and her bag, she flew back down the stairs and out into the night. The police vehicles were gone, leaving the pavement empty and the street free. She broke into a run and raced to the car park round the corner from the hotel and facing the police station. She wasn't surprised to see no panda cars or van standing in its courtyard: It had been highly unlikely from the first that Le Gallez had come with an escort to fetch Simon and to transport him less than one hundred yards to the offices of the States police.

• • •

"We rang the manor house to let her know," Le Gallez was saying to St. James as they sped through the darkness towards St. Martin, "but there was no answer."

"What do you take that to mean?"

"I hope to God it means she's gone off somewhere for the night. A concert. Church service. Meal with a friend. She's a Samaritan, and they might have something on tonight. We can only hope."

They took the turns up *Le Val des Terres*, hugging the moss-grown wall that held back the hillside and the trees. With the van close behind them, they emerged into the precinct of Fort George, where street lights shone on the empty green that edged the east side of Fort Road. The houses on the west looked strangely uninhabited at this hour, save Bertrand Debiere's. There every light was on in the front of the building, as if the architect were beaming someone home.

They coursed quickly in the direction of St. Martin, the only sound among them the periodic crackling of the police radio. Le Gallez snatched this up as they finally made the turn into one of the island's ubiquitous narrow lanes, whipping along beneath the trees until they came upon the wall that marked the boundary of *Le Reposoir*. He told the driver of the van that followed to take the turn that would direct him down to the bay. Leave the vehicle there and bring your officers back up along the footpath, he instructed. They would reconvene just on the inside of the gates to the estate.

"And for God's sake, keep out of sight," he ordered before he snapped the radio back where it belonged. To the driver of their own car he said, "Pull in at the Bayside. Go round the back."

The Bayside was a hotel, closed for the season like so many others outside of St. Peter Port. It hulked on the edge of the road in darkness, three-quarters of a mile from the gates to *Le Reposoir.* They pulled round to the back, where a rubbish bin stood next to a padlocked door. A bank of security lights blazed on immediately. Le Gallez made short work of unhooking his safety belt and throwing open the car door as soon as the vehicle stopped.

As they hiked back along the road towards the Brouard property, St. James added to Le Gallez's knowledge of the estate's layout. Once inside the walls, they ducked into the thickest growth of chestnuts along the drive, and they waited for the officers from the van to climb the footpath from the bay and join them.

"You're certain of all this?" was all Le Gallez muttered as they stood in the darkness and stamped their feet against the cold.

"It's the only explanation that works," St. James replied.

"It had better be."

Nearly ten minutes passed before the other policemen—panting heavily from their quick ascent from the bay—passed through the gates and faded into the trees to join them. At that point, Le Gallez said to St. James, "Show us where it is," and gave him the lead.

The miracle of being married to a photographer was in her sense for detail: what Deborah noticed and what Deborah remembered. So there was little challenge involved in finding the dolmen. Their main concern was to keep out of sight: of the cottage that contained the Duffys at the edge of the property, of the manor house where Ruth Brouard had failed to answer the phone. To do this, they inched their way along the east side of the drive. They circled the house at a distance of some thirty yards, clinging to the protection of the trees and feeling their way without aid of torches.

The night was extraordinarily dark; a heavy cover of clouds obscured the moon and stars. The men walked single file beneath the trees, with St. James in the lead. In this manner, they approached the shrubbery behind the stables, seeking the break in the hedge that would take them ultimately to the woods and the path, beyond which was the walled paddock where the dolmen lay.

Having no stile, the stone wall offered no easy access to the paddock which spread out beyond it. For someone unencumbered by a leg brace, mounting the wall presented very little problem. But for St. James, the situation was more complicated and made even more difficult by the darkness.

Le Gallez seemed to realise this. He clicked on a small torch that he took from his pocket and, without comment, he moved along the edge of the wall till he found a spot where the stones at the top had crumbled, offering a narrow gap through which someone might more easily lift himself. He muttered, "This'll do, I think," and he went first into the paddock.

Once within, they found themselves surrounded by a nearly prehensile growth of briars, bracken, and brambles. Le Gallez's anorak got snagged immediately, and two of the constables that followed him were soon cursing quietly as thorns from the encroaching bushes tore at them.

"Jesus," Le Gallez muttered as he ripped his jacket from the branch on which it was snagged. "You're certain this is the spot?"

"There has to be an easier access," St. James said.

"Damn right on that." Le Gallez said to one of the other men, "Give us heavier light, Saumarez."

St. James said, "We don't want to warn—"

"We're going to be good for sod all," Le Gallez said, "if we end up like bugs in a web. Saumarez, hit it. Keep it low."

The constable in question carried a powerful torch that flooded the ground with light when he switched it on. St. James groaned when he saw it— surely, it seemed, the lights would be seen from the house—but at least luck was with them when it came to the spot they'd chosen to go over the wall. For less than ten yards to their right, they could see a path that led through the paddock.

"Cut it," Le Gallez ordered, seeing this himself. The light went out. The DCI forged off through the brambles, beating them down for the men that followed. The darkness was thus both a gift and a curse. It had prevented them from easily finding the path to the middle of the paddock, leaving them instead in the middle of a botanic mire. But it also hid their passage through the overgrowth to the main path, which would have otherwise shown up only too well had the moon and the stars been visible.

The dolmen was much as Deborah had described it to St. James. It rose in the paddock's centre, as if several acres of land had been walled off generations in the past with the express intention of protecting it. To the unschooled, it might have appeared to be an inexplicable knoll plopped down without reason in the middle of a field long gone to seed. But to someone with an eye for indications of prehistory, it would have marked a spot worthy of excavation.

Access round it was by means of a narrow course hacked away from the surrounding growth. It skirted its circumference at a width of something less than two feet, and the men followed this path till they came to the thick wooden door with its combination lock hanging from a hasp.

Here Le Gallez stopped, shining his pocket torch again, this time on the lock. From there he shone it upon the bracken and the brambles. "No easy cover," he said quietly.

There was truth to that. If they were to lie in wait for their killer, it wasn't going to be easy. On the other hand, they wouldn't need to be any great distance from the dolmen since the growth of plants was so thick that it supplied plenty of cover.

"Hughes, Sebastian, Hazell," Le Gallez said with a nod towards the vegetation. "See to it. You've got five minutes. I want access without visibility. And quiet, for the love of God. You break a leg, you keep it to yourself. Hawthorne, you're by the wall. Anyone comes over, I've got my pager on vibrate. The rest of you, mobiles off, pagers off, radios off. No one talks, no one sneezes, no one burps, no one farts. We cock this up, we're back to square one and I'm not a happy man. Got it? Go."

Their advantage, St. James knew, was the hour itself. For although it seemed to be darkest night, it was not yet late. There was little chance that their killer would venture to the dolmen prior to midnight. There was too great a risk of coming upon someone else on the estate any earlier than that and too few excuses one could make for stumbling round the grounds of *Le Reposoir* without aid of torchlight after dark.

So it was with surprise that St. James heard Le Gallez stifle a curse and say tersely not fifteen minutes later, "Hawthorne's got someone on the perimeter. Shite. Damn it all to *hell*," and to the constables who were still hacking at the brambles some fifteen feet from the wooden door, "I said five *minutes,* you lot. We're coming through."

He led the way and St. James followed. Le Gallez's men had managed to establish a rough blind the size of a dog crate in the undergrowth. It was suitable for two watchers. Five squeezed into it.

Whoever was coming did so quickly, no hesitation marking a passage over the wall and along the path. In very short order a dark figure moved against the additional darkness. Only an elongating shadow against the bracken that grew on the mound marked

a progress that was defined by the certainty of someone's having been at this spot before.

Then a voice spoke quietly, firmly, and unmistakably. "Simon. Where are you?"

"What the *living* hell . . ." Le Gallez muttered.

"I know you're here and I'm not going away,"
Deborah said clearly.

St. James breathed out, half curse and half sigh.
He should have considered this. He said to Le
Gallez, "She's worked it out."

"Tell me something to surprise me," the DCI
commented. "Get her the hell out of here."

"That," St. James said, "is not going to be easy."
He edged past Le Gallez and the constables. He
worked his way back to the dolmen, saying, "Here,
Deborah."

She swung round in his direction. She said simply, "You lied to me."

He didn't reply till he reached her. He could see
her face, ghostlike in the darkness. Her eyes were
large and dark, and he was reminded at the worst
possible time of those same eyes of the child she had
been at her mother's funeral nearly two decades earlier, confused but seeking someone to trust. "I'm
sorry," he said. "I couldn't see the alternative."

"I want to know—"

"This isn't the place. You've got to go. Le Gallez's
stretched a point letting me be here. He isn't about
to stretch it further for you."

"No," she said. "I know what you think. I'm going to stay to see you proved wrong."

"This isn't about right or wrong," he told her.

"Of course," she said. "It never is for you. It's just about the facts and how you interpret them. To hell with anyone who interprets them differently. But I know these people. You don't. You never have. You see them only through—"

"You're jumping to conclusions, Deborah. We haven't the time to argue. There's too much risk. You've got to leave."

"You're going to have to carry me out of here, then." He could hear the maddening tone of finality in her voice. "You should have thought of that in advance. 'What do I do if darling Deb discovers I'm not toddling off to the police station after all?' "

"Deborah, for the love of God—"

"What in *Christ's* sake is going on?"

Le Gallez made the demand from just behind St. James. He advanced on Deborah with the best intention of intimidating her.

St. James hated to have to admit openly to someone he barely knew that he was not—and had never been, God help him—the master of this willful red-head. In another world at another time, a man might have had some sort of power over a woman like Deborah. But they, unfortunately, did not live in that long-ago world where women became the property of their men by virtue of having married them. He said, "She isn't going to—"

"I'm not leaving." Deborah spoke directly to Le Gallez.

"You'll do as you're bloody well told, Madam, or I'll have you locked up," the DCI replied.

"That's fine," she replied. "You're good at that, as I understand. You've locked up both of my friends so far with limited cause. Why not me as well?"

"Deborah . . ." St. James knew it was futile to reason with her, but he made the attempt. "You're not in possession of all the facts."

"And why is that?" she asked him pointedly.

"There hasn't been time."

"Oh, really?"

He could tell from her tone—and what was, to him, the very *scent* of emotion beneath her words— that he'd misjudged the impact it would have upon her for him to forge ahead without her knowledge. Yet he *hadn't* had the right to bring her into the picture as fully as she apparently wanted. Things had moved too swiftly for that.

She said to him in a low voice, "We came here together. To help them together."

He knew the rest that Deborah did not say: *So we were meant to finish this together.* But that was not the case and at the moment he couldn't explain why. They weren't some latter-day Tommy and Tuppence come to Guernsey, larking their way through mischief, mayhem, and murder. A real man had died, not a fairy-tale villain conveniently done in because he richly deserved it. The only form of justice that existed for that man now was to trap his killer in a single moment of self-revelation that would itself be jeopardised to hell and back if St. James could not resolve this situation with the woman standing before him.

He said, "I'm sorry. There is no time. Later, I'll explain."

She said, "Fine. I'll be waiting. You can visit me in gaol."

"Deborah, for God's sake . . ."

Le Gallez interrupted. "Jesus, man." And then to Deborah, "I'll deal with you later, Madam."

He turned on his heel and strode back to the blind. From this, St. James took it that Deborah was meant to stay with them. He didn't much like that, but he knew better than to argue with his wife any further. He, too, would have to deal with the situation at another time.

Chapter 30

THEY'D CREATED A HIDEY-HOLE for themselves. Deborah saw that it comprised a rectangle of roughly beaten down vegetation in which two other police officers were already lying in wait. There had apparently been a third, but he'd set himself up along the far perimeter of the paddock for some reason. She could see no sense in that, for there was only one way in and one way out: on the single path through the bushes.

Otherwise, she had no idea how many policemen were in the area, and she didn't much care. She was still attempting to cope with the realisation that her husband had deliberately and with plenty of forethought lied to her for the first time in their marriage. At least she *believed* it was the first time in their marriage, although she was perfectly willing to admit that anything else was possible at this point. So she alternated among seething, plotting revenge, and planning what she intended to say to him once the police had made whatever arrest they thought they were going to make that night.

The cold descended upon them like a Biblical

scourge, easing in from the bay first and then stretching across the paddock. It reached them somewhere close to midnight, or so it seemed to Deborah. No one was willing to risk the light it would take to look at the face of a watch.

They all held to silence. Minutes passed and then hours with nothing happening. Occasionally, a rustle in the bushes would strike tension throughout their little group. But when nothing followed the rustling save more rustling, the noise was put down to some creature into whose habitat they had intruded. A rat possibly. Or a feral cat, curious to investigate the interlopers.

It seemed to Deborah that they'd waited till nearly dawn, when Le Gallez finally murmured a single word, "Coming," which she might have missed altogether had not a collective rigidity seem to tighten the limbs of the men in their hiding place.

Then she heard it: the crunch of stones on the paddock wall, followed by the snap of a twig on the ground as someone approached the dolmen in the darkness. No torch lit a way that was obviously known to the person who had joined them. It was only a moment before a figure—shrouded in black like a banshee—slipped onto the path that encircled the mound.

At the door to the dolmen, the banshee risked a torch, shining it on the combination lock. From the brambles, however, all Deborah could see was the edge of a small pool of light which gave enough illumination to highlight the black silhouette of a back bent to the doorway, which gave access to the mound.

She waited for the police to make their move. No one did. No one, it seemed, even breathed as the figure at the dolmen unfastened the lock on the door and crouched, entering the prehistoric chamber.

The door remained halfway open in the banshee's wake, and in a moment a soft gleam from what Deborah knew to be a candle flickered. Then it grew brighter from a second flame. Beyond the doorway, though, they could see nothing, and whatever movement occurred within was stifled by the thickness of the stone walls of the chamber and of the earth that had covered them for generations.

Deborah couldn't understand why the police did nothing. She murmured to Simon, "What . . . ?"

His hand closed on her arm. She couldn't see his face, but she had the distinct sense that he was intent upon the dolmen's door.

Three minutes passed, no more, when the candles within were suddenly extinguished. The steady and small pool of light from the torch took their place, and it approached the door of the dolmen from within just as DCI Le Gallez whispered, "Steady now, Saumarez. Wait. Easy. Easy, man."

As the figure emerged and then stood upright, Le Gallez said, "Now." Nearby in their cramped little space, the officer in question rose and in the same movement switched on a torch so powerful that it blinded Deborah for a moment and did much the same to China River, caught both in its beam and in Le Gallez's trap.

• • •

"Stay where you are, Miss River," the DCI ordered. "The painting's not there."

"No," Deborah whispered. She heard Simon murmur, "I'm sorry, my love," but she didn't quite take it in, for things happened too quickly after that.

At the door to the dolmen, China spun as a second light from the wall behind them picked her out like a hunter's quarry. She said nothing. Instead, she ducked back inside the earthen mound and shoved the door closed behind her.

Deborah rose without thinking. She cried out, "China!" and then in a panic to her husband and to the police, "It's *not* what it seems."

As if she hadn't spoken, Simon said in answer to something to Le Gallez asked him, "Just the camp bed, some candles, a wooden box holding condoms . . ." and she knew that every word she'd spoken to her husband about the dolmen was something he had relayed to the Guernsey police.

This somehow—illogically, ridiculously, stupidly, but she could not help it, she could *not* help it— seemed like an even greater betrayal to Deborah. She couldn't think through it; she couldn't think past it. She could only charge out of their hiding spot to go to her friend.

Simon grabbed her before she got five feet.

She cried, "Let me go!" and wrested away from him. She heard Le Gallez say, "God damn it. Get her away!" and she cried, "I'll get her for you. Let me go. Let me go!"

She twisted from Simon's grasp but she didn't

leave him. They confronted each other, breathing hard. Deborah said, "She has nowhere to go. You know that. So do they. I'm going to fetch her. You must *let* me fetch her."

"I don't have that power."

"Tell them."

Le Gallez said, "You're certain?" to Simon. "No other way out?"

Deborah said, "What difference does it make if there is? How's she going to get off the island? She knows you'll phone the airport and the harbour. Is she supposed to swim to France? She'll come out when I . . . Let me tell her who's out here . . ." She heard her voice quaver and *hated* the fact that here and now she would have to battle not only with the police, not only with Simon, but also with her blasted emotions, which would never for an instant allow her to be what he was: cool, dispassionate, able to adjust his thinking in a moment on the edge of a coin, if it came down to it. Which it had.

She said brokenly to Simon, "What made you decide . . . ?" But she couldn't finish the question.

He said, "I didn't know. Not as a certainty. Just that it had to be one of them."

"What haven't you told me? No. I don't care. Let me *go* to her. I'll tell her what she's facing. I'll bring her out."

Simon studied her in silence, and Deborah could see the extent of the indecision that played on his intelligent, angular features. But she could also see the worry there of how much damage he'd done to her ability to trust him.

He said over her shoulder to Le Gallez, "Will you allow—"

"Bloody hell, no I will not. This is a killer we're talking about. We've got one corpse. I won't have another." Then to his men, "Bring the sodding bitch out."

Which was enough to spur Deborah on her way to the dolmen. She shot back through the bushes and reached the door into the mound before Le Gallez could even shout "Grab her."

Once she was there, they had little choice but to wait for what would happen next. They could storm the dolmen and risk her life if China was armed, which Deborah knew she was not, or they could wait till Deborah brought her friend out. What would happen after that—her own arrest, most likely—was something about which she did not care at the moment.

She shoved open the thick wooden door and entered the ancient chamber.

With the door shut behind her, black enveloped her, thick and silent like a tomb. The last noise she heard was a shout from Le Gallez, which the heavy door cut off when she closed it. The last sight she had was the spearpoint of light that fast extinguished at the same moment.

She said into the stillness, "China," and she listened. She tried to picture what she'd seen of the dolmen's interior when she'd been inside with Paul Fielder. The main inner chamber was straight ahead of her. The secondary chamber was to her right. There might be, she realised, further chambers within, perhaps to her left, but she hadn't seen them earlier and she couldn't recall if there were any additional fissures that might lead into one.

She put herself in the place of her friend, in the place of anyone caught in this position. Safety, she thought. The feeling of being returned to the womb. The inner side chamber, which was small and secure.

She reached for the wall. It was useless waiting for her eyes to adjust, for there was nothing to which her eyes *could* adjust. No light pierced the gloom, not a flicker, not a gleam.

She said, "China. The police are out there. They're in the paddock. There're three of them about thirty feet from the door and one on the wall and I don't know how many more in the trees. I didn't come with them. I didn't know. I followed. Simon . . ." Even at this last, she couldn't tell her friend that her own husband had apparently been the instrument of China's downfall. She said, "There's no way out of here. I don't want you to get hurt. I don't know why . . ." But her voice couldn't get through that sentence with the calm that she wanted, so she took another route. "There's an explanation for everything. I know that. There is. Isn't there. China."

She listened hard as she felt for the fissure that gave way to the small side chamber. She told herself there was nothing to fear, for this was her friend, the woman who'd seen her through a bad time that was the worst time ever, one of love and loss, of indecision, action, and action's aftermath. She'd held her and promised, "Debs, it'll pass. It *will* pass, believe me."

In the darkness, Deborah said China's name again. She added, "Let me walk you out of here. I want to help you. I want to see you through this. I'm your friend."

She gained the inner chamber, her jacket brushing against the stone wall. She heard the rustle of its material and so, apparently, did China River. She finally spoke.

"Friend," she said. "Oh yes, Debs. Aren't you ever my friend." She flicked on the torch that she'd used to illuminate the lock on the dolmen's door. The resulting light struck Deborah squarely in the face. It came low from the camp bed, where China was sitting. Behind its bright glow, her face was as white as a marble death mask hovering above the light. "You," China said to her simply, "don't know shit about friendship. You never have. So don't talk to me about what you can do to help me out."

"I didn't bring the police here. I didn't know . . ." Except Deborah couldn't quite lie, not in this final moment. For she'd been on Smith Street earlier, hadn't she? She'd returned there, and she'd seen no shop to buy the sweets that China had claimed to have secured for her brother. Cherokee himself had opened her shoulder bag in a search for money and had brought forth nothing, especially not the chocolate bars he supposedly loved. Deborah said more to herself than to China, "Was it that travel agent? Is that where you'd gone? Yes, that had to be it. You were laying your plans, where you'd go first when you got off the island because you knew they'd release you. After all, they had him. That must have been what you wanted from the first, what you planned, even. But why?"

"You'd want to know that, wouldn't you." China played the light up and down Deborah's body. She said, "Perfect in every way. Good at everything you set out to do. Always the apple of some man's eye. I can see you'd want to understand how it feels to be good for nothing and have someone oh-too-happy to prove it for you."

"You can't say you killed him because of . . . China, what did you do? Why did you do it?"

"Fifty dollars," she said flatly. "That and a surfboard. Think about it, Deborah. Fifty dollars and a banged-up surfboard."

"What're you talking about?"

"I'm *talking* about what he paid. The price tag. He thought it would be only once. They both thought that. But I was good—a whole lot better than he expected and a whole lot better than I expected—so he came back for more. The original plan was just to get his cherry taken care of, and my brother assured him that I'd go for it if he treated me right and acted like a real nice guy, if he pretended he wasn't interested in that. So that's what he did and that's what I did. Only it went on for thirteen years. Which, when you think of it, is pretty much a bargain since he shelled out only fifty dollars and a surfboard to my own brother. To my own *brother*." The torchlight trembled, but she steadied it and forced out a laugh. "Imagine. One person thinking it's love eternal and the other showing up for the best fuck he's ever going to have while all the time—all the *time,* Deborah—there's an attorney in LA and a gallery owner in New York and a surgeon in Chicago and God knows who else in the rest of the country but none of them—are you getting this, Deborah—can fuck him like I do, which is why he keeps coming back for more. And I'm so stupid as to think that in a matter of time, we'll finally be together because it's so good, my God it's so good and he's got to see that, right? And he does, he does, but there're others and there have always been others which is what he finally tells me when I confront him after my God damn brother admits he sold me to his best friend for fifty dollars and a surfboard when I was seventeen years old."

Deborah didn't move and hardly dared to breathe, knowing that to do either might be the one false move that encouraged her friend to leap over the edge she was balanced on. She said the only thing she believed. "That can't be true."

"Which part?" China asked. "The part about you, or the part about me? Because I can tell you, the part about me is fact-o amaze-o. So you must be talking about the part about you. You must be saying your life hasn't just clicked along, day one to day one hundred fucking thousand, and all of it going according to plan."

"Of course it hasn't. It doesn't. No one's does."

"Dad who adores you. Rich boyfriend willing to

do anything for you. Follow up with equally well-heeled husband. *Everything* you ever want. Not a worry in the world. Oh you go through a bad time when you come to Santa Barbara but it all works out and isn't that always the case with you. Everything always works out."

"China, nothing's that easy for anyone. You *know* that."

It was as if Deborah hadn't spoken. "And you just fade away. Like everyone else. As if I haven't put my heart and soul into being your friend when you *needed* a friend. You end up like Matt, don't you. You end up just like everyone. You take what you want and you forget what you owe."

"Are you saying . . . You can't mean you've done all this—what you've done . . . This can't be about—"

"You? Don't flatter yourself. It's time for my brother to pay the piper."

Deborah considered this. She recalled what Cherokee had told her that very first night he'd come to them in London. She said, "You didn't want to come with him to Guernsey, not at first."

"Not till I decided I could use the trip to make him pay," China acknowledged. "I wasn't sure when and I wasn't sure how, but I knew that something would come up sometime. I figured it would be dope in his suitcase when we were going through customs. We planned on Amsterdam, so I'd pick the stuff up there. That would've been nice. Not fool-proof, but a definite possibility. Or maybe a weapon. Or explosives in the carry-on. Or something. The point is I didn't care what it was. I only knew I'd find it if I kept my eyes open. And when we got here to *Le Reposoir* and he showed me . . . well, *what* he showed me . . ." Behind the torch, she offered a ghostlike smile. "There it was," she said. "Too good to pass up."

"Cherokee showed you the painting?"

"Ah," China said. "So you're the one. You and Simon the wonder-husband, I bet. Hell, no, Debs. Cherokee didn't have a clue he was carrying that painting. Neither did I. Not till Guy showed it to me. Come into the study for a nightcap, my lovely. Let me show you something that's bound to impress you more than everything else I've shown you so far or talked about so far or done so far to try to work my way into your panties because that's what I do and that's what you want and I can tell that much by looking at you. And even if you don't, there's no loss in trying, is there, because I'm rich and you're not and rich guys don't have to be anything *other* than rich to get what they want from women and you know that, Debs, more than anyone, don't you. Only this time it wasn't for fifty dollars and a surf-board and the payment didn't go to my brother. It was like killing a dozen birds, not just two. So I fucked him right here when he showed me this place because that's what he wanted, that's why he brought me, that's why he called me special—the asshole—that's why he lit the candle and patted this cot and said What d'you think of my hideaway? Whisper what you think. Come close. Let me touch you. I can make you feel and you can make me feel and the light is gentle against our skin, isn't it, and it glows to gold where we need to be touched. Like on this place and that place and God I do think you may be the one at last, my dear. So I did it with him, Deborah, and believe me, he liked it, just like Matt liked it, and this is where I put the painting when I took it the night before I killed him."

"Oh God," Deborah said.

"God had nothing to do with it. Not then. Not now. Not ever. Not in my life. Maybe in yours, but not in mine. And you know, that's not fair. It's never been fair. I'm as good as you and as good as anyone and I deserve better than what I've been handed."

"So you took the painting? Do you know what it is?"

"I do read the papers," China said. "They're not much in So-Cal and they're worse in Santa Barbara. But the big stories . . . ? Yeah. They cover the big ones."

"But what were you going to do with it?"

"I didn't know. It was an afterthought, really. Not part of the cake, just the frosting. I knew where it was in the study. He wasn't doing much to hide it away. So I took it. I put it in Guy's special place. I'd come back later for it. I knew it'd be safe."

"But anyone could have stumbled in here and found it," Deborah said. "Once they got inside the dolmen, which was only a matter of cutting off the lock if they didn't know the combination. They'd come in with a light, they'd see it, they'd—"

"How?"

"Because it was in plain sight if you went beyond the altar. You couldn't miss it."

"That's where you found it?"

"Not me . . . Paul . . . Guy Brouard's friend . . . The boy . . ."

"Ah," China said. "So he's who I have to thank."

"For what?"

"For replacing it with this." China moved into the light the hand that wasn't holding the torch. Deborah saw it was curled round an object shaped like a small pineapple. She formed the question *what is it* even as her mind made the leap to assimilate what her eyes were seeing.

Outside the dolmen, Le Gallez said to St. James, "I'll give her another two minutes. That's it."

St. James was still attempting to digest the fact that China River and not her brother had appeared at the dolmen. While he'd said to Deborah that he'd known it would have to be one of the siblings—for that was the only reasonable explanation for all that had happened, from the ring on the beach to the bottle in the field—he'd concluded from the first that it would be the brother. And this despite not having had the moral fortitude to admit to that conclusion openly, even to himself. It wasn't so much that murder was a crime he attributed to men more than to women. It was because at an atavistic level he didn't want to lay claim to, he wanted Cherokee River out of the way and had wanted him thus from the moment the American had appeared on their doorstep in London, whole and affable and calling his wife *Debs.*

So he wasn't quick to answer Le Gallez. He was too caught up in attempting to effect a mental elusion of his fallibility and his contemptible personal weakness.

"Saumarez," Le Gallez was saying next to him. "Get ready to move. You others—"

"She'll bring her out," St. James said. "They're friends. She's going to listen to Deborah. She'll bring her out. There's no other alternative."

"I'm not willing to take that risk," Le Gallez said.

The hand grenade looked ancient. Even across the chamber from it, Deborah could see that the thing was crusty with earth and discoloured with rust. It appeared to be an artifact from the Second World War and as such she couldn't believe it was dangerous. How could something so old explode?

China seemed to read her mind, because she said, "But you don't know for sure, do you? Neither do I. Tell me how they worked it all out, Debs."

"Worked what out?"

"Me. This. Here. And with you. They wouldn't have you here if they hadn't known. It doesn't make sense."

"I don't know. I told you. I followed Simon. We were at dinner and the police showed up. Simon told me—"

"Don't lie to me, all right? They had to have

found the poppy-oil bottle or they wouldn't have come for Cherokee. They figured he could have planted the other evidence to make it look like me because why would I risk planting evidence against myself on the strength of just believing they'd find that bottle? So they found it. But from there, what?"

"I don't know about a bottle," Deborah said. "I don't know about poppy oil."

"Oh, please. You know. Papa's little girl? Simon's not going to keep something important from you. So tell me, Debs."

"I have done. I don't know what they know. Simon didn't tell me. He wouldn't."

"Didn't trust you, then?"

"Apparently not." The admission struck Deborah like the unexpected slap from a parent's hand. A poppy-oil bottle. He couldn't trust her. She said, "We need to go. They're waiting. They'll be coming in if we don't—"

"I'm not," China said.

"Not what?"

"Serving time. Standing trial. Whatever they do here. I'm getting out."

"You can't . . . China, there's no place to go. There's no way you can get off the island. They've probably already given the word to . . . You can't."

"You misconstrue," China said. "Out isn't off. Out is out. You and me. Friends—in a manner of speaking—till the end." Carefully, she placed her torch to one side and she began to work at the pin on the old grenade. She murmured, "Can't remember how long it takes for these things to blow, can you?"

Deborah said, "China! No! It won't work. But if it does—"

"That's what I'm hoping," China said.

To Deborah's horror, China managed to work the pin loose. Old and rusty and exposed to God only knew what elements in the last sixty years, it should have been frozen into place, but it wasn't. Like the unexploded bombs that periodically came to light in South London, it lay like a memory in China's hand, with Deborah trying and failing to remember how much time they had—how much time *she* had—to avoid obliteration.

China murmured, "Five, four, three, two . . ."

Deborah flung herself backwards, falling mindlessly, heedlessly into the darkness. For a moment that stretched into infinity, nothing happened. Then an explosion rocked the dolmen with the roar of an Armageddon.

After that came nothing.

The door blew off. It shot like a missile into the dense vegetation, and a gust came with it, foul like a sirocco from hell. Time froze for an instant. In its suspension, all sound disappeared, sucked up by the horror of realisation.

Then after an hour a minute a second all reaction in the universe fixed itself on the head of the pin that was this spot on the island of Guernsey. Sound and movement rose round St. James like the effluence of a bursting dam which discharges water and mud as well as leaves and branches and uprooted trees and the broken corpses of animals that it finds in its path. He was aware of pushing and shoving going on within his protected vantage point of cleared-out vegetation. He felt bodies moving by him and he heard as if from a far-off planet the cursing of one man and the hoarse shouting of another. At a greater distance someone's shrieking seemed to float high above them while all round them lights swung like the limbs of hanged men, trying to pierce through the dust.

Through it all, he stared at the dolmen, knowing the blown-out door, the noise, the gust, and the aftermath all for what they were: manifestations of something that no one had even considered a possibility. When he had accepted this, he began to stumble forward. He made directly for the door without knowing he was in the brambles and caught among them. He tore at the spikes and thorns that held him fast, and if they pierced his flesh, he did not know it. He knew only the door, the interior of that place, and the unspeakable fear of what he would not name but understood all the same because no one had to spell out for him what had just occurred with his wife and a killer trapped together.

Someone grabbed him and he became aware of shouting. The words this time, not only the noise. "Jesus. Here. This way, man. Saumarez. For Christ's sake, get him. Saumarez, give us some bloody *light* over here. Hawthorne, they'll be coming from the house. Keep them *back,* for the love of God."

He was pulled and jerked and then shoved forward. Then he was free of the wild growth that filled the paddock and he was blundering in the wake of Le Gallez, their object the dolmen.

For it still stood as it had stood for one hundred thousand years already: granite hewn out of the very stuff that was this island, fitted into more granite, walled by it, floored by it, ceilinged by it. And then hidden within the earth itself which gave forth man who would attempt again and again to destroy it.

But not succeed. Even now.

Le Gallez was giving orders. He'd taken out his torch and he was shining it into the interior of the dolmen, where it lit the dust which floated out and up like liberated souls on the Day of Judgement. He spoke over his shoulder to one of his men who asked him something, and it was this question—whatever it was, because St. James could take account of nothing but what lay before him, inside that place—that made the DCI pause in the doorway to reply. That pause gave St. James access where he otherwise might not have had it, and so he took it. He took it in prayer, in a bargain with God: If she survives I'll do anything, be anything, try anything You want, accept anything. Just not this please God not this.

He didn't have a torch, but it didn't matter because he didn't need light when he had his hands. He felt his way inside, slapping his palms against the rough surface of the stones, banging his knees, in his haste smashing his head against a low lintel of some sort. He reeled from this. He felt the warmth of his blood as it seeped from the wound he'd made on his brow. He continued to bargain. Be anything, do anything, accept anything You ask of me without question, live only for others, live only for her, be faithful and loyal, listen better, attempt to understand because that's where I fail where I've always failed and You know that don't you which is why You've taken her from me haven't you haven't you haven't you.

He would have crawled but he couldn't, trapped in the brace that held him upright. But he needed to crawl, needed to kneel to make his supplication in the dark and the dust where he could not find her. So he tore at the leg of his trousers and tried to reach the hated plastic and the Velcro and he could not reach it so he cursed as much as he prayed and begged. Which was what he was doing when Le Gallez's light reached him.

"Jesus, man. Jesus," the DCI said, and he shouted behind him, "Saumarez, we need a better light."

But St. James did not. For he saw the colour first, copper it was. Then the mass and the glory of it— how he had always loved her hair.

Deborah lay sprawled just before the slightly raised stone that she had described to him as an altar, in the place where Paul Fielder told her that he had found the painting of the pretty lady with the book and the quill.

St. James stumbled to her. He was dimly aware of other movement round him and of greater light sweeping into this place. He heard voices and the sound of feet scraping against stone. He smelled the dust and the acrid stink of dead explosive. He tasted the salt and the copper of his blood and he felt first the cold hard rough stone of the altar as he reached it and then beyond it the pliant warm flesh that was the body of his wife.

All he saw was Deborah as he turned her over. The blood on her face and in her hair, her clothing torn, her eyelids closed.

Fiercely he pulled her into his arms. Fiercely he pressed her face to his neck. He found himself beyond either prayer or curse, the centre of his life—what made himself just that, himself—torn from him in an instant that he had not and could not have anticipated. Without an instant more to prepare.

He said her name. He shut his eyes against seeing anything more, and he heard nothing.

But still he could feel, not only the body that he held and swore he would not release and would never release, but after a moment the sensation of breath. Shallow, quick, and against his neck. Mercifully, dear God. Against his neck.

"My God," St. James said. "My God. *Deborah.*"

He lowered his wife to the floor and shouted hoarsely for help.

Awareness returned to her in two forms. First was the sound: a high-pitched vibration that never varied in level, tone, or intensity. It filled her ear canal, pulsating against the thin and protective membrane at its core. Then it seemed to seep past the eardrum itself to permeate her skull, and there it stayed. No room remained for ordinary sounds, cast from the world as she knew it.

After sound came sight: light and dark only, shadows posing in front of a curtain that seemed to comprise the sun. Its incandescence was so intense that she could expose herself to it for brief seconds at a time, and then she had to close her eyes again, which made the sound in her head seem louder.

Always the vibration remained. Her eyes opened or closed, herself awake or drifting in and out of consciousness, the noise was there. It became the one constant she could grasp on to, and she took it as an indication that she was alive. Perhaps children heard this as their first sensation of sound when they emerged from the womb, she thought. It was something to hold on to, so that's what she did, swimming up towards it as one would swim for the far-off surface of a lake, its undulations heavy and shifting but always sparkling with the promise of sun and air.

When she could bear the light against her eyes longer than a few seconds, Deborah saw this was because constant day had finally become night. Wherever she was had altered from the brilliance of a stage illuminated for a watching audience to the dim interior of a single room in which one thin bar of fluorescence atop her bed cast a glowing shield downward onto the form of her body, indicated by those hills and valleys in the thin blanket that covered her. Next to the bed sat her husband, in a chair drawn up to her side so that his head could rest against the mattress on which she lay. His arms cradled his head and his face was turned away from her. But she knew that it was Simon because she would always know this one man anywhere on earth that she came upon him. She would know the shape and the size of him, the way his hair curled on the back of his neck, the way his shoulder blades flattened to smooth, strong planes when he lifted his arms to pillow his head.

What she noticed was that his shirt was soiled. Copper stains smeared its collar as if he'd badly cut himself shaving and hastily daubed away the blood by means of his shirt. Streaks of dirt ran down the sleeve closer to her and more copper smudges made seeping marks on the cuffs. She could see no more of him and she lacked the strength to awaken him. All she found she could do was to move her fingers an inch nearer to him. But that was enough.

Simon raised his head. He looked like a miracle to her. He spoke but she couldn't hear him above the sound in her skull, so she shook her head, tried to talk, and found she couldn't do that either because her throat was so parched and her lips and her tongue seemed to stick to her teeth.

Simon reached for something on the table by the bed. He raised her slightly and brought a plastic glass to her lips. A straw bent from the glass and Simon gently eased it into her mouth. She drew in the water gratefully, finding it tepid but not caring. As she drank, she felt him come closer to her. She felt him trembling, and she thought the water would surely spill. She tried to steady his hand, but he stopped her. He brought her hand to his cheek and her fingers to his mouth. He bent to her and pressed his own cheek to the top of her head.

Deborah had survived, he'd been told, because she'd either never gone into the inner chamber where the explosion occurred or because she'd managed to get herself out of there and into the larger chamber seconds before the grenade went off. And it *would* have been a hand grenade, the police reported. There was evidence aplenty to verify that.

As to the other woman . . . One did not deliberately detonate a hand-held bomb packed with TNT and live to talk about it. And it had been a deliberate detonation, the police surmised. There was no other real explanation for the explosion.

"Lucky it happened in the mound," St. James had been told first by the police and then by two of the doctors who had seen his wife at Princess Elizabeth Hospital. "That sort of explosion would have brought anything else down on top of them. She would've been crushed . . . if not blown to Timbuktu. She got lucky. Everyone got lucky. A modern explosive would've taken out the mound and the paddock as well. How the hell'd that woman get her hands on a grenade, though? That's the real question."

But only one of the real questions, St. James thought. The others all began with *why*. That China River had returned to the dolmen to fetch the painting she'd placed there was not in doubt. That she'd somehow come to know the painting had been hidden for transport to Guernsey among the architectural drawings was also clear. That she'd planned and carried out the crime based on what she'd learned about Guy Brouard's habits were two facts that they could piece together from the interviews they'd conducted with the principals involved in the case. But the *why* of it all remained a mystery at first. Why steal a painting she could not hope to sell on the open market, but only to a private collector for a great deal less than it was worth . . . and only if she could find a collector who was willing to operate outside the law? Why plant evidence against herself on the slim chance that the police would find a bottle with her brother's fingerprints on it, a bottle containing traces of the opiate that had drugged the victim? And why plant that piece of evidence against her own brother? That most of all.

And then there was *how.* How had she come to get her hands on that fairy wheel that she'd used to choke Brouard? Had he shown it to her? Had she known he carried it? Had she planned to use it? Or had that merely been a moment of inspiration during which she decided to muddy the waters by using, instead of the ring she'd brought with her to the bay, something she found that morning in the pocket of his discarded clothes?

Some of these questions St. James hoped that his wife would be able to answer in time. Others, he knew, they could never answer.

Deborah's hearing would return, he was told. It might or might not have been permanently damaged by her proximity to the explosion, but they would ascertain that over time. She'd sustained a severe concussion, the complete recovery from which would take a number of months. Doubtless she would experience some memory loss about the events immediately surrounding the detonation of the hand grenade. But he wasn't to press her about those events. She would recall what she could when she could, if ever.

He phoned her father hourly with reports. When every chance of danger was passed, he spoke to Deborah about what had happened. He spoke directly into her ear, his voice low and his hand covering hers. The dressings were gone from the cuts on her face, but the stitches from a gash on her jaw were still to be removed. Her bruises were frightening to behold, but she was restless. She wanted to go home. Home to her dad, to her photography, to their dog and their cat, to Cheyne Row, to London and all that was most familiar to her.

She said, "China's dead, isn't she?" in a voice that was still uncertain of its own strength. "Tell me. I think I can hear if you get close enough."

Which was where he wanted to be anyway. So he eased himself onto the hospital bed next to her and he told her what had happened as far as he knew it. He told her all that he'd withheld from her as well. And he admitted that he'd withheld that information in part to punish her for going her own way with the skull-and-crossed-bones ring and in part for the dressing-down he himself had received from Le Gallez about that ring. He told her that once he'd spoken to Guy Brouard's American attorney and learned that the person who'd brought the architectural plans to him was not Cherokee River but a black Rastafarian, he'd managed to persuade Le Gallez to lay a trap to catch the killer. It had to be one of them, so release both of them, he'd suggested to the DCI. Let them both go free, with the proviso that they must leave the island by the first transport available to them in the morning. If this killing is about the painting that was found in the dolmen, the killer will have to fetch it before dawn . . . if the killer is one of the Rivers.

"I expected it to be Cherokee," St. James said into his wife's ear. He hesitated before admitting the rest. "I wanted it to be Cherokee."

Deborah turned her head to look at him. He didn't know if she could hear him without his lips at her ear and he didn't know if she could read his lips, but he spoke anyway while her eyes were on him. He owed her that much: that precise degree of intimate confession.

"I've asked myself over and over if it's ever *not* going to come down to that," he said.

She heard him or read him. It didn't matter which. She said, "Down to what?"

"Myself against them. As I am. As they are. What you chose as opposed to what you could have had in someone else."

Her eyes widened. "Cherokee?"

"Anyone. There he is on our doorstep, some bloke I don't even know and can't honestly remember your even mentioning in the years you've been back from America, and he's familiar to you. He's familiar *with* you. He's undeniably part of that time. Which I am not, you see. I never will be. So there's that in my head and then there's the rest: this decent-looking, able-bodied bloke coming to fetch my wife to Guernsey. Because it's going to come down to that, and I can see it, no matter what he says about the American embassy. And I know anything can come of that. But that's the last thing I want to admit."

She searched his face. "How could you ever think I would leave you, Simon? For anyone. That's not what loving someone is."

"It's not you," he said. "It's me. The person that you are . . . You've never walked away from anything, and you wouldn't because you couldn't and still be the person you are. But I see the world through the eyes of someone who did walk away, Deborah. More than once. More than just from you. So for me, the world's a place where people devastate each other all the time. Through selfishness, greed, guilt, stupidity. Or in my case, fear. Pure palm-sweating fear. Which is what comes back to haunt me when someone like Cherokee River shows up on my doorstep. Fear gains hold of me and everything I do is coloured by everything else I fear. I wanted him to be the killer because only then could I be certain of you."

"Do you really think it's that important, Simon?"

"What?"

"You know."

He lowered his head to look at his hand covering

hers so that if she *was* reading his lips, perhaps she wouldn't read it all. He said, "I couldn't even get to you easily, my love. Inside the dolmen. As I am. So yes. I think it's that important."

"But only if you feel I need to be protected. Which I don't. Simon, I stopped being seven years old so long ago. What you did for me then . . . I don't need that now. I don't even want that now. I want only you."

He took this in and tried to make it his own. He'd been damaged goods since her fourteenth year, a time long past since the day he'd sorted out the group of schoolkids who'd been bullying her. He knew that he and Deborah had arrived at a point where he was meant to trust in the strength they had together as a single unit of husband-and-wife. He was just not sure that he could do it.

This moment was like crossing a frontier for him. He could see the crossing itself but he could not make out what was on the other side. It took a leap of faith to be a pioneer. He didn't know where such faith came from.

"I'm going to have to muddle my way into your adulthood, Deborah," he said at last. "That's the best I can do at the moment and even at that, I'll probably muff things up continually. Can you bear with that? *Will* you bear with that?"

She turned her hand in his and grasped his fingers. "It's a start," she replied. "And I'm happy with a start."

Chapter 31

ST. JAMES WENT TO *Le Reposoir* on the third day after the explosion and found Ruth Brouard with her nephew. They were coming past the stables, returning from the distant paddock, where Ruth had insisted upon seeing the dolmen. She'd known it was there on the grounds, of course, but she'd known it only as "the old burial mound." That her brother had excavated it, that he'd found its entrance, that he'd both equipped it and used it as a hideaway . . . These things she didn't know. Nor did Adrian, as St. James discovered.

They'd heard the explosion in the dead of night but had not known its source or location. Awakened by it, they'd each dashed from their rooms and met in the corridor. Ruth admitted to St. James—with an embarrassed laugh—that in the first confusion she'd thought Adrian's return to *Le Reposoir* was directly related to the terrible noise. She'd intuitively known that someone had detonated a bomb somewhere, and she'd connected this to Adrian's solicitous desire that she eat a dinner which she'd found him stirring in the kitchen earlier that evening.

She'd thought that he intended her to sleep and that he'd added a little something to her meal to assist her in her slumber. So when the reverberations from the explosion rattled her bedroom windows and slammed against the house, she didn't expect to find her nephew stumbling round the upstairs corridor in his pyjamas, shouting about a plane crash, a gas leak, Arab terrorists, and the IRA.

She'd thought he meant to do damage to the estate, she admitted. If he couldn't inherit it, then he would destroy it. But she changed her mind when he took charge of the events that followed: the police, the ambulances, the fire brigade. She didn't know how she would have managed without him.

"I would have trusted it all to Kevin Duffy," Ruth Brouard said. "But Adrian said no. He said, 'He's not family. We don't know what's going on and until we do, we're handling everything that needs to be handled ourselves.' So that's what we did."

"Why did she kill my father?" Adrian Brouard asked St. James.

That brought them to the painting, for as far as St. James had been able to ascertain, the painting was China River's objective. But there by the stables was not the place to discuss a stolen seventeenth-century canvas, so he asked if they might return to the house and have their conversation in the vicinity of the pretty lady with the book and the quill. There were things to be decided about that painting.

The picture was up in the gallery, a room that extended most of the length of the east side of the house. It was paneled in walnut and hung with Guy

Brouard's collection of modern oils. The pretty lady seemed out of place among them, lying frameless on a table that held a display case of miniatures.

"What's this?" Adrian said, crossing to the table. He switched on a lamp and its glow struck the veil of hair that fell copiously round St. Barbara's shoulders. "Not exactly a piece that Dad would collect."

"It's the lady we ate our meals with," Ruth replied. "She always hung in the dining room in Paris when we were children."

Adrian looked at her. "Paris?" His voice was sombre. "But after Paris . . . Where has it come from, then?"

"Your father found it. I think he wanted to surprise me with it."

"Found it where? How?"

"I don't expect I'll ever know. Mr. St. James and I . . . We've thought he must have hired someone. It went missing after the war, but he never forgot about it. Or about any of them: the family. We just had that one picture of them—the Seder picture? the one in your father's study?—and this painting was in that picture as well. So he couldn't forget it, I suppose. And if he couldn't bring them back to us, which of course he couldn't, at least he could find our picture. So that's what he did. Paul Fielder had it. He gave it to me. I think Guy must have told him to do that if . . . Well, if anything happened to him before it happened to me."

Adrian Brouard wasn't obtuse. He looked at St. James. "Does this have to do with why he died?"

Ruth said, "I don't see how, my dear." She came to stand at her nephew's side and considered the painting. "Paul had it, so I don't see how China River could have known about it. Even if she did— if your father had told her for some reason—well, it's a sentimental thing, really, the last vestige of our family. It would have represented a promise he'd made to me in childhood, when we left France. A way of recapturing what we both knew we couldn't ever really replace. Beyond that, it's a nice enough picture, isn't it, but that's all it is at the end of the day. Just an old painting. What could it mean to anyone else?"

Of course, St. James thought, she would learn the answer to her question soon enough and if for no other reason than Kevin Duffy would tell her. If not today, then someday, he'd walk into the house and there it would be in the great stone hall or the morning room, in this gallery or in Guy Brouard's study. He'd see it and he'd have to speak . . . unless he learned from Ruth that this fragile canvas was just a memento of a time and a people that a war had destroyed.

St. James realised that the painting would be safe with her, as safe as it had been for generations when all it was was merely the pretty lady with the book and the quill, handed down from father to son and then stolen by an occupying army. It was Ruth's now. Coming to her as it had done in the aftermath of her brother's murder, it wasn't governed by the terms of his will or by any agreement between the two of them that had preceded his death. Thus, she could do with it what she liked, when she liked. Just so long as St. James held his tongue.

Le Gallez knew about the painting, but *what* did he know? Merely that China River had wanted to steal a work of art from Brouard's collection. Nothing more. What the painting was, who the artist was, where the canvas had come from, how the robbery had been carried out . . . St. James himself was the only person who knew it all. The power was his to do with as he liked.

Ruth said, "In the family, a father always handed it down to his oldest son. It was probably the way a boy metamorphosed from scion to patriarch. Would you like it, my dear?"

Adrian shook his head. "Eventually, perhaps," he told her. "But for now, no. Dad would've wanted you to have it."

Ruth touched the canvas lovingly, at the foreground where St. Barbara's robe flowed like a waterfall forever suspended. Behind her the stonemasons hewed and placed their great slabs of granite into eternity. Ruth smiled at the placid face of the saint and she murmured, *"Merci, mon frère. Merci. Tu as tenu cent fois la promesse que tu avais faite à Maman."* Then she stirred herself and gave her attention to St. James. "You wanted to see her one more time. Why?"

The answer, after all, was simplicity itself. "Because she's beautiful," he told her, "and I wanted to say goodbye."

He took his leave of them then. They walked

with him as far as the stairs. He said they had no need to accompany him farther, as he knew the way out. They came down one flight with him nonetheless, but there they stopped. Ruth wanted to rest in her room, she said. She was feeling less and less spry each day.

Adrian said he would see her safely into bed. "Take my arm, Aunt Ruth," he told her.

Deborah was expecting her final visit from the neurologist who'd been monitoring her recovery. His was the last hurdle to clear, after which she and Simon could go back to England. She'd already dressed in anticipation of being given the doctor's blessing. She'd taken up a position in an uncomfortable Scandinavian chair near the bed, and just to make sure there were no doubts about her wishes, she'd gone so far as to strip the mattress of its sheets and blanket in preparation for another patient.

Her hearing was improving by the day. A medic had removed the stitches along her jaw. Her bruises were healing and the cuts and abrasions on her face were disappearing. The inner wounds were going to take a lot longer to heal. She'd so far avoided feeling the pain of them, but she knew a day of internal reckoning was going to come.

When the door opened, she expected the doctor and she half-rose to meet him. But it was Cherokee River who stood there. He said, "I wanted to come right away, but there . . . there was too much to handle. And then, when there was less to handle, I didn't know how to face you. Or what to say. I still don't. But I needed to come. I'm leaving in a couple of hours."

She held out her hand to him but he didn't take it. She dropped it and said, "I'm so sorry."

"I'm taking her home," he said. "Mom wanted to come over and help, but I told her . . ." He gave a rueful laugh that sounded mostly of grief. He shoved his hand back through his curly hair. "She wouldn't want Mom here. She never wanted Mom to be any-where near her. Besides, there wouldn't be any point to her coming: flying all this way and then just turn-ing around and going back. She wanted to come, though. She was crying pretty bad. They hadn't talked to each other . . . I don't know. Maybe a year? Two? China didn't like . . . I don't know. I don't know for sure what China didn't like."

Deborah urged him to sit in the low and uncom-fortable chair. He said, "No. You take it."

She said, "I'll use the bed." She perched on the edge of the bare mattress, and when she had done so, Cherokee lowered himself to the chair. He sat on its edge with his elbows on his knees. Deborah waited for him to speak. She herself didn't know what to say beyond expressing her sorrow for what had hap-pened.

He said, "I don't get any of it. I still don't be-lieve . . . There was no reason. But she must have had it planned from the first. Only I can't figure out why."

"She knew you had the poppy oil."

"For jet lag. I didn't know what to expect, if we'd

be able to sleep or not when we got over here. I didn't know ... you know ... how long it would take us to get used to the time change or if we ever would. So I got the oil at home and brought it with. I told her we could both use it if we needed it. But I never did."

"So you forgot you had it?"

"Not forgot. Just didn't think about it. Whether I still had it. Whether I'd given it to her. I just didn't think." He'd been looking at his shoes, but now he looked up as he said, "When she used it on Guy, she must've forgotten that it was my bottle. She must not've realised that my fingerprints would be all over it."

Deborah moved her own gaze away from him. There was, she found, a loose thread at the edge of the mattress, and she wound it tightly round her finger. She watched her nail bed darken. She said, "China's fingerprints weren't on the bottle. Only yours."

"Sure, but there's an explanation for that. Like the way she held it. Or something." He sounded so hopeful that Deborah couldn't bear to do anything more than glance at him. She didn't have the words to reply, and when she said nothing, a silence grew. She could hear his breathing and then, beyond that, voices in the hospital corridor. Someone was arguing with a staff member, a man demanding a private room for his wife. She was "My God, a bloody *employee* of this blasted place." She was owed some special consideration, wasn't she?

Cherokee finally spoke hoarsely. "Why?"

Deborah wondered if she could come up with the words to tell him. It seemed to her that the River siblings had struck blow-for-blow upon each other, but there was no real balancing of the scales when it came to crimes committed and pain endured and there never would be, especially now. She said, "She never could forgive your mum, could she? For how it was when you two were children. Never around to *be* a mum. The string of motels. Where you had to buy your clothes. Only one pair of shoes. She couldn't ever see that this was just the *stuff* that surrounded her. It was nothing else. It didn't mean anything more than what it was: a motel, secondhand clothes shops, shoes, a mum who didn't stay round for more than a day or a week at a time. But it meant more to her. It was like . . . like a great injustice that had been done to her instead of what it was: just her hand of cards, to be done with as she liked. D'you see what I mean?"

"So she killed . . . So she wanted the cops to believe . . ." Cherokee obviously couldn't bring himself to face it, much less to say it. "I guess I don't see."

"I think she found injustice in places where other people simply found life," Deborah told him. "And she couldn't manage to get past the thought of that injustice: what had happened, what had been done—"

"To her." Cherokee completed Deborah's thought. "Yeah. Right. But what did I ever . . . ? No. When she used that oil, she didn't think . . . She didn't know . . . She didn't realise . . ." His voice died off.

"How did you know where to find us in London?" Deborah asked him.

"She had your address. If I had trouble with the embassy or anything, she said I could ask you for help. We might need it, she said, to get to the truth."

Which was what had occurred, Deborah thought. Just not the way China had anticipated. She'd doubtless reckoned that Simon would home in on her innocence, pressing the local police to continue their investigation till they found the opiate bottle she had planted. What she hadn't considered was that the local police would get to the opiate bottle on their own while Deborah's husband would take a different tack entirely, unearthing the facts about the painting and then laying a trap with that painting as bait.

Deborah said gently to China's brother, "So she sent you to fetch us. She knew how it would be if we came."

"That I'd be . . ."

"That's what she wanted."

"To pin a murder on me." Cherokee got to his feet and walked to the window. Blinds covered it, and he jerked at their cord. "So I'd end up . . . what? Like her father or something? Was this some big trip of revenge because her dad's in prison and mine isn't? Like it was my fault she got the loser for a father? Well, it wasn't my fault. It isn't my fault. And how much better was my own dad, anyway? Some

do-gooder who's spent his life saving the desert tor-
toise or the yellow salamander or what-the-hell-
ever. *Jesus.* What difference does it make? What the
hell difference did it *ever* make? I just don't get it."

"Do you need to?"

"She was my sister. So, yeah. I God damn
need to."

Deborah left the bed and joined him. Gently, she
took the cord from his hands. She raised the blinds
to fill the room with daylight, and the distant sun of
December struck their faces.

"You sold her virginity to Matthew Whitecomb,"
Deborah said. "She found out, Cherokee. She
wanted you to pay."

He made no reply.

"She thought he loved her. All this time. He
kept coming back no matter what happened between them and she thought that meant what it
didn't mean. She knew that he was cheating on her
with other women but she believed that, in the
end, he'd grow out of all that and want to be
with her."

Cherokee leaned forward. He rested his forehead
against the cool pane of the window. "He *was* cheating," Cherokee murmured. "But it was with her.
Not *on* her. *With* her. What the hell did she think?
One weekend a month? Two if she got real lucky? A
trip to Mexico five years ago and a cruise when she
was twenty-one? The asshole's *married*, Debs. Has
been for eighteen months and he wouldn't fucking
tell her. And there she was hanging on and on and I
couldn't . . . I just couldn't be the one. I couldn't do

that to her. I didn't want to see her face. So I told her how it all came about in the first place because I hoped that would be enough to piss her off and break her away from him."

"You mean . . . ?" Deborah could hardly stand to complete the thought, so horrific it was in its consequences. "You didn't sell her? She only *thought* . . . Fifty dollars and a surfboard? To Matt? You didn't do that?"

He turned his head away. He looked down into the car park of the hospital, where a taxi was pulling into the loading zone. As they watched, Simon got out of the car. He spoke to the driver for a moment, and the taxi remained behind as he approached the front doors.

"You've been sprung," Cherokee said to Deborah.

She insisted, "Did you not sell her to Matt?"

He said, "Got your things together? We c'n meet him in the lobby if you'd like."

"Cherokee," she said.

He replied, "Hell, I wanted to surf. I needed a board. It wasn't enough to borrow one. I wanted my own."

"Oh God," Deborah sighed.

"It wasn't supposed to be such a big deal," Cherokee said. "It wasn't a big deal for Matt, and with any other chick it wouldn't have been a big deal either. But how was I supposed to know how China would take it, what she'd think was supposed to grow out of it if she 'gave' herself to some loser? Jesus, Debs, it was just a screw."

"And you, in effect, were just a pimp."

"It wasn't *like* that. I could tell she had a thing for him. I didn't see the harm. She wouldn't ever have known about the deal if she hadn't become a roll of human Glad wrap throwing her life away on a stupid son of a bitch. So I had to tell her. She gave me no choice. It was for her own good."

"Like the deal itself?" Deborah asked. "That wasn't all about you, Cherokee? What you wanted and how you'd use your sister to get it? It wasn't like that?"

"Okay. Yeah. It was. But she wasn't supposed to take it so seriously. She was supposed to move on."

"Right. Well. She didn't move on," Deborah pointed out. "Because it's tough to do that when you don't have the facts."

"She *had* the damn facts. She just didn't want to see them. Jesus. Why couldn't she ever let anything go? God, *everything* festered inside her. She couldn't get past how she thought things should be."

Deborah knew he was right in at least that one respect: China had put a price tag on things, always feeling herself owed far more than was actually on offer. Deborah had finally seen that in her last conversation with the other woman: She'd expected too much of people, of life. In those expectations she had sown the seeds of her own destruction.

"And the worst of it is that she didn't need to do it, Debs," Cherokee said. "No one was holding a gun to her head. He made the moves. I put them together in the first place, yeah. But she let it happen.

She went on letting it. So how the hell could that've been my fault?"

Deborah didn't have the answer to that question. Too much fault, she thought, had been assessed upon or rejected by members of the River family through the years.

A quick knock on the door brought Simon into the room to join them. He carried what she hoped was the paperwork that would release her from Princess Elizabeth Hospital. He nodded at Cherokee but directed his question to Deborah.

"Ready to go home?" he asked her.

"More than anything else," she said.

Chapter 32

FRANK OUSELEY WAITED TILL the twenty-first of December, the shortest day and longest night of the year. Sunset would come early, and he wanted sunset. The long shadows it provided felt comfortable to him, giving him protection from any prying eyes who might inadvertently witness the final act in his personal drama.

At half past three he took up the parcel. A cardboard box, it had sat on top of the television set since he'd brought it home from St. Sampson. A band of tape kept its flaps closed, but Frank had earlier lifted this tape to check on the contents. A plastic bag now held what remained of his father. Ashes to ashes and dust to dust. The colour of the substance was somewhere between the two, lighter and darker simultaneously, ridged by the occasional fragment of bone.

Somewhere in the Orient, he knew, they picked through the ashes of the dead. The family gathered and with chopsticks in hand, they lifted out what remained of the bones. He didn't know what they did with those bones—they likely used them for family reliquaries much as the bones of martyrs had once been used to sanctify early Christian churches. But that was something he didn't intend to do with his father's ashes. What bones there were would become part of the place to which Frank had determined to deposit the rest of his father.

He'd thought first of the reservoir. The spot where his mother had drowned could have received his father with little trouble, even if he didn't scatter the remains into the water itself. Then he considered the tract of land near St. Saviour's Church, where the wartime museum had been meant to stand. But he concluded that a sacrilege existed in disposing of his father at a site where men utterly unlike him were meant to be honoured.

Carefully, he carried his father out to the Peugeot and rested him snugly on the passenger seat, cushioned all the way round by an old beach towel that he'd used as a boy. Just as carefully, he drove out of the Talbot Valley. The trees were completely bare now, with only the stands of oaks still leafy on the gentle slope of the valley's south side. And even here, many of the leaves lay on the ground, colouring the comforting, large trunks of the trees with a cape of saffron and umber.

Daylight left the Talbot Valley sooner than it did the rest of the island. Folded into a landscape of undulating hillsides eroded by centuries of stream, the occasional cottage along the road already showed bright lights in its windows. But as Frank emerged from the valley into St. Andrew, the land itself changed and so did the light. Hillside grazing for the island cows gave over to agriculture and hamlets, where cottages with a score of greenhouses behind them all drank in and reflected the last of the sun.

He headed east and came at St. Peter Port on the far side of Princess Elizabeth Hospital. From there, it was no difficult feat to get to Fort George. Although daylight was fading, it was too early for the traffic to be a problem. Besides, at this time of year, there was little enough of it. Come Easter, the roads would begin to fill.

He waited only for a tractor to lumber through the intersection at the end of Prince Albert Road. After that, he made good time to Fort George, skimming through its thick stone archway just as the sun struck the picture windows of the sprawling houses inside the fort. This place had long since been used for any military purpose, despite its name, but unlike other of the fortresses on the island—from Doyle to *le Crocq*—this was also no ruin of granite and brick. Its proximity to St. Peter Port as well as its views of Soldiers' Bay had made it a prime location for exiles from Her Majesty's revenue collectors to build their sumptuous homes. So they had done so: behind tall hedges of box and yew, behind wrought iron fences with electric gates, set back on lawns next to which stood Mercedes-Benzes and Jaguars.

A car like Frank's would have been looked upon with suspicion had he chosen to drive it anywhere within the fort other than directly to the cemetery, which was situated, as luck and irony would have it, on the most scenically advantageous part of the entire area. It occupied an east-facing slope at the southern end of the old military grounds. Its entrance was marked by a war memorial in the shape of an enormous granite cross in which a sword—embedded in the stone—duplicated the grey cruciform into which it had been placed. The irony might have been intentional. It probably was. The cemetery thrived on irony.

Frank parked in the gravel just beneath the memorial and crossed the lane to the cemetery's entrance. From there he could see the smaller islands of both Herm and Jethou rising in the mist across a placid stretch of water. From there, also, a concrete ramp—ridged against the possibility of a mourner falling in inclement weather—sloped down to the graveyard which comprised a set of terraces that had been carved out of the hillside. Set at a right angle to these terraces, a retaining wall of Rocquaine Blue held a bronze bas relief of people in profile, perhaps citizens or soldiers or victims of war. Frank could not tell. But an inscription in the relief—*Life lives beyond the grave*—suggested that those bronze figures represented the souls of the departed laid to rest in this place, and the carving itself had been fashioned into a door that, when opened, revealed the actual names of the interred.

He did not read them. He merely stopped, placed the cardboard box of his father's ashes on the ground, and opened it to remove the plastic bag.

He descended the steps to the first of the terraces. Here were buried the brave men of the island who had given their lives in World War I. They lay beneath old elms in precise lines that were marked by holly and pyracantha. Frank passed them by and continued downward.

He knew the point in the graveyard at which he would begin his solitary ceremony. The headstones there marked graves more recent than World War I, each of them identical to the other. They were simple white stone with the single decoration of a cross whose shape would have identified them unmistakably had not the names carved into them done so.

Frank descended to this group of graves. There were one hundred and eleven of them, so one hundred and eleven times would he dip his hand into the bag of ashes and one hundred and eleven times would he let what remained of his father drift through his fingers and settle on the final resting places of those German men who had come to occupy—and who had died upon—the island of Guernsey.

He began the process. At first it was hideous to him: his living flesh coming into contact with his father's incinerated remains. When the first bone fragment grazed against his palm, he shuddered and felt his stomach heave. He paused then and steeled his nerves to the rest of it. He read each name, the dates of birth and of death, as he consigned his father to the company of those he'd chosen as comrades.

He saw that some of them had been mere boys, nineteen- and twenty-year-olds who may well have been away from their homes for the very first time. He wondered how they'd experienced this small place that was Guernsey after the large land from which they'd come. Had it seemed like an outpost-ing to another planet? Or had it been a blessed res-cue from bloody combat on the front lines? How must it have felt to them to have had such power and to have been simultaneously so utterly despised?

But not by all, of course. That was the tragedy of that place and that time. Not everyone had seen them as an enemy to be scorned.

Frank moved mechanically among the graves, de-scending tier after tier until he had emptied the plas-tic sack entirely. When he was done, he walked to the marker at the bottom of the cemetery and he stood for a moment, looking back up the hill at the rows of graves, at the way he had come.

He saw that, although he'd left a small handful of his father's ashes on every German soldier's resting place, no sign of them remained. The ashes had set-tled into the ivy, the holly, and the creeper that grew in patches upon the graves, and there transformed into mere dust, a thin skin lying like an ephemeral mist that would not survive the first gust of wind.

That wind would come. It would bring with it rain. This would swell the streams which would gush from the hillsides down into the valleys and from there to the sea. Some of the dust that was his father would join it. The rest would remain, part of the earth that covered the dead. Part of the earth that gave succour to the living.

ACKNOWLEDGMENTS

As ALWAYS, I AM indebted to a number of people who assisted me during the creation of this novel.

On the lovely Channel Island of Guernsey, I must thank Inspector Trevor Coleman of the States Police, the kindly people of the Citizens Advice Bureau, and Mr. R. L. Heaume, the director of the German Occupation Museum in Forest.

In the UK, I am continually in the debt of Sue Fletcher, my editor at Hodder & Stoughton, as well as her wonderful and resourceful assistant, Swati Gamble. I extend my thanks additionally to Kate Brandice of the American embassy.

In France, the generosity of my regular translator, Marie-Claude Ferrer, enabled me to create some of the dialogue in the novel, while Veronika Kreuzhage in Germany provided me with the necessary translations related to the World War II artifacts.

In the United States, Professor Jonathan Petropolous aided my understanding of the Nazi "repatriation of art," both in person and through his invaluable book *The Faustian Bargain*. Dr. Tom

Ruben graciously supplied me with medical information when necessary, Bill Hull helped me to understand the architect's profession, and my fellow writer Robert Crais allowed me to pick his brains about money-laundering. I'm extremely grateful to Susan Berner for being willing to read an early draft of this novel, and I'm additionally grateful to my husband, Tom McCabe, for his patience and his respect of the time it takes to put a novel together. Lastly, of course, I could not have even begun this book without the constant presence, assistance, and good cheer of my assistant, Dannielle Azoulay.

Books which I found helpful during the creation of this novel were the aforementioned *The Faustian Bargain* by Jonathan Petropolous, *The Silent War* by Frank Falla, *Living with the Enemy* by Roy McLoughlin, *Buildings in the Town and Parish of St. Peter Port* by C.E.B. Brett, *Folklore of Guernsey* by Marie De Garis, *Landscape of the Channel Islands* by Nigel Jee, *Utrecht Painters of the Dutch Golden Age* by Christopher Brown, and *Vermeer and Painting in Delft* by Alex Rüger.

Finally a word about *St. Barbara.* Students of art history will know that while the painting I describe in this novel does not exist, the drawing which I attribute to Pieter de Hooch certainly does. It is, however, not by Pieter de Hooch at all but by Jan van Eyck. My purpose in callously altering its creator had to do with the period of time during which it was drawn and during which van Eyck painted. Had he actually painted *St. Barbara,* he would have composed his masterpiece on oak board, as was the practice at that time. For purposes of my novel, I needed canvas, which did not come into widespread use until a later period. I hope I'll be forgiven for this manhandling of art history.

There will, naturally, be errors in the book. These are mine alone and not attributable to any of the fine people who helped me.

About the Author

ELIZABETH GEORGE'S first novel, *A Great Deliverance*, was honored with the Anthony and Agatha Best First Novel Awards and received the Grand Prix de Littérature Policière. Her third novel, *Well-Schooled in Murder*, was awarded the prestigious German prize for suspense fiction, the MIMI. *A Suitable Vengeance, For the Sake of Elena, Missing Joseph, Playing for the Ashes, In the Presence of the Enemy, Deception on His Mind, In Pursuit of the Proper Sinner, A Traitor to Memory,* and *I, Richard* were international bestsellers. Elizabeth George divides her time between Huntington Beach, California, and London. Her novels are currently being dramatized by the BBC. Visit her website at www.ElizabethGeorgeOnline.com.